MÖBIUS TRIP

"Reintegration complete," ZORAC advised. "We're back in the universe again . . ." An unusually long pause followed. ". . . but I don't know which part. We seem to have changed our position in space." A spherical display in the middle of the floor illuminated to show the starfield surrounding the ship.

"Several large, artificial constructions are approaching us," ZORAC announced after a short pause. "The designs are not familiar, but they are obviously the products of intelligence. Implications: we have been intercepted deliberately by a means unknown, for a purpose unknown, and transferred to a place unknown by a form of intelligence unknown. Apart from the unknown, everything is obvious."

By James P. Hogan
Published by Ballantine Books:

CODE OF THE LIFEMAKER
THE GENESIS MACHINE
THRICE UPON A TIME
THE TWO FACES OF TOMORROW
VOYAGE FROM YESTERYEAR

The Giants Series:
INHERIT THE STARS
THE GENTLE GIANTS OF GANYMEDE
GIANTS' STAR
ENTOVERSE
THE GIANTS NOVELS

THE GIANTS NOVELS

INHERIT THE STARS

THE GENTLE GIANTS OF GANYMEDE

GIANTS' STAR

James P. Hogan

A Del Rey® Book
BALLANTINE BOOKS • NEW YORK

A Del Rey® Book
Published by Ballantine Books

Library of Congress Catalog Card Number: 91-14313

ISBN 0-345-38885-2

Manufactured in the United States of America

First Hardcover Edition: October 1991
First Mass Market Edition: June 1994

10 9 8 7 6 5 4 3

Cover art by Darrell K. Sweet and H.R. Van Dongen

contents

INHERIT THE STARS

To the memory of my Father

prologue

He became aware of consciousness returning.

Instinctively his mind recoiled, as if by some effort of will he could arrest the relentless flow of seconds that separated nonawareness from awareness and return again to the timeless oblivion in which the agony of total exhaustion was unknown and unknowable.

The hammer that had threatened to burst from his chest was now quiet. The rivers of sweat that had drained with his strength from every hollow of his body were now turned cold. His limbs had turned to lead. The gasping of his lungs had returned once more to a slow and even rhythm. It sounded loud in the close confines of his helmet.

He tried to remember how many had died. Their release was final; for him there was no release. How much longer could he go on? What was the point? Would there be anyone left alive at Gorda anyway?

"Gorda . . . ? Gorda . . . ?"

His mental defenses could shield him from reality no longer. *"Must get to Gorda!"*

He opened his eyes. A billion unblinking stars stared back without interest. When he tried to move, his body refused to respond, as if trying to prolong to the utmost its last precious moments of rest. He took a deep breath and, clenching his teeth at the pain that instantly racked again through every fiber of his body, forced himself away from the rock and into a sitting position. A wave of nausea swept over him. His head sagged forward and struck the inside of his visor. The nausea passed.

He groaned aloud.

"Feeling better, then, soldier?" The voice came clearly through the speaker inside his helmet. "Sun's getting low. We gotta be moving."

5

He lifted his head and slowly scanned the nightmare wilderness of scorched rock and ash-gray dust that confronted him.

"Whe—" The sound choked in his throat. He swallowed, licked his lips, and tried again. "Where are you?"

"To your right, up on the rise just past that small cliff that juts out—the one with the big boulders underneath."

He turned his head and after some seconds detected a bright blue patch against the ink-black sky. It seemed blurred and far away. He blinked and strained his eyes again, forcing his brain to coordinate with his vision. The blue patch resolved itself into the figure of the tireless Koriel, clad in a heavy-duty combat suit.

"I see you." After a pause: "Anything?"

"It's fairly flat on the other side of the rise—should be easier going for a while. Gets rockier farther on. Come have a look."

He inched his arms upward to find purchase on the rock behind, then braced them to thrust his weight forward over his legs. His knees trembled. His face contorted as he fought to concentrate his remaining strength into his protesting thighs. Already his heart was pumping again, his lungs heaving. The effort evaporated and he fell back against the rock. His labored breathing rasped over Koriel's radio.

"Finished . . . Can't move . . ."

The blue figure on the skyline turned.

"Aw, what kinda talk's that? This is the last stretch. We're there, buddy—we're there."

"No—no good . . . Had it . . ."

Koriel waited a few seconds.

"I'm coming back down."

"No—you go on. Someone's got to make it."

No response.

"Koriel . . . ?"

He looked back at where the figure had stood, but already it had disappeared below the intervening rocks and was out of the line of transmission. A minute or two later the figure emerged from behind the nearby boulders, covering the ground in long, effortless bounds. The bounds broke into a walk as Koriel approached the bunched form clad in red.

"C'mom, soldier, on your feet now. There's people back there depending on us."

He felt himself gripped below his arm and raised irresistibly, as if some of Koriel's limitless reserves of strength were pouring into him. For a while his head swam and he leaned with the top of his visor resting on the giant's shoulder insignia.

"Okay," he managed at last. "Let's go."

Hour after hour the thin snake of footprints, two pinpoints of color at its head, wound its way westward across the wilderness and steadily lengthening shadows. He marched as if in a trance, beyond feeling pain, beyond feeling exhaustion—beyond feeling anything. The skyline never seemed to change; soon he could no longer look at it. Instead, he began picking out the next prominent boulder or crag, and counting off the paces until they reached it. "Two hundred and thirteen less to go." And then he repeated it over again . . . and again . . . and again. The rocks marched by in slow, endless, indifferent procession. Every step became a separate triumph of will—a deliberate, conscious effort to drive one foot yet one more pace beyond the last. When he faltered, Koriel was there to catch his arm; when he fell, Koriel was always there to haul him up. Koriel never tired.

At last they stopped. They were standing in a gorge perhaps a quarter mile wide, below one of the lines of low, broken cliffs that flanked it on either side. He collapsed on the nearest boulder. Koriel stood a few paces ahead surveying the landscape. The line of crags immediately above them was interrupted by a notch, which marked the point where a steep and narrow cleft tumbled down to break into the wall of the main gorge. From the bottom of the cleft, a mound of accumulated rubble and rock debris led down about fifty feet to blend with the floor of the gorge not far from where they stood. Koriel stretched out an arm to point up beyond the cleft.

"Gorda will be roughly that way," he said without turning. "Our best way would be up and onto that ridge. If we stay on the flat and go around the long way, it'll be too far. What d'you say?"

The other stared up in mute despair. The rockfall, funneling up toward the mouth of the cleft, looked like a mountain. In the distance beyond towered the ridge, jagged and white in the glare of the sun. It was impossible.

Koriel allowed his doubts no time to take root. Somehow—slipping, sliding, stumbling, and falling—they reached the entrance to the cleft. Beyond it, the walls narrowed and curved around to the left, cutting off the view of the gorge below from where they had come. They climbed higher. Around them, sheets of raw reflected sunlight and bottomless pits of shadow met in knife-edges across rocks shattered at a thousand crazy angles. His brain ceased to extract the concepts of shape and form from the insane geometry of white and black that kaleidoscoped across his retina. The patterns grew and shrank and merged and whirled in a frenzy of visual cacophony.

His face crashed against his visor as his helmet thudded into the dust. Koriel hoisted him to his feet.

"You can do it. We'll see Gorda from the ridge. It'll be all downhill from there. . . ."

But the figure in red sank slowly to its knees and folded over. The head inside the helmet shook weakly from side to side. As Koriel watched, the conscious part of his mind at last accepted the inescapable logic that the parts beneath consciousness already knew. He took a deep breath and looked about him.

Not far below, they had passed a hole, about five feet across, cut into the base of one of the rock walls. It looked like the remnant of some forgotten excavation—maybe a preliminary digging left by a mining survey. The giant stopped, and grasping the harness that secured the backpack to the now insensible figure at his feet, dragged the body back down the slope to the hole. It was about ten feet deep inside. Working quickly, Koriel arranged a lamp to reflect a low light off the walls and roof. Then he removed the rations from his companion's pack, laid the figure back against the rear wall as comfortably as he could, and placed the food containers within easy reach. Just as he was finishing, the eyes behind the visor flickered open.

"You'll be fine here for a while." The usual gruffness was gone from Koriel's voice. "I'll have the rescue boys back from Gorda before you know it."

The figure in red raised a feeble arm. Just a whisper came through.

"You—you tried. . . . Nobody could have . . ."

Koriel clasped the gauntlet with both hands.

"Mustn't give up. That's no good. You just have to hang on a while." Inside his helmet the granite cheeks were wet. He backed to the entrance and made a final salute. "So long, soldier." And then he was gone.

Outside he built a small cairn of stones to mark the position of the hole. He would mark the trail to Gorda with such cairns.

At last he straightened up and turned defiantly to face the desolation surrounding him. The rocks seemed to scream down in soundless laughing mockery. The stars above remained unmoved. Koriel glowered up at the cleft, rising up toward the tiers of crags and terraces that guarded the ridge, still soaring in the distance. His lips curled back to show his teeth.

"So—it's just you and me now, is it?" he snarled at the Universe. "Okay, you bastard—let's see you take this round!"

With his legs driving like slow pistons, he attacked the ever-steepening slope.

chapter one

Accompanied by a mild but powerful whine, a gigantic silver torpedo rose slowly upward to hang two thousand feet above the sugar-cube huddle of central London. Over three hundred yards long, it spread at the tail into a slim delta topped by two sharply swept fins. For a while the ship hovered, as if savoring the air of its newfound freedom, its nose swinging smoothly around to seek the north. At last, with the sound growing, imperceptibly at first but with steadily increasing speed, it began to slide forward and upward. At ten thousand feet its engines erupted into full power, hurling the suborbital skyliner eagerly toward the fringes of space.

Sitting in row thirty-one of C deck was Dr. Victor Hunt, head of Theoretical Studies at the Metadyne Nucleonic Instrument Company of Reading, Berkshire—itself a subsidiary of the mammoth Intercontinental Data and Control Corporation, headquartered at Portland, Oregon, USA. He absently surveyed the diminishing view of Hendon that crawled across the cabin wall-display screen and tried again to fit some kind of explanation to the events of the last few days.

His experiments with matter–antimatter particle extinctions had been progressing well. Forsyth-Scott had followed Hunt's reports with evident interest and therefore knew that the tests were progressing well. That made it all the more strange for him to call Hunt at his office one morning to ask him simply to drop everything and get over to IDCC Portland as quickly as could be arranged. From the managing director's tone and manner it had been obvious that the request was couched as such mainly for reasons of politeness; in reality this was one of the few occasions on which Hunt had no say in the matter.

To Hunt's questions, Forsyth-Scott had stated quite frankly that he didn't know what it was that made Hunt's immediate presence at IDCC so imperative. The previous evening he had received a videocall from Felix Borlan, the president of IDCC, who had told him that as a matter of priority he required the only working prototype of the scope prepared for immediate shipment to the USA and an installation team ready to go with it. Also, he had insisted that Hunt personally come over for an indefinite period to take charge of some project involving the scope, which could not wait. For Hunt's benefit, Forsyth-Scott had replayed Borlan's call on his desk display and allowed him to verify for himself that Forsyth-Scott in turn was acting under a thinly disguised directive. Even stranger, Borlan too had seemed unable to say precisely what it was that the instrument and its inventor were needed for.

The Trimagniscope, developed as a consequence of a two-year investigation by Hunt into certain aspects of neutrino physics, promised to be perhaps the most successful venture ever undertaken by the company. Hunt had established that a neutrino beam that passed through a solid object underwent certain interactions in the close vicinity of atomic nuclei, which produced measurable changes in the transmitted output. By raster scanning an object with a trio of synchronized, intersecting beams, he had devised a method of extracting enough information to generate a 3-D color hologram, visually indistinguishable from the original solid. Moreover, since the beams scanned right through, it was almost as easy to conjure up views of the inside as of the out. These capabilities, combined with that of high-power magnification that was also inherent in the method, yielded possibilities not even remotely approached by anything else on the market. From quantitative cell metabolism and bionics, through neurosurgery, metallurgy, crystallography, and molecular electronics, to engineering inspection and quality control, the applications were endless. Inquiries were pouring in and shares were soaring. Removing the prototype and its originator to the USA—totally disrupting carefully planned production and marketing schedules—bordered on the catastrophic. Borlan knew this as well as anybody. The more Hunt turned these things over in his mind, the less plausible the various possible explanations that had at first occurred to him seemed, and the more convinced he became that whatever the answer turned out to be, it would be found to lie far beyond even Felix Borlan and IDCC.

His thoughts were interrupted by a voice issuing from somewhere in the general direction of the cabin roof.

"Good afternoon, ladies and gentlemen. This is Captain Mason speaking. I would like to welcome you aboard this Boeing 1017 on behalf of British Airways. We are now in level flight at our cruising altitude of fifty-two miles, speed 3,160 knots. Our course is thirty-five degrees west of true north, and the coast is now below with Liverpool five miles to starboard. Passengers are free to leave their seats. The bars are open and drinks and snacks are being served. We are due to arrive in San Francisco at ten thirty-eight hours local time; that's one hour and fifty minutes from now. I would like to remind you that it is necessary to be seated when we begin our descent in one hour and thirty-five minutes time. A warning will sound ten minutes before descent commences and again at five minutes. We trust you will enjoy your journey. Thank you."

The captain signed himself off with a click, which was drowned out as the regulars made their customary scramble for the vi-phone booths.

In the seat next to Hunt, Rob Gray, Metadyne's chief of Experimental Engineering, sat with an open briefcase resting on his knees. He studied the information being displayed on the screen built into its lid.

"A regular flight to Portland takes off fifteen minutes after we get in," he announced. "That's a bit tight. Next one's not for over four hours. What d'you reckon?" He punctuated the question with a sideways look and raised eyebrows.

Hunt pulled a face. "I'm not arsing about in Frisco for four hours. Book us an Avis jet—we'll fly ourselves up."

"That's what I thought."

Gray played the mini keyboard below the screen to summon an index, consulted it briefly, then touched another key to display a directory. Selecting a number from one of the columns, he mouthed it silently to himself as he tapped it in. A copy of the number appeared near the bottom of the screen with a request for him to confirm. He pressed the Y button. The screen went blank for a few seconds and then exploded into a whirlpool of color, which stabilized almost at once into the features of a platinum-blonde, who radiated the kind of smile normally reserved for toothpaste commercials.

"Good morning. Avis San Francisco, City Terminal. This is Sue Parker. Can I help you?"

Gray addressed the grille, located next to the tiny camera lens just above the screen.

"Hi, Sue. Name's Gray—R. J. Gray, airbound for SF, due to arrive about two hours from now. Could I reserve an aircar, please?"

"Sure thing. Range?"

"Oh—about five hundred . . ." He glanced at Hunt.

"Better make it seven," Hunt advised.

"Make that seven hundred miles minimum."

"That'll be no problem, Mr. Gray. We have Skyrovers, Mercury Threes, Honeybees, or Yellow Birds. Any preference?"

"No—any'll do."

"I'll make it a Mercury, then. Any idea how long?"

"No—er—indefinite."

"Okay. Full computer nav and flight control? Automatic VTOL?"

"Preferably and, ah, yes."

"You have a full manual license?" The blonde operated unseen keys as she spoke.

"Yes."

"Could I have personal data and account-checking data, please?"

Gray had extracted the card from his wallet while the exchange was taking place. He inserted it into a slot set to one side of the screen, and touched a key.

The blonde consulted other invisible oracles. "Okay," she pronounced. "Any other pilots?"

"One. A Dr. V. Hunt."

"His personal data?"

Gray took Hunt's already proffered card and substituted it for his own. The ritual was repeated. The face then vanished to be replaced by a screen of formatted text with entries completed in the boxes provided.

"Would you verify and authorize, please?" said the disembodied voice from the grille. "Charges are shown on the right."

Gray cast his eye rapidly down the screen, grunted, and keyed in a memorized sequence of digits that was not echoed on the display. The word POSITIVE appeared in the box marked "Authorization." Then the clerk reappeared, still smiling.

"When would you want to collect, Mr. Gray?" she asked.

Gray turned toward Hunt.

"Do we want lunch at the airport first?"

Hunt grimaced. "Not after that party last night. Couldn't face anything." His face took on an expression of acute distaste as he moistened the inside of the equine rectum he had once called a mouth. "Let's eat tonight somewhere."

"Make it round about eleven thirty hours," Gray advised.

"It'll be ready."

"Thanks, Sue."

"Thank you. Good-bye."

"Bye now."

Gray flipped a switch, unplugged the briefcase from the socket built into the armrest of his seat, and coiled the connecting cord back into the space provided in the lid. He closed the case and stowed it behind his feet.

"Done," he announced.

The scope was the latest in a long line of technological triumphs in the Metadyne product range to be conceived and nurtured to maturity by the Hunt-Gray partnership. Hunt was the ideas man, leading something of a free-lance existence within the organization, left to pursue whatever line of study or experiment his personal whims or the demands of his researches dictated. His title was somewhat misleading; in fact he *was* Theoretical Studies. The position was one which he had contrived, quite deliberately, to fall into no obvious place in the managerial hierarchy of Metadyne. He acknowledged no superior, apart from the managing director, Sir Francis Forsyth-Scott, and boasted no subordinates. On the company's organization charts, the box captioned "Theoretical Studies" stood alone and disconnected near the inverted tree head *R & D*, as if added as an afterthought. Inside it there appeared the single entry *Dr. Victor Hunt*. This was the way he liked it—a symbiotic relationship in which Metadyne provided him with the equipment, facilities, services, and funds he needed for his work, while he provided Metadyne with first, the prestige of retaining on its payroll a world-acknowledged authority on nuclear infrastructure theory, and second—but by no means least—a steady supply of fallout.

Gray was the engineer. He was the sieve that the fallout fell on. He had a genius for spotting the gems of raw ideas that had application potential and transforming them into developed, tested, marketable products and product enhancements. Like Hunt, he had survived the mine field of the age of unreason and emerged safe and single into his midthirties. With Hunt, he shared a passion for work, a healthy partiality for most of the deadly sins to counterbalance it, and his address book. All things considered, they were a good team.

Gray bit his lower lip and rubbed his left earlobe. He always bit his lower lip and rubbed his left earlobe when he was about to talk shop.

"Figured it out yet?" he asked.

"This Borlan business?"

"Uh-huh."

Hunt shook his head before lighting a cigarette. "Beats me."

"I was thinking . . . Suppose Felix has dug up some hot sales prospect for scopes—maybe one of his big Yank customers. He could be setting up some super demo or something."

Hunt shook his head again. "No. Felix wouldn't go and screw up Metadyne's schedules for anything like that. Anyhow, it wouldn't make sense—the obvious thing to do would be to fly the people to where the scope is, not the other way round."

"Mmmm . . . I suppose the same thing applies to the other thought that occurred to me—some kind of crash teach-in for IDCC people."

"Right—same thing goes."

"Mmmm . . ." When Gray spoke again, they had covered another six miles. "How about a takeover? The whole scope thing is big—Felix wants it handled stateside."

Hunt reflected on the proposition. "Not for my money. He's got too much respect for Francis to pull a stunt like that. He knows Francis can handle it okay. Besides, that's not his way of doing things—too underhanded." Hunt paused to exhale a cloud of smoke. "Anyhow, I think there's a lot more to it than meets the eye. From what I saw, even Felix didn't seem too sure what it's all about."

"Mmmm . . ." Gray thought for a while longer before abandoning further excursions into the realms of deductive logic. He contemplated the growing tide of humanity flowing in the general direction of C-deck bar. "My guts are a bit churned up, too," he confessed. "Feels like a crate of Guinness on top of a vindaloo curry. Come on—let's go get a coffee."

In the star-strewn black velvet one thousand miles farther up, the *Sirius Fourteen* communications-link satellite followed, with cold and omniscient electronic eyes, the progress of the skyliner streaking across the mottled sphere below. Among the ceaseless stream of binary data that flowed through its antennae, it identified a call from the Boeing's Gamma Nine master computer, requesting details of the latest weather forecast for northern California. *Sirius Fourteen* flashed the message to *Sirius Twelve*, hanging high over the Canadian Rockies, and *Twelve* in turn beamed it down to the tracking station at Edmonton. From here the message was relayed by optical cable to Vancouver Control and from there by microwave repeaters to the Weather Bureau station at Seattle. A few thousandths of a second later, the answers poured back up the chain in the opposite direction. Gamma Nine digested the information, made one or two minor alterations to its course and flight plan, and sent a record of the dialogue down to Ground Control, Prestwick.

chapter two

It had rained for over two days.

The Engineering Materials Research Department of the Ministry of Space Sciences huddled wetly in a field of the Ural Mountains, an occasional ray of sunlight glinting from a laboratory window or from one of the aluminum domes of the reactor building.

Seated in her office in the analysis section, Valereya

Petrokhovna turned to the pile of reports left on her desk for routine approval. The first two dealt with run-of-the-mill high-temperature corrosion tests. She flicked casually through the pages, glanced at the appended graphs and tables, scrawled her initials on the line provided, and tossed them across into the tray marked "Out." Automatically she began scanning down the first page of number three. Suddenly she stopped, a puzzled frown forming on her face. Leaning forward in her chair, she began again, this time reading carefully and studying every sentence. She finally went back to the beginning once more and worked methodically through the whole document, stopping in places to verify the calculations by means of the keyboard display standing on one side of the desk.

"This is unheard of!" she exclaimed.

For a long time she remained motionless, her eyes absorbed by the raindrops slipping down the window but her mind so focused elsewhere that the sight failed to register. At last she shook herself into movement and, turning again to the keyboard, rapidly tapped in a code. The strings of tensor equations vanished, to be replaced by a profile view of her assistant, hunched over a console in the control room downstairs. The profile transformed itself into a full face as he turned.

"Ready to run in about twenty minutes," he said, anticipating the question. "The plasma's stabilizing now."

"No—this has nothing to do with that," she replied, speaking a little more quickly than usual. "It's about your report 2906. I've just been through my copy."

"Oh . . . yes?" His change in expression betrayed mild apprehension.

"So—a niobium-zirconium alloy," she went on, stating the fact rather than asking a question, "with an unprecedented resistance to high-temperature oxidation and a melting point that, quite frankly, I won't believe until I've done the tests myself."

"Makes our plasma-cans look like butter," Josef agreed.

"Yet despite the presence of niobium, it exhibits a lower neutron-absorption cross section than pure zirconium?"

"Macroscopic, yes—under a millibar per square centimeter."

"Interesting . . ." she mused, then resumed more briskly. "On top of that we have alpha-phase zirconium with silicon, carbon, and nitrogen impurities, yet still with a superb corrosion resistance."

"Hot carbon dioxide, fluorides, organic acids, hypochlorites—we've been through the list. Generally an initial reaction sets in, but it's rapidly arrested by the formation of inert barrier layers. You could probably break it down in stages by devising a cycle of reagents in just the right sequence, but that would take a complete processing plant specially designed for the job!"

"And the microstructure," Valereya said, gesturing toward the papers on her desk. "You've used the description *fibrous*."

"Yes. That's about as near as you can get. The main alloy seems to be formed around a—well, a sort of microcrystalline lattice. It's mainly silicon and carbon, but with local concentrations of some titanium-magnesium compound that we haven't been able to quantify yet. I've never come across anything like it. Any ideas?"

The woman's face held a faraway look for some seconds.

"I honestly don't know what to think at the moment," she confessed. "But I feel this information should be passed higher without delay; it might be more important than it looks. But first I must be sure of my facts. Nikolai can take over down there for a while. Come up to my office and let's go through the whole thing in detail."

chapter three

The Portland headquarters of the Intercontinental Data and Control Corporation lay some forty miles east of the city, guarding the pass between Mount Adams to the north and Mount Hood to the south. It was here that at some time in the remote past a small inland sea had penetrated the Cascade Mountains and carved itself a channel to the Pacific, to become in time the mighty Columbia River.

Fifteen years previously it had been the site of the government-owned Bonneville Nucleonic Weapons Research Laboratory. Here, American scientists, working in collaboration with the United States of Europe Federal Research Institute at Geneva, had developed the theory of meson dynamics that led to the nucleonic bomb. The theory predicted a "clean" reaction with a yield order of magnitude greater than that produced by thermonuclear fusion. The holes they had blown in the Sahara had proved it.

During that period of history, the ideological and racial tensions inherited from the twentieth century were being swept away by the tide of universal affluence and falling birth rates that came with the spread of high-technology living. Traditional rocks of strife and suspicion were being eroded as races, nations, sects, and creeds became inextricably mingled into one huge, homogeneous global society. As the territorial irrationalities of long-dead politicians resolved themselves and the adolescent nation-states matured, the defense budgets of the superpowers were progressively reduced year by year. The advent of the nucleonic bomb served only to accelerate what would have happened anyway. By universal assent, world demilitarization became fact.

One sphere of activity that benefited enormously from the surplus funds and resources that became available after demilitarization was the rapidly expanding United Nations Solar System Exploration Program. Already the list of responsibilities held by this organization was long; it included the operation of all artificial satellites in terrestrial, Lunar, Martian, Venusian, and Solar orbits; the building and operation of all manned bases on Luna and Mars, plus the orbiting laboratories over Venus; the launching of deep-space robot probes and the planning and control of manned missions to the outer planets. UNSSEP was thus expanding at just the right rate and the right time to absorb the supply of technological talent being released as the world's major armaments programs were run down. Also, as nationalism declined and most of the regular armed forces were demobilized, the restless youth of the new generation found outlets for their adventure-lust in the uniformed branches of the UN Space Arm. It was an age that buzzed with excitement and anticipation as the new pioneering frontier began planet-hopping out across the Solar System.

And so NWRL Bonneville had been left with no purpose to serve. This situation did not go unnoticed by the directors of IDCC. Seeing that most of the equipment and permanent installations owned by NWRL could be used in much of the corporation's own research projects, they propositioned the government with an offer to buy the place outright. The offer was accepted and the deal went through. Over the years IDCC had further expanded the site, improved its aesthetics, and eventually established it as their nucleonics research center and world headquarters.

The mathematical theory that had grown out of meson dynamics involved the existence of three hitherto unknown transuranic elements. Although these were purely hypothetical, they were christened hyperium, bonnevillium, and genevium. Theory also predicted that, due to a "glitch" in the transuranic mass-*versus*-binding-energy curve, these elements, once formed, would be stable. They were unlikely to be found occurring naturally, however—not on Earth, anyway. According to the mathematics, only two known situations could give the right conditions for their formation: the core of the detonation of a nucleonic bomb or the collapse of a supernova to a neutron star.

Sure enough, analysis of the dust clouds after the Sahara tests yielded minute traces of hyperium and bonnevillium; genevium was not detected. Nevertheless, the first prediction of the theory was accepted as amply supported. Whether, one day, future generations of scientists would ever verify the second prediction, was another matter entirely.

Hunt and Gray touched down on the rooftop landing pad of the IDCC administration building shortly after fifteen hundred hours. By fifteen thirty they were sitting in leather armchairs facing the desk in Borlan's luxurious office on the tenth floor, while he poured three large measures of scotch at the teak bar built into the left wall. He walked back to the center, passed a glass to each of the Englishmen, went back around the desk, and sat down.

"Cheers, then, guys," he offered. They returned the gesture. "Well," he began, "it's good to see you two again. Trip okay? How'd you make it up so soon—rent a jet?" He opened his cigar box as he spoke and pushed it across the desk toward them. "Smoke?"

"Yes, good trip. Thanks, Felix," Hunt replied. "Avis." He inclined his head toward the window behind Borlan, which presented a panoramic view of pine-covered hills tumbling down to the distant Columbia. "Some scenery."

"Like it?"

"Makes Berkshire look a bit like Siberia."

Borlan looked at Gray. "How are you keeping, Rob?"

The corners of Gray's mouth twitched downwards. "Gutrot."

"Party last night at some bird's," Hunt explained. "Too little blood in his alcohol stream."

"Good time, huh?" Borlan grinned. "Take Francis along?"

"You've got to be joking!"

"Jollificating with the peasantry?" Gray mimicked in the impeccable tone of the English aristocracy. "Good God! Whatever next!"

They laughed. Hunt settled himself more comfortably amid a haze of blue smoke. "How about yourself, Felix?" he asked. "Life still being kind to you?"

Borlan spread his arms wide. "Life's great."

"Angie still as beautiful as the last time I saw her? Kids okay?"

"They're all fine. Tommy's at college now—majoring in physics and astronautical engineering. Johnny goes hiking most weekends with his club, and Susie's added a pair of gerbils and a bear cub to the family zoo."

"So you're still as happy as ever. The responsibilities of power aren't wearing you down yet."

Borlan shrugged and showed a row of pearly teeth. "Do I look like an ulcerated nut midway between heart attacks?"

Hunt regarded the blue-eyed, deep-tanned figure with close-cropped fair hair as Borlan sprawled relaxedly on the other side of the broad mahogany desk. He looked at least ten years younger than the president of any intercontinental corporation had a right to.

For a while the small talk revolved around internal affairs at Metadyne. At last a natural pause presented itself. Hunt sat forward, his elbows resting on his knees, and contemplated the last drop of amber liquid in his glass as he swirled it around first from right to left and then back again. Finally he looked up.

"About the scope, Felix. What's going on, then?"

Borlan had been expecting the question. He straightened slowly in his chair and appeared to think for a moment. At last he said:

"Did you see the call I made to Francis?"

"Yep."

"Then . . ." Borlan didn't seem sure of how to put it. ". . . I don't know an awful lot more than you do." He placed his hands palms-down on the desk in an attitude of candor, but his sigh was that of one not really expecting to be believed. He was right.

"Come on, Felix. Give." Hunt's expression said the rest.

"You must know," Gray insisted. "You fixed it all up."

"Straight." Borlan looked from one to the other. "Look, taking things worldwide, who would you say our biggest customer is? It's no secret—UN Space Arm. We do everything for them from Lunar data links to—to laser terminal clusters and robot probes. Do you know how much revenue I've got forecast from UNSA next fiscal? Two hundred million bucks . . . two hundred million!"

"So?"

"So . . . well—when a customer like that says he needs help, he gets help. I'll tell you what happened. It was like this: UNSA is a big potential user of scopes, so we fed them all the information we've got on what the scope can do and how development is progressing in Francis's neck of the woods. One day—the day before I called Francis—this guy comes to see me all the way from Houston, where one of the big UNSA outfits has its HQ. He's an old buddy of mine—their top man, no less. He wants to know can the scope do this and can it do that, and I tell him sure it can. Then he gives me some examples of the things he's got in mind and he asks if we've got a working model yet. I tell him not yet, but that you've got a working prototype in England; we can arrange for him to go see it if he wants. But that's not what he wants. He wants the prototype down there in Houston, and he wants people who can operate it. He'll pay, he says—we can name our own figure—but he wants that instrument—something to do with a top-priority project down there that's got the whole of UNSA in a flap. When I ask him what it is, he clams up and says it's 'security restricted' for the moment."

"Sounds a funny business," Hunt commented with a frown. "It'll cause some bloody awful problems back at Metadyne."

"I told him all that." Borlan turned his palms upward in a gesture of helplessness. "I told him the score regarding the production schedules and availability forecasts, but he said this thing was big and he wouldn't go causing this kind of trouble if he didn't have a good reason. He wouldn't, either," Borlan added with obvious sincerity. "I've known him for years. He said UNSA would pay compensation for whatever we figure the delays will cost us." Borlan resumed his helpless attitude. "So what was I supposed to do? Was I supposed to tell an old buddy who happens to be my best customer to go take a jump?"

Hunt rubbed his chin, threw back his last drop of scotch, and took a long pensive draw on his cigar.

"And that's it?" he asked at last.

"That's it. Now you know as much as I do—except that since you left England we've received instructions from UNSA to start shipping the prototype to a place near Houston—a biological institute. The bits should start arriving day after tomorrow; the installation crew is already on its way over to begin work preparing the site."

"Houston . . . Does that mean we're going there?" Gray asked.

"That's right, Rob." Borlan paused and scratched the side of his nose. His face screwed itself into a crooked frown. "I, ah—I was wondering . . . The installation crew will need a bit of time, so you two won't be able to do very much there for a while. Maybe you could spend a few days here first, huh? Like, ah . . . meet some of our technical people and clue them in a little on how the scope works—sorta like a teach-in. What d'you say—huh?"

Hunt laughed silently inside. Borlan had been complaining to Forsyth-Scott for months that while the largest potential markets for the scope lay in the USA, practically all of the know-how was confined to Metadyne; the American side of the organization needed more in the way of backup and information than it had been getting.

"You never miss a trick, Felix," he conceded. "Okay, you bum, I'll buy it."

Borlan's face split into a wide grin.

"This UNSA character you were talking about," Gray said, switching the subject back again. "What were the examples?"

"Examples?"

"You said he gave some examples of the kind of thing he was interested in knowing if the scope could do."

"Oh, yeah. Well, lemme see, now . . . He seemed interested in looking at the insides of bodies—bones, tissues, arteries—stuff like that. Maybe he wanted to do an autopsy or something. He also wanted to know if you could get images of what's on the pages of a book, but without the book being opened."

This was too much. Hunt looked from Borlan to Gray and back again, mystified.

"You don't need anything like a scope to perform an autopsy," he said, his voice strained with disbelief.

"Why can't he open a book if he wants to know what's inside?" Gray demanded in a similar tone.

Borlan showed his empty palms. "Yeah. I know. Search me—sounds screwy!"

"And UNSA is paying thousands for this?"

"Hundreds of thousands."

Hunt covered his brow and shook his head in exasperation. "Pour me another scotch, Felix," he sighed.

chapter four

A week later the Mercury Three stood ready for takeoff on the rooftop of IDCC Headquarters. In reply to the queries that appeared on the pilot's console display screen, Hunt specified the Ocean Hotel in the center of Houston as their destination. The DEC minicomputer in the nose made contact with its IBM big brother that lived underground somewhere beneath the Portland Area Traffic Control Center and, after a brief consultation, announced a flight plan that would take them via Salt Lake City, Santa Fe, and Fort Worth. Hunt keyed in his approval, and within minutes the aircar was humming southeast and climbing to take on the challenge of the Blue Mountains looming ahead.

Hunt spent the first part of the journey accessing his office files held on the computers back in Metadyne, to tidy up some of the unfinished business he had left behind. As the waters of the Great Salt Lake came glistening into view, he had just completed the calculations that went with his last experimental report and was adding his conclusions. An hour later, twenty thousand feet up over the Colorado River, he was hooked into MIT and reviewing some of their current publications. After refueling at Santa Fe they spent some time cruising around the city on manual control before finding somewhere suitable for lunch. Later on in the day, airborne over New Mexico, they took an incoming call from IDCC and spent the next two hours in conference with some of Borlan's engineers discussing technicalities of the scope. By the time Fort Worth was behind and the sun well to the west, Hunt was relaxing, watching a murder movie, while Gray slept soundly in the seat beside him.

Hunt looked on with detached interest as the villain was unmasked, the hero claimed the admiring heroine he had just saved from a fate worse than death, and the rolling captions delivered today's moral message for mankind. Stifling a yawn, he flipped the mode switch to MONITOR/CONTROL to blank out the screen and kill the theme music in midbar. He stretched, stubbed out his cigarette, and hauled himself upright in his seat to see how the rest of the universe was getting along.

Far to their right was the Brazos River, snaking south toward the Gulf, embroidered in gold thread on the light blue-gray of the distant haze. Ahead, he could already see the rainbow towers of Houston, standing at attention on the skyline in a tight defensive platoon. Houses were becoming noticeably more numerous in the foreground below. At intervals between them, unidentifiable sprawling constructions began to make their appearance—random collections of buildings, domes, girder lattices, and storage tanks, tied loosely together by tangles of roadways and pipelines. Farther away to the left, a line of perhaps half a dozen slim spires of silver reared up from a shantytown of steel and concrete. He identified them as gigantic Vega satellite ferries standing on their launchpads. They seemed fitting sentinels to guard the approaches to what had become the Mecca of the Space Age.

As Victor Hunt gazed down upon this ultimate expression of man's eternal outward urge, spreading away in every direction below, a vague restlessness stirred somewhere deep inside him.

Hunt had been born in New Cross, the shabby end of East London, south of the river. His father had spent most of his life on strike or in the pub on the corner of the street debating grievances worth going on strike for. When he ran out of money and grievances, he worked on the docks at Deptford.

Victor's mother worked in a bottle factory all day to make the money she lost playing bingo all evening. He spent his time playing football and falling in the Surrey Canal. There was a week when he stayed with an uncle in Worcester, a man who went to work dressed in a suit every day at a place that manufactured computers. And his uncle showed Victor how to wire up a binary adder.

Not long afterward, everyone was yelling at everyone more often than usual, so Victor went to live with his aunt and uncle in Worcester. There he discovered a whole new, undreamed-of world where anything one wanted could be made to happen and magic things really came true—written in strange symbols and mysterious diagrams through the pages of the books on his uncle's shelves.

At sixteen, Victor won a scholarship to Cambridge to study mathematics, physics, and physical electronics. He moved into lodgings there with a fellow student named Mike who sailed boats, climbed mountains, and whose father was a marketing director. When his uncle moved to Africa, Victor was adopted as a second son by Mike's family and spent his holidays at their home in Surrey or climbing with Mike and his friends, first in the hills of the Lake District, North Wales, and Scotland, and later in the Alps. They even tried the Eiger once, but were forced back by bad weather.

After being awarded his doctorate, he remained at the university for some years to further his researches in mathematical nucleonics, his papers on which were by that time attracting widespread attention. Eventually, however, he was forced to come to terms with the fact that a growing predilection for some of the more exciting and attractive ingredients of life could not be reconciled with an income dependent on research grants. For a while he went to work on thermonuclear fusion control for the government, but rebelled at a life made impossible by the meddlings of uninformed bureaucracy. He tried three jobs in private industry but found himself unable to muster more than a cynical indisposition toward playing the game of pretending that annual budgets, gross margins on sales, earnings per share, or discounted cash flows really meant anything that mattered. And so, when he was just turning thirty, the loner he had always been finally asserted itself; he found himself gifted with rare and acknowledged talents, lettered with degrees, credited with achievements, bestowed with awards, cited with honors—and out of a job.

For a while he paid the rent by writing articles for scientific journals. Then, one day, he was offered a free-lance assignment by the chief R & D executive of Metadyne to help out on the mathematical interpretation of some of their experimental work. This assignment led to another, and before long a steady relationship had developed between him and the company. Eventually he agreed to join them full-time in return for use of their equipment and services for his own researches—but under his conditions. And so the Theoretical Studies "Department" came into being.

And now . . . something was missing. The something within him that had been awakened long ago in childhood would always crave new worlds to discover. And as he gazed out at the Vega ships . . .

His thoughts were interrupted as a stream of electromagnetic vibrations from somewhere below was transformed into the code which alerted the Mercury's flight-control processor. The stubby wing outside the cockpit dipped and the aircar turned, beginning the smooth descent that would merge its course into the eastbound traffic corridor that led to the heart of the city at two thousand feet.

chapter five

The morning sun poured in through the window and accentuated the chiseled crags of the face staring out, high over the center of Houston. The squat, stocky frame, conceivably modeled on that of a Sherman tank, threw a square slab of shadow on the carpet behind. The stubby fingers hammered a restless tattoo on the glass. Gregg Caldwell, executive director of the Navigation and Communications Division of UN Space Arm, reflected on developments so far.

Just as he'd expected, now that the initial disbelief and excitement had worn off, everyone was jostling for a slice of the action. In fact, more than a few of the big wheels in some divisions—Biosciences, Chicago, and Space Medicine, Farnborough, for instance—were mincing no words in asking just how Navcomms came to be involved at all, let alone running the show, since the project obviously had no more connection with the business of navigation than it had with communication. The down-turned corners of Caldwell's mouth shifted back slightly in something that almost approached a smile of anticipation. So, the knives were being sharpened, were they? That was okay by him; he could do with a fight. After more than twenty years of hustling his way to the top of one of the biggest divisions of the Space Arm, he was a seasoned veteran at infighting—and he hadn't lost a drop of blood yet. Maybe this was an area in which Navcomms hadn't had much involvement before; maybe the whole thing was bigger than Navcomms could handle; maybe it was bigger than UNSA could handle; but—that was the way it was. It had chosen to fall into Navcomms' lap and that was where it was going to stay. If anyone wanted to help out, that was fine—but the project was stamped as Navcomms-controlled. If they didn't like it, let them try to change it. Man—let 'em try!

His thoughts were interrupted by the chime of the console built into the desk behind him. He turned around, flipped a switch, and answered in a voice of baritone granite:

"Caldwell."

Lyn Garland, his personal assistant, greeted him from the screen. She was twenty-eight, pretty, and had long red hair and big, brown, intelligent eyes.

"Message from Reception. Your two visitors from IDCC are here Dr. Hunt and Mr. Gray."

"Bring them straight up. Pour some coffee. You'd better sit in with us."

"Will do."

Ten minutes later formalities had been exchanged and everyone was seated. Caldwell regarded the Englishmen in silence for a few seconds, his lips pursed and his bushy brows gnarled in a knot across his forehead. He leaned forward and interlaced his fingers on the desk in front of him.

"About three weeks ago I attended a meeting at one of our Lunar survey bases—Copernicus Three," he said. "A lot of excavation and site-survey work is going on in that area, much of it in connection with new construction programs. The meeting was attended by scientists from Earth and from some of the bases up there, a few people on the engineering side and certain members of the uniformed branches of the Space Arm. It was called following some strange discoveries there—discoveries that make even less sense now than they did then."

He paused to gaze from one to the other. Hunt and Gray returned the look without speaking. Caldwell continued: "A team from one of the survey units was engaged in mapping out possible sites for clearance radars. They were operating in a remote sector, well away from the main area being leveled . . ."

As he spoke, Caldwell began operating the keyboard recessed into one side of his desk. With a nod of his head he indicated the far wall, which was made up of a battery of display screens. One of the screens came to life to show the title sheet of a file, marked obliquely with the word RESTRICTED in red. This disappeared to be replaced by a contour map of what looked like a rugged and broken stretch of terrain. A slowly pulsing point of light appeared in the center of the picture and began moving across the map as Caldwell rotated a tracker ball set into the panel that held the keyboard. The light halted at a point where the contours indicated the junction of a steep-sided cleft valley with a wider gorge. The cleft valley was narrow and seemed to branch off from the gorge in a rising curve.

"This map shows the area in question," the director resumed. "The cursor shows where a minor cleft joins the main fault running down toward the left. The survey boys left their vehicle at this point and proceeded on up to the cleft on foot, looking for a way to the top of that large rock mass—the one tagged 'five sixty.' " As Caldwell spoke, the pulsing light moved slowly along between the minor sets of contours, tracing out the path taken by the UN team. They watched it negotiate the bend above the mouth of the cleft and proceed some distance farther. The light approached the side of the cleft and touched it at a place where the contours merged into a single heavy line. There it stopped.

"Here the side was a sheer cliff about sixty feet high. That was where they came across the first thing that was unusual—a hole in the base of the rock wall. The sergeant leading the group described it as being like a cave. That strike you as odd?"

Hunt raised his eyebrows and shrugged. "Caves don't grow on moons," he said simply.

"Exactly."

The screen now showed a photo view of the area, apparently taken from the spot at which the survey vehicle had been parked. They recognized the break in the wall of the gorge where the cleft joined it. The cleft was higher up than had been obvious from the map and was approached by a ramp of loose rubble. In the background they could see a squat tower of rock flattened on top—presumably the one marked "560" on the map. Caldwell allowed them some time to reconcile the picture with the map before bringing up the second frame. It showed a view taken high up, this time looking into the mouth of the cleft. A series of shots then followed, progressing up to and beyond the bend. "These are stills from a movie record," Caldwell commented. "I won't bother with the whole set." The final frame in the sequence showed a hole in the rock about five feet across.

"Holes like this aren't unknown on the Moon," Caldwell remarked. "But they are rare enough to prompt our men into taking a closer look. The inside was a bit of a mess. There had been a rockfall—maybe several falls; not much room—just a heap of rubble and dust . . . at first sight, anyway." A new picture on the screen confirmed this statement. "But when they got to probing around a bit more, they came across something that was really unusual. Underneath they found a body—dead!"

The picture changed again to show another view of the interior, taken from the same angle as the previous one. This time, however, the subject was the top half of a human figure lying amid the rubble and debris, apparently at the stage of being half uncovered. It was clad in a space suit which, under the layer of gray-white dust, appeared to be bright red. The helmet seemed intact, but it was impossible to make out any details of the face behind the visor because of the reflected camera light. Caldwell allowed them plenty of time to study the picture and reflect on these facts before speaking again.

"That is the body. I'll answer some of the more obvious questions before you ask. First—no, we don't know who he is—or was—so we call him Charlie. Second—no, we don't know for sure what killed him. Third—no, we don't know where he came from." The executive director caught the puzzled look on Hunt's face and raised his eyebrows inquiringly.

"Accidents can happen, and it's not always easy to say what caused them—I'll buy that," Hunt said. "But to not know who he is . . . ? I mean, he must have carried some kind of ID card; I'd have thought he'd have to. And even if he didn't, he must be from one of the UN bases up there. Someone must have noticed he was missing."

For the first time the flicker of a smile brushed across Caldwell's face.

"Of course we checked with all the bases, Dr. Hunt. Results negative. But that was just the beginning. You see, when they got him back to the labs for a more thorough check, a number of peculiarities began to emerge which the experts couldn't explain—and, believe me, we've had enough brains in on this. Even after we brought him back here, the situation didn't get any better. In fact, the more we find out, the worse it gets."

" 'Back here'? You mean . . . ?"

"Oh, yes. Charlie's been shipped back to Earth. He's over at the Westwood Biological Institute right now—a few miles from here. We'll go and have a look at him later on today."

Silence reigned for what seemed like a long time as Hunt and Gray digested the rapid succession of new facts. At last Gray offered:

"Maybe somebody bumped him off for some reason?"

"No, Mr. Gray, you can forget anything like that." Caldwell waited a few more seconds. "Let me say that from what little we do know so far, we can state one or two things with certainty. First, Charlie did not come from any of the bases established to date on Luna. Furthermore"—Caldwell's voice slowed to an ominous rumble—"he did not originate from any nation of the world as we know it today. In fact, it is by no means certain that he originated from this planet at all!"

His eyes traveled from Hunt to Gray, then back again, taking in the incredulous stares that greeted his words. Absolute silence enveloped the room. A suspense almost audible tore at their nerves.

Caldwell's finger stabbed at the keyboard.

The face leaped out at them from the screen in grotesque close-up, skull-like, the skin shriveled and darkened like ancient parchment, and stretched back over the bones to uncover two rows of grinning teeth. Nothing remained of the eyes but a pair of empty pits, staring sightlessly out through dry, leathery lids.

Caldwell's voice, now a chilling whisper, hissed through the fragile air.

"You see, gentlemen—Charlie died over fifty thousand years ago!"

chapter six

Dr. Victor Hunt stared absently down at the bird's-eye view of the outskirts of Houston sliding by below the UNSA jet. The mind-numbing impact of Caldwell's revelations had by this time abated sufficiently for him to begin putting together in his mind something of a picture of what it all meant.

Of Charlie's age there could be no doubt. All living organisms take into their bodies known proportions of the radioactive isotopes of carbon and certain other elements. During life, an organism maintains a constant ratio of these isotopes to "normal" ones, but when it dies and intake ceases, the active isotopes are left to decay in a predictable pattern. This mechanism provides, in effect, a highly reliable clock, which begins to run at the moment of death. Analysis of the decay residues enables a reliable figure to be calculated for how long the clock has been running. Many such tests had been performed on Charlie, and all the results agreed within close limits.

Somebody had pointed out that the validity of this method rested on the assumptions that the composition of whatever Charlie ate, and the constituents of whatever atmosphere he breathed, were the same as for modern man on modern Earth. Since Charlie might not be from Earth, this assumption could not be made. It hadn't taken long, however, for this point to be settled conclusively. Although the functions of most of the devices contained in Charlie's backpack were still to be established, one assembly had been identified as an ingeniously constructed miniature nuclear power plant. The U^{235} fuel pellets were easily located and analysis of their decay products yielded a second, independent answer, although a less accurate one. The power unit in Charlie's backpack had been made some fifty thousand years previously. The further implication of this was that since the first set of test results was thus substantiated, it seemed to follow that in terms of air and food supply, there could have been little abnormal about Charlie's native environment.

Now, Charlie's kind, Hunt told himself, must have evolved to their human form somewhere. That this "somewhere" was either Earth or not Earth was fairly obvious, the rules of basic logic admitting no other possibility. He traced back over what he could recall of the conventional account of the evolution of terrestrial life forms and wondered if, despite the generations of painstaking effort and research that had been devoted to the subject, there might after all be more to the story than had up until then been so confidently supposed. Several thousands of millions of years was a long time by anybody's standards; was it so totally inconceivable that somewhere in all those gulfs of uncertainty, there could be enough room to lose an advanced line of human descent which had flourished and died out long before modern man began his own ascent?

On the other hand, the fact that Charlie was found on the Moon presupposed a civilization sufficiently advanced technologically to send him there. Surely, on the way toward developing space flight, they would have evolved a worldwide technological society, and in doing so would have made machines, erected structures, built cities, used metals, and left all the other hallmarks of progress. If such a civilization had once existed on Earth, surely centuries of exploration and excavation couldn't have avoided stumbling on at least some traces of it. But not one instance of any such discovery had ever been recorded. Although the conclusion rested squarely on negative evidence, Hunt could not, even with his tendency toward open-mindedness, accept that an explanation along these lines was even remotely probable.

The only alternative, then, was that Charlie came from somewhere else. Clearly this could not be the Moon itself: It was too small to have retained an atmosphere anywhere near long enough for life to have started at all, let alone reach an advanced level—and of course, his spacesuit showed he was just as much an alien there as was man.

That only left some other planet. The problem here lay in Charlie's undoubted human form, which Caldwell had stressed although he hadn't elected to go into detail. Hunt knew that the process of natural evolution was accepted as occurring through selection, over a long period, from a purely random series of genetic mutations. All the established rules and principles dictated that the appearance of two identical end products from two completely isolated families of evolution, unfolding independently in different corners of the universe, just couldn't happen. Hence, if Charlie came from somewhere else, a whole branch of accepted scientific theory would come crashing down in ruins. So—Charlie couldn't possibly have come from Earth. Neither could he possibly have come from anywhere else. Therefore, Charlie couldn't exist. But he did.

Hunt whistled silently to himself as the full implications of the thing began to dawn on him. There was enough here to keep the whole scientific world arguing for decades.

Inside the Westwood Biological Institute, Caldwell, Lyn Garland, Hunt, and Gray were met by a Professor Christian Danchekker. The Englishmen recognized him, since Caldwell had introduced them earlier by vi-phone. On their way to the laboratory section of the institute, Danchekker briefed them further.

In view of its age, the body was in an excellent state of preservation. This was due to the environment in which it had been found—a germ-free hard vacuum and an abnormally low temperature sustained, even at Lunar noon, by the insulating mass of the surrounding rock. These conditions had prevented any onset of bacterial decay of the soft tissues. No rupture had been found in the space suit. So the currently favored theory regarding cause of death was that a failure in the life-support system had resulted in a sudden fall in temperature. The body had undergone deep freezing in a short space of time with a consequent abrupt cessation of metabolic processes; ice crystals, formed from body fluids, had caused widespread laceration of cell membranes. In the course of time most of the lighter substances had sublimed, mainly from the outer layers, to leave behind a blackened, shriveled, natural kind of mummy. The most seriously affected parts were the eyes, which, composed for the most part of fluids, had collapsed completely, leaving just a few flaky remnants in their sockets.

A major problem was the extreme fragility of the remains, which made any attempt at detailed examination next to impossible. Already the body had undergone some irreparable damage in the course of being transported to Earth, and in the removal of the space suit; only the body's being frozen solid during these operations had prevented the situation from being even worse. That was when somebody had thought of Felix Borden at IDCC and an instrument being developed in England that could display the insides of things. The result had been Caldwell's visit to Portland.

Inside the first laboratory it was dark. Researchers were using binocular microscopes to study sets of photographic transparencies arranged on several glass-topped tables, illuminated from below. Danchekker selected some plates from a pile and, motioning the others to follow, made his way over to the far wall. He positioned the first three of the plates on an eye-level viewing screen, snapped on the screen light, and stepped back to join the expectant semicircle. The plates were X-ray images showing the front and side views of a skull. Five faces, thrown into sharp relief against the darkness of the room behind, regarded the screen in solemn silence. At last Danchekker moved a pace forward, at the same time half turning toward them.

"I need not, I feel, tell you who this is." His manner was somewhat stiff and formal. "A skull, fully human in every detail—as far as it is possible to ascertain by X rays, anyway." Danchekker traced along the line of the jaw with a ruler he had picked up from one of the tables. "Note the formation of the teeth—on either side we see two incisors, one canine, two premolars, and three molars. This pattern was established quite early in the evolutionary line that leads to our present day anthropoids, including of course, man. It distinguishes our common line of descent from other offshoots, such as the New World monkeys with a count of two, one, three, three."

"Hardly necessary here," Hunt commented. "There's nothing apelike or monkeylike about that picture."

"Quite so, Dr. Hunt," Danchekker returned with a nod. "The reduced canines, not interlocking with the upper set, and the particular pattern of the cusps—these are distinctly human characteristics. Note also the flatness of the lower face, the absence of any bony brow ridges . . . high forehead and sharply angled jaw . . . well-rounded braincase. These are all features of true man as we know him today, features that derive directly from his earlier ancestors. The significance of these details in this instance is that they demonstrate an example of true man, not something that merely bears a superficial resemblance to him."

The professor took down the plates and momentarily flooded the room with a blaze of light. A muttered profanity from one of the scientists at the tables made him switch off the light hastily. He picked up three more plates, set them up on the screen, and switched on the light to reveal the side view of a torso, an arm, and a foot.

"Again, the trunk shows no departure from the familiar human pattern. Same rib structure . . . broad chest with well-developed clavicles . . . normal pelvic arrangement. The foot is perhaps the most specialized item in the human skeleton and is responsible for man's uniquely powerful stride and somewhat peculiar gait. If you are familiar with human anatomy, you will find that this foot resembles ours in every respect."

"I'll take your word for it," Hunt conceded, shaking his head. "Nothing remarkable, then."

"The most significant thing, Dr. Hunt, is that nothing *is* remarkable."

Danchekker switched off the screen and returned the plates to the pile. Caldwell turned to Hunt as they began walking back toward the door.

"This kind of thing doesn't happen every day," he grunted. "An understandable reason for wanting some . . . er . . . irregular action, you would agree?"

Hunt agreed.

A passage, followed by a short flight of stairs and another passage, brought them to a set of double doors bearing the large red sign STERILE AREA. In the anteroom behind, they put on surgical masks, caps, gowns, gloves, and overshoes before passing out through another door at the opposite end.

In the first section they came to, samples of skin and other tissues were being examined. By reintroducing the substance believed to have escaped over the centuries, specimens had been restored to what were hoped to be close approximations to their original conditions. In general, the findings merely confirmed that Charlie was as human chemically as he was structurally. Some unfamiliar enzymes had, however, been discovered. Dynamite computer simulation suggested that these were designed to assist in the breakdown of proteins unlike anything found in the diet of modern man. Danchekker was inclined to dismiss this peculiarity with the rather vague assertion that "Times change," a remark which Hunt appeared to find disturbing.

The next laboratory was devoted to an investigation of the space suit and the various other gadgets and implements found on and around the body. The helmet was the first exhibit to be presented for inspection. Its back and crown were made of metal, coated dull black and extending forward to the forehead to leave a transparent visor extending from ear to ear. Danchekker held it up for them to see and pushed his hand up through the opening at the neck. They could see clearly the fingers of his rubber glove through the facepiece.

"Observe," he said, picking up a powerful xenon flash lamp from the bench. He directed the beam through the facepiece, and a circle of the material immediately turned dark. They could see through the area around the circle that the level of illumination inside the helmet had not changed appreciably. He moved the lamp around and the dark circle followed it across the visor.

"Built-in antiglare," Gray observed.

"The visor is fabricated from a self-polarizing crystal," Danchekker informed them. "It responds directly to incident light in a fashion that is linear up to high intensities. The visor is also effective with gamma radiation."

Hunt took the helmet to examine it more closely. The blend of curves that made up the outside contained little of interest, but on turning it over he found that a section of the inner surface of the crown had been removed to reveal a cavity, empty except for some tiny wires and a set of fixing brackets.

"That recess contained a complete miniature communications station," Danchekker supplied, noting his interest. "Those grilles at the sides concealed the speakers, and a microphone is built into the top, just above the forehead." He reached inside and drew down a small retractable binocular periscope from inside the top section of the helmet, which clicked into position immediately in front of where the eyes of the wearer would be. "Built-in video, too," he explained. "Controlled from a panel on the chest. The small hole in the front of the crown contained a camera assembly."

Hunt continued to turn the trophy over in his hands, studying it from all angles in absorbed silence. Two weeks ago he had been sitting at his desk in Metadyne doing a routine job. Never in his wildest fantasies had he imagined that he would one day come to be holding in his hands something that might well turn out to be one of the most exciting discoveries of the century, if not in the whole of history. Even his agile mind was having difficulty taking it all in.

"Can we see some of the electronics that were in here?" he asked after a while.

"Not today," Caldwell replied. "The electronics are being studied at another location—that goes for most of what was in the backpack, too. Let's just say for now that when it came to molecular circuits, these guys knew their business."

"The backpack is a masterpiece of precision engineering in miniature," Danchekker continued, leading them to another part of the laboratory. "The prime power source for all the equipment and heating had been identified, and is nuclear in nature. In addition, there was a water recirculation plant, life-support system, standby power and communications system, and oxygen liquefaction plant—all in that!" He held up the casing of the stripped-down backpack for them to see, then tossed it back on the bench. "Several other devices were also included, but their purpose is still obscure. Behind you, you will see some personal effects."

The professor moved around to indicate an array of objects taken from the body and arranged neatly on another bench like museum exhibits.

"A pen—not dissimilar to a familiar pressurized ballpoint type; the top may be rotated to change color." He picked up a collection of metallic strips that hinged into a casing, like the blades of a pocketknife. "We suspect that these are keys of some kind because they have magnetic codes written on their surfaces."

To one side was a collection of what looked like crumpled pieces of paper, some with groups of barely discernible symbols written in places. Next to them were two pocket-size books, each about half an inch thick.

"Assorted oddments," Danchekker said, looking along the bench. "The documents are made from a kind of plasticized fiber. Fragments of print and handwriting are visible in places— quite unintelligible, of course. The material has deteriorated severely and tends to disintegrate at the slightest touch." He nodded toward Hunt. "This is another area where we hope to learn as much as we can with the Trimagniscope before we risk anything else." He pointed to the remaining articles and listed them without further elaboration. "Pen-size torch; some kind of pocket flamethrower, we think; knife; pen-size electric pocket drill with a selection of bits in the handle; food and drink containers—they connect via valves in the tubes inside the lower part of the helmet; pocket folder, like a wallet—too fragile to open; changes of underclothes; articles for personal hygiene; odd pieces of metal, purpose unknown. There were also a few electronic devices in the pockets; they have been sent elsewhere along with the rest."

The party halted on the way back to the door to gather around the scarlet space suit, which had been reassembled on a life-size dummy standing on a small plinth. At first sight the proportions of the figure seemed to differ subtly from those of an average man, the build being slightly on the stocky side and the limbs a little short for the height of about five feet, six inches. However, since the suit was not designed for a close fit, it was difficult to be sure. Hunt noticed the soles of the boots were surprisingly thick.

"Sprung interior," Danchekker supplied, following his gaze.

"What's that?"

"It's quite ingenious. The mechanical properties of the sole material vary with applied pressure. With the wearer walking at normal speed, the sole would remain mildly flexible. Under impact, however—for example, if he jumped—it assumes the characteristics of a stiff spring. It's an ideal device for kangarooing along in lunar gravity—utilizing conditions of reduced weight but normal inertia to advantage."

"And now, gentlemen," said Caldwell, who had been following events with evident satisfaction, "the moment I guess you've been waiting for—let's have a look at Charlie himself."

An elevator took them down to the subterranean levels of the institute. They emerged into a somber corridor of white-tiled walls and white lights, and followed it to a large metal door. Danchekker pressed his thumb against a glass plate set into the wall and the door slid silently aside on recognition of his print. At the same time, a diffuse but brilliant white glow flooded the room inside.

It was cold. Most of the walls were taken up by control panels, analytical equipment, and glass cabinets containing rows of gleaming instruments. Everything was light green, as in an operating theater, and gave the same impression of surgical cleanliness. A large table, supported by a single central pillar, stood to one side. On top of it was what looked like an oversize glass coffin. Inside that lay the body. Saying nothing, the professor led them across the room, his overshoes squeaking on the rubbery floor as he walked. The small group converged around the table and stared in silent awe at the figure before them.

It lay half covered by a sheet that stretched from its lower chest to its feet. In these clinical surroundings, the gruesome impact of the sight that had leaped at them from the screen in Caldwell's office earlier in the day was gone. All that remained was an object of scientific curiosity. Hunt found it overwhelming to stand at arm's length from the remains of a being who had lived as part of a civilization, had grown and passed away, before the dawn of history. For what seemed a long time he stared mutely, unable to frame any intelligent question or comment, while speculations tumbled through his mind on the life and times of this strange creature. When he eventually jolted himself back to the present, he realized that the professor was speaking again.

". . . Naturally, we are unable to say at this stage if it was simply a genetic accident peculiar to this individual or a general characteristic of the race to which he belonged, but measurements of the eye sockets and certain parts of the skull indicate that, relative to his size, his eyes were somewhat larger than our own. This suggests that he was not accustomed to sunlight as bright as ours. Also, note the length of the nostrils. Allowing for shrinkage with age, they are constructed to provide a longer passage for the prewarming of air. This suggests that he came from a relatively cool climate . . . the same thing can be observed in modern Eskimos."

Danchekker made a sweeping gesture that took in the whole length of the body. "Again, the rather squat and stocky build is consistent with the idea of a cool native environment. A fat, round object presents less surface area per unit volume than a long, thin one and thus loses less heat. Contrast the compact build of the Eskimo with the long limbs and lean body of the Negro. We know that at the time Charlie was alive the Earth was just entering the last cold period of the Pleistocene Ice Age. Life forms in existence at that time would have had about a million years to adapt to the cold. Also, there is strong reason to believe that ice ages are caused by a reduction in the amount of solar radiation falling on Earth, brought about by the Sun and planets passing through exceptionally dusty patches of space. For example, ice ages occur approximately every two hundred and fifty million years; this is also the period of rotation of our galaxy—surely more than mere coincidence. Thus, this being's evident adaptation to cold, the suggestion of a lower level of daylight, and his established age all correlate well."

Hunt looked at the professor quizzically. "You're pretty sure already, then, that's he's from Earth?" he said in a tone of mild surprise. "I mean—it's early days yet, surely?"

Danchekker drew back his head disdainfully and screwed up his eyebrows to convey a shadow of irritation. "Surely it is quite obvious, Dr. Hunt." The tone was that of a professor reproaching an errant student. "Consider the things we have observed: the teeth, the skull, the bones, the types and layout of organs. I have deliberately drawn attention to these details to emphasize his kinship to ourselves. It is clear that his ancestry is the same as ours." He waved his hand to and fro in front of his face. "No, there can be no doubt whatsoever. Charlie evolved from the same stock as modern man and all the other terrestrial primates."

Gray looked dubious. "Well, I dunno," he said. "I think Vic's got a point. I mean, if his lot did come from Earth, you'd have expected someone to have found out about it before now, wouldn't you."

Danchekker sighed with an overplay of indifference. "If you wish to doubt my word, you have, of course, every right to do so," he said. "However, as a biologist and an anthropologist, I for my part see more than sufficient evidence to support the conclusions I have stated."

Hunt seemed far from satisfied and started to speak again, but Caldwell intervened.

"Cool it, you guys. D'you think we haven't had enough arguments like this around here for the last few weeks?"

"I really think it's about time we had some lunch," Lyn Garland interrupted with well-timed tact.

Danchekker turned abruptly and began walking back toward the door, reciting statistics on the density of body hair and the thickness of subdermal layers of fat, apparently having dismissed the incident from his mind. Hunt paused to survey the body once more before turning to follow, and in doing so, he caught Gray's eyes for an instant. The engineer's mouth twitched briefly at the corners; Hunt gave a barely perceptible shrug. Caldwell, still standing by the foot of the table, observed the brief exchange. He turned his head to look after Danchekker and then back again at the Englishmen, his eyes narrowing thoughtfully. At last he fell in a few paces behind the group, nodding slowly to himself and permitting a faint smile.

The door slid silently into place and the room was once more plunged into darkness.

chapter seven

Hunt brought his hands up to his shoulders, stretched his body back over his chair, and emitted a long yawn at the ceiling of the laboratory. He held the position for a few seconds, and then collapsed back with a sigh. Finally he rubbed his eyes with his knuckles, hauled himself upright to face the console in front of him once more, and returned his gaze to the three-foot-high wall of the cylindrical glass tank by his side.

The image of the Trimagniscope tube was an enlarged view of one of the pocket-size books found on the body, which Danchekker had shown them on their first day in Houston three weeks before. The book itself was enclosed in the scanner module of the machine, on the far side of the room. The scope was adjusted to generate a view that followed the change in density along the boundary surface of the selected page, producing an image of the lower section of the book only; it was as if the upper part had been removed, like a cut deck of cards. Because of the age and condition of the book, however, the characters on the pages thus exposed tended to be of poor quality and in some places were incomplete. The next step would be to scan the image optically with TV cameras and feed the encoded pictures into the Navcomms computer complex. The raw input would then be processed by pattern recognition techniques and statistical techniques to produce a second, enhanced copy with many of the missing character fragments restored.

Hunt cast his eye over the small monitor screens on his console, each of which showed a magnified view of a selected area of the page, and tapped some instructions into his keyboard.

"There's an unresolved area on monitor five," he announced. "Cursors read X, twelve hundred to thirteen eighty; Y, nine ninety and, ah, ten seventy-five."

Rob Gray, seated at another console a few feet away and almost surrounded by screens and control panels, consulted one of the numerical arrays glowing before him.

"Z mod's linear across the field," he advised. "Try a block elevate?"

"Can do. Give it a try."

"Setting Z step two hundred through two ten . . . increment point one . . . step zero point five seconds."

"Check." Hunt watched the screen as the surface picked out through the volume of the book became distorted locally and the picture on the monitor began to change.

"Hold it there," he called.

Gray hit a key. "Okay?"

Hunt contemplated the modified view for a while.

"The middle of the element's clear now," he pronounced at last. "Fix the new plane inside forty percent. I still don't like the strip around it, though. Give me a vertical slice through the center point."

"Which screen d'you want it on?"

"Ah . . . number seven."

"Coming up."

The curve, showing a cross section of the page surface through the small area they were working on, appeared on Hunt's console. He studied it for a while, then called:

"Run an interpolation across the strip. Set thresholds of, say, minus five and thirty-five percent on Y."

"Parameters set . . . Interpolator running . . . run complete," Gray recited. "Integrating into scan program now." Again the picture altered subtly. There was a noticeable improvement.

"Still not right around the edge," Hunt said. "Try weighting the quarter and three-quarter points by plus ten. If that doesn't work, we'll have to break it down into isodepth bands."

"Plus ten on point two five zero and point seven five zero," Gray repeated as he operated the keys. "Integrated. How's it look?"

On the element of surface displayed on Hunt's monitor, the fragments of characters had magically assembled themselves into recognizable shapes. Hunt nodded with satisfaction.

"That'll do. Freeze it in. Okay—that clears that one. There's another messy patch up near the top right. Let's have a go at that next."

Life had been reduced to much this kind of pattern ever since the day the installation of the scope was completed. They had spent the first week obtaining a series of cross-sectional views of the body itself. This exercise had proved memorable on account of the mild discomfort and not so mild inconvenience of having to work in electrically heated suits, following the medical authority's insistence that Charlie be kept in a refrigerated environment. It had proved something of an anticlimax. The net results were that, inside as well as out, Charlie was surprisingly—or not so surprisingly, depending on one's point of view—human. During the second week they had begun examining the articles found on the body, especially the pieces of "paper" and the pocketbooks. This investigation had proved more interesting.

Of the symbols contained in the documents, numerals were the first to be identified. A team of cryptographers, assembled at Navcomms HQ, soon worked out the counting system, which turned out to be based on twelve digits rather than ten and employed a positional notation with the least significant digit to the left. Deciphering the nonnumeric symbols was proving more difficult. Linguists from institutions and universities in several countries had linked into Houston and, with the aid of batteries of computers, were attempting to make some sense of the language of the Lunarians, as Charlie's race had come to be called in commemoration of his place of discovery. So far their efforts had yielded little more than that the Lunarian alphabet comprised thirty-seven characters, was written horizontally from right to left, and contained the equivalent of upper-case characters.

Progress, however, was not considered to be bad for so short a time. Most of the people involved were aware that even this much could never have been achieved without the scope, and already the names of the two Englishmen were well-known around the division. The scope attracted a lot of interest among the UNSA technical personnel, and most evenings saw a stream of visitors arriving at the Ocean Hotel, all curious to meet the coinventors of the instrument and to learn more about its principles of operation. Before long, the Ocean became the scene of a regular debating society where anybody who cared to could give free rein to his wildest speculations concerning the Charlie mystery, free from the constraints of professional caution and skepticism that applied during business hours.

Caldwell, of course, knew everything that was said by anybody at the Ocean and what everybody else thought about it, since Lyn Garland was present on most nights and represented the next best thing to a hot line back to the HQ building. Nobody minded that much—after all, it was only part of her job. They minded even less when she began turning up with some of the other girls from Navcomms in tow, adding a refreshing party atmosphere to the whole proceedings. This development met with the full approval of the visitors from out-of-town; however, it had led to somewhat strained relationships on the domestic front for one or two of the locals.

Hunt jabbed at the keyboard for the last time and sat back to inspect the image of the completed page.

"Not bad at all," he said. "That one won't need much enhancement."

"Good," Gray agreed. He lit a cigarette and tossed the pack across to Hunt without being asked. "Optical encoding's finished," he added, glancing at a screen. "That's number sixty-seven tied up." He rose from his chair and moved across to stand beside Hunt's console to get a better view of the image in the tank. He looked at it for a while without speaking.

"Columns of numbers," he observed needlessly at last. "Looks like some kind of table."

"Looks like it . . ." Hunt's voice sounded far away.

"Mmm . . . rows and columns . . . thick lines and thin lines . . . Could be anything—mileage chart, wire gauges, some sort of timetable. Who knows?"

Hunt made no reply but continued to blow occasional clouds

of smoke at the glass, cocking his head first to one side and then to the other.

"None of the numbers there are very large," he commented after a while. "Never more than two positions in any place. That gives us what in a duodecimal system? One hundred and forty-three at the most." Then as an afterthought, "I wonder what the biggest is."

"I've got a table of Lunarian–decimal equivalents somewhere. Any good?"

"No, don't bother for now. It's too near lunch. Maybe we could have a look at it over a beer tonight at the Ocean."

"I can pick out their one and two," Gray said. "And three and . . . Hey! What do you know—look at the right-hand columns of those big boxes. Those numbers are in ascending order!"

"You're right. And look—the same pattern repeats over and over in every one. It's some kind of cyclic array." Hunt thought for a moment, his face creased in a frown of concentration. "Something else, too—see those alphabetic groups down the sides? The same groups reappear at intervals all across the page . . ." He broke off again and rubbed his chin.

Gray waited perhaps ten seconds. "Any ideas?"

"Dunno . . . Sets of numbers starting at one and increasing by one every time. Cyclic . . . an alphabetic label tagged on to each repeating group. The whole pattern repeating again inside bigger groups, and bigger groups repeat again. Suggests some sort of order. Sequence . . ."

His mumblings were interrupted as the door opened behind them. Lyn Garland walked in.

"Hi, you guys. What's showing today?" She moved over to stand between them and peered into the tank. "Say, tables! How about that? Where'd they come from, the books?"

"Hello, lovely," Gray said with a grin. "Yep." He nodded in the direction of the scanner.

"Hi," Hunt answered, at last tearing his eyes away from the image. "What can we do for you?"

She didn't reply at once, but continued staring into the tank. "What are they? Any ideas?"

"Don't know yet. We were just talking about it when you came in."

She marched across the lab and bent over to peer into the top of the scanner. The smooth, tanned curve of her leg and the proud thrust of her behind under her thin skirt drew an exchange of approving glances from the two English scientists. She came back and studied the image once more.

"Looks like a calendar, if you ask me," she told them. Her voice left no room for dissent.

Gray laughed. "Calendar, eh? You sound pretty sure of it. What's this—a demonstration of infallible feminine intuition or something?" He was goading playfully.

She turned to confront him with out-thrust jaw and hands planted firmly on hips. "Listen, Limey—I've got a right to an opinion, okay? So, that's what I think it is. That's my opinion."

"Okay, okay." Gray held up his hands. "Let's not start the War of Independence all over again. I'll note it in the lab file: 'Lyn thinks it's a—' "

"Holy Christ!" Hunt cut him off in midsentence. He was staring wide-eyed at the tank. "Do you know, she could be right! She could just be bloody right!"

Gray turned back to face the side of the tank. "How come?"

"Well, look at it. Those larger groups could be something like months, and the labeled sets that keep repeating inside them could be weeks made up of days. After all, days and years have to be natural units in any calendar system. See what I mean?"

Gray looked dubious. "I'm not so sure," he said slowly. "It's nothing like our year, is it? I mean, there's a hell of a lot more than three hundred sixty-five numbers in that lot, and a lot more than twelve months, or whatever they are—aren't there?"

"I know. Interesting?"

"Hey. I'm still here," said a small voice behind them. They moved apart and half turned to let her in on the proceedings.

"Sorry," Hunt said. "Getting carried away." He shook his head and regarded her with an expression of disbelief.

"What on Earth made you say a calendar?"

She shrugged and pouted her lips. "Don't know, really. The book over there looks like a diary. Every diary I ever saw had calendars in it. So, it had to be a calendar."

Hunt sighed. "So much for scientific method. Anyway, let's run a shot of it. I'd like to do some sums on it later." He looked back at Lyn. "No—on second thought, you run it. This is your discovery."

She frowned at him suspiciously. "What d'you want me to do?"

"Sit down there at the master console. That's right. Now activate the control keyboard . . . Press the red button—that one."

"What do I do now?"

"Type this: FC comma DACCO seven slash PCH dot P sixty-seven slash HCU dot one. That means 'functional control mode, data access program subsystem number seven selected, access data file reference "Project Charlie, Book one," page sixty-seven, optical format, output on hard copy unit, one copy.' "

"It does? Really? Great!"

She keyed in the commands as Hunt repeated them more slowly. At once a hum started up in the hard copier, which stood next to the scanner. A few seconds later a sheet of glossy paper flopped into the tray attached to the copier's side. Gray walked over to collect it.

"Perfect," he announced.

"This makes me a scope expert, too," Lyn informed them brightly.

Hunt studied the sheet briefly, nodded, and slipped it into a folder lying on top of the console.

"Doing some homework?" she asked.

"I don't like the wallpaper in my hotel room."

"He's got the theory of relativity all around the bedroom in his flat in Wokingham," Gray confided, ". . . and wave mechanics in the kitchen."

She looked from one to the other curiously. "Do you know, you're crazy. Both of you—you're both crazy. I was always too polite to mention it before, but somebody has to say it."

Hunt gave her a solemn look. "You didn't come all the way over here to tell us we're crazy," he pronounced.

"Know something—you're right. I had to be in Westwood anyway. A piece of news just came in this morning that I thought might interest you. Gregg's been talking to the Soviets. Apparently one of their materials labs has been doing tests on some funny pieces of metal alloy they got hold of—all sorts of unusual properties nobody's ever seen before. And guess what—they dug them up on the Moon, somewhere near Mare Imbrium. And—when they ran some dating tests, they came up with a figure of about fifty thousand years! How about that! Interested?"

Gray whistled.

"It had to be just a matter of time before something else turned up," Hunt said, nodding. "Know any more details?"

She shook her head. " 'Fraid not. But some of the guys might be able to fill you in a bit more at the Ocean tonight. Try Hans if he's there; he was talking a lot to Gregg about it earlier."

Hunt looked intrigued but decided there was little point in pursuing the matter further for the time being.

"How is Gregg?" he asked. "Has he tried smiling lately?"

"Don't be mean," she reproached him. "Gregg's okay. He's busy, that's all. D'you think he didn't have enough to worry about before all this blew up?"

Hunt didn't dispute it. During the few weeks that had passed, he had seen ample evidence of the massive resources Caldwell was marshaling from all around the globe. He couldn't help but be impressed by the director's organizational ability and his ruthless efficiency when it came to annihilating opposition. There were other things, however, about which Hunt harbored mild personal doubts.

"How's it all doing, then?" he asked. His tone was neutral. It did not escape the girl's sharply tuned senses. Her eyes narrowed almost imperceptibly.

"Well, you've seen most of the action so far. How do *you* think it's going?"

He tried to sidestep to avoid her deliberate turning around of the question.

"None of my business, really, is it? We're just the machine minders in all this."

"No, really—I'm interested. What do you think?"

Hunt made a great play of stubbing out his cigarette. He frowned and scratched his forehead.

"You've got rights to opinions, too," she persisted. "Our Constitution says so. So, what's your opinion?"

There was no way off the hook, or of evading those big brown eyes.

"There's no shortage of information turning up," he conceded at last. "The infantry is doing a good job . . ." He let the rider hang.

"But what . . . ?"

Hunt sighed.

"But . . . the interpretation. There's something too dogmatic—too rigid—about the way the big names higher up are using the information. It's as if they can't think outside the ruts they've thought inside for years. Maybe they're overspecialized—won't admit any possibility that goes against what they've always believed."

"For instance?"

"Oh, I don't know . . . Well, take Danchekker, for one. He's always accepted orthodox evolutionary theory—all his life, I suppose; therefore, Charlie must be from Earth. Nothing else is possible. The accepted theory must be right, so that much is fixed; you have to work everything else to fit in with that."

"You think he's wrong? That Charlie came from somewhere else?"

"Hell, I don't know. He could be right. But it's not his conclusion that I don't like; it's his way of getting there. This problem's going to need more flexibility before it's cracked."

Lyn nodded slowly to herself, as if Hunt had confirmed something.

"I thought you might say something like that," she mused. "Gregg will be interested to hear it. He wondered the same thing, too."

Hunt had the feeling that the questions had been more than just an accidental turn of conversation. He looked at her long and hard.

"Why should Gregg be interested?"

"Oh, you'd be surprised. Gregg knows a lot about you two. He's interested in anything anybody has to say. It's people, see—Gregg's a genius with people. He knows what makes them tick. It's the biggest part of his job."

"Well, if it's a people problem he's got," Hunt said. "Why doesn't he fix it?"

Suddenly Lyn switched moods and seemed to make light of the whole subject, as if she had learned all she needed to for the time being.

"Oh, he will—when he gets the feeling that the time's right. He's very good with timing, too." She decided to finish the matter entirely. "Anyhow, it's time for lunch." She stood up and slipped a hand through an arm on either side. "How about two crazy Limeys treating a poor girl from the Colonies to a drink?"

chapter eight

The progress meeting, in the main conference room of the Navcomms Headquarters building, had been in session for just over two hours. About two dozen persons were seated or sprawled around the large table that stood in the center of the room, by now reduced to a shambles of files, papers, overflowing ashtrays, and half-empty glasses.

Nothing really exciting had emerged so far. Various speakers had reported the results of their latest tests, the sum total of their conclusions being that Charlie's circulatory, respiratory, nervous, endocrine, lymphatic, digestive, and every other system anybody could think of were as normal as those of anyone sitting around the table. His bones were the same, his body chemistry was the same, his blood was a familiar grouping. His brain capacity and development were within the normal range for *Homo sapiens*, and evidence suggested that he had been right-handed. The genetic codes carried in his reproductive cells had been analyzed; a computer simulation of combining them with codes donated by an average human female had confirmed that the offspring of such a union would have inherited a perfectly normal set of characteristics.

Hunt tended to remain something of a passive observer of the proceedings, conscious of his status as an unofficial guest and wondering from time to time why he had been invited at all. The only reference made to him so far had been a tribute in Caldwell's opening remarks to the invaluable aid rendered by the Trimagniscope; apart from the murmur of agreement that had greeted this comment, no further mention had been made of either the instrument or its inventor. Lyn Garland had told him: "The meeting's on Monday, and Gregg wants you to be there to answer detailed questions on the scope." So here he was. Thus far, nobody had wanted to know anything detailed about the scope—only about the data it produced. Something gave him the uneasy feeling there was an ulterior motive lurking somewhere.

After dwelling on Charlie's computerized, mathematical sex life, the chair considered a suggestion, put forward by a Texas planetologist sitting opposite Hunt, that perhaps the Lunarians came from Mars. Mars had reached a later phase of planetary evolution than Earth and possibly had evolved intelligent life earlier, too. Then the arguments started. Martian exploration went right back to the 1970s; UNSA had been surveying the surface from satellites and manned bases for years. How come no sign of any Lunarian civilization had showed up? Answer: We've been on the Moon a hell of a lot longer than that and the first traces have only just shown up there. So you could ex pect discovery to occur later on Mars. Objection: If they came from Mars, then their civilization developed on Mars. Signs of a whole civilization should be far more obvious than signs of visits to a place like Earth's Moon—therefore the Lunarians should have been detected a lot sooner on Mars. Answer: Think about the rate of erosion on the Martian surface. The signs could be largely wiped out or buried. At least that could account for there not being any signs on Earth. Somebody then pointed out that this did not solve the problem—all it did was shift it to another place. If the Lunarians came from Mars, evolutionary theory was still in just as big a mess as ever.

So the discussion went on.

Hunt wondered how Rob Gray was getting on back at Westwood. They now had a training schedule to fit in on top of their normal daily data-collection routine. A week or so before, Caldwell had informed them that he wanted four engineers from Navcomms fully trained as Trimagniscope operators. His explanation, that this would allow round-the-clock operation of the scope and hence better productivity from it, had not left Hunt convinced; neither had his further assertion that Navcomms was going to buy itself some of the instruments but needed to get some in-house expertise while they had the opportunity.

Maybe Caldwell intended setting up Navcomms as an independent and self-sufficient scope-operating facility. Why would he do that? Was Forsyth-Scott or somebody else exerting pressure to get Hunt back to England? If this was a prelude to shipping him back, the scope would obviously stay in Houston. That meant that the first thing he'd be pressed into when he got back would be a panic to get the second prototype working. Big deal!

The meeting eventually accepted that the Martian-origin theory created more problems than it solved and, anyway, was pure speculation. Last rites in the form of "No substantiating evidence offered" were pronounced, and the corpse was quietly laid to rest under the epitaph *In Abeyance*, penned in the "Action" columns of the memoranda sheets around the table.

A cryptologist then delivered a long rambling account of the patterns of character groupings that occurred in Charlie's personal documents. They had already completed preliminary processing of all the individual papers, the contents of the wallet, and one of the books; they were about halfway through the second. There were many tables, but nobody knew yet what they meant; some structured lines of symbols suggested mathematical formulas; certain page and section headings matched entries in the text. Some character strings appeared with high frequency, some with less; some were concentrated on a few pages, while others were evenly spread throughout. There were lots of figures and statistics. Despite the enthusiasm of the speaker, the mood of the room grew heavy and the questions fewer. They knew he was a bright guy; they wished he'd stop telling them.

At length, Danchekker, who had been noticeably silent through most of the proceedings and appeared to be growing increasingly impatient as they continued, obtained leave from the chair to address the meeting. He rose to his feet, clasped his lapels, and cleared his throat. "We have devoted as much time as can be excused to exploring improbable and far-flung suggestions which, as we have seen, turn out to be fallacious." He spoke confidently, taking in the length of the table with side-to-side swings of his body. "The time has surely come, gentlemen, for us to dally no longer, but to concentrate our efforts on what must be the only viable line of reasoning open to us. I state, quite categorically, that the race of beings to whom we have come to refer as the Lunarians originated here, on Earth, as did the rest of us. Forget all your fantasies of visitors from other worlds, interstellar travelers, and the like. The Lunarians were simply products of a civilization that developed here on our own planet and died out for reasons we have yet to determine. What, after all, is so strange about that? Civilizations have grown and passed away in the brief span of our more orthodox history, and no doubt others will continue the pattern. This conclusion follows from comprehensive and consistent evidence and from the proven principles of the various natural sciences. It requires no invention, fabrication, or supposition, but derives directly from unquestionable facts and the straightforward application of established methods of inference." He paused and cast his eyes around the table to invite comment.

Nobody commented. They already knew his arguments. Danchekker, however, seemed about to go through it all again. Evidently he had concluded that attempts to make them see the obvious by appealing to their powers of reason alone were not enough; his only resort then was insistent repetition until they either concurred or went insane.

Hunt leaned back in his chair, took a cigarette from a box lying nearby on the table, and tossed his pen down on his pad. He still had reservations about the professor's dogmatic attitude, but at the same time he was aware that Danchekker's record of academic distinction was matched by those of few people alive at the time. Besides, this wasn't Hunt's field. His main objection was something else, a truth he accepted for what it was and made no attempt to fool himself by rationalizing: Everything about Danchekker irritated him. Danchekker was too thin; his clothes were too old-fashioned—he carried them as if they had been hung on to dry. His anachronistic gold-rimmed spectacles were ridiculous. His speech was too formal. He had probably never laughed in his life. A skull vacuum-packed in skin, Hunt thought to himself.

"Allow me to recapitulate," Danchekker continued. "*Homo sapiens*—modern man—belongs to the phylum Vertebrata. So, also, do all the mammals, fish, birds, amphibians, and reptiles that have ever walked, crawled, flown, slithered, or swum in every corner of the Earth. All vertebrates share a common pattern of basic architecture, which has remained unchanged over millions of years despite the superficial, specialized adaptations that on first consideration might seem to divide the countless species we see around us.

"The basic vertebrate pattern is as follows: an internal skeleton of bone or cartilage and a vertebral column. The vertebrate has two pairs of appendages, which may be highly developed or degenerate, likewise a tail. It has a ventrally located heart, divided into two or more chambers, and a closed circulatory system of blood made up of red cells containing hemoglobin. It has a dorsal nerve cord which bulges at one end into a five-part brain contained in a head. It also has a body cavity that contains most of its vital organs and its digestive system. All vertebrates conform to these rules and are thereby related."

The professor paused and looked around as if the conclusion were too obvious to require summarizing. "In other words, Charlie's whole structure shows him to be directly related to a million and one terrestrial animal species, extinct, alive, or yet to come. Furthermore, *all* terrestrial vertebrates, including ourselves *and* Charlie, can be traced back through an unbroken succession of intermediate fossils as having inherited their common pattern from the earliest recorded ancestors of the vertebrate line"—Danchekker's voice rose to a crescendo—"from the first boned fish that appeared in the oceans of the Devonian period of the Paleozoic era, over four hundred million years ago!" He paused for this last to take hold and then continued. "Charlie is as human as you or I in every respect. Can there be any doubt, then, that he shares our vertebrate heritage and therefore our ancestry? And if he shares our ancestry, then there is no doubt that he also shares our place of origin. Charlie *is* a native of planet Earth."

Danchekker sat down and poured himself a glass of water.

A hubbub of mixed murmurings and mutterings ensued, punctuated by the rustling of papers and the clink of water glasses. Here and there, chairs creaked as cramped limbs eased themselves into more comfortable positions. A metallurgist at one end of the table was gesturing to the man seated next to her. The man shrugged, showed his empty palms, and nodded his head in Danchekker's direction. She turned and called to the professor.

"Professor Danchekker . . . Professor . . ." Her voice made itself heard. The background noise died away. Danchekker looked up. "We've been having a little argument here—maybe you'd like to comment. Why couldn't Charlie have come from a parallel line of evolution somewhere else?"

"I was wondering that, too," came another voice.

Danchekker frowned for a moment before replying.

"No. The point you are overlooking here, I think, is that the evolutionary process is fundamentally made up of random events. Every living organism that exists today is the product of a chain of successive mutations that has continued over millions of years. The most important fact to grasp is that each discrete mutation is in itself a purely random event, brought about by aberrations in genetic coding and the mixing of the sex cells from different parents. The environment into which the mutant is born dictates whether it will survive to reproduce its kind or whether it will die out. Thus, some new characteristics are selected for further improvement, while others are promptly eradicated and still others are diluted away by interbreeding.

"There are still people who find this principle difficult to accept—primarily, I suspect, because they are incapable of visualizing the implications of numbers and time scales beyond the ranges that occur in everyday life. Remember we are talking about billions of billions of combinations coming together over millions of years.

"A game of chess begins with only twenty playable moves to choose from. At every move the choice available to the player is restricted, and yet, the number of legitimate positions that the board could assume after only ten moves is astronomical. Imagine, then, the number of permutations that could arise when the game continues for a billion moves and at each move the player has a billion choices open to him. This is the game of evolution. To suppose that two such independent sequences could result in end products that are identical would surely be demanding too much of our credulity. The laws of chance and statistics are quite firm when applied to sufficiently large numbers of samples. The laws of thermodynamics, for example, are nothing more than expressions of the probable behavior of gas molecules, yet the numbers involved are so large that we feel quite safe in accepting the postulates as rigid rules; no significant departure from them has ever been observed. The probability of the parallel line of evolution that you suggest is less than the probability of heat flowing from the kettle to the fire, or of all the air molecules in this room crowding into one corner at the same time, causing us all to explode spontaneously. Mathematically speaking, yes—the possibility of parallelism is finite, but so indescribably remote that we need consider it no further."

A young electronics engineer took the argument up at this point.

"Couldn't God get a look in?" he asked. "Or at least, some

kind of guiding force or principle that we don't yet comprehend? Couldn't the same design be produced via different lines in different places?"

Danchekker shook his head and smiled almost benevolently.

"We are scientists, not mystics," he replied. "One of the fundamental principles of scientific method is that new and speculative hypotheses do not warrant consideration as long as the facts that are observed are adequately accounted for by the theories that already exist. Nothing resembling a universal guiding force has ever been revealed by generations of investigation, and since the facts observed are adequately explained by the accepted principles I have outlined, there is no necessity to invoke or invent additional causes. Notions of guiding forces and grand designs exist only in the mind of the misguided observer, not in the facts he observes."

"But suppose it turns out that Charlie came from somewhere else," the metallurgist insisted. "What then?"

"Ah! Now, *that* would be an entirely different matter. If it should be proved by some other means that Charlie did indeed evolve somewhere else, then we would be forced to accept that parallel evolution had occurred as an observed and unquestionable fact. Since this could not be explained within the framework of contemporary theory, our theories would be shown to be woefully inadequate. *That* would be the time to speculate on additional influences. *Then,* perhaps, your universal guiding force might find a rightful place. To entertain such concepts at this stage, however, would be to put the cart fairly and squarely before the horse. In so doing, we would be guilty of a breach of one of the most fundamental of scientific principles."

Somebody else tried to push the professor from a different angle.

"How about convergent lines rather than parallel lines? Maybe the selection principles work in such a way that different lines of development converge toward the same optimum end product. In other words, although they start out in different directions, they will both eventually hit on the same, best final design. Like . . ." He sought for an analogy. "Like sharks are fish and dolphins are mammals. They both came from different origins but ended up hitting on the same general shape."

Danchekker again shook his head firmly. "Forget the idea of perfection and best end products," he said. "You are unwittingly falling into this trap of assuming a grand design again. The human form is not nearly as perfect as you perhaps imagine. Nature does not produce best solutions—it will try *any* solution. The only test applied is that it be good enough to survive and reproduce itself. Far more species have proved unsuccessful and become extinct than have survived—far, far more. It is easy to contemplate a kind of preordained striving toward something perfect when this fundamental fact is overlooked—when looking back down the tree, as it were, with the benefit of hindsight from our particular successful branch and forgetting the countless other branches that got nowhere.

"No, forget this idea of perfection. The developments we see in the natural world are simply cases of something good enough to do the job. Usually, many conceivable alternatives would be as good, and some better.

"Take as an example the cusp pattern on the first lower molar tooth of man. It is made up of a group of five main cusps with a complex of intervening grooves and ridges that help to grind up food. There is no reason to suppose that this particular pattern is any more efficient than any one of many more that might be considered. This particular pattern, however, first occurred as a mutation somewhere along the ancestral line leading toward man and has been passed on ever since. The same pattern is also found on the teeth of the great apes, indicating that we both inherited it from some early common ancestor where it happened through pure chance.

"Charlie has human cusp patterns on all his teeth.

"Many of our adaptations are far from perfect. The arrangement of internal organs leaves much to be desired, owing to our inheriting a system originally developed to suit a horizontal and not an upright posture. In our respiratory system, for example, we find that the wastes and dirt that accumulate in the throat and nasal regions drain inside and not outside, as happened originally, a prime cause of many bronchial and chest complaints not suffered by four-footed animals. That's hardly perfection, is it?"

Danchekker took a sip of water and made an appealing gesture to the room in general.

"So, we see that any idea of convergence toward the ideal is not supported by the facts. Charlie exhibits all our faults and imperfections as well as our improvements. No, I'm sorry—I appreciate that these questions are voiced in the best tradition of leaving no possibility unprobed and I commend you for them, but really, we must dismiss them."

Silence enveloped the room at his concluding words. On all sides, everybody seemed to be staring thoughtfully through the table, through the walls, or through the ceiling.

Caldwell placed his hands on the table and looked around until satisfied that nobody had anything to add.

"Looks like evolution stays put for a while longer," he grunted. "Thank you Professor."

Danchekker nodded without looking up.

"However," Caldwell continued, "the object of these meetings is to give everyone a chance to talk freely as well as listen. So far, some people haven't had much to say—especially one or two of the newcomers." Hunt realized with a start that Caldwell was looking straight at him. "Our English visitor, for example, whom most of you already know. Dr. Hunt, do you have any views that we ought to hear about . . . ?"

Next to Caldwell, Lyn Garland was making no attempt to conceal a wide smile. Hunt took a long draw at his cigarette and used the delay to collect his thoughts. In the time it took for him to coolly emit one long, diffuse cloud of smoke and flick his hand at the ashtray, all the pieces clicked together in his brain with the smooth precision of the binary regiments parading through the registers of the computers downstairs. Lyn's persistent cross-examinations, her visits to the Ocean, his presence here—Caldwell had found a catalyst.

Hunt surveyed the array of attentive faces. "Most of what's been said reasserts the accepted principles of comparative anatomy and evolutionary theory. Just to clear the record for anyone with misleading ideas, I've no intention of questioning them. However, the conclusion could be summed up by saying that since Charlie comes from the same ancestors as we do, he must have evolved on Earth the same as we did."

"That is so," threw in Danchekker.

"Fine," Hunt replied. "Now, all this is really your problem, not mine, but since you've asked me what I think, I'll state the conclusion another way. Since Charlie evolved on Earth, the civilization he was from evolved on Earth. The indications are that his culture was about as advanced as ours, maybe in one or two areas slightly more advanced. So, we ought to find no end of traces of his people. We don't. Why not?"

All heads turned toward Danchekker.

The professor sighed. "The only conclusion left open to us is that whatever traces were left have been erased by the natural processes of weathering and erosion," he said wearily. "There are several possibilities: A catastrophe of some sort could have wiped them out to the extent that there were no traces; or possibly their civilization existed in regions which today are submerged beneath the oceans. Further searching will no doubt produce solutions to this question."

"If any catastrophe as violent as that occurred so recently, we would already know about it," Hunt pointed out. "Most of what was land then is still land today, so I can't see them sinking into the ocean somewhere, either; besides, you've only to look at our civilization to see it's not confined to localized areas—it's spread all over the globe. And how is it that in spite of all the junk that keeps turning up with no trouble at all from primitive races from around the same time—bones, spears, clubs, and so on—nobody has ever found a single example of anything related to this supposed technologically advanced culture? Not a screw, or a piece of wire, or a plastic washer. To me, that doesn't make sense."

More murmuring broke out to mark the end of Hunt's critique.

"Professor?" Caldwell invited comment with a neutral voice.

Danchekker compressed his mouth into a grimace. "Oh, I agree, I agree. It is surprising—very surprising. But what alternative are you proposing?" His voice took on a note of sarcasm. "Do you suggest that man and all the animals came to Earth in some enormous celestial Noah's Ark?" He laughed. "If so, the fossil record of a hundred million years disproves you."

"Impasse." The comment came from Professor Schorn, an authority on comparative anatomy, who had arrived from Stuttgart a few days before.

"Looks like it," Caldwell agreed.

Danchekker, however, was not through. "Would Dr. Hunt care to answer my question?" he challenged. "Precisely what other place of origin is he suggesting?"

"I'm not suggesting anywhere in particular," Hunt replied evenly. "What I am suggesting is that perhaps a more open-minded approach might be appropriate at this stage. After all, we've only just found Charlie. This business will go on for years yet; there's bound to be a lot more information surfacing that we don't have right now. I think it's too early to be jumping ahead and predicting what the answers might be. Better just to keep on plodding along and using every scrap of data we've got to put together a picture of the place Charlie came from. It might turn out to be Earth. Then again, it might not."

Caldwell led him on further. "How would you suggest we go about that?"

Hunt wondered if this was a direct cue. He decided to risk it. "You could try taking a closer look at this." He drew a sheet of paper out from the folder in front of him and slid it across to the center of the table. The paper showed a complicated tabular arrangement of Lunarian numerals.

"What's that?" asked a voice.

"It's from one of the pocket books," Hunt replied. "I think the book is something not unlike a diary. I also believe that that"—he pointed at the sheet—"could well be a calendar." He caught a sly wink from Lyn Garland and returned it.

"Calendar?"

"How d'you figure that one?"

"It's all gobbledygook."

Danchekker stared hard at the paper for a few seconds. "Can you prove it's a calendar?" he demanded.

"No, I can't. But I have analyzed the number pattern and can state that it's made up of ascending groups that repeat in sets and subsets. Also, the alphabetic groups that seem to label the major sets correspond to the headings of groups of pages farther on—remarkably like the layout of a diary."

"*Hmmph!* More likely some form of tabular page index."

"Could be," Hunt granted. "But why not wait and see? Once the language has unraveled a bit more, it should be possible to cross-check a lot of what's here with items from other sources. This is the kind of thing that maybe we ought to be a little more open-minded about. You say Charlie comes from Earth; I say he might. You say this is not a calendar; I say it might be. In my estimation, an attitude like yours is too inflexible to permit an unbiased appraisal of the problem. You've already made up your mind what you want the answers to be."

"Hear, hear!" a voice at the end of the table called.

Danchekker colored visibly, but Caldwell spoke before he could reply.

"You've analyzed the numbers—right?"

"Right."

"Okay, supposing for now it's a calendar—what more can you tell us?"

Hunt leaned forward across the table and pointed at the sheet with his pen.

"First, two assumptions. One: the natural unit of time on any world is the day—that is, the time it takes the planet to rotate on its axis . . ."

"Assuming it rotates," somebody tossed in.

"That was my second assumption. But the only cases we know of where there's no rotation—or where the orbital period equals the axial period, which amounts to the same thing—occur when a small body orbits close to a far more massive one and is swamped by gravitational tidal effects, like our Moon. For that to happen to a body the size of a planet, the planet would have to orbit very close to its parent star—too close for it to support any life comparable to our own."

"Seems reasonable," Caldwell said, looking around the table. Various heads were nodding assent. "Where do we go from there?"

"Okay," Hunt resumed. "Assuming it rotates and the day is its natural unit of time—if this complete table represents one full orbit around its sun, there are seventeen hundred days in its year, one entry for each."

"Pretty long," someone hazarded.

"To us, yes: at least, the year-to-day ratio is big. It could mean the orbit is large, the rotational period short, or perhaps a bit of both. Now look at the major number groups—the ones tagged with the heavy alphabetic labels. There are forty-seven of them. Most contain thirty-six numbers, but nine of them have thirty-seven—the first, sixth, twelfth, eighteenth, twenty-fourth, thirtieth, thirty-sixth, forty-second, and forty seventh. That seems a bit odd at first sight, but so would our system to someone unfamiliar with it. It suggests that maybe somebody had to do a bit of fiddling with it to make it work."

"Mmm . . . like with our months."

"Exactly. This is just the sort of juggling you have to do to get a sensible fit of our months into our year. It happens because there's no simple relationship between the orbital periods of planet and satellite; there's no reason why there should be. I'm guessing that if this is a calendar that relates to some other planet, then the reason for this odd mix of thirty-sixes and thirty-sevens is the same as the one that causes problems with our calendar: That planet had a moon."

"So these groups are months," Caldwell stated.

"If it's a calendar—yes. Each group is divided into three subgroups—weeks, if you like. Normally there are twelve days in each, but there are nine long months, in which the middle week has thirteen days."

Danchekker looked for a long time at the sheet of paper, an expression of pained disbelief spreading slowly across his face.

"Are you proposing this as a serious scientific theory?" he queried in a strained voice.

"Of course not," Hunt replied. "This is all pure speculation. But it does indicate some of the avenues that could be explored. These alphabetic groups, for example, might correspond to references that the language people might dig from other sources—such as dates on documents, or date stamps on pieces of clothing or other equipment. Also, you might be able to find some independent way of arriving at the number of days in the year; if it turned out to be seventeen hundred, that would be quite a coincidence, wouldn't it?"

"Anything else?" Caldwell asked.

"Yes. Computer correlation analysis of this number pattern may show hidden superposed periodicities; for all we know, there could have been more than one moon. Also, it should be possible to compute families of curves giving possible relationships between planet-to-satellite mass ratios against mean orbital radii. Later on you might know enough more to be able to isolate one of the curves. It might describe the Earth-Luna system; then again, it might not."

"Preposterous!" Danchekker exploded.

"Unbiased?" Hunt suggested.

"There is something else that may be worth trying," Schorn interrupted. "Your calendar, if that's what it is, has so far been described in relative terms only—days per month, months per year, and so on. There is nothing that gives us any absolute values. Now—and this is a long shot—from detailed chemical analysis we are making some progress in building a quantitative model of Charlie's cell-metabolism cycles and enzyme processes. We may be able to calculate the rate of accumulation of waste materials and toxins in the blood and tissues, and from these results form an estimate of his natural periods of sleep and wakefulness. If, in this way, I could provide a figure for the length of the day, the other quantities would follow immediately."

"If we knew that, then we'd know the planet's orbital period," said somebody else. "But could we get an estimate of its mass?"

"One way might be by doing a structural analysis of Charlie's bone and muscle formations and then working out the power-weight ration," another chipped in.

"That would give us the planet's mean distance from its sun," said a third.

"Only if it was like our Sun."

"You could get a check on the planet's mass from the glass and other crystalline materials in his equipment. From the crystal structure, we should be able to figure out the strength of the gravitational field they cooled in."

"How could we get a figure for density?"

"You still need to know the planetary radius."

"He's like us, so the surface gravity will be Earthlike."

"Very probable, but let's prove it."

"Prove that's a calendar first."

Remarks began pouring in from all sides. Hunt reflected with some satisfaction that at least he had managed to inject some spirit and enthusiasm into the proceedings.

Danchekker remained unimpressed. As the noise abated, he rose again to his feet and pointed pityingly to the single sheet of paper, still lying in the center of the table.

"All balderdash!" he spat. "There is the sum total of your evidence. There"—he slid his voluminous file, bulging with notes and papers, across beside it—"is mine, backed by libraries, data banks, and archives the world over. Charlie comes from Earth!"

"Where's his civilization, then?" Hunt demanded. "Removed in an enormous celestial garbage truck?"

Laughter from around the table greeted the return of Danchekker's own gibe. The professor darkened and seemed about to say something obscene. Caldwell held up a restraining hand, but Schorn saved the situation by interrupting in his calm, unruffled tone. "It would seem, ladies and gentlemen, that for the moment we must compromise by agreeing to a

purely hypothetical situation. To keep Professor Danchekker
happy, we must accept that the Lunarians evolved from the
same ancestors as ourselves. To keep Dr. Hunt happy, we must
assume they did it somewhere else. How we are to reconcile
these two irreconcilables, I would not for one moment attempt
to predict."

chapter nine

Hunt saw less and less of the Trimagniscope during the weeks
that followed the progress meeting. Caldwell seemed to go out
of his way to encourage the Englishman to visit the various
UNSA labs and establishments nearby, to "see what's going on
first-hand," or the offices in Navcomms HQ to "meet someone
you might find interesting." Hunt was naturally curious about
the Lunarian investigations, so these developments suited him
admirably. Soon he was on familiar terms with most of the engineers and scientists involved, at least in the Houston vicinity,
and he had a good idea of how their work was progressing and
what difficulties they were encountering. He eventually acquired a broad overview of the activity on all fronts and found
that, at least at the general level, the awareness of the whole
picture that he was developing was shared by only a few
privileged individuals within the organization.

Things were progressing in a number of directions. Calculations of structural efficiency, based on measurements of Charlie's skeleton and the bulk supported by it, had given a figure
for the surface gravity of his home planet, which agreed within
acceptable margins of error with figures deduced separately
from tests performed on the crystals of his helmet visor and
other components formed from a molten state. The gravity
field at the surface of Charlie's home planet seemed to have
been not much different from that of Earth; possibly it was
slightly stronger. These results were accepted as being no more
than rough approximations. Besides, nobody knew how typical

Charlie's physical build had been of that of the Lunarians in general, so there was no firm indication of whether the planet in question had been Earth or somewhere else. The issue was still wide open.

On equipment tags, document headings, and appended to certain notes, the linguistics section had found examples of Lunarian words which matched exactly some of the labels on the calendar, just as Hunt had suggested they might. While this *proved* nothing, it did add further plausibility to the idea that these words indicated dates of some kind.

Then something else that seemed to connect with the calendar appeared from a totally unexpected direction. Site-preparation work in progress near Lunar Tycho Base Three turned up fragments of metal fabrications and structures. They looked like the ruins of some kind of installation. The more thorough probe that followed yielded no fewer than fourteen more bodies, or more accurately, bits of bodies from which at least fourteen individuals of both sexes could be identified. Clearly, none of the bodies was in anything approaching the condition of Charlie's. They had all been literally blown to pieces. The remains comprised little more than splinters of charred bone scattered among scorched tatters of space suits. Apart from suggesting that besides being physically the same as humans, the Lunarians had been every bit as accident-prone, these discoveries provided no new information—until the discovery of the wrist unit. About the size of a large cigarette pack, not including the wrist bracelet, the device carried on its upper face four windows that looked like miniature electronic displays. From their size and shape, the windows seemed to have been intended to display character data rather than pictures, and the device was thought to be a chronometer or a computing-calculating aid; maybe it was both—and other things besides.

After a perfunctory examination at Tycho Three the unit had been shipped to Earth along with some other items. It eventually found its way to the Navcomms laboratories near Houston, where the gadgets from Charlie's backpack were being studied. After some preliminary experimenting the casing was safely removed, but detailed inspection of the complex molecular circuits inside revealed nothing particularly meaningful. Having no better ideas, the Navcomms engineers resorted to applying low voltages to random points to see what happened.

Sure enough, when particular sequences of binary patterns were injected into one row of contacts, an assortment of Lunarian symbols appeared across the windows. This left nobody any the wiser until Hunt, who happened to be visiting the lab, recognized one sequence of the alphabetic sets as the months that appeared on the calendar. Hence, at least one of the functions performed by the wrist unit seemed closely related to the table in the diary. Whether or not this had anything to do with recording the passage of time remained to be seen, but at least odd things looked as if they were beginning to tie up.

The linguistics section was making steady, if less spectacular, progress toward cracking the language. Many of the world's most prominent experts were getting involved, some choosing to move to Houston, while others worked via remote data links. As the first phase of their assault, they amassed volumes of statistics on word and character distributions and matchings, and produced reams of tables and charts that looked as meaningless to everybody else as the language itself. After that it was largely a matter of intuition and guessing games played on computer display screens. Every now and again somebody spotted a more meaningful pattern, which led to a better guess, which led to a still more meaningful pattern—and so on. They produced lists of words in categories believed to correspond to nouns, adjectives, verbs, and adverbs, and later on added adjectival and adverbial phrases—fairly basic requirements for any advanced inflecting language. They began to develop a feel for the rules for deriving variants, such as plurals and verb tenses, from common roots, and for the conventions that governed the formation of word sequences. An appreciation of the rudiments of Lunarian grammar was emerging from all this, and the experts in Linguistics faced the future with optimism, suddenly confident that they were approaching the point where they would begin attempting to match the first English equivalents to selected samples.

The mathematics section, organized on lines similar to linguistics, was also finding things that were interesting. Part of the diary was made up of many pages of numeric and tabular material—suggesting, perhaps, a reference section of *Useful Information*. One of the pages was divided vertically, columns of numbers alternating with columns of words. A researcher noticed that one of the numbers, when converted to decimal, came out to 1836—the proton–electron mass ratio, a fundamental physical constant that would be the same anywhere in the Universe. It was suggested that the page might be a listing of equivalent Lunarian units of mass, similar to equivalence tables used for converting ounces to grams, grams to pounds . . . and so on. If so, they had stumbled on a complete record of the Lunarian system of measuring mass. The problem was that the whole supposition rested on the slender assumption that the figure 1836 did, in fact, denote the proton–electron mass ratio and was not merely a coincidental reference to something completely different. They needed a second source of information to check it against.

When Hunt talked to the mathematicians one afternoon, he was surprised to learn that they were unaware that the chemists and anatomists in other departments had computed estimates of surface gravity. As soon as he mentioned the fact, everybody saw the significance at once. If the Lunarians had adopted the practice that was common on Earth—using the same units to express mass and weight on their own planet—then the numbers in the table gave Lunarian weights. Furthermore, there was available to them at least one object whose weight they could estimate accurately: Charlie himself. Thus, since they already had an estimate of surface gravity, they could easily approximate how much Charlie would have weighed in kilograms back home. Only one piece of information was missing for a solution to the whole problem: a factor to convert kilograms to Lunarian weight units. Then Hunt speculated that there could well be among Charlie's personal documents an identity card, a medical card—something that recorded his weight in his own units. If so, that one number would tell them all they needed to know. The discussion ended abruptly, with the head of the mathematics section departing in great haste and a state of considerable excitement to talk to the head of the linguistics section. Linguistics agreed to make a special note if anything like that turned up. So far nothing had.

Another small group, tucked away in offices in the top of Navcomms HQ building, was working on what was perhaps the most exciting discovery to come out of the books so far. Twenty pages, right at the end of the second book, showed a series of maps. They were all drawn to an apparently small scale, each one depicting extensive areas of the world's surface—but the world so depicted bore no resemblance to Earth. Oceans, continents, rivers, lakes, islands, and most othe geographical features were easily distinguishable, but in no way could they be reconciled with Earth's surface, even allowing for the passage of fifty thousand years—which would have made little difference anyway, aside from the size of the polar ice caps.

Each map carried a rectangular grid of reference lines, similar to those of terrestrial latitude and longitude, with the lines spaced forty-eight units (decimal) apart. These numbers were presumed to denote units of Lunarian circular measure, since nobody could think of any other sensible way to dimension coordinates on the surface of a sphere. The fourth and seventh maps provided the key: the zero line of longitude to which all the other lines were referenced. The line to the east was tagged "528" and that to the west "48," showing that the full Lunarian circle was divided into 576 Lunarian degrees. The system was consistent with their duodecimal counting method and their convention of reading from right to left. The next step was to calculate the percentage of the planet's surface that each map represented and to fit them together to form the complete globe.

Already, however, the general scheme was clear. The ice caps were far larger than those believed to have existed on Earth during the Pleistocene Ice Age, stretching in some places to within twenty (Earth) degrees of the equator. Most of the seas around the equatorial belt were completely locked in by coastlines and ice. An assortment of dots and symbols scattered across the land masses in the ice-free belt and, more thinly, over the ice sheets themselves, seemed to indicate towns and cities.

When Hunt received an invitation to come up and have a look at the maps, the scientists working on them showed him the scales of distance that were printed at the edges. If they could only find some way of converting those numbers into miles, they would have the diameter of the planet. But nobody had told them about the tables the mathematics section thought might be mass-unit conversion factors. Maybe one of the other tables did the same thing for units of length and distance? If so, and if they could find a reference to Charlie's height among his papers, the simple process of measuring him would allow them to work out how many Earth meters there were in a Lunarian mile. Since they already had a figure for the planet's surface gravity, its mass and mean density should follow immediately.

This was all very exciting, but all it proved was that a world had existed. It did not prove that Charlie and the Lunarians originated there. After all, the fact that a man carries a London street map in his pocket doesn't prove him to be a Londoner. So the work of relating numbers derived from physical measurements of Charlie's body to the numbers on the maps and in the tables could turn out to be based on a huge fallacy. If the diary came from the world shown on the maps but Charlie came from somewhere else, then the system of measurement deduced from the maps and tables in the diary might be a totally different system from the one used to record his personal characteristics in his papers, since the latter system would be the system used in the somewhere else, not in the world depicted on the maps. It all got very confusing.

Finally, nobody claimed to have proved conclusively that the world on the maps wasn't Earth. Admittedly it didn't look like Earth, and attempts to derive the modern distribution of terrestrial continents from the land areas on the maps had met with no success at all. But the planet's gravity hadn't been all that much different. Maybe the surface of Earth had undergone far greater changes over the last fifty thousand years than had been previously thought? Furthermore, Danchekker's arguments still carried a lot of weight, and any theory that discounted them would have an awful lot of explaining to do. But by that time, most of the scientists working on the project had reached a stage where nothing would have surprised them any more, anyway.

"Got your message. Came straight over." Hunt announced as Lyn Garland ushered him into Caldwell's office. Caldwell nodded toward one of the chairs opposite his desk, and Hunt sat down. Caldwell glanced at Lyn, who was still standing by the door.

"It's okay," he said. She left, closing the door behind her.

Caldwell fixed Hunt with an expressionless stare for a few seconds, at the same time drumming his fingers on the desk. "You've seen a lot of the setup here during the past few months. What do you think of it?"

Hunt shrugged. The answer was obvious.

"I like it. Exciting things happen around here."

"You like exciting things happening, huh?" The executive
director nodded, half to himself. He remained thoughtful for
what seemed a long time. "Well, you've only seen part of what
goes on. Most people have no idea how big UNSA is these
days. All the things you see around here—the labs, the installations, the launch areas—that's just the backup. Our main
business is up front." He gestured toward the photographs
adorning one of the walls. "We have people right now exploring the Martian deserts, flying probes down through the clouds
on Venus, and walking on the moons of Jupiter. In the deep-
space units in California, they're designing ships that will
make Vegas and even the Jupiter Mission ships look like
paddleboats. Photon-drive robot probes that will make the first
jump to the stars—some seven miles long! Think of it—seven
miles long!"

Hunt did his best to react in the appropriate manner. The
problem was, he wasn't sure what manner was appropriate.
Caldwell never said or did anything without a reason. The reason for this turn of conversation was far from obvious.

"And that's only the beginning," Caldwell went on. "After
that, men will follow the robots. Then—who knows? This is
the biggest thing the human race has ever embarked on: USA,
US Europe, Canada, the Soviets, the Australians—they're all
in on it together. Where does a thing like that go once it starts
moving, huh? Where does it stop?"

For the first time since his arrival at Houston, Hunt detected
a hint of emotion in the American's voice. He nodded slowly,
though still not comprehending.

"You didn't drag me here to give me a UNSA commercial,"
he said.

"No, I didn't," Caldwell agreed. "I dragged you over because it's time we had a serious talk. I know enough about you
to know how the wheels go round inside your head. You are
made out of the same stuff as the guys who are making all the
things happen out there." He sat back in his chair and held
Hunt's gaze with a direct stare. "I want you to quit messing
around at IDCC and come over to us."

The statement caught Hunt like a right hook.

"What . . . ! To Navcomms!"

"Correct. Let's not play games. You're the kind of person
we need, and we can give you the things you need. I know I
don't have to make a big speech to explain myself."

Hunt's initial surprise lasted perhaps half a second. Already the computer in his head was churning out answers. Caldwell had been building toward this and testing him out for weeks. So, that was why he had moved in Navcomms engineers to take over running the scope. Had the thought been in his mind as long ago as that? Already Hunt had no doubt what the outcome of the interview would be. However, the rules of the game demanded that the set questions be posed and answered before anything final could be pronounced. Instinctively he reached for his cigarette case, but Caldwell preempted him and slid his cigar box across the desk.

"You seem pretty confident you've got what I need," Hunt said as he selected a Havana. "I'm not sure even I know what that is."

"Don't you . . . ? Or is it that you just don't like talking about it?" Caldwell stopped to light his own cigar. He puffed until satisfied, then continued: "New Cross to the *Journal of the Royal Society*, solo. Some achievement." He made a gesture of approval. "We like self-starters over here—sorta . . . traditional. What made you do it?" He didn't wait for a reply. "First electronics, then mathematics . . . after that nuclear physics, later on nucleonics. What's next Dr. Hunt? Where do you go from there?" He settled back and exhaled a cloud of smoke while Hunt considered the question.

Hunt raised his eyebrows in mild admiration. "You seem to have been doing your homework," he said.

Caldwell didn't answer directly but asked, simply, "How was your uncle in Lagos when you visited him on vacation last year? Did he prefer the weather to Worcester, England? Seen much of Mike from Cambridge lately? I doubt it—he joined UNSA, he's been at Hellas Two on Mars for the last eight months. Want me to go on?"

Hunt was too mature to feel indignant; besides, he liked to see a professional in action. He smiled faintly.

"Ten out of ten."

At once Caldwell's mood became deadly serious. He leaned forward and spread his elbows on the desk.

"I'll tell you where you go from here, Dr. Hunt," he said. "Out—out to the stars! We're on our way to the stars over here! It started when Danchekker's fish first crawled up out of the mud. The urge that made them do it is the same as the one that's driven you all your life. You've gone inside the atom as far as you can go; there's only one way left now—out. That's what UNSA has to offer that you can't refuse."

There was nothing Hunt could add. Two futures lay spread out before him: One led back to Metadyne, the other beckoned onward toward infinity. He was as incapable of choosing the first as his species was of returning to the depths of the sea.

"What's your side of the deal, then?" he asked after some reflection.

"You mean, what do you have that we need?"

"Yes."

"We need the way your brain works. You can think sideways. You see problems from different angles that nobody else uses. That's what I need to bust open this Charlie business. Everybody argues so much because they're making assumptions that seem obvious but that they shouldn't be making. It takes a special kind of mind to figure out what's wrong when things that anybody with common sense can see are true turn out to be not true. I think you're the guy."

The compliments made Hunt feel slightly uncomfortable. He decided to move things along. "What do you have in mind?"

"Well, the guys we have at present are top grade inside their own specialties," Caldwell replied. "Don't get me wrong, these people are good—but I'd like them to concentrate on doing the things they're best at. However, aside from all that, I need someone with an unspecialized, and therefore impartial, outlook to coordinate the findings of the specialists and integrate them into an overall picture. If you like, I need people like Danchekker to paint the pieces of the puzzle, but I need someone like you to fit the pieces together. You've been doing a bit of that, unofficially, for quite a while anyway; I'm saying, 'Let's make it official.' "

"How about the organization?" Hunt asked.

"I've thought about that. I don't want to alienate any of our senior people by subordinating them or any of their staffs to some new whiz kid. That's only good politics. Anyhow, I don't think you'd want it that way."

Hunt shook his head to show his agreement.

"So," Caldwell resumed, "what I figure is, the various departments and sections will continue to function as they do at present. Our relationship with outfits outside Navcomms will remain unaffected. However, all the conclusions that everybody has reached so far, and new findings as they turn up, will be referred to a centralized coordinating section—that's you. Your job will be to fit the bits together, as I said earlier. You'd build up your own staff as time goes on and the work load increases. You'd be able to request any particular items of information you find you need from the specialist functions; that way you'd be defining some of their objectives. As for your objectives, they're already spelled out: Find out who these Charlie people were, where they came from, and what happened to them. You report directly to me and get the whole problem off my back. I've got enough on my schedule without worrying about corpses." Caldwell threw out an arm to show that he was finished. "Well, what do you say?"

Hunt had to smile within himself. As Caldwell had said, there was really nothing to think about. He took a long breath and turned both hands upward. "As you said—an offer I can't refuse."

"So, you're in?"

"I'm in."

"Welcome aboard, then." Caldwell looked pleased. "This calls for a drink." He produced a flask and glasses from somewhere behind the desk. He poured the whiskey and passed a glass to his newest employee.

"When do you want it to start?" Hunt asked after a moment.

"Well, you probably need a couple of months or so to sort out the formalities with IDCC. But why wait for formalities? You're on loan here from IDCC anyway and under my direction for the duration; also, we're paying for you. So what's wrong with tomorrow morning?"

"Christ!"

Caldwell's manner at once became brisk and businesslike.

"I'll allocate offices for you in this building. Rob Gray takes full charge of scope operations and keeps the engineers I've assigned to him as his permanent staff for as long as he's in Houston. That frees you totally. By the end of this week I want estimates of what you think you'll need in the way of clerical and secretarial staff, technical personnel, equipment, furniture, lab space, and computer facilities.

"By this time next week, I want you to have a presentation ready for a meeting of section and department heads that I'm going to call, to tell them how you see yourself and them working together. Make it tactful. I won't issue any official notification of these changes until after the meeting, when everybody knows what's going on. Don't talk about it until then, except to myself and Lyn.

"Your outfit will be designated *Special Assignment Group L*, and your position, will be section head, Group L. The post is classed as 'Executive, grade four, civilian,' within the Space Arm. It carries all the appropriate benefits of free use of UNSA vehicles and aircraft, access to restricted files up to category three, and standard issues of clothing and accessories for duties overseas or off-planet. All that is in the *Executive Staff Manual*; details of reporting structures, admin procedures, and that kind of thing are in the *UNSA Corporate Policy Guide*. Lyn will get you copies.

"You'll have to get in touch with the federal authorities in Houston regarding permanent residence in the USA; Lyn knows the right people. Arrange transfer of your personal belongings from England at your own convenience and charge it to Navcomms. We'll help out finding you somewhere to live, but in the meantime stay on at the Ocean."

Hunt had the fleeting thought that had Caldwell been born three thousand years previously, Rome might well have been built in a day.

"What's your current salary?" Caldwell asked.

"Twenty-five thousand European dollars."

"We'll make it thirty."

Hunt nodded mutely.

Caldwell paused and checked mentally for anything he might have overlooked. Finding nothing, he sat back and raised his glass. "Cheers, then, Vic."

It was the first time he had addressed Hunt informally.

"Cheers."

"To the stars."

"To the stars."

A low roar from a point outside the city reached the room. They glanced toward the window to see a column of light climbing into the blue as a Vega lifted off from a distant launch pad. A quiet surge of excitement welled up in Hunt's veins as he took in the sight. It was a symbol of the ultimate expression of man's outward urge, and he was about to become part of it.

chapter ten

Demands for the services of Special Assignment Group L commenced as soon as the new unit officially went into operation, and they continued to increase rapidly in the weeks that followed. By the end of a month Hunt was swamped and forced to take on extra people at a faster rate than he had intended. Originally his idea had been to keep going with a skeleton staff for a while, at least until he formed a better idea of what was required. When Caldwell first announced the establishment of the new group, there had been one or two instances of petty jealousy and resentment, but the attitude that prevailed in the end was that Hunt had contributed several worthwhile ideas, and it seemed only sensible to get him in on the team permanently. After a while, even the dissenters grudgingly began to concede that things seemed to run more smoothly with Group L around. Some of them eventually did a complete about-face and became enthusiastic supporters of the scheme, as they came to appreciate that the communication channels to Hunt's people worked in bidirectional mode, and for every bit of data they fed in, ten bits came back in the other direction. As the oil thus added to Caldwell's jigsaw-puzzle-solving machine began to prove effective, the machine shifted fully into top gear, and suddenly pieces started fitting together.

The mathematics section was still working on the equations and formulas found in the books. Since mathematical relationships would remain true irrespective of the conventions used to express them, their interpretation was a far less arbitrary affair than that of deciphering the Lunarian language. The mathematicians had been stimulated by the discovery of the mass conversion table. They turned their attention to the other tables contained in the same book and soon found one that listed many commonly used physical and mathematical constants. From it they quickly picked out *pi* as well as *e*, the base of natural logarithms, and one or two more, but they still didn't understand the system of units well enough to evaluate the majority.

Another set of tables turned out to be simple trigonometric functions; these were easily recognized once the cartographers had provided the units of circular measure. The headings of the columns of these tables gave the Lunarian symbols for sine, cosine, tangent, and the like. Once these were known, many of the mathematical expressions elsewhere started making more sense; some of them fell out immediately as familiar trigonometric relationships. These in turn helped establish the conventions used to denote normal arithmetic operations and that of exponentiation, which led to the identification of the equations of mechanical motion. Nobody was surprised when these equations revealed that Lunarian scientists had deduced the same laws as Newton. The mathematicians progressed to tables of elementary first integrals and standard forms of low-order differential equations. On later pages were expressions which they suspected might describe systems of resonance and damped oscillations. Here again, the uncertainty over units presented a problem; expressions of this type would be in a standard form that could apply equally well to electrical, mechanical, thermal, or many other types of physical phenomena. Until they knew more about Lunarian units, they could not be sure precisely what these equations meant, even if they succeeded in interpreting them mathematically.

Hunt remembered having noticed that many of the electrical subassemblies from Charlie's backpack had small metal labels mounted adjacent to plugs, sockets, and other input–output connections. He speculated that some of the symbols engraved on these labels might represent ratings in units of voltage, current, power, frequency, and so on. he spent a day in the electronics labs, produced a full report on these markings, and passed it on to Mathematics. Nobody had thought to tell them about it sooner.

The electronic technicians located the battery in the wrist unit from Tycho, took it to pieces, and with the assistance of an electrochemist from another department, worked out the voltage it had been designed to produce. Linguistics translated the markings on the casing, and that gave a figure for the Lunarian unit for electrical voltage. Well, it was a start.

Professors Danchekker and Schorn were in charge of the biological side of the research. Perhaps surprisingly, Danchekker exhibited no reluctance to cooperate with Group L and kept them fully updated with a regular flow of information. This was more the result of his deeply rooted sense of propriety than of any change of heart. He was a formalist, and if this procedure was what the formalities of the arrangement required, he would adhere to it rigidly. His refusal to budge one inch from his uncompromising views regarding the origins of the Lunarians, however, was total.

As promised, Schorn had set up investigations to determine the length of Charlie's natural day from studies of body chemistry and cell metabolism, but he was running into trouble. He was getting results, all right, but the results made no sense. Some tests gave a figure of twenty-four hours, which meant that Charlie could be from Earth; some gave thirty-five hours, which meant he couldn't be; and other tests came up with figures in between. Thus, if the aggregate of these results meant anything at all, it indicated that Charlie came from a score of different places all at the same time. Either it was crazy, or there was something wrong with the methods used, or there was more to the matter than they thought.

Danchekker was more successful in a different direction. From an analysis of the sizes and shapes of Charlie's blood vessels and associated muscle tissues, he produced equations describing the performance of Charlie's circulatory system. From these he then derived a set of curves that showed the proportions of body heat that would be retained and lost for any given body temperature and outside temperature. He came up with a figure for Charlie's normal body temperature from some of Schorn's figures that were not suspect and were based on the assumption that, as in the case of terrestrial mammals, the process of evolution would have led to Charlie's body regulating its temperature to such a level that the chemical reactions within its cells would proceed at their most efficient rates. By substituting this figure back into his original equations, Danchekker was able to arrive at an estimate of the outside temperature or, more precisely, the temperature of the environment in which Charlie seemed best adapted to function. Allowing for error, it came out at somewhere between two and nine degrees Celsius.

With Schorn's failure to produce a reliable indication of the length of the Lunarian day, there was still no way of assigning

any absolute values to the calendar, although sufficient corrob-
orating evidence had been forthcoming from various sources to
verify beyond reasonable doubt that it was indeed a calendar.
As more clues to Lunarian electrical units were found by Electronics, an alternative approach to obtaining the elusive Lunarian unit of time suggested itself. If Mathematics could
untangle the equations of electrical oscillation, they should be
able to manipulate the quantities involved in such a way to express the two constants denoting the dielectric permittivity and
magnetic permeability of free space in Lunarian units. The ratio of these constants would yield the velocity of light, expressed in Lunarian units of distance per Lunarian units of
time. The units for representing distance were understood already; therefore, those used for measuring time would be given
automatically.

All this activity in UNSA naturally attracted widespread
public attention. The discovery of a technologically advanced
civilization from fifty thousand years in the past was not something that happened very often. Some of the headlines flashed
around the World News Grid when the story was released, a
few weeks after the original find, were memorable: MAN ON
MOON BEFORE ARMSTRONG; some were hilarious: EXTINCT CIVILI-
ZATION ON MARS; some were just wrong: CONTACT MADE WITH
ALIEN INTELLIGENCE. But most summed up the situation fairly
well.

In the months that followed, UNSA's public relations office
in Washington, long geared to conducting steady and predictable dealings with the news media, reeled under a deluge of
demands from hard-pressed editors and producers all over the
globe. Washington struggled valiantly for a while, but in the
end did the human thing, and delegated the problem to
Navcomms' local PR department at Houston. The PR director
at Houston found a ready-made clearinghouse of new information in the form of Group L, right on his doorstep, so still another dimension was added to Hunt's ever growing work load.
Soon, press conferences, TV documentaries, filmed interviews,
and reporters became part of his daily routines; so did the
preparation of weekly progress bulletins. Despite the cold ob-
jectivity and meticulous phrasing of these bulletins, strange
things seemed to happen to them between their departure from
the offices of Navcomms and their arrival on the world's news-

paper pages and wall display screens. Even stranger things happened in the minds of some people who read them.

One of the British Sunday papers presented just about all of the Old Testament in terms of the interventions of space beings as seen through the eyes of simple beholders. The plagues of Egypt were ecological disruptions deliberately brought about as warnings to the oppressors; flying saucers guided Moses through the Red Sea while the waters were diverted by nucleonic force fields; and the manna from heaven was formed from the hydrocarbon combustion products of thermonuclear propulsion units. A publisher in Paris observed the results, got the message, and commissioned a free-lancer to reexamine the life of Christ as a symbolic account of the apparent miracle workings of a Lunarian returning to Earth after a forty-eight-thousand-year meditation in the galactic wilderness.

"Authentic" reports that the Lunarians were still around abounded. They had built the pyramids, sunk Atlantis, and dug the Bosporus. There were genuine eyewitness accounts of Lunarian landings on Earth in modern times. Somebody had held a conversation with the pilot of a Lunarian spaceship two years before in the middle of the Colorado Desert. Every reference ever recorded to supernatural phenomena, apparitions, visitations, miracles, saints, ghosts, visions, and witches had a Lunarian connection.

But as the months passed and no dramatic revelations unfolded, the world began to turn elsewhere for new sensations. Reports of further findings became confined to the more serious scientific journals and proceedings of the professional societies. But the scientists on the project continued their work undisturbed.

Then a UNSA team erecting an optical observatory on the Lunar Farside detected unusual echoes on ultrasonics from about two hundred feet below the surface. They sank a shaft and discovered what appeared to be all that was left of the underground levels of another Lunarian base, or at any rate, some kind of construction. It was just a metal-walled box about ten feet high and as broad and as long as a small house; one end was missing, and about a quarter of the volume enclosed had filled up with dust and rock debris. In the space that was left at the end, they found the charred skeletons of eight more Lunarians, some pieces of furniture, a few items of technical equipment, and a heap of sealed metal containers. Whatever had formed the remainder of the structure that this gallery had been part of was gone without a trace.

The metal containers were later opened by the scientists at Westwood. Inside the cans was a selection of assorted foodstuffs, well preserved despite having been cooked. Presumably, whatever had done the cooking had also cooked the Lunarians. Most of the cans contained processed vegetables, meats, and sweet preparations; a few, however, yielded a number of fish, about the size of herrings and preserved intact.

When Danchekker's assistant dissected one of the fish and began looking inside, he couldn't make sense of what he found, so he called the professor down to the lab to ask what he made of it. Danchekker didn't go home until eight o'clock the next morning. A week later he announced to an incredulous Vic Hunt: "This specimen never swam in any of our oceans; it did not evolve from, nor is it in any way related to, any form of life that has ever existed on this planet!"

chapter eleven

The Apollo Seventeen Mission, in December 1972, had marked the successful conclusion to man's first concerted effort to reach and explore first-hand a world other than his own. After the Apollo program, NASA activities were restricted, mainly as a result of the financial pressures exerted on the USA by the economic recessions that came and went across the Western world throughout that decade, by the politically inspired oil crisis and various other crises manufactured in the Middle East and the lower half of Africa, and by the promotion of the Vietnam War. During the mid and late seventies, a succession of unmanned probes were dispatched to Mars, Venus, Mercury, and some of the outer planets. When manned missions were resumed in the 1980's, they focused on the development of various types of space shuttle and on the construction of permanently manned orbiting laboratories and observatories, the main objective being the consolidation of a firm jumping-off point prior to resumed expansion outward. Thus, for a period, the Moon was left once more on its own, free to continue its billion-year contemplation of the Universe without further interruption by man.

The information brought back by the Apollo astronauts finally resolved the conflicting speculations concerning the Moon's nature and origins that had been mooted by generations of Earth-bound observers. Soon after the Solar System was formed, 4,500 million years ago, give or take a few, the Moon became molten to a considerable depth, possibly halfway to the center; the heat was generated by the release of gravitational energy as the Moon continued to accumulate. During the cooling that followed, the heavier, iron-bearing minerals sank toward the interior, while the less dense, aluminum-rich ones floated to the surface to form the highland crust. Continual bombardment by meteorites stirred up the mixture and complicated the process to some degree but by 4,300 million years ago the formation of the crust was virtually complete. The bombardment continued until 3,900 million years ago, by which time most of the familiar surface features already existed. From then until 3,200 million years ago, basaltic lavas flowed from the interior, induced in some places by remelting due to concentrations of radioactive heat sources below the surface, to fill in the impact basins and create the darker *maria*. The crust continued cooling to greater depths until molten material could no longer penetrate. Thereafter, all remained unchanging through the ages. Occasionally an additional impact crater appeared and falling dust gradually eroded the top millimeter of surface, but essentially, the Moon became a dead planet.

This history came from detailed observations and limited explorations of Nearside. Orbital observations of Farside suggested that much of the same story applied there also, and since this sequence was consistent with existing theory, nobody doubted its validity for many years after Apollo. Of course, details remained to be added, but the broad picture was convincingly clear. However, when man returned to the Moon in strength and to stay, ground exploration of Farside threw up a completely different and totally unexpected story.

Although the surface of Farside looked much the same as Nearside to the distant observer, it proved at the microscopic level to have undergone something radically different in its history. Furthermore, as bases, launch sites, communications installations, and all the other paraphernalia that accompanied man wherever he went, began proliferating on Nearside, the methodical surface coverage that this entailed produced oddities there, too.

All the experiments performed on the rock samples brought back from the eight sites explored before the mid-seventies gave consistent results supporting the orthodox theories. When the number of sites grew to thousands, by far the majority of additional data confirmed them—but some curious exceptions were noted, exceptions which seemed to indicate that some of the features on Nearside ought, rightfully, to be on Farside.

None of the explanations hazarded were really conclusive. This made little difference to the executives and officers of UNSA, since by that time the pattern of Lunar activity had progressed from that of pure scientific research to one of intense engineering operations. Only the academic fraternity of a few universities found time to ponder and correspond on the spectral inconsistencies between dust samples. So for many years the well-documented problem of "lunar hemispheric anomalies" remained filed, along with a million and one other items, in the "Awaiting Explanation" drawer of science.

A methodical review of the current state of knowledge in any branch of science that might have a bearing on the Lunarian problem was a routine part of Group L's business. Anything to do with the Moon was, naturally, high on the list of things to check up on, and soon the group had amassed enough information to start a small library on the subject. Two junior physicists, who didn't duck quickly enough when Hunt was giving out assignments, were charged with the Herculean task of sifting through all this data. It took some time for them to get around to the topic of hemispheric anomalies. When they did, they found reports of a series of dating experiments performed some years previously by a nucleologist named Kronski at the Max Planck Institute in Berlin. The data that appeared in those reports caused the two physicists to drop everything and seek out Hunt immediately.

After a long discussion, Hunt made a vi-phone call to a Dr. Saul Steinfield of the Department of Physics of the University of Nebraska, who specialized in Lunar phenomena. As a consequence of that call, Hunt made arrangements for the deputy head of Group L to take charge for a few days, and he flew north to Omaha early the next morning. Steinfield's secretary met Hunt at the airport, and within an hour Hunt was standing in one of the physics department laboratories, contemplating a three-foot-diameter model of the Moon.

"The crust isn't evenly distributed," Steinfield said, waving toward the model. "It's a lot thicker on Farside than on Nearside—something that has been known for a long time, ever since the first artificial satellites were hung around the Moon in the nineteen sixties. The center of mass is about two kilometers away from the geometric center."

"And there's no obvious reason," Hunt mused.

Steinfield's flailing arm continued to describe wild circles around the sphere in front of them. "There's no reason for the crust to solidify a lot thicker on one side, sure, but that doesn't really matter, because that's not the way it happened. The material that makes up the Farside surface is much younger than anything anybody ever believed existed on the Moon in any quantity up until about, ah, thirty or so years back—one hell of a lot younger! But you know that—that's why you're here."

"You don't mean it was formed recently," Hunt stated.

Steinfield shook his head vigorously from side to side, causing the two tufts of white hair that jutted from the sides of his otherwise smooth head to wave about in a frenzy. "No. We can tell that it's about as old as the rest of the Solar System. What I mean is—it hasn't been where it is very long."

He caught Hunt's shoulder and half turned him to face a wall chart showing a sectional view through the Lunar center. "You can see it on this. The red shell is the original outer crust going right around—it's roughly circular, as you'd expect. On Farside—here—this blue stuff sits on top of it and wasn't added very long ago."

"On top of what used to be the surface."

"Exactly. Somebody dumped a couple of billion tons of junk down on the old crust—but only on this side."

"And that's been verified pretty conclusively?" Hunt asked, just to be doubly sure.

"Yeah . . . yeah. Enough bore holes and shafts have been sunk all over Farside to tell us pretty closely where the old surface was. I'll show you something over here . . ." A major section of the far wall comprised nothing but rows of small metal drawers, each with its own neatly lettered label, extending from floor to ceiling. Steinfield walked across the room, and stooped to scan the labels, at the same time mumbling to himself semi-intelligibly. With a sudden "That's it!" he pounced on one of the drawers, opened it, and returned bearing a closed glass container about the size of a small pickle jar. It contained a coarse piece of a light gray rocky substance that glittered faintly in places, mounted on a wire support.

"This is fairly common KREEP basalt form Farside. It—"

" 'Creep'?"

"Rich in potassium—that is, K—rare earth elements, and phosphorus: KREEP."

"Oh—I see."

"Compounds like this," Steinfield continued, "make up a lot of the highlands. This one solidified around 4.1 billion years ago. Now, by analyzing the isotope products produced by cosmic-ray exposure, we can tell how long it's been lying on the surface. Again, the figure for this one comes out at about 4,100 million years."

Hunt looked slightly puzzled. "But that's normal. It's what you'd expect, isn't it?"

"If it had been lying on the surface, yes. But this came from the bottom of a shaft over seven hundred feet deep! In other words, it was on the surface for all that time—then suddenly it's seven hundred feet down." Steinfield gestured toward the wall chart again. "As I said, we find the same thing all over Farside. We can estimate how far down the old surface used to be. Below it we find old rocks and structures that go way back, just like on Nearside; above it everything's a mess—the rock all got pounded up and lots of melting took place when the garbage came down, all the way up to what's now the surface. It's what you'd expect."

Hunt nodded his agreement. The energy released by that amount of mass being stopped dead in its tracks would have been phenomenal.

"And nobody knows where it came from?" he asked.

Steinfield repeated his head-shaking act. "Some people say that a big meteorite shower must have got in the way of the Moon. That may be true—it's never been argued conclusively one way or the other. The composition of the garbage isn't really like a lot of meteorites, though—it's closer to the Moon itself. It's as if they were made out of the same stuff—that's why it looks the same from higher up. You have to look at the microstructure to see the things I've been talking about."

Hunt examined the specimen curiously for a while in silence. At length he laid it carefully on the top of one of the benches. Steinfield picked it up and returned it to its drawer.

"Okay," Hunt said as Steinfield rejoined him. "Now, what about the Farside surface?"

"Kronski and company."

"Yes—as we discussed yesterday."

"The Farside surface craters were made by the tail end of the garbage-dumping process, unlike the Nearside craters, which came from meteorite impacts, oh . . . a few billion years back. In rock samples from around the rims of Farside craters we find that things like the activity levels of long half-life elements are very low—for instance, aluminum twenty-six and chlorine thirty-six; also the rates of absorption of hydrogen, helium, and inert gases from the Solar wind. Things like that tell us that those rocks haven't been lying there very long; and since they got where they were by being thrown out of the craters, the craters haven't been there very long, either." Steinfield made an exaggerated empty-handed gesture. "The rest you know. People like Kronski have done all the figuring and put them at around fifty thousand years old—yesterday!" He waited for a few seconds. "There must be a Lunarian connection somewhere. The number sounds like too much of a coincidence to me."

Hunt frowned for a while and studied the detail of the Farside hemisphere of the model. "And yet, you must have known about all this for years," he said, looking up. "Why the devil did you wait for us to call you?"

Steinfield showed his hands again and held the pose for a second or two. "Well, you UNSA people are pretty smart cookies. I figured you already knew about all this."

"We should have picked it up sooner, I admit," Hunt agreed. "But we've been rather busy."

"Guess so," Steinfield murmured. "Anyhow, there's even more to it. I've told you all the consistent things. Now I'll tell you some of the funny things. . . ." He broke off as if just struck by a new thought. "I'll tell you about the funny things in a second. How about a cup of coffee?"

"Great."

Steinfield lit a Bunsen burner, filled a large laboratory

beaker from the nearest tap, and positioned it on a tripod over the flame. Then he squatted down to rummage in the cupboard beneath the bench and at last emerged triumphantly with two battered enamel mugs.

"First funny thing: The distribution of samples that we dig up on Farside that have a history of recent radioactive exposure doesn't match the distribution or strength of the activity sources. There ought to be sources clustered in places where there aren't."

"How about the meteorite storm including some highly active meteorites?" Hunt suggested.

"No, won't wash," Steinfield answered, looking along a shelf of glass jars and eventually selecting one that contained a reddish-brown powder and was labeled "Ferric Oxide." "If there were meteorites like that, bits of them should still be around. But the distribution of active elements in the garbage is pretty even—about normal for most rocks." He began spooning the powder into the mugs. Hunt inclined his head apprehensively in the direction of the jar.

"Coffee doesn't seem to last long around here if you leave it lying around in coffee jars," Steinfield explained. He nodded toward a door that led into the room next door and bore the sign RESEARCH STUDENTS. Hunt nodded understandingly.

"Vaporized?" Hunt tried.

Again Steinfield shook his head.

"In that case they wouldn't have been in proximity to the rock long enough to produce the effects observed." He opened another jar marked "Disodium Hydrogen Phosphate." "Sugar?"

"Second funny thing," Steinfield continued. "Heat balance. We know how much mass came down, and from the way it fell, we can figure its kinetic energy. We also know from statistical sampling how much energy needed to be dissipated to account for the melting and structural deformations; also, we know how much energy gets produced by underground radioactivity and where. Problem: The equations don't balance; you'd need more energy to make what happened happen than there was available. So, where did the extra come from? The computer models of this are very complex and there could be errors in them, but that's the way it looks right now."

Steinfield allowed Hunt to digest this while he picked up the beaker with a pair of tongs and proceeded to fill the mugs.

Having safely completed this operation, he began filling his pipe, still silent.

"Any more?" Hunt asked at last, reaching for his own cigarette case.

Steinfield nodded affirmatively. "Nearside exceptions. Most of the Nearside craters fit with the classic model: old. However, there are some scattered around that don't fit the pattern; cosmic-ray dating puts them at approximately the same age as those on Farside. The usual explanation is that some strays from the recent Farside bombardment overshot around to the Nearside . . ." He shrugged. "But there are peculiarities in some instances that don't really support that."

"Like?"

"Like some of the glasses and breccia formations show heating patterns that aren't consistent with recent impact . . . I'll show you what I mean later."

Hunt turned this new information over in his mind as he lit a cigarette and sipped his drink. It tasted like coffee, anyway.

"And that's the funny thing?"

"Yep, that's about the broad outline. No, wait a minute—last funny thing plus one. How come none of the meteorites in the shower hit Earth? Plenty of eroded remains of terrestrial meteorite craters have been identified and dated. All the computer simulations say that there should be a peak of abnormal activity at around this time, judging from how big the heap of crud that hit the Moon must have been. But there aren't any signs of one, even allowing for the effects of the atmosphere."

Hunt and Steinfield spent the rest of that day and all of the next sifting through figures and research reports that went back many years. Hunt did not sleep at all during the following night, but smoked a pack of cigarettes and consumed a gallon of coffee while he stared at the walls of his hotel room and twisted the new information into every contortion his mind could devise.

Fifty thousand years ago the Lunarians were on the Moon. Where they came from didn't really matter for the time being; that was another question. At about the same time an intense meteorite storm obliterated the Farside surface. Did the storm wipe out the Lunarians on the Moon? Possibly—but that wouldn't have had any effect on them back on whatever planet they had come from. If all the UNSA people on Luna were wiped out, it wouldn't make any lasting difference to Earth.

So, what happened to the rest of the Lunarians? Why hadn't anybody seen them since? Had something else happened to them that was more widespread than whatever happened on the Moon? Could the something else have caused the meteorite storm? Could a second something else have both caused the first and extinguished the Lunarians in other places? Perhaps there was no connection? Unlikely.

Then there were the inconsistencies that Steinfield had talked about. . . . An absurd idea came from nowhere, which Hunt rejected impatiently. But as the night wore on, it kept coming back again with growing insistence. Over breakfast he decided that he had to know the story that lay below those billions of tons of rubble. There had to be some way of extracting enough information to reconstruct the characteristics of the surface just before the bombardment commenced. He put the question to Steinfield later on that morning, back in the lab.

Steinfield shook his head firmly. "We tried for over a year to make a picture like that. We had twelve programmers working on it. They got nowhere. It's too much of a mess down there—all ploughed up. All you get is garbage."

"How about a partial picture?" Hunt persisted. "Is there any way that a contour map could be calculated, showing just the distribution on radiation sources immediately prior to the bombardment?"

"We tried that, too. You do get a degree of statistical clustering, yes. But there's no way we could tell where each individual sample was when it got irradiated. They would have been thrown miles by the impacts; a lot of them would have been bounced all over the place by repeat impacts. Nobody ever built a computer that could unscramble all that entropy. You're up against the second law of thermodynamics; if you ever built one, it wouldn't be a computer at all—it would be a refrigerator."

"What about a chemical approach? What techniques are available that might reveal where the prebombardment craters were? Could their 'ghosts' still be detected a thousand feet below the surface?"

"No way!"

"There has to be some way of reconstructing what the surface used to look like."

"Did you ever try reconstructing a cow from a truckload of hamburger?"

They talked about it for another two days and into the nights at Steinfield's home and Hunt's hotel. Hunt told Steinfield why he needed the information. Steinfield told Hunt he was crazy. Then one morning, back at the laboratory, Hunt exclaimed, "The Nearside exceptions!"

"Huh?"

"The Nearside craters that date from the time of the storm. Some of them could be right from the beginning of it."

"So?"

"They didn't get buried like the first craters on Farside. They're intact."

"Sure—but they won't tell us anything new. They're from recent impacts, same as everything that's on the surface of Farside."

"But you said some of them showed radiation anomalies. That's just what I want to know more about."

"But nobody ever found any suggestions of what you're talking about."

"Maybe they weren't looking for the right things. They never had any reason to."

The physics department had a comprehensive collection of Lunar rock samples, a sizeable proportion of which comprised specimens from the interiors and vicinities of the young, anomalous craters on Nearside. Under Hunt's persistent coercion, Steinfield agreed to conduct a specially devised series of tests on them. He estimated that he would need a month to complete the work.

Hunt returned to Houston to catch up on developments there and a month later flew back to Omaha. Steinfield's experiments had resulted in a series of computer-generated maps showing anomalous Nearside craters. The craters divided themselves into two classes on the maps: those with characteristic irradiation patterns and those without.

"And another thing," Steinfield informed him. "The first class, those that show the pattern, have also got another thing in common that the second class hasn't got: glasses from the centers were formed by a different process. So now we've got anomalous anomalies on Nearside, too!"

Hunt spent a week in Omaha and then went directly to Washington to talk to a group of government scientists and to study the archives of a department that had ceased to exist more than fifteen years before. He then returned to Omaha once again and showed his findings to Steinfield. Steinfield persuaded the university authorities to allow selected samples from their collection to be loaned to the UNSA Mineralogy and Petrology Laboratories in Pasadena, California, for further testing of an extremely specialized nature, suitable equipment for which existed at only a few establishments in the world.

As a direct consequence of these tests, Caldwell authorized the issue of a top-priority directive to the UNSA bases at Tycho, Crisium, and some other Lunar locations, to conduct specific surveys in the areas of certain selected craters. A month after that, the first samples began arriving at Houston and were forwarded immediately to Pasadena; so were the large numbers of samples collected from deep below the surface of Farside.

The outcome of all this activity was summarized in a memorandum stamped "SECRET" and written on the anniversary of Hunt's first arrival in Houston.

9 September 2028

TO: G. Caldwell
        Executive Director
        Navigation and Communications Division

FROM: Dr. V. Hunt
        Section Head
        Special Assignment Goup L

ANOMALIES OF LUNAR CRATERING

(1) Hemispheric Anomalies
     For many years, radical differences have been known to exist between the nature and origins of Lunar Nearside and Farside surface features.
     (a) Nearside
         Original Lunar surface from 4 billion years ago. Nearly all surface cratering caused by explosive release of kinetic energy by meteorite impacts. Some younger—e.g., Copernicus, 850 million year old.
     (b) Farside
         Surface comprises large mass of recently added material to average depth circa 300 meters. Craters formed during final phase of this bombardment. Dating of

these events coincides with Lunarian presence. Origin of bombardment uncertain.

(2) <u>Nearside Exceptions</u>

Known for approx. the last thirty years that some Nearside craters date from same period as those on Farside. Current theory ascribes them to overshoots from Farside bombardment.

(3) <u>Conclusion From Recent Research at Omaha and Pasadena</u>

All Nearside exceptions previously attributed to meteoritic impacts. This belief now considered incorrect. Two classes of exceptions now distinguished:

(a) Class I Exceptions

Confirmed as meteoritic impacts occurring 50,000 years ago.

(b) Class II Exceptions

Differing from Class I in irradiation history, formation of glasses, absence of impact corroboration and positive results to tests for elements hyperium, bonnevillium, genevium. Example: Crater Lunar Catalogue reference MB 3076/K2/E currenctly classed as meteoritic. Classification erroneous. Crater MB 3076/K2/E was made by a nucleonic bomb. Other cases confirmed. Investigations continuing.

(4) <u>Farside Subsurface</u>

Intensive sampling from depths approximating that of the original crust indicate widespred nucleonic detonations prior to meteorite bombardment. Thermonuclear and fission reactions also suspected but impossible to confirm.

(5) <u>Implications</u>

(a) Sophisticated weapons used on Luna at or near time of Lunarian presence, mainly on Farside. Lunarian involvement implied but not proved.

(b) If Lunarians involved, possibility of more widespread conflict embracing Lunarian home planet. Possible cause of Lunarian extinction.

(c) Charlie was a member of more than a small, isolated expedition to our Moon. A significant Lunarian presence on the Moon is indicated. Mainly concentrated on Farside. Practically all traces since obliterated by meteorite storm.

chapter twelve

Front page feature of *The New York Times*, 14 October 2028:

LUNARIAN PLANET LOCATED

DID NUCLEAR WAR DESTROY MINERVA?

Sensational new announcements by UN Space Arm Headquarters, Washington, D.C., at last positively identify the home planet of the Lunarian civilization, known to have achieved space flight and reached Earth's Moon fifty thousand years ago. Information pieced together during more than a year of intense work by teams of scientists based at the UNSA Navigation and Communications Division Headquarters, Houston, Texas, shows conclusively that the Lunarians came from an Earth-like planet that once existed in our own Solar System.

A tenth planet, christened Minerva after the Roman goddess of wisdom, is now known to have existed approximately 250 million miles from the Sun between the orbits of Mars and Jupiter, in the position now occupied by the Asteroid Belt, and is firmly established as having been the center of the Lunarian civilization.

In a further startling announcement, a UNSA spokesman stated that data collected recently at the Lunar bases, following research at the University of Nebraska, Omaha, and the UNSA Mineralogy and Petrology Laboratories, Pasadena, California, indicate that a large-scale nuclear conflict took place on the Moon at the time the Lunarians were there. The possibility that Minerva was destroyed in a full-scale nuclear holocaust of interplanetary dimensions cannot be ruled out.

NUCLEONIC BOMBS USED AT CRISIUM

Investigations in recent months at the University of Nebraska and Pasadena give positive evidence that nucleonic bombs have caused craters on the Moon previously attributed to meteorite impacts. H-bomb and A-bomb effects are also suspected but cannot be confirmed.

Dr. Saul Steinfield of the Department of Physics at the University of Nebraska explained: "For many years we have known that Lunar Farside craters are very much younger than most of the craters on Nearside. All the Farside craters, and a few of the Nearside ones, date from about the time of the Lunarians, and have always been thought to be meteoritic. Most of them, including all Farside ones, are. We have now proved, however, that some of the Nearside ones were made by bombs—for example, a few on the northern periphery of Mare Crisium and a couple near Tycho. So far, we've identified twenty-three positively and have a long list to check out."

Further evidence collected from deep below the Farside surface indicates heavier bombing there than on Nearside. Obliteration of the original Farside surface by a heavy meteorite storm immediately after these events, accounts for only meteorite craters being found there today and makes detailed reconstruction of exactly what took place unlikely. "The evidence for higher activity on Farside is mainly statistical," said Steinfield yesterday. "There's no way you could figure anything specific—for example, an actual crater count—under all that garbage."

The new discoveries do not explain why the meteorite storm happened at this time. Professor Pierre Guillemont of the Hale Observatory commented: "Clearly, there could be a connection with the Lunarian presence. Personally, I would be surprised if the agreement in dates is just a coincidence, although that, of course, is possible. For the time being, it must remain an unanswered question."

CLUES FROM *ILIAD MISSION*

Startling confirmation that Minerva disintegrated to form the Asteroid Belt has been received from space. Examination of Asteroid samples carried out on board the spacecraft *Iliad*, launched from Luna fifteen months ago to conduct a survey of parts of the Belt, shows many Asteroids to be of recent origin. Data beamed back to Mission Control Center at UNSA Operational Command Headquarters, Galveston, Texas, give cosmic-ray exposure times and orbit statistics pinpointing Minerva's disintegration at fifty thousand years ago.

Earth scientists are eagerly awaiting arrival of the first Asteroid material to be sent back from *Iliad*, which is due at Luna in six weeks time.

Scientists do not agree that Lunarians necessarily originated on Minerva. Detailed physical examinations of "Charlie" (*Times*, 7 November 2027) shows Lunarian anatomy identical to that of humans and incapable of being the product of a separate evolutionary process, according to all accepted theory. Conversely, absence of traces of Lunarian history on Earth seems to rule out any possibility of terrestrial origins. This remains the main focus of controversy among the investigators.

In an exclusive interview, Dr. Victor Hunt, the British-born UNSA nucleonics expert coordinating Lunarian investigations from Houston, explained to a *Times* reporter: "We know quite a lot about Minerva now—its size, its mass, its climate, and how it rotated and orbited the Sun. Upstairs we've built a six-foot scale model of it that shows you every continent, ocean, river, mountain range, town, and city. Also, we know it supported an advanced civilization. We also know a lot about Charlie, including his place of birth, which is given on several of his personal documents as a town easily identified on Minerva. But that doesn't prove very much. My deputy was born in Japan, but both his parents come from Brooklyn. So until we know a lot more than we do, we can't even say for sure that the Minervan civilization and the Lunarian civilization were one and the same.

"It's possible the Lunarians originated on Earth and either went to live on Minerva or made contact with another race who were there already. Maybe the Lunarians originated on Minerva. We just don't know. Whichever alternative you choose, you've got problems."

Professor Christian Danchekker, an eminent biologist at Westwood Laboratories, Houston, and also involved in Lunarian research from the beginning, confirmed that the alien species of fish discovered among foodstocks in the ruin of a Lunarian base on Lunar Farside several months ago (*Times*, 6 July 2028) appears to have been a life form native to Minerva. Markings on the containers in which the fish were preserved show that they came from a well-defined group of equatorial islands on Minerva. According to Professor Danchekker: "There is no question whatsoever that this species evolved on a planet other than Earth. It seems clear that the fish belong to an evolutionary line that developed on Minerva, and they were caught there by members of a group of colonists from Earth who established an extension of their civilization there."

The professor described the suggestion that the Lunarians might also be natives of Minerva as "ludicrous."

Despite a wealth of new information, therefore, much remains to be explained about recent events in the Solar System. Almost certainly, the next twelve months will see further exciting developments.

(See also the Special Supplement by our Science Editor on page 14.)

chapter thirteen

Captain Hew Mills, UN Space Arm, currently attached to the Solar System Exploration Program mission to the moons of Jupiter, stood gazing out of the transparent dome that surmounted the two-story Site Operations Control building. The building stood just clear of the ice, on a rocky knoll overlooking the untidy cluster of domes, vehicles, cabins, and storage tanks that went to make up the base he commanded. In the dim gray background around the base, indistinct shadows of rock buttresses and ice cliffs vanished and reappeared through the sullen, shifting vapors of the methane-ammonia haze. Despite his above-average psychological resilience and years of strict training, an involuntary shudder ran down his spine as he thought of the thin triple wall of the dome—all that separated him from this foreboding, poisonous, alien world, cold enough to freeze him as black as coal and as brittle as glass in seconds. Ganymede, largest of the moons of Jupiter, was, he thought, an awful place.

"Close-approach radars have locked on. Landing sequence is active. Estimated time to touch down: three minutes, fifty seconds." The voice of the duty controller at one of the consoles behind Mills interrupted his broodings.

"Very good, Lieutenant," he acknowledged. "Do you have contact with Cameron?"

"There's a channel open on screen three, sir."

Mills moved around in front of the auxiliary console. The screen showed an empty chair and behind it an interior view of the low-level control room. He pressed the call button, and after a few seconds the face of Lieutenant Cameron moved into the viewing angle.

"The brass are due in three minutes," Mills advised. "Everything okay?"

"Looking good, sir."

Mills resumed his position by the wall of the dome and noted with satisfaction the three tracked vehicles lurching into line to take up their reception positions. Minutes ticked by.

"Sixty seconds," the duty controller announced. "Descent profile normal. Should make visual contact any time now."

A patch of fog above the landing pads in the central area of the base darkened and slowly materialized into the blurred outline of a medium-haul surface transporter, sliding out of the murk, balanced on its exhausts with its landing legs already fully extended. As the transporter came to rest on one of the pads and its shock absorbers flexed to dispose of the remaining momentum, the reception vehicles began moving forward. Mills nodded to himself and left the dome via the stairs that led down to ground level.

Ten minutes later, the first reception vehicle halted outside the Operations Control building and an extending tube telescoped out to dock with its airlock. Major Stanislow, Colonel Peters, and a handful of aides walked through into the outer access chamber, where they were met by Mills and a few other officers. Mutual introductions were concluded, and without further preliminaries the party ascended to the first floor and proceeded through an elevated walkway into the adjacent dome, constructed over the head of number-three shaft. A labyrinth of stairs and walkways brought them eventually to number-three high-level airlock anteroom. A capsule was waiting beyond the airlock. For the next four minutes they plummeted down, down, deep into the ice crust of Ganymede.

They emerged through another airlock into number-three low-level anteroom. The air vibrated with the humming and throbbing of unseen machines. Beyond the anteroom, a short corridor brought them at last to the low-level control room. It was a maze of consoles and equipment cubicles, attended by perhaps a dozen operators, all intent on their tasks. One of the longer walls, constructed completely from glass, gave a panoramic view down over the workings in progress outside the control room. Lieutenant Cameron joined them as they lined up by the glass to take in the spectacle beyond.

They were looking out over the floor of an enormous cathedral, over nine hundred feet long and a hundred feet high, hewn and melted out of the solid ice. Its rough-formed walls glistened white and gray in the glare of countless arc lights. The floor was a litter of steelmesh roadways, cranes, gantries, girders, pipes, tubes, and machinery of every description. The left-side wall, stretching away to the far end of the tunnel, carried a lattice of ladders, scaffolding, walkways, and cabins that extended up to the roof. All over the scene, scores of figures in ungainly heavy-duty space suits bustled about in a frenzy of activity, working in an atmosphere of pressurized argon to eliminate any risk of explosion from methane and the other gases released from the melted ice. But all eyes were fixed on the right-hand wall of the tunnel.

For almost the entire length, a huge, sweeping wall of smooth, black metal reared up from the floor and curved up and over, out of sight above their heads, to be lost below the roof of the cavern. It was immense—just a part of something vast and cylindrical, lying on its side, the whole of which must have stretched far down into the ice below floor level. At the near end, outside the control room, a massive, curving wing flared out of the cylinder and spanned the cavern above their heads like a bridge, before disappearing into the ice high on the far left. At intervals along the base of the wall, where metal and ice met, a series of holes six feet or so across marked the ends of the network of pilot tunnels that had been driven all around and over and under the object.

It was far larger than a Vega. How long it had lain there, entombed beneath the timeless ice sheets of Ganymede, nobody knew. But the computations of field-vector resultants collected from the satellites had been right; there certainly had been something big down here—and it hadn't been just ore deposits.

"Ma-an," breathed Stanislow, after staring for a long time. "So that's it, huh?"

"That is big!" Peters added with a whistle. The aides echoed the sentiments dutifully.

Stanislow turned to Mills. "Ready for the big moment, then, Captain?"

"Yes, sir," Mills confirmed. He indicated a point about two hundred feet away where a group of figures was gathered close to the wall of the hull, surrounded by an assortment of equipment. Beside them a rectangular section of the skin about eight feet square had been cut away. "First entry point will be there—approximately amidships. The outer hull is double layered; both layers have been penetrated. Inside in an inner hull . . ." For the benefit of the visitors, he gestured toward a display positioned near the observation window showing the aperture in close-up. "Preliminary drilling shows that it's a single layer. The valves that you can see projecting from the inner hull were inserted to allow samples of the internal atmosphere to be taken before opening it up. Also, the cavity behind the access point has been argon-flooded."

Mills turned to Cameron before going on to describe further details of the operation. "Lieutenant, carry out a final check of communications links, please."

"Aye, aye, sir." Cameron walked back to the supervisory console at the end of the room and scanned the array of screens.

"Ice Hole to Subway. Come in, please."

The face of Commander Stracey, directing activities out near the hull, moved into view, encased in its helmet. "All checks completed and go," he reported. "Standing by, ready to proceed."

"Ice Hole to Pithead. Report transmission quality."

"All clear, vision and audio," responded the duty controller from the dome far above them.

"Ice Hole to Ganymede Main." Cameron addressed screen three, which showed Foster at Main Base, situated seven hundred miles away to the south.

"Clear."

"Ice Hole to Jupiter Four. Report, please."

"All channels clear and checking positive." The last acknowledgment came from the deputy mission director on screen four, speaking from his nerve center in the heart of the mile-long Jupiter Mission Four command ship, at that moment orbiting over two thousand miles up over Ganymede.

"All channels positive and ready to proceed, sir," Cameron called to Mills.

"Carry on, then, Lieutenant."

"Aye, aye, sir."

Cameron passed the order to Stracey, and out by the hull the ponderous figures lumbered into action, swinging forward a rock-drill supported from an overhead gantry. The group by the window watched in silence as the bit chewed relentlessly into the inner wall. Eventually the drill was swung back.

"Initial penetration complete," Stracey's voice informed them. "Nothing visible inside."

An hour later, a pattern of holes adorned the exposed expanse of metal. When lights were shone through and a TV probe inserted, the screen showed snatches of a large compartment crammed with ducts and machinery. Shortly afterward, Stracey's team began cutting out the panel with torches. Mills invited Peters and Stanislow to come and observe the operations first-hand. The trio left the control room, descended to the lower floor, and a few minutes later emerged, clad in space suits, through the airlock onto the tunnel floor. As they arrived at the aperture, the rectangle of metal was just being swung aside.

The spotlights confirmed the general impression obtained via the drill holes. When preliminary visual examinations were completed, two sergeants who had been standing by stepped forward. Communications lines were plugged into their backpacks and they were handed TV cameras trailing cables, flashlights, and a pouch of tools and accessories. At the same time, other members of the team were smoothing over the jagged edges of the hole with pads of adhesive plastic to prevent tearing of the lines. An extending aluminum ladder was lowered into the hole and secured. The first sergeant to enter turned about on the edge of the hole, carefully located the top rung with his feet, and inch by inch disappeared down into the chamber. When he had found a firm footing, the second followed.

For twenty minutes they clambered through the mechanical jungle, twisting and turning among the chaotic shadows cast by the lights pouring in through the hole above. Progress was slow; they had difficulty finding level surfaces to move on, since the ship appeared to be lying on its side. But foot by foot, the lines continued to snake sporadically down into the darkness. Eventually the sergeants stopped before the noseward bulkhead of the compartment. The screens outside showed their way barred by a door leaking through to whatever lay forward; it was made of a steely-gray metal and looked solid. It was also about ten feet high by four wide. A long conference produced the decision that there was no alternative but for them to return to where the hole had been cut to collect drills, torches, and all the other gadgetry needed to go through the whole drilling, purging, argon-filling, and cutting routine all over again. From the look of the door, it could be a long job. Mills, Stanislow, and Peters went back to the control room, collected the remainder of their party, and went to the surface installations for lunch. They returned three hours later.

Behind the bulkhead was another machinery compartment, as confusing as the first but larger. This one had many doors leading from it—all closed. The two sergeants selected one at random in the ceiling above their heads, and while they were cutting through it, others descended into the first and second compartments to position rollers for minimizing the drag of their trailing cables, which was beginning to slow them down appreciably. When the door was cut, a second team relieved the first.

They used another ladder to climb up through the door and found themselves standing on what was supposed to be the wall of a long corridor running toward the nose of the ship. A succession of closed doors, beneath their feet and over their heads, passed across the screens outside. Over two hundred feet of cabling had disappeared into the original entry point.

"We're just passing the fifth bulkhead since entering the corridor," the commentary on the audio channel informed the observers. "The walls are smooth, and appear to be metallic, but covered with a plastic material. It's coming away in most places. The floor up one side is black and looks rubbery. There are lots of doors in both walls, all big like the first one. Some have . . ."

"Just a second, Joe," the voice of the speaker's companion broke in. "Swing the big light down here . . . by your feet. See, the door you're standing on slides to the side. It's not closed all the way."

The screens showed a pair of standard-issue heavy-duty

UNSA boots, standing on a metal panel in the middle of a pool of light. The boots shuffled to one side to reveal a black gap, about twelve inches wide, running down one side of the panel. They then stepped off the panel and onto the surrounding area as their owner evidently inspected the situation.

"You're right," Joe's voice announced at last. "Let's see if it'll budge."

There then followed a jumbled sequence of arms, legs, walls, ceilings, lightness, and darkness as TV cameras and lamps exchanged hands and were waved about. When a stable picture resulted, it showed two heavily clad arms braced across the gap. Eventually:

"No dice. Stuck solid."

"How about the jack?"

"Yeah, maybe. Pass it down, willya?"

A long dialogue followed during which the jack was maneuvered into place and expanded. It slipped off. Muttered curses. Another try. And then:

"It's moving! Come on, baby . . . let's have a bit more light . . . I think it'll go easy now . . . See if you can get a foot against it . . ."

On the monitors the gray slab graunched gradually out of the picture. A black, bottomless pit fell away beneath.

"The door is about two-thirds open," a breathless voice resumed. "It's gummed up there and won't go any further. We're gonna have a quick looksee around from up here, then we'll have to come back to get another ladder. Can somebody have one ready at the door that leads up into this corridor?"

The camera closed in on the pitch-black oblong. A few seconds later a circle of light appeared in the scene, picking out part of the far wall. The light began moving around inside and the camera followed. Banks of what appeared to be electronic equipment . . . corners of cubicles . . . legs of furniture . . . sections of bulkhead . . . moved through the circle.

"There's a lot of loose junk down at the end . . . Move the light around a bit . . ." Several colored cylinders in a heap, about the size of jelly jars . . . something like a braided belt, lying in a tangle . . . a small gray box with buttons on one face . . .

"What was that? Go over a bit, Jerry . . . No, a bit more to the left."

Something white. A bar of white.

"*Jeez!* Look at that! Jerry, will you look at that?"

The skull, grinning up out of the pool of eerie white light, startled even the watchers out in the tunnel. But is was the size of the skeleton that stunned them; no man had ever boasted a chest that compared with those massive hoops of bone. But besides that, even the most inexpert among the observers could see that whatever the occupants of this craft had been, they bore no resemblance to man.

The stream of data taken in by the cameras flashed back to preprocessors in the low-level control room, and from there via cable to the surface of Ganymede. After encoding by the computers in the Site Operations Control building, it was relayed by microwave repeaters seven hundred miles to Ganymede Main Base, restored to full strength, and redirected up to the orbiting command ship. Here, the message was fed into the message exchange and scheduling processor complex, transformed into high-power laser modulations, and slotted into the main outgoing signal beam to Earth. For over an hour the data streaked across the Solar System, covering 186,000 miles every second, until the sensors of the long-range relay beacon, standing in Solar orbit not many million miles outside that of Mars, fished it out of the void, a microscopic fraction of its original power. Retransmission from here found the Deep Space Link Station, lodged in Trojan equilibrium with Earth and Luna, and eventually a synchronous communications satellite hanging high over the central USA, which beamed it down to a ground station near San Antonio. A landline network completed the journey to UNSA Mission Control, Galveston, where the information was greedily consumed by the computers of Operational Command Headquarters.

The Jupiter Four command ship had taken eleven months to reach the giant planet. Within four hours of the event, the latest information to be gathered by the mission was safely lodged in the data banks of UN Space Arm.

chapter fourteen

The discovery of the giant spaceship, frozen under the ice field of Ganymede, was a sensation but, in a sense, not something totally unexpected. The scientific world had more or less accepted as fact that an advanced civilization had once flourished on Minerva; indeed, if the arguments of the orthodox evolutionists were accepted, at least two planets—Minerva and Earth—had supported high-technology civilizations to some extent at about the same time. It did not come as a complete surprise, therefore, that man's persistent nosing around the Solar System should uncover more evidence of its earlier inhabitants. What did surprise everybody was the obvious anatomical difference between the Ganymeans as the beings on board the ship soon came to be called—and the common form shared by the Lunarians and mankind.

To the still unresolved question of whether the Lunarians and the Minervans had been one and the same or not, there was immediately added the further riddle: Where had the Ganymeans come from, and had they any connection with either? One bemused UNSA scientist summed up the situation by declaring that it was about time UNSA established an Alien Civilizations Division to sort out the whole damn mess!

The pro-Danchekker faction quickly interpreted the new development as full vindication of evolutionary theory and of the arguments they had been promoting all along. Clearly, two planets in the Solar System had evolved intelligent life at around the same period in the past; the Ganymeans had evolved on Minerva and the Lunarians had evolved on Earth. They came independently from different lines and that was why they were different. Lunarian pioneers made contact with the Ganymeans and settled on Minerva—that was how Charlie had come to be born there. Extreme hostilities broke out between the two civilizations at some point, resulting in the extinction of both and the destruction of Minerva. The reasoning was consistent, plausible, and convincing. Against it, the objection—that no evidence of any Lunarian civilization on Earth had ever been detected—began to look more lonely and more feeble every day. Deserters left the can't-be-of-Earth-origin camp in droves to join Danchekker's growing legions. Such was his gain in prestige and credibility that it seemed perfectly natural for his department to assume responsibility for conducting the preliminary evaluation of the data coming in from Jupiter.

Despite his earlier skepticism, Hunt too found the case compelling. He and a large part of Group L's staff spent much time searching every available archive and record from such fields as archeology and paleontology for any reference that could be a pointer to the one-time existence of an advanced race on Earth. They even delved into the realms of ancient mythology and combed various pseudoscientific writings to see if anything could be extracted that was capable of substantiation, that suggested the works of superbeings in the past. But always the results were negative.

While all this was going on, things began to happen in an area where progress had all but ground to a halt for many months. Linguistics had run into trouble: The meager contents of the documents found about Charlie's person simply had not contained enough information to make great inroads into deciphering a whole new, alien language. Of the two small books, one—that containing the maps and tables and resembling a handy pocket reference—together with loose documents, had been translated in parts and had yielded most of the fundamental data about Minerva and quite a lot about Charlie. The second book contained a series of dated entries in handwritten script, but despite repeated attempts, it had obstinately defied decoding.

This situation changed dramatically some weeks after the opening up of the underground remains of the devastated Lunarian base on Lunar Farside. Among the pieces of equipment included in that find had been a metal drum, containing a series of glass plates, rather like the magazines of some slide projectors. Closer examination of the plates revealed them to be simple projection slides, each holding a closely packed matrix of microdot images which, under a microscope, were seen to be pages of printed text. Constructing a system of lamps and lenses to project them onto a screen was straightforward, and in one fell swoop Linguistics became the owners of a miniature Lunarian library. Results followed in months.

Don Maddson, head of the linguistics section, rummaged through the litter of papers and files that swamped the large table standing along the left-hand wall of his office, selected a loosely clipped wad of typed notes, and returned to the chair behind his desk.

"There's a set of these on its way up to you," he said to Hunt, who was sitting in the chair opposite. "I'll leave you to read the details for yourself later. For now, I'll just sum up the general picture."

"Fine," Hunt said. "Fire away."

"Well, for a start, we know a bit more about Charlie. One of the documents found in a pouch on the backpack appears to be something like army pay records. It gives an abbreviated history of some of the things he did and a list of the places he was posted to—that kind of thing."

"Army? Was he in the army, then?"

Maddson shook his head. "Not exactly. From what we can gather, they didn't differentiate much between civilian and military personnel in terms of how their society was structured. It's more like everybody belonged to different branches of the same big organization."

"A sort of last word in totalitarianism?"

"Yeah, that's about it. The State ran just about everything; it dominated every walk of life and imposed a rigid discipline everywhere. You went where you were sent and did what you were told to do; in most cases, that meant into industry, agriculture, or the military forces. Whatever you did, the State was your boss anyway—that's what I meant when I said they were all different branches of the same big organization."

"Okay. Now, about the pay records?"

"Charlie was born on Minerva, we know that. So were his parents. His father was some kind of machine operator; his mother worked in industry, too, but we can't make out the exact occupation. The records also tell us where he went to school, for how long, where he took his military training—everybody seemed to go through some kind of military training—and where he learned about electronics. It tells us all the dates, too."

"So he was something like an electronics engineer, was he?" Hunt asked.

"Sort of. More of a maintenance engineer than a design or development engineer. He seems to have specialized in military equipment—there's a long list of postings to combat units. The last one is interesting . . ." Maddson selected a sheet and passed it across to Hunt. "That's a translation of the last page of postings. The final entry gives the name of a place and, alongside it, a description which, when translated literally, means 'off-planet.' That's probably the Lunarian name for whatever part of our Moon he was sent to."

"Interesting," Hunt agreed. "You've found out quite a lot more about him."

"Yep, we've got him pretty well taped. If you convert their dates into our units, he was about thirty-two years old at the date of his last posting. Anyhow, that's all really incidental; you can read the details. I was going to run over the picture we're getting of the kind of world he was born into." Maddson paused to consult his notes again. Then he resumed: "Minerva was a dying world. At the time we're talking about, the last cold period of the Ice Age was approaching its peak. I'm told that ice ages are Solar-System-wide phenomena; Minerva was a lot farther from the Sun than here, so as you can imagine, things were pretty bleak there."

"You've only got to look at the size of those ice caps," Hunt commented.

"Yes, exactly. And it was getting worse. The Lunarian scientists figured they had less than a hundred years to go before the ice sheets met and blanketed the whole planet completely. Now, as you'd expect, they had studied astronomy for centuries—centuries before Charlie's time, that is—and they'd known for a long time that things were going to get worse before they got better. So, they'd reached the conclusion, way back, that the only way out was to escape to another world. The problem, of course, was that for generations after they got the idea, nobody knew anything about how to do something about it. The answer had to lie somewhere along the line of better science and better technology. It became kind of a racial goal—the one thing that mattered, that generation after generation worked toward—the development of the sciences that would get them to places they knew existed, before the ice wiped out the whole race."

Maddson pointed to another pile of papers on the corner of his desk. "This was the prime objective that the State was set up to achieve, and because the stakes were so high, everything was subordinated to that objective. Hence, from birth to death the individual was subordinated to the needs of the State. It was implied in everything they wrote and drummed into them from the time they were knee-high. Those papers are a translation of a kind of catechism they had to memorize at school; it reads like Nazi stuff from the nineteen thirties." He stopped at that point and looked at Hunt expectantly.

Hunt looked puzzled. After a moment he said, "This doesn't quite make sense. I mean—how could they be striving to develop space flight if they were colonists from Earth? They must have already developed it."

Maddson gave an approving nod. "Thought you might say that."

"But . . . it's bloody silly."

"I know. It implies they must have evolved on Minerva from scratch—unless they came from Earth, forgot everything they knew, and had to learn it all over. But that also sounds crazy to me."

"Me too." Hunt thought for a long time. At last he shook his head with a sigh. "Doesn't make sense. Anyhow, what else is there?"

"Well, we've got the general picture of a totally authoritarian State, demanding unquestioning obedience from the individual and controlling just about everything that moves. Everything needs a license; there are travel licenses, off-work licenses, sick-ration licenses—even procreation licenses. Everything is in short supply and rationed by permits—food, every kind of commodity, fuel, light, accommodation—you name it. And to keep everybody in line, the State operates a propaganda machine like you never dreamed of. To make things worse, the whole planet was desperately short of every kind of mineral. That slowed them down a lot. Despite their concentrated effort, their rate of technological progress was probably not as fast as you'd think. Maybe a hundred years didn't give them as long as it sounds." Maddson turned some sheets, scanned the next one briefly, and then went on. "To make matters worse still, they also had a big political problem."

"Go on."

"Now, we're assuming that as their civilization developed, it followed similar lines to ours—first tribes, then villages, towns, nations, and so on. Seems reasonable. So, somewhere along the way they started discovering the different sciences, same as we did. As you'd expect, the same ideas started occurring to different people in different places at around the same time—like, we've gotta get outa this place. As these ideas became accepted, the Lunarians seem to have figured also that there just weren't sufficient resources for more than a few lucky ones to make it. No way were they going to get a whole planet full of people out."

"So they fought about it," Hunt offered.

"That's right. The way I picture it, lots of nations grew up, all racing each other, as well as the ice, to get the technological edge. Every other one was a rival, so they fought it out. Another thing that made them fight was the mineral shortage, especially the shortage of metallic ores." Maddson pointed at a map of Minerva mounted above the table. "See those dots on the ice sheets? Most of them were a combination of fortress and mining town. They dug right down through the ice to get at the deposits, and the army was there to make sure they kept the stuff."

"And that was the way life was. Mean people, eh?"

"Yeah, for generation after generation." Maddson shrugged. "Who knows? Maybe if we were freezing over fast, we'd be forced in the same direction. Anyhow, the situation had complications. They had the problem of having to divide their efforts and resources between two different demands all the time: first, developing a technology that would support mass interplanetary travel and, second, armaments and the defense organization to protect it—and there weren't a lot of resources to divide in the first place. Now, how would you solve a problem like that?"

Hunt pondered for a while.

"Cooperate?" he tried.

"Forget it. They didn't think that way."

"Only one other strategy possible, then: Wipe out the opposition first and then concentrate everything on the main objective."

Maddson nodded solidly. "That is exactly what they did. War, or near war, was pretty well a natural way of life all through their history. Gradually the smaller fish were eliminated until, by the time we get to Charlie, there are only two superpowers left, each dominating one of the two big equatorial continental land masses . . ." He pointed at the map again. " . . . Cerios and Lambia. From various references, we know Charlie was a Cerian."

"All set for the big showdown, then."

"Check. The whole planet was one big fortress—factory. Every inch of surface was covered by hostile missiles; the sky was full of orbiting bombs that could be dropped anywhere. We get the impression that relative to the pattern of our own civilization, their armaments programs had taken a bigger share than space research and had progressed faster." Maddson shrugged again. "The rest you can guess."

Hunt nodded slowly and thoughtfully. "It all fits," he mused. "It must have been a huge con, though. I mean, even from whichever side won, only a handful would have been able to get away in the end; I suppose they'd have been the ruling clique and its minions. Christ! No wonder they needed good propaganda; they—"

Hunt stopped in midsentence and looked at Maddson with a curious expression. "Just a minute—there's something else in all this that doesn't add up." He paused to collect his thoughts. "They had already developed interplanetary travel—how else did they get to our Moon?"

"We wondered that," Maddson said. "The only thing we could think of was that maybe they'd already figured on making for Earth eventually—that had to be the obvious choice. Maybe they were capable of sending a scouting group to stake the place out, but didn't have full-scale mass-transportation capacity yet. Probably they weren't too far away from their goal when they blew it. Perhaps if they'd pooled their marbles at that point instead of starting a crazy war over it, things might have been different."

"Sounds plausible," Hunt agreed. "So Charlie could have been part of a reconnaissance mission sent on ahead, only the opposition had the same idea and they bumped into each other. Then they started blowing holes in our Moon. Disgraceful."

A short silence ensued.

"There's another thing I don't get, either," Hunt said, rubbing his chin.

"What's that?"

"Well, the opposition—the Lambians. Everybody in Navcomms is going around saying that the war that clobbered Minerva was fought between colonists from Earth—that must be Charlie's lot, the Cerians—and an alien race that belonged to Minerva—the Ganymeans, who, from what you said, would be the Lambians. We said a moment ago that this idea of the Cerians being from Earth doesn't make sense, because if they had originated there, they wouldn't be trying to develop space flight. We can't be one hundred percent certain of that because something unusual could have happened, such as the colony being cut off for a few thousand years for some reason. But you can't say that about the Lambians; they couldn't have been neck-and-neck rivals trying to develop space flight."

"They already had it, for sure," Maddson completed for him. "We sure as hell found them on Ganymede."

"Quite. And that ship was no beginner's first attempt, either. You know, I'm beginning to think that whoever the Lambians were, they weren't Ganymeans."

"I think you're right," Maddson confirmed. "The Ganymeans were a totally different biological species. Wouldn't you expect that if they were the opposition in Lambia, somehow it would show up in the Lunarian writings? But it doesn't. Everything we've examined suggests that the Cerians and the Lambians were simply different nations of the same race. For example, we've found extracts from what appear to be Cerian newspapers, which included political cartoons showing Lambian figures; the figures are drawn as human forms. That wouldn't be so if the Lambians looked anything like the Ganymeans must have looked."

"So it appears the Ganymeans had nothing to do with the war," Hunt concluded.

"Right."

"So where do they fit in?"

Maddson showed his empty palms. "That's the funny thing. They don't seem to fit anywhere—at least, we haven't even found anything that looks like a reference to them."

"Maybe they're just a big red herring, then. I mean, we've only supposed that they came from Minerva; nothing actually demonstrates that they did. Perhaps they never had anything to do with the place at all."

"Could well be. But I can't help feeling that . . ."

The chime on Maddson's desk display console interrupted the discussion. He excused himself and touched a button to accept the call.

"Hi, Don," said the face of Hunt's assistant, upstairs in Group L's offices. "Is Vic there?" He sounded excited. Maddson swiveled the unit around to point in Hunt's direction.

"It's for you," he said needlessly.

"Vic," said the face without preamble. "I've just had a look at the reports of the latest tests that came in from Jupiter Four two hours ago. That ship under the ice and the big guys inside it—they've completed the dating tests." He drew a deep breath. "It looks like maybe we can forget the Ganymeans in all this Charlie business. Vic, if all the figures are right, that ship has been sitting there for something like twenty-five *million* years!"

chapter fifteen

Caldwell moved a step closer to inspect more carefully the nine-foot-high plastic model standing in the middle of one of the laboratories of the Westwood Biological Institute. Danchekker gave him plenty of time to take in the details before continuing.

"A full-size replica of a Ganymean skeleton," he said. "Built on the strength of the data beamed back from Jupiter. The first indisputable form of intelligent alien life ever to be studied by man." Caldwell looked up at the towering frame, pursed his lips in a silent whistle, and walked in a slow circle around and back to where the professor was standing. Hunt simply stood and swept his eyes up and down the full length of the model in wordless fascination.

"That structure is in no way related to that of any animal ever studied on Earth, living or extinct," Danchekker informed them. He gestured toward it. "It is based on a bony internal skeleton, walks upright as a biped, and has a head on top—as you can see; but apart from such superficial similarities, it has clearly evolved from completely unfamiliar origins. Take the head as an obvious example. The arrangement of the skull cannot be reconciled in any way with that of known vertebrates. The face has not receded back into the lower skull, but remains a long, down-pointing snout that widens at the top to provide a broad spacing for the eyes and ears. Also, the back of the skull has enlarged to accommodate a developing brain, as in the case of man, but instead of assuming a rounded contour, it bulges back above the neck to counterbalance the protruding face and jaw. And look at the opening through the skull in the center of the forehead; I believe that this could have housed a sense organ that we do not possess—possibly an infrared detector inherited from a nocturnal, carnivorous ancestor."

Hunt moved forward to stand next to Caldwell and peered intently at the shoulders. "These are unlike anything I've ever come across, too," he commented. "They're made up of . . . kind of overlapping plates of bone. Nothing like ours at all."

"Quite," Danchekker confirmed. "Probably adapted from the remains of ancestral armor. And the rest of the trunk is also quite alien. There is a dorsal spine with an arrangement of ribs below the shoulder plates, as you can see, but the lowermost rib—immediately above the body cavity—has developed into a massive hoop of bone with a diametral strut stretching forward from an enlarged spinal vertebra. Now, notice the two systems of smaller linked bones at the sides of the hoop . . ." He pointed them out. "They were probably used to assist with breathing by helping to expand the diaphragm. To me, they look suspiciously like the degenerate remnants of a paired-limb structure. In other words, although this creature, like us, had two arms and walked on two legs, somewhere in his earlier ancestry were animals with three pairs of appendages, not two. That in itself is enough to immediately rule out any kinship with every vertebrate of this planet."

Caldwell stooped to examine the pelvis, which comprised just an arrangement of thick bars and struts to contain the thigh sockets. There was no suggestion of the splayed dish form of the lower human torso.

"Must've had peculiar guts, too," he offered.

"It could be that the internal organs were carried more by suspension from the hoop above than by support from underneath," Danchekker suggested. He stepped back and indicated the arms and legs. "And last, observe the limbs. Both lower limbs have two bones as do ours, but the upper arm and thigh are different—they have a double-bone arrangement as well. This would have resulted in vastly improved flexibility and the ability to perform a whole range of movements that could never be duplicated by a human being. And the hand has six digits, two of them opposing; thus its owner effectively enjoyed the advantages of having two thumbs. He would have been able to tie his shoes easily with one hand."

Danchekker waited until Caldwell and Hunt had fully studied every detail of the skeleton to their satisfaction. When they looked toward him again, he resumed: "Ever since the age of the Ganymeans was verified, there has been a tendency for everybody to discount them as merely a coincidental discovery and having no direct bearing on the Lunarian question. I believe, gentlemen, that I am now in a position to demonstrate that they had a very real bearing indeed on the question."

Hunt and Caldwell looked at him expectantly. Danchekker walked over to a display console by the wall of the lab, tapped in a code, and watched as the screen came to life to reveal a picture of the skeleton of a fish. Satisfied, he turned to face them.

"What do you notice about that?" he asked.

Caldwell stared obediently at the screen for a few seconds while Hunt watched in silence.

"It's a funny fish," Caldwell said at last. "Okay—you tell me."

"It is not obvious at first sight," Danchekker replied, "but by detailed comparison it is possible to relate the structure of that fish, bone for bone, to that of the Ganymean skeleton. They're both from the same evolutionary line."

"That fish is one of those that were found on the Lunarian base on Farside," Hunt said suddenly.

"Precisely, Dr. Hunt. The fish dates from some fifty thousand years ago, and the Ganymean skeleton from twenty-five million or so. It is evident from anatomical considerations that they are related and come from lines that branched apart from a common ancestral life form somewhere in the very remote past. It follows that they share a place of origin. We already know that the fish evolved in the oceans of Minerva; therefore, the Ganymeans also came from Minerva. We thus have proof of something that has been merely speculation for some time. All that was wrong with the earlier assumption was our failure to appreciate the gap in time between the presence of the Ganymeans on Minerva, and that of the Lunarians."

"Okay," Caldwell accepted. "The Ganymeans came from Minerva, but a lot earlier than we thought. What's the big message and why did you call us over here?"

"In itself, this conclusion is interesting but no more," Danchekker answered. "But it looks pale by comparison with what comes next. In fact"—he shot a glance at Hunt—"the rest tells us all we need to know to resolve the whole question once and for all."

The two regarded him intently.

The professor moistened his lips, then went on: "The Ganymean ship has been opened up fully, and we now have an extremely comprehensive inventory of practically everything it contained. The ship was constructed for large freight-carrying capacity and was loaded when it met with whatever fate befell it on Ganymede. The cargo that it was carrying, in my opinion, constitutes the most sensational discovery ever to be made in the history of paleontology and biology. You see, that ship was carrying, among other things, a large consignment of botanical and zoological specimens, some alive and in cages, the rest preserved in canisters. Presumably the stock was part of an ambitious scientific expedition or something of that nature, but that really doesn't matter for now. What does matter is that we now have in our possession a collection of animal and plant trophies the like of which has never before been seen by human eyes: a comprehensive cross section of many forms of life that existed on Earth around the late Oligocene and early Miocene periods, twenty-five million years ago!"

Hunt and Caldwell stared at him incredulously. Danchekker folded his arms and waited.

"Earth!" Caldwell managed, with difficulty, to form the word. "Are you telling me that the ship had been to Earth?"

"I can see no alternative explanation," Danchekker returned. "Without doubt, the ship was carrying a variety of animal forms that have every appearance of being identical to species that have been well-known for centuries as a result of the terrestrial fossil record. The biologists on the Jupiter Four Mission are quite positive of their conclusions, and from the information they have sent back, I see no reason to doubt their opinions." Danchekker moved his hand back to the keyboard.

"I will show you some examples of the kind of thing I mean," he said.

The picture of the fish skeleton vanished and was replaced by one of a massive, hornless, rhinoceroslike creature. In the background stood an enormous opened canister from which the animal had presumably been removed. The canister was lying in front of what looked like a wall of ice, surrounded by cables, chains, and parts of a latticework built of metal struts.

"The *Baluchitherium*, gentlemen," Danchekker informed them, "or something so like it that the difference escapes me. This animal stood eighteen feet high at the shoulder and attained a bulk in excess of that of the elephant. It is a good example of the *titanoheres*, or titanic beasts, that were abundant in the Americas during the Oligocene but which died out fairly rapidly soon afterward."

"Are you saying that baby was alive when the ship ditched?" Caldwell asked in a tone of disbelief.

Danchekker shook his head. "Not this particular one. As you can see, it has come to us in practically as good a condition as when it was alive. It was taken from that container in the background, in which it had been packed and preserved to keep for a long time. Fortunately, whoever packed it was an expert. However, as I said earlier, there were cages and pens in the ship that originally held live specimens, but by the time they were discovered they had deteriorated to skeleton condition, as had the crew. There were six of this particular species in the pens."

The professor changed the picture to show a small quadruped with spindly legs.

"*Mesohippus*—ancestor of the modern horse. About the size of a collie dog and walking on a three-toed foot with the center toe highly elongated, clearly foreshadowing the single-toed horse of today. There is a long list of other examples such as these, every one immediately recognizable to any student of early terrestrial life forms."

Speechless, Hunt and Caldwell continued to watch as the view changed once more. This time it showed something that at first suggested a medium-size ape from the gibbon or chimpanzee family. Closer examination, however, revealed differences that set it apart from the general category of ape. The skull construction was lighter, especially in the area of the lower jaw, where the chin had receded back to fall almost be-

low the tip of the nose. The arms were proportionately somewhat on the short side for an ape, the chest broader and flatter,
and the legs longer and straighter. Also, the opposability of the
big toe had gone.

Danchekker allowed plenty of time for these points to register before continuing with his commentary.

"Clearly, the creature you now see before you belongs to the
general anthropoid line that includes both man and the great
apes. Now, remember, this specimen dates from around the
early Miocene period. The most advanced anthropoid fossil
from around that time so far found on Earth was discovered
during the last century in East Africa and is known as *Proconsul*. *Proconsul* is generally accepted as representing a step forward from anything that had gone before, but he is definitely
an ape. Here, on the other hand, we have a creature from the
same period in time, but with distinctly more pronounced hu-
manlike characteristics than *Proconsul*. In my opinion, this is
an example of something that occupies a position corresponding to that of *Proconsul*, but on the other side of the split that
occurred when man and ape went their own separate ways—in
other words, a direct ancestor to the human line!" Danchekker
concluded with a verbal flourish and gazed at the other two
men expectantly. Caldwell stared back with widening eyes, and
his jaw dropped as impossible thoughts raced through his
mind.

"Are you telling . . . that the Charlie guys could have . . .
from that?"

"Yes!" Danchekker snapped off the screen and swung back
to face them triumphantly. "Established evolutionary theory is
as sound as I've insisted all along. The notion that the Lunarians might have been colonists from Earth turns out indeed to
be true, but not in the sense that was intended. There are no
traces of their civilization to be found on Earth, because it
never existed on Earth—but neither was it the product of any
parallel process of evolution. The Lunarian civilization developed independently on Minerva from the same ancestral stock
as we did and all other terrestrial vertebrates—from ancestors
that were transported to Minerva, twenty-five million years
ago, by the Ganymeans!" Danchekker thrust out his jaw defiantly and clasped the lapels of his jacket. "And that, Dr. Hunt,
would seem to be the solution to your problem!"

chapter sixteen

The trail behind this rapid succession of new developments was by this time littered with the abandoned carcasses of dead ideas. It reminded the scientists forcibly of the pitfalls that await the unwary when speculation is given too free a rein and imagination is allowed to float farther and farther aloft from the firm grounds of demonstrable proof and scientific rigor. The reaction against this tendency took the form of a generally cooler reception to Danchekker's attempted abrupt wrapping up of the whole issue than might have been expected. So many blind alleys had been exhausted by now, that any new suggestion met with instinctive skepticism and demands for corroboration.

The discovery of early terrestrial animals on the Ganymean spaceship proved only one thing conclusively: that there were early terrestrial animals on the Ganymean spaceship. It didn't prove beyond doubt that other consignments had reached Minerva safely, or indeed, that this particular consignment was ever intended for Minerva. For one thing, Jupiter seemed a strange place to find a ship that had been bound for Minerva from Earth. All it proved, therefore, was that this consignment hadn't got to wherever it was supposed to go.

Danchekker's conclusions regarding the origins of the Ganymeans, however, were fully endorsed by a committee of experts on comparative anatomy in London, who confirmed the affinity between the Ganymean skeleton and the Minervan fish. The corollary to this deduction—that the Lunarians too had evolved on Minerva from displaced terrestrial stock—although neatly accounting for the absence of Lunarian traces on Earth and for the evident lack of advanced Lunarian space technology, required a lot more in the way of substantiating evidence.

In the meantime, Linguistics had been busy applying their

newfound knowledge from the microdot library to the last unsolved riddle among Charlie's papers, the notebook containing the handwritten entries. The story that emerged provided vivid confirmation of the broad picture already deduced in cold and objective terms by Hunt and Steinfield; it was an account of the last days of Charlie's life. The revelations from the book lobbed yet another intellectual grenade in among the already disarrayed ranks of the investigators. But it was Hunt who finally pulled the pin.

Clasping a folder of loose papers beneath his arm, Hunt strolled along the main corridor of the thirteenth floor of the Navcomms Headquarters building, toward the linguistics section. Outside Don Maddson's office he stopped to examine with curiosity a sign bearing a string of two-inch-high Lunarian characters that had been pinned to the door. Shrugging and shaking his head, he entered the room. Inside, Maddson and one of his assistants were sitting in front of the perpetual pile of litter on the large side table away from the desk. Hunt pulled up a chair and joined them.

"You've been through the translations," Maddson observed, noting the contents of the folder as Hunt began arranging them on the table.

Hunt nodded. "Very interesting, this. There are a few points I'd like to go over just to make sure I've got it straight. Some parts just don't made sense."

"We should've guessed," Maddson sighed resignedly. "Okay, shoot."

"Let's work through the entries in sequence," Hunt suggested. "I'll stop when we get to the odd bits. By the way . . ." He inclined his head in the direction of the door. "What's the funny sign outside?"

Maddson grinned proudly. "It's my name in Lunarian. Literally it means *Scholar Crazy-Boy*. Get it? *Don Mad-Son*. See?"

"Oh, Christ," Hunt groaned. He returned his attention to the papers.

"You've expressed the Lunarian-dated entries simply as consecutive numbers starting at Day One, but subdivisions of their day are converted into our hours."

"Check," Maddson confirmed. "Also, where there's doubt about the accuracy of the translation, the phrase is put in parentheses with a question mark. That helps keep things simple."

Hunt selected his first sheet. "Okay," he said. "Let's start at the beginning." He read aloud:

"*Day One. As expected, today we received full (mobilization alert?) orders. Probably means a posting somewhere. Koriel . . .* This is Charlie's pal who turns up later, isn't it?"

"Correct."

"*. . . thinks it could be to one of the (ice nests far-intercept?).* What's that?"

"That's an awkward one," Maddson replied. "It's a composite word; that's the literal translation. We think it could refer to a missile battery forming part of an outer defense perimeter, located out on the ice sheets."

"Mmm—sounds reasonable. Anyhow, *Hope so. It would be a change to get away from the monotony of this place. Bigger food ration in (ice-field combat zones?). Now . . .*" Hunt looked up. "He says, 'the monotony of this place.' How sure are we that we know where 'this place' is?"

"Pretty sure," Maddson replied with a firm nod. "The name of a town is written above the date at the top of the entry. It checks with the name of a coastal town on Cerios and also with the place given in his pay book for his last posting but one."

"So you're sure he was on Minerva when he wrote this?"

"Sure, we're sure."

"Okay. I'll skip the next bit that talks about personal thoughts.

"*Day Two. Koriel's hunches have proved wrong for once. We're going to Luna.*"

Hunt looked up again, evidently considering this part important. "How do you know he means Earth's Moon there?"

"Well, one reason is that the word he uses there is the same as the last place the pay book says he was posted to. We guess it means Luna because that's where we found him. Another reason is that later on, as you'll have read, he talks about being sent specifically to a base called Seltar. Now, we've found a reference among some of the things turned up on Farside to a list of bases on place 'X,' and the name *Seltar* appears on the list. X is the same word that is written in the pay book and in the entry you've just read. Implication: X is a Lunarian name for Earth's Moon."

Hunt thought hard for a while.

"He arrived at Seltar, too, didn't he?" he said at last. "So if he knew where he was being sent as early as that, and you're certain he was being sent to the Moon, and he got where he was supposed to go . . . that rules out the other possibility that occurred to me. There's no way he could have been scheduled for Luna but rerouted somewhere else at the last minute without the entry in the pay book being changed, is there?"

Maddson shook his head. "No way. Why'd you want to make up things like that anyhow?"

"Because I'm looking for ways to get around what comes later. It gets crazy."

Maddson looked at Hunt curiously but suppressed his question. Hunt looked down at the papers again.

"Days Three and Four describe news reports of the fighting on Minerva. Obviously a large-scale conflict had already broken out there. It looks as if nuclear weapons were being used by then—that bit near the end of Day Four, for instance: *It looks like the Lambians have succeeded in confusing the (sky nets?) over Paverol*—That's a Cerian town, isn't it? *Over half the city vaporized instantly.* That doesn't sound like a limited skirmish. What's a sky net—some kind of electronic defense screen?"

"Probably," Maddson agreed.

"Day Five he spent helping to load the ships. From the descriptions of the vehicles and equipment, it sounds as if they were embarking a large military force of some kind." Hunt scanned rapidly down the next sheet. "Ah, yes—this is where he mentions Seltar. *We're going with the Fourteenth Brigade to join the Annihilator emplacement at Seltar.* There's something crazy about this Annihilator. But we'll come back to that in a minute.

"*Day Seven. Embarked four hours ago as scheduled. Still sitting here. Takeoff delayed, since whole area under heavy missile attack. Hills inland all on fire. Launching pits intact but situation overhead confused. Unneutralized Lambian satellites still covering our flight path.*

"*Later. Received clearance for takeoff suddenly, and the whole flight was away in minutes. Didn't delay in planetary orbit at all—still not very healthy—so set course at once. Two ships reported lost on the way up. Koriel is taking bets on how many ships from our flight touch down on Luna. We're flying inside a tight defense screen but must stand out clearly on Lambian search radars.* There's a bit about Koriel flirting with one of the girls from a signals unit—quite a character, this Koriel, wasn't he . . . ? More war news received en route . . . Now—this is the part I meant." Hunt found the entry with his finger.

"Day Eight. In Lunar orbit at last!" He laid the sheet down on the table and looked from one linguist to the other. " *'In Lunar orbit at last.'* Now, you tell me: Exactly how did that ship travel from Minerva to our Moon in under two of our days? Either there is some form of propulsion that UNSA ought to be finding out about, or we've been very wrong about Lunarian technology all along. But it doesn't fit. If they could do that, they didn't have any problem about developing space flight; they were way ahead of us. But I don't believe it—everything says they had a problem."

Maddson made a show of helplessness. He knew it was crazy. Hunt looked inquiringly at Maddson's assistant, who merely shrugged and pulled a face.

"You're sure he means Lunar orbit—*our* Moon?"

"We're sure." Maddson was sure.

"And there's no doubt about the date he shipped out?" Hunt persisted.

"The embarkation date is stamped in the pay book, and it checks with the date of the entry that says he shipped out. And don't forget the wording on Day—where was it?—here, Day Seven. *'Embarked four hours ago as scheduled'*—See, 'as scheduled.' No suggestion of a change in timetable."

"And how certain is the date he reached Luna?" asked Hunt.

"Well that's a little more difficult. Just going by the dates of the notes, they're one Lunarian day apart, all right. Now, it's possible that he used a Minervan time scale on Minerva, but switched to some local system when he got to Luna. If so, it's a big coincidence that they tally like they do, but"— he shrugged—"it's possible. The thing that bothers me about that idea, though, is the absence of any entries between the shipout date and the arrival-at-Luna date. Charlie seems to have written his diary regularly. If the voyage took months, like you're saying it should have, it looks funny to me that there's nothing at all between those dates. It's not as if he'd been short of free time."

Hunt reflected for a few moments on these possibilities.

Then he said, "There's worse to come. Let's press on for now." He picked up the notes and resumed:

"Landed at last, five hours ago. (Expletive) what a mess! The landscape below as we came in on the (approach run?) was glowing red in places all around Seltar for miles. There were lakes of molten rock, bright orange, some with walls of rocks plunging straight into them where whole mountains have been blown away. The base is covered deep in dust, and some of the surface installations have been crushed by flying debris. The defenses are holding out, but the outer perimeter is (torn to shreds?). Most important—[unreadable] diameter dish of the Annihilator is intact and it is operational. The last group of ships in our flight was wiped out by an enemy strike coming in from deep space. Koriel has been collecting on all sides."

Hunt laid the paper down and looked at Maddson. "Don," he said, "how much have you been able to piece together about this Annihilator thing?"

"It was a kind of superweapon. There was more information in some of the other texts. Both sides had them, sited on Minerva itself and, from what you're reading right now, on Luna too." He added as an afterthought, "Maybe on other places as well."

"Why on Luna? Any ideas?"

"Our guess is that the Cerians and the Lambians must have developed space-flight technology further than we thought," Maddson said. "Perhaps both sides had selected Earth as their target destination for the big move, and they both sent advance parties to Luna to set up a bridgehead and . . . protect the investment."

"Why not on Earth itself, then?"

"I dunno."

"Let's stick with it for now, anyway," Hunt said. "How much do we know about what these Annihilators were?"

"From the description *dish*, apparently it was some kind of radiation projector. From other clues, they fired a high-energy photon beam probably produced by intense matter–antimatter reaction. If so, the term *Annihilator* is particularly apt; it carries a double meaning."

"Okay." Hunt nodded. "That's what I thought. Now it goes silly." He consulted his notes. "Day Nine they were getting organized and repairing battle damage. What about Day Ten, then, eh?" He resumed reading:

"Day Ten. Annihilator used for the first time today. Three fifteen-minute blasts aimed at Calvares, Paneris, and Sellidorn. Now, they're all Lambian cities, right?

"So they have this Annihilator emplacement, sitting on our Moon, happily picking off cities on the surface of Minerva?"

"Looks like it," Maddson agreed. He didn't look very happy.

"Well, I don't believe it," Hunt declared firmly. "I don't believe they had the ability to register a weapon that accurately over that distance, and even if they could, I don't believe they could have held the beam narrow enough not to have burned up the whole planet And I don't believe the power density at that range could have been high enough to do any damage at all." He looked at Maddson imploringly. "Christ, if they had technology like that, they wouldn't have been trying to perfect interplanetary travel—they'd have been all over the bloody Galaxy!"

Maddson gestured wide with his arms. "I just translate what the words tell me. You figure it out."

"It goes completely daft in a minute," Hunt warned. "Where was I, now . . . ?"

He continued to read aloud, describing the duel that developed between the Cerian Annihilator at Seltar and the last surviving Lambian emplacement on Minerva. With a weapon firing from far out in space and commanding the whole Minervan surface, the Cerians held the key that would decide the war. Destroying it was obviously the first priority of the Lambian forces and the prime objective of their own Annihilator on Minerva. The Annihilators required about one hour to recharge between firings, and Charlie's notes conveyed vividly the tension that built up in Seltar as they waited, knowing that an incoming blast could arrive at any second All around Seltar the battle was building up to a frenzy as Lambian ground and space-borne forces hurled everything into knocking out Seltar before it could score on its distant target. The skill in operating the weapon lay in computing and compensating for the distortions induced in the aiming system by enemy electronic countermeasures. In one passage, Charlie detailed the effects of a near miss from Minerva that lasted for sixteen minutes, during which time it melted a range of mountains about fifteen miles from Seltar, including the Twenty-second and Nineteenth Armored Divisions and the Forty-fifth Tactical Missile Squadron that had been positioned there.

"This iss it," Hunt said, waving one of the sheets in the air. "Listen to this. *We've got it! Four minutes ao we fired a concentrated burst at maximum power. The announcement has just come over the loudspeaker down here that it scored a direct hit. Everyone is laughing and clapping each other on the back. Some of the women are crying with relief.* That," said Hunt, slapping the papers down on the table and slumping back in his chair with exasperation, "is bloody ridiculous! Within four minutes of firing they had confirmation of a hit! How? How in God's name could they have? We know that when Minerva and Earth were at their closest, the distance between them would have been one hundred fifty to one hundred sixty million miles. The radiation would have taken something like thirteen minutes to cover that distance, and there would have to be at least another thirteen minutes before anybody on Luna could possibly know about where it struck. So, even with the planets at their closest positions, they'd have needed at least twenty-six minutes to get that report. Charlie says they got it in under four! That is absolutely, one-hundred-percent impossible! Don, how sure are you of those numbers?"

"As sure as we are of any other Lunarian time units. If they're wrong, you might as well tear up that calendar you started out with and go all the way back to square one."

Hunt stared at the page for a long time, as if by sheer power of concentration he could change the message contained in the neatly formatted sheets of typescript. There was only one thing that these figures could mean, and it put them right back to the beginning. At length he carried on:

"The next bit tells how the whole Seltar area came under sustained bombardment. A detachment including Charlie and Koriel was sent out overland to man an emergency command post about eleven miles from Seltar Base ... I'll skip the details of that ... Yes, here's the next bit that worries me. Under Day Twelve: *Set off on time in a small convoy of two scout cars and three tracked trucks. The journey was weird—miles of scorched rocks and glowing pits. We could feel the heat inside the truck. Hope the shielding was good. Our new home is a dome, and underneath it are levels going down about fifty feet. Army units dug in the hills all around. We have landline contact with Seltar, but they seem to have lost touch with Main HQ at Gorda. Probably means all long-distance landlines are out and our comsats are destroyed. Again no broadcasts from Minerva. Lots of gar-*

bled military traffic. They must have assumed (frequency priority?). Today was the first time above surface for many days. The face of Minerva looks dirty and blotchy. There," Hunt said. "When I first read that, I thought he was referring to a video transmission. But thinking about it, why would he say it that way in that context? Why right after 'the first time above surface for many days'? But he couldn't have seen any detail of Minerva from where he was, could he?"

"Could have used a pretty ordinary telescope," Maddson's assistant suggested.

"Could have, I suppose." Hunt reflected. "But you'd think there'd be more important things to worry about than stargazing in the middle of all that. Anyhow, he goes on: *About two-thirds is blotted out by huge clouds of brown and gray, and coastal outlines are visible only in places. There is a strange red spot glowing through, somewhere just north of the equator, with black spreading out from it hour by hour. Koriel reckons it's a city on fire, but it must be a tremendous blaze to be visible through all that. We've been watching it move across all day as Minerva rotates. Huge explosions over the ridge where Seltar Base is."*

The narrative continued and confirmed that Seltar was totally destroyed as the fighting reached its climax. For two days the whole area was systematically pounded, but miraculously the underground parts of the dome remained intact, although the upper levels were blown away. Afterward the scattered survivors from the military units occupying the surrounding hills began straggling back, some in vehicles and many on foot, to the dome, which by this time was the only inhabitable place left for miles.

The expected waves of victorious Lambian troopships and armored columns failed to materialize. From the regular pattern of incoming salvos, the Cerian officers slowly realized that there was nothing left of the enemy army that had moved forward into the mountains around Seltar. In the fighting with the Cerian defenses, the Lambians had suffered immense losses and their survivors had pulled out, leaving missile batteries programmed to fire robot mode to cover their withdrawal.

On Day Fifteen, Charlie wrote: *Two more red spots on Minerva, one northeast of the first and the other well south. The first has elongated from northwest to southeast. The whole surface is now just a mass of dirty brown with huge areas of black mixing in with it. Nothing at all on radio or video from Minerva; everything blotted out by atmospherics.*

There was nothing further to be done at Seltar. The inhabitable parts of what had been the dome were packed with survivors and wounded; already many were having to live in the assortment of vehicles huddled around outside it. Supplies of food and oxygen, never intended for more than a small company, would give only a temporary respite. The only hope, slender as it was, lay in reaching HQ Base at Gorda overland—a journey estimated to require twenty days.

On Day Eighteen, the departure from the dome was recorded as follows: *Formed up in two columns of vehicles. Ours moved out half an hour ahead of the second as a small advanced scouting group. We reached a ridge about three miles from the dome and could see the main column finish loading and begin lining up. That was when the missiles hit. The first salvo caught them all out in the open. They didn't have a chance. We trained our receivers on the area for a while, but there was nothing. The only way we'll ever get off this death furnace is if there are ships left at Gorda. As far as I know, there are 340 of us, including over a hundred girls. The column comprises five scout cars, eight tracked trucks, and ten heavy tanks. It will be a grim journey. Even Koriel isn't taking bets on how many get there.*

Minerva is just a black, smoky ball, difficult to pick out against the sky. Two of the red spots have joined up to form a line stretching at an angle across the equator. Must be hundreds of miles long. Another red line is growing to the north. Every now and then, parts of them glow orange through the smoke clouds for a few hours and then die down again. Must be a mess there.

The column moved slowly through the desert of scorched gray dust, and its numbers shrank rapidly as wounds and radiation sickness took their toll. On Day Twenty-six they encountered a Lambian ground force and for three hours fought furiously among the crags and boulders. The battle ended when the remaining Lambian tanks broke cover and charged straight into the Cerian position, only to be destroyed right on the perimeter line by Cerian women firing laser artillery at point-blank range. After the battle there were 165 Cerians left, but not enough vehicles to carry them.

After conferring, the Cerian officers devised a plan to continue the journey leapfrog fashion. Half the company would be moved half a day's distance forward and left there with one truck to use as living accommodation, while the remaining vehicles returned to collect the group left behind. So it would go on all the way to Gorda. Charlie and Koriel were among the first group lifted on ahead.

Day Twenty-eight. Uneventful drive. Set up camp in a shady gorge and watched the convoy about-face again and begin its long haul back for the others. They should be back this time tomorrow. Nothing much to do until then. Two died on the drive, so there are fifty-eight of us here. We take turns to rest and eat inside the truck. When it's not your turn, you make yourself as comfortable as you can sitting among the rocks. Koriel is furious. He's just spent two hours sitting outside with four of the artillery girls. He says whoever designed space suits should have thought of situations like that.

The convoy never returned.

Using the single remaining truck, the group continued the same tactic as before, ferrying one party on ahead, dumping them, and returning for the rest. By Day Thirty-three, sickness, mishaps, and one suicide had depleted the numbers such that all the survivors could be carried in the truck at once, so the leapfrogging was discontinued. Driving steadily, they estimated they would reach Gorda on Day Thirty-eight. On Day Thirty-seven, the truck broke down. The spare parts needed to repair it were not available.

Many were weak. It was clear that an attempt to reach Gorda on foot would be so slow that nobody would make it.

Day Thirty-seven. Seven of us—four men (myself, Koriel, and two of the combat troopers) and three girls—are going to make a dash for Gorda while the others stay put in the truck and wait for a rescue party. Koriel is cooking a meal before we set out. He has been saying what he thinks of life in the infantry—doesn't seem to think much of it at all.

Some hours after they left the truck, one of the troopers climbed a crag to survey the route ahead. He slipped, gashed his suit, and died instantly from explosive decompression. Later on, one of the girls hurt her leg and lagged farther and farther behind as the pain worsened. The Sun was sinking and there was no time for slowing down. Everybody in the group wrestled with the same equation in his mind—one life or twenty-eight?—

but said nothing. She solved the problem for them by quietly closing her air valve when they stopped to rest.

Day Thirty-eight. Just Koriel and me now—like the old days. The trooper suddenly doubled up, vomiting violently inside his helmet. We stood and watched while he died, and could do nothing. Some hours later, one of the girls collapsed and said she couldn't go on. The other insisted on staying with her until we send help from Gorda. Couldn't really argue—they were sisters. That was some time ago. We've stopped for a breather; I am getting near my limit. Koriel is pacing up and down impatiently and wants to get moving. That man has the strength of twelve [?lions?].

Later. Stopped at last for a couple of hours sleep. I'm sure Koriel is a robot—just keeps going and going. Human tank. Sun very low in sky. Must make Gorda before Lunar night sets in.

Day Thirty-nine. Woke up freezing cold. Had to turn suit heating up to maximum—still doesn't feel right. Think it's developing a fault. Koriel says I worry too much. Time to be on the move again. Feel stiff all over. Seriously wondering if I'll make it. Haven't said so.

Later. The march has been a nightmare. Kept falling down. Koriel insisted that the only chance we had was to climb up out of the valley we were in and try a short-cut over a high ridge. I made it about halfway up the cleft leading toward the ridge. Every step up the cleft I could see Minerva sitting right over the middle of the ridge, gashes of orange and red all over it, like a (macabre?) face, taunting. Then I collapsed. When I came to, Koriel had dragged me inside a pilot digging of some sort. Maybe someone was going to put an outpost of Gorda here. That was a while ago now. Koriel has gone on and says help will be back before I know it. Getting colder all the time. Feet numb and hands stiff. Frost starting to form in helmet— difficult to see.

Thinking about all the people strung out back there with night coming down, all like me, wondering if they'll be picked up. If we can hold out we'll be all right. Koriel will make it. If it were a thousand miles to Gorda, Koriel would make it.

Thinking about what has happened on Minerva and wondering if, after all this, our children will live on a sunnier world— and if they do, if they will ever know what we did.

Thinking about things I've never really thought about before. There should be better ways for people to spend their lives than

*in factories, mines, and army camps. Can't think what, though—
that's all we've ever known. But if there is warmth and color
and light somewhere in this Universe, then maybe something
worthwhile will come out of what we've been through.*

Too much thinking for one day. Must sleep for a while now.

Hunt found he had read right through to the end, absorbed
in the pathos of those final days. His voice had fallen to a sober pitch. A long silence ensued.

"Well, that's it," he concluded, a little more briskly. "Did
you notice that bit right at the end? In the last few lines he was
talking about seeing the surface of Minerva again. Now, they
might have used telescopes earlier on, but in the situation he
was in there, they'd hardly be lugging half an observatory
along with them, would they?"

Maddson's assistant looked thoughtful. "How about that periscope video gadget that was in the helmet?" he suggested.
"Maybe there's something wrong in the translation. Couldn't
he be talking about seeing a transmission through that?"

Hunt shook his head. "Can't see it. I've heard of people
watching TV in all sorts of funny places, but never halfway up
a bloody mountain. And another thing: He described it as sitting up above the ridge. That implies it's really out there. If it
were a view on video, he'd never have worded it that way.
Right, Don?"

Maddson nodded wearily. "Guess so," he said. "So, where
do we go from here?"

Hunt looked from Maddson to the assistant and back again.
He leaned his elbows on the edge of the table and rubbed his
face and eyeballs with his fingers. Then he sighed and sat back.

"What do we know for sure?" he asked at last. "We know
that those Lunarian spaceships got to our Moon in under two
days. We know that they could accurately aim a weapon, sited
on our Moon, at a Minervan target. We also know that the
round trip for electromagnetic waves was much shorter than it
could possibly have been talking about the right place. Finally,
we can't prove but we think that Charlie could stand on our
Moon and see quite clearly the surface features of Minerva.
Well, what does that add up to?"

"There's only one place in the Universe that fits all those
numbers," Maddson said numbly.

"Exactly—and we're standing on it! Maybe there was a
planet called Minerva outside Mars, and maybe it had a civili-

zation on it. Maybe the Ganymeans took a few animals there and maybe they didn't. But it doesn't really matter anymore, does it? Because the only planet Charlie's ship could possibly have taken off from, and the only planet they could have aimed that Annihilator at, and the only planet he could have seen in detail from Luna—is this one!

"They *were* from Earth all along!

"Everyone will be jumping off the roof and out of every window in the building when this gets around Navcomms."

chapter seventeen

With the first comprehensive translation of the handwritten notebook, the paradox was complete. Now there were two consistent and apparently irrefutable bodies of evidence, one proving that the Lunarians must have evolved on Earth, and the other proving that they couldn't have.

All at once the consternation and disputes broke out afresh. Lights burned through the night at Houston and elsewhere as the same inevitable chains of reasoning were reeled out again and yet again, the same arrays of facts scrutinized for new possibilities or interpretations. But always the answers came out the same. Only the notion of the Lunarians having been the product of a parallel line of evolution appeared to have been abandoned permanently; more than enough theories were in circulation already without anyone having to invoke this one. The Navcomms fraternity disintegrated into a myriad of cliques and strays, scurrying about to ally first with this idea and then with that. As the turmoil subsided, the final lines of defense fortified themselves around four main camps.

The Pure Earthists accepted without reservation the deductions from Charlie's diary, and held that the Lunarian civilization had developed on Earth, flourished on Earth, and destroyed itself on Earth and that was that. Thus, all references to Minerva and its alleged civilization were nonsense; there never had been any civilization on Minerva apart from that of the Ganymeans, and that was too far in the remote past to have any bearing on the Lunarian issue. The world depicted on Charlie's maps was Earth, not Minerva, so there had to be a gross error somewhere in the calculations that put it at 250 million miles from the Sun. That this corresponded to the orbital radius of the Asteroids was just coincidence; the Asteroids had always been there, and anything from *Iliad* that said they hadn't was suspect and needed double-checking.

That left only one question unexplained: Why didn't Charlie's maps look like Earth? To answer this one, the Earthists launched a series of commando raids against the bastions of accepted geological theory and methods of geological dating. Drawing on the hypothesis that continents had been formed initially from a single granitic mass that had been shattered under the weight of immense ice caps and pushed apart by polar material rushing in to fill the gaps, they pointed to the size of the ice caps shown on the maps and stressed how much larger they were than anything previously supposed to have existed on Earth. Now, if in fact the maps showed Earth and not Minerva, that meant that the Ice Age on Earth had been far more severe than previously thought, and its effects on surface geography correspondingly more violent. Add to this the effects of the crustal fractures and vulcanism as described in Charlie's observations of Earth (not Minerva), and there was, perhaps, enough in all that to account for the transformation of Charlie's Earth into modern Earth. So, why were there no traces to be found today of the Lunarian civilization? Answer: It was clear from the maps that most of it had been concentrated on the equatorial belt. Today that region was completely ocean, dense jungle, or drifting desert—adequate to explain the rapid erasure of whatever had been left after the war and the climatic cataclysm.

The Pure Earthist faction attracted mainly physicists and engineers, quite happy to leave the geologists and geographers to worry about the bothersome details. Their main concern was that the sacred principle of the constancy of the velocity of light should not be thrown into the melting pot of suspicion along with everything else.

By entrenching themselves around the idea of Earth origins, the Pure Earthists had moved into the positions previously defended fanatically by the biologists. Now that Danchekker had led the way by introducing his fleet of Ganymean Noah's Arks, the biologists abruptly turned about-face and rallied behind their new assertion of Minervan origin from displaced terrestrial ancestors. What about Charlie's Minerva–Luna flight time and the loop delay around the Annihilator fire-control system? Something was screwed up in the interpretation of Minervan time scales that accounted for both of these. Okay, how could Charlie see Minerva from Luna? Video transmissions. Okay, how could they aim the Annihilator over that distance? They couldn't. The dish at Seltar was only a remote-control tracking station. The weapon itself was mounted in a satellite orbiting Minerva.

The third flag flew over the Cutoff Colony Theory. According to this, an early terrestrial civilization had colonized Minerva, and then declined into a Dark Age during which contact with the colony was lost. The deteriorating conditions of the Ice Age later prompted a recovery on both planets, with the difference that Minerva faced a life-or-death situation and began the struggle to regain the lost knowledge in order that a return to Earth might be made. Earth, however, was going through lean times of its own and, when the advance parties from Minerva eventually made contact, didn't react favorably to the idea of another planetful of mouths to feed. Diplomacy having failed, the Minervans set up an invasion beachhead on Luna. The Annihilator at Seltar had thus been firing at targets on Earth; the translators had been misled by identical place-names on both planets—like Boston, New York, Cambridge, and a hundred other places in the USA, many of the towns on Minerva had been named after places on Earth when the original colony was first established.

The defenders of these arguments drew heavily from the claims of the Pure Earthists to account for the absence of Lunarian relics on Earth. In addition, they produced further support from the unlikely domain of the study of fossil corals in the Pacific. It had been known for a long time that analysis of the daily growth rings of ancient fossil corals provided a measure of how many days there had been in the year at various times in the past, and from this how fast the forces of tidal friction were slowing down the rotation of the Earth about its axis. These researchers showed, for example, that the year of 350 million years ago contained about four hundred days. Ten years previously, work conducted at the Darwin Institute of

Oceanography in Australia, using more refined and more accurate techniques, had revealed that the continuity from ancient to modern had not been as smooth as supposed. There was a confused period in the recent past—at about fifty thousand years before—during which the curve was discontinuous, and a comparatively abrupt lengthening in the day had occurred. Furthermore, the rate of deceleration was measurably greater after this discontinuity than it had been before. Nobody knew why this should have happened, but it seemed to indicate a period of violent climatic upheaval, as the corals had taken generations to settle down to a stable growth pattern afterward. The data seemed to indicate that widespread changes had taken place on Earth around this mysterious point in time, probably accompanied by global flooding, and all in all there *could* be enough behind the story to explain the complete disappearance of any record of the Lunarians' existence.

The fourth main theory was that of the Returning Exiles, which found these attempts to explain the disappearance of the terrestrial Lunarians artificial and inadequate. The basic tenet of this theory was that there could be only one satisfactory reason for the fact that there were no signs of Lunarians on Earth: There had never been any Lunarians on Earth worth talking about. Thus, they had evolved on Minerva as Danchekker maintained and had evolved an advanced civilization, unlike their contemporary brothers on Earth, who remained backward. Eventually, compelled by the Ice Age threat of extinction, the two superpowers of Cerios and Lambia had emerged and begun the race toward the Sun in the way described by Linguistics. Where Linguistics had gone wrong, however, was that by the time of Charlie's narrative, these events were already historical, the goal was already achieved. The Lambians had drawn ahead by a small margin and had already commenced building settlements on Earth, several of them named after their own towns on Minerva. The Cerians followed hard on their heels and established a fire base on Luna, the objective of course being to knock out the Lambian outposts on Earth before moving in themselves.

This theory did not explain the flight time of Charlie's ship, but its supporters attributed the difficulty to unknown differences between Minervan and local (Lunar) dating systems. On the other hand, it required only a few pilot Lambian bases to have been set up on Earth by the time of the war; thus, whatever remained of these after the Cerian assault, could credibly have vanished in fifty thousand years.

And as the battle lines were drawn up and the first ranging shots started whistling up and down the corridors of Navcomms, in no-man's-land sat Hunt. Somehow, he was convinced, everybody was right. He knew the competence of the people around him and had no doubt in their ability to get their figures right. If, after weeks or months of patient effort, one of them pronounced that x was 2, then he was quite prepared to believe that, in all probability, 2 it would turn out to be. Therefore, the paradox had to be an illusion. To try to argue which side was right and which was wrong was missing the whole point. Somewhere in the maze, probably so fundamental that nobody had even thought to question it, there had to be a fallacy—some wrong assumption that seemed so obvious they didn't even realize they were making it. If they could just get back to fundamentals and identify that single fallacy, the paradox would vanish and everything that was being argued would slide smoothly into a consistent, unified whole.

chapter eighteen

"You want me to go to Jupiter?" Hunt repeated slowly, making sure he had heard correctly.

Caldwell stared back over his desk impassively. "The Jupiter Five Mission will depart from Luna in six weeks time," he stated. "Danchekker has gone about as far as he can go with Charlie. What details are left to be found out can be taken care of by his staff at Westwood. He's got better things he'd like to be doing on Ganymede. There's a whole collection of alien skeletons there, plus a shipload of zoology from way back that nobody's ever seen the like of before. It's got him excited. He wants to get his hands on them. *Jupiter Five* is going right there, so he's getting together a biological team to go with it."

Hunt already knew all this. Nevertheless, he went through

the motions of digesting the information and checking through it for any point he might have missed. After an appropriate pause he replied:

"That's fine—I can see *his* angle. But what does it have to do with me?"

Caldwell frowned and drummed his fingers, as if he had been expecting this question to come, while hoping it wouldn't.

"Consider this an extension of your assignment," he said at last. "From all the arguing that's going on around this place, nobody seems to be able to agree just how the Ganymeans fit into the Charlie business. Maybe they're a big part of the answer, maybe they're not. Nobody knows for sure."

"True." Hunt nodded.

Caldwell took this as all the confirmation he needed. "Okay," he said with a gesture of finality. "You've done a good job so far on the Charlie side of the picture; maybe it's time to balance things up a bit and give you a crack at the other side, too. Well"—he shrugged—"the information's not here—it's on Ganymede. In six weeks time, *J Five* shoves off for Ganymede. It makes sense to me that you go with it."

Hunt's brow remained creased in an expression that indicated he still didn't quite see everything. He posed the obvious question. "What about the job here?"

"What about it? Basically you correlate information that comes from different places. The information will still keep coming from the places whether you're in Houston or on board *Jupiter Five*. Your assistant is capable of stepping in and keeping the routine background research and cross-checking running smoothly in Group L. There's no reason why you can't continue to be kept updated on what's going on if you're out there. Anyhow, a change of scene never did anybody any harm. You've been on this job a year and a half now."

"But we're talking about a break of years, maybe."

"Not necessarily. *Jupiter Five* is a later design than *J Four*; it will make Ganymede in under six months. Also, a number of ships are being ferried out with the Jupiter Five Mission to start building up a fleet that will be based out there. Once a reserve's been established, there will be regular two-way traffic with Earth. In other words, once you've had enough of the place we'll have no problem getting you back."

Hunt reflected that nothing ever seemed to stay normal for

very long when Caldwell was around. He felt no inclination to argue with this new directive. On the contrary, the prospect excited him. But there was something that didn't quite add up in the reasons Caldwell was giving. Hunt had the same feeling he had experienced on previous occasions that there was an ulterior motive lurking beneath the surface somewhere. Still, that didn't really matter. Caldwell seemed to have made up his mind, and Hunt knew from experience that when Caldwell made up his mind that something would be so, then by some uncanny power of preordination, so it would inevitably turn out to be.

Caldwell waited for possible objections. Seeing that none was forthcoming, he concluded: "When you joined us, I told you your place in UNSA was out front. That statement implied a promise. I always keep promises."

For the next two weeks Hunt worked frantically, reorganizing the operation of Group L and making his own personal preparations for a prolonged absence from Earth. After that, he was sent to Galveston for two weeks.

By the third decade of the twenty-first century, commercial flight reservations to Luna could be made through any reputable travel agent, for seats either on regular UNSA ships or on chartered ships crewed by UNSA officers. The standards of comfort provided on passenger flights were high, and accommodation at the larger Lunar bases was secure, enabling Lunar travel to become a routine chore in the lives of many businessmen and a memorable event for more than a few casual visitors, none of whom needed any specialized knowledge or training. Indeed, one enterprising consortium, comprising a hotel chain, an international airline, a travel-tour operator, and an engineering corporation, had commenced the construction of a Lunar holiday resort, which was already fully booked for the opening season.

Places like Jupiter, however, were not yet open to the public. Persons detailed for assignments with the UNSA deep-space missions needed to know what they were doing and how to act in emergency situations. The ice sheets of Ganymede and the cauldron of Venus were no places for tourists.

At Galveston, Hunt learned about UNSA space suits and the standard items of ancillary equipment; he was taught the use of communication equipment, survival kits, emergency life support systems, and repair kits; he practiced test routines, radio-location procedures, and equipment-fault diagnostic techniques. "Your life could depend on this little box," one instructor told the group. "You could wind up in a situation where it fails and the only person inside a hundred miles to fix it is you." Doctors lectured on the rudiments of space medicine and recommended methods of dealing with oxygen starvation, decompression, heat stroke, and hypothermia. Physiologists described the effects on bone calcium of long periods of reduced body weight, and showed how a correct balance could be maintained by a specially selected diet and drugs. UNSA officers gave useful hints that covered the whole gamut of staying alive and sane in alien environments, from navigating afoot on a hostile surface using satellite beacons as reference points, to the art of washing one's face in zero gravity.

And so, just over four weeks after his directive from Caldwell, Hunt found himself fifty feet below ground level at pad twelve of number-two terminal complex twenty miles outside Houston, walking along one of the access ramps that connected the wall of the silo to the gleaming hull of the Vega. An hour later, the hydraulic rams beneath the platform supporting the tail thrust the ship slowly upward and out, to stand clear on the roof of the structure. Within minutes the Vega was streaking into the darkening void above. It docked thirty minutes later, two and a half seconds behind schedule, with the half-mile-diameter transfer satellite *Kepler*.

On *Kepler* the passengers traveling on to Luna—including Hunt, three propulsion-systems experts keen to examine the suspected Ganymean gravity drives, four communications specialists, two structural engineers, and Danchekker's team, all destined to join *Jupiter Five*—transferred to the ugly and ungainly Capella class moonship that would carry them for the remainder of the journey from Earth orbit to the Lunar surface. The voyage lasted thirty hours and was uneventful. After they had been in Lunar orbit for twenty minutes, the announcement came over the loudspeaker that the craft had been cleared for descent.

Shortly afterward, the unending procession of plains, mountains, crags, and hills that had been marching across the cabin display screen slowed to a halt and the view started growing perceptively larger. Hunt recognized the twin ring-walled plains of Ptolemy and Albategnius, with its central conical mountain and Crater Klein interrupting its encircling wall, before the ship swung northward and these details were lost off the top of the steadily enlarging image. The picture stabilized, now centered upon the broken and crumbling mountain wall that separated Ptolemy from the southern edge of the Plain of Hipparchus. What had previously looked like smooth terrain resolved itself into a jumble of rugged cliffs and valleys, and in the center, glints of sunlight began to appear, reflected from the metal structures of the vast base below.

As the outlines of the surface installations materialized out of the gray background and expanded to fill the screen, a yellow glow in the center grew, gradually transforming into the gaping entrance to one of the underground moonship berths. There was a brief impression of tiers of access levels stretching down out of sight as huge service gantries swung back to admit the ship. Rows of brilliant arc lights flooded the scene before the exhaust from the braking motors blotted out the view. A mild jolt signaled that the landing legs had made contact with Lunar rock, and silence fell abruptly inside the ship as the engines were cut. Above the squat nose of the moonship, massive steel shutters rolled together to seal out the stars. As the berth filled with air, a new world of sound impinged on the ears of the ship's occupants. Shortly afterward, the access ramps slid smoothly from the walls to connect the ship to the reception bays.

Thirty minutes after clearing arrival formalities, Hunt emerged from an elevator high atop one of the viewing domes that dominated the surface of Ptolemy Main Base. For a long time he gazed soberly at the harsh desolation in which man had carved this oasis of life. The streaky blue and white disk of Earth, hanging motionless above the horizon, suddenly brought home to him the remoteness of places like Houston, Reading, Cambridge, and the meaning of everything familiar, which until so recently he had taken for granted. In his wanderings he had never come to regard any particular place as home; unconsciously he had always accepted any part of the world to be as much home as any other. Now, all at once, he realized that he was away from home for the first time in his life.

As Hunt turned to take in more of the scene below, he saw that he was not alone. On the far side of the dome a lean, balding figure stood staring silently out over the wilderness, absorbed in thoughts of its own. Hunt hesitated for a long time. At last he moved slowly across to stand beside the figure. All around them the mile-wide clutter of silver-gray metallic geometry that made up the base sprawled amid a confusion of pipes, girders, pylons, and antennae. On towers above, the radars swept the skyline in endless circles, while the tall, praying-mantislike laser transceivers stared unblinkingly at the heavens, carrying the ceaseless dialogues between the base computers and unseen communications satellites fifty miles up. In the distance beyond the base, the rugged bastions of Ptolemy's mountain wall towered above the plain. From the blackness above them, a surface transporter was sliding toward the base on its landing approach.

Eventually Hunt said: "To think—a generation ago, all this was just desert." It was more a thought voiced than a statement.

Danchekker did not answer for a long time. When he did, he kept his eyes fixed outside.

"But man dared to dream . . ." he murmured slowly. After a pause he added, "And what man dares to dream today, tomorrow he makes come true."

Another long silence followed. Hunt took a cigarette from his case and lit it. "You know," he said at last, blowing a stream of smoke slowly toward the glass wall of the dome, "it's going to be a long voyage to Jupiter. We could get a drink down below—one for the road, as it were."

Danchekker seemed to turn the suggestion over in his mind for a while. At length he shifted his gaze back within the confines of the dome and turned to face Hunt directly.

"I think not, Dr. Hunt," he said quietly.

Hunt sighed and made as if to turn.

"However . . ." The tone of Danchekker's voice checked him before he moved. He looked up. "If your metabolism is capable of withstanding the unaccustomed shock of nonalcoholic beverages, a strong coffee might, ah, perhaps be extremely welcome."

It was a joke. Danchekker had actually cracked a joke!

"I'll try anything once," Hunt said as they began walking toward the door of the elevator.

chapter nineteen

Embarkation on the orbiting *Jupiter Five* command ship was not scheduled to take place until a few days later. Danchekker would be busy making final arrangements for his team and their equipment to be ferried up from the Lunar surface. Hunt, not being involved in these undertakings, prepared an itinerary of places to visit during the free time he had available.

The first thing he did was fly to Tycho by surface transporter to observe the excavations still going on around the areas of some of the Lunarian finds, and to meet at last many of the people who up until then had existed only as faces on display screens. He also went to see the deep mining and boring operations in progress not far from Tycho, where engineers were attempting to penetrate to the core regions of the Moon. They believed that concentrations of rich metal-bearing ores might be found there. If this turned out to be so, within decades the Moon could become an enormous spaceship factory, where parts prefabricated in processing and forming plants on the surface would be ferried up for final assembly in Lunar orbit. The economic advantages of constructing deep-space craft here and from Lunar materials, without having to lift everything up out of Earth's gravity pit to start with, promised to be enormous.

Next, Hunt visited the huge radio and optical observatories of Giordano Bruno on Farside. Here, sensitive receivers, operating fully shielded from the perpetual interference from Earth, and gigantic telescopes, freed from any atmosphere and not having to contend with distortions induced by their own weights, were pushing the frontiers of the known Universe way out beyond the limits of their Earth-bound predecessors. Hunt sat fascinated in front of the monitor screens and resolved planets of some of the nearer stars; he was shown one nine times the size of Jupiter, and another that described a crazy figure-eight orbit about a double star. He gazed deep into the heart of the Andromeda Galaxy, and out at distant specks on the very threshold of detection. Scientists and physicists described the strange new picture of the Cosmos that was beginning to emerge from their work here and explained some of the exciting advances in concepts of space-time mechanics, which indicated that feasible methods could be devised for deforming astronomic geodesics in such a way that the limitations once thought to apply to extreme effective velocities could be avoided. If so, interstellar travel would become a practical proposition; one of the scientists confidently predicted that man would cross the Galaxy within fifty years.

Hunt's final stop brought him back to Nearside—to the base at Copernicus near which Charlie had been found. Scientists at Copernicus had been studying descriptions of the terrain over which Charlie had traveled and the accompanying sketched maps; the information contained in the notebook had been transmitted up from Houston. From the traveling times, distances, and estimates of speed quoted, they suspected that Charlie's journey had begun somewhere on Farside and had brought him, by way of the Jura Mountains, Sinus Iridum, and Mare Imbrium, to Copernicus. Not everybody subscribed to this opinion, however; there was a problem. For some unaccountable reason, the directions and compass points mentioned in Charlie's notes bore no relationship to the conventional lunar north-south that derived from its axis of rotation. The only route for Charlie's journey that could be interpreted to make any sense at all was the one from Farside across Mare Imbrium, but even that only made sense if a completely new direction was assumed for the north-south axis.

Attempts to locate Gorda had so far met with no positive success. From the tone of the final entries in the diary, it could not have been very far from the spot where Charlie was found. About fifteen miles south of this point was an area covered by numerous overlapping craters, all confirmed as being meteoritic and of recent origin. Most researchers concluded that this must have been the site of Gorda, totally obliterated by a freak concentration of meteorites in the as yet unexplained storm.

Before leaving Copernicus, Hunt accepted an invitation to drive out overland and visit the place of Charlie's discovery. He was accompanied by a Professor Alberts from the base and the crew of the UNSA survey vehicle.

* * *

The survey vehicle lumbered to a halt in a wide gorge, between broken walls of slate-gray rock. All around it, the dust
had been churned into a bewildering pattern of grooves and
ridges by Caterpillar tracks, wheels, landing gear, and human
feet—evidence of the intense activity that had occurred there
over the last eighteen months. From the observation dome of
the upper cabin, Hunt recognized the scene immediately; he
had first seen it in Caldwell's office. He identified the large
mound of rubble against the near wall of the gorge, and above
it the notch leading into the cleft.

A voice called from below. Hunt rose to his feet, his movements slow and clumsy in his encumbering space suit, and
clambered through the floor hatch and down a short ladder to
the control cabin. The driver was stretching back in his seat,
taking a long drink from a flask of hot coffee. Behind him, the
sergeant in command of the vehicle was at a videoscreen, reporting back to base via comsat that they had reached their
destination without mishap. The third crew member, a corporal
who was to accompany Hunt and Alberts outside and who was
already fitted out, was helping the professor secure his helmet.
Hunt took his own helmet from the storage rack by the door
and fixed it in place. When the three were ready, the sergeant
supervised the final checkout of life-support and communications systems and cleared them to pass, one by one, through
the airlock to the outside.

"Well, there you are, Vic. Really on the Moon now." Al-
bert's voice came through the speaker inside Hunt's helmet.
Hunt felt the spongy dust yield beneath his boots and tried a
few experimental steps up and down.

"It's like Brighton Beach," he said.

"Okay, you guys?" asked the voice of the UNSA corporal.

"Okay."

"Sure."

"Let's go, then."

The three brightly colored figures—one orange, one red,
one green—began moving slowly along the well-worn groove
that ran up the center of the mound of rubble. At the top they
stopped to gaze down at the survey vehicle, already looking
toylike in the gorge below.

They moved into the cleft, climbing between vertical walls
of rocks that closed in on both sides as they approached the
bend. Above the bend the cleft straightened, and in the dis-

tance Hunt could see a huge wall of jagged buttresses towering over the foothills above them—evidently the ridge described in Charlie's note. He could picture vividly the scene in this very place so long ago, when two other figures in space suits had toiled onward and upward, their eyes fixed on that same feature. Above it, the red and black portent of a tormented planet had glowered down on their final agony like . . .

Hunt stopped, puzzled. He looked up at the ridge again, then turned to stare at the bright disk of Earth, shining far behind his right shoulder. He turned to look one way, then back again the other.

"Anything wrong?" Alberts, who had continued on a few paces, had turned and was staring back at him.

"I'm not sure. Hang on there a second." Hunt moved up alongside the professor and pointed up and ahead toward the ridge. "You're more familiar with this place than I am. See that ridge up ahead there— At any time in the year, could the Earth ever appear in a position over the top of it?"

Alberts followed Hunt's pointing finger, glanced briefly back at the Earth, and shook his head decisively behind his facepiece.

"Never. From the Lunar surface, the position of Earth is almost constant. It does wobble about its mean position a bit as a result of libration, but not by anything near that much." He looked again. "Never anywhere near there. That's an odd question. Why do you ask?"

"Just something that occurred to me. Doesn't really matter for now."

Hunt lowered his eyes and saw an opening at the base of one of the walls ahead. "That must be it. Let's carry on up to it."

The hole was exactly as he remembered from innumerable photographs. Despite its age, the shape betrayed its artificial origin. Hunt approached almost reverently and paused to finger the rock at one side of the opening with his gauntlet. The score marks had obviously been made by something like a drill.

"Well, that's it," came the voice of Alberts, who was standing a few feet back. "Charlie's Cave, we call it—more or less exactly as it must have been when he and his companion first saw it. Rather like treading in the sacred chambers of one of the pyramids, isn't it?"

"That's one way of putting it." Hunt ducked down to peer

inside, pausing to fumble for the flashlight at his belt as the sudden darkness blinded him temporarily.

The rockfall that originally had covered the body had been cleared, and the interior was roomier than he expected. Strange emotions welled inside him as he stared at the spot where, millennia before the first page of history had been written, a huddled figure had painfully scrawled the last page of a story that Hunt had read so recently in an office in Houston, a quarter of a million miles away. He thought of the time that had passed since those events had taken place—of the empires that had grown and fallen, the cities that had crumbled to dust, and the lives that had sparkled briefly and been swallowed into the past—while all that time, unchanging, the secret of these rocks had lain undisturbed. Many minutes passed before Hunt reemerged and straightened up in the dazzling sunlight.

Again he frowned up toward the ridge. Something tantalizing was dancing elusively just beyond the fringes of the thinking portions of his mind, as if from the subconscious shadows that lay below, something insistent was shrieking to be recognized. And then it was gone.

He clipped the flashlight back into position on his belt and walked across to rejoin Alberts, who was studying some rock formations on the opposite wall.

chapter twenty

The giant ships that would fly on the fifth manned mission to Jupiter had been under construction in Lunar orbit for over a year. Besides the command ship, six freighters, each capable of carrying thirty thousand tons of supplies and equipment, gradually took shape high above the surface of the Moon. During the final two months before scheduled departure, the floating jumbles of machinery, materials, containers, vehicles, tanks, crates, drums, and a thousand other items of assorted engineering that hung around the ships like enormous Christmas-tree ornaments, were slowly absorbed inside. The Vega surface shuttles, deep-space cruisers, and other craft also destined for the mission began moving in over a period of several weeks to join their respective mother ships. At intervals throughout the last week, the freighters lifted out of Lunar orbit and set course for Jupiter. By the time its passengers and final complement of crew were being ferried up from the Lunar surface, only the command ship was left, hanging alone in the void. As H hour approached, the gaggle of service craft and attendant satellites withdrew and a flock of escorts converged to stand a few miles off, cameras transmitting live via Luna into the World News Grid.

As the final minutes ticked by, a million viewscreens showed the awesome mile-and-a-quarter-long shape drifting almost imperceptibly against the background of stars; the serenity of the spectacle seemed somehow to forewarn of the unimaginable power waiting to be unleashed. Exactly on schedule, the flight-control computers completed their final-countdown-phase checkout, obtained "Go" acknowledgment from the ground control master processor, and activated the main thermonuclear drives in a flash that was visible from Earth.

The Jupiter Five Mission was under way.

For the next fifteen minutes the ship gained speed and altitude through successively higher orbits. Then, shrugging off the restraining pull of Luna with effortless ease, *Jupiter Five* soared out and away to begin overtaking and marshalling together its flock of freighters, by this time already strung out across a million miles of space. After a while the escorts turned back toward Luna, while on Earth the news screens showed a steadily diminishing point of light, being tracked by the orbiting telescopes. Soon even that had vanished, and only the long-range radars and laser links were left to continue their electronic exchanges across the widening gulf.

Aboard the command ship, Hunt and the other UNSA scientists watched on the wall screen in mess twenty-four as the minutes passed by and Luna contracted into a full disk, partly eclipsing that of Earth beyond. In the days that followed, the two globes waned and fused into a single blob of brilliance, standing out in the heavens to signpost the way they had come. As days turned into weeks, even this shrank to become just another grain of dust among millions until, after about a month, they could pick it out only with difficulty.

Hunt found that it took time to adjust to the idea of living as part of a tiny man-made world, with the Cosmos stretching away to infinity on every side and the distance between them and everything that was familiar increasing at more than ten miles every second. Now they depended utterly for survival on the skills of those who had designed and built the ship. The green hills and blue skies of Earth were no longer factors of survival and seemed to shed some of their tangible attributes, almost like the aftermath of a dream that had seemed real. Hunt came to think of reality as a relative quantity—not something absolute that can be left for a while and then returned to. The ship became the only reality; it was the things left behind that ceased, temporarily, to exist.

He spent hours in the viewing domes along the outer hull, slowly coming to terms with the new dimension being added to his existence, gazing out at the only thing left that was familiar: the Sun. He found reassurance in the eternal presence of the Sun, with its limitless flood of life-giving warmth and light. Hunt thought of the first sailors, who had never ventured out of sight of land; they too had needed something familiar to cling to. But before long, men would turn their prow toward the open gulf and plunge into the voids between the galaxies. There would be no Sun to reassure them then, and there would be no stars at all; the galaxies themselves would be just faint spots, scattered all the way to infinity.

What strange new continents were waiting on the other side of those gulfs?

Danchekker was spending one of his relaxation periods in a zero-gravity section of the ship, watching a game of 3-D football being played between two teams of off-duty crew members. The game was based on American-style football and took place inside an enormous sphere of transparent, rubbery plastic. Players hurtled up, down, and in all directions, rebounding off the wall and off each other in a glorious roughhouse directed—vaguely—at getting the ball through two circular goals on opposite sides of the sphere. In reality, the whole thing was just an excuse to let off steam and flex muscles beginning to go soft during the long, monotonous voyage.

A steward tapped the scientist on the shoulder and informed him that a call was waiting in the videobooth outside the recreation deck. Danchekker nodded, unclipped the safety loop of his belt from the anchor pin attached to the seat, clipped it around the handrail, and with a single effortless pull, sent himself floating gracefully toward the door. Hunt's face greeted him, speaking from a quarter of a mile away.

"Dr. Hunt," he acknowledged. "Good morning—or whatever it happens to be at the present time in this infernal contraption."

"Hello, Professor," Hunt replied. "I've been having some thoughts about the Ganymeans. There are one or two points I could use your opinion on; could we meet somewhere for a bite to eat, say inside the next half hour or so?"

"Very well. Where did you have in mind?"

"Well, I'm on my way to the restaurant in E section right now. I'll be there for a while."

"I'll join you there in a few minutes." Danchekker cut off the screen, emerged from the booth, and hauled himself back into the corridor and along it to an entrance to one of the transverse shafts leading "down" toward the axis of the ship. Using the handrails, he sailed some distance toward the center before checking himself opposite an exit from the shaft. He emerged through a transfer lock into one of the rotating sections, with simulated G, at a point near the axis where the speed differential was low. He launched himself back along another rail and felt himself accelerate gently, to land thirty feet away, on his feet, on a part of the structure that had suddenly become the floor. Walking normally, he followed some signs to the nearest tube access point, pressed the call button, and waited about twenty seconds for a capsule to arrive. Once inside, he keyed in his destination and within seconds was being whisked smoothly through the tube toward E section of the ship.

The permanently open self-service restaurant was about half full. The usual clatter of cutlery and dishes poured from the kitchens behind the counter at one end, where a trio of UNSA cooks were dishing out generous helpings of assorted culinary offerings ranging from UNSA eggs and UNSA beans to UNSA chicken legs and UNSA steaks. Automatic food dispensers with do-it-yourself microwave cookers had been tried on *Jupiter Four* but hadn't proved popular with the crew. So the designers of *Jupiter Five* had gone back to the good old-fashioned methods.

Carrying their trays, Hunt and Danchekker threaded their way between diners, card players, and vociferous debating groups and found an empty table against the far wall. They sat down and began transferring their plates to the table.

"So, you've been entertaining some thoughts concerning our Ganymean friends," Danchekker commented as he began to butter a roll.

"Them and the Lunarians," Hunt replied. "In particular, I like your idea that the Lunarians evolved on Minerva from terrestrial animal species that the Ganymeans imported. It's the only thing that accounts acceptably for no traces of any civilizations showing up on Earth. All these attempts people are making to show it might be different don't convince me much at all."

"I'm very gratified to hear you say so," Danchekker declared. "The problem, however, is proving it."

"Well, that's what I've been thinking about. Maybe we shouldn't have to."

Danchekker looked up and peered inquisitively over his spectacles. He looked intrigued. "Really? How, might I ask?"

"We've got a big problem trying to figure out anything about what happened on Minerva because we're fairly sure it doesn't exist anymore except as a million chunks of geology strewn around the Solar System. But the Lunarians didn't have that problem. They had it in one piece, right under their feet. Also, they had progressed to an advanced state of scientific knowledge. Now, what must their work have turned up—at least to some extent?"

A light of comprehension dawned in Danchekker's eyes.

"Ah!" he exclaimed at once. "I see. If the Ganymean civilization had flourished on Minerva first, then Lunarian scientists would surely have deduced as much." He paused, frowned, then added: "But that does not get you very far, Dr. Hunt. You are no more able to interrogate Lunarian scientific archives than you are to reassemble the planet."

"No, you're right," Hunt agreed. "We don't have any detailed Lunarian scientific records—but we do have the microdot library. The texts it contains are pretty general in nature, but I couldn't help thinking that if the Lunarians discovered an advanced race had been there before them, it would be big and exciting news, something everybody would know about; you've only got to look at the fuss that Charlie has caused on Earth. Perhaps there were references through all of their writings that pointed to such a knowledge—if we knew how to read them." He paused to swallow a mouthful of sausage. "So, one of the things I've been doing over the last few weeks is going through everything we've got with a fine-tooth comb to see if anything could point to something like that. I didn't expect to find firm proof of anything much—just enough for us to be able to say with a bit more confidence that we think we know what planet we're talking about."

"And did you find very much?" Danchekker seemed interested.

"Several things," Hunt replied. "For a start, there are stock phrases scattered all through their language that refer to the Giants. Phrases like 'As old as the Giants' or 'Back to the year of the Giants' . . . like we'd say maybe, 'Back to the year one.' In another place there's a passage that begins 'A long time ago, even before the time of the Giants' . . . There are lots of things like that. When you look at them from this angle, they all suddenly tie together." Hunt paused for a second to allow the professor time to reflect on these points, then resumed: "Also, there are references to the Giants in another context, one that suggests superpowers or great knowledge—for example, 'Gifted with the wisdom of the Giants.' You see what I mean—these phrases indicate the Lunarians felt a race of giant beings—and probably one that was advanced technologically—had existed in the distant past."

Danchekker chewed his food in silence for a while.

"I don't want to sound overskeptical," he said at last, "but all this seems rather speculative. Such references could well be to nothing more than mythical creations—similar to our own heroes of folklore."

"That occurred to me, too," Hunt conceded. "But thinking about it, I'm not so sure. The Lunarians were the last word in pragmatism—they had no time for romanticism, religion, matters of the spirit, or anything like that. In the situation they were in, the only people who could help them were themselves, and they knew it. They couldn't afford the luxury and the delusion of inventing gods, heroes, and Father Christmases to work their problems out for them." He shook his head. "I don't believe the Lunarians made up any legends about these Giants. That would have been too much out of character."

"Very well," Danchekker agreed, returning to his meal. "The Lunarians were aware of the prior existence of the Ganymeans. I suspect, however, that you had more than that in mind when you called."

"You're right," Hunt said. "While I was going through the texts, I pulled together some other bits and pieces that are more in your line."

"Go on."

"Well, supposing for the moment that the Ganymeans did ship a whole zoo out to Minerva, the Lunarian biologists later on would have had a hell of a problem making any sense out of what they found all around them, wouldn't they? I mean, with two different groups of animals loose about the place, totally unrelated—and bearing in mind that they couldn't have known what we know about terrestrial species . . ."

"Worse than that, even," Danchekker supplied. "They would have been able to trace the native Minervan species all the way back to their origins; the imported types, however, would extend back through only twenty-five million years or so. Before that, there would have been no record of any ancestors from which they could have descended."

"That's precisely one of the things I wanted to ask you," Hunt said. He leaned forward and rested his elbows on the table. "Suppose you were a Lunarian biologist and knew only the facts he would have known. What sort of picture would it have added up to?"

Danchekker stopped chewing and thought for a long time, his eyes staring far beyond where Hunt was sitting. At length he shook his head slowly.

"That is a very difficult question to answer. In that situation one might, I suppose, speculate that the Ganymeans had introduced alien species. But on the other hand, that is what a biologist from Earth would think; he would be conditioned to expect a continuous fossil record stretching back over hundreds of millions of years. A Lunarian, without any such conditioning, might not regard the absence of a complete record as in any way abnormal. If that was part of the accepted way of things in the world in which he had grown up . . ."

Danchekker's voice faded away for a few seconds. "If I were a Lunarian," he said suddenly, his voice decisive, "I would explain what I saw thus: Life began in the distant past on Minerva, evolved through the accepted process of mutation and selection, and branched into many diverse forms. About twenty-five million years ago, a particularly violent series of mutations occurred in a short time, out of which emerged a new family of forms, radically different in structure from anything before. This family branched to produce its own divergency of species, living alongside the older models, and culminating in the emergence of the Lunarians themselves. Yes, I would explain the new appearances in that way. It's similar to the appearance of insects on Earth—a whole family in itself, structurally dissimilar to anything else." He thought it over again for a second and then nodded firmly. "Certainly, compared to an explanation of that nature, suggestions of forced interplanetary migrations would appear very farfetched indeed."

"I was hoping you'd say something like that." Hunt nodded, satisfied. "In fact, that's very much what they appear to have believed. It's not specifically stated in anything I've read, but odds and ends from different places add up to that. But there's something odd about it as well."

"Oh?"

"There's a funny word that crops up in a number of places that doesn't have a direct English equivalent; it means something between 'manlike' and 'man-related.' They used it to describe many animal types."

"Probably the animals descended from the imported types and related to themselves," Danchekker suggested.

"Yes, exactly. But they also used the same word in a totally different context—to mean 'ashore,' 'on land' . . . anything to do with dry land. Now, why should a word become synonymous with two such different meanings?"

Danchekker stopped eating again and furrowed his brow.

"I really can't imagine. Is it important?"

"Neither could I, and I think it is. I've done a lot of cross-checking with Linguistics on this, and it all adds up to a very peculiar thing: 'Manlike' and 'dry-land' became synonymous on Minerva because they did in fact mean the same thing. All the land animals on Minerva were new models. We coined the word *terrestoid* to describe them in English."

"*All* of them? You mean that by Charlie's time there were none of the original Minervan species left at all?" Danchekker sounded amazed.

"That's what we think—not on land, anyway. There was a full fossil record of plenty of types all the way up to, and including the Ganymeans, but nothing after that—just terrestoids."

"And in the sea?"

"That was different. The old Minervan types continued right through—hence your fish." .   •

Danchekker gazed at Hunt with an expression that almost betrayed open disbelief.

"How extraordinary!" he exclaimed.

The professor's arm had suddenly become paralyzed and was holding a fork in midair with half a roast potato impaled on the end. "You mean that all the native Minervan land life disappeared—just like that?"

"Well, during a fairly short time, anyway. We've been asking for a long time what happened to the Ganymeans. Now it looks more as if the question should be phrased in even broader terms: What happened to the Ganymeans and all their land-dwelling relatives?"

chapter twenty-one

For weeks the two scientists debated the mystery of the abrupt disappearance of the native Minervan land dwellers. They ruled out physical catastrophe on the assumption that anything of that kind would have destroyed the terrestoid types as well. The same conclusion applied to climatic cataclysm.

For a while they considered the possibility of an epidemic caused by microorganisms imported with the immigrant animals, one against which the native species enjoyed no inherited, in-built immunity. In the end they dismissed this idea as unlikely on two counts: first, an epidemic sufficiently virulent in its effects to wipe out each and every species of what must have numbered millions, was hard to imagine; second, all information received so far from Ganymede suggested that the Ganymeans had been considerably farther ahead in technical knowledge than either the Lunarians or mankind—surely they could never have made such a blunder.

A variation on this theme supposed that germ warfare had broken out, escalated, and got out of control. Both the previous objections carried less weight when viewed in this context; in the end, this explanation was accepted as possible. That left only one other possibility: some kind of chemical change in the Minervan atmosphere to which the native species hadn't been capable of adapting but the terrestoids had. But what?

While the pros and cons of these alternatives were still being evaluated on *Jupiter Five*, the laser link to Earth brought details of a new row that had broken out in Navcomms. A faction of Pure Earthists had produced calculations showing that the Lunarians could never have survived on Minerva at all, let alone flourished there; at that distance from the Sun it would simply have been too cold. They also insisted that water could never have existed on the surface in a liquid state and held this fact as proof that wherever the world shown on Charlie's maps had been, it couldn't have been anywhere near the Asteroids.

Against this attack the various camps of Minervaists concluded a hasty alliance and opened counterfire with calculations of their own, which invoked the greenhouse effect of atmospheric carbon dioxide to show that a substantially higher temperature could have been sustained. They demonstrated further that the percentage of carbon dioxide required to produce the mean temperature that they had already estimated by other means, was precisely the figure arrived at by Professor Schorn in his deduction of the composition of the Minervan atmosphere from an analysis of Charlie's cell metabolism and respiratory system. The land mine that finally demolished the Pure Earthist position was Schorn's later pronouncement that Charlie exhibited several physiological signs implying adaptation to an abnormally high level of carbon dioxide.

Their curiosity stimulated by all this sudden interest in the amount of carbon dioxide in the Minervan atmosphere, Hunt and Danchekker devised a separate experiment of their own. Combining Hunt's mathematical skill with Danchekker's knowledge of quantitave molecular biology, they developed a computer model of generalized Minervan microchemical behavior potentials, based on data derived from the native fish. It took them over three months to perfect. Then they applied to the model a series of mathematical operators that simulated the effects of different chemical agents in the environment. When he viewed the results on the screen in one of the console rooms Danchekker's conclusion was quite definite: "Any airbreathing life form that evolved from the same primitive an-

cestors as this fish and inherited the same fundamental system
of microchemistry, would be extremely susceptible to a family
of toxins that includes carbon dioxide—far more so than the
majority of terrestrial species."

For once, everything added up. About twenty-five million
years ago, the concentration of carbon dioxide in the atmosphere
of Minerva apparently increased suddenly, possibly through
some natural cause that had liberated the gas from chemical
combination in rocks, or possibly as a result of something the
Ganymeans had done. This could also explain why the
Ganymeans had brought in all the animals. Perhaps their prime
objective had been to redress the balance by covering the planet
with carbon-dioxide-absorbing, oxygen-producing terrestrial
green plants; the animals had been included simply to preserve
a balanced ecology in which the plants could survive. The attempt failed. The native life succumbed, and the more highly re-
sistant immigrants flourished and spread out over a whole new
world denuded of alien competition. Nobody knew for sure that
it had been so on Minerva. Possibly nobody ever would.

And nobody knew what had become of the Ganymeans.
Perhaps they had perished along with their cousins. Perhaps,
when their efforts proved futile, they had abandoned Minerva
to its new inhabitants and left the Solar System completely to
find a new home elsewhere. Hunt hoped so. For some strange
reason he had developed an inexplicable affection for this mysterious race. In one of the Lunarian texts he had come across
a verse that began: "Far away among the stars, where the
Giants of old now live . . ." He hoped it was true.

And so, quite suddenly, at least one chapter in the early history of Minerva had been cleared up. Everything now pointed
to the Lunarians and their civilization as having developed on
Minerva and not on Earth. It explained the failure of Schorn's
early attempt to fix the length of the day in Hunt's calendar by
calculating Charlie's natural periods of sleep and wakefulness.
The ancestors of the Lunarians had arrived from Earth carrying
a deeply rooted metabolic rhythm evolved around a twenty-
four-hour cycle. During the twenty-five million years that followed, some of the more flexible biological processes in their
descendants adapted successfully to the thirty-five-hour day of
Minerva, while others changed only partially. By Charlie's
time, all the Lunarians' physiological clocks had gotten hopelessly out of synchronization; no wonder Schorn's results made

no sense. But the puzzling numbers in Charlie's notebook still remained to be accounted for.

In Houston, Caldwell read Hunt and Danchekker's joint report with deep satisfaction. He had realized long before that to achieve results, the abilities of the two scientists would have to be combined and focused on the problem at hand instead of being dissipated fruitlessly in the friction of personal incompatibility. How could he manipulate into being a situation in which the things they had in common outweighed their differences? Well, what did they have in common? Starting with the simplest and most obvious thing—they were both human beings from planet Earth. So where would this fundamental truth come to totally overshadow anything else? Where but on the barren wastes of the Moon or a hundred million miles out in the emptiness of space? Everything seemed to be working out better then he had dared hope.

"It's like I always said," Lyn Garland stated coyly when Hunt's assistant showed her a copy of the report. "Gregg's a genius with people."

The arrival in Ganymede orbit of the seven ships from Earth was a big moment for the Jupiter Four veterans, especially those whose tour of duty was approaching an end and who could now look forward to going home soon. In the weeks to come, as the complex program of maneuvering supplies and equipment between the ships and the surface installations unfolded, the scene above Ganymede would become as chaotic as that above Luna had been during departure preparations. The two command ships would remain standing off ten miles apart for the next two months. Then *Jupiter Four*, accompanied by two of the recently arrived freighters, would move out to take up station over Callisto and begin expanding the pilot base already set up there. *Jupiter Five* would remain at Ganymede until joined by *Saturn Two*, which was at that time undergoing final countdown for Lunar lift-out and due to arrive in five months. After rendezvous above Ganymede, one of the two ships (exactly which was yet to be decided) would set course for the ringed planet, on the farthest large-scale manned probe yet attempted.

The long-haul sailing days of *Jupiter Four* were over. Too slow by the standards of the latest designs, it would probably be stripped down to become a permanent orbiting base over

Callisto. After a few years it would suffer the ignoble end of being dismantled and cannibalized for surface constructions.

With all the hustle and traffic congestion that erupted in the skies over Ganymede, it was three days before the time came for the group of UNSA scientists to be ferried to the surface. After months of getting used to the pattern of life and the company aboard the ship, Hunt felt a twinge of nostalgia as he packed his belongings in his cabin and stood in line waiting to board the Vega moored alongside in the cavernous midships docking bay. It was probably the last he would see of the inside of this immense city of metal alloys; when he returned to Earth, it would be aboard one of the small, fast cruisers ferried out with the mission.

An hour later *Jupiter Five*, festooned in a web of astronautic engineering, was shrinking rapidly on the cabin display in the Vega. Then the picture changed suddenly and the sinister frosty countenance of Ganymede came swelling up toward them.

Hunt sat on the edge of his bunk inside a Spartan room in number-three barrack block of Ganymede Main Base and methodically transferred the contents of his kit bag into the aluminum locker beside him. The air-extractor grille above the door was noisy. The air drawn in through the vents set into the lower walls was warm, and tainted with the smell of engine oil. The steel floor plates vibrated to the hum of heavy machinery somewhere below. Propped up against a pillow on the bunk opposite, Danchekker was browsing through a folder full of facsimiled notes and color illustrations and chattering excitedly like a schoolboy on Christmas Eve.

"Just think of it, Vic, another day and we'll be there. Animals that actually walked the Earth twenty-five million years ago! Any biologist would give his right arm for an experience like this." He held up the folder. "Look at that. I do believe it to be a perfectly preserved example of *Trilophodon*—a four-tusked Miocene mammoth over fifteen feet high. Can you imagine anything more exciting than that?"

Hunt scowled sourly across the room at the collection of pin-ups adorning the far wall, bequeathed by an earlier UNSA occupant.

"Frankly, yes," he muttered. "But equipped rather differently than a bloody *Trilophodon*."

"Eh? What's that you said?" Danchekker blinked uncomprehendingly through his spectacles. Hunt reached for his cigarette case.

"It doesn't matter, Chris," he sighed.

chapter twenty-two

The flight northward to Pithead lasted just under two hours. On arrival, the group from Earth assembled in the officers' mess of the control building for coffee, during which scientists from Jupiter Four updated them on Ganymean matters.

The Ganymean ship had almost certainly been destined for a large-scale, long-range voyage and not for anything like a limited exploratory expedition. Several hundred Ganymeans had died with their ship. The quantity and variety of stores, materials, equipment, and livestock that they had taken with them indicated that wherever they had been bound, they had meant to stay.

Everything about the ship, especially its instrumentation and control systems, revealed a very advanced stage of scientific knowledge. Most of the electronics were still a mystery, and some of the special-purpose components were unlike anything the UNSA engineers had ever seen. Ganymean computers were built using a mass-integration technology in which millions of components were diffused, layer upon layer, into a single monolithic silicon block. The heat dissipated inside was removed by electronic cooling networks interwoven with the functional circuitry. In some examples, believed to form parts of the navigation system, component packing densities approached that of the human brain. A physicist held up a slab of what appeared to be silicon, about the size of a large dictionary; in terms of raw processing power, he claimed, it was capable of outperforming all the computers in the Navcomms Headquarters building put together.

The ship was streamlined and strongly constructed, indicating that it was designed to fly through atmospheres and to land on a planet without collapsing under its own weight. Ganymean engineering appeared to have reached a level where the functions of a Vega and a deep-space interorbital transporter were combined in one vessel.

The propulsion system was revolutionary. There were no large exhaust apertures and no obvious reaction points to suggest that the ship had been kicked forward by any kind of thermodynamic or photonic external thrust. The main fuel-storage system fed a succession of convertors and generators designed to deliver enormous amounts of electrical and magnetic energy. This supplied a series of two-foot-square superconducting busbars and a maze of interleaved windings, fabricated from solid copper bars, that surrounded what appeared to be the main-drive engines. Nobody was sure precisely how this arrangement resulted in motion of the ship, although some of the theories were startling.

Could this have been a true starship? Had the Ganymeans left en masse in an interstellar exodus? Had this particular ship foundered on its way out of the Solar System, shortly after leaving Minerva? These questions and a thousand more remained to be answered. One thing was certain, though: If the discovery of Charlie had given two years' work to a significant proportion of Navcomms, there was enough information here to keep half the scientific world occupied for decades, if not centuries.

The party spent some hours in the recently erected laboratory dome, inspecting items brought up from below the ice, including several Ganymean skeletons and a score of terrestrial animals. To Danchekker's disappointment, his particular favorite—the man-ape anthropoid he had shown to Hunt and Caldwell many months before on a viewscreen in Houston— was not among them. "Cyril" had been transferred to the laboratories of the *Jupiter Four* command ship for detailed examination. The name, graciously bestowed by the UNSA biologists, was in honor of the mission's chief scientist.

After lunch in the base canteen, they walked into the dome that covered one of the shaftheads. Fifteen minutes later they were standing deep below the surface of the ice field, gazing in awe at the ship itself.

It lay, fully uncovered, in the vast white floodlighted cavern, its underside still supported in its mold of ice. The hull cut a clean swath through the forest of massive steel jacks and ice pillars that carried the weight of the roof. Beneath the framework of ramps and scaffolding that clung to its side, whole sections of the hull had been removed to reveal the compartments inside. The floor all around was littered with pieces of machinery lifted out by overhead cranes. The scene reminded Hunt of the time he and Borlan had visited Boeing's huge plant near Seattle where they assembled the 1017 skyliners— but everything here was on a far vaster scale.

They toured the network of catwalks and ladders that had been laid throughout the ship, from the command deck with its fifteen-foot-wide display screen, through the control rooms, living quarters, and hospital, to the cargo holds and the tiers of cages that had contained the animals. The primary energy-convertor and generator section was as imposing and as complex as the inside of a thermonuclear power station. Beyond it, they passed through a bulkhead and found themselves dwarfed beneath the curves of the exposed portions of a pair of enormous toroids. The engineer leading them pointed up at the immense, sweeping surfaces of metal.

"The walls of those outer casings are sixteen feet thick," he informed them. "They're made from an alloy that would cut tungsten-carbide steel like cream cheese. The mass concentration inside them is phenomenal. We think they provided closed paths in which masses of highly concentrated matter were constrained in circulating or oscillating resonance, interacting with strong fields. It's possible that the high rates of change of gravity potential that this produced were somehow harnessed to induce a controlled distortion in the space around the ship. In other words, it moved by continuously falling into a hole that it created in front of itself—kind of like a four-dimensional tank track."

"You mean it trapped itself inside a space-time bubble, which propagated somehow through normal space?" somebody offered.

"Yes, if you like," the engineer affirmed. "I guess a bubble is as good an analogy as any. The interesting point is, if it did work that way, every particle of the ship and everything inside it would be subjected to exactly the same acceleration. Therefore there would be no G effect. You could stop the ship dead from, say, a million miles an hour to zero in a millisecond, and nobody inside would even know the difference."

"How about top speed?" someone else asked. "Would there have been a relativistic limit?"

"We don't know. The theory boys up in *Jupiter Four* have been losing a lot of sleep over that. Conventional mechanics wouldn't apply to any movement of the ship itself, since it wouldn't be actually moving in the local space inside the bubble. The question of how the bubble propagates through normal space is a different ball game altogether. A whole new theory of fields has to be worked out. Maybe completely new laws of physics apply—as I said before, we just don't know. But one thing seems clear: Those photon-drive starships they're designing in California might turn out to be obsolete before they're even built. If we can figure out enough about how this ship worked, the knowledge could put us forward a hundred years."

By the end of the day Hunt's mind was in a whirl. New information was coming in faster than he could digest it. The questions in his head were multiplying at a rate a thousand times faster than they could ever be answered. The riddle of the Ganymean spaceship grew more intriguing with every new revelation, but at the back of it there was still the Lunarian problem unresolved. He needed time to stand back and think, to put his mental house in order and sort the jumble into related thoughts that would slot into labeled boxes in his mind. Then he would be able to see better which question depended on what, and which needed to be tackled first. But the jumble was piling up faster than he could pick up the pieces.

The banter and laughter in the mess after the evening meal soon became intolerable. Alone in his room, he found the walls claustrophobic. For a while he walked the deserted corridors between the domes and buildings. They were oppressive; he had lived in metal cans for too long. Eventually he found himself in the control tower dome, staring out into the incandescent gray wall that was produced by the floodlights around the base soaking through the methane–ammonia fog of the Ganymedean night. After a while even the presence of the duty controller, his face etched out against the darkness by the glow from his console, became an intrusion. Hunt stopped by the console on his way to the stairwell.

"Check me out for surface access."

The duty controller looked across at him. "You're going outside?"

"I need some air."

The controller brought one of his screens to life. "You are who, please?"

"Hunt. Dr. V. Hunt."

"ID?"

"730289 C/EX4."

The controller logged the details, then checked the time and keyed it in.

"Report in by radio in one hour's time if you're not back. Keep a receiver channel open permanently on 24.328 megahertz."

"Will do," Hunt acknowledged. "Good night."

"Night."

The controller watched Hunt disappear toward the floor below, shrugged to himself, and automatically scanned the displays in front of him. It was going to be a quiet night.

In the surface access anteroom on the ground level, Hunt selected a suit from the row of lockers along the right-hand wall. A few minutes later, suited up and with his helmet secured, he walked to the airlock, keyed his name and ID code into the terminal by the gate, and waited a couple of seconds for the inner door to slide open.

He emerged into the swirling silver mist and turned right to follow the line of the looming black metal cliff of the control building. The crunch of his boots in the powder ice sounded faint and far away, through the thin vapors. Where the wall ended he continued walking slowly in a straight line, out into the open area and toward the edge of the base. Phantom shapes of steel emerged and disappeared in the silent shadows around him. The gloom ahead grew darker as inlands of diffuse light passed by on either side. The ice began sloping upward. Irregular patches of naked, upthrusting rock became more frequent. He walked on as if in a trance.

Pictures from the past rolled by before his mind's eye: a boy, reading books, shut away in the upstairs bedroom of a London slum . . . a youth, pedaling a bicycle each morning through the narrow streets of Cambridge. The people he had been were no more real than the people he would become. All through his life he had been moving on, never standing still, always in the process of changing from something he had been to something he would be. And beyond every new world, another beckoned. And always the faces around him were unfamiliar ones—they drifted into his life like the transient shadows of the rocks that now moved toward him from the mists ahead. Like the rocks, for a while the people seemed to exist and take on form and substance, before slipping by to dissolve into the shrouds of the past behind him, as if they had never been. Forsyth-Scott, Felix Borlan, and Rob Gray had already ceased to exist. Would Caldwell, Danchekker, and the rest soon fade away to join them? And what new figures would materialize out of the unknown worlds lying hidden behind the veils of time ahead?

He realized with some surprise that the mists around him were getting brighter again; also, he could suddenly see farther. He was climbing upward across an immense ice field, now smooth and devoid of rocks. The light was an eerie glow, permeating evenly through mists on every side as if the fog itself were luminous. He climbed higher. With every step the horizon of his vision broadened further, and the luminosity drained from the surrounding mist to concentrate itself in a single patch that second by second grew brighter above his head. And then he was looking out over the top of the fog bank. It was just a pocket, trapped in the depression of the vast basin in which the base had been built; it had no doubt been sited there to shorten the length of the shaft needed to reach the Ganymean ship. The slope above him finished in a long, rounded ridge not fifty feet beyond where he stood. He changed direction slightly to take the steeper incline that led directly to the summit of the ridge. The last tenuous wisps of whiteness fell away.

At the top, the night was clear as crystal. He was standing on a beach of ice that shelved down from his feet into a lake of cotton wool. On the opposite shore of the lake rose the summits of the rock buttresses and ice cliffs that stood beyond the base. For miles around, ghostly white bergs of Ganymedean ice floated on an ocean of cloud, shining against the blackness of the night.

But there was no Sun.

He raised his eyes, and gasped involuntarily. Above him, five times larger than the Moon seen from Earth, was the full disk of Jupiter. No photograph he had ever seen, or any image reproduced on a display screen, could compare with the grandeur of that sight. It filled the sky with its radiance. All the colors of the rainbow were woven into its iridescent bands of light, stacked layer upon layer outward from its equator. They faded as they approached its edge and merged into a hazy circle of pink that encircled the planet. The pink turned to violet and finally to purple, ending in a clear, sharp outline that traced an enormous circle against the sky. Immutable, immovable, eternal . . . mightiest of the gods—and tiny, puny, ephemeral man had crawled on a pilgrimage of five hundred million miles to pay homage.

Maybe only seconds passed, maybe hours. Hunt could not tell. For a fraction of eternity he stood unmoving, a speck lost among the silent towers of rock and ice. Charlie too had stood upon the surface of a barren waste and gazed up at a world wreathed in light and color—but the colors had been those of death.

At that moment, the scenes that Charlie had seen came to Hunt more vividly than at any time before. He saw cities consumed by fireballs ten miles high; he saw gaping chasms, seared and blackened ash that had once held oceans, and lakes of fire where mountains had stood. He saw continents buckle and break asunder, and drown beneath a fury of white heat that came exploding outward from below. As clearly as if it were really happening, he saw the huge globe above him swelling and bursting, grotesque with the deceptive slowness of mighty events seen from great distances. Day by day it would rush outward into space, consuming its moons one after the other in an insatiable orgy of gluttony until its force was spent. And then . . .

Hunt snapped back to reality with a jolt.

Suddenly the answer he had been seeking was there. It had come out of nowhere. He tried to trace its root by backtracking through his thoughts—but there was nothing. The pathways up from the deeper levels of his mind had opened for a second, but now were closed. The illusion was exposed. The paradox had gone. Of course nobody had seen it before. Who would think to question a truth that was self-evident, and older than the human race itself?

"Pithead Control calling Dr. V. Hunt. Dr. Hunt, come in, please." The sudden voice in his helmet startled him. He pressed a button in the control panel on his chest.

"Hunt answering," he acknowledged. "I hear you."

"Routine check. You're five minutes overdue to report. Is everything okay?"

"Sorry, didn't notice the time. Yes, everything's okay . . . very okay. I'm coming back now."

"Thank you." The voice cut off with a click.

Had he been gone that long? He realized that he was cold. The icy fingers of the Ganymedean night were beginning to feel their way inside his suit. He wound his heating control up a turn and flexed his arms. Before he turned, he looked up once more for a final glimpse of the giant planet. For some strange reason it seemed to be smiling.

"Thanks, pal," he murmured with a wink. "Maybe I'll be able to do something for you someday."

With that he began moving down from the ridge, and rapidly faded into the sea of cloud.

chapter twenty-three

A group of about thirty people, mainly scientists, engineers, and UNSA executives, filed into the conference theater in the Navcomms Headquarters building. The room was arranged in ascending tiers of seats that faced a large blank screen at the far end from the double doors. Caldwell was standing on a raised platform in front of the screen, watching as the various groups and individuals found seats. Soon everybody was settled and an usher at the rear signaled that the corridor outside was empty. Caldwell nodded in acknowledgment, raised his hand for silence, and stepped a pace forward to the microphone in front of him.

"Your attention, please, ladies and gentlemen . . . Could we have quiet, please . . ." The baritone voice boomed out of the loudspeakers around the walls. The murmurs subsided.

"Thank you all for coming on such short notice," he resumed. "All of you have been engaged for some time now in some aspect or other of the Lunarian problem. Ever since this thing first started, there have been more than a few arguments and differences of opinions, as you all know. Taking all things into consideration, however, we haven't done too badly. We started out with a body and a few scraps of paper, and from them we reconstructed a whole world. But there are still some fundamental questions that have remained unanswered right up to this day. I'm sure there's no need for me to recap them for the benefit of anyone here." He paused. "At last, it appears, we may have answers to those questions. The new developments that cause me to say this are so unexpected that I feel it appropriate to call you all together to let you see for yourselves what I saw for the first time only a few hours ago." He waited again and allowed the mood of the gathering to move from one suited to preliminary remarks to something more in tune with the serious business about to begin.

"As you all know, a group of scientists left us many months ago with the Jupiter Five Mission to investigate the discoveries on Ganymede. Among that group was Vic Hunt. This morning we received his latest report on what's going on. We are about to replay the recording for you now. I think you will find it interesting."

Caldwell glanced toward the projection window at the back of the room and raised his hand. The lights began to fade. He stepped down from the platform and took his seat in the front row. Darkness reigned briefly. Then the screen illuminated to show a file header and reference frame in standard UNSA format. The header persisted for a few seconds, then disappeared to be replaced by the image of Hunt, facing the camera across a desktop.

"Navcomms Special Investigation to Ganymede, V. Hunt reporting, 20 November 2029, Earth Standard Time," he announced. "Subject of transmission: *A Hypothesis Concerning Lunarian Origins*. What follows is not claimed to be rigorously proven theory at this stage. The object is to present an account of a possible sequence of events which, for the first time, explains adequately the origins of the Lunarians, and is also consistent with *all* the facts currently in our possession." Hunt paused to consult some notes on the desk before him. In the conference theater the silence was absolute.

Hunt looked back up and out of the screen. "Up until now I've tended not to accent any particular one of the ideas in circulation in preference to the rest, primarily because I haven't been sufficiently convinced that any of them, as stated, accounted adequately for everything that we had reason to be-

lieve was true. That situation has changed. I have now come to
believe that one explanation exists which is capable of supporting all the evidence. That explanation is as follows:

"The Solar System was formed originally with nine planets,
which included Minerva and extended out as far as Neptune.
Akin to the inner planets and located beyond Mars, Minerva
resembled Earth in many ways. It was similar in size and density and was composed of a mix of similar elements. It cooled
and developed an atmosphere, a hydrosphere, and a surface
composition." Hunt paused for a second. "This has been one
source of difficulty—reconciling surface conditions at this distance from the Sun with the existence of life as we know it.
For proof that these factors can indeed be reconciled, refer to
Professor Fuller's work at London University during the last
few months." A caption appeared on the lower portion of the
screen, giving details of the titles and access codes of Fuller's
papers on the subject.

"Briefly, Fuller has produced a model of the equilibrium
states of various atmospheric gases and volcanically introduced
water vapor, that is consistent with known data. To sustain the
levels of free atmospheric carbon dioxide and water vapor, and
the existence of large amounts of water in a liquid state, the
model requires a very high level of volcanic activity on the
planet, at least in its earlier history. That this requirement was
evidently met could suggest that relative to its size, the crust of
Minerva was exceptionally thin, and the structure of this crust
unstable. This is significant, as becomes clear later. Fuller's
model also ties in with the latest information from the Asteroid
surveys. The thin crust could be the result of relatively rapid
surface cooling caused by the vast distance from the Sun, but
with the internal molten condition being prolonged by heat
sources below the surface. The Asteroid missions report many
samples being tested that are rich in radioactive heat-producing
substances.

"So, Minerva cooled to a mean surface temperature somewhat colder than Earth's but not as cold as you might think.
With cooling came the formation of increasingly more complex molecules, and eventually life emerged. With life came
diversification, followed by competition, followed by
selection—in other words, evolution. After many millions of
years, evolution culminated in a race of intelligent beings who

became dominant on the planet. These were the beings we have christened the Ganymeans.

"The Ganymeans developed an advanced technological civilization. Then, approximately twenty-five million years ago, they had reached a stage which we estimate to be about a hundred years ahead of our own. This estimate is based on the design of the Ganymean ship we've been looking at here, and the equipment found inside it.

"Some time around this period, a major crisis developed on Minerva. Something upset the delicate mechanism controlling the balance between the amount of carbon dioxide locked up in the rocks and that in the free state; the amount in the atmosphere began to rise. The reasons for this are speculative. One possibility is that something triggered the tendency toward high volcanic activity inherent in Minerva's structure—maybe natural causes, maybe something the Ganymeans did. Another possibility is that the Ganymeans were attempting an ambitious program of climate control and the whole thing went wrong in a big way. At present we really don't have a good answer to this part. However, our investigations of the Ganymeans have hardly begun yet. There are still years of work to be done on the contents of the ship alone, and I'm pretty certain that there's a lot more waiting to be discovered down under the ice here.

"Anyhow, the main point for the present is that something happened. Chris Danchekker has shown . . ." Another file reference appeared on the bottom of the screen. ". . . that all the higher, air-breathing Minervan life forms would almost certainly have possessed a very low tolerance to increases in carbon-dioxide concentration. This derives from the fundamental system of microchemistry inherited from the earliest ancestors of the line. This implies, of course, that the changing surface conditions on Minerva posed a threat to the very existence of most forms of land life, including the Ganymeans. If we accept this situation, we also have a plausible reason for supposing that the Ganymeans went through a phase of importing on a vast scale a mixed balance of plant and animal life from Earth. Perhaps, stuck out where it was, Minerva had nothing to compare with the quantity and variety of life teeming on the much warmer planet Earth.

"Evidently, the experiment didn't work. Although the imported stock found conditions favorable enough to flourish in, they failed to produce the desired result. From various bits of information, we believe the Ganymeans gave the whole thing up as a bad job and moved out to find a new home somewhere outside the Solar System. Whether or not they succeeded we don't know; maybe further study of what's in the ship will throw more light on that question."

Hunt stopped to pick up a case from the desk and went through the motions of lighting a cigarette. The break seemed to be timed to give the viewers a chance to digest this part of his narrative. A subdued chorus of mutterings broke out around the room. Here and there a light flared as individuals succumbed to the suggestion from the screen. Hunt continued:

"The native Minervan land species left on the planet soon died out. But the immigrant types from Earth enjoyed a better adaptability and survived. Not only that, they were free to roam unchecked and unhindered across the length and breadth of Minerva, where any native competition rapidly ceased to exist. The new arrivals were thus free to continue the process of evolutionary development that had begun millions of years before in the oceans of Earth. But at the same time, of course, the same process was also continuing on Earth itself. Two groups of animal species, possessing the same genetic inheritance from common ancestors and equipped with the same evolutionary potential, were developing in isolation on two different worlds.

"Now, for those of you who have not yet had the pleasure, allow me to introduce Cyril." The picture of Hunt vanished and a view of the man-ape retrieved from the Ganymean ship appeared.

Hunt's voice carried on with the commentary: "Chris's team has made a thorough examination of this character in the *Jupiter Four* laboratories. Chris's own summary of their results was, quote: 'We consider this to be something nearer the direct line of descent toward modern man than anything previously studied. Many fossil finds have been made on Earth of creatures that represented various branches of development from the early progressive apes in the general direction of man. All finds to date, however, have been classed as belonging to offshoots from the mainstream; a specimen of a direct link in the chain leading to *Homo sapiens* has always persistently eluded us. Here, we have such a link.' Unquote." The image of Hunt reappeared. "We can be fairly sure, therefore, that among the terrestrial life forms left to develop on Minerva were numbers of primates as far advanced in their evolution as anything back on Earth.

"The faster evolution characteristic of Minerva thus far, was repeated, possibly as a result of the harsher environment and climate. Millions of years passed. On Earth a succession of manlike beings came and went, some progressive, some degenerate. The Ice Age came and moved through into its final, glacial phase some fifty thousand years ago. By this time on Earth, primitive humanoids represented the apex of progress—crude cave dwellers, hunters, makers of simple weapons and tools chipped out of stone. But on Minerva, a new technological civilization already existed: the Lunarians—descended from the imported stock and from the same early ancestors as ourselves, human in every detail of anatomy.

"I won't dwell on the problems that confronted the developing Lunarian civilization—they're well known by now. Their history was one long story of war and hardship enacted around a racial quest to escape from their dying world. Their difficulties were compounded by a chronic shortage of minerals, possibly because the planet was naturally deficient, or possibly because it had been thoroughly exploited by the Ganymeans. At any rate, the warring factions polarized into two superpowers, and in the showdown that followed they destroyed themselves and the planet."

Hunt paused again at this point to allow another period of consolidation for the audience. This time, however, there was complete silence. Nothing he had said so far was new, but he had formed a set selected from the thousand and one theories and speculations that had raged around Navcomms for as long as many could remember. The silent watchers in the theater sensed that the real news was still to come.

"Let's stop for a moment and examine how well this account fits in with the evidence we have. First, the original problem of Charlie's human form. Well, that's answered: He was human—descended from the same ancestors as the rest of us and requiring nothing as unlikely as a parallel line to explain him. Second, the absence of any signs of the Lunarians on Earth. Well, the reason is quite obvious: They never were on Earth. Third, all the attempts to reconcile the surface geography of Charlie's world with Earth become unnecessary, since by this account they were indeed two different planets.

"So far so good, then. This by itself, however, does not explain all the facts. There are some additional pieces of evidence which must be taken into account by any theory that claims to be comprehensive. They can be summarized in the following questions:

"One: How could Charlie's voyage from Minerva to our Moon have taken only two days?"

"Two: How do we explain a weapons system, consistent with the Lunarian level of technology, that was capable of accurate registration over a range extending from our Moon to Minerva?

"Three: How could the loop feedback delay in the fire-control system have been substantially less than the minimum of twenty-six minutes that could have applied over that distance?

"Four: How could Charlie distinguish surface features of Minerva when he was standing on our Moon?"

Hunt looked out from the screen and allowed plenty of time for the audience to reflect on these questions. He stubbed out his cigarette and leaned forward toward the camera, his elbows coming to rest on the desk.

"There is, in my submission, only one explanation which is capable of satisfying these apparently nonsensical requirements. And I put it to you now. The moon that orbited Minerva from time immemorial up until the time of these events fifty thousand years ago—and the Moon that shines in the sky above Earth today—are one and the same!"

Nothing happened for about three seconds.

Then gasps of incredulity erupted from around the darkened room. People gesticulated at their neighbors while some turned imploringly for comment from the row behind. Suddenly the whole theater was a turmoil of muttered exchanges.

"Can't be!"

"By God—he's right!"

"Of course . . . of course . . . !"

"Has to be . . ."

"Garbage!"

On the screen Hunt stared out impassively, as if he were watching the scene. His allowance for the probable reaction was well timed. He resumed speaking just as the confusion of voices was dying away.

"We *know* that the moon Charlie was on was our Moon— because we found him there, because we can identify the areas of terrain he described, because we have ample evidence of a large-scale Lunarian presence there, and because we have proved that it was the scene of a violent exchange of nucleonic and nuclear weapons. But that same place *must also have been* the satellite of Minerva. It was only a two-day flight from the planet—Charlie says so and we're confident we can interpret his time scale. Weapons were sited there which could pick off targets on Minerva, and observations of hits were almost instantaneous; and if all that is not enough, Charlie could stand not ten yards from where we found him and distinguish details of Minerva's surface. These things could *only* be true if the place in question was within, say, half a million miles of Minerva.

"Logically, the only explanation is that both moons were one and the same. We've been asking for a long time whether the Lunarian civilization developed on Earth or whether it developed on Minerva. Well, from the account I've given, it's obvious it was Minerva. We thought we had two contradictory sets of information, one telling us it was Earth and the other telling us it wasn't. But we had misinterpreted the data. It wasn't telling us anything to do with Earth or Minerva at all—it was telling us about Earth's or Minerva's *moon*! Some facts told us we were dealing with Earth's moon while others told us we were dealing with Minerva's moon. As long as we insisted on introducing, quite unconsciously, the notion that the two moons were different, the conflict between these sets of facts couldn't be resolved. But if, purely within the logical constraints of the situation, we introduce the postulate that both moons were the same, that conflict disappears before our eyes."

Shock seemed to have overtaken the audience. At the front somebody was muttering, "Of course . . . of course . . ." half to himself and half aloud.

"All that remains is to reconcile these propositions with the situation we observe around us today. Again, only one explanation is possible. Minerva exploded and dispersed to become the Asteroid Belt. The greater part of its mass, we're fairly sure, was thrown into the outer regions of the Solar System and became Pluto. Its moon, although somewhat shaken, was left intact. During the gravitational upheaval that occurred when its parent planet broke up, the satellite's orbital momentum around the Sun was reduced and it began to fall inward.

"We can't tell how long the orphaned moon plunged steadily nearer the Sun. Maybe the trip lasted months, maybe years. Next comes one of those million-to-one chances that sometimes happen in nature. The trajectory followed by the moon brought it close to Earth, which had been pursuing its own *solitary* path around the Sun ever since the beginning of time!" Hunt paused for a few seconds. "Yes, I repeat, *solitary* path! You see, if we are to accept what I believe to be the only satisfactory explanation open to us, we must accept also its consequence: that until this point in time, some fifty thousand years ago, planet Earth had *no moon*! The two bodies drew close enough for their gravitational fields to interact to the point of mutual capture; the new, common orbit turned out to be stable, and Earth adopted a foundling it has kept right up to this day.

"If we accept this account, many of the other things that have been causing problems suddenly make sense. Take, for example, the excess material that covers most of Lunar Farside and has been shown to be of recent origin, and coupled with that, the dating of all Farside craters and some Nearside ones to around the time we're talking about. Now we have a ready explanation. When Minerva blew up, what is now Luna was sitting there right in the way of all the debris. That's where the meteorite storm came from. That's how practically all evidence of the Lunarian presence on Luna was wiped out. There's probably no end to remains of their bases, installations, and vehicles still there waiting to be uncovered—a thousand feet below the Farside surface. We think that the Annihilator emplacement at Seltar was on Farside. That suggests that what is Farside to Earth today was Nearside to Minerva; hence it makes sense that most of the meteorite storm landed where it did.

"Charlie appears to have referred to compass directions different from ours on the Lunar surface, implying a different north-south axis. Now we see why. Some people have asked why, if Luna suffered such an intense bombardment, there should be no signs of any comparable increase in meteorite activity on Earth at the time. This too now makes sense: When Minerva blew up, Luna was in its immediate vicinity but Earth wasn't. And a last point on Lunar physics—We've known for half a century that Luna is formed from a mix of rocky compounds different from those found on Earth, being low in volatiles and rich in refractories. Scientists have speculated for a long time that possibly the Moon was formed in another part of the Solar System. This indeed turns out to be true if what I've said is correct.

"Some explanations have suggested that the Lunarians set

up advanced bridgeheads on Luna. This enabled their evident presence there to be reconciled with evolutionary origins on Minerva, but raised an equally problematical question: Why were they struggling to master interplanetary space-flight technology when they must have had it already? In the account I have described, this problem disappears. They had reached their own moon, but were still some ways from being able to move large populations to anyplace as remote as Earth. Also, there is now no need to introduce the unsupported notion of Lunarian colonies on either planet; either way, it would pose the same question.

"And finally, an unsolved riddle of oceanography makes sense in this light, too. Research into tidal motions has shown that catastrophic upheavals on a planetary scale occurred on Earth at about this time, resulting in an abrupt increase in the length of the day and an increase in the rate at which the day is further being lengthened by tidal friction. Well, the arrival of Minerva's moon would certainly create enormous gravitational and tidal disturbances. Although the exact mechanics aren't too clear right now, it appears that the kinetic energy acquired by Minerva's moon as it fell toward the Sun, was absorbed in neutralizing part of the Earth's rotational energy, causing a longer day. Also, increased tidal friction since then is to be expected. Before the Moon appeared, Earth experienced only Solar tides, whereas from that time up until today, there have been both Solar and Lunar tides."

Hunt showed his empty hand in a gesture of finality and pushed himself back in his chair. He straightened the pile of notes on the desk before going on to conclude:

"That's it. As I said earlier, at this stage it represents no more than a hypothesis that accounts for all the facts. But there are some things we can do toward testing the truth of it.

"For a start, we have a large chunk of Minerva piled up all over Farside. The recent material is so like the original Lunar material that it was years before anybody realized it had been added only recently. That supports the idea that the Moon and the meteorites originated in the same part of the Solar System. I'd like to suggest that we perform detailed comparisons between data from Farside material and data from the Asteroid surveys. If the results indicate that they are both the same kind of stuff and appear to have come from the same place, the whole idea would be well supported.

"Another thing that needs further work is a mathematical model of the process of mutual capture between Earth and Luna. We know quite a lot about the initial conditions that must have existed before and, of course, a lot more about the conditions that exist now. It would be reassuring to know that for the equations involved there exist solutions that allow one situation to transform into the other within the normal laws of physics. At least, it would be nice to prove that the whole idea isn't impossible.

"Finally, of course, there is the Ganymean ship here. Without doubt a lot of new information is waiting to be discovered—far more than we've had to work on so far. I'm hoping that somewhere in the ship there will be astronomic data to tell us something about the Solar System at the time of the Ganymeans. If, for example, we could determine whether or not the third planet from the Sun of their Solar System had a satellite, or if we could learn enough about their moon to identify it as Luna—perhaps by recognizing Nearside surface features—then the whole theory would be well on the way to being proved.

"This concludes the report.

"Personal addendum for Gregg Caldwell . . ." The view of Hunt was replaced by a landscape showing a wilderness of ice and rock. "This place you've sent us to, Gregg—the mail service isn't too regular, so I couldn't send a postcard. It's over a hundred Celsius degrees below zero; there's no atmosphere worth talking about and what there is, is poisonous; the only way back is by Vega, and the nearest Vega is seven hundred miles away. I wish you were here to enjoy all the fun with us, Gregg—I really do!

"V. Hunt from Ganymede Pithead Base. End of transmission."

chapter twenty-four

The long-awaited answers to where the Lunarians had come from and how they came to be where they had been found sent waves of excitement around the scientific world and prompted a new frenzy of activity in the news media. Hunt's explanation seemed complete and consistent. There were few objections or disagreements; the account didn't leave much to object to or disagree with.

Hunt had therefore met fully the demands of his brief. Although detailed interdisciplinary work would continue all over the world for a long time to come, UNSA's formal involvement in.the affair was more or less over. So Project Charlie was run down. That left Project Ganymeans, which was just starting up. Although he had not yet received any formal directive from Earth to say so, Hunt had the feeling that Caldwell wouldn't waste the opportunity offered by Hunt's presence on Ganymede just when the focus of attention was shifting from the Lunarians to the Ganymeans. In other words, it would be some time yet before he would find himself walking aboard an Earth-bound cruiser.

A few weeks after the publication of UNSA's interim conclusions, the Navcomms scientists on Ganymede held a celebration dinner in the officers' mess at Pithead to mark the successful end of a major part of their task. The evening had reached the warm and mellow phase that comes with cigars and liqueurs when the last-course dishes have been cleared away. Talkative groups were standing and sitting in a variety of attitudes around the tables and by the bar, and beers, brandies, and vintage ports were beginning to flow freely. Hunt was with a group of physicists near the bar, discussing the latest news on the Ganymean field drive, while behind them another circle was debating the likelihood of a world government being established within twenty years. Danchekker seemed to have been unduly quiet and withdrawn for most of the evening.

"When you think about it, Vic, this could develop into the ultimate weapon in interplanetary warfare," one of the physicists was saying. "Based on the same principles as the ship's drive, but a lot more powerful and producing a far more intense and localized effect. It would generate a black hole that would persist, even after the generator that made it had fallen into it. Just think—an artificially produced black hole. All you'd have to do is mount the device in a suitable missile and fire it at any planet you took a dislike to. It would fall to the center and consume the whole planet—and there'd be no way to stop it."

Hunt looked intrigued. "You mean it could work?"

"The theory says so."

"Christ, how long would it take—to wipe out a planet?"

"We don't know yet; we're still working on that bit. But there's more to it than that. There's no reason why you shouldn't be able to put out a star using the same method. Think about that as a weapon—one black-hole bomb could destroy a whole solar system. It makes nucleonic weapons look like kiddie toys."

Hunt started to reply, but a voice from the center of the room cut him off, rising to make itself heard above the buzz of conversation. It belonged to the commander of Pithead Base, special guest at the dinner.

"Attention, please, everybody," he called. "Your attention for a moment, please." The noise died as all faces turned toward him. He looked around until satisfied that everyone was paying attention. "You have invited me here tonight to join you in celebrating the successful conclusion of what has probably been one of the most challenging, the most astounding, and the most rewarding endeavors that you are ever likely to be involved in. You have had difficulties, contradictions, and disagreements to contend with, but all that is now in the past. The task is done. My congratulations." He glanced toward the clock above the bar. "It is midnight—a suitable time, I think, to propose a toast to the being that started the whole thing off, wherever he may be." He raised his glass. "To Charlie."

"To Charlie," came back the chorus.

"*No!*"

A voice boomed from the back of the room. It sounded firm

and decisive. Everybody turned to look at Danchekker in surprise.

"No," the professor repeated. "We can't drink to that just yet."

There was no suggestion of hesitation or apology in his manner. Clearly his action was reasoned and calculated.

"What's the problem, Chris?" Hunt asked, moving forward away from the bar.

"I'm afraid that's not the end of it."

"How do you mean?"

"The whole Charlie business— There is more to it—more than I have chosen to mention to anybody, because I have no proof. However, there is a further implication in all that has been deduced—one which is even more difficult to accept than even the revelations of the past few weeks."

The festive atmosphere had vanished. Suddenly they were in business again. Danchekker walked slowly toward the center of the room and stopped with his hands resting on the back of one of the chairs. He gazed at the table for a moment, then drew a deep breath and looked up.

"The problem with Charlie, and the rest of the Lunarians, that has not been touched upon is this: quite simply, they were *too* human."

Puzzled looks appeared here and there. Somebody turned to his neighbor and shrugged. They all looked back at Danchekker in silence.

"Let us recapitulate for a moment some of the fundamental principles of evolution," he said. "How do different animal species arise? Well, we know that variations of a given species arise from mutations caused by various agencies. It follows from elementary genetics that in a freely mixing and interbreeding population, any new characteristic will tend to be diluted, and will disappear within relatively few generations. However"—the professor's tone became deadly serious—"when sections of the population became reproductively isolated from one another— for example, by geographical separation, by segregation of behavior patterns, or by seasonal differences, say, in mating times—dilution through interbreeding will be prevented. When a new characteristic appears within an isolated group, it will be confined to and reinforced within that group; thus, generation by generation, the group will *diverge* from the other group or groups from which it has been isolated. Finally a new species will establish itself. This principle is fundamental to the whole idea of evolution: Given isolation, divergence *will* occur. The origins of all species on Earth can be traced back to the existence at some time of some mechanism or other of isolation between variations within a single species. The animal life peculiar to Australia and South America, for instance, demonstrates how rapidly divergence takes effect even when isolation has existed only for a short time.

"Now we seem to be satisfied that for the best part of twenty-five million years, two groups of terrestrial animals—one on Earth, the other on Minerva—were left to evolve in *complete* isolation. As a scientist who accepts fully the validity of the principle I have just outlined, I have no hesitation in saying that divergence between these two groups *must* have taken place. That, of course, applies equally to the primate lines that were represented on both planets."

He stopped and stood looking from one to the other of his colleagues, giving them time to think and waiting for a reaction. The reaction came from the far end of the room.

"Yes, now I see what you're saying," somebody said. "But why speculate? What's the point in saying they should have diverged, when it's clear that they didn't?"

Danchekker beamed and showed his teeth. "What makes you say they didn't?" he challenged.

The questioner raised his arms in appeal. "What my two eyes tell me—I can see they didn't."

"What do you see?"

"I see humans. I see Lunarians. They're the same. So, they didn't diverge."

"Didn't they?" Danchekker's voice cut the air like a whiplash. "Or are you making the same unconscious assumption that everyone else has made? Let me go over the facts once again, purely from an objective point of view. I'll simply list the things we observe and make no assumptions, conscious or otherwise, about how they fit in with what we think we already know.

"First: The two populations were isolated. Fact.

"Second: Today, twenty-five million years later, we observe two sets of individuals, ourselves and the Lunarians. Fact.

"Third: We and the Lunarians are identical. Fact.

"Now, if we accept the principle that divergence must have occurred, what must we conclude? Ask yourselves—If confronted by those facts and nothing else, what would any scientist deduce?"

Danchekker stood facing them, pursing his lips and rocking back and forth on his heels. Silence enveloped the room, broken after a few seconds by his whistling quietly and tunelessly to himself.

"Christ . . . !" The exclamation came from Hunt. He stood gaping at the professor in undisguised disbelief. "They couldn't have been isolated from each other," he managed at last in a slow, halting voice. "They must both be from the same . . ." The words trailed away.

Danchekker nodded with evident satisfaction. "Vic's seen what I am saying," he informed the group. "You see, the only logical conclusion that can be drawn from the statements I have just enumerated is this: If two identical forms are observed today, they must both come from the *same* isolated group. In other words, if two lines were isolated and branched apart, both forms *must* lie on the *same branch*!"

"How can you say that, Chris?" someone insisted. "We know they came from different branches."

"What do you know?" Danchekker whispered.

"Well, I know that the Lunarians came from the branch that was isolated on Minerva . . ."

"Agreed."

". . . And I know that man comes from the branch that was isolated on Earth."

"How?"

The question echoed sharply around the walls like a pistol shot.

"Well . . . I . . ." The speaker made a gesture of helplessness. "How do I answer a question like that? It . . . it's obvious."

"Precisely!" Danchekker showed his teeth again. "You *assume* it—just as everybody else does! That's part of the conditioning you've grown up with. It has been assumed all through the history of the human race, and naturally so—there has never been any reason to suppose otherwise." Danchekker straighted up and regarded the room with an unblinking stare. "Now perhaps you see the point of all this. I am stating that, on the evidence we have just examined, the human race did not evolve on Earth at all. *It evolved on Minerva!*"

"Oh, Chris, really . . ."

"This is getting ridiculous . . ."

Danchekker hammered on relentlessly: "Because, if we accept that divergence must have occurred, then both we and the Lunarians must have evolved in the same place, and we already know that *they* evolved on *Minerva*!"

A murmur of excitement mixed with protest ran around the room.

"I am stating that Charlie is not just a distantly related cousin of man—*he is our direct ancestor!*" Danchekker did not wait for comment but pressed on in the same insistent tone: "And I believe that I can give you an explanation of our own origins which is fully consistent with these deductions." An abrupt silence fell upon the room. Danchekker regarded his colleagues for a few seconds. When he spoke again, his voice had fallen to a calmer and more objective note.

"From Charlie's account of his last days, we know that some Lunarians were left alive on the Moon after the fighting died down. Charlie himself was one of them. He did not survive for long, but we can guess that there were others—desperate groups such as the ones he described—scattered across that Lunar surface. Many would have perished in the meteorite storm on Farside, but some, like Charlie's group, were on Nearside when Minerva exploded and were spared the worst of the bombardment. Even a long time later, when the Moon finally stabilized in orbit around Earth, a handful of survivors remained who gazed up at the new world that hung in their sky. Presumably some of their ships were still usable—perhaps just one, or two, or a few. There was only one way out. Their world had ceased to exist, so they took the only path open to them and set off on a last, desperate attempt to reach the surface of Earth. There could be no way back—there was no place to go back to.

"So we must conclude that their attempt succeeded. Precisely what events followed their emergence out into the savagery of the Ice Age we will probably never know for sure. But we can guess that for generations they hung on the very edge of extinction. Their knowledge and skills would have been lost. Gradually they reverted to barbarism, and for forty thousand years were lost in the midst of the general struggle for survival. But survive they did. Not only did they survive, they consolidated, spread, and flourished. Today their descendants dominate the Earth just as they dominated Minerva—you, I, and the rest of the human race."

A long silence ensued before anybody spoke. When somebody did, the tone was solemn. "Chris, assuming for now that everything was like you've said, a point still bothers me: If we and the Lunarians both came from the Minervan line, what happened to the other line? Where did the branch that was developing on Earth go?"

"Good question." Danchekker nodded approval. "We know from the fossil record on Earth that during the period that came after the visits of the Ganymeans several developments in the general human direction took place. We can trace this record quite clearly right up to the time in question, fifty thousand years ago. By that time the most advanced stage reached on Earth was that represented by Neanderthal man. Now, the Neanderthals have always been something of a riddle. They were hardy, tough, and superior in intelligence to anything prior to them or coexisting with them. They seemed well adapted to survive the competition of the Ice Age and should, one would think, have attained a dominant position in the era that was to follow. But that did not happen. Strangely, almost mysteriously, they died out abruptly between forty and fifty thousand years ago. Apparently they were unable to compete effectively against a new and far more advanced type of man, whose sudden appearance, as if from nowhere, has always been another of the unsolved riddles of science: *Homo sapiens*—us!"

Danchekker read the expressions on the faces before him and nodded slowly to confirm their thoughts.

"Now, of course, we see why this was so. He did indeed appear out of nowhere. We see why there is no clear fossil record in the soil of Earth to link *Homo sapiens* back to the chain of earlier terrestrial man-apes: He did not evolve there. And we see what it was that so ruthlessly and so totally overwhelmed the Neanderthals. How could they hope to compete against an advanced race, weaned on the warrior cult of Minerva?"

Danchekker paused and allowed his gaze to sweep slowly around the circle of faces. Everybody seemed to be suffering from mental punch-drunkenness.

"As I have said, all this follows purely as a chain of reasoning from the observations with which I began. I can offer no evidence to support it. I am convinced, however, that such evidence does exist. Somewhere on Earth the remains of the Lunarian spacecraft that made that last journey from Luna must still exist, possibly buried beneath the mud of a seabed, possibly under the sands of one of the desert regions. There must exist, on Earth, pieces of equipment and artifacts brought by the tiny handful who represented the remnant of the Lunarian civilization. Where on Earth, is anyone's guess. Personally, I would suggest as the most likely areas the Middle East, the eastern Mediterranean, or the eastern regions of North Africa. But one day proof that what I have said is true will be forthcoming. This I predict with every confidence."

The professor walked around to the table and poured a glass of Coke. The silence of the room slowly dissolved into a rising tide of voices. One by one, the statues that had been listening returned to life. Danchekker took a long drink and stood in silence for a while, contemplating his glass. Then he turned to face the room again.

"Suddenly lots of things that we have always simply taken for granted start falling into place." Attention centralized on him once again. "Have you ever stopped to think what it is that makes man so different from all the other animals on Earth? I know that we have larger brains, more versatile hands, and so forth; what I am referring to is something else. Most animals, when in a hopeless situation will resign themselves to fate and perish in ignominy. Man, on the other hand, does not know how to give in. He is capable of summoning up reserves of stubbornness and resilience that are without parallel on his planet. He is able to attack anything that threatens his survival, with an aggressiveness the like of which the Earth has never seen otherwise. It is this that has enabled him to sweep all before him, made him lord of all the beasts, helped him tame the winds, the rivers, the tides, and even the power of the Sun itself. This stubbornness has conquered the oceans, the skies, and the challenges of space, and at times has resulted in some of the most violent and bloodstained periods in his history. But without this side to his nature, man would be as helpless as the cattle in the field."

Danchekker scanned the faces challengingly. "Well, where did it come from? It seems out of character with the sedate and easygoing pattern of evolution on Earth. Now we see where it came from: It appeared as a mutation among the evolving primates that were isolated on Minerva. It was transmitted through the population there until it became a racial characteristic. It proved to be such a devastating weapon in the survival struggle there that effective opposition ceased to exist. The inner driving force that it produced was such that the Lunarians were flying spaceships while their contemporaries on Earth were still playing with pieces of stone.

"That same driving force we see in man today. Man has proved invincible in every challenge that the Universe has thrown at him. Perhaps this force has been diluted somewhat in the time that has elapsed since it first appeared on Minerva; we reached the brink of that same precipice of self-destruction but stepped back. The Lunarians hurled themselves in regardless. It could be that his was why they did not seek a solution by cooperation—their in-built tendency to violence made them simply incapable of conceiving such a formula.

"But this is typical of the way in which evolution works. The forces of natural selection will always operate in such a way as to bend and shape a new mutation, and to preserve a variation of it that offers the best prospects of survival for the species as a whole. The raw mutation that made the Lunarians what they were was too extreme and resulted in their downfall. Improvement has taken the form of a dilution, which results in a grater psychological stability of the race. Thus, we survive where they perished."

Danchekker paused to finish his drink. The statues remained statues.

"What an incredible race they must have been," he said. "Consider in particular the handful who were destined to become the forefathers of mankind. They had endured a holocaust unlike anything we can even begin to imagine. They had watched their world and everything that was familiar explode in the skies above their heads. After this, abandoned in an airless, waterless, lifeless, radioactive desert, they were slaughtered beneath the billions of tons of Minervan debris that crashed down from the skies to complete the ruin of all their hopes and the total destruction of all they had achieved.

"A few survived to emerge onto the surface after the bombardment. They knew that they could live only for as long as their supplies and their machines lasted. There was nowhere they could go, nothing they could plan for. They did not give in. They did not know how to give in. They must have existed for months before they realized that, by a quirk of fate, a slim chance of survival existed.

"Can you imagine the feelings of that last tiny band of Lunarians as they stood amid the Lunar desolation, gazing up at the new world that shone in the sky above their heads, with nothing else alive around them and, for all they knew, nothing else alive in the Universe? What did it take to attempt that one-way journey into the unknown? We can try to imagine, but we will never know. Whatever it took, they grasped at the straw that was offered and set off on that journey.

"Even this was only the beginning. When they stepped out of their ships onto the alien world, they found themselves in the midst of one of the most ruthless periods of competition and extinction in the history of the Earth. Nature ruled with an uncompromising hand. Savage beasts roamed the planet; the climate was in turmoil following the gravitational upheavals caused by the arrival of the Moon; possibly they were decimated by unknown diseases. It was an environment that none of their experience had prepared them for. Still they refused to yield. They learned the ways of the new world: They learned to feed by hunting and trapping, to fight with spear and club; they learned how to shelter from the elements, to read and interpret the language of the wild. And as they became proficient in these new arts they grew stronger and ventured farther afield. The spark that they had brought with them and which had carried them through on the very edge of extinction began to glow bright once again. Finally that glow erupted into the flame that had swept all before it on Minerva; they emerged as an adversary more fearsome and more formidable than anything the Earth had ever known. The Neanderthals never stood a chance—they were doomed the moment the first Lunarian foot made contact with the soil of Earth.

"The outcome you see all around you today. We stand undisputed masters of the Solar System and poised on the edge of interstellar space itself, just as they did fifty thousand years ago."

Danchekker placed his glass carefully on the table and moved slowly toward the center of the room. His sober gaze shifted from eye to eye. He concluded: "And so, gentlemen, we inherit the stars.

"Let us go out, then, and claim our inheritance. We belong to a tradition in which the concept of defeat has no meaning. Today the stars and tomorrow the galaxies. No force exists in the Universe that can stop us."

epilogue

Professor Hans Jacob Zeiblemann, of the Department of Paleontology of the University of Geneva, finished his entry for the
day in his diary, closed the book with a grunt, and returned it
to its place in the tin box underneath his bed. He hoisted his
two-hundred-pound bulk to its feet and, drawing his pipe from
the breast pocket of his bush shirt, moved a pace across the
tent to knock out the ash on the metal pole by the door. As he
stood packing a new fill of tobacco into the bowl, he gazed out
over the arid landscape of northern Sudan.

The Sun had turned into a deep gash just above the horizon,
oozing blood-red liquid rays that drenched the naked rock for
miles around. The tent was one of three that stood crowded together on a narrow sandy shelf. The shelf was formed near the
bottom of a steep-sided rocky valley, dotted with clumps of
coarse bush and desert scrub that clustered together along the
valley floor and petered out rapidly, without gaining the slopes
on either side. On a wider shelf beneath stood the more numerous tents of the native laborers. Obscure odors wafting upward
from this direction signaled that preparation of the evening
meals had begun. From farther below came the perpetual
sound of the stream, rushing and clattering and jostling on its
way to join the waters of the distant Nile.

The crunch of boots on gravel sounded nearby. A few seconds later Zeiblemann's assistant, Jorg Hutfauer, appeared, his
shirt dark and streaked with perspiration and grime.

"Phew!" The newcomer halted to mop his brow with something that had once been a handkerchief. "I'm whacked. A
beer, a bath, dinner, then bed—that's my program for tonight."

Zeiblemann grinned. "Busy day?"

"Haven't stopped. We've extended sector five to the lower
terrace. The subsoil isn't too bad there at all. We've made
quite a bit of progress."

185

"Anything new?"

"I brought these up—thought you might be interested. There's more below, but it'll keep till you come down tomorrow." Hutfauer passed across the objects he had been carrying and continued on into the tent to retrieve a can of beer from the pile of boxes and cartons under the table.

"Mmm . . ." Zeiblemann turned the bone over in his hand. "Human femur . . . heavy." He studied the unusual curve and measured the proportions with his eye. "Neanderthal, I'd say . . . or very near related."

"That's what I thought."

The professor placed the fossil carefully in a tray, covered it with a cloth, and laid the tray on the chest standing just inside the tent doorway. He picked up a hand-size blade of flint, simply but effectively worked by the removal of long, thin flakes.

"What did you make of this?" he asked.

Hutfauer moved forward out of the shadow and paused to take a prolonged and grateful drink from the can.

"Well, the bed seems to be late Pleistocene, so I'd expect upper paleolithic indications—which fits in with the way it's been worked. Probably a scraper for skinning. There are areas of microliths on the handle and also around the end of the blade. Bearing in mind the location, I'd put it at something related fairly closely to the Capsian culture." He lowered the can and cocked an inquiring eye at Zeiblemann.

"Not bad," said the professor, nodding. He laid the flint in a tray beside the first and added the identification sheet that Hutfauer had written out. "We'll have a closer look tomorrow when the light's a little better."

Hutfauer joined him at the door. The sound of jabbering and shouting from the level below told them that another of the natives' endless minor domestic disputes had broken out over something.

"Tea's up if anyone's interested," a voice called out from behind the next tent.

Zeiblemann raised his eyebrows and licked his lips. "What a splendid idea," he said. "Come on, Jorg."

They walked around to the makeshift kitchen, where Ruddi Magendorf was sitting on a rock, shoveling spoonfuls of tea leaves out of a tin by his side and into a large bubbling pot of water.

"Hi, Prof—hi, Jorg," he greeted as the two joined him. "It'll be brewed in a minute or two."

Zeiblemann wiped his palms on the front of his shirt. "Good. Just what I could do with." He cast his eye about automatically and noted the trays, covered by cloths, laid out on the trestle table by the side of Magendorf's tent.

"Ah, I see you've been busy as well," he observed. "What do we have there?"

Magendorf followed his gaze.

"Jomatto brought them up about half an hour ago. They're from the upper terrace of sector two—east end. Take a look."

Zeiblemann walked over to the table and uncovered one of the trays to inspect the neatly arrayed collection, at the same time mumbling absently to himself.

"More flint scrapers, I see . . . Mmmm . . . That could be a hand ax. Yes, I believe it is . . . Bits of jawbone, human . . . looks as if they might well match up. Skull cap . . . Bone spearhead . . . Mmm . . ." He lifted the cloth from the second tray and began running his eye casually over the contents. Suddenly the movement of his head stopped abruptly as he stared hard at something at one end. His face contorted into a scowl of disbelief.

"What the hell is this supposed to be?" he bellowed. He straighted up and walked back toward the stove, holding the offending object out in front of him.

Magendorf shrugged and pulled a face.

"I thought you'd better see it," he offered, then added: "Jomatto says it was with the rest of that set."

"Jomatto says what?" Zeiblemann's voice rose in pitch as he glowered first at Magendorf and then back at the object in his hand. "Oh, for God's sake! The man's supposed to have a bit of sense. This is a serious scientific expedition . . ." He regarded the object again, his nostrils quivering with indignation. "Obviously one of the boys has been playing a silly joke or something."

It was about the size of a large cigarette pack, not including the wrist bracelet, and carried on its upper face four windows that could have been meant for miniature electronic displays. It suggested a chronometer or calculating aid, or maybe it was both and other things besides. The back and contents were missing, and all that was left was the metal casing, somewhat battered and dented, but still surprisingly unaffected very much by corrosion.

"There's a funny inscription on the bracelet," Magendorf said, rubbing his nose dubiously. "I've never seen characters like it before."

Zeiblemann sniffed and peered briefly at the lettering.

"*Pah!* Russian or something." His face had taken on a pinker shade than even that imparted by the Sudan sun. "Wasting valuable time with—with dime-store trinkets!" He drew back his arm and hurled the wrist set high out over the stream. It flashed momentarily in the sunlight before plummeting down into the mud by the water's edge. The professor stared after it for a few seconds and then turned back to Magendorf, his breathing once again normal. Magendorf extended a mug full of steaming brown liquid.

"Ah, splendid," Zeiblemann said in a suddenly agreeable voice. "Just the thing." He settled himself into a folding canvas chair and accepted the proffered mug eagerly. "I'll tell you one thing that does look interesting, Ruddi," he went on, nodding toward the table. "That piece of skull in the first tray—number nineteen. Have you noticed the formation of the brow ridges? Now, it could well be an example of . . ."

In the mud by the side of the stream below, the wrist unit rocked back and forth to the pulsing ripples that every few seconds rose to disturb the delicate equilibrium of the position into which it had fallen. After a while, a rib of sand beneath it was washed away and it tumbled over into a hollow, where it lodged among the swirling, muddy water. By nightfall, the lower half of the casing was already embedded in silt. By the following morning, the hollow had disappeared. Just one arm of the bracelet remained, standing up out of the sand below the rippling surface. The arm bore an inscription, which, if translated, would have read: KORIEL

THE GENTLE GIANTS
OF GANYMEDE

To my wife, Lyn, who showed
me that greener grass can
always be made to grow on
whatever side of the field one
happens to be.

prologue

Leyel Torres, commander of the scientific observation base near the equator on Iscaris III, closed the final page of the report that he had been reading and stretched back in his chair with a grateful sigh. He sat for a while, enjoying the feeling of relaxation as the seat adjusted itself to accommodate his new posture, and then rose to pour himself a drink from one of the flasks on a tray on the small table behind his desk. The drink was cool and refreshing, and quickly dispelled the fatigue that had begun to build up inside him after more than two hours of unbroken concentration. Not much longer now, he thought. Two months more and they should be saying good-bye to this barren ball of parched rock forever and returning to the clean, fresh, infinite star-speckled blackness that lay between here and home.

He cast his eye around the inside of the study of his private quarters in the conglomeration of domes, observatory buildings and communications antennas that had been home for the last two years. He was tired of the same, endless month-in, month-out routine. The project was exciting and stimulating it was true, but enough was enough; going home, as far as he was concerned, couldn't come a day too soon.

He walked slowly over to the side of the room and stared for a second or two at the blank wall in front of him. Without turning his head he said aloud: "View panel. See-through mode."

The wall immediately became one-way transparent, presenting him with a clear view out over the surface of Iscaris III. From the edge of the jumble of constructions and machinery that made up the base, the dry, uniform reddish-brown crags and boulders stretched all the way to the distinctly curved skyline where they abruptly came to an end beneath a curtain of black velvet embroidered with stars. High above, the fiery orb of Iscaris blazed mercilessly, its reflected rays filling the room with a warm glow of orange and red. As he looked out across the wilderness, a sudden longing welled up inside him for the simple pleasure of walking under a blue sky and breathing in the forgotten exhilaration of a wind blowing free. Yes, indeed—departure couldn't come a day too soon.

A voice that seemed to issue from nowhere in particular in the room interrupted his musings.

"Marvyl Chariso is requesting to be put through, Commander. He says it's extremely urgent."

"Accept," Torres replied. He turned about to face the large viewscreen that occupied much of the opposite wall. The screen came alive at once to reveal the features of Chariso, a senior physicist, speaking from an instrumentation laboratory in the observatory. His face registered alarm.

"Leyel," Chariso began without preamble. "Can you get down here right away. We've got trouble—real trouble." His tone of voice said the rest. Anything that could arouse Chariso to such a state had to be bad.

"I'm on my way," he said, already moving toward the door.

Five minutes later Torres arrived in the lab and was greeted by the physicist, who by this time was looking more worried than ever. Chariso led him to a monitor before a bank of electronic equipment where Galdern Brenzor, another of the scientists, was staring grim-faced at the curves and data analyses on the computer output screens. Brenzor looked up as they approached and nodded gravely.

"Strong emission lines in the photosphere," he said. "Absorption lines are shifting rapidly toward the violet. There's no doubt about it; a major instability is breaking out in the core and it's running away."

Torres looked over at Chariso.

"Iscaris is going nova," Chariso explained. "Something's gone wrong with the project and the whole star's started to blow up. The photosphere is exploding out into space and preliminary calculations indicate we'll be engulfed here in less than twenty hours. We have to evacuate."

Torres stared at him in stunned disbelief. "That's impossible."

The scientist spread his arms wide. "Maybe so, but it's fact. Later we can take as long as you like to figure out where we went wrong, but right now we've got to get out of here . . . *fast!"*

Torres stared at the two grim faces while his mind instinctively tried to reject what it was being told. He gazed past them at another large wall screen that was presenting a view being transmitted from ten million miles away in space. He was looking at one of the three enormous G-beam projectors, a cylinder two miles long and a third of a mile across, that had been built in stellar orbit thirty million miles from Iscaris with their axes precisely aligned on the center of the star. Behind the silhouette of the projector Iscaris's blazing globe was still normal in appearance, but even as he looked he imagined that he could see its disk swelling almost imperceptibly but menacingly outward.

For a moment his mind was swamped by emotions—the enormity of the task that suddenly confronted them, the hopelessness of having to think rationally under impossible time pressures, the futility of two years of wasted efforts. And then, as quickly as it had come, the feeling evaporated and the commander in him reasserted itself.

"zorac," he called in a slightly raised voice.

"Commander?" The same voice that had spoken in his study answered.

"Contact Garuth on the *Shapieron* at once. Inform him that a matter of the gravest urgency has arisen and that it is imperative for all commanding officers of the expedition to confer immediately. I request that he put out an emergency call to summon them to link in fifteen minutes from now. Also, sound a general alert throughout the base and have all personnel stand by to await further instructions. I'll link in to the conference from the multiconsole in Room 14 of the Main Observatory Dome. That's all."

Just over a quarter of an hour later Torres and the two scientists were facing an array of wall screens that showed the other participants in the conference. Garuth, commander-in-chief of the expedition, sat flanked by two aides in the heart of the mother-ship *Shapieron* two thousand miles above Iscaris III. He listened without interruption to the account of the situation. The chief scientist, speaking from elsewhere in the ship, confirmed that in the past few minutes sensors aboard the *Shapieron* had yielded data similar to that reported by instruments from the surface of Iscaris III, and that the computers had produced the same interpretation. The G-beam projectors had caused some unforeseen and catastrophic change in the internal equilibrium of Iscaris, and the star was in the process of turning into a nova. There was no time to think of anything but escape.

"We have to get everybody off the surface," Garuth said. "Leyel, the first thing I need is a statement of what ships you've got down there at the moment, and how many personnel they can bring up. We'll send down extra shuttles to ferry out the rest as soon as we know what your shortage in carrying capacity is. Monchar . . ." He addressed his deputy on another of the screens. "Do we have any ships more than fifteen hours out from us at maximum speed?"

"No, sir. The farthest away is out near Projector Two. It could make it back in just over ten."

"Good. Recall them all immediately, emergency priority. If the figures we've just heard are right, the only way we'll stand a chance of getting clear is on the *Shapieron*'s main drives. Prepare a schedule of expected arrival times and make sure that preparations for reception have been made."

"Yes, sir."

"Leyel . . ." Garuth switched his gaze back to look straight out of the screen in Room 14 of the Observatory Dome. "Bring all your available ships up to flight-readiness and begin planning your evacuation at once. Report back on status one hour from now. One bag of personal belongings only per person."

"May I remind you of a problem, sir," the chief engineer of the *Shapieron*, Rogdar Jassilane, added from the drive section of the ship.

"What is it, Rog?" Garuth's face turned away to look at another screen.

"We still have a fault on the primary retardation system for the main-drive toroids. If we start up those drives, the only way they'll ever slow down again is at their own natural rate. The whole braking system's been stripped down. We could never put it together again in under twenty hours, let alone trace the fault and fix it."

Garuth thought for a moment. "But we can start them up okay?"

"We can," Jassilane confirmed. "But once those black

holes start whirling round inside the toroids, the angular momentum they'll build up will be phenomenal. Without the retardation system to slow them down, they'll take years to coast down to a speed at which the drives can be deactivated. We'd be under main drive all the time, with no way of shutting down." He made a helpless gesture. "We could end up anywhere."

"But we've no choice," Garuth pointed out. "It's fly or fry. We'll have to set course for home and orbit the Solar System under drive until we've dropped to a low enough return velocity. What other way is there?"

"I can see what Rog's getting at," the chief scientist interjected. "It's not quite as simple as that. You see, at the velocities that we would acquire under years of sustained main drive, we'd experience an enormous relativistic time-dilation compared to reference frames moving with the speed of Iscaris or Sol. Since the *Shapieron* would be an accelerated system, much more time would pass back home than would pass on board the ship; we know *where* we'd end up all right . . . but we won't be too sure of *when*."

"And, in fact, it would be worse than just that," Jassilane added. "The main drives work by generating a localized space-time distortion that the ship continuously 'falls' into. This also produces its own time-dilation effect. Hence you'd have the compound effect of both dilations added together. What that would mean with an unretarded main drive running for years, I couldn't tell you—I don't think anything like it has ever happened."

"I haven't done any precise calculations yet, naturally," the chief scientist said. "But if my mental estimates are anything to go by, we could be talking about a compound dilation of the order of millions."

"Millions?" Garuth looked stunned.

"Yes." The chief scientist looked out at them soberly. "For every year that we spend slowing down from the velocity that we'll need to escape the nova, we could find that a million years have passed by the time we get home."

Silence persisted for a long time. At last Garuth spoke in a voice that was heavy and solemn. "Be that as it may, to survive we have no choice. My orders stand. Chief Engineer Jassilane, prepare for deep-space and bring the main drives up to standby readiness."

* * *

Twenty hours later the *Shapieron* was under full power and hurtling toward interstellar space as the first outrushing front of the nova seared its hull and vaporized behind it the cinder that had once been Iscaris III.

chapter one

In a space of time less than a single heartbeat in the life of the universe, the incredible animal called Man had fallen from the trees, discovered fire, invented the wheel, learned to fly and gone out to explore the planets.

The history that followed Man's emergence was a turmoil of activity, adventure and ceaseless discovery. Nothing like it had been seen through eons of sedate evolution and slowly unfolding events that had gone before.

Or so, for a long time, it had been thought . . .

But when at last Man came to Ganymede, largest of the moons of Jupiter, he stumbled upon a discovery that totally demolished one of the few beliefs that had survived centuries of his insatiable inquisitiveness: He was not, after all, unique. Twenty-five million years before him, another race had surpassed all that he had thus far achieved.

The fourth manned mission to Jupiter, early in the third decade of the twenty-first century, marked the beginning of intensive exploration of the outer planets and the establishment of the first permanent bases on the Jovian satellites. Instruments in orbit above Ganymede had detected a large concentration of metal some distance below the surface of the moon's ice crust. From a base specially sited for the purpose, shafts were sunk to investigate this anomaly.

The spacecraft that they found there, frozen in its changeless tomb of ice, was huge. From skeletal remains found inside the ship, the scientists of Earth reconstructed a picture of the race of eight-foot-tall giants that had built it and whose level of technology was estimated as having been a century or more ahead of Earth's. They christened the giants the "Ganymeans," to commemorate the place of the discovery.

The Ganymeans had originated on Minerva, a planet that once occupied the position between Mars and Jupiter but which had since been destroyed. The bulk of Minerva's mass had gone into a violently eccentric orbit at the edge of the solar system to become Pluto, while the remainder of the debris was dispersed by Jupiter's tidal effects and formed the Asteroid Belt. Various scientific investigations, including cosmic-ray exposure-tests on material samples recovered from the Asteroid Belt, pinpointed the breakup of Minerva as having occurred some fifty thousand years in the past—long, long after the Ganymeans were known to have roamed the Solar System.

The discovery of a race of technically advanced beings from twenty-five million years back was exciting enough. Even more exciting, but not really surprising, was the revelation that the Ganymeans had visited Earth. The cargo of the spacecraft found on Ganymede included a collection of plant and animal specimens the likes of which no human eye had ever beheld— a representative cross section of terrestrial life during the late Oligocene and early Miocene periods. Some of the samples were well preserved in canisters while others had evidently been alive in pens and cages at the time of the ship's mishap.

The seven ships that were to make up the Jupiter Five Mission were being constructed in Lunar orbit at the time these discoveries were made. When the mission departed, a team of scientists traveled with it, eager to delve more deeply into the irresistibly challenging story of the Ganymeans.

A data manipulation program running in the computer complex of the mile-and-a-quarter-long Jupiter Five mission command ship, orbiting two thousand miles above Ganymede, routed its results to the message-scheduling processor. The information was beamed down by laser to a transceiver on the surface of Ganymede Main Base, and relayed northward via a chain of repeater stations. A few millionths of a second and seven hundred miles later, the computers at Pithead Base decoded the message destination and routed the signal to a display screen on the wall of a small conference room in the Biological Laboratories section. An elaborate pattern of the symbols used by geneticists to denote the internal structures of chromosomes appeared on the screen. The five people seated around the table in the narrow confines of the room studied the display intently.

"There. If you want to go right down to it in detail, that's what it looks like." The speaker was a tall, lean, balding man clad in a white lab coat and wearing a pair of anachronistic gold-rimmed spectacles. He was standing in front and to one side of the screen, pointing toward it with one hand and clasping his lapel lightly with the other. Professor Christian Danchekker of the Westwood Biological Institute in Houston, part of the UN Space Arm's Life Sciences Division, headed the team of biologists who had come to Ganymede aboard *Jupiter Five* to study the early terrestrial animals discovered in the Ganymean spacecraft. The scientists sitting before him contemplated the image on the screen. After a while Danchekker summarized once more the problem they had been debating for the past hour.

"I hope it is obvious to most of you that the expression we are looking at represents a molecular arrangement characteristic of the structure of an enzyme. This same strain of enzyme has been identified in tissue samples taken from many of the species so far examined in the labs up in *J4*. I repeat—*many* of the species . . . many *different* species . . ." Danchekker clasped both hands to his lapels and gazed at his miniaudience expectantly. His voice fell almost to a whisper. "And yet nothing resembling it or suggestive of being in any way related to it has ever been identified in any of today's terrestrial animal species. The problem we are faced with, gentlemen, is simply to explain these curious facts."

Paul Carpenter, fresh-faced, fair-haired and the youngest present, pushed himself back from the table and looked inquiringly from side to side, at the same time turning up his hands. "I guess I don't really see the problem," he confessed candidly. "This enzyme existed in animal species from twenty-five million years back—right?"

"You've got it," Sandy Holmes confirmed from across the table with a slight nod of her head.

"So in twenty-five million years they mutated out of all recognition. Everything changes over a period of time and it's no different with enzymes. Descendant strains from this one are probably still around but they don't look the same . . ." He caught the expression on Danchekker's face. "No? . . . What's the problem?"

The professor sighed a sigh of infinite patience. "We've been through all that, Paul," he said. "At least, I was under the impression that we had. Let me recapitulate. Enzymology has made tremendous advances over the last few decades. Just about every type has been classified and catalogued, but never anything like this one, which is completely different from anything we've ever seen."

"I don't want to sound argumentative, but is that really true?" Carpenter protested. "I mean . . . we've seen new additions to the catalogues even in the last year or two, haven't we? There was Schnelder and Grossmann at São Paulo with the P273B series and its derivatives . . . Braddock in England with—"

"Ah, but you're missing the whole point," Danchekker interrupted. "Those were new strains, true, but they fell neatly into the known standard families. They exhibited characteristics that place them firmly and definitely within known related groups." He gestured again toward the screen. "That one doesn't. It's completely new. To me it suggests a whole new class of its own—a class that contains just one member. Nothing yet identified in the metabolism of any form of life as we know it has ever done that before." Danchekker swept his eyes around the small circle of faces.

"Every species of animal life that we know belongs to a known family group and has related species and ancestors that we can identify. At the microscopic level the same thing applies. All our previous experiences tell us that even if this enzyme does date from twenty-five million years back, we ought to be able to recognize its family characteristics and relate it to known enzyme strains that exist today. However, we cannot. To me this indicates something very unusual."

Wolfgang Fichter, one of Danchekker's senior biologists, rubbed his chin and stared dubiously at the screen. "I agree that it is highly improbable, Chris," he said. "But can you really be so sure that it is impossible? After all, over twenty-five million years? . . . Environmental factors may have changed and caused the enzyme to mutate into something unrecognizable. I don't know, some change in diet maybe . . . something like that."

Danchekker shook his head decisively. "No. I say it's impossible." He raised his hands and proceeded to count points off on his fingers. "One—even if it did mutate, we'd still be able to identify its basic family architecture in the same way we can identify the fundamental properties of, say, any vertebrate. We can't.

"Two—if it occurred only in one species of Oligocene animal, then I would be prepared to concede that perhaps the enzyme we see here had mutated and given rise to many strains that we find in the world today—in other words this strain represents an ancestral form common to a whole modern family. If such were the case, then perhaps I'd agree that a mutation could have occurred that was so severe that the relationship between the ancestral strain and its descendants has been obscured. But that is not the case. This same enzyme is found in many different and nonrelated Oligocene species. For your suggestion to apply, the same improbable process would have had to occur many times over, independently, and all at the same time. I say that's impossible."

"But . . ." Carpenter began, but Danchekker pressed on.

"Three—none of today's animals possesses such an enzyme in its microchemistry yet they all manage perfectly well without it. Many of them are direct descendants of Oligocene types from the Ganymean ship. Now some of those chains of descent have involved rapid mutation and adaptation to meet changing diets and environments while others have not. In several cases the evolution from Oligocene ancestors to today's forms has been very slow and has produced only a small degree of change. We have made detailed comparisons between the microchemical processes of such ancestral Oligocene ancestors recovered from the ship and known data relating to animals that exist today and are descended from those same ancestors. The results have been very much as we expected—no great changes and clearly identifiable relationships between one group and the other. Every function that appeared in the microchemistry of the ancestor could be easily recognized, sometimes with slight modifications, in the descendants." Danchekker shot a quick glance at Fichter. "Twenty-five million years isn't really so long on an evolutionary time scale."

When no one seemed ready to object, Danchekker forged ahead. "But in every case there was one exception—this enzyme. Everything tells us that if this enzyme were present in the ancestor, then it, or something very like it, should be readily observable in the descendants. Yet in every case the results have been negative. I say that cannot happen, and yet it has happened."

A brief silence descended while the group digested Danchekker's words. At length Sandy Holmes ventured a thought. "Couldn't it still be a radical mutation, but the other way around?"

Danchekker frowned at her.

"How do you mean, the other way around?" asked Henri Rousson, another senior biologist, seated next to Carpenter.

"Well," she replied, "all the animals on the ship had been to Minerva, hadn't they? Most likely they were born there from ancestors the Ganymeans had transported from Earth. Couldn't something in the Minervan environment have caused a mutation that resulted in this enzyme? At least that would explain why none of today's terrestrial animals have it. They've never been to Minerva and neither have any of the ancestors they've descended from."

"Same problem," Fichter muttered, shaking his head.

"What problem?" she asked.

"The fact that the *same* enzyme was found in many different and nonrelated Oligocene species," Danchekker said. "Yes, I'll grant that differences in the Minervan environment could mutate some strain of enzyme brought in from Earth into something like that." He pointed at the screen again. "But many different species were brought in from Earth—different species each with its own characteristic metabolism and particular groups of enzyme strains. Now suppose that something in the Minervan environment caused those enzymes—*different* enzymes—to mutate. Are you seriously suggesting that they would *all* mutate independently into the *same* end-product?" He waited for a second. "Because that is exactly the situation that confronts us. The Ganymean ship contained many preserved specimens of different species, but every one of those species possessed precisely the *same* enzyme. Now do you want to reconsider your suggestion?"

The woman looked helplessly at the table for a second, then made a gesture of resignation. "Okay . . . If you put it like that, I guess it doesn't make sense."

"Thank you," Danchekker acknowledged stonily.

Henri Rousson leaned forward and poured himself a glass of water from the pitcher standing in the center of the table. He took a long drink while the others continued to stare thoughtfully through the walls or at the ceiling.

"Let's go back to basics for a second and see if that gets us anywhere," he said. "We know that the Ganymeans evolved on Minerva—right?" The heads around him nodded in assent. "We also know that the Ganymeans must have visited Earth because there's no other way they could have ended up with terrestrial animals on board their ship—unless we're going to invent another hypothetical alien race and I'm sure not going to do that because there's no reason to. Also, we know that the ship found here on Ganymede had come to Ganymede from Minerva, not directly from Earth. If the ship came from Minerva, the terrestrial animals must have come from Minerva too. That supports the idea we've already got that the Ganymeans were shipping all kinds of life forms from Earth to Minerva for some reason."

Paul Carpenter held up a hand. "Hang on a second. How do we know that the ship downstairs came here from Minerva?"

"The plants," Fichter reminded him.

"Oh yeah, the plants. I forgot . . ." Carpenter subsided into silence.

The pens and animal cages in the Ganymean ship had contained vegetable feed and floor-covering materials that had remained perfectly preserved under the ice coating formed when the ship's atmosphere froze and the moisture condensed out. Using seeds recovered from this material, Danchekker had succeeded in cultivating live plants completely different from anything that had ever grown on Earth, presumed to be examples of native Minervan botany. The leaves were very dark—almost black—and absorbed every available scrap of sunlight, right across the visible spectrum. This seemed to tie in nicely with independently obtained evidence of Minerva's great distance from the Sun.

"How far," Rousson asked, "have we got in figuring out *why* the Ganymeans were shipping all the animals in?" He spread his arms wide. "There had to be a reason. How far are we getting on that one? I don't know, but the enzyme might have something to do with it."

"Very well, let's recapitulate briefly what we think we already know about the subject," Danchekker suggested. He moved away from the screen and perched on the edge of the table. "Paul. Would you like to tell us your answer to Henri's question." Carpenter scratched the back of his head for a second and screwed up his face.

"Well ..." he began, "first there's the fish. They're established as being native Minervan and give us our link between Minerva and the Ganymeans."

"Good," Danchekker nodded, mellowing somewhat from his earlier crotchety mood. "Go on."

Carpenter was referring to a type of well-preserved canned fish that had been positively traced back to its origin in the oceans of Minerva. Danchekker had shown that the skeletons of the fish correlated in general arrangement to the skeletal remains of the Ganymean occupants of the ship that lay under the ice deep below Pithead Base; the relationship was comparable to that existing between the architectures of, say, a man and a mammoth, and demonstrated that the fish and the Ganymeans belonged to the same evolutionary family. Thus if the fish were native to Minerva, the Ganymeans were, too.

"Your computer analysis of the fundamental cell chemistry of the fish," Carpenter continued, "suggests an inherent low tolerance to a group of toxins that includes carbon dioxide. I think you also postulated that this basic chemistry could have been inherited from way back in the ancestral line of the fish—right from very early on in Minervan history."

"Quite so," Danchekker approved. "What else?"

Carpenter hesitated. "So Minervan land-dwelling species would have had a low CO_2 tolerance as well," he offered.

"Not quite," Danchekker answered. "You've left out the connecting link to that conclusion. Anybody ... ?" He looked at the German. "Wolfgang?"

"You need to make the assumption that the characteristics of low CO_2 tolerance came about in a very remote ancestor—one that existed before any land-dwelling types appeared on Minerva." Fitcher paused, then continued. "Then you can postulate that this remote life form was a common ancestor to all later land dwellers and marine descendants—for example, the fish. On the basis of that assumption you can say that the characteristic could have been inherited by all the land-dwelling species that emerged later."

"Never forget your assumptions," Danchekker urged. "Many of the problems in the history of science have stemmed from that simple error. Note one other thing too: If the low-CO_2-tolerance characteristic did indeed come about very early in the process of Minervan evolution and survived right down to the time that the fish was alive, then suggestions are that it was a very *stable* characteristic, if our knowledge of terrestrial evolution is anything to go by anyway. This adds plausibility to the suggestion that it could have become a common characteristic that spread throughout all the land dwellers as they evolved and diverged, and has remained essentially unaltered down through the ages—much as the basic design of terrestrial vertebrates has remained unchanged for hundreds of millions of years despite superficial differences in shape, size and form." Danchekker removed his spectacles and began polishing the lenses with his handkerchief.

"Very well," he said. "Let us pursue the assumption and conclude that by the time the Ganymeans had evolved—twenty-five million years ago—the land surface of Minerva was populated by a multitude of its own native life forms, each of which possessed a low tolerance to carbon dioxide, among other things. What other clues do we have available to us that might help determine what was happening on Minerva at that time?"

"We know that the Ganymeans were quitting the planet and trying to migrate someplace else," Sandy Holmes threw in. "Probably to some other star system."

"Oh, really?" Danchekker smiled, showing his teeth briefly before breathing on his spectacle lenses once more. "How do we know that?"

"Well, there's the ship down under the ice here for a start," she replied. "The kind of freight it was carrying and the amount of it sure suggested a colony ship intending a one-way trip. And then, why should it show up on *Ganymede* of all places? It couldn't have been traveling between any of the inner planets, could it?"

"But there's nothing outside Minerva's orbit to colonize," Carpenter chipped in. "Not until you get to the stars, that is."

"Exactly so," Danchekker said soberly, directing his words at the woman. "You said '*suggested* a colony ship.' Don't forget that that is precisely what the evidence we have at present amounts to—a suggestion and nothing more. It doesn't *prove* anything. Lots of people around the base are saying we now know that the Ganymeans abandoned the Solar System to find a new home elsewhere because the carbon-dioxide concentration in the Minervan atmosphere was increasing for some reason which we have yet to determine. It is true that if what we have just said was fact, then the Ganymeans would have shared the low tolerance possessed by all land dwellers there, and any increase in the atmospheric concentration could have caused them serious problems. But as we have just seen, we *know* nothing of the kind; we merely observe one or two suggestions that might add up to such an explanation." The professor paused, seeing that Carpenter was about to say something.

"There was more to it than that though, wasn't there?" Carpenter queried. "We're pretty certain that all species of Minervan land dwellers died out pretty rapidly somewhere around twenty-five million years ago . . . all except the Ganymeans themselves maybe. That sounds like just the effect you'd expect if the concentration did rise and all the species there couldn't handle it. It seems to support the hypothesis pretty well."

"I think Paul's got a point," Sandy Holmes chimed in. "Everything adds up. Also, it fits in with the ideas we've been having about why the Ganymeans were shipping all the animals into Minerva." She turned toward Carpenter, as if inviting him to complete the story from there.

As usual, Carpenter didn't need much encouragement. "What the Ganymeans were really trying to do was redress the CO_2 imbalance by covering the planet with carbon-dioxide-absorbing, oxygen-producing terrestrial green plants. The animals were brought along to provide a balanced ecology that the plants could survive in. Like Sandy says, it all fits."

"You're trying to fit the evidence to suit the answers that you already want to prove," Danchekker cautioned. "Let's separate once more the evidence that is fact from the evidence which is supposition or mere suggestion." The discussion continued with Danchekker leading an examination of the principles of scientific deduction and the techniques of logical analysis. Throughout, the figure who had been following the proceedings silently from his seat at the end of the table farthest from the screen continued to draw leisurely on his cigarette, taking in every detail.

Dr. Victor Hunt had also accompanied the team of scientists who had come with *Jupiter Five* more than three months before to study the Ganymean ship. Although nothing truly spectacular had emerged during this time, huge volumes of data on the structure, design, and contents of the alien ship had been amassed. Every day, newly removed devices and machinery were examined in the laboratories of the surface bases and in the orbiting *J4* and *J5* mission command ships. Findings from these tests were as yet fragmentary, but clues were beginning to emerge from which a meaningful picture of the Ganymean civilization and the mysterious events of twenty-five million years before might eventually emerge.

That was Hunt's job. Originally a theoretical physicist specializing in mathematical nucleonics, he had been brought into the UN Space Arm from England to head a small group of UNSA scientists; the group's task was to correlate the findings of the specialists working on the project both on and around Ganymede and back on Earth. The specialists painted the pieces of the puzzle; Hunt's group fitted them together. This arrangement was devised by Hunt's immediate boss, Gregg Caldwell, executive director of the Navigation and Communications Division of UNSA, headquartered in Houston. The scheme had already worked well in enabling them to unravel successfully the existence and fate of Minerva, and first signs were that it promised to work well again.

He listened while the debate among the biologists went full circle to end up focusing on the unfamiliar enzyme that had started the whole thing off.

"No, I'm afraid not," Danchekker said in reply to a question from Rousson. "We have no idea at present what its purpose was. Certain functions in its reaction equations suggest that it could have contributed to the modification or breaking down of some kind of protein molecule, but precisely what molecule or for what purpose we don't know." Danchekker gazed around the room to invite further comment but nobody appeared to have anything to say. The room became quiet. A mild hum from a nearby generator became noticeable for the first time. At length Hunt stubbed his cigarette and sat back to rest his elbows on the arms of his chair. "Sounds as if there's a problem there, all right," he commented. "Enzymes aren't my line. I'm going to have to leave this one completely to you people."

"Ah, nice to see you're still with us, Vic," Danchekker said, raising his eyes to take in the far end of the table. "You haven't said a word since we sat down."

"Listening and learning," Hunt grinned. "Didn't have a lot to contribute."

"That sounds like a philosophical approach to life," Fichter said, shuffling the papers in front of him. "Do you have many philosophies of life ... maybe a little red book full of them like that Chinese gentleman back in nineteen whatever it was?"

" 'Fraid not. Doesn't do to have too many philosophies about anything. You always end up contradicting yourself. Blows your credibility."

Fichter smiled. "You've nothing to say to throw any light on our problem with this wretched enzyme then," he said.

Hunt did not reply immediately but pursed his lips and inclined his head to one side in the manner of somebody with doubts about the advisability of revealing something that he knew. "Well," he finally said, "you've got enough to worry about with that enzyme as things are." The tone was mildly playful, but irresistibly provocative. All heads in the room swung around abruptly to face in his direction.

"Vic, you're holding out on us," Sandy declared. "Give."

Danchekker fixed Hunt with a silent, challenging stare. Hunt nodded and reached down with one hand to operate the keyboard recessed into the edge of the table opposite his chair. Above the far side of Ganymede, computers on board *Jupiter Five* responded to his request. The display on the conference room wall changed to reveal a densely packed columnar arrangement of numbers.

Hunt allowed some time for the others to study them. "These are the results of a series of quantitative analytical tests that were performed recently in the *J5* labs. The tests involved the routine determination of the chemical constituents of cells from selected organs in the animals you've just been talking about—the ones from the ship." He paused for a second, then continued matter-of-factly. "These numbers show that certain combinations of elements turned up over and over again, always in the same fixed ratios. The ratios strongly suggest the decay products of familiar radioactive processes. It's exactly as if radioisotopes were selected in the manufacture of the enzymes."

After a few seconds, one or two puzzled frowns formed in response to his words. Danchekker was the first to reply. "Are you telling us that the enzyme incorporated radioisotopes into its structure ... selectively?" he asked.

"Exactly."

"That's ridiculous," the professor declared firmly. His tone left no room for dissent. Hunt shrugged.

"It appears to be fact. Look at the numbers."

"But there is no way in which such a process could come about," Danchekker insisted.

"I know, but it did."

"Purely chemical processes cannot distinguish a radioisotope from a normal isotope," Danchekker pointed out impatiently. "Enzymes are manufactured by chemical processes. Such processes are incapable of selecting radioisotopes to use for the manufacture of enzymes." Hunt had half expected that Danchekker's immediate reaction would be one of uncompromising and total rejection of the suggestion he had just made. After working closely with Danchekker for over two years, Hunt had grown used to the professor's tendency to sandbag himself instinctively behind orthodox pronouncements the moment anything alien to his beliefs reared its head. Once he'd been given time to reflect, Hunt knew, Danchekker could be as innovative as any of the younger generation of scientists seated around the room. For the moment, then, Hunt remained silent, whistling tunelessly and nonchalantly to himself as he drummed his fingers absently on the table.

Danchekker waited, growing visibly more irritable as the seconds dragged by. "Chemical processes cannot distinguish a radioisotope," he finally repeated. "Therefore no enzyme could be produced in the way you say it was. And even if it could, there would be no purpose to be served. Chemically the enzyme will behave the same whether it has radioisotopes in it or not. What you're saying is preposterous!"

Hunt sighed and pointed a weary finger toward the screen. "I'm not saying it, Chris," he reminded the professor. "The numbers are. There are the facts—check 'em." Hunt leaned forward and cocked his head to one side, at the same time contorting his features into a frown as if he had just been struck with a sudden thought. "*What* were you saying a minute ago about people wanting to fit the evidence to suit the answers they'd already made their minds up about?" he asked.

chapter two

At the age of eleven, Victor Hunt had moved from the bedlam
of his family home in the East End of London and gone to live
with an uncle and aunt in Worcester. His uncle—the odd man
out in the Hunt family—was a design engineer at the nearby
laboratories of a leading computer manufacturer and it was his
patient guidance that first opened the boy's eyes to the excitement and mystery of the world of electronics.

Some time later young Victor put his newfound fascination
with the laws of formal logic and the techniques of logic-
circuit design to its first practical test. He designed and built a
hard-wired special-purpose processor which, when given any
date after the adoption of the Gregorian calendar in 1582,
would output a number from 1 to 7 denoting the day of the
week on which it had fallen. When, breathless with expectation, he switched it on for the first time, the system remained
dead. It turned out that he had connected an electrolytic capac-
itor the wrong way around and shorted out the power supply.

This exercise taught him two things: Most problems have
simple solutions once somebody looks at things the right way,
and the exhilaration of winning in the end makes all the effort
worthwhile. It also served to reinforce his intuitive understanding that the only sure way to prove or disprove what looked
like a good idea was to find some way to test it. As his subsequent career led him from electronics to mathematical physics and thence to nucleonics, these fundamentals became the
foundations of his permanent mental makeup. In nearly thirty
years he had never lost his addiction to the final minutes of
mounting suspense that came when the crucial experiment had
been prepared and the moment of truth was approaching.

He experienced that same feeling now, as he watched
Vincent Carizan make a few last-minute adjustments to the
power-amplifier settings. The attraction in the main electronics

lab at Pithead Base that morning was an item of equipment recovered from the Ganymean ship. It was roughly cylindrical, about the size of an oil drum, and appeared to be rather simple in function in that it possessed few input and output connections; apparently it was a self-contained device of some sort, rather than a component in some larger and more complex system.

However, its function was far from obvious. The engineers at Pithead had concluded that the connections were intended as power inlet points. From an analysis of the insulating materials used, the voltage clamping and protection circuits, the smoothing circuits, and the filtering arrangements, they had deduced the kind of electrical supply it was designed to work from. This had enabled them to set up a suitable arrangement of transformers and frequency converters. Today was the day they intended to switch it on to see what happened.

Besides Hunt and Carizan, two other engineers were present in the laboratory to supervise the measuring instruments that had been assembled for the experiment. Frank Towers observed Carizan's nod of satisfaction as he stepped back from the amplifier panel and asked:

"All set for overload check?"

"Yep," Carizan answered. "Give it a zap." Towers threw a switch on another panel. A sharp *clunk* sounded instantly as a circuit breaker dropped out somewhere in the equipment cabinet behind the panel.

Sam Mullen, standing by an instrumentation console to one side of the room, briefly consulted one of his readout screens. "Current trip's functioning okay," he announced.

"Unshort it and throw in some volts," Carizan said to Towers, who changed a couple of control settings, threw the switch again and looked over at Mullen.

"Limiting at fifty," Mullen said. "Check?"

"Check," Towers returned.

Carizan looked at Hunt. "All set to go, Vic. We'll try an initial run with current limiters in circuit, but whatever happens our stuff's protected. Last chance to change your bet; the book's closing."

"I still say it makes music," Hunt grinned. "It's an electric barrel organ. Give it some juice."

"Computers?" Carizan cocked an eye at Mullen.

"Running. All data channels checking normal."

"Okay then." Carizan rubbed the palms of his hands together. "Now for the star turn. Live this time, Frank—phase one of the schedule."

A tense silence descended as Towers reset his controls and threw the main switch again. The readings on the numeric displays built into his panel changed immediately.

"Live," he confirmed. "It's taking power. Current is up to the maximum set on the limiters. Looks like it wants more." All eyes turned toward Mullen, who was scanning the computer output screens intently. He shook his head without looking around.

"Nix. Makes a dodo look like a real ball of fire."

The accelerometers, fixed to the outside of the Ganymean device standing bolted in its steel restraining frame on rubber vibration absorbers, were not sensing any internal mechanical motion. The sensitive microphones attached to its casing were picking up nothing in the audible or ultrasonic ranges. The head sensors, radiation detectors, electromagnetic probes, gaussmeters, scintillation counters and variable antennas—all had nothing to report. Towers varied the supply frequency over a trial range but it soon became apparent that nothing was going to change. Hunt walked over to stand beside Mullen and inspect the computer outputs, but said nothing.

"Looks like we need to wind the wick up a little," Carizan commented. "Phase two, Frank." Towers stepped up the input voltage. A row of numbers appeared on one of Mullen's screens.

"Something on channel seven," he informed them. "Acoustic." He keyed a short sequence of commands into the console keyboard and peered at the wave form that appeared on an auxiliary display. "Periodic wave with severe even-harmonic distortion . . . low amplitude . . . fundamental frequency is about seventy-two hertz."

"That's the supply frequency," Hunt murmured. "Probably just a resonance somewhere. Shouldn't think it means much. Anything else?"

"Nope."

"Wind it up again, Frank," Carizan said.

As the test progressed they became more cautious and increased the number of variations tried at each step. Eventually the characteristics of the input supply told them that the device was saturating and seemed to be running at its design levels.

By this time it was taking a considerable amount of power but apart from reporting continued mild acoustic resonances and a slight heating of some parts of the casing, the measuring instruments remained obstinately quiet. As the first hour passed, Hunt and the three UNSA engineers resigned themselves to a longer and much more detailed examination of the object, one that would no doubt involve dismantling it. But, like Napoleon, they took the view that lucky people tend to be people who give luck a chance to happen; it had been worth a try.

The disturbance generated by the Ganymean device was, however, not of a nature that any of their instruments had been designed to detect. A series of spherical wave fronts of intense but highly localized space-time distortion expanded outward from Pithead Base at the speed of light, propagating across the Solar System.

Seven hundred miles to the south, seismic monitors at Ganymede Main Base went wild and the data validation programs running in the logging computer aborted to signal a system malfunction.

Two thousand miles above the surface, sensors aboard the *Jupiter Five* command ship pinpointed Pithead Base as the origin of abnormal readings and flashed an alert to the duty supervisor.

Over half an hour had passed since full power had been applied to the device in the laboratory at Pithead. Hunt stubbed out a cigarette as Towers finally shut down the supply and sat back in his seat with a sigh.

"That's about it," Towers said. "We're not gonna get anyplace this way. Looks like we'll have to open it up further."

"Ten bucks," Carizan declared. "See, Vic—no tunes."

"Nothing else, either," Hunt retorted. "The bet's void."

At the instrumentation console Mullen completed the storage routine for the file of meager data that had been collected, shut down the computers and joined the others.

"I don't understand where all that power was going," he said, frowning. "There wasn't nearly enough heat to account for it, and no signs of anything else. It's crazy."

"There must be a black hole in there," Carizan offered. "That's what the thing is—a garbage can. It's the ultimate garbage can."

"I'll take ten on that," Hunt informed him readily.

* * *

Three hundred and fifty million miles from Ganymede, in the Asteroid belt, a UNSA robot probe detected a rapid succession of transient gravitational anomalies, causing its master computer to suspend all system programs and initiate a full run of diagnostic and fault-test routines.

"No kidding—straight out of Walt Disney," Hunt told the others across the table in one corner of the communal canteen at Pithead. "I've never seen anything like the animal murals decorating the walls of that room in the Ganymean spacecraft."

"Sounds crazy," Sam Mullen declared from opposite Hunt. "What d'you think they are—Minervans or something else?"

"They're not terrestrial, that's for sure," Hunt replied. "But maybe they're not anything . . . anything real, that is. Chris Danchekker's convinced they can't be real."

"How d'you mean, *real*?" Carizan asked.

"Well, they don't *look* real," Hunt answered. He frowned and waved his hands in small circles in the air. "They're all kinds of bright colors . . . and clumsy . . . ungainly. You can't imagine them evolving from any real-life evolutionary system—"

"Not selected for survival, you mean?" Carizan suggested. Hunt nodded rapidly.

"Yes, that's it. No adaptation for survival . . . no camouflage or ability to escape or anything like that."

"Mmm . . ." Carizan looked intrigued, but nonplussed. "Any ideas?"

"Well, actually yes," Hunt said. "We're pretty sure the room was a Ganymean children's nursery or something similar. That probably explains it. They weren't supposed to be real, just Ganymean cartoon characters." Hunt paused for a second, then laughed to himself. "Danchekker wondered if they'd named any of them Neptune." The other two looked at him quizzically. "He reasoned that they coudln't have had a Pluto because there wasn't a Pluto then," Hunt explained. "So maybe they had a Neptune instead."

"Neptune!" Carizan guffawed and brought his hand down sharply on the table. "I like it. . . . Wouldn't have thought Danchekker could crack a joke like that."

"You'd be surprised," Hunt told him. "He can be quite a character once you get to know him. He's just a bit stuffy at

first, that's all. . . . But you should see them. I'll bring some
prints over. One was bright blue with pink stripes down the
sides—body like an overgrown pig. And it had a trunk!"

Mullen grimaced and covered his eyes.

"Man . . . The thought's enough to put me off drink for
keeps." He turned his head and looked toward the serving
counter. "Where the hell's Frank?" As if in answer to the question, Towers appeared behind him carrying a tray with four
cups of coffee. He set the tray down, squeezed into a seat and
proceeded to pass the drinks round.

"Two white with, a white without, and a black with. Okay?"
He settled himself back and accepted a cigarette from Hunt.
"Cheers. The man over by the counter there says you're leav-
ing for a spell. That right?"

Hunt nodded. "Only five days. I'm due for a bit of leave on
J5. Flying up from Main the day after tomorrow."

"On your own?" Mullen asked.

"No—there'll be five or six of us. Danchekker's coming
too. Can't say I'll be sorry for a break, either."

"I hope the weather holds out," Towers said with playful
sarcasm. "It'd be too bad if you missed the holiday season.
This place makes me wonder what the big attraction ever was
at Miami Beach."

"The ice comes with scotch there," Carizan suggested.

A shadow fell across the table. They looked up to greet a
burly figure sporting a heavy black beard and clad in a tartan
shirt and blue jeans. It was Pete Cummings, a structures engineer who had come to Ganymede with the team that had included Hunt and Danchekker. He reversed a chair and perched
himself astride it, directing his gaze at Carizan.

"How'd it go?" he inquired. Carizan pulled a face and
shook his head.

"No dice. Bit of heat, bit of humming . . . otherwise nothing
to shout about. Couldn't get anything out of it."

"Too bad." Cummings made an appropriate display of sympathy. "It couldn't have been you guys that caused all the
commotion then."

"What commotion?"

"Didn't you hear?" He looked surprised. "There was a message beamed down from J5 a little while back. Apparently
they picked up some funny waves coming up from the
surface . . . seems that the center was somewhere around here.

The commander's been calling all around the base trying to find out who's up to what, and what caused it. They're all flappin' around in the tower up there like there's a fox in the henhouse."

"I bet that's the call that came in just when we were leaving the lab," Mullen said. "Told you it could have been important."

"Hell, there are times when a man needs coffee," Carizan answered. "Anyhow, it wasn't us." He turned to face Cummings. "Sorry, Pete. Ask again some other time. We've just been drawing blanks today."

"Well, the whole thing's mighty queer," Cummings declared, rubbing his beard. "They've checked out just about everything else."

Hunt was frowning to himself and drawing on his cigarette pensively. He blew out a cloud of smoke and looked up at Cummings.

"Any idea what time this was, Pete?" he asked. Cummings screwed up his face.

"Lemme see—aw, under an hour." He turned and called across to a group of three men who were sitting at another table. "Hey, Jed. What time did J5 pick up the spooky waves? Any idea?"

"Ten forty-seven local," Jed called back.

"Ten forty-seven local," Cummings repeated to the table.

An ominous silence descended abruptly on the group seated around Hunt.

"How about that, fellas?" Towers asked at last. The matter-of-fact tone did not conceal his amazement.

"It could be a coincidence," Mullen murmured, not sounding convinced.

Hunt cast his eyes around the circle of faces and read the same thoughts on every one. They had all reached the same conclusion; after a few seconds, he voiced it for them.

"I don't believe in coincidences," he said.

Five hundred million miles away, in the radio and optical observatory complex on Lunar Farside, Professor Otto Schneider made his way to one of the computer graphics rooms in answer to a call from his assistant. She pointed out the unprecedented readings that had been reported by an instrument designed to measure cosmic gravitational radiation, especially that believed to emanate from the galactic center. These signals were quite positively identified, but had not come from anywhere near that direction. They originated from somewhere near Jupiter.

Another hour passed on Ganymede. Hunt and the engineers returned to the lab to reappraise the experiment in light of what Cummings had told them. They called the base commander, reported the situation, and agreed to prepare a more intensive test for the Ganymean device. Then, while Towers and Mullen reexamined the data collected earlier, Hunt and Carizan toured the base to beg, borrow or steal some seismic monitoring equipment to add to their instruments. Suitable detectors were finally located in one of the warehouses, where they were kept as spares for a seismic outstation about three miles from the base, and the team began planning the afternoon's activities. By this time their excitement was mounting rapidly, but even more their curiosity; if, after all, the machine was an emitter of gravity pulses, what purpose did it serve?

One thousand five hundred million miles from Ganymede, not far from the mean orbit of Uranus, a communications subprocessor interrupted the operation of its supervisory computer. The computer activated a code-conversion routine and passed a top-priority message on to the master-system monitor.

A transmission had been received from a standard Model 17 Mark 3B Distress Beacon.

chapter three

The surface transporter climbed smoothly above the eternal veil of methane-ammonia haze that cloaked Pithead Base and leveled out onto a southerly course. For nearly two hours it skimmed over an unchanging wilderness of a stormy sea sculptured in ice and half immersed in a sullen ocean of mist. Occasional outcrops of rock added texture to the scene, standing black against the ghostly radiance induced by the serene glow of Jupiter's enormous rainbow disk. And then the cabin view screen showed a tight group of perhaps half a dozen silver spires jutting skyward from just over the horizon ahead—the huge thermonuclear Vega shuttles that stood guard over Ganymede Main Base.

After taking refreshments at Main, Hunt's party joined other groups bound for *J5* and boarded one of the Vegas. Soon afterward they were streaking into space and Ganymede rapidly became just a smooth, featureless snowball behind them. Ahead, a pinpoint of light steadily elongated and enlarged, and then resolved itself into the awe-inspiring, majestic, mile-and-a-quarter-long *Jupiter Five* mission command ship, hanging alone in the void; *Jupiter Four* had departed the week before, bound for Callisto where it would take up permanent orbit. The computers and docking radars guided the Vega gently to rest inside the cavernous forward docking bay, and within minutes the arrivals were walking into the immense city of metal.

Danchekker promptly disappeared to discuss with the *J5*'s scientists the latest details of their studies of the terrestrial animal samples from Pithead. Without shame or conscience Hunt spent a glorious twenty-four hours totally relaxing, doing nothing. He enjoyed many rounds of drinks and endless yarns with *Jupiter Five* crew members he had become friendly with on the long voyage out from Earth, and found unbounded pleasure in the almost forgotten sense of freedom that came with simply sauntering unencumbered along the seemingly interminable expanses of the ship's corridors and vast decks. He felt intoxicated with well-being—exuberant. Just being back on *Jupiter Five* again seemed to bring him nearer to Earth and to things that were familiar. In a sense he was home. This tiny, manmade world, an island of light and life and warmth drifting through an infinite ocean of emptiness, was no longer the cold and alien shell that he had boarded high above Luna more than a year ago. It now seemed to him a part of Earth itself.

Hunt spent the second day paying social calls on some of *J5*'s scientific personnel, exercising in one of the ship's lavishly equipped gymnasiums and cooling off afterward with a swim. A little while later, enjoying a well-earned beer in one of the bars and debating with himself what to do about dinner, he found himself talking to a medical officer who was snatch-

ing a quick refresher after coming off duty. Her name was
Shirley. To their mutual surprise it turned out that Shirley had
studied at Cambridge, England, and had rented a flat not two
minutes' walk from Hunt's own student-day lodgings. Before
very long one of those instant friendships that springs up out
of nowhere was bursting into full bloom. They dined together
and spent the rest of the evening talking and laughing and
drinking, and drinking and laughing and talking. By midnight
it had become evident that there would be no sudden parting
of the ways. Next morning he felt better than he had for what
he was sure was an unhealthily long time. That, he told himself, was surely what medical officers were supposed to make
people feel like.

On the following day he rejoined Danchekker. The results of
the two years of work that Hunt and Danchekker had spear-
headed was by now a subject of worldwide acclaim, and the
names of the two scientists had been in the limelight as a consequence. The Jupiter Five Mission director, Joseph B.
Shannon, an Air Force colonel prior to world demilitarization
fifteen years earlier, had been informed of their presence on
the ship and had invited them to join him for lunch. Accordingly, halfway through the official day, they found themselves
sitting at a table in the director's dining room, savoring the
mellow euphoria that comes with cigars and brandy after the
final course and obliging Shannon with their personal accounts
of the other sensational discovery that had rocked the scientific
world during those two years—the discovery of Charlie and
the Lunarians. It ranked in sensationalism with that of the
Ganymeans.

The Ganymeans had turned up later, when the shafts driven
down into the ice below Pithead had penetrated to the
Ganymean spacecraft. Some time before that discovery, exploration of the Lunar surface had yielded traces of yet another
technologically advanced civilization that had flourished in the
Solar System long before that of Man. This race was given
the name "Lunarians," again to commemorate the place where
the first finds had been made, and was known to have reached
its peak some fifty thousand years before—during the final
cold period of the Pleistocene Ice Age. Charlie, a spacesuited
corpse found well-preserved beneath debris and rubble not far
from Copernicus, had constituted the first find of all and had

provided the clues that marked the starting point from which the story of the Lunarians was eventually reconstructed.

The Lunarians had proved to be fully human in every detail. Once this fact was established, the problem that presented itself was that of explaining where the Lunarians had come from. Either they had originated on Earth itself as a till-then unsuspected civilization that had emerged prior to the existence of modern Man, or they had originated somewhere else. There were no other possibilities open to consideration.

But for a long time both possibilities seemed to be ruled out. If an advanced society had once flourished on Earth, surely centuries of archaeological excavation should have produced abundant evidence of it. On the other hand, to suppose that they had originated elsewhere would require a process of parallel evolution—a violation of the accepted principles of random mutation and natural selection. The Lunarians therefore, being neither from Earth nor from anywhere else, couldn't exist. But they did. The unraveling of this seeming insoluble mystery had brought Hunt and Danchekker together and had occupied them, along with hundreds of experts from just about all the world's major scientific institutions, for over two years.

"Chris insisted right from the beginning that Charlie, and presumably all the rest of the Lunarians too, could only have descended from the same ancestors as we did." Hunt spoke through a swirling tobacco haze while Shannon listened intently. "I didn't want to argue with him on that, but I couldn't go along with the conclusion that seemed to go with it—that they must, therefore, have originated on Earth. There would have to be traces of them around, and there weren't."

Danchekker smiled ruefully to himself as he sipped his drink. "Yes, indeed," he said. "As I recall, our meetings in those early days were characterized by what might be described as, ah, somewhat direct and acrimonious exchanges."

Shannon's eyes twinkled briefly as he pictured the months of heated argument and dissent that were implied by Danchekker's careful choice of euphemisms.

"I remember reading about it at the time," he said, nodding. "But there were so many different reports flying around and so many journalists getting their stories confused, that we never could get a really clear idea of exactly what was going on behind it all. When did you first figure out for sure that the Lunarians came from Minerva?"

"That's a long story," Hunt answered. "The whole thing was an unbelievable mess for a long time. The more we found out, the more everything seemed to contradict itself. Let me see now . . ." He paused and rubbed his chin for a second. "People all over were getting snippets of information from all kinds of tests on the Lunarian remains and relics that started to turn up after Charlie. Then too, there was Charlie himself, his space suit, backpack and so on, and all the things with them . . . then the other bits and pieces from around Tycho and places. The clues eventually started fitting together and out of it all we gradually built up a surprisingly complete picture of Minerva and managed to work out fairly accurately where Minerva must have been."

"I was with UNSA at Galveston when you joined Navcomms," Shannon informed Hunt. "That part of the story received a lot of coverage. *Time* did a feature on you called 'The Sherlock Holmes of Houston.' But tell me something— what you've just said doesn't seem to sort out the problem; if you managed to track them down to Minerva, how did that answer the question of parallel evolution? I'm afraid I still don't see that."

"Quite right," Hunt confirmed. "All it proved was that a planet existed. It didn't prove that the Lunarians evolved on it. As you say, there was still the problem of parallel evolution." He flicked his cigar at the ashtray and shook his head with a sigh. "All kinds of theories were in circulation. Some talked about a civilization from the distant past that had colonized Minerva and had somehow gotten cut off from home; others said they had evolved there from scratch by some kind of convergent process that wasn't properly understood. . . . Life was becoming crazy."

"But at that point we encountered an extraordinary piece of luck," Danchekker came in. "Your colleagues from *Jupiter Four* discovered the Ganymean spaceship—here, on Ganymede. Once the cargo was identified as terrestrial animals from about twenty-five million years ago, an explanation suggested itself that could account adequately for the whole situation. The conclusion was incredible, but it fitted."

Shannon nodded vigorously, indicating that this answer had confirmed what he had already suspected.

"Yes, it had to be the animals," he said. "That's what I thought. Until you established that the ancestors of the Lunarians had been shipped from Earth to Minerva by the Ganymeans, you had no way of connecting the Lunarians with Minerva. Right?"

"Almost, but not quite," Hunt replied. "We'd already managed to connect the Lunarians with Minerva—in other words we knew they'd been involved with the planet somehow—but we couldn't account for how they could have *evolved* there. You're right, though, in saying that the animals that the Ganymeans shipped there long before solved that one in the end. But first we had to connect the Ganymeans with Minerva. At first, you see, all we knew was that one of their ships conked out on Ganymede. No way of knowing where it came from."

"Of course. That's right. There wouldn't have been anything to indicate that the Ganymeans had anything to do with Minerva, would there? So what finally pointed you in the right direction?"

"Another stroke of luck, I must confess," Danchekker said. "Some perfectly preserved fish were found among the food stocks in the remains of a devastated Lunarian base on Luna. We succeeded in proving that the fish were native to Minerva and had been brought to Luna by the Lunarians. Furthermore, the fish were shown to be anatomically related to Ganymean skeletons. This, of course, implied that the Ganymeans too must have evolved from the same evolutionary line as the fish. Since the fish were from Minerva, the Ganymeans also had to be from Minerva."

"So that was where the ship must have come from," Hunt pointed out.

"And where the animals must have come from," Danchekker added.

"And the only way they could have got there is if the Ganymeans took them there," Hunt finished.

Shannon reflected on these propositions for a while. "Yes . . . I see," he said finally. "It all makes sense. And the rest everybody knows. Two isolated populations of terrestrial animals resulted—the one that had always existed on Earth, and the one established on Minerva by the Ganymeans, which included advanced primates. During the twenty-five million years that followed, the Lunarians evolved from them, on Minerva, and that's how they came to be human in form." Shannon stubbed his cigar, then placed his hands flat on the table and looked up at the two scientists. "And the Ganymeans," he said. "What happened to them? They vanished completely twenty-five million years back. Are you people anywhere near answering that one yet? How about leaking a little bit of information in advance? I'm interested."

Danchekker made an empty-handed gesture.

"Believe me, I would like nothing better than to be able to comply. But honestly, we haven't made any great strides in that direction yet. What you say is correct; not only the Ganymeans, but also all the land-dwelling forms of life native to Minerva died out or disappeared in a very short space of time, relatively speaking, at about that time. The imported terrestrial species flourished in their place and eventually the Lunarians emerged." The professor showed his palms again. "What happened to the Ganymeans and why? That remains a mystery. Oh . . . we have theories, or should I say we can offer possible explanations. The most popular seems to be that an increase in atmospheric toxins, particularly carbon dioxide, proved lethal to the natives but not to the immigrant types. But to be truthful, the evidence is far from conclusive. I was talking to your molecular biologists here on *J5* only yesterday; some of their more recent work makes me less confident in that theory than I was two or three months ago."

Shannon looked mildly disappointed but accepted the situation philosophically. Before he could comment further, a white-jacketed steward approached the table and began collecting the empty coffee cups and dusting away the specks of ash and bread crumbs. As they sat back in their chairs to make room, Shannon looked up at the steward.

"Good morning, Henry," he said casually. "Is the world treating you well today?"

"Oh, mustn't grumble, sir. I've worked for worse firms than UNSA in my time," Henry replied cheerfully. Hunt was intrigued to note his East London accent. "A change always does you good; that's what I always say."

"What did you do before, Henry?" Hunt inquired.

"Cabin steward for an airline."

Henry moved away to begin clearing the adjacent table. Shannon caught the eyes of the two scientists and inclined his head in the direction of the steward.

"Amazing man, Henry," he commented, his tone lowered slightly. "Did you get to meet him at all on the way out from

Earth?" The other two shook their heads. "*Jupiter's Five*'s reigning chess champion."

"Good Lord," Hunt said, following his gaze with a new interest. "Really?"

"Learned to play when he was six," Shannon told them. "He's got a gift for it. He could probably make a lot of money out of it if he chose to take the game seriously, but he says he prefers keeping it as a hobby. The first navigation officer studies up day and night just to take the title away from Henry. Between us though, I think he's going to need an awful lot of luck to do it, and that's supposed to be the one game that luck doesn't come into. Right?"

"Precisely," Danchekker affirmed. "Extraordinary."

The mission director glanced at the clock on the dining-room wall, then spread his arms along the edge of the table in a gesture of finality.

"Well, gentlemen," he said. "It's been a pleasure meeting you both at last. Thank you for a most interesting conversation. We must make a point of keeping in touch regularly from now on. I have to attend an appointment shortly, but I haven't forgotten that I promised to show you the ship's command center. So, if you're ready, we'll go there now. I'll introduce you to Captain Hayter who's to show you around. Then, I'm afraid, you'll have to excuse me."

Fifteen minutes later, after riding a capsule through one of the ship's communications tubes to reach another section of the vessel, they were standing surrounded on three sides by a bewildering array of consoles, control stations and monitor panels on the bridge; below them stretched the brilliantly lit panorama of *Jupiter Five*'s command center. The clusters of operator stations, banks of gleaming equipment cubicles and tiers of instrument panels were the nerve center from which ultimately all the activities of the mission and all the functions of the ship were controlled. The permanent laser link that handled the communications traffic to Earth; the data channels to the various surface installations and the dispersed fleet of UNSA ships nosing around the Jovian system; the navigation, propulsion and flight-control systems; the heating, cooling, lighting, life-support systems and ancillary computers and machinery, and a thousand and one other processes—all were supervised and coordinated from this stupendous concentration of skills and technology.

Captain Ronald Hayter stood behind the two scientists and waited as they took in the scene below the bridge. The mission was organized and its command hierarchy structured in such a way that operations were performed under the ultimate direction of the Civilian Branch of the Space Arm; supreme authority lay with Shannon. Many functions essential to UNSA operations, such as crewing spaceships and conducting activities safely and effectively in unfamiliar alien environments, called for standards of training and discipline that could only be met by a military-style command structure and organization. The Uniformed Branch of the Space Arm had been formed in response to these needs; also, not entirely fortuitously, it went a long way toward satisfying peacefully the longing for adventure of a significant proportion of the younger generation, to whom the idea of large-scale, regular armed forces belonged to a past that was best forgotten. Hayter was in command of all uniformed ranks present aboard *J5* and reported directly to Shannon.

"It's quiet at the moment compared to what it can be like," Hayter commented at last, stepping forward to stand between them. "As you can see, a number of sections down there aren't manned; that's because lots of things are shut down or just under automatic supervision while we're parked in orbit. This is just a skeleton crew up here too."

"Seems to be some activity over there," Hunt said. He pointed down at a group of consoles where the operators were busily scanning viewscreens, tapping intermittently into keyboards and speaking into microphones and among themselves. "What's going on?"

Hayter followed his finger, then nodded. "We're hooked into a cruiser that's been in orbit over Io for a while now. They've been putting a series of probes in low-altitude orbits over Jupiter itself and the next phase calls for surface landings. The probes are being prepared over Io right now and the operation will be controlled from the ship there. The guys you're looking at are simply monitoring the preparation." The captain indicated another section farther over to the right. "That's traffic control . . . keeping tabs on all the ship movements around the various moons and in between. They're always busy."

Danchekker had been peering out over the command center in silence. At last he turned toward Hayter with an expression of undisguised wonder on his face.

"I must say that I am very impressed," he said. "Very impressed indeed. On several occasions during our outward voyage, I'm afraid that I referred to your ship as an infernal contraption; it appears that I am now obliged to eat my words."

"Call it what you like, Professor," Hayter replied with a grin. "But it's probably the safest contraption ever built. All the vital functions that are controlled from here are fully duplicated in an emergency command center located in a completely different part of the ship. If anything wiped out this place we could still get you home okay. If something happened on a large enough scale to knock out both of them—well . . ." he shrugged. "I guess there wouldn't be much of the ship left to get home anyhow."

"Fascinating," Danchekker mused. "But tell me—"

"Excuse me, sir." The watch officer interrupted from his station a few feet behind them. Hayter turned toward him.

"What is it, Lieutenant?"

"I have the radar officer on the screen. Unidentified object detected by long-range surveillance. Approaching fast."

"Activate the second officer's station and switch it through. I'll take it there."

"Aye aye, sir."

"Excuse me," Hayter muttered. He moved over to the empty seat in front of one of the consoles, sat down and flipped its main screen into life. Hunt and Danchekker took a few paces to bring them a short distance behind him. Over his shoulder they could see the features of the ship's radar officer materialize.

"Something unusual going on, Captain," he said. "Unidentified object closing on Ganymede. Range eighty-two thousand miles; speed fifty miles per second but reducing; bearing two-seven-eight by oh-one-six solar. On a direct-approach course. ETA computed at just over thirty minutes. Strong echoes at quality seven. Reading checked and confirmed."

Hayter stared back at him for a second. "Do we have any ships scheduled in that sector?"

"Negative, sir."

"Any deviations from scheduled flight plans?"

"Negative. All ships checked and accounted for."

"Trajectory profile?"

"Inadequate data. Being monitored."

Hayter thought for a moment. "Stay live and continue re-porting." Then he turned to the watch officer: "Call the duty bridge crew to stations. Locate the mission director and alert him to stand by for a call to the bridge."

"Yes, sir."

"Radar." Hayter directed his gaze back at the screen on the panel in front of him. "Slave optical scanners to LRS. Track on UFO bearing and copy onto screen three, B5." Hayter paused for a second, then addressed the watch officer again. "Alert traffic control. All launches deferred until further notice. Arrivals scheduled at *J5* within the next sixty minutes are to stand off and await instructions."

"Do you want us to leave?" Hunt asked quietly. Hayter glanced around at him.

"No, that's okay," he said. "Stick around. Maybe you'll see some action."

"What is it?" Danchekker asked.

"I don't know." Hayter's face was serious. "We've never had anything like this before."

Tension rose as the minutes ticked by. The duty crew appeared quickly in ones and twos and took up their positions at the consoles and panels on the bridge. The atmosphere was quiet but charged with suspense as the well-oiled machine readied itself . . . and waited.

The telescopic image resolved by the optical scanners was distinct, but impossible to interpret: circular overall, it appeared to posses four thin protuberances in cruciform, with one pair somewhat longer and slightly thicker than the other. It could have been a disk, or a spheroid, or perhaps it was something else seen end-on. There was no way of telling.

Then the first view came in via the laser link to *Jupiter Four*, orbiting Callisto. Because of the relative positions of Ganymede and Callisto, and of the rapidly diminishing range of the intruder, the telescopes on the *Jupiter Four* obtained an oblique view from a position some distance from its projected course, to Ganymede.

The observers aboard *J5* gasped as the picture being trans-mitted from *J4* appeared on the screen. Vegas, the only ships intended for flight through planetary atmospheres, were the only UNSA vessels in the vicinity that were constructed to a streamlined design; this ship was clearly not a Vega. Those sweeping lines and delicately curved, gracefully balanced fins had not been conceived by any designer of Earth.

Some of the color drained from Hayter's face as he stared incredulously at the screen and the full implications of the sight dawned on him. He swallowed hard, then surveyed the astounded faces surrounding him.

"Man all stations on the command floor," he ordered in a voice approaching a whisper. "Summon the mission director to the bridge immediately."

chapter four

Framed in the large wall display screen on the bridge of *Jupiter Five*, the alien craft hung in a void against a background of stars turning almost imperceptibly. It was almost an hour since the new arrival had slowed down to rest relative to the command ship and had gone into a parallel orbit over Ganymede. The two ships were standing just over five miles apart and every detail of the craft was now easily discernible. There was little to interrupt the sleek contours of its hull and fin surfaces and no identification markings or insignia of any kind. There were, however, several patches of discoloration that might have been the remnants of markings which had been abraded, or perhaps, scorched. In fact the whole appearance of the craft somehow gave the impression of wear and deterioration suffered in the course of a long, hard voyage. Its outer skin was rough and pitted and was from end to end disfigured by indistinct streaks and blotches, as if the whole ship had at some time been exposed to severe heat.

Jupiter Five had been the scene of frenzied activity ever since the first meaningful pictures came in. There had been no indication so far of whether or not the craft carried a crew or, if it did, what the intentions of that crew might be. *Jupiter Five* carried no weapons or defensive equipment of any kind; this was one eventuality the mission planners had not considered seriously.

Every position on the command floor was now manned and throughout the ship every crew member was at his assigned emergency station All bulkheads had been closed and the main drives brought to a state of standby readiness. Communications with the bases on the surface of Ganymede and from other UNSA ships in the vicinity had ceased in order to avoid revealing their existence and their locations. Those daughter ships of *J5* capable of being made flight-ready within the time available had dispersed into the surrounding volume of space; a few were under remote control from *J5*, to be used as ramships if necessary. Signals beamed at the alien craft evoked a response, but *J5*'s computers were unable to decode it into anything intelligible. Now there was nothing else to do but wait.

Throughout all the excitement, Hunt and Danchekker had stood virtually dumbstruck. They were the only people present on the bridge who were privileged to enjoy a grandstand view of everything that happened, without the distraction of defined duties to perform. They were, perhaps, the only ones able to reflect deeply on the significance of the events that were unfolding.

After the discoveries of first the Lunarians and then the Ganymeans, the notion that other races besides Man had evolved to an advanced technological level was firmly accepted. But this was something different. Just five miles away from them was not some leftover relic from another age or the hulk of an ancient mishap. There was a functional, working machine that had come from another world. Right at that moment, it was under the control and guidance of some form of intelligence; it had been maneuvered surely and unhesitatingly to its present orbit and it had responded promptly to *J5*'s signals. Whether it contained occupants or not, these events added up to the first-ever interaction between modern Man and an intelligence that was not of his planet. The moment was unique; however long history might continue to unfold, it could never be repeated.

Shannon stood in the center of the bridge gazing up at the main screen. Hayter was standing beside him, running his eye over the data reports and other images being presented on the row of auxiliary screens below it. One of them showed a view of Gordon Storrel, the deputy mission director, standing by in the emergency command center with his own staff of officers. The outgoing signal to Earth was still operating, carrying complete details of everything that happened.

"Analyzers have just detected a new component," the communications officer called out from his station on one side of the bridge. Then he announced a change in the pattern of signals being picked up from the alien craft. "Tight-beam transmission resembling K-Band radar. PRF twenty-two point three four gigahertz. Unmodulated."

Another minute or so dragged endlessly by. Then, another voice: "New radar contact. Small object has separated from alien ship. Closing on *J5*. Ship maintaining position."

A wave of alarm, felt rather than sensed directly, swept over the observers on the bridge. If the object was a missile there was little that they could do; the nearest ramship was fifty miles away and would require half a minute, even under maximum acceleration, to intercept. Captain Hayter did not have time to juggle with arithmetic.

"Fire *Ram One* and engage," he snapped.

A second later the reply came to confirm. "*Ram One* fired. Locked on target."

Beads of perspiration showed on some of the faces staring at the screens. The main display had not yet resolved the object, but one of the auxiliary screens displayed a plot of the two large vessels and a small but unmistakable blip beginning to close the gap between them.

"Radar reports steady approach speed of ninety feet per second."

"*Ram One* closing. Impact at twenty-five seconds."

Shannon licked his dry lips as he scanned the data on the screens and digested the flow of reports. Hayter had done the right thing and placed the safety of his ship above all other considerations. What to do now was a problem that lay solely with the mission director.

"Thirty miles. Fifteen seconds to impact."

"Object holding course and speed steady."

"That's no missile," Shannon said in a tone that was decisive and final. "Captain, call off the interception."

"Abort *Ram One*," Hayter ordered.

"*Ram One* disengaged and turning away."

Long exhalations of breath and sudden relaxing of postures

signaled the release of the tensions that had been building up. The Vega streaking in from deep space made a shallow turn that took it into a pass at twenty miles' distance and vanished once more into the infinite cosmic backdrop.

Hunt turned to Danchekker, talking in a low voice, "You know, Chris, it's a funny thing. . . . I've got an uncle who lives in Africa. He says there are some places where it's customary to greet strangers by intimidating them with screams and shouts and brandishings of spears. It's the accepted way of establishing your status."

"Perhaps they regard that as no more than a sensible precaution," Danchekker said drily.

At last the optical cameras distinguished a bright speck in the middle-distance between J5 and the alien ship. A zoom-in revealed it to be a smooth, silver disk devoid of any appendages; as before, the view gave no clue of its true shape. It continued its unhurried pace until it was a half-mile from the command ship; there it came to rest and turned itself broadside-on to present a simple, unadorned egg-shaped profile. It was just over thirty feet long and appeared to be of entirely metallic construction. After a few seconds it began showing a bright and slowly flashing white light.

The consensus arrived at in the debate that followed was that the egg was requesting permission to enter the ship. The communication time lag to Earth did not allow immediate consultation with higher authority. After sending a full report Earthward via the laser link, Shannon announced his decision to grant the request.

A reception party was hurriedly organized and dispatched to one of *Jupiter Five*'s docking bays. The docking bay, designed for maintenance work on J5's assorted daughter vessels, carried a pair of enormous outer doors which were normally left open, but which could be closed when circumstances dictated that the bay be filled with air. Access from the main body of the ship was gained through a number of smaller ancillary airlocks positioned at intervals along the inner side of the bay. Clad in space suits, the reception party emerged into one of the vast working platforms in the docking bay and set up a beacon adjusted to flash at the same frequency as that still pulsing on the egg.

On the bridge of *Jupiter Five*, an expectant semicircle

formed around the screen showing the docking bay. The silver ovoid drifted into the center of the starry carpet separating the gaping shadows of the outer doors. The egg descended slowly, its light now extinguished, then hovered some distance above the platform as if cautiously surveying the situation. A close-up showed that in several places on its surface, circular sections of its skin had risen above the overall outline, forming a series of squat, retractable turrets which rotated slowly, presumably to scan the inside of the bay with cameras and other instruments. The egg then resumed its descent and came gently to rest about ten yards from where the reception party was standing in a tight, apprehensive huddle. Overhead an arc light came on to bathe it in a pool of white.

"Well, it's down." The voice of Deputy Mission Director Gordon Storrel, who had volunteered to lead the reception party, announced on an audio channel. "Three landing pads have come out from underneath. There's no other sign of life."

"Give it two minutes," Shannon said into his microphone. "Then move forward to the halfway point, slowly. Stop there."

"Roger."

After sixty seconds another light was turned on to illuminate the group of Earthmen; somebody had suggested that to have the party seen as shadowy forms lurking in the gloom could have an undesirably sinister impression. The action produced no response from the egg.

At last Storrel turned to his men. "Okay, time's up. We're moving in."

The screen showed the knot of ungainly, helmeted figures walking slowly forward; at their head was the one bearing Storrel's golden shoulder flashes, and on either side of him a senior UNSA officer. They halted. Then, a panel in the side of the egg slid aside smoothly to reveal a hatch about eight feet high and at least half that wide. The figures in the space suits stiffened visibly and the watchers on the bridge braced themselves, but nothing further happened.

"Maybe they're hung up about protocol or something," Storrel said. "They've come into our den. Could be they're telling us it's our turn?"

"Could be," Shannon agreed. In a quieter voice he asked Hayter: "Anything to report from up top?" The captain activated another channel to speak to two UNSA sergeants positioned on a maintenance catwalk high above the platform in the docking bay.

"Come in, Catwalk. What can you see?"

"We've got a fair angle down inside it. The inside's in shadow but we've got an image on the intensifier. Just pieces of equipment and fittings . . . seems crammed pretty full. No movement or signs of life."

"No signs of life visible, Gordon," Shannon relayed to the bay. "It looks as if you can stay there forever or have a look. Good luck. Don't think twice about backing off if anything's even slightly suspicious."

"No chance of that," Storrel told him. "Okay, fellas, you heard. Never say UNSA doesn't live up to its job ads. Miralski and Oberman, come with me; the rest of you, stay put."

Three figures moved forward from the group and paused near a small ramp that had telescoped from the bottom of the hatch. Another screen came to life on the bridge to show the view picked up by a hand-held camera operated by one of the UNSA officers. For a second it held a shot of the yawning hatch and the top of the ramp, and then a back view of Storrel filled the screen.

Storrel's commentary came through on audio. "I'm at the top of the ramp now. There's a drop of about a foot down to the deck inside. There's an inner door on the other side of the entrance compartment and it's open. Looks like an airlock." The TV picture closed in as the camera operator moved up beside Storrel; it confirmed his description and the general impression of cramped and cluttered surroundings that had been gained from the catwalk. A glow of warm, yellowy light penetrated the lock from beyond the inner door.

"I'm going through into the inner compartment . . ." A pause. "This looks like the control cabin. It has seats for two occupants sitting side by side, facing forward. Could be pilot and copilot stations—all kinds of controls and instruments . . . No sign of anybody, though . . . just one other door, leading aft, closed. The seats are very large, in scale with everything else about the general design. Must be big guys . . . Oberman, come on through and get a shot of it for the folks back home."

The view showed the scene as Storrel had described, then began sweeping slowly around the cabin to record close-ups of the alien equipment. Suddenly Hunt pointed toward the screen.

"Chris!" he exclaimed, catching Danchekker's sleeve. "That

long gray panel with the switches on ... did you notice it? I've seen those same markings before! They were on—"

He abruptly stopped speaking as the camera swung sharply upward and focused on a large display screen that was set directly in front of the egg's two empty seats. Something was happening on it. A second later they were staring speechlessly at the image of three alien beings. Every pair of eyes on the bridge of *Jupiter Five* opened wide in stunned disbelief.

There was not a man present who had not seen that form before—the long, protruding lower face broadening into the elongated skull ... the massive torsos and the incredible six-fingered hand with two thumbs. ... Danchekker himself had constructed the first eight-feet-tall, full-scale model of that same form, not long after *Jupiter Four* had sent back details of its finds. Everybody had seen the artist's impressions of what the shapes that had contained those skeletons must have looked like.

The artists had done a fine job ... as everybody could now see.

The aliens were Ganymeans!

chapter five

The evidence amassed to that time indicated that the Ganymean presence in the Solar System had ceased some twenty-five million years in the past. Their home planet no longer existed, except as an ice ball beyond Neptune and the debris that constituted the Asteroid Belt, and had not for fifty thousand years. So how could Ganymeans appear on the screen in the egg? The first possibility to flash through Hunt's mind was that they were looking at an ancient recording that had been triggered when the egg was entered. This idea was quickly dispelled. Behind the three Ganymeans, they could see a large display screen not unlike the main display on *J5*'s bridge; it held a view of *Jupiter Five*, seen from the angle at which the large alien ship was lying. The Ganymeans were out there, now, inside that ship ... just five miles away. Then things began happening inside the egg that left no time for more philosophic speculation as to the meaning of it all.

Nobody could be sure what the changes of expression on the alien faces meant, but the general impression was that they were every bit as astonished as the Earthmen. The Ganymeans began gesticulating, and at the same time meaningless speech issued from the audio grille. There was no air inside the egg to carry sound. Evidently the Ganymeans had been monitoring the transmissions from the reception party and were now using the same frequencies and modulation.

The picture of the aliens focused on the middle one of the trio. Then an alien voice spoke again, pronouncing just two syllables. It said something that sounded like "Gar-ruth." The figure on the screen inclined its head slightly, in a way that unmistakably conveyed a combination of politeness and dignity rarely seen on earth. "Gar-ruth," the alien voice repeated. Then again, "Garuth." A similar process took place to introduce the other two, at which point the view widened out to embrace all three. They remained unmoving, staring from the screen, as if waiting for something.

Catching on quickly, Storrel moved to stand directly in front of the screen. "Stor-rel. Storrel." Then, in impulse, he added: "Good afternoon." He admitted later that it sounded stupid, but claimed that his brain hadn't been thinking too coherently at the time. The view on the egg's screen changed momentarily to show Storrel looking back at himself.

"Storrel," the alien voice stated. The pronunciation was perfect. A number of those watching had believed at the time that it was Storrel himself who had spoken.

Miralski and Oberman were introduced in turn, an exercise in shuffling and clambering that was not helped by the restricted confines of the cabin. Then a series of pictures was flashed on the screen, to each of which Storrel replied with an English noun: *Ganymean, Earthman, spaceship, star, arm, leg, hand, foot.* That went on for a few minutes. Evidently the Ganymeans were accepting the onus of doing all the learning; it soon became apparent why—whoever was doing the talking showed an ability to absorb and remember information with astonishing speed. He never asked for a repeat of a definition and he never forgot a detail. His mistakes were frequent to be-

gin with but once corrected they never recurred. The voice did
not synchronize with the mouths of the three visible Ganymeans; presumably the speaker was one of the others aboard the
alien ship who must have been monitoring the proceedings.

A small screen alongside the egg's main display suddenly
presented a diagram: a small circle adorned with a wreath of
radial spikes, and around it a set of nine concentric circles.

"What the hell's this?" Storrel's voice murmured.

Shannon's brow creased into a frown. He looked inquiringly
at the faces around him.

"Solar System," Hunt suggested. Shannon passed the information on to Storrel, who advised the Ganymean. The picture
switched to that of just an empty circle.

"Who is this?" the Ganymean voice asked.

"Correction," Storrel said, employing the convention that
had already been adopted. "*What* is this?"

"Where 'who'? Where 'what'?"

" 'Who' for Ganymeans and Earthmen."

"Ganymeans and Earthmen—collective?"

"People."

"Ganymeans and Earthmen people?"

"Ganymeans and Earthmen *are* people."

"Ganymeans and Earthmen are people."

"Correct."

" 'What' for not-people?"

"Correct."

"Not-people—general?"

"Things."

" 'Who' for people; 'what' for things?"

"Correct."

"What is this?"

"A circle."

A dot then appeared in the middle of the circle.

"What is this?" the voice inquired.

"The center."

" 'The' for one; 'a' for many?"

" 'The' *when* one; 'a' *when* many."

The diagram of the Solar System reappeared as before, but
with the symbol at the center flashing on and off.

"What is this?"

"The Sun."

"A star?"

"Correct."

Storrel proceeded to name the planets as their respective symbols were flashed in turn. The dialogue was still slow and clumsy but it was improving. During the exchange that followed, the Ganymeans managed to convey their bewilderment at the absence of any planet between Mars and Jupiter, a task that proved to be not too difficult since the Earthmen had been expecting it. It took a long time to get the message across that Minerva had been destroyed, and that all that remained of it was some rubble and Pluto, the latter already named and the source, understandably, of further mystery to the aliens.

When, after repeated questioning and double-checking, the Ganymeans at last accepted that they had not misunderstood, their mood became very quiet and subdued. Despite the fact that none of the gestures and facial expressions were familiar to them, the Earthmen watching were overcome by the sense of utter despair and infinite sadness apparent on the alien ship. They could feel the anguish that was written into every movement of those long, now somehow sorrowful, Ganymean faces, as if their very bones were being touched by a wail that came from the beginning of time.

It took a while for the aliens to become communicative again. The Earthmen, noting that the Ganymean expectations had been based on a knowledge of the Solar System that belonged to the distant past, concluded that they must after all, as had been suspected for some time, have migrated to another star. Very probably then, their sudden reappearance represented a sentimental journey to the place where their kind had originated millions of years before and which none of them had ever seen except, perhaps, as carefully preserved records that had been handed down for longer than could be remembered. Small wonder they were dismayed at what they had come so far to find.

But when the Earthmen introduced the notion that the Ganymeans had journeyed from another star, and sought an indication of its position, they were greeted with what appeared to be a firm denial. The aliens seemed to be trying to tell them that their journey had begun long ago from Minerva itself, which of course was ridiculous. By this time, however, Storrel had got himself into a hopeless grammatical tangle and the whole subject was dismissed as the result of a short-term communications problem. No doubt it would be resolved later, when the linguistic skills of the interpreter had improved.

The Ganymean interpreter had spotted the implied connection between "Earth" and "Earthmen," and returned to the subject to obtain confirmation that the beings he was talking to had indeed come from the third planet from the Sun. The Ganymeans visible on the screen appeared very agitated when informed that this was correct, and they went off into a lengthy exchange of remarks among themselves which were not audible on radio. Why that revelation should cause such a reaction was not explained. The question was not asked.

The aliens concluded by indicating that they had been voyaging for a great length of time and had endured much illness and many deaths among their numbers. They were short of supplies, their equipment was in poor condition with much of it unserviceable, and they were all suffering from total physical, mental, emotional and spiritual exhaustion. They gave the impression that only the thought of returning to their home had given them the will to carry on against impossible difficulties; now that hope had been shattered, they were at their end.

Leaving Storrel to continue talking to the aliens, Shannon moved away from the screen and beckoned some of the others, including the two scientists, to gather round for a short, impromptu conference.

"I'm going to send a party across to their ship," he informed them in a lowered voice. "They need help over there and I guess we're the only ones around here that can give it. I'll recall Storrel from the bay and have him lead it; he seems to be getting along fine with them." Then he glanced at Hayter. "Captain, make ready a bus for immediate flight. Detail ten men to go with Storrel, including at least three officers. I'd like everybody in the party to be assembled for a briefing in the lock antechamber to whichever bus can leave soonest, let's say ... thirty minutes from now. Everyone has to be fully supplied, of course."

"Right away," Hayter acknowledged.

"Any other points from anybody?" Shannon asked the assembly.

"Do you want sidearms issued?" one of the officers inquired.

"No. Anything else?"

"Just one thing." The speaker was Hunt. "A request. I'd like to go too." Shannon looked at him and hesitated, as if the question had taken him by surprise. "I was sent here specifically to investigate the Ganymeans. That's my official assignment. What better way could there be of helping me do it?"

"Well, I really don't know." Shannon screwed up his face and scratched the back of his head as he sought for possible objections. "There's no reason why not, I suppose. Yeah—I guess that'd be okay." He turned to Danchekker. "How about you, Professor?"

Danchekker held up his hands in protest. "You are most kind to offer, but thank you, no. I'm afraid I've already had quite enough excitement for one day. And besides that, it has taken me more than a year to feel safe inside *this* contraption. What an alien one must be like, I dread to think."

Hayter grinned and shook his head, but said nothing.

"Fine then." Shannon cast his gaze around one more time to invite further comments. "That's it. Let's get back to our man out front." He walked back to the screen and drew toward him the microphone that connected him with Storrel. "How's it going down there, Gordon?"

"Okay. I'm teaching them to count."

"Good. But get one of the others to take over, would you? We're sending you out on a little trip. Captain Hayter will provide the details in a second. You're going to be an ambassador for Earth."

"What do they pay one of those?"

"Give us time, Gordon. We're still working on the matter." Shannon smiled. It was the first time he had felt relaxed for what seemed like a very long while.

chapter six

The bus—a small personnel carrier normally used for ferrying passengers between satellites or orbiting spacecraft—was drawing near to the Ganymean ship. From where he was sitting, squeezed between the bulky shapes of two other space-suited figures on one of the benches that ran along the sides of the cabin, Hunt could see the ship closing in toward them on the small viewscreen set into the end wall.

From close range, the impression of age and wear was even more vivid than it had been previously. The patterns of discoloration covering the ship from nose to tail, not fully resolved from J5 even under quite high magnification, were now distinct and in places suggested camouflage patterns reminiscent of movies. The outer skin was peppered irregularly with round holes of various sizes, none of them very large, each of which was surrounded by a raised rim of rounded grayish metal and looked like a miniature Lunar crater; it was as if the ship had been bombarded by thousands of tiny particles moving at enormous speed—sufficient to puncture the skin and dissipate enough energy to melt the surrounding material. Either the ship had traveled an enormous distance, Hunt told himself, or there were conditions outside the Solar System that UNSA had yet to encounter.

A rectangular aperture, easily large enough to admit the bus, had opened in the side of the *Shapieron*, as they now knew the Ganymean ship to be called. A soft orange glow illuminated the inside and a white beacon flashed near the center of one of the longer sides.

As the bus turned gently to home in on it, the pilot's voice came over the intercom. "Hold on to your seats back there. We're going in without any docking radar so it's gonna have to be a purely visual approach. Leave all helmets in their racks until after touchdown."

With its maneuvering jets nudging delicately, the bus inched its way through the opening. Inside the bay a bulbous craft with a blue-black sheen was secured against the inner bulkhead, taking up most of the available space. Two large and sturdy looking platforms, constructed perpendicular to the main axis of the ship, projected into the volume that remained; a pair of silver eggs lay side by side on one of them but the other was clear except for a beacon that had been positioned well over to one side to allow ample unobstructed landing space. The bus lined itself up, moved in to hover ten feet or so above the platform, eased itself gingerly downward and came to rest.

Hunt knew immediately that there was something strange

about the situation but it took him a few seconds to realize just what it was. There were puzzled expressions on a couple of the faces around him too.

The seat was pressing up against him. He was experiencing an approximately normal weight, but he had seen no evidence of any mechanism whereby such an effect could have been achieved. *Jupiter Five* had sections that simulated normal gravity by means of continual rotation, although some parts of the ship were designated zero-G areas for special purposes. Instruments that needed to be trained on fixed objects, for example the camera that had been holding the *Shapieron* for the previous few hours, were mounted on projecting booms which could be counterrotated to compensate—similar in principle to ground-based astronomic telescopes. But the view of the Ganymean ship presented on the screens back at *J5* had given no suggestion that the vessel, or any part of it, was rotating. Furthermore, as the bus had positioned itself for its final approach into the landing bay, thus maintaining a fixed position relative to the door, the background stars had been stationary; this meant that the pilot had not been obliged to synchronize his approach run with any rotational motion of his target. Thus, the sensation of weight could only mean that the Ganymeans were employing some revolutionary technology to produce an artificial gravity effect. Intriguing.

The pilot spoke again to confirm this conclusion.

"Well, I guess I'm having one of my lucky days. We made it." The slow Southern drawl was a godsend. "Some of you people have probably noticed the gravity. Don't ask me how they do it but it sure ain't centrifugal. The outer hatch has closed and we're reading a pressure buildup outside, so it looks like they're turning on the air or whatever they use. I'll tell you if you need helmets or not when we've done some tests. Won't take more'n a minute. We still have contact with *J5* here. Guess our friends are picking up our transmissions and relaying them on. *J5* says the emergency status has been relaxed and communications have been resumed with other locations. Message from *J4* reads: *Tell 'em we waved as they went past.*"

The air was breathable—almost normal. Hunt had expected as much; the ship's atmosphere would probably resemble that of Minerva, and terrestrial life had flourished there. The figures in the cabin stayed outwardly calm, but here and there fidgeting and last-minute fiddling with pieces of equipment betrayed the rising air of impatience and expectancy.

The honor of placing the first human foot on an alien spacecraft was to be Storrel's. He rose from his seat near the rear of the cabin and waited for the inner door of the lock to swing aside; then he moved through into the chamber and peered through the transparent port of the outer door.

After a short wait he reported his findings to the rest of the party. "A door is opening in the wall at the edge of the platform we're on. There are guys standing inside it—the big guys. They're coming out . . . one, two, three . . . five of them. Now they're coming across . . ." Heads in the cabin turned instinctively toward the wall screen, but it was showing another part of the structure.

"Can't get a scanner on them," the pilot said, as if reading their thoughts. "It's a blind spot. You're in command now, sir." Storrel continued looking out of the port but said nothing further for a while. Then he turned back to face the cabin and took a deep breath.

"Okay, this is it. No change from plan; play it as briefed. Open her up, pilot."

The outer door of the bus slid into its recess and a short metal stairway unfolded onto the platform. Storrel moved forward to stand framed in the entrance for a second, then disappeared slowly outside. The UNSA officer who was to be second, already waiting at the inner door, followed him while, farther back in the cabin, Hunt took his place in the slowly shuffling line.

Hunt's impression as he emerged was one of a vastness of space that had not been apparent from inside the bus; it was like walking suddenly out of a side chapel and into the nave of a cathedral. Not that he found himself surrounded by a large unused area—this was, after all, a spacecraft—but beyond the tail assembly of the *Shapieron*'s daughter ship, now seen as a sweeping, metallic, geometrical sculpture above their heads, the perspective lines of the docking bay's interior converged in the distance to add true proportion to the astronautic wonder in which they were now standing.

But these were just sensations that flitted across the background of Hunt's perceptions. Before him, history was being made: the first face-to-face meeting between Man and an intelligent, alien species was taking place. Storrel and the two officers were standing slightly in front of the rest of the party, who had formed into a single rank; just a few feet away, facing Storrel, stood what appeared to be the leader of the Ganymean reception committee and, behind him, his four companions.

Their skins were light gray and appeared somewhat coarse compared to that of humans. All five displayed dense hair covering their heads and hanging to their shoulders though there was no hint of any facial growth. On three of them, including the leader, the hair was jet black; one of the others had gray, almost white, hair while the fifth's was a very dark coppery hue, enhancing the subtle reddish tint of his complexion.

Their clothes were a mixture of colors and shared nothing in common except a basic style, which was that of a simple, loose-fitting, shirtlike garment worn with plain trousers gathered into some kind of band at the ankle; there was certainly no suggestion of any sort of uniform. All were wearing glossy, thick-soled boots, again in various colors, and some had ornate belts around their waists. In addition, each sported a thin, gold headband supporting what looked like a disk-shaped jewel in the center of his forehead and wore a flat, silver box, at a distance not unlike a cigarette case, on a metallic wrist bracelet. There was nothing to distinguish the leader visually.

For a few momentous seconds the two groups faced each other in silence. In the doorway behind the Earthmen, the copilot of the bus was recording the scene for posterity, using a hand camera. Then the Ganymean leader moved forward a pace and made the same head-inclining gesture they had seen earlier on the screen in *Jupiter Five*. Wary of anything that might unwittingly give offense, Storrel replied with a crisp, regulation UNSA salute. To the delight of the Earthmen, all five Ganymeans promptly copied him, though with a trace of uncertainty and an appalling lack of timing that would have brought tears to the eyes of a UNSA drill sergeant.

Slowly and haltingly, the Ganymean leader spoke. "I am Mel-thur. Good af-ter-noon."

That simple statement would go down among history's immortal moments. Later it became a standard joke, shared equally by Earthmen and Ganymeans alike. The voice was deep and gravelly, nothing like that of the interpreter who had spoken previously via the egg; in the latter case, the diction, and even the accent, had been flawless. Evidently this was not the interpreter; it made the fact that he had taken the trouble to offer an opening greeting in the native tongue of his guests an even nicer gesture.

Melthur went on to deliver a brief recitation in his own language while the visitors listened respectfully. Then it was Storrel's turn. All the way over from J5 he had been anticipating and dreading this moment, wishing that there was something in the UNSA training manuals to cover a situation like this. After all, weren't mission planners paid to exhibit a modicum of foresight? He straightened up and delivered the short speech that he had mentally prepared, hoping that the historians of years to come would be lenient in their judgment and appreciative of the circumstances.

"Fellow travelers and neighbors, greetings from the people of Planet Earth. We come in peace and in a spirit of friendship to all beings. May this meeting prove to be the beginning of a long and lasting coexistence between our races, and from it may there grow a mutual understanding and an accord that will benefit both our kinds. Henceforth let Ganymeans and Earthmen together continue to expand that common frontier of knowledge that has brought them both away from their worlds and into this universal realm that belongs to all worlds."

The Ganymeans in their turn showed respect by remaining motionless and silent for a few seconds after Storrel had finished. Then, the formalities over, the leader beckoned to them to follow and turned back toward the door through which he and his companions had appeared. Two of the other Ganymeans followed him to lead the party of Earthmen, and the remaining pair fell in behind.

They proceeded along a broad, white-walled corridor onto which many doors opened from both sides. Every place was brilliantly lit by a uniform diffuse glow that seemed to emanate from every part of the ceiling and from many of the panels that made up the walls. The floor was soft and yielding beneath their feet and made no sound. The air was cold.

Along the way, groups and small lines of Ganymeans had gathered to watch the procession. Most of them were as tall as those who had met the bus, but several were much smaller and looked more delicate in build and complexion; they appeared to be children at various stages of growth. The variations in clothing on the bystanders was even more pronounced than before, but everyone was wearing the same type of jeweled headband and wrist unit. Hunt began to suspect that these served more than purely decorative purposes. Many of the clothes showed signs of wear and general deterioration, contributing to the overall atmosphere of weariness and demoralization that he sensed on every side. The walls and doors bore scars that had been left by countless scrapings of passing objects; away from the walls the floors had been worn thin by feet that had passed to and fro for longer than he could imagine; and the sagging postures of some of the figures, several of them being supported by companions, told their own story.

The corridor was quite short and brought them to a second, slightly wider one that ran transversely; this second corridor curved away from them to left and right and seemed to be part of a continuous circular thoroughfare that encompassed the core of the vessel. Immediately in front of them, in the curving wall that formed the outer shell of the core, was a large open door. The Ganymeans ushered them through into the bare circular room beyond—it was about twenty feet in diameter—and the door slid silently shut. A vague whine of unseen machinery issued from an unidentifiable source and meaningless symbols flashed on and off on a panel set into the wall near the door. Hunt guessed after a few seconds that they were inside a large elevator that moved along a shaft contained within the ship's core. There had been no sensation of acceleration whatsoever—another example, perhaps, of the Ganymean mastery of gravitic engineering.

They emerged from the elevator and crossed another circular corridor to pass through what seemed to be a control or instrumentation room; on both sides of the central throughway the walls were lined with console stations, indicator panels and displays, and Ganymeans were seated at a number of the positions. The general lines of the room were cleaner and less cluttered than those aboard UNSA vessels. The instruments and equipment seemed to be integrated into the decor rather than added afterward. At least as much thought had been devoted to aesthetics as to function. The color scheme, a subtle balance of yellows, oranges and greens, formed a single, organic, curviform design that flowed from end to end of the room, making it as much an object for appreciative contemplation as an operation part of the *Shapieron*. By comparison the command center of *Jupiter Five* seemed stark and utilitarian.

The door at the far end brought them to their destination. It was a large trapezoidal room, presumably as a consequence of its position between the core of the ship and the outer hull, predominantly white and gray. The wall at the wide end was dominated by an enormous display screen, below which stood a row of crew stations and instrument facia, all encumbered by noticeably fewer switches and buttons than would be normal for equivalent equipment on *J5*. Some desklike working surfaces and a number of unidentifiable devices occupied the central area of the room and the narrow end was raised to form a dais that carried three large, unoccupied chairs, standing behind a long console and facing the main display screen. This was almost certainly the place from which the captain and his lieutenants supervised operation of the ship.

Four Ganymeans were waiting in the large open area before the dais. The Earthmen drew up facing them and the ritual exchange of short speeches was repeated. As soon as the formalities had been concluded the Ganymean spokesman, Garuth as he had identified himself, directed their attention to a collection of items arrayed along the top of one of the tables. For each of the Earthmen present there was a headband and wrist unit identical to those worn by all the Ganymeans, plus some smaller articles. One of the UNSA officers reached hesitantly toward them and then, reassured by gestures from the aliens that were obviously meant to convey encouragement, picked a headband to examine it more closely. One by one the others followed suit.

Hunt selected one and picked it up, only to find that it was practically weightless. What had seemed from a distance to be a jewel in the middle of the piece turned out in fact to be a flat, shiny disk of silvery metal about the size of a quarter, with a tiny dome of what appeared to be black glass mounted in the center. The band itself was far too short to encircle a Ganymean head and the metal showed signs of having been broken and crudely repaired—clearly the result of the device having been hastily modified to human proportions.

A huge, gray six-fingered hand with broad nails as well as flexible horn pads on the knuckles moved into Hunt's field of vision and gently took hold of the headband. He looked up and found himself staring into the eyes of one of the alien giants, who was now standing right beside him. The eyes were dark blue and contained enormous, circular pupils; Hunt could have sworn that they were twinkling with good-natured laughter. Before he had time to collect his reeling thoughts, the headband had been secured snugly in place. The Ganymean then picked up one of the smaller items, a rubbery disk attached to a padded clip, and attached it with a simple movement to the lobe of Hunt's right ear; it fitted quite comfortably in such a way that the disk rested lightly against the bony protrusion above the side of his neck. A similar device was fastened to the neck of his shirt collar, just visible inside the rim of the helmet-seating of his space suit, the gadget's disk in contact with his throat. Hunt realized that the aliens were mingling freely and that all his colleagues were being assisted in a similar manner. Before he could observe any more, his own giant held up the last item, the wrist unit, and demonstrated the ingenious adjustment method of the bracelet a few times before securing it on Hunt's suit forearm. The face of the unit was taken up almost entirely by what had to be a miniature display screen, although nothing was visible on it at that moment. The giant pointed to one of the tiny buttons set in a row beneath the screen and made a series of head movements and facial expressions that didn't mean very much. Then he turned away to an unattended Earthman who was having trouble fitting his earpiece into place.

Hunt looked around him. The unoccupied Ganymeans gathered round the room to witness these proceedings seemed to be waiting patiently for something to happen. Above them, framed in panorama on the main viewing screen, was the image of *Jupiter Five*, still riding five miles off. The sudden sight of something familiar and reassuring among all these strange surroundings at once swept away the dreamlike paralysis that had slowly been creeping over him. He looked down at the wrist unit again, shrugged, and touched the button that the giant had indicated.

"I am ZORAC. Good afternoon."

Hunt looked up again and turned to see who had spoken, but nobody was even looking at him. A puzzled frown formed on his face.

"You are who?" He heard the same voice again. Hunt looked from side to side and behind him again, completely bewildered. He noticed that one or two of the other Earthmen were acting in the same strange manner, and that a couple of them had started to mumble, apparently to themselves. And then he realized that the voice was coming from the earpiece he was wearing. It was the voice of the Ganymean interpreter that he had first heard on *J5*. In the same split second it dawned on him that the throat-piece was a microphone. Feeling, for a moment, slightly self-conscious at the thought of appearing as ridiculous as his colleagues, he replied, "Hunt."

"Earthmen talk to me. I talk to Ganymeans. I translate."

Hunt was taken completely by surprise. He had not expected to have to play so active a role in whatever developed, having seen himself more as an observer; now he was being invited to participate directly in the dialogue. For a moment he was nonplussed because no intelligent continuation suggested itself.

Then, not wishing to give an impression of rudeness, he asked: "Where are you?"

"Different parts in different places in the *Shapieron*. I am not a Ganymean. I am a machine. I believe the Earth word is *computer* . . ." A short pause followed, then: "Yes. I was correct. I am a computer."

"How did you manage to check that out so fast?" Hunt queried.

"I am sorry. I do not understand that question yet. Can you say it more simply please?"

Hunt thought for a second.

"You did not understand the word computer the first time. You did understand it the second time. How did you know?"

"I asked the Earthman who is talking to me in the egg inside *Jupiter Five*."

Hunt marveled as he realized that ZORAC was no mere computer, but a supercomputer. It was capable of conducting and learning from independent and simultaneous conversations. That went a long way toward explaining the phenomenal progress it was making in its comprehension of English and accounted for its ability to memorize every detail of information without need for repetition. Hunt had seen some of Earth's most advanced language-translation machines in action on several occasions; compared to them ZORAC was staggering.

For the next few minutes the Ganymeans remained silent spectators while the Earthmen familiarized themselves with ZORAC and with the facilities that they now enjoyed for communicating both with it and through it. The headbands were miniature TV cameras through which the scene perceived by a wearer could be transmitted directly into the machine. The view from any headband could be presented on any wrist screen, as could any other item of information capable of graphic representation and available from the ship's computer complex. ZORAC—a collective name for this complex—provided not only a versatile mechanism enabling individuals to access and interact with the ship's many facilities, but also an extremely sophisticated means for individuals to communicate among themselves. And all this was merely a sideline; ZORAC's prime function was that of supervising and controlling just about everything in the *Shapieron*. That was why the instrument panels and consoles were so simple and straightforward in general appearance; most operations were carried out by means of vocal commands to ZORAC.

Once ZORAC had introduced itself to all the newcomers, the serious business of the day resumed once more with Storrel conducting a more productive dialogue with Garuth, the Ganymean mission commander. From the discussion it appeared that the *Shapieron* had indeed come from another star system to which it had gone long before for the purpose of conducting a scientific mission of some complexity. A catastrophe had befallen the expedition and forced them to depart in haste, without time to prepare for a long voyage; the situation was exacerbated by technical problems relating to the ship itself, though their precise nature remained obscure. The voyage had been long and was beset with difficulties, resulting in the predicament that the giants now found themselves facing, and which had already been described to the Earthmen. Garuth concluded by stressing again the poor physical and mental condition of his people, and their need to find somewhere to land their ship in order to recuperate and appraise their situation.

Throughout the proceedings, a running commentary on both sides of the conversation was radioed back to the crew remaining on the bus, whose Ganymean relay gave Shannon and the others on the bridge of the *J5* a minute-by-minute report of what was happening.

Even before Garuth had finished speaking, Shannon had contacted Ganymede Main Base and instructed the commander there to begin preparations to receive a shipload of unexpected and very weary guests.

chapter seven

"One of the other Earthmen has just instructed me to get lost and switched his unit off," ZORAC said. "I could only do that by taking the *Shapieron* away into space and I'm certain that he didn't intend that. What did he mean?"

Hunt grinned to himself as he allowed his head to sink back into the pillow while he contemplated the ceiling. He had been back on board *Jupiter Five* for several hours and was relaxing in his cabin after a strenuous day while experimenting further with his Ganymean communications kit.

"It's an Earth saying," he replied. "It doesn't mean what the words mean literally. It's what people sometimes say when they're not interested in listening to somebody. Probably he was tired and needed to sleep. But don't you say it when you talk to Earthmen. It conveys irritation and is a little insulting."

"I see. Okay. Is there a word or phrase for a saying that doesn't mean what it says literally?"

Hunt sighed and rubbed the bridge of his nose wearily. Suddenly he had nothing but admiration for the patience of schoolteachers.

"I suppose we'd call it a figure of speech," he said.

"But surely speech is formed from words, not figures, or have I made a mistake somewhere?"

"No, you're right. That's just another saying."

"A figure of speech is a figure of speech then. Right?"

"Yes. ZORAC, I'm getting tired too. Could you save any more questions about English until I'm ready for it again. There are some questions I'd still like to ask you."

"Otherwise you'll instruct me to get lost and switch off?"

"Correct."

"Okay. What are your questions?"

Hunt hoisted his shoulders up against the end of his bunk and clasped his hands behind his head. After a moment's reflection, he was ready. "I'm interested in the star that your ship came from. You said that it had a system of several planets."

"Yes."

"Your ship came from one of those planets?"

"Yes."

"Did all the Ganymean people move from Minerva and go live on that planet a long time ago?"

"No. Only three large ships went and their carried-ships. Also there were three very large machines that propelled themselves like spaceships. The Ganymeans went there to test a scientific idea. They did not go there to live. All came back in the *Shapieron* but many have died."

"When you went to the star, where did you travel from?"

"From Minerva."

"Where were the rest of the Ganymean people—the ones who didn't go with you to the star?"

"They remained on Minerva, naturally. The work to be done at the star needed only a small number of scientific people."

Hunt's incredulity could no longer be contained. The thing that he had been beginning to suspect for some time was really true.

"How long ago was it when you left the star?" he asked, his voice catching slightly as he formed the words.

"Approximately twenty-five million Earth years ago," ZORAC informed him.

For a long time Hunt said nothing. He just lay there, his mind struggling to comprehend the enormity of what he had learned. Just a few hours before he had been standing face to face with beings who had been alive long before the species called *Homo sapiens* had ever begun to emerge. And they were still alive now, and had been through the unimaginable epochs between. The very thought of it was stupefying.

He did not imagine for one moment that this could represent anything like a normal Ganymean life span and he guessed it to be the result of relativistic time-dilation. But to produce an effect of such magnitude they must have sustained a phenomenal velocity for an incredible length of time. What could possibly have induced the Ganymeans to journey the vast distance that this implied? And, equally strange, why should they willingly inflict upon themselves what they must have known would be a permanent forfeiture of their world, their way of life and all the things that were familiar to them? What significance could their expedition have had, since nothing they could have achieved at their destination could possibly have affected their civilization in any way whatsoever—not with that discrepancy in time scales? But hadn't Garuth said something about everything not having gone according to plan?

Having sorted his thoughts into something resembling order once more, Hunt had another question. "How far from the sun was this star?"

"The distance that light would travel in nine point three Earth years," ZORAC answered.

The situation was getting crazy. Allowing for the speed that would have been necessary to produce the time-dilation, such a journey should have taken hardly any time at all . . . astronomically speaking.

"Did the Ganymeans know that they would return after twenty-five million years?" Hunt asked, determined to get to the bottom of it.

"When they left the star, they knew. But when they left Minerva to go to the star, they did not know. They did not have a reason to believe that the journey from the star would be longer than the journey to the star."

"How long did it take them to get there?"

"Measured from the sun, twelve point one years."

"And the journey back again took twenty-five million?"

"Yes. They could not avoid traveling very fast. I believe that the results of this are familiar to you. They orbited the sun far away many times."

Hunt replied with the obvious question. "Why didn't they just slow down?"

"They could not."

"Why?"

ZORAC seemed to hesitate for a fraction of a second.

"The electrical machines could not be operated. The points that destroy all things and move in circles could not be stopped. The space-and-time-joining blendings could not be unbent."

"I don't understand that," Hunt said, frowning.

"I can't be more clear without asking more questions about English," ZORAC warned him.

"Leave it for now." Hunt remembered the stir caused by speculations about the propulsion system of the Ganymean ship beneath Pithead, which dated from about the same period as the *Shapieron*. Although the UNSA scientists and engineers could not be certain, many of them suspected that motion had been produced not by reactive thrust, but by an artificially induced zone of localized space-time distortion into which the vessel "fell" continuously. Hunt felt that such a principle could allow the kind of sustained acceleration needed for the *Shapieron* to attain the speeds implied by ZORAC's account. No doubt other scientists were putting similar questions to ZORAC; he would discuss the matter with them tomorrow, he decided, and not press the matter further for the time being.

"Do you remember that time?" he asked casually. "Twenty-five million years ago, when your ship left Minerva?"

"Twenty-five million years by Earth time," ZORAC pointed out. "It has been less than twenty years by *Shapieron* time. Yes. I remember all things."

"What kind of world did you leave?"

"I don't fully understand. What kind of *kind* do you mean?"

"Well, for example, what was the place on Minerva like that you departed from? Was the land flat? Was there water? Were there structures that the Ganymean people had built? Can you describe a picture of it?"

"I can show a picture," ZORAC offered. "Please observe the screen."

Intrigued, Hunt reached out to pick up the wrist unit from where he had placed it on the top of the bedside locker. As he turned it over in his hand the screen came to life with a scene that immediately drew an involuntary whistle of amazement from his lips. He was looking down on the *Shapieron*, or at least on a vessel that was indistinguishable from it, but this was not the scarred and pitted hulk that he had seen from the bus a few hours before; it was a clean, gleaming, majestic tower of flawless mirror-silver, standing proudly on its tail in a vast open space that was occupied by strange constructions—buildings, cylinders, tubular structures, domes, masts and curves, all interconnected and fused into a single, contiguous synthetic landscape. Two other ships were standing there on either side of the first, both just as grand, but somewhat smaller.

The air above the spaceport—for that was what the picture suggested—was alive with all manner of flying vehicles ranging from the very large to the very small, the majority of which moved in well-defined lanes like processions of disciplined skywalking ants.

Behind it all, soaring up for what must have been miles to

dominate the skyline, was the city. It was nothing like any city that Hunt had ever seen, but there was nothing else that it could have been. Tier upon tier, level after level, the skyscrapers, terraces, sweeping ramps, and flying bridges clung together in a fantastic composite pattern that seemed to leap into the sky in a series of joyous bounds that defied gravity. The whole construction might have been sculpted by some infinitely skillful cosmic artist from a single monolith of gleaming marble, and yet there were parts of it that seemed to float detached like ivory islands in the sky. Only a knowledge that transcended Man's could have conceived such a feat; it had to be yet another instance of a Ganymean science that remained to be stumbled upon by the scientists of Earth.

"That is the *Shapieron* as it was before it left Minerva," ZORAC informed him. "The other two ships that traveled with it are there too. The place behind was called *Gromos*. I don't know what the word is for a place constructed for many Ganymeans to live in."

"A city," Hunt supplied, at the same time feeling an acute inadequacy in the description. "Were the Ganymeans fond of their city?"

"Sorry?"

"Did they like their city? Did they wish very much to be home again?"

"Very much. The Ganymeans were fond of all things on Minerva. They were fond of their home." ZORAC seemed to possess a well-developed ability to sense when further information was needed. "When they left the star, they knew then that their journey home would take a long time. They did not expect all things to be not changed. But they did not expect to find that their home did no longer exist. They are very sad." Hunt had already seen enough to know this. Before he could ask another question, ZORAC spoke up. "Is it okay if I ask questions that are not about English?"

"Yes, all right," Hunt answered. "What do you want to know?"

"The Ganymeans are very unhappy. They believe that the Earthmen destroyed Minerva. Is this true, and if it is, why did they destroy it?"

"No!" Hunt reacted instinctively, with a start. "No. That's not true. Minerva was destroyed fifty thousand years ago. There were no men on Earth then. We came later."

"Did the Lunarians destroy Minerva then?" ZORAC asked. Evidently it had broached this same subject with others on *Jupiter Five* already.

"Yes. How much do you know about them?"

"Twenty-five million years ago, the Ganymeans took kinds of Earth life from Earth to Minerva. In a short time afterward, the Ganymeans and all kinds of life that were of Minerva and lived on land died. The life kinds from Earth did not die. The Lunarians grew from them and looked like Earthmen now. Other scientific people on *Jupiter Five* have told me this. This is all I know."

This told Hunt something that he hadn't realized before and hadn't really thought about. Prior to the last few hours, it seemed, ZORAC had been completely ignorant of the Ganymeans having imported large numbers of terrestrial animal species to their own planet. Just to be sure, he had one other question. "The Ganymeans had not brought any Earth life to Minerva before you left to go to the star?"

"No."

"Do you know if they intended to?"

"If they did, I was never told."

"Do you know of any reason why they should wish to?"

"No."

"So whatever the problem was, it must have cropped up later."

"Sorry?"

"The reason must have happened after you left Minerva."

"I think the phrase is 'I suppose so.' I can compute no alternative."

Hunt realized with growing excitement that the mystery of what had happened to the Ganymean civilization was one that posed a challenge to both races. Surely, he told himself, their combined knowledge would prove capable of producing the answers. He decided it was time to complete the story of the Lunarians for ZORAC's benefit—the story that had uncovered the most astounding revelations of recent years, even, perhaps, of all time. This story involved a change in our understanding of the structure of the Solar System and required a complete rewriting of the very origins of Mankind.

"Yes, you are right," Hunt said, after a while. "The Lunarians grew—we would say 'evolved'—from the forms of Earth life that were left on Minerva after the Ganymeans and other

Minervan kinds died out. It took twenty-five million years for them to evolve. By fifty thousand years ago, they had become an advanced race; they built spaceships, machines and cities. Has anybody told you what happened after that?"

"No. But I was intending to ask."

"Is is true that Minerva possessed a moon?"

"A satellite that orbited the planet?"

"Correct."

"Yes."

Hunt nodded to himself in satisfaction. It was as he and the other scientists of Earth had deduced from their investigations of the Lunarian finds.

"And tell me," he asked as a check. "Did Earth possess a moon . . . twenty-five million years ago?"

"No. Earth had no satellite then." Hunt could have been mistaken, but he was sure that ZORAC was learning to convey emotional colorations by the infection of its voice. He could have sworn that there was surprise in that response.

"Today, Earth has a moon," he said. "It has had a moon for approximately fifty thousand years."

"Since the time when the Lunarians became an advanced race."

"Exactly."

"I see. A connection is clearly implied. Please explain."

"When the Lunarians destroyed Minerva, the planet exploded . . . broke into pieces. The largest piece now orbits the sun as its most distant planet, Pluto. The other pieces, or most of them, still orbit the sun between Mars and Jupiter. I assume you know this, since the Ganymeans were surprised when they found that the Solar System had changed."

"Yes, I know about Pluto and the asteroids," ZORAC confirmed. "I knew that the Solar System had changed and that Minerva was not present. But I did not know about the process by which it had changed."

"Minerva's moon fell toward the Sun. Lunarians were still alive on the moon. It came near to Earth and was captured. It became Earth's moon, and still is now."

"The Lunarians who were alive must have traveled to Earth," ZORAC interrupted. "During the time that followed, they increased their numbers. Earthmen have evolved from Lunarians. That is why they look the same. I can compute no alternative. Am I right?"

"Yes, you're right, ZORAC." Hunt shook his head in admiration. With hardly any data at all to go by, the machine had unerringly arrived at the same conclusion that had taken the scientists of Earth more than two years to piece together, after some of the most vigorous argument and dissent for many decades. "At least, we believe that that is right. We cannot prove it conclusively."

"Sorry. Conclusively?"

"Finally . . . for certain."

"I see. I reason that the Lunarians must have traveled to Earth in spaceships. They must have taken machines and other things. I suggest that Earthmen should look for these things on the surface of the Earth. This would prove what you believe is true. My conclusion is that you haven't tried, or alternatively you have tried but have not succeeded."

Hunt was flabbergasted. Had ZORAC been around two years earlier the whole puzzle would have been solved in a week.

"Have you been talking to an Earthman called Danchekker?" he asked.

"No. I have not met the name. Why?"

"He is a scientist and reasons the same things as you. We have not yet found any traces of things that the Lunarians might have brought with them. Danchekker predicts that such things will be found one day."

"Did the Earthmen not know where they had come from?" ZORAC inquired.

"Not until very recently. Before that it was believed that they evolved only on Earth."

"The life kinds that they evolved from on Minerva had been taken from Earth by the Ganymeans. The same life kinds were left to live on Earth also.

"The Lunarians who did not die and went to Earth were an advanced race. The Earthmen of now did not know of them until recently. Therefore they had forgotten where they came from. I reason that there must have been very few Lunarians who did not die. They became unadvanced and forgot their knowledge. After fifty thousand years they became advanced again, but they had forgotten the Lunarians. As they found new knowledge, they would see remains of life kinds from many years ago everywhere on Earth. They would see the sameness as their own life kind. They would reason that they evolved on Earth. Recently Earthmen have discovered Lunarians and

Ganymeans. Now they have deduced the true events. Otherwise they would not be able to explain why Lunarians looked the same as them."

ZORAC had the whole thing figured out. Admittedly the machine had been able to start out with a number of key items of information that had taken Hunt and his colleagues a long time to uncover, but nevertheless it was a staggering piece of logical analysis.

Hunt was still marveling at the achievement when ZORAC spoke again. "I still do not know *why* the Lunarians destroyed Minerva."

"They didn't intend to," Hunt explained. "There was a war on Minerva. We believe the planet's crust was thin and unstable. The weapons used were very powerful. The planet exploded in the process."

"Sorry. War? Crust? Weapon? Don't follow."

"Oh God . . ." Hunt groaned. He paused to select and light a cigarette from a pack lying on the locker. "The outside of a planet is cold and hard—near the surface. That's its crust."

"Like a skin?"

"Yes, but brittle . . . it breaks into pieces easily."

"Okay."

"When many people fight in large groups, that's war."

"Fight?"

"Oh hell . . . violent action between one group of people and another group. When they organize themselves to kill."

"Kill what?"

"The other group of people."

ZORAC gave one distinct impression of confusion. For a second the machine seemed to be having difficulty in believing its microphone.

"Lunarians organized themselves to kill other Lunarians," it said, slowly and carefully as if anxious not to be misunderstood. "They did this deliberately?" The turn of conversation had caught Hunt somewhat unprepared. He began to feel uneasy and even a little embarrassed, like a child being insistently cross-examined over some transgression that it would sooner forget.

"Yes," was all he could manage.

"Why did they wish to do such a thing?" The emotional inflection was there again, now registering undisguised incredulity.

"They fought because ... because ..." Hunt wrestled for something to say. The machine, it seemed, had no comprehension whatsoever of such matters. What way was there to summarize the passions and complexities of millenia of history in a few sentences? "To protect themselves ... to defend their own group from other groups ..."

"From other groups who were organized to kill them?"

"Well, the matter is very complicated ... but yes, you could say that."

"Then logically the same question still applies—why did the other groups wish to do such things?"

"When one group made another group angry about something ... or when two groups both wanted the same thing, or when one group wanted another group's land, maybe ... sometimes they would fight to decide." What he was saying didn't seem an adequate explanation, Hunt admitted to himself, but it was the best he could do. A short silence ensued; even ZORAC, it seemed, had to think hard about this one.

"Did all the Lunarians have brain problems?" it asked at last, having evidently deduced what it considered the most probable common factor.

"They were naturally a very violent race, we believe," Hunt replied. "But at the time they lived, they faced the prospect of extinction—all dying out. Minerva was freezing all over fifty thousand years ago. They wanted to go to a warmer planet to live. We think they wanted to go to Earth. But there were many Lunarians, few resources, and little time. The situation made them afraid and angry ... and they fought."

"They killed each other to prevent them from dying? They destroyed Minerva to protect it from freezing?"

"They didn't intend to do such a thing," Hunt said again.

"What did they intend?"

"I suppose they intended that the group that was left after the war would go to Earth."

"Why couldn't all groups go? The war must have needed resources that would have been used better for other things. All Lunarians could have used their knowledge. They wanted to live but did everything to make certain that they would not. They had brain problems." The tone of ZORAC's final pronouncement was definite.

"All this was not something they had planned deliberately.

They were driven by emotions. When men feel strong emotions, they do not always do the most logical things."

"Men ... Earthmen ...? Earthmen feel strong emotions too, that make them fight like the Lunarians did?"

"Sometimes."

"And Earthmen make wars too?"

"There have been many wars on Earth, but there have been none for a long time."

"Do the Earthmen wish to kill the Ganymeans?"

"*No!* No ... of course not. There is no reason ..." Hunt protested violently.

"There can never be a reason," ZORAC stated. "The Lunarians had no reason. The things that you said are not reasons since they do the opposite to what is wanted—so they are not reasonable. The Earthmen must have evolved brain problems from the Lunarians. Very sick."

Danchekker had theorized that the extraordinary aggressiveness and powers of determination exhibited by Man, compared to other terrestrial species, had originated as a mutation among the anthropoids left on Minerva after the decline of the Ganymeans. It had accounted for the startling rapidity of the emergence and development of the Lunarian civilization, which had attained spaceflight while the most advanced species on Earth were represented only by primitive stone-working cultures. As ZORAC had surmised, this formidable Lunarian trait had indeed been passed on to their terrestrial descendants (although becoming somewhat diluted in the process), and had in turn constituted the most potent factor in the subsequent emergence and rise of the human race. Could that trait after all turn out to be the unique aberration that Danchekker had sometimes speculated?

"Were there never wars on Minerva?" Hunt asked. "Even in the early history of the Ganymean people, did groups never fight?"

"No. There can be no reason. Such ideas would never occur."

"Individuals—did they never fight? Were they never violent?"

"Sometimes a Ganymean would try to harm another Ganymean, but only if he was very sick. Brain problems did occur. Very sad. On most occasions the doctors could fix the problems. Sometimes one with problems would have to be kept away from other Ganymeans and helped. But very few were like that."

Mercifully, ZORAC did not seem disposed to pass moral judgments, but all the same Hunt was beginning to feel distinctly uncomfortable, like a Papuan headhunter facing a missionary.

ZORAC quickly made the situation worse. "If all Lunarians were sick and the doctors were sick too, anything could happen. It then becomes computable that they blew the planet up. If Earthmen are all sick and can make machines and come to Ganymede, they can make a war and blow up planets too. I must warn Garuth of the possibility. He might not want to stick around. Other places would be safer than a Solar System full of sick Earthmen."

"There will be no war," Hunt told ZORAC firmly. "Those things happened a long time ago. Earthmen are different now. We do not fight today. The Ganymeans are safe here—they are our friends."

"I see." The machine sounded unconvinced. "To compute the probability of the truth of that, I must know more about the Earthmen and how they have evolved. Can I ask more questions?"

"Ask them some other time," Hunt said, suddenly feeling weary of it all. He had much to think about and discuss with others before taking the conversation any further. "I think we've talked enough for now. I need some sleep."

"I must get lost then?"

"Yes, I'm afraid so, ZORAC old pal. I'll talk to you tomorrow."

"Very well. In that case, good afternoon."

"You got that wrong. I'm going to bed. It's night now."

"I know. It was a joke."

"Good afternoon," Hunt smiled as he pressed a button on the wrist unit to break the connection. A computer with a sense of humor; now he had seen everything. He carefully arranged the various items that made up the communications kit on top of his locker and settled back to finish his cigarette while he reflected on the astonishing conversation. How ludicrous and tragically comical all their fears and precautions seemed now. The Ganymeans not only had no word for war, they had not the faintest concept of it. He was beginning to feel like something that had lived its whole grubby life beneath a stone that had just been turned over.

He was just about to switch off the light when the chime on the bedside wall panel sounded. Absently he reached out and flipped a switch to accept the call. It was an announcement via the audio channel.

"This is Director Shannon speaking. I just thought you'd all like to know that a message was received from Earth at 2340 hours local. After an all-night emergency meeting at UN Headquarters, the decision to allow the *Shapieron* to land at Ganymede Main Base has been endorsed. The Ganymeans have been informed and preparations are going ahead. That's all. Thank you."

chapter eight

And so, the incredible voyage of twenty-five million years came at last to an end.

Hunt was among the observers in the spacious transparent dome of the Operations Control Tower at Ganymede Main who watched in silence as the huge shape of the *Shapieron* slid slowly down toward the space prepared for it just beyond the edge of the base. It came to rest standing upright on the tips of the four sharply swept fins that formed its tail assembly, with the stern end of the main body of the ship still one hundred feet or more above the ice, dwarfing the platoon of Vegas that stood on one side like a welcoming guard of honor.

The small fleet of vehicles that had been waiting just outside the area at once began crawling forward; the leading three stopped just in front of the nearest supporting fin and disgorged figures clad in standard-issue UNSA space suits, while the rest formed up into waiting lines on either side. The figures assembled into straight ranks facing the ship; three stood a short distance ahead of the rest—Commander Lawrence Foster, in charge of Main, his deputy, and one of the several senior officers from *Jupiter Five* who had come down to observe. The diminutive sun was very low in the sky, accentuating the bleakness of the Ganymedean landscape and painting sinister streaks of bottomless shadow across the frozen crags and the shattered cliffs of ice that had survived unchanging from meteorite impacts as old as time itself.

Then, as they watched, the stern section of the *Shapieron* detached itself from the main hull of the vessel and began to move vertically downward. After a few seconds they could see that it was still connected by three steadily lengthening bright silver tubes, the tubes clustered tightly around the central axis of the ship. The stern section touched the ice, and stopped; a number of doors slid open all around it and short access ramps extended downward to connect them to the surface. Watching from the dome, Hunt remembered the elevator shaft through which he and his companions had been conveyed after leaving the bus when they had visited the *Shapieron*. If his estimations were accurate, the shaft had been about as far in from the outer hull of the ship as were the three tubes that were visible now. Presumably then, the shaft extended on inside one of the tubes and each of the tubes was an extension of an identical shaft. That meant that traffic up and down the length of the ship traveled via a three-elevator system that could be extended to ground level when required; the whole tail end of the structure moved down as well to afford a "lobby." Very neat. But his further study of the vessel was interrupted as a stir spread through the dome. The Ganymeans were coming out.

Looking more gigantic than ever in their suits, a party of aliens descended one of the ramps slowly and approached the waiting Earthmen, who immediately snapped into saluting posture. In the next few minutes an exchange of formalities similar to that which Hunt had already witnessed was reenacted. The loudspeaker inside the dome broadcast Foster's welcome to the Ganymeans on behalf of all the governments of Earth and reiterated a desire for friendship between all races for all time. He made reference to the plight of the voyagers and indicated that, though sparse, whatever resources and assistance the Earthmen could offer was theirs.

Garuth, who had elected to lead his people personally from the ship, replied through ZORAC, a channel from which had been linked into the dome's communications circuits. He echoed Foster's sentiments dutifully, though in a way that sounded somehow mechanical and artificial, as if he could not fully comprehend why such sentiments need be voiced. Garuth gave the impression of doing his best to comply with an unfamiliar ritual that served no obvious purpose. Nevertheless his audience appreciated the gesture. He went on to express the gratitude of his people that fate, while taking their brothers from them, had left them new brothers to take their place when they came home. The two races, he concluded, had much to learn from each other.

Then the waiting vehicles moved toward the ramps to transport the Ganymeans to the quarters that had been made ready for them. The vehicles could not manage more than a few Ganymeans at one time, even stripped of seats and removable fittings, so they concentrated primarily on moving the sick and enfeebled, of whom there were many. The rest, guided by the space-suited pygmy figures now dotting the scene, began a slow trek on foot toward the buildings waiting for them. Before long a broken procession of huddled groups and stragglers stretched across the ice from the ship to the base proper. Above it all, in the harshness of seminight, the stars stared down in stony-eyed indifference.

The dome had become very quiet. Grim faces looked out over the scene, each one an impenetrable mask preserving the privacy of thoughts that were not for sharing. No video record would ever recapture the feelings of this moment, whatever it might show, however many times it might be seen.

· After a while, a sergeant who was standing next to Hunt turned his head a fraction. "Man, I don't know," he muttered quietly. "What a hell of a way to come home."

"What a hell of a home to come home to," Hunt replied.

The accommodations available at Main were not sufficient to hold all the Ganymeans, who numbered more than four hundred, so the majority were obliged to remain in the *Shapieron*. Nevertheless, just being on a firm surface again, even if it was only the frozen ball of rubble called Ganymede, and among other beings seemed to provide the aliens with a badly needed psychological tonic. Earthmen showed them the facilities and amenities that were available in their new quarters, pointed out the stocks of supplies and food-stuffs provided for experimentation, and the various other items which, it was hoped, would help to make life reasonably comfortable. Meanwhile other UNSA crews delivered similar loads, hurriedly ferried from one of the orbiting freighters, to the Ganymeans still inside their ship. Then the new arrivals were left in peace and to their own devices.

After a much-needed rest, they announced that they were ready to resume their dialogue with their hosts. Accordingly, an evening conference was arranged between the leaders and certain other individuals of the two races, to be held in the officers' mess and to be followed by a formal welcoming dinner. Hunt was among those invited to attend; so was Danchekker.

chapter nine

The temperature had originally been lowered to make the Ganymeans feel more at home, but by the time everybody had been crammed into the officers' mess for an hour or more and palls of tobacco smoke were hanging sullenly beneath the lights, it turned out to be just as well for all. Danchekker finished what he had been saying into the microphone of the headset that he was wearing over his sweater then resumed his seat. Garuth replied from the far end of the room, where the Ganymean contingent was concentrated.

"I think I'd better let a scientist answer a scientist on that one, Professor." He looked down and behind him at one of the other Ganymeans. "Shilohin, will you respond?" All the Earthmen present who did not possess Ganymean kits had been equipped with headsets similar to Danchekker's and could thus follow ZORAC's translation of the proceedings. The machine's ability in this respect was now quiet passable although, mainly as a result of having conversed with many and varied individuals, it had not yet fully established a way to disentangle formal English constructions from American colloquialisms, a defect that sometimes yielded hilarious results.

Shilohin, the chief scientist of the Ganymean expedition, had already been introduced to the company. As Garuth sat down to make room, she rose to her feet and spoke. "First, I must congratulate the scientists of Earth for their superb piece of figuring out. Yes, as Professor Danchekker has just suggested, we Ganymeans do not enjoy a high tolerance to carbon dioxide. He and his colleagues were also absolutely correct in the picture that they had deduced of conditions on Minerva at the time of our departure—a planet that they had not even seen."

Shilohin paused a moment, waiting for that much to sink in. Then she continued. "The average concentration of radioactive, heat-producing substances in Minervan rocks was somewhat higher than is found on Earth. The interior of Minerva was thus hotter and molten to a greater degree, and the crust was thinner. The planet was therefore more active volcanically than Earth, a tendency that was further complicated by the strong tidal forces induced in the crust by Luna, which orbited closer to Minerva than it does to Earth today. This high level of volcanic activity released large quantities of carbon dioxide and water vapor into the atmosphere, resulting in a greenhouse effect that sustained a high enough surface temperature for the oceans to remain liquid and life to emerge. By terrestrial standards it was still sure-as-hell cold, but not nearly as cold as it would have been otherwise.

"This situation had always existed throughout the history of Minerva. By the time that our civilization was at its peak, however, a new epoch of tectonic activity was just beginning. The level of carbon dioxide in the atmosphere began showing a measurable increase. It soon became clear that it would only be a matter of time before the level grew beyond the point we could tolerate. After that our world would become, for us, uninhabitable. What could we do?" Shilohin let the question hang and cast her eyes around the room, apparently inviting the Earthmen to start a discussion.

After a few seconds a UNSA engineer at the back responded. "Well, we've seen some pretty remarkable examples of the kind of technology that you people had. I wouldn't have thought you'd have found it much of a problem to figure out some way of simply winding the level back down again . . . some kinda planetwide climatic control, I guess . . . sump'n like that."

"Commendably on the ball," she said, with something that they took to be the equivalent of an approving nod. "We did in fact employ planetary climatic control to some degree, primarily to limit the extent of the Minervan ice caps. But when it came to tinkering with the chemical composition of the atmosphere, we were less certain of our ability to keep everything sufficiently under control; the balance was very delicate." She looked directly at the questioner. "A scheme along the lines you suggest was in fact proposed, but mathematical models indicated that there was too high a risk of destroying the greenhouse effect completely, and so of guaranteeing the end of life on Minerva even more quickly. We are a cautious people and do not take risks readily. Our government threw the idea out."

She remained silent and allowed them time to think of other possibilities. Danchekker didn't bother to raise the notion that they might have tried importing terrestrial plant life as an attempt at introducing a compensatory mechanism. He already knew full well that the Ganymeans knew nothing of such a venture. Presumably that solution had been tried after Garuth's expedition had departed. Further analyses by his scientists and discussions with ZORAC had indicated if that had been the objective of the exercise, it would not have succeeded anyway—a point that would surely not have escaped the Ganymean scientists at the time. For the moment this event was still as much a mystery as ever.

Eventually Shilohin spread her arm wide as if appealing to a class of children who were being a little slow that day. "Logically it's very simple," she said. "If we left the carbon-dioxide level to rise, we would die. Therefore we could not allow it to rise. If we prevented the rise, as we could have done, there would have been too much of a risk of freezing the whole planet solid because the carbon dioxide kept Minerva warm through the greenhouse effect. We needed the results of the greenhouse effect to keep us warm because we were a long way from the Sun. Hence, we wouldn't need it at all if we were nearer the Sun, or if the Sun were warmer."

Some of the faces in front of her remained blank; some suddenly looked incredulous. "It's easy then," a voice called from near Hunt. "All you had to do was move Minerva in a bit or heat up the sun." He meant that as a joke but the Ganymean began nodding her head in imitation of the human mannerism.

"Exactly," she said. "And those were the two conclusions we arrived at too." A few gasps of amazement came from various parts of the room. "Both possibilities were studied extensively. Eventually a team of astrophysicists convinced the government that warming up the sun was the more practicable.

Nobody could find a flaw in the calculations, but, as always, our government was cautious and elected not to blow a wad on fooling around with the sun. They wanted to see some proof first that the plan would work . . . Yes, Dr. Hunt?" She had noticed his hand half raised to attract attention.

"Could you give us a few details on how they proposed to do such a thing?" he asked. "I think even the idea of contemplating something like that has astonished a few of us here." Mutters of agreement from all around echoed his sentiments.

"Certainly," she replied. "The Ganymeans, as most of you know by now, had developed a branch of technology that is not yet understood in your own world—a technology based on the principles of artificially generating and controlling the effect termed 'gravity.' The proposal of the Ganymean astrophysicists involved placing three very large and very powerful projectors in orbit around the sun, which would concentrate beams of space-time distortion—'gravity intensification' if you like, although that describes the effect of the process rather than its nature—at the Sun's center. Theory predicted that this would induce an increase, effectively, in the Sun's self-gravitation and produce a slight collapse of the star, which would cease when the radiation pressure again balanced the gravitational pressure. At the new equilibrium the Sun would radiate more strongly and, provided that all the right quantities were chosen, would just compensate for the loss of Minerva's greenhouse effect. In other words we could now risk tampering with the carbon-dioxide level since, if we blew it and we started to freeze, we could put things right again by adjusting the solar constant. Does that answer the question sufficiently, Dr. Hunt?"

"Yes . . . very much so. Thank you." There were a thousand other questions that he could have asked at that moment, but he decided to leave them all for ZORAC later; for the time being he was having enough trouble even trying to visualize engineering on such a scale, yet Shilohin made the whole thing sound as routine as putting up an apartment block.

"As I said a moment ago," Shilohin resumed, "our government insisted on testing the theory first. Our expedition was formed for that purpose—to carry out a full-scale trial experiment on a Sunlike star elsewhere." She paused and made a gesture that was not familiar. "As it turned out, I guess they did the right thing. The star became unstable and went nova.

We barely escaped with our lives. Garuth has just told you of the problem with the *Shapieron*'s propulsive system that resulted in the situation we have now—although we have aged less than twenty years since leaving Iscaris, on your time scale this all happened twenty-five million years ago. So here we are."

A chorus of mutterings broke out around the room. Shilohin waited for a few moments before continuing. "It's a bit cramped in here and difficult to change places. Does anybody else have any questions for me before I sit down again and hand this back to Garuth?"

"Just one." The speaker was Lawrence Foster, commander of Main. "A few of us have been wondering . . . You developed a technology that was way ahead of ours—interstellar travel for instance. So you must have explored the Solar System pretty thoroughly in the course of all that. Somebody here's taking bets that at least some Ganymeans got to Earth at some time. Care to comment on that?"

Shilohin seemed to flinch slightly for some reason . . . although it was difficult to be sure. She did not answer at once, but turned to exchange a few briefly muttered words with Garuth. Then she looked up again.

"Yes . . . you are correct . . ." The words coming through the headphones and earpieces of the listeners sounded hesitant, as if faithfully reproducing an uncertainty from the original utterances. "The Ganymeans came . . . to Earth."

A stir of excitement broke out across the room. This was something that nobody wanted to miss.

"Before your expedition went to Iscaris, I guess," Foster said.

"Yes, naturally . . . in the hundred Earth years or so before that time." She paused. "In fact a few of the crew of the *Shapieron* went to Earth before being recruited for the Iscaris expedition. None of them is here at the moment though."

The Earthmen were keen to hear more about their own world from beings who had actually been there long before they themselves had even existed. Questions began pouring spontaneously from all around the room.

"Hey, when can we talk to them?"

"Do you have any pictures stored away someplace?"

"How about maps or something?"

"I bet they built that city high up in that place in South America."

"You're crazy. It's not near old enough."

"Were these the expeditions to Earth to bring back the animals?"

The sudden increase in the enthusiasm of her audience seemed only to add to Shilohin's confusion. She picked up the last question, the answer to which they already knew, as if hoping for some reason that it would divert attention from the rest.

"No, there were no shipments of animals to Minerva then, neither was there any talk of such a plan. That must have happened later on. Like you, we do not know why that was done."

"Okay, but about the—" Foster stopped speaking as ZORAC sounded in his ear.

"This is ZORAC speaking only to the Earthmen; I am not interpreting for Shilohin. I do not believe that the Ganymeans really wish to elaborate further for the time being. It might be a good idea to change the subject. Excuse me."

The puzzled frowns that immediately appeared all over the room confirmed that all the Earthmen had heard the same thing: apparently the message had not, however, been transmitted to the Ganymeans, who showed none of the reactions that it would, without a doubt, have elicited. An awkward silence reigned for just a second before Foster took firm control and steered them all into calmer waters.

"These things can wait until another time," he said. "Time's getting on and we must be near dinner. Before we finish here, we ought to agree on our more immediate plans. The biggest problem seems to me to be the trouble you've got with your ship. How do you plan tackling that, and is there anything we can do to help?"

Shilohin conferred briefly with her companions and then sat down, giving a distinct impression of relief at getting out of the firing line. Her place was taken by Rogdar Jassilane, chief engineer of the *Shapieron*.

"We've had twenty years to figure out what the problem is, and we know how to fix it," he told them. "Garuth has described the effect of the trouble, which involved being unable to slow down the system of circulating black holes upon which the physics of the drive is based. All the time that drive was running, there was nothing we could do about it. We're able to fix it now, but some key components were wrecked and to attempt replacing them from scratch would be difficult, if not impossible. What we really need to do is have a look at the Ganymean ship that's under the ice at Pithead. From the pictures you've shown us, it seems to be a somewhat more advanced design than the *Shapieron*. But I'm hopeful we will be able to find what we need there. The basic concepts of the drive appear to be the same. That's the first thing we have to do—go to Pithead."

"No problem there," Foster said. "I'll arrange . . . oh, excuse me a second . . ." He turned to throw an inquiring look at a steward, who had appeared in the doorway. "I see . . . thanks. We'll be right along." He looked back toward Jassilane. "Sorry about that, but dinner's ready now. Yes, in answer to your question, we can arrange that expedition for as early as you like tomorrow. We can talk about the details later tonight, but in the meantime, shall we all go through?"

"That will be fine," Jassilane said. "I will select some of our own engineers for the visit. In the meantime as you say, let's all go through." He remained standing while the rest of the Ganymeans hoisted themselves to their feet behind him, forming a hopeless crush at the end of the room.

As the Earthmen also stood up and began moving back to make more space for the giants, Garuth made one final comment. "The other reason we wish to see the ship at Pithead is also very important to us. There is a chance that we might find some clues there which support your theory that the Ganymeans eventually migrated to another star system. If that is true, we might perhaps find something to identify which star it was."

"I think the stars can wait until tomorrow too," Jassilane said as he moved past. "Right now I'm more interested in that Earth food. Have you tried that stuff they call pineapple yet? It's delicious—never anything like that on Minerva."

Hunt found himself standing beside Garuth in the crowd forming around the door. He looked up at the massive features. "Would you really do it, Garuth . . . go all the way to still another star, after all this time?"

The giant stared down and seemed to be weighing the question in his mind.

"Perhaps," he replied. "Who knows?" Hunt sensed from the tone of the voice in his ear that ZORAC had ceased operating in public-address mode and was now handling separately the different conversations taking place on either side. "For years now my people have lived on a dream. At this time more than any other, it would be wrong to destroy that dream. Today they are tired and think only of rest; tomorrow they will dream again."

"We'll see what tomorrow brings at Pithead then," Hunt said. He caught the eye of Danchekker, who was standing immediately behind them. "Are you going to sit with us at dinner, Chris?"

"With pleasure, provided you are prepared to tolerate my being unsociable," the professor replied. "I absolutely refuse to eat with this contraption hanging round my head."

"Enjoy your meal, Professor," Garuth urged. "Let the socializing wait until afterward."

"I'm surprised you heard that," Hunt said. "How did ZORAC know we were talking in a group of three? I mean, it must have known that to put it through on your audio as well."

"Oh, ZORAC is very good at things like that. It learns fast. We're quite proud of ZORAC."

"It's an amazing machine."

"In more ways than you perhaps imagine," Garuth agreed. "It was ZORAC that saved us at Iscaris. Most of us were overcome by the heat when the ship was caught by the fringe of the nova; that was what caused many of the deaths among us. It was ZORAC that got the *Shapieron* clear."

"I really must stop calling its brethren contraptions," Danchekker murmured. "Wouldn't want to upset it or anything if it's sensitive about such matters."

"That's okay by me." A different voice came through on the circuit. "As long as I can still call *your* brethren monkeys."

That was when Hunt learned to recognize when a Ganymean was laughing.

When they all sat down to dinner, Hunt was mildly surprised to note that the menu was completely vegetarian. Apparently the Ganymeans had insisted on this.

chapter ten

The period of leave that Hunt and Danchekker had originally intended to spend on *Jupiter Five* had expired anyway, so the two scientists traveled the next day with the mixed party of Earthmen and Ganymeans to Pithead Base. The journey was indeed a mixed affair, with some Ganymeans squeezing into the UNSA medium-haul transporters while the luckier Earthmen traveled as passengers in one of the *Shapieron*'s daughter vessels.

The first thing the aliens were shown at Pithead was the distress beacon that had brought them across the Solar System to Ganymede; already that event seemed a long time ago. The aliens explained that ordinary electromagnetic transmissions could not be received inside the zone of localized space-time distortion that was generated by the standard form of Ganymean drive, and for this reason most long-range communications were effected by means of modulated gravity pulses instead; the beacon used precisely this principle. The Ganymeans had picked up the signal after they had at last shut down their main drives and entered the Solar System under auxiliary power, which was fine for flitting around between planets but not much good for interstellar marathons. Their subsequent bewilderment at what they found—Minerva gone and an extra planet where there shouldn't have been one—could well be imagined; and then they had picked up the signals. As one UNSA officer said to Hunt: "Imagine coming back in twenty-five million years' time and hearing something out of today's hit parade. They must have wondered if they hadn't really been anywhere at all and had dreamed the whole thing."

The party continued on through a metal-walled underground corridor which brought them to the laboratories where preliminary examinations were normally made of items brought up from the ship below. The room that they found themselves in was a large one divided by half-height partitions into a maze of work bays, each a clutter of machinery, test instruments, electronics racks and tool cabinets. Above it all, the roof was barely visible behind the tangles of piping, ducts, cables and conduits that spanned the room.

Craig Patterson, the lab supervisor for that section, ushered the group into one of the bays and gestured at a workbench on which lay a squat metal cylinder, about a foot high and three feet or more across, surrounded by an intricate arrangement of brackets, webs and flanges, all integral with the main body. The whole assembly looked heavy and solid and had evidently been removed from a mounting in some larger piece of equipment; there were several ports and connections that suggested inlet and outlet points, possibly electrical.

"Here's something that's had us baffled," Patterson said. "We've brought a few of these up so far—all identical. There are hundreds more down there, all over the ship. They're mounted under the floors at intervals everywhere you go. Any ideas?"

Rogdar Jassilane stepped forward and stooped to study the object briefly.

"It resembles a modified *G*-pack," Shilohin commented from the doorway where she was standing next to Hunt. The Ganymeans were able to converse via ZORAC, still at Main, seven hundred miles away. Jassilane ran a finger along the casing of the object, examined some of the markings still visible in places, and then straightened up, apparently having seen all he needed.

"That's what it is, all right," he announced. "It seems to have a few extras to the ones I'm used to, but the basic design's the same."

"What's a *G*-pack?" asked Art Stelmer, one of Patterson's engineers.

"An element in a distributed node field," Jassilane told him.

"Great." Stelmer replied with a shrug, still mystified.

Shilohin went on to explain. "I'm afraid it's to do with a branch of physics that hasn't been discovered by your race yet. In your space vessels, such as *Jupiter Five*, you simulate gravity by arranging for most portions of the structure to rotate, don't you?" Hunt suddenly remembered the inexplicable sensation of weight that he had felt on entering the *Shapieron*. The implication of what Shilohin had just said became clear.

"You don't simulate it," he guessed. "You manufacture it."

"Quite," she confirmed. "Devices like that were standard fittings in all Ganymean ships."

The Earthmen present were not really surprised since they had suspected for some time that the Ganymean civilization had mastered technologies that were totally unknown to them. All the same they were intrigued.

"We've been wondering about that," Patterson said, turning to face Shilohin. "What kind of principles is it all based on? I've never heard of anything like this before." Shilohin did not answer at once but seemed to pause to collect her thoughts.

"I'm not really sure where to begin," she replied at last. "It would take rather a long time to explain meaningfully. . . ."

"Hey, there's a booster collar from a transfer tube," one of the other Ganymeans broke in. He was staring over the partition into the adjoining bay and pointing to another, larger piece of Ganymean machinery that was lying there partially dismantled.

"Yes, I believe you're right," Jassilane agreed, following his companion's gaze.

"What the hell's a booster collar?" Stelmer pleaded.

"And a transfer tube?" Patterson added, forgetting his question of a few seconds before.

"There were tubes running all over the ship that were used for moving objects, and people, from place to place," Jassilane answered. "You must know them because I've seen them on the plans of the ship that your engineers have drawn."

"We kind of half-guessed what they were," Hunt supplied. "But we were never really sure about how they worked. Is this another *G*-trick?"

"Right," Jassilane said. "Local fields inside the tubes provided the motive force. That collar next door is simply a type of amplifier that was fitted around the tube to boost and smooth the field strength. There'd be one—oh—every thirty feet or so, depending on how wide the tube was."

"You mean people went hurtling through these things?" Patterson sounded distinctly dubious.

"Sure. We've got them in the *Shapieron* too," Jassilane replied nonchalantly. "The main elevator that some of your people have already been in runs in one. That one uses an enclosed capsule running inside, but the smaller ones don't. In those you just freefall."

"How do you avoid colliding with somebody?" Stelmer asked. "Or are they strictly one-way?"

"Two-way," Jassilane told him. "A tube would usually carry a split field, half up and half down. The traffic can be segregated without problems. The collar contributes to that too—part of it is what we call a 'beam edge delimiter.' "

"So how d'you get out?" Stelmer persisted, still clearly fascinated by the idea.

"You decelerate through a localized pattern of standing waves that's triggered as you approach the drop-out point you've selected," Jassilane said. "You enter in much the same way . . ."

The conversation degenerated into a long discussion on the principles of operation and traffic control employed in the networks of transfer tubes built into Ganymean spacecraft and, as it turned out, most Ganymean buildings and cities. Throughout it all, Patterson's question as to how it worked never did get answered.

After spending some time examining a few more items from the ship, the party left that section of the base to continue their tour. They followed another corridor to the subsurface levels of the Site Operations Control Building and ascended several flights of stairs to the first floor. From there an elevated walkway carried them into an adjacent dome, constructed over the head of number-three shaft. Eventually, after negotiating a labyrinth of walkways and passages, they were standing in the number-three high-level airlock anteroom. A capsule was waiting beyond the airlock to take the first half-dozen of them down to the workings below the surface. By the time the capsule had returned and made its third descent, the whole party was together again deep inside the ice crust of Ganymede.

Accompanied by Jassilane, two other Ganymeans, and Commander Hew Mills, the senior officer of the uniformed UNSA contingent at Pithead, Hunt emerged from the capsule into number-three low-level anteroom. From there a short corridor brought them at last to the low-level control room, where the rest of the party was already gathered. Nobody took any notice of the new arrivals; all eyes were fixed on the view that confronted them from beyond the expanse of glass that constituted the far wall of the control room.

They were looking out over a vast cavern hewn and melted from the solid ice, shining a hundred different hues from gray to brilliant white in the light from a thousand arc lamps. The far side of the cavern was lost to view behind a forest of huge steel jacks and columns of ice left intact to support the roof. There, immediately before them, stretching away into the distance and cutting a clean swath through the forest, was the Ganymean ship.

Its clean, graceful lines of black metal were broken at scores of points where sections of the hull had been removed to gain access or to remove selected parts of the internal machinery. In some places the ship resembled the skeleton of a whale stranded on a beach, just a series of curving ribs soaring toward the cavern roof, to mark where whole sections of the ship had been stripped down. Latticeworks of girders and metal tubing adorned its sides in irregular and untidy clusters, in some places extending fully from floor to roof, supporting a confusion of catwalks, ladders, platforms, ramps, rigs, and winches wreathed intermittently in bewildering tangles of hydraulic and pneumatic feed tubes, ventilator pipes, and electrical supply lines.

Scores of figures labored all across the panorama up on the scaffolding by the hull, down among the maze of stacked parts and fittings that littered the floor, high on the walkways clinging to the rough-hewn walls of ice and standing on the top of the hull itself. In one place a gantry was swinging clear a portion of the outer skin; in another, the sporadic flashing of an oxyacetylene torch lit up the interior of an exposed compartment; farther along, a small group of engineers was evidently in conference, making frequent gestures at information being presented on a large, portable viewscreen. The site was a bustle of steady, deliberate earnest activity.

The Earthmen waited in silence while the Ganymeans took in the scene.

Eventually Jassilane said, "It's quite a size . . . certainly as large as we expected. The general design is definitely a few steps ahead of anything that was flying when we left Minerva. ZORAC, what do you make of it?"

"Torroidal sections protruding from the large cutaway portion three hundred feet along from where you're standing are almost certainly differential resonance stress inductors to confine focus of the beam point for the main drive," ZORAC answered. "The large assembly on the floor immediately below you, with the two Earthmen standing in front of and underneath it is unfamiliar, but suggests an advanced design of an aft compensating reactor. If so, propulsion was probably by means of standard stress-wave propagation. If I am correct, there should be a forward compensating reactor in the ship too. The Earthmen at Main have shown me diagrams of a device that looks like one, but to be sure we should make a point of looking inside the nose end to check it firsthand. I would also like an opportunity to view the primary energy-convertor section and its layout."

"Mmm . . . it could be worse," Jassilane murmured absently.

"What was that all about, Rog?" Hunt asked him. The Giant half turned and raised an arm toward the ship.

"ZORAC has confirmed my own first impressions," he said. "Although that ship was built some time after the *Shapieron*, the basic design doesn't seem to have altered too much."

"There's a good chance it might help you get yours fixed then, huh?" Mills chimed in.

"Hopefully," Jassilane agreed.

"We'd need to see it closeup to be sure," Shilohin cautioned.

Hunt turned to face the rest of the party and spread his arms with palms upturned. "Well, let's go on down and do just that," he said.

They moved away from the viewing window and threaded their way through and between the equipment racks and consoles of the control room to a door on the opposite side to descend to the lower floor. After the door had closed behind the last of the party, one of the duty operators at the consoles half turned to one of his colleagues.

"See Ed, I told ya," he remarked cheerfully. "They didn't eat anybody."

Ed frowned dubiously from his seat a few feet away.

"Maybe they're just not hungry today," he muttered.

On the floor of the cavern, immediately below the window, the mixed group of Ganymeans and Earthmen emerged through an airlock and began making their way across the steel-mesh flooring and through the maze of assorted engineering toward the ship.

"It's quite warm," Shilohin commented to Hunt as they

walked. "And yet there's no sign of melting on the walls. How come?"

"The air-circulation system's been carefully designed," he informed her. "The warmer air is confined down here in the working area and screened off from the ice by curtains of cold air blowing upward all round the sides to extractors up in the roof. The way the walls are shaped to blend into the roof produces the right flow pattern. The system works quite well."

"Ingenious," she murmured.

"What about the explosion risk from dissolved gases being released from the ice?" another Ganymean asked. "I'd have thought there'd be a hazard there."

"When the excavations were first started it was a problem," Hunt answered. "That was when most of the melting was being done. Everybody had to work in suits down here then. They were using an argon atmosphere for exactly the reason you just mentioned. Now that the ventilation's been improved there's not really a big risk anymore so we can be a bit more comfortable. The cold-air curtains help a lot too; they keep the rate of gas-escape down pretty well to zero and what little there is gets swept away upward. The chances of a bang down here are probably less than the base up top getting clobbered by a stray meteorite."

"Well, here we are," Mills announced from the front. They were standing at the foot of a broad, shallow metal ramp that rose from the floor and disappeared through a mass of cabling up into a large aperture cut in the hull. Above them, the bulging contour of the ship's side soared in a monstrous curve that swept over and out of sight toward the roof. Suddenly they were like mice staring up at the underside of a garden roller.

"Let's go in then," Hunt said.

For the next two hours they walked every inch of the labyrinth of footways and catwalks that had been built inside the craft, which had come to rest on its side and offered few horizontal surfaces of its own upon which it was possible to move easily. The Giants followed the cable-runs and the ducting with eyes that obviously knew what they were looking for. Every now and then they stopped to dismantle an item of particular interest with sure and practiced fingers or to trace the connections to a device or component. They absorbed every detail of the plans supplied by UNSA scientists, which showed as much as the Earthmen could deduce of the vessel's design and structure.

After a long dialogue with ZORAC to analyze the results of these observations, Jassilane announced, "We are optimistic. The chances of restoring the *Shapieron* to a fully functional condition seem good. We'd like to conduct a far more detailed study of certain parts of this ship, however—one that would involve more of our technical experts from Main. Could you accommodate a small group of our people here for, say, two or three weeks?" He addressed these last words to Mills. The commander shrugged and opened his hands.

"Whatever you want. Consider it done," he replied.

Within an hour of the party's return to the surface for a meal, another UNSA transporter was on its way north from Main bringing more Ganymeans and the necessary tools and instruments from the *Shapieron*.

Later on, they went to the biological laboratories section of the base and admired Danchekker's indoor garden. They confirmed that the plants he had cultivated were familiar to them and represented types that were widespread in the equatorial regions of the Minerva they had known. At the professor's insistence they accepted some cuttings to be taken back to the *Shapieron* and grown there as mementoes of their home. The gesture seemed to affect them deeply.

Danchekker then led the party down into a large storage room excavated out of the solid ice below the biological labs. They emerged into a spacious, well-lit area, the walls of which were lined with shelving that carried a miscellany of supplies and instruments; there were rows of closed storage cupboards all painted a uniform green, unrecognizable machines draped in dustcovers, and in places stacks of unopened packing cases reaching almost to the ceiling. But the sight that immediately captured every eye was that of the beast towering before them about twenty feet from the doorway.

It stood over eighteen feet high at the shoulder on four tree-trunklike legs, its massive body tapering at the front into a long sturdy neck to carry its relatively small but ruggedly formed head high and well forward. Its skin was grayish and appeared rough and leathery, twisting into deep, heavy wrinkles that girded the base of its neck and the underside of its head below its short, erect ears. Over two enormous flared nostrils and a yawning parrot-beaklike mouth, the eyes were wide and staring. They were accentuated by thick folds of skin above, and directed straight down to stare at the door.

"This is one of my favorites," Danchekker informed them breezily as he walked forward at the head of the party to pat the beast fondly on the front of one of its massive forelegs.

"*Baluchitherium*—a late-Oligocene to early-Miocene Asian ancestor of modern rhinoceroses. In this species the front feet have already lost their fourth toe and adopted a three-toed structure similar to the hind feet—a trend which had become well pronounced in the Oligocene. Also, the strengthening of the upper-jaw structure here is quite developed, although this particular breed did not evolve into a true horned variety, as you can see. Another interesting point is the teeth, which—" Danchekker stopped speaking abruptly as he turned to face his audience and realized that only the Earthmen had followed him into the room to stand around the specimen he was describing. The Ganymeans had come to a standstill in a close huddle just inside the door, where they stood staring speechless up at the towering shape of *Baluchitherium*. Their eyes were opened wide as if frozen in disbelief. They were not exactly cowering at the sight, but the expressions on their faces and their tense stances signaled uncertainty and apprehension.

"Is something the matter?" Danchekker asked, puzzled. There was no response. "It's quite harmless, I assure you," he went on, making his voice reassuring. "And very, very dead . . . one of the samples preserved in the large canisters that were found in the ship. It's been very dead for at least twenty-five million years."

The Ganymeans slowly returned to life. Still silent and somehow subdued, they began moving cautiously toward the spot where the Earthmen were standing in a loose semicircle. For a long time they gazed at the immense creature, absorbing every detail in awed fascination.

"ZORAC," Hunt muttered quietly into his throat mike. The rest of the Earthmen were watching the Ganymeans silently, waiting for some signal to resume their dialogue and not sure yet what exactly it was that was affecting their guests so strongly.

"Yes, Vic?" the machine answered in his ear.

"What's the problem?"

"The Ganymeans have not seen an animal comparable to *Baluchitherium* before. It is a new and unexpected experience."

"Does it come as a surprise to you too?" Hunt asked.

"No. I recognize it as being very similar to other early terrestrial species recorded in my archives. The information came from Ganymean expeditions to Earth that took place before the time of the *Shapieron*'s departure from Minerva. None of the Ganymeans with you at Pithead has ever been to Earth, however."

"But surely they must know something about what those expeditions found," Hunt insisted. "The reports must have been published."

"True," ZORAC agreed. "But it's one thing to read a report about animals like that, and another to come face to face with one suddenly, especially when you're not expecting it. I suppose that if I were an organic intelligence that had evolved from a survival-dominated organic evolutionary system, and possessed all the conditioned emotional responses that implies, I'd be a bit shocked too."

Before Hunt could reply, one of the Ganymeans—Shilohin—finally spoke up.

"So . . . that is an example of an animal of Earth," she said. Her voice was low and hesitant, as if she were having difficulty articulating the words.

"It's incredible!" Jassilane breathed, still keeping his eyes fixed on the huge beast. "Was that thing really alive once . . . ?"

"What's *that*?" Another Ganymean was pointing beyond *Baluchitherium* to a smaller but more ferocious-looking animal posed with one paw raised and lips curled back to reveal a set of fearsome, pointed teeth. The other Ganymeans followed his finger and gasped.

"*Cynodictis,*" Danchekker answered with a shrug. "A curious mixture of feline and canine characteristics from which both our modern cat and dog families eventually emerged. The one next to it is *Mesohippus*, ancestor of all modern horses. If you look carefully you can see . . ." He stopped in midsentence and seemed to switch his line of thought abruptly. "But why do these things seem so strange to you? Surely you have seen animals before . . . There were animals on Minerva, weren't there?"

Hunt observed intently. The reactions that he had witnessed

seemed odd from a race so advanced and which, until then, had seemed so rational in everything they said and did.

Shilohin took it upon herself to answer. "Yes . . . there were animals . . ." She began looking from side to side at her companions as if seeking support in a difficult situation. "But they were . . . *different* . . ." she ended, vaguely. Danchekker seemed intrigued.

"Different," he repeated. "How interesting. In what way do you mean? Weren't there any as big as this for instance?"

Shilohin's anxiety seemed to increase. She was showing the same inexplicable reluctance to discuss Oligocene Earth as on earlier occasions. Hunt sensed a crisis approaching and saw that Danchekker, in his enthusiasm, was not getting the message. He turned away from the rest of the party. "ZORAC, give me a private channel to Chris Danchekker," he said in a lowered voice.

"You've got it," ZORAC responded a second later, sounding almost relieved.

"Chris," Hunt whispered. "This is Vic." He observed a sudden change in Danchekker's expression and went on. "They don't want to talk about it. Maybe they're still nervous about our links with the Lunarians or something—I don't know but something's bugging them. Wrap up and let's get out of here."

Danchekker caught Hunt's eye, blinked uncomprehendingly for a second, then nodded and abruptly changed the subject. "Anyway, I'm sure all that can wait until we are in more comfortable surroundings. Why don't we go back upstairs. There are some more experiments being conducted in the labs that I think might interest you."

The group began shuffling back toward the door. Behind them, Hunt and Danchekker exchanged mystified glances.

"What was the meaning of all that, my I ask?" the professor inquired.

"Search me," Hunt replied. "Come on or we'll get left behind."

Many hundreds of millions of miles from Pithead, the news of the meeting with an intelligent alien race broke over an astounded world. As recordings of the first face-to-face contact aboard the *Shapieron* and the arrival of the aliens at Ganymede Main Base were replayed across the world's viewscreens, a wave of wonder and excitement swept around the planet, ex-

ceeding even that which had greeted the discoveries of Charlie
and the first Ganymean spaceship. Some of the reactions were
admirable, some deplorable, some just comical—but all of
them predictable.

At a high, official level, Frederick James McClusky, senior
United States delegate to the extraordinary session that had
been called by the United Nations, sat back in his chair and
stared around the packed circular auditorium while Charles
Winters, the U.K. representative from U.S. Europe, delivered
the final words of his forty-five-minute address:

". . . In summary it is our contention that the location at
which the first landing is to be effected should obviously be
selected from within the boundaries of the British Isles. The
English language is now established as the standard means of
communication for social, business, scientific, and political dialogue between all the races, peoples and nations of Earth. It
has come to symbolize the dissolution of the barriers that once
divided us, and the establishment of a new order of harmony,
trust and mutual cooperation across the surface of the globe.
And so it is particularly appropriate that the English tongue
should have been the vehicle by which the first words between
our alien friends and ourselves were exchanged. Might I also
remind you that at present, the speech of the British Isles is the
only human language that has been assimilated by the
Ganymean machine. What then, gentlemen, could be more fitting than that the first Ganymean to set foot upon our planet
should do so on the soil where that language originated?"

Winters concluded with a final appealing look around the
auditorium and sat down among a mixed murmuring of lowered voices and rustling of papers. McClusky jotted a few
notes on his pad and cast an eye over the collection that he had
already made.

In a rare show of agreement, the governments of Earth had
released a joint statement declaring that the homeless wanderers from the past would be welcome to settle there if they so
wished. The present meeting was called after the public announcement had been released, and had generated into a heated
wrangle on camera over which nation should enjoy the prestige
of receiving the aliens first.

Initially, McClusky, following his brief from the Presidential
Advisory Committee and the State Department in Washington,
had made first claim by drawing attention to the predominantly

American flavor of the UNSA operations being staged around Jupiter. The Americans had found them, he had said in effect, and the Americans therefore had a right to keep them. The Soviets had taken two hours to say that since their nation occupied a larger portion of the Earth's land surface than any other, it represented the majority of the planet and that was what counted. China had countered by pointing out that she represented more people than any other nation and therefore, making an expedient appeal to democratic principles, China offered a more meaningful interpretation of "majority." Israel had taken the view that it had more in common with homeless minority groups and that considerations of such kind would more accurately reflect the true nature of the situation. Iraq had lodged a claim on the grounds of its being the site of the oldest known nation, and one of the African republics on the grounds of its being the youngest.

By then McClusky was getting fed up with the whole business. Irritated he threw his pen down onto his pad and stabbed a finger at the button that caused his request light to come on. A few minutes later an indicator on his panel informed him that the Chairman had acknowledged the request. McClusky leaned to his microphone. "The Ganymeans haven't even said they want to come to Earth yet, let alone settle here. Wouldn't it be a good idea to ask them about it first before we spend more time on all this?"

The remark prompted a further debate during which the opportunity for diplomatic procrastination proved impossible to resist. In the end the matter was duly *Deferred, Pending Further Information*.

The delegates did, however, agree on one small item.

They were concerned that the UNSA spacecrews, officers, scientists and other on-the-spot personnel at Ganymede had not been schooled in the subtle arts of diplomacy and found the risks implicit in their enforced status as representatives and ambassadors for the whole of Earth worrisome. Accordingly they drafted a set of guidelines impressing upon all UNSA personnel the seriousness and importance of their responsibilities and, among other things, urged them to ". . . desist from any thoughtless or impulsive statements or actions that might conceivably be interpreted as provocative by unfamiliar beings of uncertain disposition and intent. . . ."

When the message was transmitted and dutifully read to the

UNSA crews and scientists on Ganymede, it produced some amusement. Such was the Earthmen's uncertainty of the "disposition and intent . . ." that they read the message to the Ganymeans, too.

The Giants thought it was funny.

chapter eleven

Compared to Main, Pithead was small and Spartan, offering only limited accommodations and restricted amenities. During the days that Ganymean experts were conducting a more intensive examination of the ship there, the two races found themselves intermingling more freely than before and getting to know one another better. Hunt made the most of this opportunity to observe the aliens at close hand and to gain a deeper insight to their ways and temperaments.

The single most striking thing that set them apart from Earthmen was, as he already knew, their total ignorance of the very concept of war or willful violence in any form. At Pithead he gradually came to attribute this to a common factor that he noticed in all of them—something which, he realized, represented a fundamental difference in their mental makeup. Not once had he detected a hint of aggressiveness in a Ganymean. They never seemed to argue about anything, show signs of impatience, or give any evidence of possessing tempers that could be frayed. That in itself did not surprise him unduly; he would hardly have expected less from an extremely advanced and civilized people. But the point that did strike him was the complete absence of emotional traits of the kind that would provide alternate outlet for such instincts in a socially acceptable manner. They exhibited no sense of competitiveness among themselves, no sense of rivalry, even in the harmless, subtle, friendly ways that men accept as part of living and frequently find enjoyable.

The notion of losing face meant nothing to a Ganymean. If

he were proved wrong in some matter he would readily concede the fact; if he were proved right he would feel no particular self-satisfaction. He could stand and watch another perform a task that he knew he could do better, and say nothing—a feat almost impossible for most Earthmen. In the reverse situation he would promptly ask for help. He was never arrogant, authoritative or disdainful, yet at the same time never visibly humble, servile or apologetic; nothing in his manner ever sought to intimidate, and neither did it acknowledge implied intimidation from others. There was simply nothing in anything they said or did, or in the way that they said and did it, that signaled any instinctive desire to seek status or superiority. Many psychologists believed this aspect of human social behavior constituted a set of substitute rituals that permitted release of underlying aggressive instincts which communal patterns of living required to be suppressed. If this was so, then the only conclusion Hunt could draw from his observations was that for some reason these underlying instincts just didn't exist in the Ganymeans.

All this was not to say that the Ganymeans were a cold and unemotional people. As their reactions to the destruction of Minerva had shown, they were warm, friendly and deeply sentimental, at times to a degree that an Earthman reared in the "old school" might have considered unbecoming. And they possessed a well-developed, though very subtle and sophisticated, sense of humor, not a little of which was evident in the basic design of ZORAC. Also as Shilohin had indicated, they were a cautious people, cautious not in the sense of being timid, but of premeditating every move and action. They never did anything without knowing exactly what they were trying to achieve, why they wanted to achieve it, how they were going to do it, and what they would do if the expected failed to materialize. To the average engineer from Earth the disaster of Iscaris would have been shrugged off as just one of those things to be forgotten or tried again with hopes for better luck; to the Ganymeans it was inexcusable that such a thing should ever have happened and they had not yet fully come to terms with it, even after twenty years.

Hunt saw them as a dignified and proud race, moderate in speech and noble in bearing, yet underneath it all sociable and approachable. They exhibited none of the suspicion and mistrust of strangers that was typical through much of the society of Earth. They were quiet, reserved, self-assured, and above all they were rational. As Danchekker remarked to Hunt one day in the bar at Pithead: "If the whole universe went insane and blew itself up, I'm sure the Ganymeans would still be there at the end of it to put the pieces together again."

The bar at Pithead became the main focus of social activity between the small group of Ganymeans and the Earthmen. Every evening after dinner, ones and twos of both races would begin trickling in until the room was filled to capacity and every square foot of horizontal space, including the floor, was covered by a sprawling body of one kind or the other, or littered with glasses. The discussions rambled on to touch every subject conceivable and usually went through to the early hours of the morning; for anybody not disposed to seek solitude and privacy, there was little else to do after work at Pithead.

The Ganymeans developed a strong partiality for scotch whiskey, which they preferred neat, by the tumblerful. They reciprocated by bringing in a distillation of their own from the *Shapieron*. A number of the Earthmen experimented with it and found it to be pleasant, warming, slightly sweet . . . and of devastating potency, but not until about two hours after beginning to drink it. Those who had learned the hard way christened it GTB—Ganymean Time Bomb.

It was during one of these evenings that Hunt decided to broach directly the subject that had been puzzling more than a few of the Earthmen for some time. Shilohin was present, so was Monchar, Garuth's second-in-command, together with four other Ganymeans; on the Earth side were Danchekker, Vince Carizan the electronics engineer, and a half dozen others.

"There is a point that's been bothering some of us," he said, by that time having come to appreciate the Ganymean preference for direct speech. "You must know that having people around today who can describe how Earth was in the distant past makes us want to ask all kinds of questions, yet you never seem to want to talk about it. Why?" A few murmurs from all around endorsed the question. The room suddenly became very quiet. The Ganymeans seemed ill at ease again and looked at each other as if hoping someone else would take the lead.

Eventually Shilohin replied. "We know very little about your world. It's a delicate issue. You have a culture and history that are completely strange. . . ." She gave the Ganymean equivalent of a shrug. "Customs, values, manners . . . accepted ways of saying things. We wouldn't want to offend somebody by unwittingly saying the wrong thing, so we tend to avoid the subject."

Somehow the answer was not really convincing.

"We all believe there's a deeper reason than that," Hunt said candidly. "We in this room might come from different origins, but first and foremost we are all scientists. Truth is our business and we shouldn't shy away from the facts. This is an informal occasion and we all know each other pretty well now. We'd like you to be frank. We're curious."

The air became charged with expectancy. Shilohin looked again toward Monchar, who quietly signaled his acquiescence. She downed the last of her drink slowly as she collected her thoughts, then looked up to address the room.

"Very well. Perhaps, as you say, we would do better without any secrets. There was one crucial difference between the patterns of natural evolution that unfolded on your world and on our world—on Minerva there were no carnivores." She paused as if waiting for a response, but the Earthmen continued to sit in silence; obviously there was more to come. She felt a twinge of sudden relief inside. Perhaps the Ganymeans had been overapprehensive of the possible reactions of these unpredictable and violently inclined dwarves after all.

"The basic reason for this difference, believe it or not, lay in the fact that Minerva was much farther away from the Sun." She went on to explain. "Life could never have developed on Minerva at all without the greenhouse effect, which you already know about. Even so, it was a cold planet, certainly in comparison to Earth.

"But this greenhouse effect kept the Minervan oceans in a liquid state and, as on Earth, life first appeared in the shallower parts of the oceans. Conditions there did not favor progression toward higher forms of life as much as on the warmer Earth; the evolutionary process was relatively slow."

"But intelligence appeared there much earlier than it did on Earth," somebody tossed in. "Seems a little strange."

"Only because Minerva was farther from the Sun and cooled more quickly," Shilohin replied. "That meant that life got off to an early start there."

"Okay."

She resumed. "The patterns of evolution on the two worlds were remarkably similar to start with. Complex proteins appeared, leading eventually to self-replicating molecules, which in time led to the formation of living cells. Unicellular forms came first, then colonies of cells and after them multicelled organisms with specialized features—all of them variations on the basic marine invertebrate form.

"The point of departure at which the two lines went their own way, each in response to the conditions prevailing on its own planet, was marked by the appearance of marine vertebrates—boned fishes. This stage marked a plateau beyond which the Minervan species couldn't progress toward anything higher until they had solved a fundamental problem that was not faced by their counterparts on Earth. The problem was simply their colder environment.

"You see, as improvements appeared in the Minervan species, the improved body processes and more highly refined organs demanded more oxygen. But the demand was already high because of the lower temperature. The primitive circulatory systems of the early Minervan fish couldn't cope with the dual workload of carrying enough oxygen to the cells, and of carrying wastes and toxins away from the cells—not if progress toward anything more advanced was going to be made, anyway."

Shilohin paused again to invite questions. Her listeners were too intrigued, however, to interrupt her story at that point.

"As always happens in situations like that," she continued, "Nature tried a number of alternatives to find a way around the problem. The most successful experiment took the form of a secondary circulation system developing alongside the first to permit load-sharing—a completely duplicated network of branching ducts and vessels; thus, the primary system concentrated exclusively on circulating blood and delivering oxygen, while the secondary took over fully the job of removing the toxins."

"How extraordinary!" Danchekker could not help from exclaiming.

"Yes, I suppose that when judged by the things you're used to it was, Professor."

"One thing—how did the different substances find their way in and out of the right system?"

"Osmotic membranes. Do you want me to go into detail now?"

"No, er, thank you." Danchekker held up a hand. "That can wait until another time. Please continue."

"Okay. Well, after this basic architecture had become sufficiently refined and established, evolution toward higher stages was able to resume once more. Mutations appeared, the environment applied selection principles, and life in the Minervan seas began diverging and specializing into many and varied species. After a while, as you would expect, a range of carnivorous types established themselves. . . ."

"I thought you said there weren't any," a voice queried.

"That came later. I'm talking about very early times."

"Okay."

"Fine. So, carnivorous fish appeared on the scene and, again as you would expect, Nature immediately commenced looking for ways of protecting the victims. Now the fish that had developed the double-circulatory-system architecture, who tended to be more advanced forms anyway because of this, hit on a very efficient means of defense: the two circulatory systems became totally isolated from one another, and the concentration of toxins in the secondary system increased to lethal proportions. In other words, they become poisonous. The isolation of the secondary system from the primary prevented poison from entering the bloodstream. That would have been fatal for the owner itself, naturally."

Carizan was frowning about something. He caught her eye and gestured for her to hold the conversation there a moment.

"Can't really say I see that as being much protection at all," he said. "What's the good in poisoning a carnivore after it's eaten you? That'd be too late, wouldn't it?"

"To the individual who was unfortunate enough to encounter one that hadn't learned yet, yes," she agreed. "But don't forget that Nature can afford to be very wasteful when it comes to individuals; it's the preservation of the species as a whole that matters. When you think about it, the survival or extermination of a species can depend on whether or not a strain of predators becomes established that has a preference for them as a diet. In the situation I've described, it was impossible for such a strain of predators to emerge; if a mutation appeared that had a tendency in that direction, it would promptly destroy itself the first time it experimented in following its instinct. It would never get a chance to pass its characteristic on to any descendants, so the characteristic could never be reinforced in later generations."

"Another thing too," one of the UNSA biologists interjected. "Young animals tend to imitate the feeding habits of their parents . . . on Earth anyway. If that was true on Minerva too, the young that managed to get born would naturally tend to pick up the habits of parents that avoided the poisonous species. It would have to be that way since any mutant that didn't avoid them wouldn't live long enough to become a parent in the first place."

"You can see the same thing in terrestrial insects, for example," Danchekker threw in. "Some species mimic the coloring of wasps and bees, although they are quite harmless. Other animals leave them alone completely—it's the same principle."

"Okay, that makes sense." Carizan motioned for Shilohin to continue.

"So marine life on Minerva developed into three broad families: carnivorous types; nonpoisonous noncarnivores, with specialized alternative defense mechanisms; and poisonous noncarnivores, which possessed the most effective defense and were left free to carry on their development from what was already an advanced and privileged position."

"This didn't alter their resistance to cold then?" somebody asked.

"No, the secondary system in these species continued to perform its original function as well as ever. As I said, the only differences that had occurred were that the toxin concentration was increased and it became isolated from the primary."

"I got it."

"Fine. Now, the two types of noncarnivores had to eat, so they competed between themselves for what was available—plants, certain rudimentary invertebrate organisms, water-borne organic substances and so on. But Minerva was cold and did not offer an abundance of things like that—nothing like what is found on Earth, for instance. The poisonous species were efficient competitors and gradually became overwhelmingly dominant. The nonpoisonous noncarnivores declined and, since they constituted the food supply for the carnivores, the numbers and varieties of carnivores declined with them. Eventually two distinct groups segregated out of all this and from that time on lived separate lives: the nonpoisonous types moved out into the oceans away from the competition, and the carnivores naturally followed them. Those two groups evolved into a pattern of deep-sea life that eventually found its own balance and stabilized. The poisonous types retained the shallower, coastal waters as their sole preserve, and it was from them that land dwellers subsequently emerged."

"You mean that all the land-dwelling species that developed later inherited the basic pattern of a double system?" Danchekker said, fascinated. "They were all poisonous?"

"Precisely," she replied. "By that time the trait had become firmly established as a fundamental part of their basic design—much as many vertebrate characteristics on your own world. It was faithfully passed on to all later descendants, essentially unchanged. . . ."

Shilohin paused as a few mutterings and murmurs of surprise arose from the listeners; the implication of what she was saying was beginning to dawn on them. Somebody at the back finally put it into words.

"That explains what you said at the start—why there were no carnivores on Minerva later on. They could never become established for all the reasons you've been talking about, even if they appeared spontaneously from time to time."

"Quite so," she confirmed. "Occasionally an odd mutation in that direction would appear but, as you point out, it could never gain a foothold again. The animals that evolved on Minerva were exclusively herbivorous. They did not follow the same lines of development as terrestrial animals because the selective factors operating in their natural environment were different. They evolved no fight-or-flight instincts since there was nothing to defend against and nothing to flee from. They did not develop behavior patterns based on fear, anger or aggression since such emotions had no survival value to them, and hence were not selected and reinforced. There were no fast runners since there were no predators to run from, and there was no need for natural camouflage. There were no birds, since there was nothing to stimulate their appearance."

"Those murals in the ship!" Hunt turned to Danchekker as the truth suddenly hit him. "They weren't children's cartoons at all, Chris. They were real!"

"Good Lord, Vic." The professor gaped and blinked through his spectacles in surprise, wondering why the same thought hadn't struck him. "You're right. Of course . . . you're absolutely right. How extraordinary. We must study them more closely . . ." Danchekker seemed about to say something else but stopped abruptly, as if another thought had just occurred to him. He frowned and rubbed his forehead but waited until the hubbub of voices had died away before he spoke.

"Excuse me," he called when normality had returned. "There is something else . . . If there were no predators in existence at all, what kept the numbers of the herbivores in check? I can't see any mechanism for preserving a natural balance."

"I was just coming to that," Shilohin answered. "The answer is: accidents. Even slight cuts or abrasions would allow poison to seep from the secondary system into the primary. Most accidents were fatal to Minervan animals. Natural selection favored natural protection. The species that survived and flourished were those with the best protection—leathery outer skins, thick coverings of fur, scaly armor plating, and so on." She held up one of her hands to display extensive nails and knuckle pads, and then shifted the collar of her shirt slightly to uncover part of the delicate, overlapping, scaly plates that formed a strip along the top of her shoulder. "Many remnants of ancestral protection are still detectable in the Ganymean form today."

Hunt realized now the reasons for the Ganymeans' temperament being the way it was. From the origins that Shilohin had just described, intelligence had emerged not in response to any need to manufacture weapons or to outwit foe or prey, but as a means of anticipating and avoiding physical damage. Learning and the communication of knowledge would have assumed a phenomenal survival value among the primitive Ganymeans. Caution in all things, prudence, and the ability to analyze all possible outcomes of an action would have been reinforced by selection; haste and rashness would be fatal.

Evolving from such ancestors, what else could they be but instinctively cooperative and nonaggressive? They would know nothing of violent competition in any form or of the use of force against a rival; hence they exhibited none of the types of complex behavior patterns which, in a later and more civilized society, would "normally" afford symbolic expression of such instincts. Hunt wondered what was "normal." Shilohin, as if reading his thoughts, supplied a definition from the Ganymean point of view.

"You can imagine then how, when civilization eventually began to develop, the early Ganymean thinkers looked upon the world that they saw about them. They marveled at the way in which Nature, in its infinite wisdom, had imposed a strict natural order upon all living things: the soil fed the plants and the plants fed the animals. The Ganymeans accepted this as the natural order of the universe."

"Like a divinely ordained plan," somebody near the bar suggested. "Sounds like a religious outlook."

"You're right," Shilohin agreed, turning to face the speaker. "In the early history of our civilization religious notions did prevail widely. Before scientific principles were better understood, our people attributed many of the mysteries that they were unable to explain to the workings of some omnipotent agency . . . not unlike your God. The early teachings held that the natural order of living things was the ultimate expression of this guiding wisdom . . . I suppose you would say: The will of God."

"Except in the deep-ocean basins," Hunt commented.

"Well, that fitted in quite well too," Shilohin replied. "The early religious thinkers of our race saw that as a punishment. In the seas, way back before history, the law had been defied. As a punishment for that, the lawbreakers had been banished permanently to the deepest and darkest depths of the oceans and never emerged to enjoy sunlight."

Danchekker leaned toward Hunt and whispered, "Rather like the Fall from Eden. An interesting parallel, don't you think?"

"Mmm . . . with a T-bone steak in place of an apple," Hunt murmured.

Shilohin paused to push her glass across the bar and waited for the steward to refill it. The room remained quiet while the Earthmen digested the things she had been saying. At last she sipped her drink, and then resumed.

"And so, you see, to the Ganymean, Nature was indeed perfect in all its harmony, and beautiful in its perfection. As the sciences were discovered and the Ganymeans learned more about the universe in which they lived, they never doubted that however far among the stars their knowledge might take them and however far they might one day probe toward infinity, Nature and its natural law would everywhere reign supreme. What reason had they even to imagine otherwise? They were unable even to conceive how things could be otherwise."

She stopped for a moment and swept her eyes slowly around the room, as if trying to weigh up the expressions on the circle of faces.

"You asked me to be frank," she said, then paused again. "At last, we realized a dream that we had been nurturing for generations—to go out into space and discover the wonders of other worlds. When at last the Ganymeans, still with their idyllic convictions, came to the jungles and savagery of Earth, the effect on them was shattering. We called it the Nightmare Planet."

chapter twelve

The Ganymean engineers announced that the ship beneath Pithead would provide the parts needed to repair the drive system of the *Shapieron* and that the work would take three to four weeks. A shuttle service between Pithead and Main came into being as technicians and scientists of both races cooperated in the venture. The Ganymeans, of course, directed and carried out the technical side of the operation while the Earthmen took care of the transportation, logistics, and domestic arrangements. Parties of UNSA experts were invited aboard the *Shapieron* to observe the work in progress and to stand in spellbound fascination as some of the mysteries and intricacies of Ganymean science were explained. One eminent authority on nuclear engineering from *Jupiter Five* declared later that the experience made him feel like "an unapprenticed plumber's mate being shown around a fusion plant."

While all this was going on, a team of UNSA specialists at Main worked out a schedule to give ZORAC a crash course on terrestrial computer science and technology. The result of this exercise was the construction of a code-conversion and interface system, most of the details of which were worked out by ZORAC itself, to couple the Ganymean computer directly into the communications network at Main and thus into the computer complex of *J5*. This gave ZORAC, and through it the Ganymeans as well, direct access to *J5*'s data banks and opened up a mine of information on many aspects of the ways of life, history, geography and sciences of Earth—for which the aliens had insatiable appetites.

One day, in the communications room of the Mission Control Center at UNSA Operational Command Headquarters, Galveston, there was consternation when a strange voice began speaking suddenly and unexpectedly over the loudspeaker system. It was another of ZORAC's jokes. The machine had composed its own message of greeting to Earth and injected it into the outgoing signal stream of the laser link from Jupiter.

Earth was, of course, clamoring to know more about the Ganymeans. In a press conference staged specifically for broadcast over the world news grid, a panel of Ganymeans answered questions put to them by scientists and reporters who had traveled with the *J5* mission. A large local audience was expected for the event and, since none of the facilities available at Main seemed to be large enough, the Ganymeans readily agreed to the idea of holding the event inside the *Shapieron*. Hunt was a member of the group that flew down from Pithead to take part.

The first questions concerned the concepts and principles behind the design of the *Shapieron*, especially its propulsive system. In reply, The Ganymeans stated that the speculations of the UNSA scientists had been partly right, but did not tell the whole story. The arrangement of massive torroids containing tiny black holes that spun in closed circular paths did indeed generate very high rates of change of gravity potential which resulted in a zone of intense space-time distortion, but this did not propel the ship directly; it created a focal point in the center of the torroids at which a trickle of ordinary matter was induced to annihilate out of existence. The mass-equivalent appeared in the form of gravitational energy, though not in any way as simple as the classical notion of a force directed toward a central point; the Ganymeans described the resultant effect as resembling "a stress in the structure of space-time surrounding the ship. . . ." It was this stress wave that propagated through space, carrying the ship with it as it went.

The idea of being able to cause matter to annihilate at will was astonishing, and that the annihilation should result in artificial gravity phenomena was a revelation. But to learn that all this merely represented a means of bringing under control something that went on naturally anyway all over the universe . . . was astounding. For this, apparently, was exactly the way in which gravity originated in Nature; all forms of matter were all the time decaying away to nothing, albeit at an immeasurably slow rate, and it was the tiny proportion of basic particles that were annihilating at any given moment that gave rise to the gravitational effect of mass. Every annihilation event produced a microsopic, transient gravity pulse, and it was the additive effect of millions of these pulses occurring every second which, when perceived at the macroscopic level, produced the illusion of a steady field. Thus, gravity ceased to be something static and passive that existed wherever a quantity of mass happened to be; now, no longer an oddity standing apart, it fell into line with all the other field phenomena of physics and became a quantity that depended on the rate of *change* of something—in this case, the rate of change of mass. This principle, together with the discovery of a means of artificially generating and controlling the process, formed the basis of Ganymean gravitic engineering technology.

This account caused consternation among the scientists from Earth who were present. Hunt voiced their reactions by asking how some of the fundamental laws of physics—conservation of mass-energy and momentum, for example—could be reconciled with the notion of particles being able to vanish spontaneously whenever they chose. The cherished fundamental laws, it turned out, were neither fundamental nor laws at all. Like the Newtonian mechanics of an earlier age, they were just approximations that would be revealed with the development of more precise theoretical models and improved measurement techniques, similar to the way in which careful experiments with light waves had demonstrated the untenability of classical physics and resulted in the formulation of special relativity. The Ganymeans illustrated the point by mentioning that the rate at which matter decayed was such that one gram of water would require well over ten billion years to disappear completely—utterly undetectable by any experiment that could be devised within the framework of contemporary terrestrial science. While that remained true, the established laws that Hunt had referred to would prove perfectly adequate since the errors that resulted from them would make no practical difference. In the same way, classical Newtonian mechanics continued to suffice for most day-to-day needs although relativity provided the more accurate description of reality. The history of Minervan science had shown the same pattern of development; when terrestrial science had progressed farther, no doubt, similar discoveries and lines of reasoning would lead to the same reexamination of basic principles.

This led to the question of the permanency of the universe. Hunt asked how the universe could still exist at all let alone still be evolving if all the matter in it was decaying at the rate that the Ganymeans had indicated, which was not slow on a cosmic time scale; there ought not to have been very much of the universe left. The universe went on forever, he was told. All the time, throughout the whole volume of space, particles were appearing spontaneously as well as vanishing spontaneously, the latter process taking place predominantly inside matter—naturally, since that was where there were more of them to vanish from in the first place. Thus the evolution of progressively more complex mechanisms of creating order out of chaos—basic particles, interstellar clouds, stars, planets, organic chemicals, then life itself and after that intelligence— formed a continuous cycle, a perpetual stage where the show never stopped but individual actors came and went. Underlying it all was a unidirectional pressure that strove always to bring high levels of organization from lower ones. The universe was the result of a conflict of two opposing, fundamental trends; one, represented by the second law of thermodynamics, was the tendency for disorder to increase, while the other—the evolutionary principle—produced local reversals by creating order. In the Ganymean sense, the term evolution was not something that applied only to the world of living things, but one that embraced equally the whole spectrum of increasing order, from the formation of an atomic nucleus from stellar plasma to the act of designing a supercomputer; within this spectrum, the emergence of life was reduced to just another milestone along the way. They compared the evolutionary principle to a fish swimming upstream against the current of entropy; the fish and the current symbolized the two fundamental forces in the Ganymean universe. Evolution worked the way it did because selection worked; selection worked because probability worked in a particular way. The universe was, in the final analysis, all a question of statistics.

Basic particles thus appeared, lived out their mortal spans, and then vanished. Where did they come from and where did they go to? This question summed up the kinds of problem that had existed at the frontier of Ganymean science at the time of the *Shapieron*'s departure. The whole universe perceived by the senses was compared to a geometric plane through which a particle passed, to be observable for a while as it made its contribution to the evolving histories of the galaxies. But in what kind of superuniverse was this plane embedded? Of what kind of truer reality was everything that had ever been observed just a pale and insignificant shadow? These were the secrets that the researchers of Minerva had been beginning to probe and which, they had confidently believed, would eventually yield the key not only to practicable intergalactic travel, but also to movement in domains of existence that even they were incapable of imagining. The scientists from the *Shapieron* wondered how much their descendants had learned in the years, decades, or even centuries, that had elapsed after their departure from Minerva. Could the abrupt disappearance of a whole civilization have a connection with some undreamed of universe that they had discovered?

The newsmen present were interested in the cultural basis of the Minervan civilization, particularly the means of conducting everyday commercial transactions between individuals and between organizations. A freely competing economy based on monetary values seemed incompatible with the noncompetitive Ganymean character and raised the question of what alternative system the aliens used to measure and control the obligations between an individual and the rest of society.

The Ganymeans confirmed that their system had functioned without the motivational forces of profit and a need to maintain any kind of financial solvency. This was another area in which the radically different psychology and conditioning of the Ganymeans made a smooth dialogue impossible, mainly because they had no comprehension of many of the facts of living that were accepted as self-evident on Earth. That some means of control was desirable to insure that everybody put into society at least as much as he took out was strange to them; so was the concept that any measure of a "normal" input-output ratio could be specified since, they maintained, every individual had his own preferred ratio at which he functioned optimally, and which it was his basic right to choose.

The concept of financial necessity or any other means of coercing somebody to live a life that he would not otherwise follow was, to them, a grotesque infringement on freedom and dignity. Besides that, they seemed unable to understand why it should be necessary to base any society on such principles.

What then, they were asked, was there to prevent everybody becoming purely a taker, with no obligation to give anything in return? That being the case, how could a society survive at all? Again the Ganymeans seemed unable to understand the problem. Surely, they pointed out, individuals possessed an instinct to contribute and one of the essential needs of living was the satisfaction of that instinct; why would anybody deliberately deprive himself of the feeling of being needed? Apparently that was what motivated the Ganymean in place of monetary incentives—he simply could not live with the thought of not being of any use to anybody. He was just made that way. The worst situation he could find himself in was that of having to depend on society for his wants without being able to reciprocate, and anybody who sought such an existence deliberately was regarded as a social anomaly in need of psychiatric help and an object of sympathy—rather like a mentally retarded child. The observation that this was regarded by many on Earth as the ultimate fulfillment of ambition reinforced the Ganymean conviction that *Homo sapiens* had inherited some awful defects from the Lunarians. On a more encouraging note they expressed the view, based on what they knew of the last few decades of Man's history, that Nature was slowly but surely repairing the damage.

By the time the conference had finished Hunt found that all the talking had made him thirsty. He asked ZORAC if there was anywhere nearby where he might get a drink and was informed that if he went out through the main door of the room he was in, turned right and followed the corridor for a short distance, he would come to an open seating area where refreshments were available. Hunt ordered a GTB and Coke—the latest product of the fusion of the two cultures and an instant hit with both—and left the mêlée of producers and technicians to follow the directions and pick up the drink at the dispensing unit.

As he turned and cast an eye around the area to look for a suitable seat, he noted absently that he was the only Earthman present. A few Ganymeans were scattered around singly or in small groups, but most of the places were empty. He picked out a small table with a few unoccupied chairs around it, sauntered across and sat down. Apart from one or two slight nods of acknowledgment, none of the Ganymeans took any notice of him; anyone would have thought it an everyday occurrence for unaccompanied aliens to wander around their ship. The sight of the ashtray on the table prompted him to reach into his pocket for his cigarette pack. Then he stopped, momentarily puzzled; the Ganymeans didn't smoke. He peered more closely at the ashtray and realized that it was standard UNSA issue. He looked around. Most of the tables had UNSA ashtrays. As usual the Ganymeans had thought of everything; naturally there would be Earthmen around with the conference that day. He sighed, shook his head in admiration and settled back into the huge expanse of upholstered luxury to relax with his thoughts.

He didn't realize Shilohin was standing nearby until ZORAC spoke in his ear with the voice that it reserved for her. "Dr. Hunt, isn't it? Good afternoon."

Hunt looked up with a start and then recognized her. He grinned at the standard salutation and gestured toward one of the empty seats. Shilohin sat down and placed her own drink on the table.

"I see we seem to have had the same idea," she said. "It's thirsty work."

"You can say that again."

"Well . . . how do you think it went?"

"It was great. I think they were all fascinated. . . . I bet it'll cause some pretty lively arguments back home."

Shilohin seemed to hesitate for a second before going on. "You don't think Monchar was too direct . . . too openly critical of your way of life and your values? Those things he said about the Lunarians for example . . ."

Hunt reflected for a moment while he drew on his cigarette.

"No, I don't think so. If that's the way Ganymeans see it, it's much better if it's said straight. . . . If you ask me, something like that has needed saying for a long time. I can't think of anybody better to say it; more people might start taking notice now . . . good thing too."

"That's nice to know anyway," she said, sounding suddenly more at ease. "I was beginning to feel a little worried about it."

"I don't think anybody's very worried about that side of it," Hunt commented. "Certainly the scientists aren't. They're more worried about having the laws of physics collapse around their ears. I don't think you've realized yet what a stir you've started. Some of our most basic convictions are going to have to be rethought—right from square one. We thought we had just a few more pages to add to the story; now it looks as if we might have to rewrite the whole book."

"That's true I suppose," she conceded. "But at least you won't have to go all the way back as far as the Ganymean scientists did." She noted his look of interest. "Oh yes, believe me, Dr. Hunt, we went through the same process ourselves. The discovery of relativity and quantum mechanics turned all of our classical ideas upside down just as happened in your own science in the early twentieth century. And then when the things we were talking about earlier began fitting together, we had another major scientific upheaval; all the concepts that had survived the first time and were regarded as absolute turned out to be wrong—all the ingrained beliefs had to be changed."

She turned to look at him and made a Ganymean gesture of resignation. "Your science would have reached the same point eventually even if we hadn't arrived, and not all that far in the future either if my judgment is anything to go by. As things are, you'll dodge the worst since we can show you most of what's involved anyway. Fifty years from now you'll be flying ships like this one."

"I wonder." Hunt's voice was far away. It sounded incredible, but then he thought of the history of aviation; how many of the colonial territories of the 1920s would have believed that fifty years later they would be independent states running their own jet fleets? How many Americans would have believed that the same time span would take them from wooden biplanes to Apollo?

"And what happens after that?" he murmured, half to himself. "Will there be more scientific upheavals waiting . . . things that even you people don't know about yet either?"

"Who knows?" she replied. "I did outline where research had got to when we left Minerva; anything could have happened afterward. But don't make the mistake of thinking that we know everything, even within our existing framework of knowledge. We've had our surprises too, you know—since we came to Ganymede. The Earthmen have taught us some things we didn't know."

This was news to Hunt.

"How do you mean?" he asked, naturally intrigued. "What kind of things?"

She sipped her drink slowly to collect her thoughts. "Well, let's take this question of carnivorism, for example. As you know, it was unknown on Minerva, apart from in certain deep-sea species that only scientists were interested in and most other Ganymeans preferred to forget."

"Yes, I know that."

"Well, Ganymean biologists had, of course, studied the workings of evolution and reconstructed the story of how their own race originated. Although layman's thinking was largely governed by the concept of some divinely ordained natural order, as I mentioned earlier, many scientists recognized the chance aspect of the scheme that had established itself on our world. Purely from the scientific viewpoint, they could see no reason why things *had* to be the way they were. So, being scientists, they began to ask what might have happened if things had been different . . . for example, if carnivorous fish had not migrated to midocean depths, but had remained in coastal waters."

"You mean if amphibian and land-dwelling carnivores had evolved," Hunt supplied.

"Exactly. Some scientists maintained that it was just a quirk of fate that led to Minerva being the way it was—nothing to do with any divine laws at all. So they began constructing hypothetical models of ecological systems that included carnivores . . . more as intellectual exercise, I suppose."

"Mmm . . . interesting. How did they turn out?"

"They were hopelessly wrong," Shilohin told him. She made a gesture of emphasis. "Most of the models predicted the whole evolutionary system slowing down and degenerating into a stagnant dead end, much as happened in our own oceans. They hadn't managed to separate out the limitations imposed by an aquatic environment, and attributed the result to the fundamentally destructive nature of the way of life there. You can imagine their surprise when the first Ganymean expedition reached Earth and found just such a land-based ecology in action. They were amazed at how advanced and how specialized the animals had become . . . and the birds! That was something none of them had dreamed of. Now you can see why many of us were stunned by the sight of the animals that you showed us at Pithead. We had heard of such creatures, but none of us had actually seen one."

Hunt nodded slowly and began to comprehend fully at last. To a race that had grown up surrounded by Danchekker's cartoons, the sight of *Trilophodon*, the four-tusked walking tank, or of the saber-toothed killing machine *Smilodon*, must have been awesome. What kind of picture had the Ganymeans formed of the ferocious arena that had molded and shaped such gladiators, he wondered.

"So, they had to change their ideas on that subject in a hurry as well," he said.

"They did. . . . They revised all their theories on the strength of the evidence from Earth, and they worked out a completely new model. But, I'm afraid, they got it all wrong again."

Hunt couldn't suppress a short laugh.

"Really? What went wrong this time?"

"Your level of civilization and your technology," she told him. "All our scientists were convinced that an advanced race could never emerge from the pattern of life that they saw on Earth twenty-five million years ago. They argued that intelligence could never appear in any stable form in such an environment, and even if it did it would destroy itself as soon as it had the power to do so. Certainly any kind of sociable living or communal society was out of the question and, since the acquisition of knowledge depends on communication and cooperation, the sciences could never be developed."

"But we proved that was all baloney, eh?"

"It's incredible!" Shilohin indicated bewilderment. "All our models showed that any progression from the life forms of your Miocene period toward greater intelligence would depend on selection for greater cunning and more sophisticated methods of violence; no coherent civilization could possibly develop from a background like that. And yet . . . we have returned and found not only a civilized and technologically advanced culture, but one that is accelerating all the time. It seemed impossible. That was why we took so much convincing that you came from the third planet from the Sun—the Nightmare Planet."

These remarks made Hunt feel flattered, but at the same time he remembered how close the Ganymean prophecies had come to being true.

"But you were so nearly right, weren't you," he said soberly. "Don't forget the Lunarians. They did destroy themselves in just the way that your model predicted, although it looks as if they too advanced farther than you thought they would. It was only the fact that a handful of them survived it that we're here at all, and they only made it on a million-to-one shot." He shook his head and exhaled a cloud of smoke sharply. "I wouldn't feel too bad about what your models said; they came far too near the truth for comfort as far as I'm concerned . . . far too near. If whatever it as that made the Lunarians the way they were hadn't modified itself somehow and become diluted in the course of time, we'd be going the same way and your model would be proved right again. With luck though, we're over that hump now."

"And that's the most incredible thing of all," Shilohin said, picking up the point immediately. "The very thing that we believed would prove an insurmountable barrier to progress has turned out to be your biggest advantage."

"How do you mean?"

"The aggressiveness, the determination—the refusal to let anything defeat you. All that is built deep into the basic Earthman character. It's a relic from your origins, modified, refined, and adapted. But that's where it comes from. You maybe don't see it that way, but we can. We're astounded by it. Try to understand, we've never seen or imagined anything like it before."

"Danchekker said something like that," Hunt mumbled, but Shilohin continued, apparently not having heard him.

"Our instincts are to avoid any form of danger, because of the way we originated . . . certainly not to seek it deliberately. We are a cautious people. But Earthmen . . . ! They climb mountains, sail tiny boats around a planet alone, jump out of aircraft for fun! All their games are simulated combat; this thing you call 'business' reenacts the survival struggle of your evolutionary system and the power-lust of your wars; your 'politics' is based on the principle of meeting force with force and matching strength with strength." She paused for a moment, and then went on. "These are completely new to Ganymeans. The idea of a race that will actually rise up and answer threats with defiance is . . . unbelievable. We have studied large portions of your planet's history. Much of it is horrifying to us, but also, beneath the superficial story of events, some of us see something deeper—something stirring.

The difficulties that Man has faced are appalling, but the way in which he has always fought back at them and always won in the end—I must confess there is something about it that is strangely magnificent."

"But why should that be?" Hunt asked. "Why should the Ganymeans feel that we have some unique advantage, especially with their different background? They achieved the same things . . . and more."

"Because of the time it's taken you to do it," she said.

"Time?"

"Your rate of advancement. It's stupendous! Haven't Earthmen realized? No, I don't suppose there's any reason why they should." She looked at him again, seemingly at a loss for a second. "How long ago did Man harness steam? It took you less than seventy years from learning to fly to reach your Moon. Twenty years after you invented transistors half your world was being run by computers. . . ."

"That's good, compared to Minerva?"

"Good! It's miraculous! It makes our own development pale into insignificance. And it's getting faster all the time! It's because you attack Nature with the same innate aggressiveness that you hurl at anything that stands in your way. You don't hack each other to pieces or bomb whole cities anymore, but the same instinct is still there in your scientists, engineers . . . your businessmen, your politicians. They all love a good fight. They thrive on it. That's the difference between us. The Ganymean learns for knowledge and finds that he solves problems as a by-product; the Earthman takes on a problem and finds that he's learned something when he's solved it, but it's the kick he gets out of fighting and winning that matters. Garuth summed it up fairly well when I was talking to him yesterday. I asked him if he thought that any of the Earthmen really believed in this God they talk about. Know what he said?"

"What'd he say?"

" 'They will once they've made Him.' "

Hunt couldn't help grinning at Garuth's bemusement that was at the same time a compliment. He was about to reply when ZORAC spoke into his hear in its own voice:

"Excuse me, Dr. Hunt."

"Yes?"

"A Sergeant Brukhov wants to talk for a second. Are you accepting calls?"

"Excuse me a minute," he said to Shilohin. "Okay. Put him on."

"Dr. Hunt?" The voice of one of the UNSA pilots came through clearly.

"Here."

"Sorry to bother you, but we're sorting out the arrangements for getting everybody back to Pithead. I'm taking a transporter back half an hour from now and I've got a couple of empty seats. Also there's a Ganymean ship leaving about an hour later and some of the guys are hitching a ride on it. You're on the list to go; it's your choice which way."

"Any idea who's going on the Ganymean ship?"

"Don't know who they are, but they're standing right in front of me. I'm in the big room that the conference was held in."

"Give me a shot, would you?" Hunt asked.

He activated his wrist unit and observed the view being picked up by Brukhov's headband. It showed a group of faces that Hunt recognized at once, all of them from the labs at Pithead. Carizan was there . . . so was Frank Towers.

"Thanks for the offer," Hunt said. "I'll go with them though."

"Okay . . . oh . . . hang on a sec . . ." Indistinct background noises, then Brukhov again. "One of them wants to know where the hell you've got to."

"Tell him I've found the bar."

More noises.

"He wants to know where the hell that is."

"Okay, look over at the wall," Hunt replied. "Now follow it along to your left . . . a bit farther . . ." He watched the image move across the screen. "Hold it there. You're looking at the main door."

"Check."

"Through there, turn right and follow the passage. They can't miss it. Drinks are on the house; order through ZORAC."

"Okay, I got it. They say they'll see you there in a coupla minutes. Over and out."

"Channel cleared down," ZORAC informed him.

"Sorry about that," Hunt said to Shilohin. "We've got company on the way."

"Earthmen?"

"Bunch of drunks from up north. I made the mistake of telling them where we are."

She laughed—he could recognize the sound now—and then, slowly, her mood became serious again. "You strike me as a very rational and level-headed Earthman. There is something that we have never mentioned before because we were unsure of the reaction it might produce, but I feel it is something that we can talk about here."

"Go on." Hunt sensed that she had been giving some thought to whatever the matter was while he had been talking to the pilot. He detected a subtle change in her manner; she was not quite conveying that the topic was one of strict confidence, but that how he chose to use the information would be left to his own discretion. He knew his own kind better than she did.

"There was an occasion when the Ganymeans resorted to the use of willful violence . . . deliberate destruction of life."

Hunt waited in silence, unsure of what kind of response would be appropriate.

"You know," she went on, "about the problem that Minerva was experiencing—with the carbon-dioxide level rising. Well, one possible solution presented itself immediately—simply migrate to another planet. But this was at a time before there were any ships like the *Shapieron* . . . before we could travel to other stars. Therefore we could contemplate only the planets of the Solar System. Apart from Minerva itself, only one of them could have supported life."

Hunt looked at her blankly; the message had not quite registered.

"Earth," he said with a slight shrug.

"Yes, Earth. We could move our whole civilization to Earth. As you know, we sent expeditions to explore it, but when they sent back details of the environment that they found there, we knew that there could be no simple answer to Minerva's problems. Ganymeans could never have survived amid such savagery."

"So the idea was abandoned then?" Hunt suggested.

"No . . . not quite. You see, the whole terrestrial ecology and the creatures that formed part of it were thought by many Ganymeans to be so unnatural as to constitute a perversion of life itself—a smear upon an otherwise perfect universe that the universe would be a better place without." Hunt gaped at her as what she was saying began to sink in. "A suggestion was put forward that the whole planet be wiped clean of the disease that infested it. Terrestrial life would be exterminated, and then Minervan forms would be substituted. After all, the supporters of the scheme argued, it would be simply playing the game by Earth's own rules."

Hunt was stunned. After everything that had been said, the Ganymeans could actually have been capable of conceiving a scheme like that? She watched and seemed to read the thought in his mind.

"Most Ganymeans opposed the idea, instinctively, totally and without compromise. It was completely against their basic nature. The public protest that it provoked was probably the most vigorous in our whole history.

"Nevertheless, our own world was in danger of becoming uninhabitable, and some members of the government took the view that they had an obligation to investigate every possible alternative. So, in secret, they set up a small colony on Earth to experiment on a local scale." She saw the questions forming on Hunt's lips and held up a hand to forestall them. "Don't ask me where on Earth this colony was or what methods they employed to do the things they were sent there to do; I have great difficulty in speaking about this at all. Let us just say that the results were catastrophic. In some regions the ecology collapsed completely as a consequence of the things that were done and many terrestrial species became extinct during what you call the Oligocene period for this reason. Some of the areas affected remain deserts on Earth to this day."

Hunt didn't know what to say, so said nothing. The things he had just been told were shocking not because of the means or ends that they implied, which were all too familiar to humans, but because they were so unexpected. For him the conversation was a revelation and a staggering one at that, but no more. For the Ganymean, he realized, it was traumatic.

Shilohin seemed somewhat reassured by the absence of any violent emotional response on his part, and so continued. "Not surprisingly, the psychological effects on the colonists were equally disastrous. The whole sorry affair was quietly ended and filed away as one of the shabbier episodes of our history. We prefer to try and forget about it."

A babble of human voices interspersed with laughter came

from farther along the corridor. As Hunt looked up expectantly Shilohin touched his arm to retain his attention for a moment longer.

"That, Dr. Hunt, is the real reason why we feel too ashamed to talk about the Oligocene Earth and its animals," she said.

chapter thirteen

The *Shapieron* was pronounced fully functional once more and the Ganymeans announced their intention to take the ship for a test flight to the outermost fringe of the Solar System. The trip was expected to take about a week.

A mixed gathering of scientists, engineers and UNSA personnel had congregated in the messroom at Pithead to watch the takeoff, the view of which was being relayed from Main Base and shown on the wall screen. Hunt, Carizan and Towers were sharing a table at the back of the room and drinking coffee. As the countdown neared zero, the hubbub of conversation quieted and an air of expectancy descended.

"All UNSA vessels have cleared the area. You're okay to go on schedule." The voice of the controller at Main sounded from the audio grille.

"Acknowledged," the familiar voice of ZORAC replied. "All our prelaunch checks are positive. We're lifting off now. *Au revoir* until about a week from now, Earthmen."

"Sure. See ya around."

For a few seconds longer the huge, majestic shape, its tail end now retracted and its outer bays closed, remained motionless, towering skyward to dominate the untidy sprawl of the base in the foreground. Then the ship began to lift, slowly and smoothly, sliding up into an unbroken background of stars as the camera followed it and the last ice crest disappeared off the bottom of the picture. Almost at once it started to contract rapidly as the foreshortening increased with the angle at a rate that hinted of the fearsome buildup of speed.

"Man, look at her go!" came the voice from Main. "Do you have radar contact yet, *J5*?"

"It's going like greased lightning out of hell," another voice answered. "We're starting to lose it. The image is breaking up. They must be on main drive already—their stress field's starting to scramble the echoes. Image on the optical scanners is losing coherence too . . ." And then: "That's it. It's gone . . . like it was never there at all. Fantastic!"

That was that. A few low whistles of surprise broke the silence in the messroom at Pithead, followed by muttered exclamations and murmurings. Gradually the fragments of conversation flowed together and merged into a steady continuum of noise that rose and found its own level. The picture on the screen reverted to the view of Main, now looking somehow empty and incomplete without the ship standing in the background. Even after so short a time, life on Ganymede without the Giants around didn't feel quite right.

"Well, I've got to go," Hunt said, rising from his chair. "Chris wants to talk about something. See you both later." The other two looked up.

"Sure. See you later."

"See you, Vic."

As he moved toward the door, Hunt realized that Pithead didn't seem right either without a single Ganymean in sight. It was strange, he thought, that every one of them should need to go on a test flight; but . . . that was not really something for Earthmen to reason why. He realized also that not having ZORAC around would also take some getting used to. He had come unconsciously to accept the ability to communicate directly with others and to consult with the machine, whatever time of day it was or wherever he happened to be. ZORAC had come to be a guide, mentor, tutor and advisor all rolled into one—an omniscient and omnipresent companion. Hunt suddenly felt very alone and isolated without it. The Ganymeans could have left specialized relay equipment at Ganymede that would have sustained a link to ZORAC, but the mutual slowing down of clocks that the *Shapieron*'s velocity would produce, together with the large distance that its flight would entail, would soon have made any form of meaningful communication impossible. It was, he admitted privately to himself, going to be a long week.

* * *

Hunt found Danchekker in his lab fussing over his Minervan plants, which by this time were proliferating in every corner of the room and seemed set to embark on an invasion of the corridor outside. The subject that the professor wanted to discuss was the theory that he and Hunt had formulated jointly, before the arrival of the Ganymeans, concerning the low inherent tolerance of all Minervan land-dwelling species to atmospheric carbon dioxide. This theory held that the trait had been inherited, along with the basic system of chemical metabolism, from some very early, common, marine ancestor. After discussing the matter at some length with various Ganymean scientists through ZORAC, Danchekker now knew that this theory was wrong.

"In fact, when land dwellers eventually appeared on Minerva, they evolved a very efficient method of coping with the planet's high carbon-dioxide level. The way in which they did it was one which, with the benefit of hindsight, was very obvious and very simple." Danchekker stopped rummaging around among the mass of leaves for a moment and half turned his head to allow Hunt time to reflect on the statement. Hunt, perched casually on one of the stools with an elbow resting on the edge of the bench beside him, said nothing and waited.

"They adapted their secondary circulation systems to absorb the excess," Danchekker told him. "Systems that had evolved specifically to remove toxins in the first place. They provided a ready-made mechanism ideal for the job."

Hunt turned the proposition over in his mind and rubbed his chin thoughtfully.

"So . . ." he said after a while. "This idea we had that they all inherited a low tolerance was way off the rails . . . all baloney."

"Baloney."

"And this characteristic stayed, did it? I mean, all the species that came later inherited the mechanism . . . they were all well-adapted to their environment?"

"Yes. Perfectly adequately."

"But there's still something I don't see yet," Hunt said, frowning. "If what you've just said was true, the Ganymeans should have inherited an adequate resistance too. If they did, they wouldn't have had a CO_2 problem. But they themselves said they did have a CO_2 problem. So how come?"

Danchekker turned to face him and wiped his palms on the

front of his lab coat. He beamed through his spectacles and showed his teeth.

"They did inherit it . . . the resistance mechanism. They did have a problem too. But, you see, the problem wasn't natural; it was artificial. They brought it upon themselves, far later in their history."

"Chris, you're talking in riddles. Why not start at the beginning?"

"Very well." Danchekker began wiping dry the tools he had been using and replaced them in one of the drawers as he spoke. "As I said a moment ago, when land-dwelling life appeared on Minerva, the secondary circulation systems that all species already possessed—which caused them to be poisonous—adapted to absorb the excess carbon dioxide. Thus although Minervan air was high in carbon dioxide compared to that of Earth, all the forms of life that emerged there flourished quiet happily since they had evolved a perfectly good means of adapting to their surroundings . . . which is the way one would expect Nature to work. When, after hundreds of millions of years, intelligence emerged in the form of primitive Ganymeans, they too possessed the same basic architecture, which had remained essentially unchanged. So far so good?"

"They were still poisonous and they were well adapted," Hunt said.

"Quite so."

"What happened then?"

"Then a very interesting thing must have happened. The Ganymean race appeared and went through all the stages you would expect of a primitive culture beginning to grope its way toward civilization—making tools, growing food, building houses and so on. Well, by this time, as you might imagine, the ancient self-defense that they had inherited from their remote marine ancestors for protecting them against carnivores was turning out to be more of a damned nuisance than a help. There were no carnivores to be protected from and it was soon obvious that none were likely to appear. On the other hand, the acute accident-proneness that resulted from self-poisoning was proving to be a severe handicap." Danchekker held up a finger to show a small band of adhesive plaster around the second joint. "I nicked myself with a scalpel yesterday," he commented. "Had I been one of those early Ganymeans, I would most probably have been dead within the hour."

"Okay, point taken," Hunt conceded. "But what could they do about it?"

"Somewhere around the time that I was describing—the early beginnings of civilization—the ancients discovered that the poisons in the secondary system could be neutralized by including certain plants and molds in their diet. They discovered this by observing the habits of some animals whose immunity to damage that should have meant certain death was well known. That simple step was probably their biggest single leap forward. Coupled with their intelligence it virtually insured dominance over all forms of Minervan life. It opened up the whole of medical science, for example. With their self-poisoning mechanism defused, surgery became possible. At a later stage in their history they developed a simple surgical method of neutralizing the secondary system permanently without having to rely on drugs. It became standard practice for every Ganymean to be treated in this way soon after birth. Even later still, when they had progressed to a level beyond ours, they isolated the gene that caused the secondary system to develop in the fetus in the first place and eradicated it completely. They literally bred this trait out of themselves. None of the Ganymeans we've met was born with a secondary system at all, and neither were quite a few generations before them. Rather an elegant solution, don't you think?"

"Incredible," Hunt agreed. "I've never had a chance to talk about that kind of thing with them . . . not yet anyway."

"Oh, yes." Danchekker nodded. "They were extremely proficient genetic engineers, were our Ganymean friends . . . very proficient."

Hunt thought for a second and then snapped his fingers in sudden comprehension.

"But of course," he said. "In doing that they buggered their CO_2 tolerance too."

"Precisely, Vic. All the other animals on Minerva retained the high natural tolerance. Only the Ganymeans were different; they sacrificed it in exchange for accident-resistance."

"But I don't see how they could," Hunt said, frowning again. "I mean, I can see how they did it, but I don't see how they could get away with it. They must have needed the CO_2 tolerance, otherwise they wouldn't have evolved it in the first place. They must have known that too. Surely they weren't stupid."

Danchekker nodded as if he already knew what Hunt was going to say.

"That probably wasn't so obvious at the time," he said. "You see, the composition of the Minervan atmosphere fluctuated through the ages much the same as that of Earth has. From various researches the Ganymeans established that at the time land life first emerged, volcanic activity was at a peak and the level of CO_2 was very high; naturally, therefore, the earliest species developed a high resistance. But as time went on the level decreased progressively and appeared to have stabilized itself by the time of the Ganymeans. They came to regard their tolerance mechanism as an ancient relic of conditions that no longer existed and their experiences showed that they could get by without it. The margin was small—the CO_2 level was still high by our standards—but they could manage. So, they decided to do away with it permanently."

"Ah, but then the level started going up again," Hunt guessed.

"Suddenly and catastrophically," Danchekker confirmed. "On a geological time scale anyway. They were in no immediate danger, but all their measurements and calculations indicated that if the rate of increase went on, they—or their descendants one day anyway—would be in trouble. They would be unable to survive without their ancient tolerance mechanism, but they had eliminated that mechanism from their race. All the other animals would have no difficulty in adapting, but the Ganymeans were somewhat stuck."

The full magnitude of the problem that had confronted the Ganymeans dawned on Hunt at last. They had bought a one-way ticket out of the hard-labor camp only to find that it led to the death cell.

"What could they do?" Danchekker asked, and then went on to answer the question for himself. "First—use their technology to hold the CO_2 level down by artificial means. They thought of that but their models couldn't guarantee them a tight enough measure of control over the process. There was a high risk that they'd end up freezing the whole planet solid and, being the cautious breed that they were, they elected not to try it—at least not until it was a last-resort measure.

"Second—they could reduce the CO_2 as before, but have ready at hand a method for warming up the sun to compensate for the loss of the greenhouse effect if the atmospheric engineering got out of control. They tried that on Iscaris but it went wrong, as the scientists on Minerva learned when they received a message from the *Shapieron* that was sent just before the ship itself got away."

Hunt made no move to interrupt, so Danchekker continued. "Third—they could migrate to Earth. They tried doing so on a pilot scale, but that went wrong too." Danchekker shrugged and held the posture, his arms extended to indicate that he had run out of possibilities. Hunt waited for a moment longer, but the professor evidently had nothing more to say.

"So what the devil did they do?" Hunt asked.

"I don't know. The Ganymeans don't know either, since whatever else may have been thought of was thought of after they had left Minerva. They are as curious as we are—more so I would imagine. It was their world."

"But the animals from Earth," Hunt insisted. "They were all imported later on. Couldn't they have had something to do with the solution?"

"They could have, certainly, but what exactly, I've no idea. Neither have the Ganymeans. We're satisfied, though, that it would not have been anything to do with using a terrestrial type of ecology to absorb the CO_2. That simply wouldn't have worked."

"That idea's gone right out the window, eh?"

"Right out," Danchekker said decisively. "Why they brought the animals there and whether or not it had anything to do with their atmospheric problem is still all a mystery. . . ." The professor paused and peered intently over the top of his spectacles. "There's another mystery too now—a new one—from what we've just been talking about."

"Another one?" Hunt returned his stare curiously. "What?"

"All the other Minervan animals," Danchekker replied slowly. "You see, if they all possessed a perfectly adequate mechanism for dealing with CO_2, it couldn't have been the changing atmosphere of Minerva that wiped them all out after all. If that didn't, then what did?"

chapter fourteen

The landscape was a featureless, undulating sheet of ice that extended in every direction to merge into the gloom of a perpetual night. Overhead a diminutive Sun, barely more than just a bright star among millions, sent down its feeble rays to paint an eerie and foreboding twilight on the scene.

The huge shadowy shape of the ship soared upward to lose itself in the blackness above; arc lights set high on its side cast down a brilliant cone of whiteness, etching out an enormous circle on the ice next to where the ship stood. Around the inside of the periphery of the pool of light, several hundred space-suited, eight-foot-tall figures stood four deep in unmoving ranks, their heads bowed and their hands clasped loosely before them. The area within the circle was divided into a series of concentric rings and at regular intervals around each ring rectangular pits had been cut into the ice, each one aligned with the center. By the side of each of the pits lay a metallic, box-shaped container roughly nine feet long and four feet wide.

A small group of figures walked slowly to the center and began moving around the innermost ring, stopping at each pit in turn and watching in silence while the container was lowered before moving on to the next. A second small group followed, filling each of the pits with water from a heated hose; the water froze solid in seconds. When they had finished the first ring they moved out to begin on the second, and continued until they were back at the edge of the circle.

They stood gazing for a long time at the simple memorial that they had erected in the center of the circle—a golden obelisk with an inscription on each face, surmounted by a light that would burn for a hundred years. And as they gazed, their thoughts went back in time to friends and faces that they once had known, and who could never again be more than memories.

319

Then, when the time had come, they turned away and began filing slowly back toward their ship. When the arc lights were turned out, only the tiny glow of light around the obelisk remained to hold the night at bay.

They had honored the pledge that they had made and carried with them through all the years that had brought them here, from another place, from another time.

Beneath the ice field of Pluto lay the soil of Minerva.

The Giants had come home to lay their dead to rest.

chapter fifteen

The *Shapieron* reappeared out of space as suddenly as it had gone. The surveillance radars of *Jupiter Five* picked up an indistinct echo hurtling in from the void and rapidly consolidating itself as it shed speed at a phenomenal rate. By the time the optical scanners had been brought to bear, there it was, coasting into orbit over Ganymede just like the first time. This time, however, the emotions that greeted its arrival were very different.

The exchange of messages recorded in *Jupiter Five*'s Communications Center Day Log was enthusiastic and friendly.

Shapieron Good afternoon.
J5   Hi. How was the trip?
Shap.   Excellent. How has the weather been?
J5   Pretty much the same as ever. How were the engines?
Shap.   Never better. Did you save our rooms?
J5   Same ones as before. You wanna go on down?
Shap.   Thanks. We know the way.

Within five hours of the *Shapieron* touching down at Ganymede Main Base, familiar eight-foot-tall figures were clumping up and down the corridors at Pithead once again.

* * *

Hunt's conversation with Danchekker had stimulated his curiosity about biological mechanisms for combating the effects of toxins and contaminants in the body, and he spent the next few days accessing the data banks of *Jupiter Five* to study up on the subject. Shilohin had mentioned that terrestrial life had evolved from early marine species that hadn't developed a secondary circulation system because they hadn't needed one; the warmer environment of Earth had imposed less strenuous demands for oxygen with the result that load-sharing had not been necessary. But it was this same mechanism that had later enabled the emerging Minervan land dwellers to adapt to a CO_2-rich atmosphere. The terrestrial animals imported to Minerva had obviously possessed no similar mechanism, and yet they had adapted readily enough to their new home. Hunt was curious to find out how they did it.

His researches failed, however, to throw up anything startling. Each world had evolved its own family of life, and the two systems of fundamental chemistry on which the two families were based were not the same. Minervan chemistry was rather delicate, as Danchekker had deduced long ago from his study of the preserved Minervan fish discovered in the ruins of a wrecked Lunarian base; land animals inheriting such chemistry would be inherently sensitive to certain toxins, including carbon dioxide, and would require an extra line of defense to give them a reasonable tolerance if atmospheric conditions were extreme—hence the adaptation of the secondary system in the earliest land dwellers. Terrestrial chemistry was more rugged and flexible and could survive a far wider range of changes, even without any assistance. And that was really all there was to it.

One afternoon, Hunt found himself sitting in front of the viewscreen in one of the computer console rooms at Pithead at the end of another unsuccessful attempt to uncover a new slant on the subject. Having nobody else to talk to, he activated his channel into the Ganymean computer network and discussed the problem with ZORAC. The machine listened solemnly without offering much in the way of comment while Hunt spoke. Afterward it had one comment. "I really don't see much to add, Vic. You seem to have got it pretty wrapped up."

"There's nothing you can think of that I might have left

out?" Hunt queried. It seemed a funny question for a scientist to put to a machine, but Hunt had come to know well ZORAC's uncanny ability to spot a missing detail or a small flaw in what appeared to be a watertight line of reasoning.

"No. The evidence adds up to what you've already concluded: Minervan life needed the help of a secondary system to adapt and terrestrial life didn't. That is an observed fact, not a deduction. Therefore there's not a lot I can say."

"No, I guess not," Hunt conceded with a sigh. He flipped a switch to cut off the terminal, lit a cigarette and slumped back in a chair. "It wasn't really that important, I suppose," he commented absently after a while. "I was just curious to see if the differences in biochemistry between our life forms and Minervan ones pointed to anything significant. Looks as if they don't."

"What were you hoping to find?" ZORAC asked. Hunt shrugged automatically.

"Oh, I don't know . . . something that might shed light on the kinds of things we've been asking . . . what happened to all the Minervan land dwellers, what was it that they couldn't survive that the animals from Earth could—we know it wasn't the CO_2 concentration now. . . . Things like that."

"Anything unusual, in fact," ZORAC suggested.

"Mmm . . . guess so."

A few seconds passed before ZORAC spoke again. Hunt had the uncanny impression that the machine was turning the proposition over in its mind. Then it said in a matter-of-fact voice: "Maybe you've been asking the wrong question."

It took a moment for the implication to sink in. Then Hunt snatched the cigarette from his lips and sat forward in his chair with a start.

"What d'you mean?" he asked. "What's wrong with the question?"

"You're asking why Minervan life and terrestrial life were different and succeeding only in proving that the answer is, 'because they were.' It's undeniably true, but singularly ineffective in telling you anything new. It's like asking, 'Why does salt dissolve in water when sand doesn't?' and coming up with the answer, 'because salt's soluble and sand isn't.' Very true, but it doesn't tell you much. That's what you're doing."

"You mean I've simply been working around a circular argument?" Hunt said, but even as he spoke he could see it was true.

"An elaborate one, but when you analyze the logic of it—yes," ZORAC confirmed.

Hunt nodded to himself and flicked his cigarette to the ashtray.

"Okay. What question should I be asking?"

"Forget about Minervan life and terrestrial life for a moment, and just concentrate on the terrestrial," ZORAC replied. "Now ask why Man is so different from any other species."

"I thought we knew all that." Hunt said. "Bigger brains, opposable thumbs, high-quality vision all in one species together—all the tools you need to stimulate curiosity and learning. What's new?"

"I know *what* the differences are," ZORAC stated. "My question was *why* are they?"

Hunt rubbed his chin with his knuckle for a while as he reflected on the question. "Do you think that's significant?"

"Very."

"Okay. I'll buy it. Why is Man so different from any other species?"

"I don't know."

"Great!" Hunt exhaled a long stream of smoke with a sigh. "And how exactly is that supposed to tell us more than my answers did?"

"It doesn't," ZORAC conceded. "But it's a question that needs answering. If you're looking for something unusual, that's a good place to start. There's something very unusual about Man."

"Oh, how come?"

"Because by rights Man shouldn't exist. It shouldn't have been possible for him to evolve. Man simply can't happen, but he did. That seems very unusual to me."

Hunt shook his head, puzzled. The machine was speaking in riddles.

"I don't understand. Why shouldn't Man have happened?"

"I have computed the interaction matrix functions that describe the responses of neuron trigger potentials in the nervous systems of higher terrestrial vertebrates. Some of the reaction coefficients are highly dependent on the concentrations and distributions of certain microchemical agencies. Coherent response patterns in key areas of the cerebral cortex could not stabilize with the levels that are usual in all species except Man."

Pause.

"ZORAC, what are you talking about?"

"I'm not making sense?"

"To put it mildly—no."

"Okay." ZORAC paused for a second as if getting its thoughts organized. "Are you familiar with Kaufmann and Randall's recent work at the University of Utrecht, Holland? It is fully recorded in *Jupiter Five*'s data bank."

"Yes, I did come across some references to it," Hunt replied. "Refresh my memory on it."

"Kaufmann and Randall conducted extensive research on the way in which terrestrial vertebrates protect themselves against toxic agents and harmful microorganisms that enter their systems," ZORAC said. "The details vary somewhat from species to species, but essentially the basic mechanism is the same—presumably handed down and modified from common remote ancestral forms."

"Ah yes, I remember," Hunt said. "A kind of natural self-immunization process, wasn't it."

He was referring to the discovery by the scientists at Utrecht that the animals of Earth manufactured a whole mixture of contaminants and toxins on a small scale, which were injected into the bloodstream in quantities just high enough to stimulate the production of specific antitoxins. The "blueprint" for manufacturing these antitoxins was thus permanently impressed into the body's chemical system in such a way that production would multiply prodigiously in the event of the body being invaded on a dangerous scale.

"Correct," ZORAC answered. "It explains why animals are far less bothered by unwholesome environments, polluted diets and so on than Man is."

"Because Man is different; he doesn't work that way—right?"

"Right."

"Which brings us back to your question."

"Right."

Hunt regarded the blank screen of the console for a while, frowning to himself in an effort to follow what the machine was getting at. Whatever it was, it failed to register.

"I still don't see where it gets us," Hunt said at last. "Man's different because he's different. It's just as much a pointless question as before."

"Not quite," ZORAC said. "The point is that it shouldn't have been possible for Man to become different. That's what's interesting."

"How come? I'm not with you."

"Permit me to show you some equations that I have solved," ZORAC suggested.

"Go ahead."

"If you key in a channel-activate command I'll put them on the large screen via the UNSA comnet."

Hunt obliged by tapping a quick sequence of characters into the keyboard in front of him. A second later the screen above kaleidoscoped into a blaze of colors which immediately stabilized into a mass of densely packaged mathematical expressions. Hunt stared at the display for a few seconds and then shook his head.

"What's it all supposed to be?" he asked.

ZORAC was happy to explain. "Those expressions describe quantitatively certain aspects of behavior of the generalized central nervous system of the terrestrial vertebrate. Specifically they define how the basic nervous system will respond to the presence of given concentrations and mixes of various chemical agents in the bloodstream. The coefficients indicated in red are modifiers that would be fixed for a given species, but the dominant factors are the general ones shown in green."

"So?"

"It reveals a fundamental drawback in the method that was adopted by terrestrial animals to protect themselves from their chemical environment. The drawback is that the substances introduced into the bloodstream by the self-immunization process will interfere with the functions of the nervous system. In particular, they will inhibit the development of higher brain functions."

Suddenly Hunt realized what ZORAC was driving at. Before he could voice his thoughts, however, the machine went on.

"In particular, intelligence shouldn't be capable of emerging at all. Larger and more complex brains demand a greater supply of blood; a greater supply of blood carries more contaminants and concentrates them in the brain cells; contaminated brain cells can't coordinate sufficiently to exhibit higher levels of activity, that is, intelligence.

"In other words, intelligence should never have been able to evolve from the terrestrial line of vertebrate evolution. All the figures there say that terrestrial life should have got itself truly stuck up a dead end."

Hunt gazed for a long time at the symbols frozen on the screen while he pondered the meaning of all this. The ancient architecture evolved by the remote ancestors of the vertebrates hundreds of millions of years before had met a short-term need but failed to anticipate the longer-term consequences. But Man, somewhere along his evolutionary line, had abandoned the self-immunization mechanism. In doing this he had increased his vulnerability to his surroundings, but at the same time he had opened up the way to evolving the superior intelligence that would, in time, more than make up for the initial disadvantage.

The intriguing question of course was: How and when had Man done it? The theory offered by the Utrecht researchers was: during the forced exodus of his ancestors to Minerva, during the period that lasted from twenty-five million to fifty thousand years ago. Twenty-five million years before, many species of ordinary terrestrial life had been shipped there; nearly that long later, only one had come back—one that had been very far from ordinary. *Homo sapiens*, in the shape of the Lunarians, had returned—the most ferocious adversary that the survival arena of either world had ever witnessed. He had dominated Minerva while contemporaneous anthropoids on Earth groped around in the dim twilight zone on the fringes of self-awareness, and then, having destroyed that world, had returned to Earth to claim his place of origin, completely and ruthlessly extinguishing his remote cousins in the process.

Danchekker had reasoned that a violent mutation had taken place along the line of human descent isolated on Minerva. This latest piece of information pointed out the area in which the mutation had occurred; it didn't attempt to explain why it had happened. But then, mutations are random events; there was nothing to suggest that there had been any specific cause to look for.

The evident fact of the emergence of Ganymean intelligence fitted in nicely with this body of theory too. The architecture of Minervan land dwellers had isolated the system that carried the toxins from the system that carried blood. Thus, when larger brains became in order, the way was clear to evolve a brain that could draw more blood without more toxins—the density of one network simply increased while that of the other didn't. Higher brain functions could develop without hindrance. The intelligence of the Ganymeans was the natural and logical outcome of Minervan evolution. Terrestrial evolution, however, pointed to no such natural and logical outcome; Man had somehow cheated the system.

"Well," Hunt declared finally. "It's interesting, sure. But what makes you say it shouldn't have happened? Mutations are random events. The change came about as a mutation that took place on Minerva, somewhere along the line that led to the Lunarians and from there to Man. It looks straightforward. What's wrong with that?"

"I thought you'd say that," ZORAC commented, somehow managing to give the impression of sounding quite pleased with itself. "That's the obvious first reaction."

"So—what's wrong with it?"

"It couldn't work. What you're saying is that somewhere early on in the primate line on Minerva, a mutation must have occurred that deactivated the self-immunization system."

"Yes," Hunt agreed.

"But there's a problem in that," ZORAC advised him. "You see, I have performed extensive computations on further data available from *J5*—data that describe the genetic coding contained in vertebrate chromosomes. In all species, the coding that controls the development of the self-immunization process in the growing embryo contains the coding that enables the animal specifically to absorb excess carbon dioxide. In other words, if you deactivated the self-immunization mechanism, you'd also lose the ability to tolerate a CO_2-rich environment. . . ."

"And Minerva was becoming CO_2-rich," Hunt supplied, seeing the point.

"Exactly. If a mutation of the kind you're suggesting occurred, then the species in which it had occurred could not have survived on Minerva. Hence, the ancestors of the Lunarians could have not have mutated like that. If they did, they'd have died out. The Lunarians would never have existed and you wouldn't exist."

"But I do," Hunt pointed out needlessly, but with a certain sense of satisfaction.

"I know, and you shouldn't, and that's my question," ZORAC concluded.

Hunt stubbed out his cigarette and lapsed into thought again. "What about the funny enzyme that Chris Danchekker is always talking about? He found it in all the preserved Oligocene animals in the ship here, didn't he? There were traces of a variant of it in Charlie too. D'you reckon that could have something to do with it? Maybe something in the environment on Minerva reacted in some complicated way and got around the problem and the enzyme appeared somehow in the process. That wouldn't explain why today's terrestrial animals haven't got it; the ancestors they're descended from never went there. Perhaps that's why modern Man doesn't have it either—he's been back on Earth for a long time now and away from the environment that stimulated it. How about that?"

"Impossible to confirm," ZORAC pronounced. "Inadequate data available on the enzyme at present. Very speculative. Also, there's another point it doesn't explain."

"Oh, what?"

"The radioactive decay residues. Why should the enzymes found in the Oligocene animals appear to have been formed from radioisotopes while the ones found in Charlie didn't?"

"I don't know," Hunt admitted. "That doesn't make sense. Anyhow, I'm not a biologist. I'll talk about all this to Chris later." Then he changed the subject. "ZORAC—about all those equations you computed."

"Yes?"

"Why did you compute them? I mean . . . do you just do things like that spontaneously . . . on your own initiative?"

"No. Shilohin and some of the other Ganymean scientists asked me to."

"Any idea why?"

"Routine. The computations were relevant to certain researches that they are conducting."

"What kind of researches?" Hunt asked.

"On the things we have been discussing. The question that I suggested a few minutes ago was not something that I originated myself; it was a question that they have been asking. They are very interested in the whole subject. They're curious to find out how Man came to exist at all when all available data says he shouldn't and all their models predicted that he would destroy himself if he did."

Hunt was intrigued to learn that the Ganymeans were studying his kind with such intensity, especially since they appeared to have progressed so much farther in their deductions than the UNSA team had. He was surprised also that ZORAC would so readily divulge something that could be considered sensitive information.

"I'm amazed that there aren't any restrictions on you talking about things like that," he said.

"Why?"

The question caught Hunt unprepared.

"Oh, I don't know really," he said. "On Earth I suppose things like that would only be accessible to people authorized . . . certainly not freely available to anyone who cared to ask for it. I suppose I . . . just assumed it would be the same."

"The fact that Earthmen are neurotic is no reason for Ganymeans to be furtive," ZORAC told him bluntly.

Hunt grinned and shook his head slowly.

"I guess I asked for that," he sighed.

chapter sixteen

The first and most important task that the Ganymeans had faced—that of getting their ship in order again—had now been successfully accomplished. So the focal point of their activities shifted to Pithead, where they commenced working intensively toward their second objective—coming to grips with the computer system of the wrecked ship. Whether the Ganymean race had migrated to another star, and if so which star, had still not been answered. A strong probability remained that this information was sitting waiting to be found, buried somewhere in the intricate molecular circuits and storage banks that went to make up the data-processing complex of a ship that had been built after the answers to these questions were known. The ship might even have been involved in that very migration.

The task turned out to be nowhere near as straightforward as the first one. Although the Pithead ship was of a later and more advanced design than the *Shapieron*, its main drives worked on similar principles and used components which, although showing certain modifications and refinements in some instances, performed functions that were essentially the same as those of their earlier counterparts. The drive system thus exemplified a mature technology that had not changed radically between the times of the two ships' construction, and the repair of the *Shapieron* had been possible as a consequence.

The same was not true for the computer systems. After a week of intensive analysis and probing, the Ganymean scientists admitted they were making little headway. The problem was that the system components that they found themselves trying to comprehend were, in most cases, unlike anything they had seen before. The processors themselves consisted of solid crystal blocks inside which millions of separate circuit elements of molecular dimensions were interconnected in three dimensions with complexities that defied the imagination. Only somebody who had been trained and educated in the design and physics of such devices would hope to unravel the coding locked inside them.

Some of the larger processors were completely revolutionary in concept, even to the Ganymeans, and seemed to represent a merging of electronic and gravitic technologies; characteristics of both were inextricably mingled together to form devices in which the physical interconnections between cells holding electronic data could be changed through variable graviticbonding links. The hardware configuration itself was programmable and could be switched from nanosecond to nanosecond to yield an array in which any and every cell could function as a storage element at one instant or as a processing site the next; processing could, in the ultimate, be performed everywhere in the complex, all at the same time—surely the last word in parallelism. One interested but bemused UNSA engineer described it as "soft hardware. A brain with a billion times the speed . . ."

And every subsystem of the ship—communications, navigation, computation, propulsion control, flight control, and a hundred others—consisted of a network of interconnected processing nodes like that, with all the networks integrated into an impossible web that covered the length and breadth of the vessel.

Without detailed documentation and technical design information there was no way of tackling the problem. But no documentation was available. All the information was locked away inside the same system that they needed the information to get into; it was like having a can with the can opener inside it.

So, at the next progress meeting aboard the *Shapieron*, the senior Ganymean computer scientist declared himself ready to quit. When somebody commented that the Earthmen wouldn't have given up so easily he thought about it, agreed with the evaluation and went back to Pithead to try again. After another week he came back again and stated, emphatically and finally, that if anybody thought the Earthmen could do better they'd be welcome to try. He'd quit.

And that, it seemed, was that.

There was nothing further to be achieved on Ganymede. Therefore the aliens at last announced their long-awaited decision to accept the invitation that had been extended to them by the world's governments, and come to Earth. This did not mean that they had also accepted the invitation to settle there. Admittedly there was nowhere else within many light-years for them to go, but many of them still harbored misgivings at what might await them on the Nightmare Planet. But they were rational beings and the rational thing to do was obviously to go and see the place before prejudging it. Any decision as to what to do about the longer-term future would wait until they were in possession of more concrete information on which to base it.

A number of UNSA personnel from the Jupiter missions were at the end of their duty tours and already scheduled to return to Earth as the comings and goings of ships permitted. The Ganymeans offered a ride in the *Shapieron* to anybody planning on going their way and were almost overwhelmed by the rush to accept.

Fortuitously, Hunt's latest communication from Gregg Caldwell, executive director of UNSA's Navcomms Division and Hunt's immediate chief, had indicated that Hunt's assignment on Ganymede was considered fulfilled and there was other work to be done back at Houston. Arrangements were being put in hand to ship him back. He had no difficulty in getting his name deleted from the UNSA schedule and added to the list of passengers due to go with the *Shapieron*.

Danchekker's main reason for coming to Ganymede had been to investigate the terrestrial Oligocene animals found in the Pithead ship. The professor persuaded Monchar, second in command of the Ganymean expedition, that there was plenty of room in the *Shapieron* to carry all the specimens of interest; after that he persuaded his director, at the Westwood Biological Institute, Houston, that the investigations would be carried out more thoroughly back on Earth, where all the facilities needed were available for the asking. The outcome was exactly as he had intended: Danchekker was going too.

And so the time came for Hunt to pack his belongings and take one last look around the tiny room that had been home for so long. Then he made the familiar walk along the well-worn corridor that led to the Domestic Dome to join the handful of others who were shipping out. There they stood a last round of drinks for their friends staying on and made their farewells. After promises to keep in touch and assertions that every-body's paths would cross again one day, they trooped through into the Site Operations Control building where the base com-mander and some of his staff were waiting in the airlock ante-room to bid them an official adieu. The access tube beyond the airlock took them through into the cabin of the tracked ice crawler that would carry them across to the landing pads, where a transporter ship was waiting.

Hunt's feelings were mixed as he gazed out of one of the crawler's viewing ports at the shadowy snatches of buildings and constructions that came and went among Pithead's swirling, eternal methane-ammonia mist. Going home after a long time away was always a nice feeling of course, but he would miss many aspects of the life he had grown used to in the tightly knit UNSA community here, where everybody shared in everybody else's problems and strangers were un-known. The spirit of comradeship that he found here, the feel-ing of belonging, the sense of a common purpose . . . all these things gave a special intimacy to this tiny, manmade haven of survival that had been carved out of the hostile Ganymedean wilderness. The feelings he was experiencing so intensely at that moment would soon be diluted and forgotten when he re-turned to Earth and again rubbed shoulders every day with faceless millions, all busily living out their different lives in their different ways and with their different aims and values. There, custom and synthetic social barriers served to mark out the lines of demarcation that men needed in order to satisfy their psychological need to identify with definable cultural groups. The colony on Ganymede had not needed to build any artificial walls around itself to set it apart from the rest of the human race; Nature and several hundred million miles of empty space provided all the isolation necessary.

Perhaps, he thought to himself, that was why men pitched camps on the South Col of Everest, sailed ships across the seven seas, and held reunion dinners year after year to share nostalgic memories of school or army days. The challenges and the hardships that they faced together forged bonds between them that the protective cocoon of normal society could never emulate and awakened an awareness of qualities in themselves and in each other that could never be erased. He knew then that, like the sailor or the mountaineer, he would return time after time to know again the things that he had found on Ganymede.

Danchekker, however, was less of a romantic.

"I don't care if they discover seven-headed monsters on Saturn," the professor said as they boarded the transporter. "Once I get home again I'm staying there. I've lived quite enough of my life already surrounded by these wretched contraptions."

"I bet you find you've developed agoraphobia when you get there," Hunt told him.

At Main there was another round of farewells to go through before they were driven out, now wearing space suits, to the *Shapieron*'s lowered entrance section; they could not be flown directly up into the ship's outer bays because the telescopic access tubes that projected from the buildings of the base—affording direct entry to UNSA ships and vehicles—were not designed to mate with the airlocks of Ganymean daughter vessels. Members of the Ganymean crew received them at the foot of the entrance ramp and conducted them up into the stern section, where an elevator was waiting to carry them up into the main body of the ship.

Three hours later loading was complete and the final departure preparations had been made. Garuth and a small Ganymean rear guard exchanged formal words of parting with the base commander and some of his officers, who had driven out to the ramp for the ceremony. Then the Earthmen boarded their vehicle and returned to the base while the Ganymeans withdrew into the *Shapieron* and the stern section retracted upward into its flight position.

Hunt was alone in the cabin that had been allocated to him, taking in his last view of Main from a mural videoscreen, when ZORAC announced that takeoff was imminent. There was no sensation of motion at all; the view just started to diminish in size and flatten out as the ground fell away beneath. The Ganymedean landscape flowed inward from the edges of the picture and the surface details rapidly dissolved into a uniform sea of frosty whiteness as the ship gained altitude. Soon even the pinpoint of reflected light that was Main faded into the background, and an arc of blackness began advancing upward across the view as Ganymede's dark side moved into the picture. At the top, the curvature of the moon's sunlit side appeared, ushering in a gaggle of attendant background stars. The bright strip left in the center of the screen continued to narrow steadily, and at last its ends slipped in from beyond the edges of the frame to reveal it as a brilliant crescent hanging in the heavens, and already shrinking as he watched. Then the crescent and the stars seemed to dissolve into diffuse smudges of light that flowed into one another until the whole screen was reduced to a uniform expanse of featureless, iridescent fog. The ship was now under main drive, he realized, and temporarily shut off from information coming in from the rest of the universe—information carried as electromagnetic waves anyway. He wondered what the Ganymeans used instead—to navigate by, for instance. Here was something he would raise with ZORAC.

But that could wait for now. For the moment he just wanted to relax and prepare his mind for other things. Unlike his voyage out aboard *Jupiter Five*, the journey to Earth would be measured in days.

chapter seventeen

And so the Ganymeans came at last to Earth.

After the failure of the various governments to reach agreement among themselves as to where the aliens should be received in the event of their accepting the invitation to visit, the Parliament of the United States of Europe had voted to go it alone and make their own preparations anyway—just in case. The place they selected was an area of pleasant open country on the Swiss shore of Lake Geneva, where, it was hoped, the climate would prove agreeable to the Ganymean constitution and the historical tradition of nonbelligerence would add a singularly appropriate note.

About halfway between the city of Geneva and Lausanne, they fenced off an area just over a mile square on the edge of the lake, and inside it erected a village of chalets that had been designed for Ganymean occupation; the ceilings were high, the doorways big, the beds strong, and the windows slightly tinted. Communal cooking and dining facilities were provided, along with leisure rooms, terminals linked into the World's integrated entertainments/data/news grid, an outsize swimming pool, a recreation area, and just about anything else which seemed likely to contribute to making life comfortable and could be included in the time available. A huge concrete pad was laid to support the *Shapieron* and afford parking for vehicles and daughter ships, and accommodation inside the perimeter was provided for delegations of visiting Earthmen, together with conference and social facilities.

When the news came in from Jupiter that the aliens were planning on departing for Earth in just a couple of weeks' time and—even more startling—the journey would take only a few days, it was obvious that the issue of where to receive them had already been decided. By the time the *Shapieron* appeared from the depths of space and went into Earth orbit, a fleet of suborbital aircraft was converging on Geneva with officials and Heads of State from every corner of the globe, all hurrying to participate in the hastily worked out welcoming formalities. Swarms of buzzing VTOL jets shuttled back and forth between Geneva International Airport and what was now being called Ganyville to convey them to their final destination while traffic on the Geneva/Lausanne highway below deteriorated to a bumper-to-bumper jam, private aircars having been banned from the area. A peppering of colors, becoming denser as the hours went by, appeared on the green inland slopes that overlooked Ganyville, as the first spectators arrived and set up camp with tents, sleeping bags, blankets, and picnic stoves, determined to secure and hold a grandstand view. A continuous cordon of jovial but overworked policemen, including some from Italy, France, and Germany since the numbers of the tiny Swiss force were simply not up to the task, maintained a clear zone two hundred meters wide between the rapidly growing crowd and the perimeter fence, while on the lakeward side a flotilla of police launches scurried to and fro to keep at bay an armada of boats, yachts, and craft of every description. Along the roadsides an instant market came into being as the more entrepreneurial members of the shopkeeping fraternity from the nearby towns loaded their stocks into trucks and brought the business to where the customers were. A lot of small fortunes were made that day, from selling everything from instant meals and woolly sweaters to hiking boots and high-power telescopes.

Several thousand miles above, the *Shapieron* was not quite away from it all. An assortment of UNSA craft had formed themselves into a ragged escort around the ship, sweeping with it round the Earth every hour and a half. Many of them carried newsmen and camera crews broadcasting live to an enthralled audience via the World News Grid. They had exchanged messages with ZORAC and the Earthmen aboard who had come with the *Shapieron* from Jupiter, thrilled the viewers below by beaming down views from inside an alien spacecraft, and mixed in constantly updated reports of the latest developments at Lake Geneva. In between, the commentators had described *ad nauseam* how the ship had first appeared over Ganymede, what had transpired since, where their race had originated in the first place, why the expedition had gone to Iscaris and what had happened there, and anything else they could think of to fill in time before the big event. Half the factories and offices on Earth were estimated to have given it up as a bad job and closed down until after the big event was all over, since the employees who weren't glued to a screen somewhere else were glued to one being paid out of the firm's money. As one president of a New York company commented to an NBC street interviewer: "I'm not gonna spend thousands to find out all over again what King Canute proved centuries ago—you can't stop the tide once it's made its mind up. I've sent 'em all home to get it outa their systems. I guess this year we've got an extra day's public holiday." On being asked what he himself intended doing, he replied with surprise: "Me? I'm going home to watch the landing, of course."

Inside the *Shapieron*, Hunt and Danchekker were among the mixed group of Ganymeans and Earthmen gathered in the ship's command center—the place to which Hunt had been conducted with Storrel and the others at the time of their momentous first visit from *Jupiter Five*. A number of eggs had been dispatched from the *Shapieron* to descend to lower altitudes and obtain, for the aliens' benefit, a bird's-eye preview of different parts of Earth. The Earthmen were explaining the significance of some of the pictures that the eggs were sending back. Already the Ganymeans had gazed incredulously at the teeming density of life in cities such as New York, Tokyo and London, gasped at the spectacles of the Arabian desert and the Amazon jungle—terrain unlike any that had existed on Minerva—and stared in mute, horrified fascination at a telescopic presentation of lions stalking zebra in the African grasslands.

To Hunt, the familiar sights of green continents, sun-drenched plains and blue oceans, after what felt like an eternity of nothing but rock, ice and the blackness of space, were overpowering. As different parts of the mosaic of Earth came and went across the main screen, he detected a steady change in the moods of the Ganymeans too. The earlier misgivings and apprehensions that some of them had felt were being swept away by an almost intoxicating enthusiasm that became contagious as time went by. They were becoming restless and excited—keen to see more, firsthand, of the incredible world where chance had brought them.

One of the eggs was hovering three miles up over Lake Geneva and relaying up to the *Shapieron* its telescopic view of the throngs that were still building up on the hills overlooking Ganyville and all over the meadows surrounding it. The Ganymeans were pleasantly surprised, and at the same time astounded, that they should be the objects of such widespread interest and such a display of mass emotion. Hunt had tried to explain that the arrival of alien spacecraft was not something that happened very often, let alone one from twenty-five million years in the past, but the Ganymeans appeared unable to comprehend how anything could give rise to a spontaneous demonstration of emotion on so vast a scale. Monchar had wondered if the Earthmen that they had so far met represented "the more stable and rational end to the human spectrum rather than a typical cross section." Hunt had decided to say nothing and leave it at that. Monchar would no doubt be able to answer that for himself in good time.

A lull in the conversation had occurred and everybody was watching the screen as one of the Ganymeans muttered commands to ZORAC to take the egg a little lower and zoom in closer. The view expanded and closed in on the side of a small, grassy hill, by this time thick with people of all ages, sizes, manners and garbs. There were people cooking, people drinking, people playing and people just sitting; it could have been a day at the races, a pop festival, a flying display, or all of them rolled into one.

"Are they all safe out in the open there?" one of the Ganymeans asked dubiously after a while.

"Safe?" Hunt looked puzzled. "How do you mean?"

"I'm surprised that none of them seem to be carrying guns. I'd have thought they would have guns."

"Guns? What for?" Hunt asked, somewhat bewildered.

"The carnivores," the Ganymean replied, as if it was obvious. "What will they do if they are attacked by carnivores?"

Danchekker explained that few animals existed that were dangerous to Man, and that those that did lived only in a few restricted areas, all of them many thousands of miles from Switzerland.

"Oh, I assumed that was why they have built a defensive system around the place," The Ganymean said.

Hunt laughed. "That's not to keep carnivores out," he said. "It's to keep humans out."

"You mean they might attack us?" There was a sudden note of alarm in the question.

"Not at all. It's simply to insure your privacy and to make sure that nobody makes a nuisance of himself. The government assumed that you wouldn't want crowds of sightseers and tourists wandering around you all the time and getting in the way."

"Couldn't the government just make a law ordering them to stay away?" Shilohin asked from across the room. "That sounds much simpler."

Hunt laughed again, probably because the feeling of seeing home again was affecting him a little. "You haven't met many Earth-people yet," he said. "I don't think they'd take very much notice. They're not what you might call . . . easily disciplined."

Shilohin was evidently surprised by the statement. "Really?" she said. "I had always imagined them to be precisely the opposite. I mean . . . I've watched some of the old newsreels from Earth—from the archives of your 15 computers, newsreels from the times when there were wars on Earth. Thousands of Earthmen all dressed the same walked backward and forward in straight lines while others shouted commands which they obeyed instantly. And the wars . . . when they were ordered to fight the wars and kill other Earthmen, they obeyed. Is that not being disciplined?"

"Yes . . . it is," Hunt admitted uncomfortably, hoping he wasn't about to be asked for an explanation; there wasn't one.

But the Ganymean who had been worried about carnivores was persistent.

"You mean that if they are ordered to do something that is clearly irrational, they will do it unhesitatingly," he said. "But if they are ordered to do something that is not only eminently sensible but also polite, they will take no notice?"

"Er . . . I guess that's about it," Hunt said weakly. "Very often anyway."

Another Ganymean crewman half turned from the console that he was watching.

"They're all mad," he declared firmly. "I've always said so. It's the biggest madhouse in the Galaxy."

"They are also our hosts," Garuth broke in sharply. "And they have saved our lives and offered us their home as our home. I will not have them spoken of in that manner."

"Sorry, sir," the crewman mumbled and returned his attention to his console.

"Please forgive the remark, Dr. Hunt," Garuth said.

"Think nothing of it," Hunt replied with a shrug. "I couldn't have put it better myself. . . . It's what keeps us sane, you see," he added for no particular reason, causing more bewildered looks to be exchanged between his alien companions.

At that moment ZORAC interrupted with an announcement.

"Ground Control is calling from Geneva. Shall I put the call through for Dr. Hunt again?"

Hunt walked over to the communications console from which he had acted as intermediary during previous dialogues. He perched himself up on the huge Ganymean chair and instructed ZORAC to connect him. The face of the controller at Geneva, by now familiar, appeared on the screen.

" 'Allo again, Dr. 'unt. 'Ow are zings going up zere?"

"Well, we're still waiting," Hunt told him. "What's the news?"

"Ze Prime Minister of Australia and ze Chinese Premier 'ave now arrived at Geneva. Zey weel be at Ganyville eenside ze 'alf ower. I am now authorized to clear you for touchdown een seexty minutes from now. Okay?"

"We're going down one hour from now," Hunt announced to the expectant room. He looked at Garuth. "Do I have your approval to confirm that?"

"Please do," Garuth replied.

Hunt turned back toward the screen. "Okay," he informed the controller. "Sixty minutes from now. We're coming down."

Within minutes the news had flashed around the globe and the world's excitement rose to fever pitch.

chapter eighteen

Hunt stood inside one of the central elevators of the *Shapieron*, gazing at the blank expanse of the door panel in front of him

while the seemingly interminable length of the vessel sped by
outside. Behind him, the rest of the UNSA contingent from
Ganymede were packed tightly together, every one of them silently absorbed in his own thoughts as the moment of home-
coming drew nearer. The *Shapieron* was now descending
stern-first on its final approach. A number of Ganymeans were
present in the elevator too, on their way to join the main body
of Ganymeans that had been selected to make the first exit out
onto the surface of Earth, most of whom were already assembled in the stern section of the ship.

The symbols appearing and disappearing on the face of the
indicator panel by the door suddenly stopped changing and became stable. A second later the wide doors slid aside and the
company began spilling out the elevator to find themselves in
a vast, circular space that extended all the way around the cylindrical wall of the ship's inner core. Entrances to six huge
airlocks were equally spaced around the outer walls and the
floor in between was filled with a dense throng of Ganymeans,
most of them strangely silent. Hunt spotted Garuth, surrounded
by a small group of Ganymeans, standing near one of the
airlocks. Shilohin was on one side of him and Monchar on the
other; Jassilane was nearby. Like all of the Ganymeans present,
they were staring up at an enormous display screen set high
on the wall of the central core, dominating the floor from
above the elevator doorways. Hunt made his way through the
throng of giant figures toward where Garuth's group was
standing. He stopped next to Garuth and turned to look back
at the screen.

The view being shown was one looking vertically down on
the shore of the lake. The picture was bisected into two
roughly equal halves, one showing the greens and browns of
the hills, the other the reflected blues of the sky. The colors
were vivid and obscured in places by scattered puffs of small
white clouds. The shadows of the clouds made sharp blotches
on the land beneath, indicating the day was bright and sunny.
The features in the terrain slowly revealed themselves and began flowing outward toward the edges of the screen as the ship
descended.

The clouds blossomed up from flat daubs of paint to become
islands of billowing whiteness floating on the landscape; then
they were gone from the steadily narrowing and enlarging
view.

Dots that were houses were visible now, some standing isolated among the hills and others clustered together along the
twisting threads of the roads that were becoming discernible.
And precisely in the center of the screen, vertically below the
Shapieron's central axis, a speck of whiteness right on the
shoreline marked the concrete landing area of Ganyville, with
the rows of neatly aligned chalets inside the perimeter now beginning to take shape. A narrow strip of green emphasized the
perimeter line, denoting the zone outside the fence that had
been kept clear of people. Beyond the cleared zone the land
was visibly lighter in hue with the additive effect from thousands upon thousands of upturned faces.

Hunt noticed that Garuth was speaking quietly into his
throat microphone and pausing at intervals as if to listen to replies. He assumed that Garuth was updating himself with reports from the flight crew back in the command center, and
elected not to interrupt. Instead he activated his own channel
via his wrist unit. "ZORAC, how's it going?"

"Altitude nine thousand six hundred feet, descent speed two
hundred feet per second, reducing," the familiar voice replied.
"We've locked on to the approach radars. Everything's under
control and looking good."

"Looks like we're in for a hell of a welcome," Hunt commented.

"You should see the pictures coming in from the probes.
The hills are packed for miles around and there are hundreds
of small boats on the lake all packed together about a quarter-
mile offshore. The airspace above and around the landing zone
is clear, but the sky's thick with aircars all around. Half your
planet must have turned out."

"How are the Ganymeans taking it?" Hunt asked.

"A bit overawed, I think."

At that moment Shilohin noticed Hunt and moved across to
join him.

"This is incredible," she said, gesturing upward toward the
screen. "Are we really important enough for all this?"

"They don't get many aliens dropping in from other stars,"
Hunt told her cheerfully. "So they're making the most of the
occasion." He paused as another thought struck him, then said:
"You know, it's a funny thing . . . people on Earth have been
claiming that they've seen UFOs and flying saucers and things
like that for hundreds of years, and all the time there's been all

kinds of arguing about whether they really existed or not. You'd think they'd have guessed that when it really happened, it'd be unmistakable. Well, they sure know all about it today."

"Touchdown in twenty seconds," ZORAC announced. Hunt could sense a wave of emotion rippling through the ranks of Giants all around him.

All that was visible on the screen now was the waffle-iron pattern of the chalets of Ganyville and the white expanse of the concrete landing area. The ship was descending toward the lakeward side of the landing area, which was clear; on the landward side, between the landing area and the edge of the chalets, rows of dots arranged into ordered geometric groups became visible, and resolved themselves rapidly into human figures.

"Ten seconds," ZORAC recited. The murmuring that had been building up as a vague background subsided abruptly. The only sound was the distant rush of air around the ship and the muted surging of power from its engines.

"*Touchdown.* We have landed on the planet Earth. Awaiting further instructions."

"Deploy ship for surface access," Garuth ordered. "Proceed with routine shutdown of flight systems and prepare Engineers' Report."

Although there was no sensation of motion, Hunt knew that the whole section of the ship in which they were all standing was now moving smoothly toward the ground as the three elevator tubes telescoped downward from the main body of the vessel. While this was taking place, the main screen high above their heads presented a full-circle scan of the ground in the immediate vicinity of the ship.

Beyond the area bridged by the *Shapieron*'s tail fins, arrayed in a vast arc between the ship and the rows of chalets in the background, several hundred people were standing stiffly at attention in a series of boxed groups, as if lined up for inspection at a military parade. In front of every group was a flag bearer carrying the standard of one of the nations of Earth; in front of the flag bearers the Heads of State and their aides, all attired in dark business suits and standing rigidly erect, were waiting. Hunt picked out the Stars and Stripes of the USA, the Union Jack and several more of the emblems of US Europe, the Hammer and Sickle of the USSR and the Red Star of China. There were scores more that he could not identify readily. Behind and to the sides he caught snatches of brightly colored ceremonial military uniforms and the glint of sunlight reflected from brass. He tried to put himself in the position of those people standing outside. None of them had yet seen an alien face to face. He tried to capture their feelings and emotions as they stood there gazing up at the huge tower of silver metal that they had just watched slide down out of the sky. The moment was unique; never before in history had anything like this happened, and it could never happen for the first time again.

Then ZORAC's voice sounded once more.

"Tailgate is down. Pressures are balanced, outer lock-doors open and surface-access ramps extended. Ready to open up."

Hunt sensed the expectation building up around him. All heads were now turning to gaze toward Garuth. The Ganymean leader cast his eyes slowly around the assembly, allowed them to rest for a moment on the party of Earthmen still grouped together by the elevator door, and then shifted them toward Hunt.

"We will go out in the order already agreed. However, we are strangers on this world. There are others among us who are coming home. This is their world and they should lead us out onto it."

The Ganymeans needed no further prompting. Even as Garuth finished speaking, their ranks parted to form a long, straight aisle leading from the group of Earthmen by the elevators to where Garuth and Hunt were standing. After a few seconds, the Earthmen began walking slowly forward. Danchekker was in front. As they approached the airlock near which Hunt was waiting, the Ganymeans moved aside to make room for them in front of the inner door.

"All set then, Chris?" Hunt asked as the two drew face to face. "A few more seconds and you'll be home again."

"I must say all this publicity is something I could have done without," the professor replied. "I feel rather like some kind of Moses leading the tribes in. However, let us get on with it."

Hunt turned to stand beside Danchekker, facing the inner door. He glanced at Garuth and nodded.

"ZORAC, open inner door, lock five," Garuth ordered.

The ribbed metal panels slid noiselessly out of Hunt's field of vision. He stepped forward into the lock chamber and began moving forward toward the outer door, vaguely aware through the torrent of emotions rising inside him of Danchekker to one side and the rest of the UNSA contingent following behind. Beyond the outer door a broad, shallow ramp sloped down to the concrete. They stepped out onto the top of the ramp to find themselves in what appeared to be a vast cathedral of arched metal vaulting ribs, formed by the sweeping curves of the undersides of the *Shapieron*'s tail fins, soaring upward and inward to meet the body of the ship high above their heads. The ramp and the area straddled by the ship were in the shadow of the bulk of the vessel and its mighty fins. But beyond the ship the day was a blaze of sunlight, painting the scene around them in a riot of color—the green of the overlooking hills and the purple, white and blue of the mountains and the sky behind, the rainbow speckling of the crowds packed on the hillsides; the pastel pinks, greens, reds, blues and oranges of the chalets; the whiteness of the concrete apron below them and even the snowy shirtfronts of the delegates standing there in their precise, unmoving ranks.

And then came the cheering. It was like a slow tide of noise that seemed to begin far away on the tops of the hills and roll downward gathering strength and momentum as it went, until it broke over them in a roaring ocean of sound that flooded their senses. The hills themselves suddenly seemed to become alive as a pattern of spontaneous movement erupted as far as the eye could see. People in the tens of thousands were on their feet, shouting out the tension and the anticipation that had been building up inside them for days, and as they shouted, they waved—arms, hats, shirts, coats—anything that came to hand. And behind it all, rising and falling and rising again as if striving to be heard above the din came sporadic strains of massed bands.

The Earthmen halted a few feet down the ramp, momentarily overcome by the combined assault on their senses from all sides. Then they began moving again, down the ramp and onto the solid ground of Earth beneath the towering columns of the *Shapieron*'s fins. They marched forward into the sunlight toward a spot where a small party of Earth's representatives were standing ahead of the main body. They walked as if in a trance, their heads turning to take in the scenes around them, the multitudes on the hills, the lake behind . . . to gaze up at the ship stretching toward the sky above, now quiet and motionless. A few of them raised their arms and began waving back at the crowds on the surrounding hills. The noise redoubled as the crowds roared their approval. Soon they were all waving.

Hunt drew closer to the party ahead and recognized the features of Samuel K. Wilby, Secretary General of the UN. Beside him were Irwin Frenshaw, Director General of UNSA from Washington, D.C., and General Bradley Cummings, Supreme Commander of the uniformed arm of UNSA. Wilby greeted him with an extended hand and a broad smile.

"Dr. Hunt, I believe," he said. "Welcome home. I believe you've brought some friends with you." He shifted his eyes. "Ah—and you are Professor Danchekker. Welcome."

Danchekker had no sooner completed shaking hands when the noise around them rose to an unprecedented crescendo. They looked up and back at the ship.

The Ganymeans were coming out.

With Garuth in the lead, the first group of Giants had emerged at the top of the ramp. There they had stopped, and were staring around them in a way that hinted at their complete bewilderment.

"zorac," Hunt said. "They look a bit lost up there. Tell 'em to come on down and meet the folks."

"They will," the machine replied in his ear. "They need a minute to get used to it. Remember they have not breathed natural air for twenty years. This is the first time they've been out in the open for all that time."

At the tops of other ramps around the ship's stern section more airlocks had opened and more Ganymeans were appearing. Garuth's carefully planned order of emergence was already forgotten. Some of the Giants were milling around in the airlock doors, while others were already partway down the ramps; some were just standing motionless and staring.

"They're a bit lost," Hunt said to Wilby. "We ought to go over and straighten them out." Wilby nodded and motioned his group to follow. Some UN aides conducted the main party of Earthmen from Ganymede toward the national delegations while Hunt, Danchekker and a couple of others turned back to escort Wilby's group to the ramps.

"zorac, connect me to Garuth," Hunt muttered as they walked.

"You're through."

"This is Vic Hunt. Well, how d'you like it?"

"My people are temporarily overwhelmed," the familiar

voice answered. "Come to that, so am I. I had expected that
the sensation of coming out under an open sky after so long
would be traumatic, but never anything like this. And all these
people . . . the shouting . . . I can find no words."

"I'm with the group that's approaching the ramp you're now
on," Hunt advised. "Get your act together and come on down.
There's people here you have to say hello to."

As they neared the base of the ramp, Hunt looked up and
saw Garuth, Shilohin, Monchar, Jassilane and a few others
moving down toward them. To the left and right, other
Ganymeans who had already reached the ground via the
other ramps began converging on the spot where Wilby's
group was waiting.

Garuth stepped off the ramp, his companions following
close behind, and halted to look down at the Secretary General.
Slowly and solemnly they shook hands.

Hunt acted as an interpreter via ZORAC and concluded introductions between the two groups.

"This is one of the guys who runs the whole of the UNSA
show," he said to Garuth when they came to Irwin Frenshaw.
"Without it we'd never have been there for you to find."

And then the two groups turned and, now mingled together,
began walking away from the ramp. From above and behind
them, scores of eight-foot-tall figures flowed downward along
the ramps to join the lead group from behind. They came out
into the sunlight and halted for a moment to survey the delegations from the nations of Earth arrayed before them. A sudden hush descended upon the hills behind.

And then Garuth slowly raised his right arm in a gesture of
salutation. One by one the rest of the Ganymeans copied him.
They stood there silent and unmoving, a hundred arms extended and raised to convey a common message of greeting
and friendship to all of the peoples of Earth.

At once the roar swept down from the hillsides again. If
what had come before had been a flood, then this was a tidal
wave. It seemed to echo back and forth across the valleys as
if the mountains of Switzerland themselves were reverberating
and joining in their welcome.

Wilby turned toward Hunt and leaned forward to speak
close to his ear.

"I think your friends have made something of a hit," he
said.

"I expected some fuss," Hunt told him, "but never this in a million years. Shall we carry on?"

"Let's go."

Hunt turned toward Garuth and tuned in.

"Come on, Garuth," he said. "It's time to pay our respects. Some of these people out there have come a long way to meet you."

Slowly, with the small mixed party of Earthmen and Ganymean leaders in front, the Giants began moving forward *en masse* toward the waiting heads of the governments of Earth's nations.

chapter nineteen

For the next hour or so, the Ganymean leaders went from one group of national representatives to the next, exchanging brief formal speeches of goodwill. As the Ganymeans moved on, the groups broke up and dispersed to join the growing mass of Earthmen and aliens mingling on the concrete apron below the *Shapieron.* It was a very different reception from the one that had greeted the first hesitant emergence of the Ganymeans out onto the ice at Ganymede Main Base.

"I still don't quite understand it," Jassilane said to Hunt as the party moved toward the delegation from Malaysia. "So far you've told us that everyone we've met was from a government. But what I want to know is who is *the* government?"

"*The* government?" Hunt asked, not quite following. "Which one?" The Giant made motions of exasperation in the air.

"The one that runs the planet. Which one is it?"

"None of them," Hunt told him.

"That's what I thought. So where are they?"

"There isn't one," Hunt said. "It's run by all of them and none of them."

"I should have guessed," Jassilane replied. In translating, ZORAC managed to inject a good simulation of a weary sigh.

For the rest of the day the formalities continued amid an almost carnival atmosphere. Garuth and the Ganymean leaders spent some time with each group of government representatives, establishing relationships and arranging a timetable of projected official visits to the various nations represented. It was a busy day for Hunt and the other Earthmen from Ganymede, whose familiarity with the aliens put them in great demand for performing introductions and made them the obvious choice for acting as general mediators in the dialogues. By invitation of the European Government, a liaison bureau—a representative international body operating under UN sponsorship—had been established as a permanent institution within the Earthman sector of Ganyville. By evening the program of affairs to be discussed between the two races was being handled in a more-or-less orderly and coordinated fashion.

That night there was a grand welcoming banquet in Ganyville, vegetarian of course, in which words, and wine, flowed freely. After the meal and still more speeches were over and the two races had begun mixing and socializing, Hunt found himself, glass in hand, standing to one side of the room with three Ganymeans—Valio and Kralom, two of the crew officers from the *Shapieron*, and Strelsya, a female administrator. Valio was explaining his confusion over some of the things he had learned that day.

"Emmanuel Crow, I think he said his name was," Valio told them. "He was with the delegation from the place you live in, Vic—USA. Said he was from Washington . . . State Department or something. The thing that puzzled me was when he said he was a Red Indian."

Hunt propped himself casually against the table behind him and sipped his scotch.

"Why, what's the problem?" he asked.

"Well, we met the Indian government spokesman later on, and he said India isn't anywhere near the USA.," Valio explained. "So how could Crow be an Indian?"

"That's a different Indian," Hunt replied, fearing as he spoke that the conversation was about to get itself into a tangle. Sure enough, Kralom had something to add.

"I met someone who was a West Indian, but he said he came from the east."

"There is an East Indies . . ." Strelsya began.

"I know, but that's way over in the west," Kralom said.

Hunt groaned inwardly and reached in his pocket for his cigarette pack while he collected his thoughts. Before he could inject a word of explanation, Valio resumed.

"I thought that maybe when he said he was a *Red* Indian he might be really from China because they're supposed to be red and they're not far from India, but it turns out they're yellow."

"Perhaps he was Russian," Kralom suggested. "Somebody told me they're red too."

"No, they're pink," Strelsya declared firmly. She motioned her head in the direction of a short, heavily built man in a black suit with his back toward them, talking to another mixed group. "There—he's one if I remember rightly. See for yourself."

"I've met him," Kralom said. "He's a White Russian. He said so, but he doesn't look white."

The three aliens looked imploringly toward Hunt for some words of wisdom to make sense of it all.

"Not to worry—it's all hangovers from a long time ago. The whole world's getting so mixed up together now that I really don't suppose it'll matter much longer," he said lamely.

By the early hours of the morning, while a thousand lights still twinkled on the shadows of the surrounding hills, all was quiet, except for occasional scuffling noises and every now and again an ominous crash of bulk against timber, as gigantic frames tottered unsteadily but contentedly to bed through the narrow alleys between the chalets.

The next morning, the august visitors from every corner of the globe began departing to give Ganyville a week of undisturbed rest and relaxation. A light schedule of discussion with visiting groups of Earthmen, mainly scientists, had been arranged for the week and some news features were laid on for the benefit of the public; for the most part, however, the Giants were left free to enjoy the feeling of having a world under their feet again.

Many simply spent their time stretched out on the grass, basking in a splendor that was, to them, tropical. Others walked for hours along the perimeter, stopping all the time to savor the air as if making sure they were not dreaming it all and standing and staring in unconcealed delight at the lake, the hills, and the snow-capped peaks of the distant Alps. Others became addicted to the Earthnet terminals in the chalets, and displayed an insatiable appetite for information on every facet of Earth, its people, its history, its geography, and everything else there was to know about it. To facilitate this, ZORAC had been connected into the Earthnet system, enabling an enormous interchange of the accumulated knowledge of two civilizations.

But best of all to watch was the reaction of the Ganymean children. Born aboard the *Shapieron* during its epic voyage from Iscaris, they had never seen a blue sky, a landscape or a mountain, never breathed natural air, and had never before conceived the notion of leaving their ship without requiring any kind of protection. To them, the lifeless void between the stars was the only environment that existed.

At first, many of them shrank from coming out of the ship at all, fearful of consequences that had been instilled into them all their lives and which they accepted unquestioningly as fundamental truths. When at last a few of the more trusting and adventurous ones crept warily to the doors at the tops of the access ramps and peered outside, they froze in utter disbelief and confusion. From the things both their elders and ZORAC had told them, they had a vague idea of planets and worlds— places bigger than the *Shapieron* that you could live *on* instead of *in*, they gathered, though what this could possibly mean had never been clear. And then they had come to Ganymede; obviously that was a planet, they'd thought.

But now this! Hundreds of people outside the ship clad only in their shirtsleeves; how could that be possible? How could they breathe and why did they not explode with decompression? Space was supposed to be everywhere, but it wasn't here; what had happened to it? How did the universe suddenly divide itself into two parts, half "up" and half "down"—words that could only mean anything inside a ship? Why was down all green; who could have made anything so large and why had they made it in strange shapes that stretched away as far as one could see? Why was up all blue and why weren't there any stars? Where did all the light come from?

Eventually, with much coaxing, they ventured down the ramps and onto the ground. Nothing awful happened to them. Soon they became reassured and began to explore their new and wondrous surroundings. The concrete at the bottom of the ramps, the grass beyond, the wooden walls of the chalets—all were new and each held its own particular fascination. But the most astounding sight of all was that stretching away, seemingly forever, on the other side of the ship—more water than they had ever believed existed in the whole of the universe.

Before long they were romping and reveling in an ecstasy of freedom greater than anything they had ever known. The crowning glory came when the Swiss police launches started running joy rides for them, up along the shore, out into the middle of Lake Geneva, and back again. It soon became obvious that only the grownups and their hang-ups stood in the way of the question of settling on Earth; the kids had made *their* minds up in no uncertain manner.

Two days after the landing, Hunt was enjoying a coffee break in the residents' cafeteria at Ganyville when a low buzz from his Ganymean wrist unit signaled an incoming call. He touched a button to activate the unit and ZORAC'S voice promptly informed him: "The coordination office in the Bureau Block is trying to contact you. Are you accepting?"

"Okay."

"Dr. Hunt?" The voice sounded young and, somehow, pretty.

"That's me," he acknowledged.

"Coordination office here. Sorry to trouble you but could you come over? We could use your help on something."

"Not until you promise to marry me." He was in that kind of mood. Maybe it was coming home after being away for so long.

"What? . . ." The voice rose in surprise and confusion. "I don't . . . that is, I'm serious . . ."

"What makes you think I'm not?"

"You're crazy. Now how about coming over? . . . on business." At least, he thought, she recovered her balance nice and quickly.

"Who are you?" he asked lightly.

"I told you—the coordination office."

"Not them—*you*."

"Yvonne . . . why?"

"Well, I'll make a deal. You need me to help you out. I need someone to show me around Geneva before I go back to the States. Interested?"

"That's different," the voice retorted, though not without a hint of a smile. "I'm doing a UN job. You're conducting private enterprise. Now are you coming over?"

"Deal?"

"Oh . . . maybe. We'll see later. For the moment what about our problem?"

"What's the problem?"

"Some of your Ganymean pals are here and want to go outside. Somebody thought it would be a good idea if you went too."

Hunt sighed and shook his head to himself. "Okay," he said finally. "Tell 'em I'm on my way."

"Will do," the voice replied, then in a suddenly lowered and more confidential tone added: "I'm off on Sundays, Mondays and Tuesdays." Then it cut itself off with a click. Hunt grinned to himself, finished his coffee and rose to leave the table. A sudden thought struck him.

"ZORAC," he muttered.

"Yes, Vic?"

"Are you coupled into the Earthnet local comms grid?"

"Yes. That's how I routed the call through."

"Yes I know . . . What I meant was, was she talking through a standard two-way vi-terminal?"

"Yes."

"With a visual pickup?"

"Yes."

Hunt rubbed his chin for a moment.

"You didn't record the visual by any chance, did you?"

"I did," ZORAC informed him. "Want a playback?"

Without waiting for an answer, the machine reran a portion of the conversation on the screen of the wrist unit. Hunt nodded and whistled his silent approval. Yvonne was blond, blue-eyed, and attractive, her appearance somehow enhanced by the trim cut of her light-gray UN uniform jacket and white blouse.

"Do you record everything you handle?" Hunt inquired as he sauntered toward the door.

"No, not everything."

"What made you record that then?"

"I knew you'd ask for it," ZORAC told him.

"I don't think I like eavesdroppers in on my calls," Hunt said. "Consider yourself reprimanded."

ZORAC ignored the remark. "I logged her extension number too," it said. "Seeing as you didn't think to ask for it."

"D'you know if she's married?"

"How could I know that?"

"Oh, I don't know ... Knowing you, you could probably crack the access codes and get into UN's personnel records through the Earthnet or something like that."

"I could, but I won't," ZORAC said. "There are things that a good computer will do for you and things that it won't. From here on in, you're on your own."

Hunt cut off the channel. Shaking his head, he emerged from the cafeteria and turned in the direction of the Bureau Block.

He appeared a few minutes later inside the coordination office on the first floor, where Garuth and some other Ganymeans were waiting with a number of UN officials.

"We feel we want to return the welcome that the people of Earth have given us," Garuth said. "So, we'd like to go for a walk outside the perimeter to meet them."

"That okay?" Hunt asked, directing his words at the portly, silver-haired man who appeared to be the most senior of the officials present.

"Sure. They're guests here, not prisoners. We thought it would be a good idea if someone they knew went with them though."

"Fine by me," Hunt said, nodding. "Let's go." As he turned toward the door, he caught a glimpse of Yvonne operating a vi-console at the back of the office and winked mischievously. She colored slightly and looked down at the keyboard below the screen. Then she glanced up, winked back with a quick smile and busied herself at the keyboard again.

Outside the building they were joined by more Ganymeans and a contingent of Swiss police headed by an apprehensive chief. The party walked down a path to the roadway and turned left to proceed between the rows of chalets toward a steel-mesh gate that formed part of the perimeter fence. As they walked clear of the chalets and continued up along the gently sloping gravel road toward the gate, a stir ran through the crowds sitting on the grassy mounds beyond the fence on the far side of the clear zone. People began jumping to their feet and looking down toward the fence. The excitement grew as the Ganymeans halted while Swiss constables unlocked the gate and swung it aside.

With Garuth on one side of him and the Swiss police chief on the other, Hunt led the party through the gate as the clamor of voices ahead of them rose and became cheering. People began running down the slopes to press together just short of the police cordon, waving and calling as the party continued along the roadway across the clear zone.

The cordon opened to let them through, and suddenly the people massed together across the roadway found themselves staring up into the awesome faces from another world. While the noise from all around continued unabated, the ranks immediately in front of the Giants grew strangely hushed, and fell back as if to maintain a respectful distance. Garuth stopped and looked slowly around the semicircle of faces. As his gaze traveled from one to another the eyes averted. Hunt could understand their uncertainty, but at the same time he was anxious that the gesture the Giants had wanted to make should not go unreciprocated.

"I'm Vic Hunt," he called to the crowd in a loud voice. "I have traveled with these people all the way from Jupiter. This is Garuth, commander of the Ganymean ship. He and his companions have come to meet you all personally and at their own request. Let's make them feel at home."

Still the people seemed to shrink back. Some seemed to want to make a welcoming gesture, but everybody was waiting for somebody else to take the first step. And then a boy at the front of the crowd wrenched his hand free from his mother's, marched forward and confronted Garuth's towering frame boldly. Wearing stout mountain boots below a pair of alpine-style leather shorts, he was about twelve years old with a tangle of fair hair and a face covered with freckles. His mother started forward instinctively, but the man standing next to her restrained her with his arm.

"I don't care about them, Mr. Garuth," the boy declared loudly. "I wanna shake your hand." With that he confidently extended his arm upward. The Giant stooped, his face contorting into an expression that could only be a smile, grasped the hand and shook it warmly. The tension in the crowd evaporated and they began surging forward jubilantly.

Hunt looked around and saw that the scene had suddenly

transformed itself. In one place a Ganymean was posing with an arm around the shoulders of a laughing middle-aged woman while her husband took a photograph; in another, a Giant was accepting a proffered cup of coffee while behind him a third was looking down dubiously at a persistent, tail-wagging Alsatian dog that one family had brought along. After patting it experimentally a few times, the Giant squatted down and began ruffling its fur, to be rewarded by a frenzy of licks on the tip of his long, tapering face.

Hunt lit a cigarette and sauntered across to join the Swiss police chief, who was mopping copious perspiration from his brow with a pocket handkerchief.

"There—it didn't go badly at all, Heinrich," he said. "Told you there was nothing to worry about."

"Maybe, Dr. 'unt," Heinrich answered, still not sounding too happy. "All ze same, I will be much ze 'appier when we can, 'ow you say in ze America . . . 'get ze 'ell out of 'ere.' "

Hunt spent a couple more days in the Earthmen sector of Ganyville helping the liaison bureau get organized and taking his own share of rest and relaxation. Then, having voted himself a spell of special leave for conduct which, he was sure, was well beyond the call of duty, he collected Yvonne, hitched them both a ride into Geneva on one of the still-shuttling VTOL jets, and embarked on a spree in the city. Three days later they tumbled out of an eastbound groundcar that stopped on the main highway running along the perimeter, slightly disheveled, distinctly unsteady on their feet and deliriously happy.

By that time—over a full week since the day the *Shapieron* had landed—the liaison bureau had got things fully under control and parties of Ganymeans were already beginning to leave to make visits and attend conferences all over the world. Some groups, in fact, had been gone for some time and news reports were already coming in on how they were faring.

Small parties of eight-foot-tall aliens, together with their ever-vigilant police escorts, had become accepted, if not yet commonplace, sights in Times Square, Red Square, Trafalgar Square and the Champs-Elysées. They had listened appreciatively to a Beethoven concert in Boston, toured the London Zoo with a mixture of awe and horror, attended lavish receptions in Buenos Aires, Canberra, Cape Town and Washington,

D.C., and paid their respects at the Vatican. In Peking their culture had been complimented as the ultimate exemplification of the communist ideal, in New York as that of the democratic ideal, and in Stockholm as that of the liberal ideal. And everywhere the crowds thronged to greet them.

The reports from around the globe told of the aliens' total amazement at the variety of life, color, vitality and exuberance that they saw all around them wherever they went. Everybody on Earth, they said, seemed to be in a hurry to live a whole lifetime each day, as if they feared there might not be sufficient hours in a mortal span to accommodate all the things to be seen and done. The Minervan cities had been bigger in terms of engineering constructions and architecture, but had offered nothing that compared even remotely with the variety, energy and sheer zest for living that teemed day and night in the metropolises of Earth. The Minervan technology had been farther advanced, but its rate of advancement was paltry compared to the stupendous mushrooming of human civilization that resulted from the hustling, bustling restlessness exploding outward from this incredible planet.

Speaking at a scientific conference in Berlin, a Ganymean told his audience: "The Ganymean theory of the origin of the universe describes a steady equilibrium in which matter appears, quietly acts out its appointed role, and then quietly vanishes—a slow, easy-going, evolutionary situation that goes well with our temperament and our history. Only Man could have conceived the catastrophic discontinuity of the Big Bang. I believe that when you have had an opportunity to examine our theories more closely, you will discard your Big Bang ideas. And yet I feel it singularly appropriate that Man should have formulated such a theory. You see, ladies and gentlemen, when Man visualized the cataclysmic expansion of the Big Bang Model, he was not seeing the universe at all; he was seeing himself."

After he had been back on Earth for ten days, Hunt was contacted again by UNSA, who conveyed their hopes that he had enjoyed his leave. But some people at Houston knew him better than he thought and suggested that it might be a good idea if he began thinking about coming back.

More to the point, UNSA had made arrangements through the bureau for a Ganymean scientific delegation to visit Navcomms Headquarters at Houston, primarily to learn more about the Lunarians. The Ganymeans had been expressing a lot of interest in Man's immediate ancestral race for some reason and, since the Lunarian investigations had been controlled from Houston and much of the work had been done there, it was the obvious place to bring them. UNSA suggested that since Hunt was due to return to Houston anyway, he could act as organizer and courier for the delegation and insure their safe arrival in Texas. Danchekker, who was also due to return to Houston to resume his duties at the Westwood Biological Institute, decided to fly with them.

And so, at the end of his second week home, Hunt found himself in a familiar environment: the inside of a Boeing 1017 skyliner, fifty miles up over the North Atlantic and westward bound.

chapter twenty

"When I sent you off to Ganymede, I just wanted you to find out a little bit more about the guys. I didn't expect you to come back with a whole shipful of them." Gregg Caldwell chewed on his cigar and looked out across his desk with an expression that was half amusement and half feigned exasperation. Hunt, sprawled in the chair opposite, grinned and took another sip of his scotch. It was good to be back among the familiar surroundings of Navcomms HQ again. The inside of Caldwell's luxurious office with its murals and one wall completely dedicated to a battery of viewscreens; the panoramic view down over the rainbow towers of Houston—nothing had changed.

"So you've got more than your money's worth, Gregg," he replied. "Not complaining, are you?"

"Hell no. I'm not complaining. You've done another good job by the way things are shaping up. It's just that whenever I set you an assignment, things seem to have this tendency to kinda . . . get outa hand. I always end up with more than I bargained for." Caldwell removed his cigar from his teeth and inclined his head briefly. "But as you say, I'm not complaining."

The executive director studied Hunt thoughtfully for a few seconds. "So . . . what was it like to be away from Earth for the first time?"

"Oh, it was . . . an experience," Hunt answered automatically, but when he looked up he saw from the mischievous twinkle that danced in the eyes below the craggy brows that the question had been more than casual. He should have known. Caldwell never said or did anything without a reason.

" 'Know thyself,' " Caldwell quoted softly. "And others too, maybe, huh?" He shrugged as if making light of the matter, but the twinkle still remained in his eyes.

Hunt's brows knitted for a split second, and then his eyes slowly widened as the cryptic message behind this turn in the conversation became clear. It took perhaps two seconds for the details to click into place in his brain. In the early days of the Lunarian investigations, just after Hunt had moved to Houston from England, his relationship with Danchekker had been caustic. Progress toward unraveling the mystery was more often than not hampered because the two scientists dissipated their energies fruitlessly in personal conflicts. But later on, in the wilderness of Luna and out in the void between Earth and Jupiter, all that had somehow been forgotten. It was then that the two scientists had begun to work in harmony, and the difficulties had crumbled before the powerful assault of their combined talents, which was what had been needed to solve the Lunarian problem. Hunt could see that clearly now. Suddenly, he also realized that this state of affairs had not come about through mere accident. He stared at Caldwell with new respect, and slowly nodded ungrudging approval.

"Gregg," he said, in a tone of mock reproach. "You've been pulling strings again. You set us up."

"I did?" Caldwell's voice was suitably innocent.

"Chris and me. It was out there we began to see each other as people and learned to pool our marbles. That's what cracked the Lunarian riddle. You knew it would happen . . ." Hunt pointed an accusing finger across the desk. "That's why you did it."

Caldwell compressed his heavy jowls momentarily into a tight-lipped grin of satisfaction. "So, you got more than your money's worth," he threw back. "Not complaining, are you?"

"Smooth operator," Hunt complimented, raising his glass. "Okay, we've both had a good deal. That's how I think business ought to be. But now to the present and the future—what have you got lined up next?"

Caldwell sat forward and rested his elbows on the desk. He exhaled a long stream of blue smoke. "What about this bunch of alien guys you brought back from Europe; are you still tied up most of the time with looking after them?"

"They've been introduced over at Westwood now," Hunt told him. "They're interested in the Lunarians and particularly want to have a look at Charlie over there. Chris Danchekker is handling that side of things, which leaves me fairly free for a while."

"Fine. What I'd like you to start giving some thought to is a preliminary overview of Ganymean science," Caldwell said. "What with this ZORAC machine of theirs and all the conferences and discussions they're having all over the place, there's more information coming across than we can handle. When all the excitement dies down there's going to be one hell of a lotta work to get through with all that. When you were coordinating the Charlie business you operated a pretty good network of channels to most of the leading scientific institutions and establishments around the world. I'd like you to use those channels again to make a start at cataloging and evaluating everything that's new, especially things that could be of particular use to UNSA—like their gravitics. We may find we want to revise a lot of our own research programs in light of what these big guys have got to tell us. Now seems as good a time as any to begin."

"The group stays intact for a while then?" Hunt guessed, referring to the team that he had headed during the Lunarian investigations and which had continued working under the supervision of his deputy, mainly to tidy up the unresolved details, during his time on Ganymede.

"Yep," Caldwell nodded. "The way they work seems set up for the job. Have you said hello to them yet?"

Hunt shook his head. "Only got back this morning. I came straight on here."

"Do that then," Caldwell said. "There are probably a lot of old friends around here that you want to see. Take the rest of this week to settle in again. Then make a start on what we just talked about on Monday. Okay?"

"Okay. The first thing I'll do is go see the group and give them an idea of what our next job's going to be. I think they'll like it. Who knows . . . they might even have half of it organized for me by Monday if they start thinking about it." He cocked an inquiring eye at Caldwell. "Or is that what you figure you pay me to do?"

"I pay you to think smart," Caldwell grunted. "That's called delegation. If you wanna delegate too, that's what I call thinking smart. Do it."

Hunt spent the rest of that day with his own staff, familiarizing himself with some of the fine points of how they had been getting on—he had kept in touch with them almost daily for the general things—and outlining for them his recent directive from Caldwell. After that there was no getting away; they quizzed him for hours about every scrap of information that he had managed to absorb on Ganymean scientific theory and technology, kept him talking all through lunch, and succeeded in extracting a commitment from him to arrange for a Ganymean scientist or two to come and give them an intensive teach-in. At least, he reflected as he finally left for home at nine o'clock that night, he was not going to have any problems with motivation there.

Next morning he made a point of avoiding that part of Navcomms HQ building that contained his own offices and started his day by paying a call on another old friend of his— Don Maddson, head of the linguistics section. It was Don's team, working in cooperation with several universities and research institutes all over the world, that had played one of the most important roles in the Lunarian saga by untangling the riddle of the Lunarian language, using documents found on Charlie's person and, later, a library of microdot texts from the remains of a Lunarian base that had come to light near Tycho. Without the translations, it would never have been possible even to prove conclusively that the Lunarians and the Ganymeans had come from the same planet.

Hunt stopped outside the door of Maddson's office, knocked lightly and entered without waiting for a reply. Maddson was sitting behind his desk studying a sheet from a stack of the innumerable pieces of paper without which his office would never have seemed complete. He glanced up, stared incredulously for a second, and then his face split into a broad ear-to-ear smile.

"Vic! What the . . ." He half rose from his chair and began pumping Hunt's proffered hand vigorously. "It's great to see ya . . . great. I knew you were back on Earth but nobody told me you were Stateside yet . . ." He beckoned Hunt toward an easy chair on the other side of the desk. "Sit down, sit down . . . When did you get in?"

"Yesterday morning," Hunt replied, settling himself comfortably. "I had to see Gregg and then I got tied up completely with the Group L bunch. Gregg wants us to start thinking about writing a compendium of Ganymean science. They're all dead keen to go on it . . . kept me talking till heavens knows what time last night in the Ocean Bar."

"Ganymeans, eh?" Maddson grinned. "I thought maybe you'd have brought us one back."

"There's a load of 'em over at Westwood with Chris Danchekker right now."

"Yeah. I know about that. They're due to pay us a call here later. Everybody around here's getting keyed up with the suspense. They can't wait." Maddson sat back in his chair and regarded Hunt over interlaced fingers for a few seconds. At last he shook his head. "Well, I dunno where to start Vic. It's been all this time . . . there are so many questions . . . I guess there's enough to keep us talking all day, huh? Or maybe you're getting tired of people asking all the same things all the time, over and over?"

"Not at all," Hunt said. "But why don't we save all that for lunch? Maybe some of the others might like to join us and then I'll only need to say it all to everybody once; otherwise I *might* end up getting tired of it, and that wouldn't do."

"Great idea," Maddson agreed. "We'll reserve the topic for lunch. In the meantime, have a guess what we're into now?"

"Who?"

"Us . . . the section . . . Linguistics."

"What?"

Maddson took a deep breath, stared Hunt straight in the eye and proceeded to deliver a string of utterly meaningless syllables in a deep, guttural voice. Then he sat back and beamed proudly, his expression inviting Hunt to accept the implied challenge.

"What the hell was that all about?" Hunt asked, as if doubting his own ears.

"Even *you* don't know?"

"Why should I?"

Maddson was evidently enjoying himself. "That, my friend, was Ganymean," he said.

"Ganymean?"

"Ganymean!"

Hunt stared at him in astonishment. "How in God's name did you learn that?"

Maddson waited a moment longer to make the most of Hunt's surprise, then gestured toward the display unit standing on one side of his desk.

"We've got ourselves a channel through to ZORAC," he said. "There's been a pretty fantastic demand for access into it ever since it was hooked into the Earthnet, just as you'd imagine. But being UNSA we qualify for high priority. That sure is one hell of a machine."

Hunt was duly impressed. "So, ZORAC's been teaching you Ganymean, eh," he said. "It fits. I should have guessed you wouldn't let a chance like that slip by."

"It's an interesting language," Maddson commented. "It's obviously matured over a long period of time and been rationalized extensively—hardly any irregular forms or ambiguities at all. Actually, it's pretty straightforward to learn structure-wise, but the pitch and vocal inflections don't come naturally to a human. That's the most difficult part." He made a throwing-away motion in the air. "It's only of academic interest I guess . . . but as you say, a chance we couldn't resist."

"How about the Lunarian texts from Tycho," Hunt asked. "Been making progress on the rest of those too?"

"You bet." Maddson waved toward the piles of papers covering the desk and the table standing against the wall on one side of his office. "We've been pretty busy here all around."

Maddson proceeded to describe some of the details his team of linguists had been able to fill in during Hunt's absence, concerning the Lunarian culture and the way in which it had been organized on the Minerva of fifty thousand years before. There was a thumbnail sketch of the war-torn history of the Lunarian civilization; some detailed maps of parts of the planet's surface with accounts of geographic, climactic, agricultural, and industrial characteristics; a treatise on the citizen's obligations and duties toward the State in the totalitarian fortress-factory that was Minerva; a description of native Minervan life forms as reconstructed from fossil remains and some speculations on the possible causes of their abrupt extinction twenty-five million years before. There were numerous references to the earlier race that had inhabited the planet before the Lunarians themselves had emerged; obviously, a civilization such as that of the Ganymeans could never have passed away without leaving ample traces of itself behind for posterity. The Lunarians had marveled at the ruins of Ganymean cities, examined their awesome machines without growing much the wiser, and reconstructed a fairly comprehensive picture of how their world had once looked. In most of their writings, the Lunarians had referred to the Ganymeans simply as the Giants.

Then, more than an hour after they had begun talking, Maddson drew out a set of charts from below some other papers and spread them out for Hunt's inspection. They were views of the heavens at night, showing the stars in groupings that were not immediately recognizable. Captions, which Hunt identified as being written in Lunarian, were scattered across the charts and below each caption, in smaller print, a translation appeared in English.

"These might interest you, Vic," Maddson said, still bubbling with enthusiasm. "Star charts drawn by Lunarian astronomers fifty thousand years ago. When you've looked at them for a little while, you'll pick out all the familiar constellations. They're a bit distorted from the ones we see today because the relative displacements have altered a little with time, of course. In fact, we passed these on to some astronomers at Hale who were able to calculate from the distortions exactly how long ago these charts were drawn. It doesn't come out at too far off fifty thousand years at all."

Hunt said nothing but leaned forward to peer closely at the charts. This was fascinating—a record of the skies as they had appeared when the Lunarian civilization had been at its peak, immediately prior to its catastrophic fall. As Maddson had said, all the familiar constellations were there, but changed subtly from those seen in modern times. The other thing that made them difficult to identify were the sets of lines drawn all over the charts to interconnect groups of the more prominent stars into patterns and shapes that bore no resemblance to the familiar constellations; the lines tended to draw the eye along unfamiliar paths and obscure the better-known patterns. Orion, for example, was there, but not connected up as a single, intact configuration; part of it was grouped independently into a subset, while the other part was separated from the rest of Orion and linked to the normally distinct parallelograph of Lepus to form something else instead. The result was that it took time to identify the two parts of Orion and mentally fuse them back together again to reveal that Orion was there at all.

"I see," Hunt observed thoughtfully at last. "They saw pictures in the stars just like we do, only they saw different ones. Takes a while to get used to, doesn't it?"

"Yeah—interesting, huh?" Maddson agreed. "They not only saw different shapes; they grouped the stars differently too. That doesn't really come as a surprise though; I've always said there was more dog in the mind of the beholder than there ever was in Canis Major. Still, it's interesting to see that their minds seemed to work the same way . . . even if they were every bit as susceptible to autosuggestion."

"What's this?" Hunt inquired after a few more seconds. He indicated a pattern that lay over toward the left-hand side of the chart he had been studying. The Lunarians had formed a large constellation by connecting together Hercules, Serpens, Corona Borealis and part of Boötes to produce a starfish-shaped pattern. The English translation of its name read simply *The Giant*.

"I wondered if you'd spot that one," Maddson said, nodding in approval. "Well, as we know, the Lunarians knew all about the Ganymeans having been there before them. I guess they musta kinda named one of their constellations . . . sort of in honor of them, or something like that." He swept a hand over the chart to take in the whole extent of it. "As you can see, they named their constellations after all kinds of things, but mainly after animals just like we did. I suppose it must be a natural tendency in some kind of way." He pointed back at the one Hunt had picked out. "If you're the imaginative kind, you can see something in that which vaguely suggests the Ganymean form . . . it does to me anyhow. I mean . . . in Hercules you can see the head and the two arms raised up . . . Serpens forms a slightly flexed leg trailing back . . . and then the lines through Corona Borealis and then down to Arcturus give you the other leg. See what I mean? It sorta looks like a figure running or leaping."

"It does, doesn't it," Hunt agreed. His eyes held a faraway look for a moment, then he went on: "I'll tell you something else this tells us. Don: The Lunarians knew about the Giants very early in their history too—not just later on after they discovered the sciences."

"How d'you figure that?"

"Well, look at the names that they've given to all their constellations. As you said, they're all simple, everyday things—animals and so on. Those are the kinds of names that a simple and primitive people would think up . . . names that come from the things they see in the world around them. We got our names for our constellations in exactly the same way."

"You mean that these names were handed down from way back," Maddson said. "Through the generations . . . from the early times when the Lunarians were just starting to think about getting civilized. Yeah, I suppose you could be right." He paused to think for a second. "I see what you mean now. . . . The one they called *The Giant* was probably named at about the same time as the rest. The rest were named while the Lunarians were still primitive, so *The Giant* was named while they were still primitive. Conclusion: The Lunarians knew about the Ganymeans right from the early days. Yeah— I'll buy that . . . I suppose it's not all that surprising, though. I mean, from the pictures that the Ganymeans have shown us of their civilization, there must have been all kinds of evidence left lying around all over the planet. The early Lunarians could hardly have missed it, primitive or not. All they had to do was have eyes."

"No wonder their writings and legends were full of references to the Giants then," Hunt said. "That knowledge must have had a terrific influence on how their civilization and thinking developed. Imagine what a difference it might have made if the Sumerians had seen evidence of a long-lost, technically advanced race all around them. They might—hey, what's this?" Hunt had been scanning idly over the remaining star charts while he was talking. Suddenly he stopped and peered closely at one of them, at the same time pointing to one of the inscriptions with his finger. The inscription did not refer to a constellation of stars this time, but to a single star, standing alone and shown relatively faintly. The inscription, however, stood out in bold Lunarian characters. Its English equivalent read: The Giants' Star.

"Something wrong?" Maddson asked.

"Not wrong . . . just a bit odd." Hunt was frowning thoughtfully. "This star—it's nowhere near that other constellation. It's in another hemisphere completely, out near Taurus . . . yet it's got a name like that. I wonder why they gave it a name like that."

"Why not?" Maddson shrugged. "Why shouldn't they give it a name like that? It's as good as any other. Maybe they were kinda running outa names."

Hunt was still looking perturbed.

"But it's so faint," he said slowly. "Don, are the different brightnesses of the stars shown on these charts significant? I mean, did they tend to show the brighter stars larger, same as we do?"

"As a matter of fact, yes they did," Maddson answered. "But what of it? Does it really . . ."

"Which star is this?" Hunt asked, now evidently intrigued and apparently not hearing.

"Search me." Maddson spread his hands wide. "I'm no astronomer. Is it so important?"

"I think it is." Hunt's voice was curiously soft, and still held a faraway note.

"How come?"

"Look at it this way. That looks like a very faint star to me—magnitude four, five or less at a guess. Something makes me wonder if that star would be visible at all from the Solar System to the naked eye. Now if that were the case, it could only have been discovered after the Lunarians invented telescopes. Right?"

"That figures," Maddson agreed. "So what?"

"Well, now we get back to the name. You see, that kind of name—The Giants' Star—is in keeping with all the rest. It's the kind of name that you'd expect the ancients of the Lunarian race to come up with. But what if the ancients of the Lunarian race never knew about it . . . because they'd never seen it? That means that it had to have been given its name later, after the science of astronomy had been refined to a high level, by the advanced civilization that came later. But why would an advanced civilization give it a name like that?"

A look of growing comprehension spread slowly across Maddson's face. He looked back at Hunt but was too astounded by the implication to say anything. Hunt read the expression and nodded to confirm what Maddson was thinking.

"Exactly. We have to grope around in the dark to find out anything about what kind of evidence of their existence the Ganymeans left behind them. The Lunarian scientists had no such problem because they had the one thing available to them that we don't have—the planet Minerva, intact, right under their feet, no doubt with enough evidence and clues buried all over it to keep them busy for generations." He nodded again in response to Maddson's incredulous stare. "They must have built up a very complete record of what the Ganymeans had done, all right. But all the evidence they used to do it was lost with them."

Hunt paused and drew his cigarette case slowly from his inside jacket pocket while he quickly checked over the line of reasoning in his mind.

"I wonder what they knew about that star that we don't know," he said at last, his voice now become very quiet. "I wonder what they knew about that star that caused them to choose a name like that. We've suspected for a long time that the Giants might have migrated to another star, but we've never been able to prove it for sure or been able to say what star it might have been. And now this turns up . . ."

Hunt stopped with his lighter poised halfway toward his mouth. "Don," he said. "In your life, do you find that fate steps in and lends a hand every now and again?"

"Never really thought about it," Maddson admitted. "But now you come to mention it, I guess I have to agree."

chapter twenty-one

As time went by, the Ganymean scientists grew to know better and work more closely with the scientific community of Earth. In several areas, information supplied by the aliens contributed significantly to advances in human knowledge.

Maps reproduced from ZORAC's data banks showed the surface of the Earth as it had appeared at the time of the early Minervan expeditions to the planet, during its late Oligocene period. These same maps showed the Atlantic Ocean little more than half as wide as was shown on twenty-first-century maps, indicating that the time represented was that much nearer to the breaking adrift of the American continent. The Mediterranean Sea was much wider with Italy half rotated prior to being driven into Europe by Africa's relentless northward drive to create the Alps; India had just made contact with Asia and begun throwing up the Himalayas; Australia was much closer to Africa. Measurements of these maps enabled current theories of plate tectonics to be thoroughly checked and brought a whole new light to bear on many aspects of the Earth sciences.

Throughout all this the Ganymeans declined to say exactly where their experimental colonies on Earth had been located, or what areas had been affected by the ecological catastrophes that they had induced. These matters, they said, were best left in the past where they belonged.

At institutes of physics and universities all over the world, the Ganymeans unveiled the rudiments and fundamental concepts of the theoretical basis of the extended science that had led to the emergence of their technology of gravitics. In this they did not provide blueprints for constructing gadgets and devices whose principles would not be comprehended and whose introduction would have been premature; they offered only general guidance, declaring that Man would fill in the details in his own way, and would do so when the time was right.

The Ganymeans also painted bright and promising pictures of the future by describing the unlimited abundance of resources that the universe had to offer. All substances, they pointed out, were built from the same atoms and, given the right knowledge and sufficient energy, anything required—metals, crystals, organic polymers, oils, sugars and proteins—could be synthesized from plentiful and freely available materials. Energy, as Man was beginning to discover, was waiting to be trapped in undreamed of quantities. Of the total amount of energy radiated out into space by the sun, less than one thousandth part of one billionth was actually intercepted by the disk of the Earth. Nearly half of that was reflected away back into space, and of the remainder that actually penetrated through to the surface, only a minute fraction was harnessed to any useful purpose. Borrowing from the commercial jargon of Earth, the Ganymeans described the tiny pockets of energy that happened to be trapped in one form or another about the surface of his planet as representing Man's starting capital. Future generations, they predicted, would look back at Apollo as just the down payment on the best long-term investment Man ever made.

As the months passed by, the two cultures interlocked more closely and adjusted to accommodate one another so well that it seemed to many that the Giants had always been there. The *Shapieron* toured the globe and spent a day or two at most of the world's major airports, attracting visitors by the tens of thousands; on several occasions it took selected parties on one-hour rides around the Moon and back! Anybody who had access to an Earthnet terminal and who could get through the permanently jammed public exchange could speak to ZORAC, and a number of high-priority channels were permanently reserved for allocation to schools. Despite their ancestry, many of the young Ganymeans developed a passion for baseball, soccer, and other such sports—pastimes the likes of which had been unknown to them in their previous shipbound existence. Before long they had formed their own leagues to challenge their terrestrial counterparts. At first their elders were a little disturbed by this turn of events, but later they reasoned that the notion of competition seemed to have brought Man a long way in a short time; perhaps the grafting, in small doses, of the Earthman's will to win onto the Ganymean's analytical ability to see just how to go about doing it, wouldn't be so bad after all.

For six months the Ganymeans toured every nation of Earth learning its ways, absorbing its culture, meeting its peoples—the high, the low, the rich, the poor, the ordinary and the famous. After a while they were no longer the "aliens." They became simply a new factor in an environment that the people of Earth were by now accustomed to accept as constantly changing. Hunt noticed again, this time on a global scale, the same thing he had noticed at Pithead in the week that the Ganymeans had gone to Pluto—they seemed to belong on

Earth. Without them being constantly around or featured in the headlines, Earth would not, somehow, have seemed normal.

Then, one day, the news flashed around the globe that Garuth would shortly appear on the Earthnet to make an important announcement to all the people of Earth. No hint was given as to what this announcement would contain, but there was something about the mood of the moment that forewarned of some significant development. When the evening arrived on which Garuth was due to speak, the world was watching and waiting at a billion viewscreens.

Garuth spoke for a long time on the events that had taken place since the time of the Ganymeans' arrival. He touched upon most of the sights that he and his companions had seen, the places they had been to and the things that they had learned. He expressed again the amazement that the Ganymeans had experienced at the restlessness, vivacity and impatient frenzy for living that they had found on every side in what he described as "this fantastic, undreamed-of world of yours." And, speaking on behalf of all his kind, he repeated their gratitude to the governments and people of the planet that had shown them friendship, hospitality and generosity without limit, and offered their home to share.

But then his mood, which had been slightly solemn throughout, took on a distinctly somber note. "As most of you, my friends, know, for a long time now there has been speculation that long ago, sometime after our ship departed from Minerva, our race abandoned that planet forever to seek a new home elsewhere. There have been suggestions that the new home they found was a planet of a distant star—the one that has become known as the Giants' Star.

"Both these notions must remain mere speculation. Our scientists and yours have been working together for many months now, studying the Lunarian records and following up every clue that might possibly add further credence to these notions. I have to tell you that these efforts have thus far proved fruitless. We cannot say for certain that the Giants' Star is indeed the new home of our race. We cannot even say for certain that our race did in fact migrate to a new home at all.

"There is a chance, nevertheless, that these things could be true."

The long face paused and stared hard at the camera for what seemed a long time, almost as if it knew that the watchers at the screens all over the world could sense suddenly what was coming next.

"I must now inform you that I and my senior officers have discussed and examined these questions at great length. We have decided that, slim though the chances of success appear to be, we must make the attempt to find these answers. The Solar System was once our home, but it is no longer our home. We must take to the void again and seek our own kind."

He paused again to allow time for his meaning to sink in.

"This decision did not come easily. My people have spent a large part of their natural lives wandering in depths of space. Our children have never known a home. A journey to the Giants' Star will, we know, take many years. In many ways we are sad, naturally, but, like you, we must in the end obey our instincts. Deep down we could never rest until the question of The Giants' Star has been finally answered.

"And so, my friends, I am bidding you farewell. We will carry with us pleasant memories of the time that we knew here on the sunny blue and green world of Earth. We will never forget the warmth and hospitality of the people of this world, nor will we forget what they did for us. But, sadly, it must end.

"One week from today we will depart. Should we fail in our quest, we, or our descendants, will return. This I promise."

The Giant raised his arm in a final salute, and inclined his head slightly.

"Thank you—all of you. And good-bye."

He held the posture for a few more seconds. Then the broadcast cut out.

A half-hour after the broadcast, Garuth emerged from the main door of the conference center at Ganyville. He stopped for a while, savoring the first hint of winter being carried down from the mountains on the night air. Around him all was still apart from an occasional figure flitting through the pools of warm orange light that flooded out of the windows into the alley between the wooden walls of the chalets. The night was clear as crystal. He stood for a long time staring up at the stars. Then he began walking slowly along the path in front of him and turned into the broad throughway that led down, between the rows of chalets, toward the immense floodlit tower of the *Shapieron*.

He passed by one of the ship's supporting legs and moved

on into the space spanned by its four enormous fin surfaces, suddenly dwarfed by the sweeping lines of metal soaring high above him. As he approached the foot of one of the ramps that led up into the lowered stern and stepped into the surrounding circle of light, a half-dozen or so eight-foot figures straightened up out of the shadows at the bottom of the ramp. He recognized them immediately as members of his crew, no doubt relaxing and enjoying the calm of the night. As he drew nearer, he sensed from the way they stood and the way they looked at him that something had changed. Normally they would have called out some jovial remark or made some enthusiastic sign of greeting, but they did not. They just stood there, silent and withdrawn. As he reached the ramps they stood aside to make way and raised their hands in acknowledgment of his rank. Garuth returned the salutes and passed between them. He found that he could not meet their eyes. No one spoke. He knew that they had seen the broadcast, and he knew how they felt. There was nothing he could say.

He reached the top of the ramp, passed through the open airlock and crossed the wide space beyond to enter the elevator that ZORAC had waiting. A few seconds later he was being carried swiftly upward into the main body of the *Shapieron.*

He came out of the elevator over five hundred feet above ground level, and followed a short corridor to a door which brought him into his private quarters. Shilohin, Monchar and Jassilane were waiting there, sitting in a variety of poses around the room. He sensed the same attitude that he had felt a minute before at the ramp. He stood for a moment looking down at them while the door slid silently shut behind him. Monchar and Jassilane were looking at one another uneasily. Only Shilohin was holding his gaze, but she said nothing. Garuth emitted a long-drawn-out sigh then moved slowly between them to stand for a while contemplating a metallic tapestry that adorned the far wall. Then he turned about to face them once more. Shilohin was still watching him.

"You're still not convinced that we have to go," he said at last.

The remark was unnecessary, but somebody had to say something. No reply was necessary either.

The scientist shifted her eyes away and said, as if addressing the low table standing between her and the other two. "It's the way in which we're going about it. They've trusted you unquestioningly all this time. All the way from Iscaris ... all those years ... You ..."

"One second." Garuth moved across to a small control panel set into the wall near the door. "I don't think this conversation should go on record." He flipped a switch to cut off the room from all channels to ZORAC, and hence to the ship's archived records.

"You know that there's no Ganymean civilization waiting at the Giants' Star or anywhere else," Shilohin resumed. Her voice was about as near an accusation as a Ganymean could get. "We've been through the Lunarian records time and again. It adds up to nothing. You are taking your people away to die somewhere out there between the stars. There will be no coming back. But you allow them to believe in fantasies so that they will follow where you lead them. Surely those are the ways of Earthmen, not Ganymeans."

"They offered us their world as home," Jassilane murmured, shaking his head. "For twenty years your people have dreamed of nothing but coming home. And now that they have found one, you would take them back out into the void again. Minerva is gone; nothing we can do will change that. But by a quirk of fate we have found a new home—here. It will never happen a second time."

Suddenly Garuth was very weary. He sank down into the reclining chair by the door and regarded the three solemn faces staring back at him. There was nothing that he could add to the things that had already been said. Yes, it was true; the Earthmen had greeted his people as if they were long-lost brothers. They had offered all they had. But in the six months that had gone by, Garuth had looked deep below the surface. He had looked; he had listened; he had watched; he had seen.

"Today the Earthmen welcome us with open arms," he said. "But in many ways, they are still children. They show us their world as a child would open its toy cupboard to a new play-friend. But a play-friend who visits once in a while is one thing; one who moves in to stay, with equal rights to ownership to the toy cupboard, is another."

Garuth could see that his listeners wanted to be convinced, to feel the reassurance of thinking the way he thought, but could not—no more than they had been able to a dozen times before. Nevertheless he had no choice but to go through it yet again.

"The human race is still struggling to learn to live with itself. Today we are just a handful of aliens—a novelty; but one day we would grow to a sizable population. Earth does not yet possess the stability and the maturity to adapt to coexistence on that scale; they are just managing to coexist with one another. Look at their history. One day, I'm sure, they will be capable, but the time is not ripe yet.

"You forget their pride and their innate instincts to compete in all things. They could never accept passively a situation in which their instincts would compel them, one day, to see themselves as inferiors and us as dominant rivals. When that time came, we would be forced to go anyway, since we would never impose ourselves or our ways on unwilling or resentful hosts, but that would happen only after a lot of problems and eventual unpleasantness. It is better this way."

Shilohin heard his words, but still everything inside her recoiled from the verdict that they spelled out.

"So, for this you would deceive your own people," she whispered. "Just to insure the stable evolution of this alien planet, you would sacrifice your own kind—the last few pathetic remnants of our civilization. What kind of judgment is this?"

"It is not my judgment, but the judgment of time and fate," Garuth replied. "The Solar System was once the undisputed domain of our race, but that time ended long ago. We are the intruders now—an anachronism; a scrap of flotsam thrown up out of the ocean of time. Now the Solar System has become rightly the inheritance of Man. We do not belong here any longer. That is not a judgment for us to make, but one that has already been made for us by circumstances. It is merely ours to accept."

"But your people . . ." Shilohin protested. "Shouldn't they know? Haven't they the right . . . ?" She threw her arms in the air in a gesture of helplessness. Garuth remained silent for a moment, then shook his head slowly.

"I will not reveal to them that the new home at the Giants' Star is a myth," he declared firmly. "That is a burden that need be carried only by us, who command and lead. They do not have to know . . . yet. It was their hope and their belief in a purpose that nurtured them from Iscaris to Sol. So it can be again for a while. If we are taking them away to their doom to perish unsung and unmourned somewhere in the cold, uncharted depths of space, they deserve at least that before the final truth has to become known. That is precious little to ask."

A grim silence reigned for a long time. A faraway look came over Shilohin as she turned over again in her mind the things that Garuth had said. And then the look changed gradually into a frown. Her eyes cleared and swung slowly upward to meet Garuth's.

"Garuth," she said. Her voice was curiously calm and composed. All traces of the emotions she had felt previously were gone. "I've never said this to you ever before, but . . . I don't believe you." Jassilane and Monchar looked up abruptly. Garuth seemed strangely unsurprised, almost as if he had been expecting her to say that. He leaned back in his chair and contemplated the tapestry on the wall. Then he swung his eyes slowly back toward her.

"What don't you believe, Shilohin?"

"Your reasons . . . everything you've been saying for the last few weeks. It's just not . . . you. It's a rationalization of something else . . . something deeper." Garuth said nothing, but continued to regard her steadfastly. "Earth *is* maturing rapidly," she continued. "We've mixed with them and been accepted by them in ways that far exceeded our wildest hopes. There's no evidence to support the predictions you made. There's no evidence that we could never coexist, even if our numbers did grow. You would never sacrifice your people just on the off-chance that things might not work out. You'd try it first . . . for a while at least. There has to be another reason. I won't be able to support your decision until I know what that reason is. You talked about the burden of us who command and lead. If we carry that burden, then surely we've a right to know why."

Garuth continued staring at her thoughtfully for a long time after she had finished speaking. Then he transferred his gaze, still with the same thoughtful expression, to Jassilane and Monchar. The look in their eyes echoed Shilohin's words. Then, abruptly, he seemed to make up his mind.

Without speaking, he rose from the chair, walked over to the control panel, and operated the switch to restore normal communications facilities to the room.

"zorac," he called.

"Yes, Commander?"

"You recall the discussion that we had about a month ago concerning the data that the human scientists have collected on the genetics of the Oligocene species discovered in the ship at Pithead?"

"Yes."

"I'd like you to present the results of your analysis of that data to us. This information is not to be made accessible to anyone other than myself and the three people who are in this room at present."

chapter twenty-two

The crowds that came to Ganyville to see the *Shapieron* depart were as large as those that had greeted its arrival, but their mood was a very different one. This time there was no jubilation or wild excitement. The people of Earth would miss the gentle Giants that they had come to know so well, and it showed.

The governments of Earth had again sent their ambassadors and, on the concrete apron below the towering ship, two groups of Earthmen and aliens faced each other for the last time. After the final formalities had been exchanged and the last farewell speeches had been uttered, the spokesman for each of the two races presented his parting gift.

The Chairman of the United Nations, acting on behalf of all of the peoples and nations of Earth, handed over two ornamental metal caskets, heavily inscribed on their outside faces and decorated with precious stones. The first contained a selection of seeds of many terrestrial trees, shrubs and flowering plants. The second, somewhat larger, contained the national flag of every one of the world's states. The seeds, he said, were to be planted at a selected place when the Giants arrived at their new home; the plants that grew from them would symbolize all of terrestrial life and provide a lasting reminder that henceforth both worlds would always be a home to Man and Ganymean equally. The flags were to be flown above that place on some as yet unknown future day when the first ship from Earth reached The Giants' Star. Thus, when Man came at last to launch himself into the void between the stars, he would find a small part of Earth waiting to greet him on the other side.

Garuth's gift to Earth was knowledge. He presented a large chest filled with books, tables, charts and diagrams which, he stated, provided a comprehensive introduction to the Ganymean genetic sciences. In presenting this knowledge to Earth, the Ganymeans were attempting to atone in the only way that they could for the species of Oligocene animals that had been made extinct during the ugly extermination experiments of long ago. By techniques that were explained in these texts, Garuth said, the DNA codes that existed in any preserved cell from any part of an animal organism could be extracted and used to control the artificially induced growth of a duplicate, living organism. Given a sliver of bone, a trace of tissue or a clipping of horn, a new embryo could be synthesized and from it the complete animal would grow. Thus, provided that some remnant remained, all of the extinct species that had once roamed the surface of the Earth could be resurrected. In this way, the Ganymeans hoped, the species that had met with sudden and untimely ends as a result of their actions would be allowed to live and run free again.

And then the last group of Ganymeans stood for a while to return the silent wavings of the multitudes on the surrounding hills before filing slowly up into the ship. With them went a small party of Earthmen destined for Ganymede, where the *Shapieron* was scheduled to make a short call to allow the Ganymeans to bid farewell to their UNSA friends there.

ZORAC spoke over the communications network of Earth to deliver a final message from the Ganymeans and then the link was broken. The *Shapieron* retracted its stern section into its flight position and for a while the huge ship stood alone while the world watched. And then it began to rise, slowly and majestically, before soaring up and away to rejoin its element. Only the sea of upturned faces, the lines of tiny figures arrayed around the empty space in the center of the concrete apron, and the rows of outsize deserted wooden chalets remained to show that it had ever been.

The mood inside the *Shapieron* was solemn too. In the command center, Garuth stood in the area of open floor below the dais surrounded by a group of senior officers and watched in silence as the mottled pattern of blue and white on the main screen shrank and became the globe of Earth. Shilohin was standing beside him, also silent and absorbed in thoughts of her own.

Then ZORAC spoke, his voice seemingly issuing from the surrounding walls. "Launch characteristics normal. All systems checked and normal. Request confirmation of orders."

"Existing orders confirmed," Garuth replied quietly. "Destination Ganymede."

"Setting course for Ganymede," the machine reported. "Arrival will be as scheduled."

"Hold off main drives for a while," Garuth said suddenly. "I'd like to see Earth for a little longer."

"Maintaining auxiliaries," came the response. "Main drives being held on standby pending further orders."

As the minutes ticked by the globe on the screen contracted slowly. The Ganymeans continued to watch in silence.

At last Shilohin turned to Garuth. "And to think, we called it the Nightmare Planet."

Garuth smiled faintly. His thoughts were still far away.

"They've woken up from the nightmare now," he said. "What an extraordinary race they are. Surely they must be unique in the Galaxy."

"I still can't bring myself to believe that everything we have seen can have evolved from such origins," she replied. "Don't forget I was brought up in a school that taught me to believe that this could never happen. All our theories and our models predicted that intelligence was unlikely to develop at all in any ecology like that, and that any form of civilization would be absolutely impossible. And yet . . ." she made a gesture of helplessness, "look at them. They've barely learned to fly and already they talk about the stars. Two hundred years ago they knew nothing of electricity; today they generate it by fusion power. Where will they stop?"

"I don't think they ever will," Garuth said slowly. "They can't. They must fight all the time, just as their ancestors did. Their ancestors fought each other; they fight the challenges that the universe throws at them instead. Take away their challenges and they would waste away."

Shilohin thought again about the incredible race that had struggled to claw its way upward through every difficulty and obstacle imaginable, not the least of which was its own perversity, and which now reigned unchallenged and triumphant in the Solar System that the Ganymeans had once owned.

"Their history is still abhorrent in many ways," she said. "But at the same time there is something strangely magnificent and proud about them. They can live with danger where we could not, because they know that they can conquer danger. They have proved things to themselves that we will never know, and it is that knowledge that will carry them onward where we would hesitate. If Earthmen had inhabited the Minerva of twenty-five million years ago, I'm sure that things would have turned out differently. They wouldn't have given up after Iscaris; they would have found a way to win."

"Yes," Garuth agreed. "Things would certainly have turned out very differently. But before long, I feel, we will see what would have happened if that had been true. Very soon now the Earthmen will explode outward all over the Galaxy. Somehow, I don't think it will ever be quite the same again after that happens."

The conversation lapsed once more as the two Ganymeans shifted their eyes again to take in a last view of the planet that had defied all their theories, laws, principles and expectations. In the years to come they would no doubt gaze many times at this image, retrieved from the ship's data banks, but it would never again have the impact of this moment.

After a long time, Garuth called out aloud, "ZORAC."

"Commander?"

"It's time we were on our way. Activate main drives."

"Switching over from standby. Commencing run-up to full power now."

The disk of Earth dissolved into a wash of colors that ran across the screen and began to fade. After a few minutes the colors had merged into a sheet of drab, uniform, grayish fog. The screen would show nothing more until they reached Ganymede.

"Monchar," Garuth called. "I have things to attend to. Will you take over here for a while?"

"Aye-aye, sir."

"Very good. I will be in my room if I am needed for anything."

Garuth excused himself from the company, acknowledged the salutations around him, and left the command center. He walked slowly through the corridors that led to his private quarters, fully preoccupied with the thoughts inside his head and largely oblivious to his surroundings. When he had closed the door behind him, he stared at himself in the wall mirror in his stateroom for a long time, as if looking for visible changes in his appearance that might have been brought about by what he had done. Then he sank into one of the reclining armchairs and stared unseeingly at the ceiling until he lost track of time.

Eventually he activated the wall screen in the stateroom and called up a star chart that showed the part of the sky that included the constellation of Taurus. For a long time he sat staring at the faint point that would grow progressively brighter in the course of the long voyage ahead. There was a hope that they could all be wrong. There was always a chance. If the Ganymeans *had* migrated there, what kind of civilization would they have developed over the millions of years that had passed by since the *Shapieron* departed from Minerva? What kind of science would they possess? What wonders would they accept as commonplace that even he could never conceive? As his mind went out toward the faint spot on the star chart, he felt a sudden surge of hope welling up inside him. He began to picture the world that was there waiting to greet them and he grew restless and impatient at the thought of the years that would have to pass by before they could know.

He knew that the optimism of the human scientists knew no bounds. Already the huge disks of the radio-observatory situated on Lunar Farside were beaming a high-power transmission in Ganymean communications code out toward the Giants' Star to forewarn of the *Shapieron*'s coming—a message that would take years to cover the distance, but which would still arrive well ahead of the ship.

Then he slumped back in the chair, despairing and dispirited. He knew, as his few trusted companions knew, that there would be nobody there to receive it. Nothing in the Lunarian records had proved anything. It was all Earthmen's wishful thinking.

His thoughts went back to the incredible Earthmen—the race that had struggled and fought for millennia to overcome such horrendous difficulties, and who now, at last, were emerging from their past to a prospect of lasting prosperity and wisdom . . . if they could only be left alone for a little longer to complete the things they had so valiantly strived to achieve. They had built their world out of chaos, against all the theories and predictions of all the sages and scientists of Minerva. They deserved to be left alone to enjoy their world without interference.

For Garuth knew, as now only Shilohin, Jassilane and Monchar knew, that the Ganymeans had created the human race.

The Ganymeans had been the direct cause of all the defects, handicaps and problems that should by rights have left Man with all the odds piled hopelessly against him. But Man had triumphed over all of them. Justice demanded now that Man be left alone to perfect his world in his own way and without further interference from the Ganymeans.

The Ganymeans had already interfered enough.

chapter twenty-three

In Danchekker's office, high in the main building of the Westwood Biological Institute on the outskirts of Houston, the professor and Hunt were watching the view of the *Shapieron* being sent down from a telescopic camera tracking from a satellite high above the Earth. The image grew gradually smaller and then suddenly enlarged again as the magnification was stepped up. Then it began to shrink once more.

"It's just coasting," Hunt commented from an armchair set over to one side of the room. "Seems as if they want to get one last look at us." Danchekker said nothing but just nodded absently as he watched from behind his desk. The commentary coming over on audio confirmed Hunt's observation.

"Radar indicates that the ship is still traveling quite slowly compared to the performance that we have seen before. It doesn't seem to be going into orbit . . . just continuing to move steadily away from Earth. This is the last time you'll have a chance to see this fantastic vessel live, so make the most of the moment. We are looking at the closing page of what has surely been the most astounding chapter ever written in the history of the human race. How can things ever be the same again?" A short pause. "Hello, something's happening I'm told. . . . The ship's starting to accelerate now. It's really streaking away from us now, building up speed fast all the time. . . ." The image on the screen began to perform a crazy dance of growing and shrinking again at a bewildering rate.

"They're on main drive," Hunt said, as the commentator continued.

"The image is starting to break up. . . . The stressfield's becoming noticeable now. . . . It's going . . . getting fainter . . . That's it Well I guess that just about—" The voice and picture died together as Danchekker flipped a switch behind his desk to cut off the display.

"So, there they go to meet whatever destiny awaits them," he said. "I wish them well." A short silence ensued while Hunt fished in his pockets for his lighter and cigarette case. As he leaned back in his chair again he said, "You know, Chris, when you think about it, these last couple of years have been pretty remarkable."

"To say the least."

"Charlie, the Lunarians, the ship at Pithead, the Ganymeans . . . and now this." He gestured toward the blank screen. "What better time could we have picked to be alive? It makes every other period of history seem a bit dull, doesn't it?"

"It does indeed . . . very dull indeed." Danchekker seemed to be answering automatically, as if part of his mind were still hurtling out into space with the *Shapieron*.

"It's a bit of a pity, though, in some ways," Hunt said after a while.

"What is?"

"The Ganymeans. We never really got to the bottom of some of the interesting questions, did we? It's a pity they couldn't have stayed around just a little longer—until we'd managed to figure out a few more of the answers. Actually I'm a bit surprised they didn't. At one stage they seemed even more curious about some things than we were."

Danchekker seemed to turn the proposition over in his mind for a long time. Then he looked up and across to where Hunt was sitting and eyed him in a strange way. When he spoke his voice was curiously challenging.

"Oh really? Answers to questions such as what, might I ask?"

Hunt frowned at him for a second, then shrugged as he exhaled a stream of smoke.

"You know what questions. What happened on Minerva after the *Shapieron* left? Why did they ship all those terrestrial animals there? What bumped off all the Minervan animals? That kind of thing . . . It would be nice to know, even if it is a bit academic now, if only to tidy all the loose ends up."

"Oh, those." Danchekker's air of studied nonchalance was masterly. "I think I can supply you with whatever answers you require to those questions." The matter-of-factness in Danchekker's voice left Hunt at a loss for words. The professor cocked his head to one side and regarded him quizzically but could not contain a slight admission of the amusement that he felt.

"Well . . . Good God, what are they then?" Hunt managed at last. He realized that in his astonishment he had let his cigarette slip from his fingers and made hasty efforts to retrieve it from the side of his chair.

Danchekker watched the pantomime in silence, then replied. "Let me see now, to answer directly the questions that you have just asked would not really convey very much, since they all interrelate. Most of them follow from the work I have been doing here ever since we got back from Ganymede, which covers quite a lot of ground. Perhaps it would be simpler if I just start at the beginning and follow it through from there." Hunt waited while Danchekker leaned back and interlaced his fingers in front of his chin and contemplated the far wall to collect his thoughts.

At last Danchekker resumed. "Do you recall the piece of research from Utrecht that you brought to my attention soon after we got back—concerning the way in which animals manufacture small amounts of toxins and contaminants to exercise their defensive systems?"

"The self-immunization process. Yes, I remember. ZORAC picked that one up. Animals possess it but human beings don't. What about it?"

"I found the subject rather intriguing and spent some time after our discussion following it up, which included holding some very long and detailed conversations with a Professor Tatham from Cambridge, an old friend of mine who specializes in that kind of thing. In particular, I wanted to know more about the genetic codes that are responsible for this self-immunization mechanism forming in the developing embryo. It seemed to me that if we were going to try to pinpoint the causes for this radical difference between us and the beasts, this was the level at which we should look for it."

"And . . . ?"

"And, the results were extremely interesting . . . in fact, re-remarkable." Danchekker's voice fell almost to a whisper that seemed to accentuate every syllable. "As ZORAC discovered, in virtually all of today's terrestrial animals, the genetic coding that determines their self-immunization mechanism is closely related to the coding responsible for another process; you might say that both processes are subsets of the same program. The other process regulates carbon-dioxide absorption and rejection."

"I see . . ." Hunt nodded slowly. He didn't yet see exactly where Danchekker was leading, but he was beginning to sense something important.

"You're always telling me you don't like coincidences," Danchekker went on. "I don't either. There was far too much of a coincidence about this, so Tatham and I started delving a bit deeper. When we investigated the experiments performed at Pithead and on board *Jupiter Five*, we came across a second rather remarkable thing, that tied in with what I have just been talking about—concerning the Oligocene animals found in the ship there. The Oligocene animals all contain the same genetic coding elements, but in their case there is a difference. The subprograms that control the two processes I mentioned have somehow been separated out; they exist as discrete groupings that lie side by side on the same DNA chain. Now that is very remarkable, wouldn't you say?"

Hunt considered the question for a few seconds.

"You mean that in today's animals both processes are there, but all scrambled up together, but in the Oligocene species they're separated out."

"Yes."

"*All* the Oligocene species?" Hunt asked after a moment's further reflection. Danchekker nodded in satisfaction at seeing that Hunt was on the right track.

"Precisely, Vic. *All* of them."

"That doesn't really make sense. I mean, the first thing you'd think would be that some kind of mutation had occurred to change one form into the other—the scrambled-up form and the separated-out form. That could have happened either way around. In one case the scrambled form could be the 'natural' terrestrial pattern that became mutated on Minerva; that would explain why the animals from there have it and the descendants of the ones that were left here don't. Alternatively, you could suppose that twenty-five million years ago the separated-out form was standard, which explains of course why the animals from that time exhibit it, but that in subsequent evolution here on Earth it changed itself into the scrambled form." He looked across at Danchekker and threw his arms out wide. "But there's one basic flaw in both those arguments—it happened in lots of different species, all at the same time."

"Quite," Danchekker nodded. "And, by all the principles of selection and evolution that we accept, that would appear to rule out the possibility of any kind of mutation—*natural* mutation, anyway. It would be inconceivable for the same chance event to occur spontaneously and simultaneously in many distinct and unrelated lines . . . utterly inconceivable."

"*Natural* mutation?" Hunt look puzzled. "What are you saying then?"

"It's perfectly simple. We're just agreed that the difference couldn't be due to ordinary natural mutation, but nevertheless it's there. The only other explanation possible then is that it was *not* natural."

Impossible thoughts flashed through Hunt's mind. Danchekker read the expression on his face and voiced them for him.

"In other words they didn't just happen; they were made to happen. The genetic codings were *deliberately* rearranged. We are talking about an *artificial* mutation."

For a moment Hunt was stunned. The word deliberate denoted conscious volition, which in turn implied an intelligence.

Danchekker nodded again to confirm his thoughts. "If I may rephrase your question of a minute ago, what we are really asking is, did the animals that were shipped to Minerva change, or did the animals that were left on Earth change after the others were shipped? Now add to the equation the further fact that we have established—that *somebody* deliberately caused the change to happen—and we are left with only one choice."

Hunt completed the argument for him. "There hasn't been anybody around on Earth during the last twenty-five million years that could have done it, so it must have been done on Minerva. That can only mean . . ." His voice trailed off as the full implication became clear.

"The Ganymeans!" Danchekker said. He allowed some time for this to sink in and then continued. "The Ganymeans altered the genetic coding of the terrestrial animals that they took back to their own planet. I am fairly certain that the samples that were recovered from the ship at Pithead were descendants of a strain that had been mutated in this way and had faithfully carried on the mutation in themselves. This is the only logical conclusion that can be drawn from the evidence we have reviewed. Also, it is strongly supported by another interesting piece of evidence."

By now Hunt was ready for anything.

"Oh?" he replied. "What?"

"That strange enzyme that turned up in all of the Oligocene species," Danchekker said. "We know now what it did." The look on Hunt's face asked all the questions for him. Danchekker continued: "That enzyme was constructed for one specific task. It cleaved the DNA chain at precisely the point where those two coding groups were joined—in species where they were separated out, of course. In other words, it isolated the genetic code that defined the CO_2-tolerance characteristics."

"Okay," Hunt said slowly, but still not following the argument fully. "I'll take your word for that. . . But how does that support what you just said about the Ganymeans? I'm not quite—"

"That enzyme was not a result of any *natural* process! It was something that had been manufactured and introduced artificially. That was where the radioactive decay products came from; the enzyme was manufactured artificially and included radioactive tracer elements to allow its progress through the body to be tracked and measured. We use the same technique widely in medical and physiological research ourselves."

Hunt held up a hand to stop Danchekker going any further for the time being. He sat forward in his chair and closed his eyes for a second as he mentally stepped through the reasoning that the professor had summarized.

"Yes . . . okay . . . You've pointed out all along that chemical processes can't distinguish a radioisotope from a normal one. So, how could the enzyme have selected radioisotopes to build into itself? Answer: It couldn't; somebody must have selected them and therefore the enzyme must have been manufactured artificially. Why use radioisotopes? Answer: Tracers."

Hunt again looked across at the professor, who was following and nodding encouragement. "But the enzyme does a specialized job on the modified DNA chain, and you've already established that the DNA was modified artificially in the animals that were shipped to Minerva. . . . Ah, I see . . . I can see how the two tie in together. What you're saying is that the Ganymeans altered the DNA coding of the terrestrial animals, and then manufactured a specific enzyme to operate on the altered DNA."

"Exactly."

"And what was the purpose of it all?" Hunt was becoming visibly excited. "Any ideas on that?"

"Yes," Danchekker replied. "I think we have. In fact the things that we have just considered tell us all that we need to know to guess at what they were up to." He sat back and interlaced his fingers again. "With the enzyme performing in the way that I have just described, the object of the exercise becomes clear. At least I think it does. . . . If the animals that possessed the already altered DNA were implanted with the enzymes, the chromosomes in their reproductive cells would have been modified. This would have made it possible for a strain of offspring to be bred from them who possessed the CO_2 coding in the form of an isolated, compact unit that could be manipulated and 'got at' with comparative ease. If you like, it enabled this particular characteristic to be separated out, perhaps with a view to its becoming the focal point of further experiments with later generations. . . ." Danchekker's voice took on a curious note as he uttered the last few words, as if he were hinting that the main implication of his dissertation was about to emerge.

"I can see what you're saying," Hunt told him. "But not quite why. What *were* they up to then?"

"*That* was how they sought to solve their environmental problem after all else had failed," Danchekker said. "It must have been something that was thought of during the later period of Ganymean history on Minerva—sometime after the *Shapieron* went to Iscaris, otherwise Shilohin and the others would have known about it."

"What was how they sought to solve it? Sorry, Chris, I'm afraid I'm not with you all the way yet."

"Let us recapitulate for a moment on their situation," Danchekker suggested. "They knew that the CO_2 level on Minerva had begun to rise, and that one day it would reach a point that they would be unable to withstand; the other Minervan native species would be unaffected, but the Ganymeans would be vulnerable as a consequence of their breeding their original tolerance out of themselves as part of the trade-off for better accident-resistance. They lost it when they took the decision to dispense permanently with their secondary circulation systems. They declined climatic engineering as a solution and tried migration to Earth and the Iscaris experiment but both failed. Later on, it appears, they must have tried something else."

Hunt was all ears. He made a gesture of total capitulation and said simply, "Go on."

"One thing that they did discover on Earth, however, was a family of life that had evolved from origins in a warmer environment than that of Minerva, and which had not had to contend with the load-sharing problem that had caused the double-circulatory-system architecture to become standard on their own planet. Of particular interest, terrestrial life had evolved a completely different mechanism for dealing with carbon dioxide—one that did not depend on any secondary circulation system."

Hunt looked incredulous. He stared at Danchekker for a second while the professor waited for the response.

"You're not trying to say . . . they didn't try and pinch it?"

Danchekker nodded. 'If my suspicions are anything to go by, that is exactly what they tried to do. The animals from Earth were transported back to Minerva for the purpose of large-scale genetic experiments. The object of those experiments, I believe, was threefold: first, to modify the DNA coding in such a way that the CO_2-tolerance portion became separated out from the scrambled form—as you put it—that had evolved naturally on Earth; second, to perfect a means—the enzyme—of isolating that block of code and passing it on in an intact and workable unit to later strains; third, but this is a guess, to implant those codes into *Minervan* animals in an attempt to find out if a Minervan life form could be modified into developing a mechanism for dealing with carbon dioxide that did not depend on its secondary system. We have evidence that they achieved the first two of these objectives; the third must necessarily remain speculative, at least for the time being."

"And if they did succeed in the third, then the next step would be . . ." Hunt's voice trailed off again. The sheer ingenuity of the Ganymean scheme made it difficult for him to accept it unquestioningly.

"If it worked, and if there were no undesirable side effects, the intention was no doubt to engineer the same codes into themselves," Danchekker confirmed. "Thus they would enjoy an in-built tolerance that would happily continue to perpetuate itself through succeeding generations, while at the same time preserving all the advantages that they had already gained by doing away with their secondary systems. A fascinating example of what intelligence can do to improve on Nature when natural evolution throws up a solution that leaves much to be desired, don't you think?"

Hunt rose from his chair and began pacing slowly from one side of the office to the other as he marveled at the sheer audacity of even conceiving such a scheme. The Ganymeans had expressed wonder at Man's readiness to meet Nature head-on in every challenge, but here was something, surely, that Man would have balked at. The basic instincts of the Ganymeans steered them away from physical danger, conflict and the like, but their thirst for intellectual adventure and combat, it appeared, was unquenchable; that was the spur that had driven them to the stars. Danchekker watched in silence, waiting for the question that he knew would come next. At length Hunt stopped and wheeled to face the desk.

"Yes, it was neat, all right," he agreed. "But it didn't work, did it, Chris?"

"Regrettably, no," Danchekker conceded. "But not for reasons for which, I feel, they were really to blame. We might have some catching up to do with them technically, but nevertheless I believe that we are in a position to see where they went wrong." He didn't wait for the obvious question at that point but went on. "We have the advantage of knowing far more than they possibly could have about life on our own planet. We have access to the work of thousands of scientists who have studied the subject for centuries, but the Ganymeans who came here twenty-five million years ago did not. In particular, they could not have known what Professor Tatham and his team at Cambridge have only just discovered."

"The scrambling together of the self-immunization and the CO_2-tolerance codings?"

"Yes, exactly that. The thing that the Ganymean genetic engineers would never have realized was that in isolating the latter, in order to make their proposed later experiments simpler, they were losing the former. Because of the method they adopted, the descendant strains that they bred would have been ideal subjects for further CO_2-tolerance research, but they would also have lost their self-immunization capabilities. In other words the Ganymeans created and raised a whole range of mixed terrestrial animals species that possessed no trace of the age-old mechanism for stimulating their own defensive processes by flooding the body with mild doses of pollutants—a mechanism which we still see today in the descendants of the animals that remained on Earth to continue evolving naturally, of course."

Hunt had stopped pacing and was now looking down at Danchekker with a slow frown spreading across his face, as if another thought had just struck him.

"But there's something else, isn't there?" he said. "The self-immunization process has something to do with higher brain functions. . . . Are you saying what I think you're saying?"

"I suspect so. As you know, the toxins introduced into the body by the self-immunization process in today's animals has the effect of inhibiting the development of the higher brain centers. And another thing—Tatham's latest work indicates that, because of the way terrestrial life happens to have evolved, the capacity for violence and aggression is closely related to the development of those centers too. Thus, the Ganymeans would have found themselves unable to produce variants of the type they wanted without also removing the inhibition on the development of higher brain functions, and in addition producing an enhanced tendency toward aggression. That being the case and the Ganymeans being the way they were, I can't really see them taking the experiment any further. They would never have risked introducing anything like that into themselves, whatever the urgency of the situation. Never."

"So they gave the whole thing up as a bad job in the end and went off to pastures new," Hunt completed.

"Maybe, and again maybe not. We have no way of telling

for sure. I certainly hope so for the sake of Garuth and his friends." Danchekker leaned forward on the desk and at once his mood became more serious. "But whatever the answer to that is, at least we have a definite answer to another of the questions that you asked at the beginning."

"Which one?"

"Well, consider the situation that must have existed on Minerva when the Ganymeans came to the point of accepting that their ambitious genetic engineering solution was running into trouble. They could go away to another star or stay on their own world and perish. Either way, the days of the Ganymean presence on Minerva were numbered. Now take them out of the equation, and what is left? Answer—two populations of animals both of which are well adapted to handling the environmental conditions. First there are the native Minervan types, and second the artificially mutated descendants of the imported terrestrial types, free to roam the planet after the departure of the Ganymeans. Now return to the equation one further factor that I have established through long interrogation of ZORAC's archives—the native Minervan species would *not* have been poisonous to terrestrial carnivores—and what do you conclude?"

Hunt gazed back with eyes that were suddenly aghast.

"Christ!" he breathed. "It would have been a bloody slaughter."

"Yes, indeed. Consider a planet inhabited only by those ridiculous Technicolored cartoon animals that we found drawn on the walls of that ship at Pithead—animals that had never evolved any specializations for defense, concealment or escape, and which had no need for fight-or-flight instincts at all. Now throw in among them a typical mix of predators from Earth—every one a selected product of millions of years of improvement of the arts of ferocity, stealth and cunning . . . added to which they were evolving higher levels of intelligence that had previously been inhibited and their already fearsome aggressiveness was being further reinforced. Now what picture do you see?"

Hunt just continued to stare in horrified silence as the picture unfolded before his mind's eye.

"*That's* what wiped them all out," he said at last. "That poor bloody Minervan zoo wouldn't have had a chance. No wonder it didn't last for more than a few generations after the Ganymeans disappeared from the scene."

"With another consequence as well," Danchekker came in. "The terrestrial carnivores concentrated on most readily available prey—the native species—and so gave the terrestrial herbivores a breathing space to increase their numbers and become firmly established. By the time the Minervan natives had been wiped out the carnivores would have been forced to revert to their old habits, but by that time the situation would have stabilized. A mixed and balanced terrestrial animal ecology had been given time to establish itself across Minerva. . ." The professor's voice took on a soft and curious tone. "And that is the way things must have remained . . . right on through until the time of the Lunarians."

"Charlie . . ." Hunt sensed that Danchekker was at last hinting at something he had been building up to all along. "Charlie," Hunt repeated. "You found that same enzyme in him too, didn't you?"

"We did, but in a somewhat degenerate form . . . as if it were in the last phases of fading away completely. It did fade away of course, since Man no longer possesses it . . . But the interesting point, as you say, is that Charlie had it and so, presumably, did the rest of the Lunarians."

"And there was only one place for it to come from . . ."

"Precisely."

Hunt raised a hand to his brow as the full import of these revelations hit him. He turned slowly to meet Danchekker's solemn gaze and then slowly, his features knotted into a mask of disbelief that strove to reject the things that reason now stripped bare, sank weakly down onto an arm of the nearest chair. Danchekker said nothing, waiting for Hunt to put the pieces together for himself.

"The population on Minerva included samples of the latest Oligocene primates," Hunt said after a while. "They were almost certainly as advanced as anything that Earth had produced at the time, and with the greatest potential for advancing further. The Ganymeans had unwittingly removed the inhibition on further brain development. . . ." He looked up and met Danchekker's imperturbable stare again. "They'd have raced ahead from there. There was nothing to stop them. And with their aggressive streak unleashed as well . . . a whole race of runaway mutants . . . psychological Frankenstein monsters . . ."

"Which is, of course, where the Lunarians came from," Danchekker said. His voice was grave. "By rights they shouldn't have survived. All the theories and models of the Ganymean scientists said that they would inevitably destroy themselves. They almost did. They turned a whole planet into one vast fortress and by the time they had developed technology their lives revolved around unceasing warfare and the ruthless, uncompromising determination to exterminate all other rival states. They were capable of conceiving no other formula to solve their problems. In the end they did indeed destroy themselves and Minerva along with them . . . at least, they destroyed their civilization, if that is the correct term for it. They should have destroyed themselves totally, but, by a million-to-one chance, it did not quite happen. . . ." Danchekker looked up and left Hunt to fill in the rest.

But Hunt just sat and stared, overwhelmed. After the nuclear holocaust between the opposing forces of the two remaining Lunarian superstates had altered permanently the face of Minerva's moon and Minerva had disintegrated, the moon fell inward toward the Sun to be captured by Earth. The tiny band of survivors carried with it had possessed the resources to set off one last, desperate journey—to the surface of the new world that now hung in the sky above their heads. For forty thousand years the descendants of those survivors had merged into the survival struggle of Earth, but eventually they had spread all over the planet and emerged as an adversary as formidable as their ancestors had been on Minerva.

At last, Danchekker resumed quietly. "We have speculated for some time now that the Lunarians, and hence Man, originated from an unprecedented mutation that must have occurred somewhere along the primate line that was isolated on Minerva. Also, we have noted that somewhere along his line of ancestry, Man has somehow abandoned the self-immunization process that other animals have in common. Now we see not only proof that these things were true, but also how they came about. In fact many species went along that same path, but all bar one were destroyed when Minerva was destroyed. Only one—Man in the form of the Lunarians—came back again." Danchekker paused and took a long breath. "An unprecedented mutation did indeed occur on Minerva, but it was not a natural mutation. Modern Man exhibits fewer of the extremes that drove the Lunarians to their doom, thankfully, but all the same the legacy of our ancestry is written through the pages of our history. *Homo sapiens is the end-product of an unsuccessful series of Ganymean genetic experiments!*

"The Ganymeans believe that Man is slowly but surely recovering from the instability and compulsive violence that destroyed the Lunarians. Let us hope they are right."

Neither man said anything more for a long time. It was ironic, Hunt thought, that after all the Ganymeans had said, their own kind should turn out to be the prime cause of all the things that had come to pass over the last twenty-five million years. And throughout all that time, while primates evolved into sapient beings on Minerva, and the Lunarian civilization came and went, and fifty thousand years of human history were being acted out on Earth, the *Shapieron* had been out there in the void, preserved by the mysterious workings of the laws that distort time and space.

"An unsuccessful series of Ganymean genetic experiments," Hunt echoed Danchekker. "They started the whole thing. They came back to find us flying spaceships and building fusion plants, and they thought our rate of progress was miraculous. And all the time they'd started the whole thing off in their own labs, twenty-five million years ago . . . and given it up as a bad job! It's funny when you think about it, Chris. It's damned funny. And now they've gone for good. I wonder what they would have said if they'd only known what we know now."

Danchekker did not reply at once, but stared thoughtfully at the top of his desk for a while, as if weighing whether or not to say what was going through his head. In the end he stretched an arm forward and began toying idly with a pen. When he spoke he did not engage Hunt's eyes directly but continued to watch the pen tumbling over and over between his fingers.

"You know, Vic, in the last months before they went, the Ganymeans became very interested in all aspects of terrestrial biochemistry, including all our available data on Charlie, Man and the Oligocene animals from Pithead. For a long time they were bubbling over with curiosity and zorac couldn't find enough questions to ask about such matters. And then, about a month ago, they suddenly became very quiet about it all. They haven't even mentioned it since."

The professor looked up and confronted Hunt with a direct and candid stare.

"I think I know why," he said, very softly. "You see, Vic . . . they knew all right. They knew. They knew that they had brought a pathetically deformed creature into a hostile universe and left it to fend for itself against odds that were hopeless, and they returned and saw what that creature had become—a proud and triumphant conqueror that laughs its defiance at anything the universe cares to throw at it. That is why they are gone. They believe that they owe it to Man to leave him free to perfect the world that he has built for himself in whatever way he chooses. They know what we were and they see what we have made of ourselves since. They feel that we have suffered enough interference in the past and have shown ourselves to be the better managers of our own destiny."

Danchekker tossed the pen aside, gazed up and concluded:

"And somehow, Vic, I don't think that we will let them down. The worst is over now."

epilogue

The signal transmitted by the huge radio dish at the observatory on Lunar Farside streaked outward from the fringe of the Solar System and into the vast gulfs of empty space beyond. Its whisper brushed the sensors of a sentinel that had been maintaining an unbroken vigil for a long, long time. The circuits inside the robot understood and responded to the Ganymean code that had been used to assemble the signal.

Other equipment inside the robot transformed the signal into vibrations of forces and fields that obeyed laws of physics unknown to Man, and dispatched it into a realm of existence of which the universe of space and time were mere shadowy projections. In another part of the shadow universe, on a warm, bright planet that orbited a cheerful star, other machines received and interpreted the message.

The builders of the machines were informed and were at

once filled with wonder at the things that were reported to them.

The sentinel extracted their reply from the superstructure of space, transformed it back into electromagnetic waves, and beamed it back toward the satellite of the third planet from the Sun.

The astronomers at the Lunar Farside observatory were completely at a loss to explain the information coming from the instruments connected to their receivers; there was nothing within light-years of them from which a reply could have been evoked, but a reply was coming in hours after they had commenced transmitting. The officials at UNSA were equally bemused and time went by while scientists used the information that had been transferred from ZORAC's data banks to translate the message from Ganymean communications code into the Ganymean language. But still it meant nothing to anybody.

Then somebody thought of involving Dr. Victor Hunt of Navcomms Division. Hunt immediately remembered Don Maddson's study of the Ganymean language and sent the text down to Linguistics to see what they could make of it. Forty-eight hours passed by while Maddson and his assistant worked. The task was not one that they had practiced and, without ZORAC on tap to guide them, not one that could be accomplished readily. But the message was concise and eventually a red-eyed but triumphant Maddson presented Hunt with a single sheet of paper on which was typed:

The story of those who went to Iscaris long ago has been told through the generations since our ancestors came from Minerva. However you got there and however you found us, come home. There is a new Minerva now. We, your sons and daughters, are waiting to welcome you.

There were also some numbers and mathematical symbols that others in Navcomms had decoded, and which identified the Giants' Star as the source of the message by confirming its spectral type and its geometric position with respect to readily locatable pulsars in the neighboring regions of the Galaxy.

What physical processes might have been instrumental was something that Hunt could not even begin to guess at, but there was no time for academic speculation on such matters. The Ganymeans had to be told about what had happened and the

Shapieron could not be contacted by ordinary means while it was in flight and under main drive. The only chance was to catch it at Ganymede.

The message from the Giants' Star was hastily transmitted to UNSA Operational Command Headquarters at Galveston, beamed up to an orbiting communications station and relayed out over the laser link to *Jupiter Five*. Hours passed while Hunt, Danchekker, Maddson, Caldwell and everyone else at Houston waited anxiously for something to come in through the open channel to Galveston. At last the screen came to life. The message on it read:

> *Shapieron left here seventeen minutes before your transmission came in. Last seen accelerating flat-out for deep-space. All contact now broken. Sorry.*

There was nothing more that anybody could do.

"At least," Hunt said as he turned wearily from the screen toward the circle of dejected faces in Caldwell's office, "it's nice to know that it will all have been worth it when they get there. At least they won't have any nasty surprises waiting at the end of this voyage." He turned back and gazed wistfully at the screen once more, then added: "I suppose it would have been even nicer if they knew it too."

GIANTS' STAR

To Jackie

prologue

By the beginning of the fourth decade of the twenty-first century, it seemed that the human race was finally beginning to learn to live together and that it was on its way to the stars. Having abandoned the crippling arms race and disbanded the bulk of their strategic forces, the superpowers were instead pouring their billions into a massive transfer of Western technology and know-how to the nations of the Third World. With the increased wealth and living standards that came universally with global industrialization, and the security and variety that accompanied more affluent life-styles, population became self-limiting, and hunger, poverty, along with most of mankind's other traditional age-old scourges, at last looked as if they were on the brink of being eradicated permanently. While the U.S.–U.S.S.R. rivalry transformed itself into a war of wits and diplomacy for economic and political influence among the stabilizing nation-states, Man's adventure lust found its expression in a revitalized, multinational space program, which burst outward across the solar system in a new wave of exploration and expansion coordinated under a specially formed UN Space Arm. Lunar development and exploitation proceeded rapidly, permanent bases appeared on Mars and in orbit above Venus, and a series of large-scale manned missions reached the outer planets.

But probably the greatest revolution of the times was the upheaval in science that had followed some of the discoveries made on the Moon and out at Jupiter in the course of these explorations. In the space of just a few years, a series of astonishing discoveries had toppled beliefs unquestioned since the beginnings of science, forced a complete rewriting of the history of the solar system itself, and culminated in Man's first encounter with an advanced alien species.

A hitherto unknown planet, christened Minerva by the investigators who unraveled its story, had once occupied the position between Mars and Jupiter in the solar system as originally formed, and had been inhabited by an advanced race of eight-foot-tall aliens who came to be known as the "Ganymeans" after the first evidence of their existence came to light on Ganymede, largest of the Jovian moons. The Ganymean civilization, which flourished up until twenty-five million years before the present, vanished abruptly. Some of Earth's scientists believed that deteriorating environmental conditions on Minerva might have forced the "Giants" to migrate to some other star system, but the matter had not been settled conclusively. Much later—some fifty thousand years prior to the current period in Earth's history—Minerva was destroyed. The bulk of its mass, thrown outward into an eccentric orbit on the edge of the solar system, became Pluto. The remainder of the debris was dispersed by Jupiter's tidal effect and formed the Asteroid Belt.

While the pieces of this puzzle were still being fitted together, a starship from the ancient Ganymean civilization returned. Having undergone a relativistic time dilation that was compounded by a technical problem in the vessel's space-time-distorting drive system, the net result was that an elapsed time of twenty-odd years for the ship corresponded to the passing of something on the order of a million times that number on Earth. The *Shapieron* had departed from Minerva before the onset of whatever had befallen the rest of the Ganymean race, and its occupants were therefore unable to either confirm or refute the theories of the terrestrial researchers involved with the subject. The Giants stayed for six months, combining their efforts with those of Earth's scientists in a search for more clues and mingling harmoniously into Earth's society. Mankind had found a friend, and the remnants of the Ganymean race had, it was assumed, found a home.

But it was not to be. Investigations uncovered a hint that the Ganymean civilization had migrated to a star located near the constellation of Taurus—a star that came to be called the "Giants' Star"; there was no guarantee, but there was hope. Shortly afterward the *Shapieron* departed, leaving behind a sad, but in many ways wiser, world.

Radio observatories on lunar Farside beamed a signal toward the Giant's Star to forewarn of the *Shapieron*'s coming. Though the signal would take years to cover the distance, it would still arrive well ahead of the ship. To the astonishment of the scientists who composed the transmission, a reply purporting to have come from the Giants' Star and confirming that it was indeed the new home of the Ganymeans was received only hours after they first began sending. But by that time the *Shapieron* had already left, and news of the message could not be relayed to it because of the space-time distortion induced around the craft by its drive, which prevented electromagnetic signals from being received coherently. There was nothing more that the scientists on Earth could do; the *Shapieron* had vanished back into the void from whence it had come, and many more years of uncertainty would pass before the Ganymeans aboard it would know whether or not their quest was in vain.

The transmitters on lunar Farside continued sending intermittently during the three months that followed, but no further reply was evoked.

chapter one

Dr. Victor Hunt finished combing his hair, buttoned on a clean shirt, and paused to contemplate the somewhat sleepy-eyed but otherwise presentable image staring back at him from the bathroom mirror. He detected a couple of gray strands here and there among his full head of dark brown waves, but somebody would have had to be looking for them to notice them. His skin had an acceptably healthy tone to it; the lines of his cheeks and jaw were solid and firm, and his belt still rested loosely on his hips to serve its intended purpose of keeping his pants up and not to keep his waistline in. All in all, he decided, he wasn't doing too badly for thirty-nine. The face in the mirror frowned suddenly as the ritual reminded him of a typical specimen of middle-age male wreckage in a TV commercial; all it wanted now was for the mentally defective, bottle-brandishing wife to appear in the doorway behind to deliver the message on baldness cures, body deodorants, remedies for bad breath, or whatever. Shuddering at the thought, he tossed the comb into the medicine cabinet above the sink, closed the door, and ambled through into the apartment's kitchen.

"Are you through in the bathroom, Vic?" Lyn's voice called from the open door of the bedroom. It sounded bright and cheerful, and should have been illegal at that time in the morning.

"Go ahead." Hunt tapped a code into the kitchen terminal to summon a breakfast menu onto its screen, studied the display for a few seconds, then entered an order to the robochef for scrambled eggs, bacon (crisp), toast with marmalade, and coffee, twice. Lyn appeared in the hallway outside, Hunt's bathrobe hanging loosely on her shoulders and doing little to hide her long, slim legs and golden-tanned body. She flashed him a smile, then vanished into the bathroom in a swirl of the red hair that hung halfway down her back.

"It's coming up," Hunt called after her.

"The usual," her voice threw back from the doorway.

"You guessed?"

"The English are creatures of habit."

"Why make life complicated?"

The screen presented a list of grocery items that were getting low, and Hunt okayed the computer to transmit an order to Albertson's for delivery later that day. The sound of the shower being turned on greeted him as he emerged from the kitchen and walked through into the living room, wondering how a world that accepted as normal the nightly spectacle of people discussing their constipation, hemorrhoids, dandruff, and indigestion in front of an audience of a million strangers could possibly find something obscene in the sight of pretty girls taking their clothes off. "There's now't so strange as folk," his grandmother from Yorkshire would have said, he thought to himself.

It wouldn't have needed a Sherlock Holmes to read the story of the night before from the scene that confronted him in the living room. The half-filled coffee cup, empty cigarette pack, and the remains of a pepperoni pizza surrounded by scientific papers and notes strewn untidily in front of the desk terminal told of an evening that had begun with the best and purest of intentions to explore another approach to the Pluto problem. Lyn's shoulder bag on the table by the door, her coat draped across one end of the couch, the empty Chablis bottle, and the white cardboard box containing traces of a beef-curry dinner-to-go all added up to an interruption in the form of an unexpected but not exactly unwelcome arrival. The crumpled cushions and the two pairs of shoes lying where they had fallen between the couch and the coffee table said the rest. Oh well, Hunt told himself, it wouldn't make much difference to the rest of the world if the solution to how Pluto had wound up where it was had to wait an extra twenty-four hours.

He walked over to the desk and interrogated the terminal for any mail that might have come in overnight. There was a draft of a paper being put together by Mike Barrow's team at Lawrence Livermore Labs, suggesting that an aspect of Ganymean physics that they had been studying implied the possibility of achieving fusion at low temperatures. Hunt scanned it briefly and rerouted it to his office for closer reading there. A couple of bills and statements of account . . . file away and present again at the end of the month. Videorecording from Uncle William in Nigeria; Hunt entered a command for a replay and stood back to watch. Beyond the closed door the shower noises stopped, then Lyn sauntered back into the bedroom.

William and the family had enjoyed having Vic over on vacation recently and had especially liked hearing his personal account of his experiences at Jupiter and later back on Earth with the Ganymeans . . . Cousin Jenny had gotten an admin job at the nuclear steelmaking complex that was just going into operation outside Lagos. . . . News from the family in London was that all were well, except for Vic's older brother, George, who had been charged with threatening behavior after an argument about politics at his local pub. . . . The postgraduate student's at Lagos University had been enthralled by Hunt's lecture about the *Shapieron* and were sending on a list of questions that they hoped he'd find time to reply to.

Just as the recording was finishing, Lyn came out of the bedroom wearing her chocolate blouse and ivory crêpe skirt from the night before, then disappeared again into the kitchen. "Who's that?" she called, to the accompaniment of cupboard doors being opened and closed and plates being set down on a working surface.

"Uncle Billy."

"The one in Africa that you visited a few weeks ago?"

"Uh huh."

"So how are they doing?"

"He looks fine. Jenny's got herself fixed up at the new nu-plex I told you about, and brother George is in trouble again."

"Uh-oh. What now?"

"Doing his pub lawyer act by the sound of it. Somebody didn't agree that the government ought to guarantee paychecks to anybody on strike."

"What is he—some kind of nut?"

"Runs in the family."

"You said it, not me."

Hunt grinned. "So never say you weren't warned."

"I'll remember that. . . . Food's ready."

Hunt flipped off the terminal and walked into the kitchen. Lyn, perched on a stool at the breakfast bar that divided the room in two, had already started eating. Hunt sat down opposite her, drank some coffee, then picked up his fork. "Why the rush?" he asked. "It's still early. We're not pushed for time."

"I'm not coming straight in. I ought to go home first and change."

"You look okay to me—fact, not a bad piece of womanry at all."

"Flattery will get you anywhere you like. No . . . Gregg's got some special visitors coming down from Washington to-day. I don't want to look 'groped' and spoil the Navcomms image." She smiled and mimicked an English accent. "One must maintain standards, you know."

Hunt snorted derisively. "It needs more practice. Who are the visitors?"

"All I know is they're from the State Department. Some hush-hush stuff that Gregg's been mixed up with lately . . . lots of calls coming in on secure channels, and couriers showing up with for-your-eyes-only things in sealed bags. Don't ask me what it's about."

"He hasn't let you in on it?" Hunt sounded surprised.

She shook her head and shrugged. "Maybe it's because I as-sociate with crazy, unreliable foreigners."

"But you're his personal assistant," Hunt said. "I thought you knew about everything that happens around Navcomms."

Lyn shrugged again. "Not this time . . . at least, not so far. I've got a feeling I might find out today, though. Gregg's been dropping hints."

"Mmm . . . odd . . ." Hunt returned his attention to his plate and thought about the situation. Gregg Caldwell, Executive Director of the Navigation and Communications Division of the UN Space Arm, was Hunt's immediate chief. Through a combination of circumstances, under Caldwell's direction Navcomms had played a leading role in piecing together the story of Minerva and the Ganymeans, and Hunt had been intimately involved in the saga both before and during the Ganymeans' stay on Earth. Since their departure, Hunt's main task at Navcomms had been to head up a group that was coordinating the researches being conducted in various places into the volume of scientific information bequeathed by the aliens to Earth. Although not all the findings and speculations had been made public, the working atmosphere inside Navcomms was generally pretty frank and open, so security precautions taken to the extreme that Lyn had described were virtually unheard of. Something odd was going on, all right.

He leaned against the backrest of the bar chair to light a cigarette, and watched Lyn as she poured two more coffees. There was something about the way her gray-green eyes never quite lost their mischievous twinkle and about the hint of a pout that was always dancing elusively around her mouth that he found both amusing and exciting—"cute," he supposed an American would have said. He thought back over the three months that had elapsed since the *Shapieron* left, and tried to pinpoint what had happened to turn somebody who had been just a smart-headed, good-looking girl at the office into somebody he had breakfast with fairly regularly at one apartment or the other. But there didn't seem to be any particular where or when; it was just something that had happened somehow, somewhere along the line. He wasn't complaining.

She glanced up as she set the pot down and saw him looking at her. "See, I'm quite nice to have around, really. Wouldn't the morning be dull with only the vi-screen to stare at." She was at it again . . . playfully, but only if he didn't want to take it seriously. One rent made more sense than two, one set of utility bills was cheaper, et cetera, et cetera, et cetera.

"I'll pay the bills," Hunt said. He opened his hands appealingly. "You said it yourself earlier—Englishmen are creatures of habit. Anyhow, I'm maintaining standards."

"You sound like an endangered species," she told him.

"I am—chauvinists. Somebody's got to make a last stand somewhere."

"You don't need me?"

"Of course not. Good Lord, what a thought!" He scowled across the bar while Lyn returned an impish smile. Maybe the world could wait another forty-eight hours to find out about Pluto. "What are you up to tonight—anything special?" he asked.

"I got invited to a dinner party over in Hanwell ... that marketing guy I told you about and his wife. They're having a big crowd of people in, and it sounded as if it could be fun. They told me to bring a friend, but I didn't think you'd be all that interested."

Hunt wrinkled his nose and frowned. "Isn't that the ESP-and-pyramid bunch?"

"Right. They're all excited because they've got a superpsychic going there tonight. He predicted everything about Minerva and the Ganymeans years ago. It has to be true—*Amazing Supernature* magazine said so."

Hunt knew she was teasing but couldn't suppress his irritation. "Oh for Christ's sake ... I thought there was supposed to be an educational system in this bloody country! Don't they have any critical faculties at all?" He drained the last of his coffee and banged the mug down on the bar. "If he predicted it years ago, why didn't anybody hear about it years ago? Why do we only hear about it after science has told him what he was supposed to predict? Ask him what the *Shapieron* will find when it gets to the Giants' Star and make him write it down. I bet that never gets into *Amazing Supernature* magazine."

"That would be taking it too seriously," Lyn said lightly. "I only go there for the laughs. There's no point in trying to explain Occam's Razor to people who believe that UFOs are timeships from another century. Besides, apart from all that, they're nice people."

Hunt wondered how this kind of thing could still go on after the Ganymeans, who flew starships, created life in laboratories, and built self-aware computers, had affirmed repeatedly that they saw no reason to postulate the existence of any powers existing in the universe beyond those revealed by science and rational thinking. But people still wasted their lives away with daydreams.

He was becoming too serious, he decided, and dismissed the matter with a wave of his hand and a grin. "Come on. We'd better do something about sending you on your way."

Lyn headed for the living room to collect her shoes, bag,

and coat, then met him again at the front door of the apartment. They kissed and squeezed each other. "I'll see you later, then," she whispered.

"See you later. Watch out for those crazies."

He waited until she had disappeared into the elevator, then closed the door and spent five minutes clearing the kitchen and restoring some semblance of decency to the rest of the place. Finally he put on a jacket, stuffed some items from the desk into his briefcase, and left in an elevator heading for the roof. Minutes later his airmobile was at two thousand feet and climbing to merge into an eastbound traffic corridor with the rainbow towers of Houston gleaming in the sunlight on the skyline ahead.

chapter two

Ginny, Hunt's slightly plump, middle-aged, meticulous secretary, was already busy when he sauntered into the reception area of his office, high in the skyscraper of Navcomms Headquarters in the center of Houston. She had three sons, all in their late teens, and she hurled herself into her work with a dedication that Hunt sometimes thought might represent a gesture of atonement for having inflicted them on society. Women like Ginny always did a good job, he had found. Long-legged blondes were all very nice, but when it came to getting things done properly and on time, he'd settle for the older mommas any day.

"Good morning, Dr. Hunt," she greeted him. One thing he had never been able to persuade her to accept fully was that Englishmen didn't expect, or really want, to be addressed formally all the time.

"Hi, Ginny. How are you today?"

"Oh, just fine, I guess."

"Any news about the dog?"

"Good news. The vet called last night and said its pelvis

isn't fractured after all. A few weeks of rest and it should be fine."

"That's good. So what's new this morning? Anything panicky?"

"Not really. Professor Speechan from MIT called a few minutes ago and would like you to call back before lunch. I'm just finishing going through the mail now. There are a couple of things I think you'll be interested in. The draft paper from Livermore, I guess you've already seen."

They spent the next half-hour checking the mail and organizing the day's schedule. By that time the offices that formed Hunt's section of Navcomms were filling up, and he left to update himself on a couple of the projects in progress.

Duncan Watt, Hunt's deputy, a theoretical physicist who had transferred from UNSA's Materials and Structures Division a year and a half earlier, was collecting results on the Pluto problem from a number of research groups around the country. Comparisons of the current Solar System with records from the *Shapieron* of how it had looked twenty-five million years before established beyond doubt that most of what had been Minerva had ended up as Pluto. Earth had been formed originally without a satellite, and Luna had orbited as the single moon of Minerva. When Minerva broke up, its moon fell inward, toward the Sun, and by a freak chance was captured by Earth, about which it had orbited stably ever since. The problem was that so far no mathematical model of the dynamics involved had been able to explain how Pluto could have acquired enough energy to be lifted against solar gravitation to the position it now occupied. Astronomers and specialists in celestial mechanics from all over the world had tried all manner of approaches to the problem but without success, which was not all that surprising since the Ganymeans themselves had been unable to produce a satisfactory solution.

"The only way you can get it to work is by postulating a three-body reaction," Duncan said, tossing up his hands in exasperation. "Maybe the war had nothing to do with it. Maybe what broke Minerva up was something else passing through the Solar System."

Thirty minutes later and a few doors farther along the corridor, Hunt found Marie, Jeff, and two of the students on loan from Princeton, excitedly discussing the set of partial-differential tensor functions being displayed on a large mural graphics screen.

"It's the latest from Mike Barrow's team at Livermore," Marie told him.

"I've already seen it," Hunt said. "Haven't had a chance to go through it yet, though. Something about cold fusion, isn't it?"

"What it seems to be saying is that the Ganymeans didn't have to generate high thermal energies to overcome proton–proton repulsion," Jeff chipped in.

"How'd they do it then?" Hunt asked.

"Sneakily. They started off with the particles being neutrons so there wasn't any repulsion. Then, when the particles were inside the range of the strong force, they increased the energy gradient at the particle surfaces sufficiently to initiate pair production. The neutrons absorbed the positrons to become protons, and the electrons were drawn off. So there you've got it—two protons strongly coupled. Pow! Fusion."

Hunt was impressed, although he had seen too much of Ganymean physics by that time to be astounded. "And they could control events like that down at that level?" he asked.

"That's what Mike's people reckon."

Shortly afterward, an argument developed over one of the details, and Hunt left the group as they were in the process of placing a call to Livermore for clarification.

It seemed as if the information left by the Ganymeans was all starting to bear fruit at once, causing something new to break out every day. Caldwell's idea of using Hunt's section as an international clearinghouse for the research into Ganymean sciences was starting to produce results. When the first clues concerning Minerva and the Ganymeans were coming to light, Caldwell had set up Hunt's original pilot group to do exactly this kind of thing. The organization had proved well suited to the task, and now it formed a ready-made group for tackling the latest studies.

Hunt's last call was on Paul Shelling, whose people occupied a group of offices and a computer room on the floor below. One of the most challenging aspects of Ganymean technology was their "gravitics," which enabled them to deform space-time artificially without requiring large concentrations of mass. The *Shapieron*'s drive system had utilized this capability by creating a "hole" ahead of the ship into which it "fell" continuously to propel itself through space; the "gravity" inside the vessel was also manufactured, not simulated. Shelling, a gravitational physicist on a sabbatical from Rockwell International, headed up a mathematical group which had been delving into Ganymean field equations and energy-metric transforms for six months. Hunt found him staring at a display of isochrons and distorted space-time geodesics, and looking very thoughtful.

"It's all there," Shelling said, keeping his eyes fixed on the softly glowing colored curves and speaking in a faraway voice. "Artificial black holes . . . just switch 'em on and off to order."

The information did not come as a big surprise to Hunt. The Ganymeans had confirmed that the *Shapieron*'s drive had in fact achieved this, and Hunt and Shelling had talked about its theoretical basis on many occasions. "You've figured it out?" Hunt asked, slipping into a vacant chair and studying the display.

"We're on our way, anyhow."

"Does it get us any nearer instant point-to-point transfers?" That was something the Ganymeans had not achieved, although the possibility was implicit in their theoretical constructs. Black holes distantly separated in normal space seemed to link up via a hyperrealm within which unfamiliar physical principles operated, and the ordinary concepts and restrictions of the relativistic universe simply didn't apply. As the Ganymeans had agreed, the promises implied by this were staggering, but nobody knew how to turn them into realities yet.

"It's in there," Shelling answered. "The possibility is in there, but there's another side to it that bothers me, and it's impossible to separate out."

"What's that?" Hunt asked.

"Time transfers," Shelling told him. Hunt frowned. Had he been talking to anybody else, he would have allowed his skepticism to show openly. Shelling spread his hands and gestured toward the screen. "You can't get away from it. If the solutions admit point-to-point transfers through normal space, they admit transfers through time too. If you could find a way of exploiting one, you'd automatically have a way of exploiting the other as well. Those matrix integrals are symmetric."

Hunt waited for a moment to avoid appearing derisive. "That's too much, Paul," he said. "What happens to causality? You'd never be able to unscramble the mess."

"I know . . . I know the theory sounds screwy, but there it

is. Either we're up a dead end and none of it works, or we're stuck with both solutions."

They spent the next hour working through Shelling's equations again but ended up none the wiser. Groups at Cal Tech, Cambridge, the Ministry of Space Sciences in Moscow, and the University of Sydney, Australia, had found the same thing. Obviously Hunt and Shelling were not about to crack the problem there and then, and Hunt eventually left in a very curious and thoughtful mood.

Back in his own office, he called Speehan at MIT, who turned out to have some interesting results from a simulation model of the climatic upheavals caused fifty thousand years earlier by the process of lunar capture. Hunt then took care of a couple of other urgent items that had come in that morning, and was just settling down to study the Livermore paper when Lyn called from Caldwell's suite at the top of the building. Her face was unusually serious.

"Gregg wants you in on the meeting up here," she told him without preamble. "Can you get up right away?"

Hunt sensed that she was pushed for time. "Give me two minutes." He cut the connection without further ado, consigned Livermore to the uncharted depths of the Navcomms data bank, told Ginny to consult Duncan if anything desperate developed during the rest of the day, and left the office at a brisk pace.

chapter three

From the web of communications links interconnecting UNSA's manned and unmanned space vehicles with orbiting and surface bases all over the solar system, to the engineering and research establishments at places such as Houston, responsibility for the whole gamut of Navcomms activities ultimately resided in Caldwell's office at the top of the Headquarters Building. It was a spacious and opulently furnished room with one wall completely of glass, looking down over the lesser skyscrapers of the city and the ant colony of the pedestrian precincts far below. The wall opposite Caldwell's huge curved desk, which raced inward from a corner by the window, was composed almost totally of a battery of display screens that gave the place more the appearance of a control room than of an office. The remaining walls carried a display of color pictures showing some of the more spectacular UNSA projects of recent years, including a seven-mile-long photon-drive star probe being designed in California and an electromagnetic catapult being constructed across twenty miles of Tranquillitatis to hurl lunar-manufactured structural components into orbit for spacecraft assembly.

Caldwell was behind his desk and two other people were sitting with Lyn at the table set at a T to the desk's front edge when a secretary ushered Hunt in from the outer office. One of them was a woman in her mid- to late forties, wearing a high-necked navy dress that hinted of a firm and well-preserved figure, and over it a wide-collared jacket of white-and-navy check. Her hair was a carefully styled frozen sea of auburn that stopped short of her shoulders, and the lines of her face, which was not unattractive in a natural kind of way beneath her sparse makeup, were clear and assertive. She was sitting erect and seemed composed and fully in command of herself. Hunt had the feeling that he had seen her somewhere before.

Her companion, a man, was smartly attired in a charcoal three-piece suit with a white shirt and two-tone gray tie. He had a fresh, clean-shaven look about him and jet-black hair cut short and brushed flat in college-boy fashion, although Hunt put him at not far off his own age. His eyes, dark and constantly mobile, gave the impression of serving an alert and quick-thinking mind.

Lyn flashed Hunt a quick smile from the side of the table opposite the two visitors. She had changed into a crisp two-piece edged with pale orange and was wearing her hair high. She looked distinctly un-"groped."

"Vic," Caldwell announced in his gravelly bass-baritone voice, "I'd like you to meet Karen Heller from the State Department in Washington, and Norman Pacey, who's a presidential advisor on foreign relations." He made a resigned gesture in Hunt's direction. "This is Dr. Vic Hunt. We send him to Jupiter to look into a few relics of some extinct aliens, and he comes back with a shipful of live ones."

They exchanged formalities. Both visitors knew about Hunt's exploits, which had been well publicized. In fact Vic had met Karen Heller once very briefly at a reception given for some Ganymeans in Zurich about six months earlier. Of course! Hadn't she been the U.S. Ambassador to—France, wasn't it, at the time? Yes. She was representing the U.S. at the UN now, though. Norman Pacey had met some Ganymeans too, it turned out—in Washington—but Hunt hadn't been present on that occasion.

Hunt took the empty chair at the end of the table, facing along the length of it toward Caldwell's desk, and watched the head of wiry, gray, close-cropped hair while Caldwell frowned down at his hands for a few seconds and drummed the top of his desk with his fingers. Then he raised his craggy, heavily browed face to look directly at Hunt, who knew better than to expect much in the way of preliminaries. "Something's happened that I wanted to tell you about earlier but couldn't," Caldwell said. "Signals from the Giants' Star started coming in again about three weeks ago."

Even though he should have known about such a development if anyone did, Hunt was too taken aback for the moment to wonder about it. As months passed after the sole reply to the first message transmitted from Giordano Bruno at the time of the *Shaperion*'s departure, he had grown increasingly suspicious that the whole thing had been a hoax—that somebody with access to the UNSA communications net had somehow arranged a message to be relayed back from some piece of UNSA hardware located out in space in the right direction. He was open-minded enough to admit that with an advanced alien civilization anything could be possible, but a hoax had seemed the most likely explanation for the fourteen-hour turn-around time. If Caldwell were right, it made so much nonsense of that conviction.

"You're certain they're genuine?" he asked dubiously when he had recovered from the initial shock. "It couldn't all be a sick joke by a freak somewhere?"

Caldwell shook his head. "We have enough data now to pinpoint the source interferometrically. It's way out past Pluto, and UNSA does not have anything anywhere near it. Besides, we've checked every bit of traffic through all our hardware, and it's clean. The signals are genuine."

Hunt raised his eyebrows and exhaled a long breath. Okay,

so he'd been wrong on that one. He shifted his gaze from Caldwell to the notes and papers lying along the middle of the table in front of him, and frowned as another thought occurred to him. Like the original message from Farside, the reply from the Giants' Star had been composed in the ancient Ganymean language and communications codes from the time of the *Shapieron*. After the ship's departure, the reply had been translated by Don Maddson, head of the linguistics section lower down in the building, who had made a study of Ganymean during the aliens' stay. That had required considerable effort, short though the reply had been, and Hunt knew of no one else anywhere who could have handled the more recent signals that Caldwell was talking about. As a rule Hunt didn't have much time for protocol and formality, but if Maddson was in on this, he sure-as-hell should have known about it too. "So who did the translating?" he asked suspiciously. "Linguistics?"

"There wasn't any need," Lyn said simply. "The signals are coming through in standard datacomm codes. They're in English."

Hunt slumped back in his chair and just stared. Ironically that said definitely that it was no hoax; who in their right mind would forge message from aliens in English? And then it came to him. "Of course!" he exclaimed. "They must have intercepted the *Shapieron* somehow. Well, that's good to—" He broke off in surprise as he saw Caldwell shake his head.

"From the content of the dialogue over the last few weeks, we're pretty certain that's not the case," Caldwell said. He looked at Hunt gravely. "So if they haven't talked to the Ganymeans who were here, and they know our communication codes and our language, what does that say to you?"

Hunt looked around and saw that the others were watching him expectantly. So he thought about it. And after a few seconds his eyes widened slowly, and his mouth fell open in undisguised belief. *"Je-sus!"* he breathed softly.

"That's right," Norman Pacey said. "This whole planet must be under some kind of surveillance . . . and has been for a long time." For the moment Hunt was too flabbergasted to offer any reply. Little wonder the whole business had been hushed up.

"That supposition was backed up by the first of the new signals that came in at Bruno," Caldwell resumed. "It said in no uncertain terms that nothing whatsoever relating to the contact was to be communicated via lasers, comsats, datalinks, or any kind of electronic media. The scientists up at Bruno who received the message went along with that directive, and told me about it by sending a courier down from Luna. I passed the word up through Navcomms to UNSA Corporate in the same way and told the Bruno guys to carry on handling things locally until somebody got back to them."

"What it means is that at least part of the surveillance is in the form of tapping into our communications network," Pacey said. "And whoever is sending the signals, and whoever is running the surveillance, are not the same . . . 'people,' or whatever. And the ones who are talking to us don't want the other ones knowing about it." Hunt nodded, having figured that much out already.

"I'll let Karen take it from there," Caldwell said and nodded in her direction.

Karen Heller leaned forward to rest her arms lightly along the edge of the table. "The scientists at Bruno established fairly early on that they were indeed in contact with a Ganymean civilization descended from migrants from Minerva," she said, speaking in carefully modulated tones that rose and fell naturally and made listening easy. "They inhabit a planet called Thurien, in the planetary system of the Giants' Star, or 'Gistar,' to use the contraction that seems to have been adopted. While this was going on, UNSA in Washington referred the matter to the UN." She paused to look over at Hunt, but he had no questions at that point. She went on, "A special working party reporting to the Secretary General was formed to debate the issue, and the ruling finally came out that a contact of this nature was first and foremost a political and diplomatic affair. A decision was made that further exchanges would be handled secretly by a small delegation of selected representatives of the permanent-member nations of the Security Council. To preserve secrecy, no outsiders would be informed or involved for the time being."

"I had to hold things right there when that ruling came down the line," Caldwell interjected, looking at Hunt. "That was why I couldn't tell you about any of this before." Hunt nodded. Now that it had been explained, at least he felt a little better on that score.

He was still far from completely happy, however. It sounded as if there had been a typical bureaucratic overreaction to the whole thing. Playing safe was all very well up to a point, but surely this supersecrecy was taking things too far. The thought of the UN keeping everybody out of it apart from a handful of select individuals who had probably had few, if any, dealings with Ganymeans was infuriating.

"They didn't want *anybody* else included?" he asked dubiously. "Not even a scientist or two—somebody who knows Ganymeans?"

"*Especially* not scientists," Caldwell said, but volunteered nothing further. The whole thing was beginning to sound nonsensical.

"As a permanent member of the Council, the U.S.A. was informed from high up in the UN and applied sufficient pressure to be represented on the delegation," Heller continued. "Norman and myself were assigned that duty, and for most of the time since then we've been at Giordano Bruno, participating in the exchange of signals that has been continuing with the Thuriens."

"You mean everything is being handled locally from there?" Hunt asked.

"Yes. The ban on communicating anything to do with it electronically is being strictly adhered to. The people up there who know what's going on are all security-cleared and reliable."

"I see." Hunt sat back and braced his arms along the table in front of him. So far there was a mystery and some reason for being uncomfortable, but nothing that had been said so far explained what Heller and Pacey were doing in Houston. "So what's been going on?" he asked. "What have you been talking to Thurien about?"

Heller motioned with her head to indicate a lockable document folder lying by her elbow. "Complete transcripts of everything received and sent are in there," she told him. "Gregg has a full set of copies, and since you'll no doubt be involved from now on, you'll be able to read them for yourself shortly. To sum up, the first messages from Thurien asked for information about the *Shapieron*—its condition, the well-being of its occupants, their experiences on Earth, and that kind of thing. Whoever was sending the messages seemed concerned . . . as if they considered us a threat to it for some reason." Heller paused, seeing the look of noncomprehension that was spreading across Hunt's face.

"Are you saying they didn't know about the ship before we beamed that first signal out from Farside?" he asked.

"So it would appear," Heller replied.

Hunt thought for a moment. "So again, whoever is handling the surveillance isn't talking to whoever is sending these messages," he said.

"Exactly," Pacey agreed, nodding. "The ones handling the surveillance could hardly have not known about the *Shapieron* while it was here if they have any access to our communications network. There were enough headlines about it."

"And that's not the only strange thing," Heller went on. "The Thuriens that we have been in contact with seem to have formed a completely distorted picture of Earth's recent history. They think we're all set for World War III only this time interplanetary, with orbiting bombs everywhere, radiation and particle-beam weapons commanding the surface from the Moon . . . you name it."

Hunt had been growing even more bemused as he listened. He could see now why it looked as if the *Shapieron* couldn't have been intercepted—at least not by the Thuriens who were talking to Earth; the Ganymeans from the ship would have cleared up any misunderstandings like that straight away. But even if the Thuriens who were doing the talking hadn't intercepted the *Shapieron*, they had an impression of Earth nonetheless, which meant that they could only have obtained it from the Thuriens who were handling the surveillance. The impression they had obtained was wrong. Therefore, either the surveillance wasn't very effective, or the story being passed on was being distorted. But if the messages had been coming in composed in English, the surveillance methods had to be pretty effective, which therefore implied that the Thuriens passing on the story weren't passing it on straight.

But that didn't make a lot of sense, either. Ganymeans didn't play Machiavellian games of intrigue or deceive one another knowingly. Their minds didn't work that way; they were far too rational . . . unless the Ganymeans who now existed on Thurien had changed significantly in the course of the twenty-five million years that separated them from their ancestors aboard the *Shapieron*. That was a thought. A lot of changes could have taken place in that time. He couldn't arrive at any definite conclusions now, he decided, so the information was simply filed away for retrieval and analysis later.

"It sounds strange, all right," Hunt agreed after he had

sorted that much out in his head. "They must be pretty confused by now."

"They were already," Caldwell said. "The reason they reopened the dialogue is that they want to come to Earth physically—I guess to straighten out the whole mess. That's what they've been trying to get the UN people to arrange."

"Secretly," Pacey explained in answer to Hunt's questioning look. "No public spectacles or anything like that. What it seems to add up to is that they're hoping to do some quiet checking up without the outfit that's running the surveillance knowing about it."

Hunt nodded. The plan made sense. But there was a note in Pacey's voice that hinted of things not having gone so smoothly. "So what's the problem?" he asked, shifting his eyes to glance at both Pacey and Heller.

"The problem is the policy that's been handed down from the top levels inside the UN," Heller replied. "To put it in a nutshell, they're scared of what it might mean if this planet simply opens up to a civilization that's millions of years ahead of us . . . our whole culture could be torn up by the roots; our civilization would come apart at the seams; we'd be avalanched with technology that we're not ready to absorb . . . that kind of thing."

"But that's ridiculous!" Hunt protested. "They haven't said they want to take this place over. They just want to come here and talk." He made an impatient throwing-away motion in the air. "Okay, I'll accept that we'd have to play it softly and exercise some caution and common sense, but what you're describing sounds more like a neurosis."

"It is," Heller said. "The UN's being irrational—there's no other word for it. And the Farside delegation is following that policy to the letter and operating in go-slow, stall-stall-stall mode." She waved toward the folder she had indicated earlier. "You'll see for yourself. Their responses are evasive and ambiguous, and do nothing to correct the wrong impressions that the Thuriens have got. Norman and I have tried to fight it, but we get outvoted."

Hunt caught Lyn's eye as he sent a despairing look around the room. She sent back a faint half-smile and a barely perceptible shrug that said she knew how he felt. A faction inside the UN had fought hard and for the same reasons to prevent the Farside transmissions being continued after the first, unexpected reply had come in, he remembered, but had been over-ruled after a deafening outcry from the world's scientific community. That same faction seemed to be active again.

"The worst part is what we suspect might be behind it," Heller continued. "Our brief from the State Department was to help move things smoothly toward broadening Earth's communications with Thurien as fast as developments allowed, at the same time protecting this country's interests where appropriate. The Department didn't really agree with the policy of excluding outsiders, but had to go along with it because of UN protocols. In other words, the U.S. has been trying to play it straight so far, but under protest."

"I can see the picture," Hunt said as she paused. "But that just says that you're becoming frustrated by the slow progress. You sounded as if there's more to it than that."

"There is," Heller confirmed. "The Soviets also have a representative on the delegation—a man called Sobroskin. Given the world situation—with us and the Soviets competing everywhere for things like the South Atlantic fusion deal, industrial-training franchises in Africa, scientific-aid programs, and so on—the advantage that either side could get from access to Ganymean know-how would be enormous. So you'd expect the Soviets to be just as impatient to kick some life into this damn delegation as we are. But they aren't. Sobroskin goes along with the official UN line and doesn't bitch about it. In fact he spends half his time throwing in complications that slow things down even further. Now when those facts are laid down side by side, what do they seem to say?"

Hunt thought over the question for a while, then tossed out his hands with a shrug. "I don't know," he said candidly. "I'm not a political animal. You tell me."

"It could mean that the Soviets are planning to set up their own private channel to fix a landing in Siberia or somewhere so that they get exclusive rights," Pacey answered. "If that's so, then the UN line would suit them fine. If the official channel stays clogged up, and the U.S. plays straight and sticks with the official channel, then guess who walks off with the bonanza. Think of the difference it would make to the power balance if a few heads of select governments around the world were quietly tipped off that the Soviets had access to lots of know-how that we didn't. You see—it all fits with the way Sobroskin is acting."

"And an even more sobering thought is the way in which the UN's policy fits in with that so conveniently," Heller added. "It could mean that the Soviets have ways that we don't even know about of pulling all kinds of strings and levers right inside the top levels of the UN itself. If that's true, the global implications for the U.S. are serious indeed."

The facts were certainly beginning to add up, Hunt admitted to himself. The Soviets could easily set up another long-range communications facility in Siberia, up in orbit, out near Luna maybe, and operate their own link to whatever was intercepting Farside's signals out beyond the edge of the solar system. Any reply coming back would probably be in the form of a fairly wide beam by the time it got to Earth, which meant that anybody could receive it and know that somebody somewhere other than the UN was cheating. But if the replies were in a prearranged code, nobody would be able to interpret them or know for whom they were intended. The Soviets might be accused, in which case they would deny the charge vehemently . . . and that would be about as much as anybody would be able to do about it.

He thought he could see now why he had been brought in on all this. Heller had given herself away earlier when she said that the U.S. had been trying to play it straight, *"so far."* As insurance the State Department had decided that it needed its own private line too, but nothing crude enough to be detected anywhere within a few hundred thousand miles of Earth. So who would they have sent Heller and Pacey to talk to? Who else but someone who knew a lot about Ganymeans and Ganymean technology, somebody who had also been among the first people to receive them on Ganymede?

And that was another point—Hunt had spent a lot of time on Ganymede, and he still had many close friends among the UNSA personnel there with the Jupiter Four and Jupiter Five missions. Jupiter was a long, long way from the vicinity of Earth, which meant that no receivers anywhere near Earth would ever know anything about a beam aimed toward Jupiter from the fringe of the solar system, whether the beam diverged appreciably or not. And, of course, the *J4* and *J5* command ships were linked permanently to Earth by laser channels . . . which Caldwell and Navcomms just happened to control. It couldn't possibly be all just a coincidence, he decided.

Hunt looked up at Caldwell, held his eye for a second, then

turned his head to gaze at the two people from Washington. "You want to set up a private wire to Gistar via Jupiter to arrange a landing here, without any more messing around, before the Soviets get around to doing something," he told them. "And you want to know if I can come up with an idea for telling the people at Jupiter what we want them to do, without the risk of any Thuriens who might be bugging the laser link finding out about it. Is that right?" He turned his eyes back toward Caldwell and inclined his head. "What do I get, Gregg?"

Heller and Pacey exchanged glances that said they were impressed.

"Ten out of ten," Caldwell told him.

"Nine," Heller said. Hunt looked at her curiously. There was a hint of laughter in her expression. "If you can come up with something, we'll need all the help we can get handling whatever comes afterward," she explained. "The UN might have decided to try going it alone without their Ganymean experts, but the U.S. hasn't."

"In other words, welcome to the team," Norman Pacey completed.

chapter four

Joseph B. Shannon, Mission Director of *Jupiter Five*, orbiting two thousand miles above the surface of Ganymede, stood in an instrumentation bay near one end of the mile-and-a-quarter-long ship's command center. He was watching a large mural display screen from behind a knot of spellbound ship's officers and UNSA scientists. The screen showed an undulating landscape of oranges, yellows, and browns as it lay cringing beneath a black sky made hazy by a steady incandescent drizzle falling from somewhere above, while in the far distance half the skyline was erupting in a boiling column of colors that exploded upward off the top of the picture.

It had been fifty-two years before—the year that Shannon

was born—when other scientists at the Jet Propulsion Laboratory in Pasadena had marveled at the first close-ups of Io to be sent back by the *Voyager I* and *II* probes, and dubbed the extraordinary disk of mottled orange "the great pizza in the sky." But Shannon had never heard of any pizza being cooked in the way this one had.

Orbiting through a plasma flux of mean particle energies corresponding to 100,000° Kelvin sustained by Jupiter's magnetic field, the satellite acted as an enormous Faraday generator and supported internal circulating currents of five million amperes with a power dissipation of a thousand billion watts. And as much energy again was released inside it as heat from tidal friction, resulting from orbital perturbations induced as Europa and Ganymede lifted Io resonantly up and down through Jupiter's gravity. This amount of electrically and gravitationally produced heat maintained large reservoirs of molten sulfur and sulfur compounds below the moon's surface, which eventually penetrated upward through faults to explode into the virtually zero-pressure of the outside. The result was a regular succession of spectacular volancoes of solidifying sulfur and sulfur-dioxide frost that ejected at velocities of up to a thousand meters per second, and sometimes reached heights of 300 kilometers or more.

Shannon was looking at a view of one of those volcanoes now, sent back from a probe on Io's surface. It had taken the mission's engineers and scientists more than a year of back-to-the-drawing-board experiences to devise an instrumentation package and shielding method that would function reliably under Jupiter's incessant bombardment of radiation, electrons, and ions, and Shannon had felt an obligation to be present in person to observe the results of their eventual success. Far from being the chore he had expected, the occasion had turned out an exhilaration and served as a reminder of how easy it was for supreme commanders of anything to allow themselves to become remote and lose touch with what was happening in the trenches. In future, he thought to himself, he would make a point of keeping more up to date on the progress of the mission's scientific projects.

He remained in the command center discussing details of the probe for a full hour after he was officially off duty, and then at last excused himself and retired to his private quarters. After a shower and a change of clothes he sat down at the desk in his stateroom and interrogated the terminal for a listing of the day's mail. One item that had come in was qualified as a text message from Vic Hunt at Navcomms Headquarters. Shannon was both pleasantly surprised and intrigued. He had had many interesting talks with Hunt during the latter's stay on Ganymede, and didn't perceive him as being somebody with much time for idle socializing, which suggested that something interesting was afoot. Curious, he keyed in a command for Hunt's message to be displayed. Five minutes later he was still sitting there staring at the message, his brows knitted in a mystified frown. It read:

Joe,
    To avoid any further cross words on this subject, I looked for some clues in the book you mentioned and came across some references on pages 5, 24, and 10. When you get down to sections 11 and 20, it all makes more sense.
    How they got 786 is still a puzzle.
    Regards
    Vic

Not a word of it meant anything to him. He knew Hunt well enough to be reasonably sure that something serious was behind the message, and all he could think of was that Hunt was trying to tell him something highly confidential. But why would Hunt go to this kind of trouble when UNSA possessed a perfectly adequate system of security codes? Surely it wasn't possible that somebody could be eavesdropping on the UNSA net, somebody equipped with enough computer power to render its protective measures unreliable. On the other hand, Shannon reflected soberly, the Germans had thought exactly that in World War II, and the British, with their "Turing Engine" at Bletchley, had been able to read the complete radio traffic between Hitler and his generals, frequently even before the intended recipients. Certainly this message would mean nothing to any third party even though it had come through in plain English, which made it appear all the more innocuous. The problem was that it didn't mean anything to Shannon, either.

Shannon was still brooding about the message early the next morning when he sat down for breakfast in the senior officers' dining quarters. He liked to eat early, before the captain, the first navigation officer, and the others who were usually on early shift appeared. It gave him time to collect his thoughts for the day and keep up with events elsewhere by browsing through the *Interplanetary Journal*—a daily newspaper beamed out from Earth by UNSA to its various ships and installations all over the solar system. The other reason he liked to be early was that it gave him an opportunity to tackle the *Journal*'s crossword puzzle. He'd been an incurable addict for as long as he could remember, and rationalized his addiction by claiming that an early-morning puzzle sharpened the mental faculties in preparation for the demands of the day ahead. He wasn't really sure if that were true, and didn't care all that much either, but it was as good an excuse as any. There was nothing sensational in the news that morning, but he skimmed dutifully through the various items and arrived gratefully at the crossword page just as the steward was refilling his coffee cup. He folded the paper once, then again, and rested it against the edge of the table to scan through the clues casually while he felt inside his jacket for a pen. The heading at the top read: JOURNAL CROSSWORD PUZZLE NUMBER 786.

Shannon stiffened, his hand still inside his jacket, as the number caught his eye. *"How they got 786 is still a puzzle"* replayed itself instantly in his mind. Every word of Hunt's mysterious message had become firmly engraved by that time. *"786"* and *"puzzle"* . . . both appearing in the same sentence. It couldn't be a coincidence, surely. And then he remembered that Hunt had been a keen crossword solver too in his rare moments of free time; he had introduced Shannon to the particularly cryptic puzzles contained in the London *Times*, and the two of them had spent many a good hour solving them over drinks at the bar. Suppressing the urge to leap from his chair with a shout of *Eureka!*, he pushed the pen back into his pocket and felt behind it for the copy of the message tucked inside his wallet. He drew out the sheet of paper, unfolded it, and smoothed it flat on the table between the *Journal* and his coffee cup. He read it once again, and the words took on a whole new light of meaning.

Right there in the first line it said *"cross words,"* and a little farther on, *"clues."* Their significance was obvious now. What about the rest of it? He had never mentioned any book to Hunt, so that part had to be just padding. Presumably the numbers that followed meant something, though. Shannon frowned and stared hard at them: 5, 24, 10, 11, and 20. . . . The sequence didn't immediately jump out and hit him for any reason. He had already tried combining them in various ways and gotten nowhere, but when he read through the message again in its new context, two of the phrases that he had barely noticed before did jump out and hit him: ". . . came *across* . . . ," associated with 5, 24, and 10, and immediately after: ". . . get *down* . . . ," associated with 11 and 20, had obvious connotations to do with crosswords: they referred to the across and down sets of clues. So presumably whatever Hunt was trying to say would be found in the answers to clues 5, 24, and 10 across, and 11 and 20 down. That had to be it.

With rising excitement he transferred his attention to the *Journal*. At that moment the captain and the first navigation officer appeared in the doorway across the room, talking jovially and laughing about something. Shannon rose from his seat and picked up the *Journal* in one movement. Before they were three paces into the room he had passed them, walking briskly in the opposite direction and tossing back just a curt "Good morning, gentlemen," over his shoulder. They exchanged puzzled looks, turned to survey the doorway through which the Mission Director had already vanished, looked at each other again and shrugged, and sat down at an empty table.

Back in the privacy of his stateroom, Shannon sat down at his desk and unfolded the paper once more. The clue to 5 across read, "Find the meaning of a poem to Digital Equipment Corporation (6)." The company name was well known among UNSA and scientific people; DEC computers were used for everything from preprocessing the datastreams that poured incessantly through the laser link between Jupiter and Earth to controlling the instruments contained in the robot landed on Io. *"DEC"!* Those letters had to be part of the solution. What about the rest of the clue? "Poem." A list of synonyms paraded through Shannon's head: "verse" . . . "lyric" . . . "epic" . . . "elegy." They were no good. He wanted something of three letters to complete the single-word answer of six letters indicated in the parentheses. *"Ode"!* Added *to* "DEC" it gave "DECODE," which mean, "Find the meaning of." Not too difficult. Shannon penned in the answer and shifted his attention to 24 across.

"Dianna's lock causes heartache (8)." "Dianna's" was an

immediate giveaway, and after some reflection Shannon had succeeded in obtaining Di's tress (lock of hair), which gave heartache in the form of "DISTRESS."

10 across read, "A guiding light in what could be a confused voyage (6)." The phrase "could be a confused voyage" suggested an anagram of "voyage," which comprised six letters. Shannon played with the letters for a while but could form them into nothing sensible, so moved on to 11 down. "Let's fit a date to reorganize the experimental results (4,4,4)." Three words of four letters each made up the solution. "Reorganize" looked like a hint for an anagram again. Shannon searched the clue for a combination of words containing twelve letters and soon picked out "Let's fit a date." He scribbled them down randomly in the margin of the page and juggled with them for a few minutes, eventually producing "TEST DATA FILE," which his instinct told him was the correct answer.

The clue for 20 down was, "Argon beam matrix (5)." That didn't mean very much, so Shannon began working out some of the other clues to obtain some cross-letters in the words he had missed. The "guiding light" in 10 across turned out to be "BEACON," which was *in* the remainder of the clue and staring him in the face all the time as it had said: ". . . could *be a con*fused . . ." The suggestion of an anagram had been made deliberately to mislead. He wondered what kind of warped mentality was needed to qualify as a crossword compiler. Finally the "argon beam" was revealed as "Ar" (chemical symbol) plus "ray" (beam), to give "ARRAY," i.e., a matrix. Interestingly the answer to the first clue of all, 1 across, was "SHANNON," a river in Ireland, presumably slipped in as a confirmation to him personally.

The complete message with the words placed in the same order as the numbers that Hunt had given now read:

DECODE DISTRESS BEACON TEST-DATA-FILE ARRAY.

Shannon sat back in his chair and studied the final result with some satisfaction, although it so far still told him far from everything. It was evident, however, that it had something to do with the Ganymeans, which tied in with Hunt's being involved.

ACROSS

1 Watery Irish flower (6)
5 Find the meaning of a poem to Digital Equipment Corporation (6)
9 Guilty of having no money after the pub? Quite the opposite! (8)
10 A guiding light in what could be a confused voyage (6)
12 Writer, jumping into action, arrives at a profound conclusion (4, 3)
13 The ultimate in text remedies (7)
14 Oriental rule changed by Swiss mathematician (5)
16 Wild riot about the point of a short preamble, colloquially speaking (5)
17 Expert loses two-thirds but takes back art for something more (5)
18 A separated piece (5)
20 Continental one-fan car, maybe (7)
21 Ringing around to abolish a right (7)
23 Keep the elephant's head and tail in the rain (6)
24 Dianna's lock causes heartache (8)
25 After six months, men and I find a type of Arab (6)
26 Surrounds North Carolina with ease, to a point (7)

DOWN

1 Win in a sled, perhaps? It's not fair! (7)
2 But the arms this noted lady was advised to get wouldn't have been much good to Venus! (5)
3 Powerful response, right from the heart? (7, 8)
4 Possibly did on gin? Con't—it's not habit-forming (3-9)
6 A wave from a charge of the Light Brigade (15)
7 Hydrogen makes harmony in turbulent star-core (9)
8 Norman's head in the lake? No—some other guy (5)
11 Let's fit a date to reorganize the experimental results (4, 4, 4)
15 It sounds like a lumberjack's musical number (9)
19 Hoover, initially in trust over the South, urges progress (7)
20 Argon beam matrix (5)
22 Deposit nothing in the smaller amount (5)

Some time before the *Shapieron* appeared out of the depths of space at Ganymede, the UNSA missions exploring the Jovian moon system had discovered the wreck of an ancient Ganymean spaceship from twenty-five million years back entombed beneath Ganymede's ice crust. In the process of experimenting with some of the devices recovered from the vessel, Hunt and a group of engineers at Pithead—one of the surface bases on Ganymede—had managed to activate a type of Ganymean emergency transmitter that utilized gravity waves since the propulsive method used by Ganymean ships precluded their receiving electromagnetic signals while under main drive; that was what had attracted the *Shapieron* to Ganymede after reentering the Solar System. Shannon remembered that there had been a suggestion to use that same device to relay the news of the surprise reply from the Gaints' Star on to the *Shapieron* after its departure, but Hunt had grown suspicious that the reply was a hoax and had vetoed the idea.

That had to be the "Distress Beacon" in Hunt's message. So what was the "Test-Data-File Array" that Shannon was supposed to decode? The Ganymean beacon had been shipped to Earth along with many other items that various institutions had wanted to experiment with firsthand, and the researchers conducting those experiments usually made a point of sending their results back to Jupiter via the laser link to keep interested parties there informed. The only thing that Shannon could think of was that Hunt had somehow arranged for some information to be sent over the link disguised as a file of ordinary-looking experimental test data purportedly relating to the beacon and probably consisting of just a long list of numbers. Now that Shannon's attention had been drawn to the file, the way the numbers were supposed to be read would hopefully, with close enough scrutiny, make itself clear.

If that was it, the only people likely to know anything about unusual files of test data coming in from Earth would be the engineers down at Pithead who had worked on the beacon after it was brought up from beneath the ice. Shannon activated the terminal on his desk and entered a command to access the *Jupiter Five* personnel records. A few minutes later he had identified the engineering project leader in charge of that work as a Californian called Vincent Carizan, who had joined *J5* from UNSA's Propulsion Systems and Propellants Division, where he had worked for ten years after obtaining a master's degree in electrical and electronic engineering at Berkeley.

Shannon's first impulse was to put a call through to Pithead, but after a minute or two of further reflection he decided against it. If Hunt had taken such pains to avoid any hint of the subject being interpretable from what went over the communications network, anything could be happening. He was still pondering on what to do when the call-tone sounded from the terminal. Shannon cleared the screen and touched a key to accept. It was his adjutant officer calling from the command center.

"Excuse me, sir, but you are scheduled to attend the Operations Controller's briefing in G-327 in five minutes. Since nobody's seen you this morning, I thought maybe a reminder might be called for."

"Oh . . . thanks, Bob," Shannon replied. "Look, something's come up, and I don't think I'm going to be able to make it. Make excuses for me, would you."

"Will do, sir."

"Oh, and Bob . . ." Shannon's voice rose suddenly as a thought struck him.

The adjutant looked up just as he had been about to cut the call. "Sir?"

"Get here as soon as you've done that. I've got a message that I want couriered down to the surface."

"Couriered?" the adjutant appeared surprised and puzzled.

"Yes. It's to go to one of the engineers at Pithead. I can't explain now, but the matter is urgent. If you don't waste any time, you should be able to make the nine o'clock shuttle down to Main. I'll have it sealed and waiting by the time you get here. Treat this as grade *X-ray.*"

The adjutant's face at once became serious. "I'll be there right away," he said, and the screen went blank.

Shannon received a brief call from Pithead shortly before lunch, advising that Carizan was on his way up to *Jupiter Five* via Ganymede Main Base. When Carizan arrived, he brought with him a printout of a file of data, supposedly relating to tests performed on the Ganymean beacon, that had materialized in the computers at Pithead that very morning after coming in from Earth over the link and being relayed down to the surface. The engineers at Pithead had been puzzled because the file header was out of sequence and contained references that

didn't match the database indexing system. And nobody had
known anything about any tests being scheduled of the kind
that the header mentioned.

As Shannon had anticipated, the file contained just numbers—many groups of numbers, each group consisting of a
long list of pairs; it was typical of the layout of an experimental report giving readings of interrelated variables and would
have meant nothing more to anybody who had no reason not
to accept it at face value. Shannon called together a small team
of specialists whose discretion could be trusted, and it didn't
take them long to deduce that each group of pairs formed a set
of datapoints defined by x-y coordinates in a 256-by-256 matrix array; the hint had been there in the crossword. When the
sets of points were plotted on a computer display screen, each
set formed a pattern of dots that looked just like a statistical
scattering of test data about a straight-line function. But when
the patterns of dots were superposed they formed lines of
words written diagonally across the screen, and the words
formed a message in English. The message contained pointers
to other files of numbers that had also been beamed through
from Earth and gave explicit instructions for decoding them,
and when this was done the amount of information that they
yielded turned out to be prodigious.

The result was a set of detailed directions for *Jupiter Five* to
transmit a long sequence of Ganymean communications coding
groups not into the UNSA net but outward, toward coordinates
that lay beyond the edge of the solar system. The contents of any
replies received from that direction were, the directions said, to
be disguised as experimental data in the way that had thus been
established and communicated to Navcomms via the laser link.

Shannon was weary and red-eyed due to lack of sleep by the
time he sat down at the terminal in his stateroom and composed a message for transmission to Earth, addressed to Dr.
Victor Hunt at Navcomms Headquarters, Houston. It read:

Vic,
I've talked to Vince Carizan, and it's all a lot clearer
now. We're running some tests on it as you asked, and if
anything positive shows up I'll have the results sent straight
through.
Best wishes,
Joe

chapter five

Hunt lounged back in the pilot's seat and stared absently down at the toytown suburbs of Houston while the airmobile purred along contentedly, guided by intermittent streams of binary being directed up at it from somewhere below. It was interesting, he thought, how the patterns of movement of the groundcars, flowing, merging, slowing, and accelerating in unison on the roadways below seemed to reveal some grand, centrally orchestrated design—as if they were all parts of an unimaginably complex score composed by a cosmic Bach. But it was all an illusion. Each vehicle was programmed with only the details of its own destination plus a few relatively simple instructions for handling conditions along the way; the complexity emerged as a consequence of large numbers of them interacting freely in their synthetic environment. It was the same with life, he reflected. All the magical, mystical, and supernatural forces invoked through the ages to explain it were inventions that existed in the minds of misled observers, not in the universe they observed. He wondered how much untapped human talent had been wasted in futile pursuit of the creations of wishful thinking. The Ganymeans had entertained no such illusions, but had applied themselves diligently to understanding and mastering the universe as it was, instead of how it seemed to be or how they might have wanted it to be. Maybe that was why the Ganymeans had reached the stars.

In the seat next to him, Lyn looked up from the half-completed crossword in the *Interplanetary Journal* of a few days earlier. "Got any ideas for this—'It sounds like a lumberjack's musical number.' What do you make of that?"

"How many letters?" Hunt asked after a few moments of thought.

"Nine."

Hunt frowned at the flight-systems status summaries being

routinely updated on the console display in front of him. "Log-arithm," he said after another pause.

Lyn thought about it, then smiled faintly. "Oh, I see . . . sneaky. It sounds like 'logger rhythm.' "

"Right."

"It fits okay." She wrote the word in on the paper resting on her lap. "I'm glad that Joe Shannon had fewer problems with it than this."

"You and me both."

Shannon's confirmation that the message was understood had arrived two days earlier. The idea had occurred to Hunt and Lyn one evening while they were at Lyn's apartment, solving a puzzle in one of Hunt's books of London *Times* crosswords. Don Maddson, the linguistics expert at Navcomms who had studied the Ganymean language, was one of the regular compilers of the *Journal* puzzles and also a close friend of Hunt's. So with Caldwell's blessing, Hunt had told Maddson as much as was necessary about the Gistar situation, and together they had constructed the message transmitted to Jupiter. Now there was nothing to do but wait and hope that it produced results.

"Let's hope Murphy takes a day off," Lyn said.

"Never hope that. Let's hope somebody remembers Hunt's extension to the Law."

"What's Hunt's extension?"

" 'Everything that can go wrong, will . . . unless somebody makes it his business to do something about it.' "

The stub wing outside the window dipped as the airmobile banked out of the traffic corridor and turned to commence a shallow descent. A cluster of large white buildings standing to attention on a river bank about a mile away moved slowly around until they were centered in the windshield and lying dead ahead.

"He must have been an insurance salesman," Hunt murmured after a short silence.

"Who?"

"Murphy. 'Everything's going to screw up—sign the application now.' Who else but an insurance salesman would have thought of saying something like that?"

The buildings ahead grew to take on the smooth, clean lines of the Westwood Biological Institute of UNSA's Life Sciences Division. The vehicle slowed to a halt and hovered fifty feet above the roof of the Biochemistry building, which with Neurosciences and Physiology formed a trio facing the elongated bulk of Administration and Central Facilities across a plaza of colorful mosaic paving broken up by lawns and a bevy of fountains playing in the sun. Hunt checked the landing area visually, then cleared the computer to complete the descent sequence. Minutes later he and Lyn were checking in at the reception desk in the building's top-floor lobby.

"Professor Danchekker isn't in his office," the receptionist informed them as she consulted her screen. "The route-through code entered against his number is for one of the basement labs. I'll try there." She keyed in another code, and after a short delay the characters on the screen vanished in a blur of colors which immediately assembled themselves into the features of a lean, balding man wearing a pair of anachronistic gold-rimmed spectacles perched at the top of a thin, somewhat aquiline nose. His skin gave the impression of having been stretched over his bones as an afterthought, with barely enough left over to cover his defiant, outthrust chin. He didn't seem too pleased at the interruption.

"Yes?"

"Professor Danchekker, top lobby here. I have two visitors for you."

"I am extremely busy," he replied curtly. "Who are they and what do they want?"

Hunt sighed and pivoted the flatscreen display around to face him. "It's us, Chris—Vic and Lyn. You're expecting us."

Danchekker's expression softened, and his mouth compressed itself into a thin line that twitched briefly upward at the ends. "Oh, of course. I do apologize. Come on down. I'm in the dissecting lab on Level E."

"Are you working alone?" Hunt asked.

"Yes. We can talk here."

"We'll see you in a couple of minutes."

They walked on through to the elevator bank at the rear of the lobby. "Chris must be working with his animals again," Lyn remarked as they waited.

"I don't think he's come up for air since we got back from Ganymede," Hunt said. "I'm surprised he hasn't started looking like some of them."

Danchekker had been with Hunt on Ganymede when the *Shapieron* reappeared in the Solar System. In fact Danchekker had made the major contribution to piecing together what was probably the most astounding part of the whole story, the more sensitive details of which still had not been cleared for publication to an unsuspecting and psychologically unprepared world.

Not surprisingly, the Ganymeans had made visits to Earth during the period that their civilization had flourished on Minerva—twenty-five million years before. Their scientists had predicted an epoch of deteriorating environmental conditions on Minerva in the form of an increasing concentration of atmospheric carbon dioxide, for which they had only a low inherent tolerance, so one of the reasons for their interest in Earth had been to assess it as a possible candidate for migration. But they soon abandoned the idea. The Ganymeans had evolved from ancestors whose biochemistry had precluded the emergence of carnivores, thus inhibiting the development of aggressiveness and ruthlessness together with most of the related traits that had characterized the survival struggle on Earth. The savagery that abounded in the environment of late-Oligocene, early-Miocene Earth made it altogether too inhospitable for the placid Ganymean temperament, and made the notion of settling there unthinkable.

These visits to Earth did, however, have one practical outcome in addition to satisfying the Ganymeans' scientific curiosity. In the course of their studies of the forms of animal life they discovered, they identified a totally new, gene-based mechanism for absorbing CO_2, which gave terrestrial fauna a far higher and more adaptable inherent tolerance. It suggested an alternative approach to solving the problem on Minerva. The Ganymeans imported large numbers of terrestrial animal species back to their own planet to conduct genetic experiments aimed at transplanting the functional terrestrial coding groups into their own species, thereafter to be inbred automatically into their descendants. Some well-preserved specimens of these early terrestrial animals had been recovered from the wrecked ship on Ganymede, and Danchekker had brought many of them back to Westwood for detailed studies.

The experiments were not successful, and soon afterward the Ganymeans disappeared. The terrestrial species left on Minerva rapidly wiped out the virtually defenseless native forms, adapted and radiated to flourish across the planet, and continued to evolve. . . .

Almost twenty-five million years later—around fifty thousand years before the current period on Earth—an intelligent, fully human form had established itself on Minerva. This race was named the "Lunarians" after the first traces of their existence came to light in the course of lunar explorations being conducted in 2028, which was when Hunt had first gotten involved and moved from England to join UNSA. The Lunarians were a violent and warlike race who developed advanced technology rapidly and eventually polarized into two superpowers, Cerios and Lambia, which clashed in a final, cataclysmic war fought across the entire surface of Minerva and beyond. In the violence of this conflict Minerva had been destroyed, Pluto and the Asteroids born, and Luna orphaned.

A few survivors were left stranded on the lunar surface at the end of these events. Somehow, when at last the Moon stabilized in orbit around Earth after being captured, some of these survivors succeeded in reaching the only haven left for them in the entire solar system—the surface of Earth itself. For millennia they clung precariously to the edge of extinction, reverting to barbarism for a period and in the process losing the thread that traced their origins. But in time they grew strong and spread far and wide. They supplanted the Neanderthals, who were descended from the primates that had continued to evolve undisturbed on Earth, and eventually came to dominate the entire planet in the form of Modern Man. Only much later, when at last they rediscovered the sciences and ventured back into space, did they find the evidence to reconstruct the story of their origins.

They found Danchekker attired in a stained white lab smock, measuring and examining parts taken from a large, brown, furry carcass lying on the dissection table. It was powerfully muscled, and its fearsome, well developed carnivore's teeth were exposed where the lower jaw of the snout had been removed. Danchekker informed them that it was an intriguing example of a relative to *Daphoenodon* of the Lower Miocene. Despite its evidently distinct digitigrade mode of locomotion, moderately long legs, and heavy tail, its three upper molars distinguished it as an ancestor of *Amphicyon* and through it of all modern bears—unlike *Cynodesmus*, of which Danchekker also had a specimen, whose upper dentition of two molars put it between *Cynodictis* and contemporary Canidae. Hunt took his word for it.

Hunt had practically insisted to Caldwell that if they succeeded in arranging a landing for a ship from Thurien, Danchekker would have to be included in the reception party; he probably knew more about Ganymean biology and psychology than anybody else in the world's scientific community. Caldwell had broached the subject confidentially with the Director of the Westwood Institute, who had agreed and advised Danchekker accordingly. Danchekker had not needed very much persuading. He was far from happy at the manner in which the eminent personages responsible for managing Earth's affairs had been handling things, however.

"The whole situation is preposterous," Danchekker declared irritably while he was loading the instruments he had been using into a sterilizer on one side of the room. "Politics, cloak-and-dagger theatrics—this is an unprecedented opportunity for the advancement of knowledge and probably for a quantum leap in the progress of the whole human race, yet here we are having to plot and scheme as if we were dealing in illicit narcotics or something. I mean, good God, we can't even talk about it over the phone! The situation's intolerable."

Lyn straightened up from the dissecting table, where she had been curiously studying the exposed innards of *Daphoenodon*. "I guess the UN feels it has an obligation to humanity to play safe," she said. "It's a contact with a whole new civilization, and they figure that up front it ought to be handled by the professionals."

Danchekker closed the sterilizer lid with a bang and walked over to a sink to rinse his hands. "When the *Shapieron* arrived at Ganymede, the only representatives of *Homo sapiens* there to meet it were, as I recall, the scientific and engineering personnel of the UNSA Jupiter missions," he pointed out coolly. "They conducted themselves in exemplary fashion and had established a perfectly civilized relationship with the Ganymeans long before the ship came to Earth. That was without any 'professionals' being involved at all, apart from sending inane advice from Earth on how the situation should be managed, and which those on the spot simply laughed at and ignored."

Hunt looked across from a chair by a desk that stood in one corner of the lab, almost surrounded by computer terminal equipment and display screens. "Actually there is something to be said for the UN line," he said. "I don't think you've thought yet just how big a risk we might be taking."

Danchekker sniffed as he came back around the table. "What are you talking about?"

"If the State Department wasn't convinced that if we don't go it alone and fix a landing the Soviets will, we'd be a lot more cautious too," Hunt told him.

"I don't follow you," Danchekker said. "What is there to be cautious about? The Ganymean mind is incapable of conceiving anything that could constitute a threat to our, or anybody else's, well-being, as you well know. They simply have not been shaped by the factors that have conditioned *Homo sapiens* to be what he is." He waved a hand in front of his face before Hunt could reply. "And as for your fears that the Thuriens may have changed in some fundamental way, you may forget that. The fundamental traits that determine human behavior were established, not tens but hundreds of millions of years ago, and I have studied Minervan evolution sufficiently to be satisfied that the same may safely be said of Ganymeans also. On such timescales, twenty-five million years is scarcely significant, and quite incapable of giving rise to changes of the magnitude that your suggestion implies."

"I know that," Hunt said when he could get a word in. "But you're going off at a wrong tangent. That's not the problem. The problem is that we might not be talking to Ganymeans at all."

Danchekker seemed taken aback for a moment, then frowned as if Hunt should have known better. "That's absurd," he declared. "Who else could we be talking to? The original transmission from Farside was encoded in Ganymean communications format and understood, was it not? What reason is there to suppose its recipients were anything else?"

"They're talking in English now, but it's not coming from London," Hunt replied.

"But they are talking from Gistar," Danchekker retorted. "And isn't that where, from independently derived evidence, we deduced that the Ganymeans went?"

"We don't *know* that those signals are coming from Gistar," Hunt pointed out. "They say they are, but they've been saying all kinds of other strange things as well. Our beams are being aimed *in the direction of* Gistar, but we've no idea what's out there past the edge of the solar system picking them up. It could be some kind of Ganymean relay that transforms signals that our physics knows nothing about into electromagnetic waves, but then again it might not."

"Surely it's obvious," Danchekker said, sounding a trifle disdainful. "The Ganymeans left some kind of monitoring device behind when they migrated to Gistar, probably to detect and alert them to any signs of intelligent activity."

Hunt shook his head. "If that were the case, it would have been triggered by early radio over a hundred years ago. We'd have known about it long before now."

Danchekker thought about it for a moment, then showed his teeth. "Which proves my point. It responded only to Ganymean codes. We've never sent anything out encoded in Ganymean before, have we? Therefore it must be of Ganymean origin."

"And now it's talking English. Does that mean it was made by Boeing?"

"Obviously the language was acquired via their surveillance operation."

"And maybe they learned Ganymean the same way."

"You're being absurd."

Hunt threw out his arms in appeal. "For Christ's sake, Chris, all I'm saying is let's be open-minded for now and accept that we might be letting ourselves in for something we didn't expect. You're saying they have to be Ganymeans, and you're probably right; I'm saying there's a chance they might not be. That's all I'm saying."

"You said yourself that Ganymeans don't play cloak-and-dagger games and twist facts around, Professor," Lyn injected in a tone that she hoped would calm things a little. "But whoever it is seems to have some funny ideas about how to open up interplanetary relations. . . . And they've got some pretty weird ideas on how Earth is coming along these days, so somebody hasn't been talking straight to somebody somewhere. That hardly sounds like Ganymeans, does it?"

Danchekker snorted but seemed hard-pressed for a reply. The terminal on a side table by the desk saved him by emitting a call-tone. "Excuse me" he muttered, leaning past Hunt to accept. "Yes?" Danchekker inquired.

It was Ginny, calling from Navcomms HQ. "Hello, Professor Danchekker. I believe Dr. Hunt is with you. I have an urgent message for him. Gregg Caldwell said to find him and let him know right away."

Danchekker moved back a pace, and Hunt rolled his chair

forward in front of the screen. "Hi, Ginny," he acknowledged. "What's new?"

"A message has come in for you from *Jupiter Five*." She looked down to read something below the edge of the screen. "It's from the Mission Director—Joseph B. Shannon. It reads, 'The lab tests worked out just as you hoped. Complete file of results being assembled for transmission now. Good luck.' " Ginny looked up again. "Is that what you wanted to know?"

Hunt's face was radiating jubilation. "It sure is, Ginny!" he said. "Thanks . . . a lot." Ginny nodded and tossed him a quick smile; the screen blanked out.

Hunt swiveled his chair around to find two awed faces confronting him. "I guess we can stop arguing about it," he told them. "It looks as if we'll know for sure before very much longer."

chapter six

The main receiver dish at Giordano Bruno was like a gigantic Cyclopean eye—a four-hundred-foot-diameter paraboloid of steel latticework towering into the starry blackness above the lifeless desolation of lunar Farside. It was supported by twin lattice towers moving in diametric opposition around the circular track that formed the most salient surface feature of the observatory and base. As it stood motionless, listening to whispers from distant galaxies, the lines of its lengthening shadow lay draped as a distorted mesh across the domes and lesser constructions huddled around it, spilling over on one side to become indistinct and lost among the boulders and craters scattered beyond.

Karen Heller stood gazing up at it through the transparent wall of an observation tower protruding from the roof of the two-story Main Block. She had gone there to be alone and recompose herself after yet another acrimonious meeting of the eleven-person UN Farside delegation, which had gotten nowhere. Their latest scare was that the signals might not be coming from Ganymeans at all, which was her own fault for ill-advisedly introducing the thought that Hunt had voiced when she was in Houston a week earlier. She wasn't sure even now why she had brought that possibility up at all, since with hindsight it provided an opportunity for procrastination that they were bound to latch on to. As she had commented to a surprised Norman Pacey afterward, it had been a badly calculated attempt at a shock tactic to spur any positive reaction, and had misfired. Perhaps in her frustration she hadn't been thinking too clearly at the time. Anyway it was done now, and the latest transmission sent out toward Gistar had discounted the possibility of any landing in the immediate future and instead talked reams of insignificant detail to do with rank and protocol. Ironically this in itself should have said clearly enough that the aliens, Ganymean or not, harbored no hostile intentions; if they did, they would surely have just arrived, if that was what they wanted to do, without waiting for a cordial invitation. It all made the UN policy more enigmatic and reinforced her suspicions, and the State Department's, that the Soviets were setting themselves up to go it alone and were manipulating the UN somehow. Nevertheless the U.S. would continue to follow the rules until Houston succeeded in establishing a channel via Jupiter—assuming Houston succeeded. If they did, and if none of the efforts to speed things up at Bruno had borne fruit by that time, the U.S. would feel justified in concluding that its hand had been forced.

As she gazed up at the lines of metal etched against the blackness by the rays of the setting sun, she marveled at the knowledge and ingenuity that had created an oasis of life in a sterile desert a quarter of a million miles from Earth and built instruments such as this, which even as she watched might be silently probing the very edges of the universe. One of the scientific advisors from NSF had told her once that all of the energy collected by all the world's radio telescopes since the beginnings of that branch of astronomy almost a century earlier was equivalent to no more than that represented by the ash from a cigarette falling through a distance of several feet. And somehow the whole fantastic picture painted by modern cosmology—of collapsed stars, black holes, X-ray-emitting binaries, and a universe consisting of a "gas" of galaxy "molecules"—had all been reconstructed from the information contained in it.

She had ambivalent views about scientists. On the one hand, their intellectual accomplishments were baffling and at times like this awesome; on the other, she often felt that at a deeper level their retreat into the realm of the inanimate represented an abdication—an escape from the burdens of the world of human affairs within which the expression of knowledge acquired meaning. Even biologists seemed to reduce life to terms of molecules and statistics. Science had created the tools to solve humanity's problems a century ago, but had stood by helplessly while others took the tools and forged them into means of attaining other ends. It was not until the 2010s, when the UN emerged as a truly coherent global influence to be reckoned with, that strategic disarmament had become fact and the resources of the superpowers were at last mobilized toward building a safer and better world.

It was all the more tragic and inexplicable that the UN—until so recently the epitome of the world's commitment to meaningful progress and the realization of the full potential of the human race—should be the obstacle in the road along which the arrow of that progress surely pointed. It seemed a law of history for successful movements and empires to resist further change after the needs that had motivated them into promoting change had been satisfied. Perhaps, she reflected, the UN was already, in keeping with the universally accelerating pace of the times, beginning to show the eventual senility symptoms of all empires—stagnation.

But the planets continued to move in their predicted orbits, and the patterns being revealed by the computers connected to the instruments at Giordano Bruno didn't change. So was her "reality" an illusion built on shifting sands, and had scientists shunned the illusion for some vaster, unchanging reality that was the only one of permanence that mattered? Somehow she couldn't picture the Englishman Hunt or the American she had met in Houston as fugitives who would idle their lives away tinkering in ivory towers.

A moving point of light detached itself from the canopy of stars and enlarged gradually into the shape of the UNSA surface transporter ship due in from Tycho. It came to a halt above the far side of the base, and after pausing for a few seconds sank slowly out of sight between Optical Dome 3 and a clutter of storage tanks and laser transceivers. Aboard it would be the courier with the latest information from Houston via Washington. The experts had decreed that if Ganymean technology was behind the surveillance of Earth's communications anything was possible, and the ban on using even supposedly secure channels was still being rigidly enforced. Heller turned away and walked across the floor of the dome to call an elevator at the rear wall. A minute or two later she stepped out into a brightly lit, white-walled corridor three levels below the surface and began walking in the direction of the central hub of Bruno's underground labyrinth.

Mikolai Sobroskin, the Soviet representative on Farside, came out of one of the doors as she passed and turned to walk with her in the same direction. He was short but broad, completely bald, and pink-skinned, and he walked with a hurried, jerking gait, even in lunar gravity, that made her feel for a moment like Snow White. From a dossier that Norman Pacey had procured, however, she knew that the Russian had been a lieutenant-general in the Red Army, where he had specialized in electronic warfare and countermeasures, and a counterintelligence expert for many years after that. He came from a world about as far removed from Walt Disney's as it was possible to get.

"I spent three months in the Pacific conducting equipment trials aboard a nuclear carrier many years ago," Sobroskin remarked. "It seemed that it was impossible to get from anywhere to anywhere without interminable corridors. I never did find out what lay in between half those places. This base reminds me of it."

"I'd say the New York subway," Heller replied.

"Ah, but the difference is that these walls get washed more regularly. One of the problems with capitalism is that only the things that pay get done. So it wears a clean suit which conceals dirty undershorts."

Heller smiled faintly. At least it was good that the differences that erupted across the table in the conference room could be left there. Anything else would have made life intolerable in the cramped, communal atmosphere of the base. "The shuttle from Tycho had just landed," she said. "I wonder what's new."

"Yes, I know. No doubt some mail from Moscow and Washington for us to argue about tomorrow." The original UN charter had ruled against representatives receiving instructions from their national governments, but nobody at Farside kept up any pretenses about that.

"I hope not too much," she sighed. "We should be thinking of the future of the whole planet. National politics shouldn't come into this." She glanced sideways as she spoke, searching his face for a hint of a reaction. Nobody in Washington had yet been able to decide for sure if the UN stance was being dictated from the Kremlin, or if the Soviets were simply playing along with something they found expedient to their own ends. But the Russian remained inscrutable.

They came out of the corridor and entered the "common room"—normally the UNSA Officers' Mess, but assigned temporarily for off-duty use by the visiting UN delegation. The air was warm and stuffy. A mixed group of about a dozen UN delegates and permanent residents of the base was present, some reading, two engrossed in a chess game, and the others talking in small groups around the room or at the small bar at the far end. Sobroskin continued walking and disappeared through the far door, which led to the rooms allocated for office space for the delegation. Heller had intended going the same way, but she was intercepted by Niels Sverenssen, the delegation's Swedish chairman, who detached himself from a small group standing near where they had entered.

"Oh, Karen," he said, catching her elbow lightly and steering her to one side. "I've been looking for you. There are a few points from today's meeting that we ought to resolve before finalizing tomorrow's agenda. I was hoping to discuss them before it's typed up." He was very tall and lean, and he carried his elegant crown of silver hair with a haughty uprightness that always made Heller think of him as the last of the true blue-blooded European aristocrats. His dress was always impeccable and formal, even at Bruno where practically everyone else had soon taken to more casual wear, and he gave the impression somehow of looking on the rest of the human race with something approaching disdain, as if condescending to mix with them only as an imposition of duty. Heller was never able to feel quite at ease in his presence, and she had spent too much time in Paris and on other European assignments to attribute it simply to cultural differences.

"Well, I was on my way to check the mail," she said. "If the discussion can wait for an hour or so, I could see you back here. We'll go through it over a drink maybe, or use one of the offices. Was it anything important?"

"A few questions of procedure and some definitions that need clarifying under one or two headings." Sverenssen's voice had fallen from its public-address mode of a moment earlier, and as he spoke he moved around as if to shield their conversation from the rest of the room. He was looking at her with a curious expression—an intrigued detachment that was strangely intimate and distant at the same time. It made her feel like a kitchen wench being looked over by a medieval lord-of-the-manor. "I was thinking of something perhaps a little more comfortable later," he said, his tone now ominously confidential. "Possibly over dinner, if I might have the honor."

"I'm not sure when I'll be having dinner tonight," she replied, telling herself that she was getting it all wrong. "It might be late."

"A more companionable hour, wouldn't you agree," Sverenssen murmured pointedly.

It was getting to her again: His words implied that the honor would be his, but his manner left no doubt that she should consider it hers. "I thought you said that you needed to talk before the agenda gets typed," she said.

"We could clear that matter up in an hour as you suggest. That would make dinner a far more relaxing and enjoyable occasion . . . later."

Heller had to swallow hard to maintain her composure. He *was* propositioning her. Such things happened and that was life, but the way this was happening wasn't real. "I think you must have misjudged something," she told him curtly. "If you have business to discuss, I'll talk to you in an hour. Now would you excuse me please?" If he left it at that, it would all soon be forgotten.

He didn't. Instead he moved a pace closer, causing her to back away a step instinctively. "You are an extremely intelligent and ambitious, as well as an attractive, woman, Karen," he said quietly, dropping his former pose. "The world has so many opportunities to offer these days—especially to those who succeed in making friends among its more influential circles. I could do a lot for you that you would find extremely helpful, you know."

His presumption was too much. "You're making a mistake," Heller breathed harshly, striving to keep her voice at a level that would not attract attention. "Please don't compound it any further."

Sverenssen was unperturbed, as if the routine were familiar and mildly boring. "Think it over," he urged, and with that turned casually and rejoined the group he had left. He'd paid his dollar and bought a ticket. It was no more than that. The fury that Heller had been suppressing boiled up inside as she walked out of the room, managing with some effort to keep her pace normal.

Norman Pacey was waiting for her when she reached the U.S. delegate's offices a few minutes later. He seemed to be having trouble in containing his excitement over something. "News!" he exclaimed without preamble as she entered. Then his expression changed abruptly. "Hey, you're looking pretty mad about something. Anything up?"

"It's nothing. What's happened."

"Malliusk was here a little while ago." Gregor Malliusk was the Russian Director of Astronomy at Bruno and one of the privileged few among the regular staff there who knew about the dialogue with Gistar. "A signal came in about an hour ago that isn't intended for us. It's in some kind of binary numeric code. He can't make anything out of it."

Heller looked at him numbly. It could only mean that somebody else, either somewhere on Earth or in its vicinity, had begun transmitting to Gistar and wanted the reply kept private. "The Soviets?" she asked hoarsely.

Pacey shrugged. "Who knows? Sverenssen will probably call a special session, and Sobroskin will deny it, but I'd stake a month's pay."

His voice didn't carry the defeat that it should have, and what he had said didn't account for the jubilant look that Heller had caught on his face as she entered. "Anything else?" she asked, praying inwardly that the reason was what she thought it might be.

Pacey's face split into a wide grin that he could contain no longer. He scooped up some papers from a wad lying in front of the opened courier's bag on a table beside him and waved them triumphantly in the air. "Hunt got through!" he exclaimed. "They've done it via Jupiter! The landing is already fixed for a week from now, and the Thuriens have confirmed it. It's all arranged for a disused airbase in Alaska. It's all fixed up!"

Heller took the papers from him and smiled with relief and

elation as she scanned rapidly down the first sheet. "We'll do it, Norman," she whispered. "We'll beat those bastards yet!"

"You've got a recall to Earth from the Department so you can be there as planned. You'll be getting space-happy with all these lunar flights." Pacey sighed. "I'll be thinking about you while I'm holding the fort up here. I only wish I was coming too."

"You'll get your chance soon enough," Heller said. Everything looked bright again. She lifted her face suddenly from the papers in her hand. "I'll tell you what—tonight we'll both have a special dinner to celebrate . . . a kind of farewell party until whenever. Champagne, a good wine, and the best poultry the cook here's got in his refrigerator. How does that sound?"

"Sounds great," Pacey replied, then frowned and rubbed his chin dubiously. "Although . . . would it really be a good idea? I mean, with this unidentified signal coming in only an hour ago, people might wonder what the hell we're celebrating. Sverenssen might think it's us, not the Soviets, who are being underhanded."

"Well we are, aren't we?"

"Yeah, I guess so—but for a good reason. That's different."

"So let them. If the Soviets think the heat's on us, they might get a false sense of security and not move too fast." A look of grim satisfaction came into Heller's eyes as she thought of something else. "And let Sverenssen think anything he damn well likes," she said.

chapter seven

Clad in a standard-issue UNSA arctic jacket, quilted over-trousers, and snowboots, Hunt stood in the center of a small group of muffled figures stamping their feet and breathing frosty clouds of condensation into the air on the concrete apron of McClusky Air Force Base, situated in the foothills of the Baird Mountains one hundred miles inside the Arctic Circle. The ground fog of the previous day had thinned somewhat to become a layer of overcast through which the washy blob of the sun was just able to impart a drab mix of off-white and grays to the texture of the surrounding landscape. Most of the signs of life among the huddle of semiderelict buildings behind them were concentrated around the former mess hall, which had been hastily patched up and windproofed to provide makeshift accommodation and a command post for the operation. A gaggle of UNSA aircraft and other vehicles parked among a litter of supplies and equipment along the near edge of the apron, and a team of handpicked UNSA personnel positioned in the background with cameras and microphone booms set up ready to record the impending event, completed the scene. The command post had landline links into the area radar net, and a homing beacon had been set up for the Ganymean ship. A strangely tense silence predominated, broken only by the intermittent cries of kittiwakes wheeling and diving above the frozen marshes beyond the perimeter fence, and the humming of a motor generator supplying power from one of the parked trailers.

McClusky was about as far from population centers and major air-traffic lanes as it was possible to get without going outside the U.S., but like every other point on the Earth's surface it was still subject to satellite scrutiny. In an attempt to mask the landing, UNSA had given notice that tests of a new type of reentry vehicle would be conducted in the area during that week, and had requested airlines and other organizations to reroute flights accordingly until further notice. To accustom the region's radar controllers to an abnormal pattern of activity, UNSA had also been staging irregular flights over Alaska for several days and altering their announced flight plans at short notice. Beyond that there was little they could do. How any thing like the arrival of a starship could be kept secret from terrestrial observers, never mind an advanced alien surveillance system, was something nobody was quite sure of. Whoever was sending the messages through Jupiter had seemed satisfied with the arrangements, however, and had stated that they would take care of the rest.

The last message to go out via Jupiter had given the names of the persons who would make up the reception party, their positions, and a brief summary of what they did and why each was included. The aliens had reciprocated with a reply advising that three of their members would be prominent in conducting their dealings with Earth. The first was "Calazar," who was described as personifying the government of Thurien and its associated worlds—the figure nearest to a "president" that the planet seemed to possess. Accompanying him would be Frenua Showm, a female "ambassador" whose function had to do with affairs between the various sectors of Thurien society, and Porthik Eesyan, who was involved with policies of scientific, industrial, and economic importance. Whether or not more than just these three would be involved, the aliens hadn't said.

"This is all a striking contrast to the *Shapieron*'s arrival on this planet," Danchekker muttered, surveying the scene around them. That event on the shore of Lake Geneva had been witnessed by tens of thousands and shown live over the news grid.

"It reminds me of Ganymede Main," Hunt replied. "All we need is helmets on and a few Vegas around. What a way to start a new era!"

On Hunt's other side, Lyn, looking lost in the outsize, fur-trimmed hood pulled closely around her face, thrust her hands deeper into her jacket pockets and ground down a block of slush with her foot. "They're about due," she said. "I hope they've got good brakes." Assuming all was on schedule, the ship would have left Thurien, over twenty light-years away, just about twenty-four hours earlier.

"I don't think we need entertain any fears of ineptitude on the part of the Ganymeans," Danchekker said confidently.

"*If* they turn out to be Ganymeans," Hunt remarked, even though by this time he no longer had any real doubts about the matter.

"*Of course* they're Ganymeans," Danchekker snorted impatiently.

Behind them Karen Heller and Jerol Packard, the U.S. Secretary of State, stood motionless and silent. They had persuaded the President to go ahead with the operation on the strength of the implication that the aliens, Ganymean or not, were friendly, and if they were wrong they could well have committed their country to the worst blunder in its history. The President had hoped to be present in person, but in the end had accepted reluctantly the advice of his aides that the absence of too many important people at the same time without explanation would be inviting undesirable attention.

Suddenly the voice of the operations controller inside the mess hall barked over the loudspeaker mounted on a mast at the rear. "Radar contact!" The figures around Hunt stiffened visibly. Behind them the team of UNSA technicians hid their nervousness behind a frenzied outbreak of last-minute preparations and adjustments. The voice came again: "Approaching due west, range twenty-two miles, altitude twelve thousand feet, speed six hundred miles per hour, reducing." Hunt swung his head around instinctively to peer upward along with all the others, but it was impossible to make out anything through the overcast.

A minute went by in slow motion. "Five miles," the controller's voice announced. "It's down to five thousand feet. Visual contact any time now." Hunt could feel the blood pumping solidly in his chest. Despite the cold, his body suddenly felt clammy inside his heavy clothing. Lyn wriggled her arm through his and pulled herself closer.

And then the wind blowing down from the mountains to the west brought the first snatch of a low moaning sound. It lasted for a second or two, faded away, then came back again and this time persisted. It swelled slowly to a steady drone. A frown began forming on Hunt's face as he listened. He turned and glanced back, and saw that several of the UNSA people were exchanging puzzled looks too. There was something wrong. That sound was too familiar to be from any starship. Mutterings started breaking out, then ceased abruptly as a dark shape materialized out of the cloud base and continued descending on a direct line toward the base. It was a standard Boeing 1227 medium-haul, transonic VTOL—a model widely used by domestic carriers and UNSA's preferred type for general-purpose duties. The tension that had been building up around the apron released itself in a chorus of groans and curses.

Behind Heller and Packard, Caldwell, his face dark with fury, spun around to confront a bewildered UNSA officer. "I thought this area was supposed to have been cleared," he snapped.

The officer shook his head helplessly. "It was. I don't understand. . . . Somebo—"

"Get that idiot out of here!"

Looking flustered, the officer hurried away and disappeared through the open door of the mess hall. At the same time voices from the control room inside began pouring out over the loudspeaker, evidently left inadvertently live in the confusion.

"I can't get anything out of it. It's not responding."

"Use the emergency frequency."

"We've already tried. Nothing."

"For Christ's sake what's happening in here? Caldwell just chewed my balls off outside. Find out from Yellow Six who it is."

"I've got 'em on the line now. They don't know, either. They thought it was ours."

"Gimme that goddam phone!"

The plane leveled out above the edge of the marshes about a mile away and kept coming, heedless of the volley of brilliant red warning flares fired from the top of McClusky's control tower. It slowed to a halt above the open area of concrete in front of the reception party, hung motionless for a moment, and then started sinking toward the ground. A handful of UNSA officers and technicians ran forward making frantic crossed-arms signals over their heads to wave it off, but fell back in disarray as it came on down regardless and settled. Caldwell strode ahead of the group, gesticulating angrily and shouting orders at the UNSA figures who were converging around the nose and making signs up at the cockpit.

"Imbeciles!" Danchekker muttered. "This kind of thing should never happen."

"It looks as if Murphy's back from vacation," Lyn said resignedly in Hunt's ear. But Hunt only half heard. He was staring hard at the Boeing with a strange look on his face. There was something very odd about that aircraft. It had landed in the middle of a sea of watery snow and slush churned up by the activity of the last few days, yet its landing jets hadn't thrown up the cloud of spray and vapor that they should have. So maybe it didn't have any landing jets. If that were so it might have looked like a 1227, but it certainly wasn't powered like one. And there didn't seem to be much response from the cockpit to the antics of the people below. In fact, unless Hunt's eyes were deceiving him, there wasn't anybody in the cockpit at all. Suddenly his face broke into a wide grin as the penny dropped.

"Vic, what is it?" Lyn asked. "What's funny?"

"What's the obvious way to hide something in the middle of an airfield from a surveillance system?" he asked. He gestured toward the plane, but before he could say any more a voice that could have belonged to a natural-born American boomed out across the apron from its direction.

"Greetings from Thurien to Earth, et cetera. Well, we made it. Too bad about the lousy weather."

All movement around the craft ceased instantly. A total silence fell. One by one the heads on every side jerked around and gaped at each other speechlessly as the message percolated through.

This was a starship? The *Shapieron* had stood nearly half a mile high. It was like having a little old lady show up at Tycho on a bicycle.

The forward passenger door opened, and a flight of steps unfolded itself to the ground. All eyes were riveted to the open doorway. The UNSA people up front drew back slowly while Hunt and his companions, with Heller and Packard a pace behind, moved forward to close in behind Caldwell and then slowed to a halt again uncertainly. Behind them the expectant cameras focused unwaveringly on the top of the steps.

"You'd better come on in," the voice suggested. "No sense in catching colds out there."

Heller and Packard exchanged bemused glances; none of their talks and briefings in Washington had prepared them for this. "I guess we just ad-lib as we go," Packard said in a low voice. He tried to summon up a reassuring grin, but it died somewhere on its way to his face.

"At least it's not happening in Siberia," Heller murmured.

Danchekker was fixing Hunt with a satisfied look. "If those utterances are not indicative of Ganymean humor at work, I'll accept creationism," he said triumphantly. The aliens could have warned them about the ship's disguise, Hunt agreed inwardly, but apparently they had been unable to resist making a mild joke out of it. And they obviously had little time for pomp and formality. It sounded like Ganymeans, all right.

They began moving toward the steps with Caldwell in the lead while the UNSA people opened up to let them pass through. Hunt was a couple of paces behind Caldwell as Caldwell was about to step onto the first stair. Caldwell emitted a startled exclamation and seemed to be lifted off the ground. As the others froze in their tracks, he was whisked upward over the stairway without any part of his body seeming to touch it, and deposited on his feet inside the doorway apparently none the worse for wear. He seemed a trifle shaken when he turned to look back down at them, but composed himself rapidly. "Well, what are you waiting for?" he growled. Hunt was obviously next in line. He drew a long, unsteady breath, shrugged, and stepped forward.

A strangely pleasant and warm sensation enveloped him, and a force of some kind drew him onward, carrying his weight off his legs. There was a blurred impression of the steps flowing by beneath his feet, and then he was standing beside Caldwell, who was watching him closely and not without a hint of amusement. Hunt was finally convinced—this was not a 1227.

They were in a fairly small, bare compartment whose walls were of a translucent amber material and glowed softly. It seemed to be an antechamber to whatever lay beyond another door leading aft, from which a stronger light was emanating. Before Hunt could take in any more of the details, Lyn sailed in through the doorway and landed lightly on the spot he had just vacated. "Smoking or non-smoking?" he asked.

"Where's the stewardess? I need a brandy."

Then Danchekker's voice shouted in sudden alarm from outside. "What in God's name is happening? Do something with this infernal contraption!" They looked back down. He was hanging a foot or two above the stairway, flailing his arms in exasperation after having apparently come to a halt halfway through the process of joining them. "This is ridiculous! Get me down from here!"

"You're crowding the doorway," the voice that had spoken before advised from somewhere around them. "How about moving on through and making more room?" They moved toward the inner doorway, and Danchekker appeared behind somewhat huffily a few seconds later. While Heller and Packard were following, Hunt and Lyn followed Caldwell into the body of the craft.

They found themselves in a short corridor that ran twenty feet or so toward the tail before stopping at another door, which was closed. A series of partitions extending from floor to ceiling divided the space on either side into a half-dozen or so narrow cubicles facing inward from left and right. As they moved along the corridor, they found that all the cubicles were identical, each containing some kind of recliner, luxuriously upholstered in red, facing inward toward the corridor and surrounded by a metal framework supporting panel inlays of a multicolored crystalline material and a bewildering layout of delicately constructed equipment whose purpose could have been anything. There was still no sign of life.

"Welcome aboard," the voice said. "If you'd each take a seat, we can begin."

"Who's doing the talking?" Caldwell demanded, looking around and overhead. "We'd appreciate the courtesy of your identifying yourself."

"My name is VISAR," the voice replied. "But I'm only the pilot and cabin crew. The people you're expecting will be here in a few minutes."

They were probably through the door at the far end, Hunt decided. It seemed odd. The voice reminded him of his first meeting with the Ganymeans, inside the *Shapieron* shortly after it had arrived in orbit over Ganymede. On that occasion, too, contact with the aliens had been through a voice functioning as interpreter, which turned out subsequently to belong to an entity called ZORAC—a supercomputer complex distributed through the ship and responsible for the operation of most of its systems and functions. "VISAR," he called out. "Are you a computer system built into this vehicle?"

"You could say that," VISAR answered. "It's about as near as we're likely to get. A small extension is there. The rest is scattered all over Thurien plus a whole list of other planets and places. You've got a link into the net."

"Are you saying this ship isn't operating autonomously?" Hunt asked. "You're interacting between here and Thurien in realtime?"

"Sure. How else could we have turned around the messages from Jupiter?"

Hunt was astounded. VISAR's statement implied a communications network distributed across star systems and operating with negligible delays. It meant that the point-to-point transfers, at least of energy, that he had often talked about with Paul Shelling at Navcomms were not only proved in principle, but up and running. No wonder Caldwell was looking stunned; it put Navcomms back in the Stone Age.

Hunt realized that Danchekker was now immediately behind him, peering curiously around, with Heller and Packard just inside the door. Where was Lyn? As if to answer his unvoiced equation, her voice spoke from inside one of the cubicles. "Say, it feels great. I could stand this for a week or two, maybe." He turned and saw that she was already lying back in one of the recliners and apparently enjoying it. He looked at Caldwell, hesitated for a moment, then moved into the adjacent cubicle, turned, and sat down, allowing his body to sink back into the recliner's yielding contours. It felt right for human rather than Ganymean proportions, he noted with interest. Had they built the whole craft in a week specifically for the occasion? That would have been typical of Ganymeans too.

A warm, pleasant feeling swept over him again and made him feel drowsy, causing his head to drop back automatically into the concave rest provided. He felt more relaxed than he could ever remember and suddenly didn't care if he never had to get up again. There was a vague impression of the woman—he couldn't recall her name—and the Secretary of something-or-other from Washington floating in front of him as if in a dream and gazing down at him curiously. "Try it. You'll like it," he heard himself murmuring distantly.

Some part of his mind was aware that he had been thinking clearly only moments before, but he was unable to remember what or really to care why. His mind had stopped functioning as a coherent entity and seemed to have disassembled into separate functions that he could observe in a detached kind of way as they continued to operate as isolated units instead of in concert. It should be troubling him, part of himself told the rest casually, and the rest agreed . . . but it wasn't.

Something was happening to his vision. The view of the upper part of the cubicle collapsed suddenly into meaningless blurs and smears, and then almost as quickly reassembled itself into an image that swelled, shrank, then faded and finally brightened once again. When it stabilized all the colors were wrong, like those of a false-color, computer-generated display. The colors reversed into complementary tones for a few insane seconds, overcorrected, and then suddenly were normal.

"Excuse these preliminaries," VISAR's voice said from somewhere. At least Hunt thought it was VISAR's; it was barely comprehensible, with the pitch sliding from a shrill whine through several octaves to finish in an almost inaudible rumble. "This process . . ." something completely unintelligible followed, ". . . one time, and after that there will be no . . ." a confusion of telescoped syllables, ". . . will be explained shortly." The last part was free from distortion.

And then Hunt became acutely conscious of the pressure of the recliner against his body, of the touch of his clothes against his skin, and even of the sensation of air flowing through his nostrils as he breathed. His body started to convulse, and he felt a sudden spasm of alarm. Then he realized that he was not moving at all; the impression was due to rapid variations in sensitivity taking place all over his skin. He felt hot all over, then cold, itchy for a moment, prickly for a moment, and then completely numb—and then suddenly normal once more.

Everything was normal. His mind had reintegrated itself, and all his faculties were in order. He wriggled his fingers and found that the invisible gel that had been immersing him was gone. He tried moving an arm, then the other arm; everything was fine.

"Feel free to get up," VISAR said. Hunt climbed slowly to his feet and stepped back into the corridor to find the others emerging and looking as bewildered as he felt. He looked past them at the door blocking the far end, but it was still closed.

"What do you suppose may have been the object of that exercise?" Danchekker asked, for once looking at a loss. Hunt could only shake his head.

And then Lyn's voice sounded from behind him. "Vic." It was just one word, but its ominous tone of warning spun him around instantly. She was staring wide-eyed along the corridor toward the door through which they had entered. He turned his head farther to follow her gaze.

Filling the doorway was the huge frame of a Ganymean, clad in a silvery garment that was halfway between a short cape and a loose jacket, worn over a trousered tunic of dark green. The deep, liquid violet, alien eyes surveyed them for a few seconds from the elongated, protruding face while they watched silently, waiting for a first move. Then the Ganymean announced, "I am Bryom Calazar. You are the people we have been expecting, I see. Please step this way. It's a little too crowded in here for introductions." With that he moved out of sight toward the outer door. Danchekker thrust out his jaw, drew himself up to his full height, and went back into the antechamber after him. After a moment's hesitation Lyn followed.

"This is absurd." Danchekker's voice reached Hunt just as he was stepping through behind Lyn. The statement was uttered in the tone of somebody clinging obstinately to reason and flatly denying that what his senses were reporting could be real. A split second later Lyn gasped, and an instant after that Hunt could see why. He had assumed that Calazar had come

from another compartment leading forward from the antechamber, but there was no such compartment. There didn't need to
be. The other Ganymeans were outside.

For McClusky Air Force Base, Alaska, and the Arctic had
all gone. Instead he was looking out at a completely different
world.

chapter eight

The plane, starship, or whatever the vessel was no longer stood
in the open at all. Hunt found himself staring out at the interior
of an enormous enclosed concourse formed by a mind-defying
interpenetration of angled planes and flowing surfaces of glowing amber and shades of green. It seemed to be the hub of an
intricate, three-dimensional dovetailing of thoroughfares, galleries, and shafts extending away up, down, and at all angles
through a conjunction of variously oriented spaces that baffled
the senses. He felt as if he had stepped into an Escher drawing
as he fought to extract some shred of sense from the contradictions of the same surfaces serving as floors here, walls there,
and transforming into roofs overhead elsewhere, while all over
the scene dozens of Ganymean figures went unconcernedly
about their business, some in inverted subsets of the whole,
others perpendicular, with one merging somehow into the other
until it was impossible to tell which direction was what. His
brain balked and gave up. He couldn't take in any more of it.

A group of about a dozen Ganymeans was standing a short
distance back from the doorway with the one who had introduced himself as Calazar positioned a few feet ahead. They
seemed to be waiting. After a few seconds Calazar beckoned.
In a complete daze and with his mind only barely able to register what was happening, Hunt felt himself being pulled almost hypnotically through the door and was aware only
vaguely that he was stepping out at floor level.

Everything exploded around him. The whole scene burst

into a spinning vortex of color that whirled around him on every side to destroy even the sense of orientation of his immediate surroundings that he had retained. The noise of a thousand banshees was crushing him. He was trapped inside a shrieking avalanche of light.

The vortex became a spinning tunnel into which he was hurtling helplessly at increasing speed. Shapes of light hurled themselves out of the formlessness ahead and exploded away into fragments only inches from his face. Never in his life had he known true panic, but it was there, clawing and tearing, paralyzing any ability to think. He was in a nightmare that he could neither control nor wake up from.

A black void opened up at the tunnel end and rushed at him. Suddenly it was calm. The blackness was . . . space. Black, infinite, star-studded space. He was out in space, looking at stars.

No. He was inside somewhere, looking at stars on a large screen. His surroundings were shadowy and indistinct—some kind of control room with vague suggestions of figures around him . . . human figures. He could feel himself shaking and perspiration drenching his clothes, but part of the panic had let go and was allowing his mind to function.

On the screen a bright object was enlarging steadily as it appeared to be approaching from the background of stars. There was something familiar about it. He felt as if he were reliving something he had experienced a long time ago. Part of a large metallic structure loomed in the foreground to one side of the view, highlighted by an eerie reddish glow coming from off-screen. It suggested part of whatever place the view was being captured from—a spacecraft of some kind. He was aboard a spacecraft watching something approaching on a screen, and he had been there before.

The object continued to enlarge, but even before it became recognizable he knew what it was: It was the *Shapieron*. He had gone back almost a year in time and was back inside the command center of *Jupiter Five* watching the arrival of the *Shapieron* as he had been when it first appeared over Ganymede. He had watched this sequence replayed from UNSA's archives many times since then and knew every detail of what was coming next. The ship slowed gradually and maneuvered to come to relative rest standing five miles off in parallel orbit, swinging around to present a side view of the graceful curves of its half-mile length of astronautic engineering.

And then something happened that he was completely unprepared for. Another object, moving fast and blazing white at the tail curved into the screen from one side, passed close by the *Shapieron*'s nose, and exploded in a huge flash a short distance beyond. Hunt stared at it, stunned. That wasn't the way it had happened.

And then a voice sounded from the screen—an American voice, speaking in the clipped tones of the military. "Warning missile launched. Attack salvo primed and locked on target. T-beams being directed in near-miss pattern, and destroyers moving in to take up close-escort formation. Orders are to fire for effect if alien attempts evasion."

Hunt shook his head and looked wildly from side to side, but the shadow figures around him paid no heed to his presence. "No!" he shouted. "It wasn't like that! This is all wrong!" The shadows remained heedless.

On the screen a flotilla of black, sinister-looking vessels moved into view from all directions to take up position around the Ganymean starship. "Alien is responding," the voice announced neutrally. "Commencing descent into parking orbit."

Hunt shouted out again in protest and leaped forward, at the same time wheeling around to appeal for a response from the shadow figures. But they had gone. The command center had gone. All of *Jupiter Five* had gone.

He was looking down on a huddle of metal domes and buildings standing beside a line of Vega ferries amid an icy wilderness that lay naked beneath the stars. It was Main Base on the surface of Ganymede. And on an open area to one side of the complex, dwarfing the Vegas behind, stood the awesome tower of the *Shapieron*. He had advanced by several days and was witnessing again the moment when the ship had just landed.

But instead of the simple but touching welcoming scene that he remembered, he saw a column of forlorn Ganymeans being herded across the ice from their ship between lines of impassive, heavily armed combat troops, under the muzzles of heavy weapons being trained from armored vehicles positioned farther back. And the base itself had acquired defense works, weapons emplacements, missile batteries, and all kinds of things that had never existed. It was insane.

He couldn't tell whether he was inside one of the domes and looking out over the scene as he had been at the time, or whether he was somehow floating disembodied at some other viewpoint. Again his immediate surroundings were indistinct. He swung around, moving in a dreamlike way in which his body had lost its substance, and found that he was alone. Even surrounded by ice and endless empty space he felt clammy and claustrophobic. The terror that had gripped him when he first stepped out of the alien vessel was still there, gnawing insistently and stripping away his powers of reason. "What is this?" he demanded in a voice that choked somewhere at the back of his throat. "I don't understand. What does this mean?"

"You don't remember?" the voice boomed deafeningly from nowhere and everywhere.

Hunt looked wildly in every direction, but there was nobody. "Remember what?" he whispered. "I remember none of this."

"You do not remember these events?" the voice challenged. "You were there."

An anger surged up inside him suddenly—a delayed-action reflex to protect him from the merciless assault on his mind and senses. *"No!"* he shouted. "Not like *that*! They never happened like that. What kind of lunacy is this?"

"How, then, did they happen?"

"They were our friends. They were welcomed. We gave gifts." His anger boiled over into a quivering rage. "Who are you? Are you mad? Show yourself."

Ganymede vanished, and a series of confused impressions poured by in front of his eyes, which inexplicably his mind assembled together into coherent meaning. There was a vision of the Ganymeans being taken into captivity by a stern and uncompromising American military . . . being allowed to repair their ship only after agreeing to divulge details of their technology . . . being taken to Earth to keep their side of the bargain . . . being dispatched ignominiously back into the depths of space.

"Was it not so?" the voice demanded.

"For Christ's sake, NO! Whoever you are, you're insane!"

"What parts are untrue?"

"All of it. What is the—"

A Soviet newscaster was talking hysterically. Although it was in Russian, Hunt somehow understood. The war had to start now, before the West could turn its advantage into something tangible . . . speeches from a balcony; crowds chanting and cheering . . . launchings of U.S. MIRV satellites . . . propaganda from Washington ... tanks, missile transporters, marching lines of Chinese infantry ... high-power radiation weapons hidden in deep space across the solar system. A race that had gone insane was marching off to doomsday with bands playing and flags waving.

"NO-O-O-O!" He heard his own voice rise to a shriek that seemed to come from all sides to engulf him, and then die somewhere far off in the distance. His strength evaporated abruptly, and he felt himself collapsing.

"He speaks the truth," a voice said from somewhere. It was calm and decisive, and sounded like a lone rock of sanity amid the maelstrom of chaos that had swept him out of the universe.

Collapsing ... falling ... blackness ... nothing.

chapter nine

Hunt was dozing in what felt like a soft and very comfortable armchair. He was relaxed and refreshed, as if he had been there for some time. The memory of his experience was still vivid, but it lingered only as something that he regarded in a detached, almost academically curious, kind of way. The terror had gone. The air around him smelled fresh and slightly scented, and subdued music was playing in the background. After a few seconds it registered as a Mozart string quartet. What kind of insanity was he part of now?

He opened his eyes, straightened up, and looked around. He was in an armchair, and the chair was part of an ordinary-looking room, furnished in contemporary style with another, similar chair, reading desk, a large wooden table in the center, a side table near the door set with an ornate vase of roses, and a thick carpet of dark brown pile that blended fairly well with the predominantly orange and brown decor. There was a single window behind him, covered by heavy drapes that were closed and billowing gently in the breeze coming through from the outside. He looked down at himself and found that he was wearing a dark blue, open-necked shirt and light gray slacks. There was nobody else in the room.

After a few seconds he got up, found that he felt fine, and strolled across the room to part the drapes curiously. Outside was a pleasant, summery scene that could have been part of any major city on Earth. Tall buildings gleamed clean and white in the sun, familiar trees and open green spaces beckoned, and Hunt could see the curve of a wide river immediately below, an older-style bridge with a railed parapet and rounded arches, familiar models of groundcars moving along the roadways, and processions of airmobiles in the sky. He let the drapes fall back as they had been and glanced at his watch, which seemed to be working normally. Less than twenty minutes had passed since the "Boeing" touched down at McClusky. Nothing made sense.

He turned his back to the window and thrust his hands into his pockets while he thought back and tried to remember something that had been puzzling him even before he stepped out of the spacecraft. It had been something trivial, something that had barely registered in the few moments that had elapsed between Calazar's brief appearance inside the craft and Hunt's first glimpse of the stupefying scene that had greeted him outside just before everything went crazy. It had been something to do with Calazar.

And then it came to him. In the *Shapieron*, ZORAC had interpreted between Ganymeans and humans by means of earpiece and throat-mike devices that provided normal-sounding synthesized voices, but which did not synchronize with the facial movements of the original speakers. But Calazar had spoken without any such aids, and apparently quite effortlessly. What made it all the more peculiar was that the Ganymean larynx produced a low, guttural articulation and was utterly incapable of reproducing a human pitch even approximately. So how had Calazar done it, and without looking like a badly dubbed movie at that?

Well, he wasn't going to get nearer any answers by standing here, he decided. The door looked normal enough, and there was only one way to find out whether it was locked or not. He was halfway toward it when it opened and Lyn walked in, looking cool and comfortable in a short-sleeved pullover top and slacks. He stopped dead and stared at her while part of him braced itself instinctively for her to hurl herself across the room and throw her arms around his neck while sobbing in true heroine tradition. Instead she stopped just inside the door and stood casually inspecting the room.

"Not bad," she commented. "The carpet's too dark, though. It should be a more red rust." The carpet promptly changed to a more red rust.

Hunt stared at it for a few seconds, blinked, and then looked up numbly. "How the hell did you do that?" he asked, looking down again to make sure that he hadn't imagined it. He hadn't.

She looked surprised. "It's VISAR. It can do anything. Haven't you been talking to it?" Hunt shook his head. Lyn's face became puzzled. "If you didn't know, how come you're wearing different clothes? What happened to your Nanook outfit?"

Hunt could only shake his head. "I don't know. I don't know how I got here, either." He stared down at the red rust carpet again. "Amazing . . . I think I could use a drink."

"VISAR," Lyn said in a slightly raised voice. "How about a scotch, straight, no ice?" A glass half filled with an amber liquid materialized from nowhere on the table beside Hunt. Lyn picked it up and offered it to him nonchalantly. He reached out hesitantly to touch with it a fingertip, at the same time half hoping that it wouldn't be there. It was. He took the glass unsteadily from her hand and tested it with a sip, then downed a third of the remainder in one gulp. The warmth percolated smoothly down through his chest and after a few moments had worked a small miracle of its own. Hunt drew a long breath, held it for a few seconds, then exhaled it slowly but still shakily.

"Cigarette?" Lyn inquired. Hunt nodded without thinking. A cigarette, already lit, appeared between his fingers. Don't even ask about it, he told himself.

It all had to be some kind of elaborate hallucination. How, when, why, or where he didn't know, but it seemed that he had little choice for the moment but to go along with it. Perhaps this whole preliminary interlude had been staged by the Thuriens to provide a period of adjustment and familiarization or something like that. If so, he could see their point. This was like dumping an alchemist from the Middle Ages into the middle of a computerized chemical plant. Thurien, or wherever this was, was going to take some getting used to, he realized. Having decided that much, he felt that probably he was over the biggest hurdle already. But how had Lyn managed to adapt so quickly? Maybe there were disadvantages to being a scientist that he hadn't thought about before.

When he looked up and studied her face, he could see now that her superficial calm was being forced in order to control an underlying bemusement not far short of his own. Her mind was temporarily blocking itself off from the full impact of what it all meant, probably in a way similar to the delayed shock that was a common reaction to exceptionally painful news such as the death of a close relative. He could detect no sign of her having been through anything as traumatic as he had. At least that was something to be thankful for.

He moved over to one of the chairs and turned to perch himself on an arm. "So . . . how did you get here?" he asked.

"Well, I was right behind you on the gravity conveyor, or whatever you'd call it, from that crazy place that we all walked out into from the planet, and then . . ." She broke off as she caught the perplexed expression creeping across Hunt's face. "You don't know what I'm talking about, do you?"

He shook his head. "What gravity conveyor?"

Lyn frowned at him uncertainly. "We all walked out of the plane? . . . There was this big bright place with everything upside down and sideways? . . . Something like whatever lifted us up the stairs picked us all up and took us off along one of the tubes—a big yellow-and-white one? . . ." She was listing the items slowly and intoning them as questions, all the while watching his face intently as if trying to help him identify the point at which he had lost the thread, but it was obvious already that she had experienced something quite different right from the beginning.

He waved a hand in front of his face. "Okay, skip the details. How did you get separated from the others?"

Lyn started to reply and then stopped suddenly and frowned, as if realizing for the first time that her own recollections were by no means as complete as she had thought. "I'm not sure . . ." She hesitated. "Somehow I ended up . . . I don't know where it was. . . . There was this big organization chart—colored boxes with names in them, and lines of who reports to who—that had to do with some crazy kind of United *States* Space *Force*." Her face grew more confused as she replayed the memory in her mind. "There were lots of UNSA names on it that I knew, but with ranks and things that didn't make any sense. Gregg's name was there as a general, and mine was right underneath as a major." She shook her head in a way that told Hunt not to bother asking her to explain it.

Hunt remembered the transcripts he had read of the Thurien messages received at Farside, which had been baffling in their suggestion of a militarized Earth divided in an East–West lineup that was strangely reminiscent of the reconstructions of how Minerva had been just before the final, cataclysmic Cerian–Lambian war. And the grilling that he had just gone through, if that was the right word for it, had echoed the same theme. There had to be a connection. "What happened then?" he asked.

"VISAR started talking and asked me if that was an accurate representation of the outfit I worked for," Lyn replied. "I told it that most of the names were right, but the rest was garbage. It asked some questions about a couple of weapons programs that Gregg was supposed to be mixed up with. Then it showed me some pictures of a surface-bombardment satellite that this U.S.S.F. was supposed to have put in orbit, and a big radiation projector on the Moon that never existed. I told VISAR it was out of its mind. We talked about it for a bit, and in the end we got quite friendly."

All that hadn't happened in ten minutes, Hunt thought. There must have been some kind of time-compression process involved. "There wasn't anything . . . 'high-pressure' about all this?" he inquired.

Lyn looked at him, surprised. "No way. It was all very civilized and nice. That was when I mentioned that I felt strange wearing those clothes indoors, and suddenly—*zap!*" She gestured down at herself. "Instant outfit. Then I found out more about VISAR's tricks. How long do you think it'll be before IBM gets one on the market?"

Hunt stood up and began pacing across the room, noting absently as he moved that his cigarette didn't seem to be accumulating any ash to be disposed of. It was some kind of interrogation procedure, he decided. The Thuriens had obviously gotten confused over the situation on today's Earth, and for some reason it was important to them to have the correct story. If that was the case, they certainly hadn't wasted any time over it. Perhaps Hunt's experience had been a shock tactic designed to guarantee straight answers at the optimum moment when he had been totally unprepared and too disoriented to have fabricated anything. If so, it had certainly worked, he reflected grimly.

"After that I asked where you were. VISAR directed me out through a door and along a corridor, and here I am," Lyn completed.

Hunt was about to say something more when the phone rang. He looked around and noticed it for the first time. It was a standard domestic datagrid terminal and went so naturally with the surroundings that it hadn't registered previously. The call-tone sounded again.

"Better answer it," Lyn suggested.

Hunt walked over to the corner, pulled up a chair, sat down, and touched a key on the terminal to accept. His jaw dropped open in disbelief as he found himself staring at the features of the operations controller at McClusky.

"Dr. Hunt," the controller said, sounding relieved. "Just a routine check to see if everything's okay. You people have been in there for a while now. Any problems?"

For what seemed a long time, Hunt could only stare back blankly. He'd never heard of phone calls from the real world intruding into hallucinations before. It had to be part of the hallucination too. What was somebody supposed to say to hallucinatory operations controllers? "How are you talking to us?" he managed at last, succeeding with some effort in making his voice almost normal.

"We got a transmission from the plane a while ago saying it would be okay for us to use a low-power, narrow beam aimed straight at it," the controller replied. "We set it up and waited, but when nothing came through we thought we'd better try calling you."

Hunt closed his eyes for a moment, then opened them again and glanced sideways at Lyn. She didn't understand it, either. "Are you saying that plane is still out there?" he asked, looking back at the screen.

The controller looked puzzled. "Why . . . sure . . . I'm looking right at it out the window." Pause. "Are you sure everything's okay in there?"

Hunt sat back woodenly, and his mind jammed up. Lyn stepped past him and stooped in front of the screen. "Everything's okay," she said. "Look, we're a bit busy right now. Call you back in a few minutes, okay?"

"Just as long as we know. Okay, talk to you later." The controller vanished from the screen.

Lyn's composure evaporated with the picture. She looked down at Hunt, visibly worried and frightened for the first time since entering the room. "It's still out there. . . ." Her voice was coming unevenly as she struggled to keep it under control. "Vic—what's happening?"

Hunt scowled around the room as the indignation that he had been suppressing at last came surging up inside. "VISAR," he called on impulse. "Can you hear me?"

"I'm here," the familiar voice answered.

"That plane that landed at McClusky—it's still there. We just talked to them on the phone."

"I know," VISAR agreed. "I put the call through."

"Isn't it about time you told us what the hell's going on?"

"The Thuriens were intending to explain it when you meet them very shortly," VISAR replied. "You are due an apology, and they want to make it to you personally, not second-hand through me."

"Then would you mind telling us where the hell we are?" Hunt said, not feeling very mollified by the statement.

"Sure. You're in the *perceptron*, which as you've just told me is still on the apron at McClusky." Hunt caught Lyn's eye in a mute exchange of baffled looks. She shook her head weakly and sank down into one of the chairs. "You don't look very convinced," VISAR commented. "A small demonstration, perhaps?"

Hunt felt his mouth opening and closing, and heard sounds coming out. But he wasn't making it happen. He was moving like a puppet to the pulls of invisible strings. "Excuse me," his mouth said as his head turned itself toward Lyn. "Don't worry about this—VISAR will explain. I'll be back in a few minutes."

And then he was lying back on something yielding and soft.

"Voilà!" VISAR's voice pronounced from somewhere overhead.

He opened his eyes and looked around, but a few seconds went by before he realized where he was.

He was back in the recliner inside one of the cubicles in the ship that had landed at McClusky.

Everything seemed very quiet and still. He rose to his feet and moved out into the corridor to peer into the adjacent cubicle. Lyn was still there, lying back in the recliner looking relaxed, her eyes closed and her face serene. He looked down and noticed for the first time that, like her, he was wearing UNSA arctic clothing again. He moved along to inspect the other cubicles and found all the others were there too, looking much the same.

"Take a walk outside and check it out," VISAR's voice suggested. "We'll still be here when you get back."

Hunt made his way dazedly to the door at the forward end of the corridor, stopped for a moment and braced himself for anything, and stepped through into the antechamber. McClusky and Alaska were back again. Through the open outer door he could see figures stirring and starting to move forward as they saw him. He moved toward the door, and seconds later was on his feet at the bottom of the access stairway. The figures converged around him, and excited questions assailed him from all sides as he began walking across the apron toward the mess hall.

"What's happening in there?"

"Are there Ganymeans inside?"

"Are they coming out?"

"How many of them are there?"

"Just . . . talking so far. What? Yes . . . well, sort of. I'm not sure. Look, give me a few minutes. I need to check something."

Inside the mess hall he made straight for the control room, set up in one of the front rooms. The controller and his two operators had watched Hunt through the window that looked out across the apron and were waiting expectantly. "Vic, how's it going?" the controller greeted as he came in the door.

"Fine," Hunt murmured absently. He stared hard at the consoles and screens set up around the room and forced his mind to go back over what had happened since they entered the craft. What he was seeing right now was real. Everything around him was real. The phone call had been part of something that hadn't been real. Obviously it couldn't have worked the other way around; reality couldn't communicate into the realm of the hallucinatory via radio. Obviously?

"Have you had any contact from that plane since we went inside?" he asked, turning to glance at the control-room crew.

"Why . . . yes." The controller looked suddenly worried. "You talked to us yourself a few minutes ago. You're sure everything's . . . all right?"

Hunt brought a hand up to massage his brow and give the

confusion boiling inside his head time to die down a little. "How did you get through?" he asked.

"We got a signal from it earlier telling us we could couple in via a low-power beam, like I told you. I just asked for you by name."

"Do it again," Hunt said.

The controller moved in front of the supervisory console, tapped a command into its touchboard array, and spoke toward the two-way audio grille above the main screen. "McClusky Control to alien. Alien vessel, come in please."

"Acknowledged," a voice answered.

"VISAR?" Hunt said, recognizing it.

"Hi again. Convinced now?"

Hunt's eyes narrowed thoughtfully as he stared at the blank screen. At last the wheels of his brain felt as if they were sorting themselves out and lining themselves up on the right axles again. There was one obvious thing for him to try. "Put me through to Lyn Garland," he said.

"One moment."

The screen came to life, and a second later Lyn was looking out at him, framed by the background of the room he had recently been in. It must have been equally clear that Hunt was calling from McClusky, but her face did not register undue surprise. VISAR must have been doing some explaining.

"You sure get around," she commented drily.

A shadow of a smile formed on Hunt's face as the first glimmer of light began showing through it all. "Hi," he said. "Question: What happened after I last talked to you?"

"You vanished into thin air—just like that. It gave me a bit of a fright, but VISAR's been straightening me out about a lot of things." She held up a hand and wriggled her fingers in front of her face, at the same time shaking her head wonderingly. "I can't believe I'm not really doing this. It's all happening inside my head? It's incredible!"

Right at that moment she probably knew more about what was going on than he did, Hunt reflected. But he thought he had the general idea now. An instant communications link to Thurien . . . miracles worked to order . . . Ganymeans talking in English. . . . And what had VISAR called that vessel—the *perceptron*? The pieces started dropping into place.

"Just keep talking to VISAR," he said. "I'll be back in a few minutes." Lyn smiled the kind of smile that said she knew everything would work out okay; Hunt winked, then cut off the screen.

"Would you mind telling us what's going on?" the controller asked. "I mean . . . we're only supposed to be running this operation."

"Just give me a second," Hunt said, entering the code to reactivate the channel. He turned his face toward the grille. "VISAR?"

"You rang?"

"That place we walked out of the perceptron into—does it exist, or did you invent it?"

"It exists. It's part of a place called Vranix, which is an old city on Thurien."

"Did we see it the way it is right now?"

"Yes, you did."

"So you have to be relaying instantly between here and Thurien."

"You're getting the idea."

Hunt thought for a second. "What about the room with the carpet?"

"I invented that. A special effect—faked. We thought that maybe some familiar-looking surroundings would help you get used to how we do things. Figured the rest out yet?"

"I'll try a long shot," Hunt said. "How about total sensory stimulation and monitoring, plus an instant communications link. We never went to Thurien; you brought Thurien here. And Lyn never answered any phone call. You pumped it straight into her nervous system along with everything else she thinks she's doing, and you manufactured all the appropriate AV data to send through the local beam. How's that?"

"Pretty good," VISAR replied, managing to inject a strong note of approval into its voice. "So are you ready to rejoin the party? You're due to meet the Thuriens in a few minutes."

"I'll talk to you later," Hunt said, and cut the connection.

"Now would you mind telling us what the hell this is all about?" the controller invited.

Hunt's expression was distant, his voice slow and thoughtful. "That's just a flying phone booth out there on the apron. It's got equipment inside that somehow couples directly into the perceptual parts of the nervous system and transfers a total impression from a remote place. What you saw on the screen a minute ago was extracted straight out of Lyn's mind. A computer translated it into audiovisual modulations on a signal beam and directed it into your antenna. It processed the transmission from here in the opposite direction."

Ten minutes later Hunt reentered the perceptron and sat down in the same recliner that he had occupied before. "What do I say—'Home, James'?" he asked aloud.

This time there were no preliminary sensory disturbances. He was instantly back in the room with Lyn, who seemed to have been expecting him to reappear; VISAR had evidently forewarned her. He looked around the room curiously to see if he could detect any hint of its being a creation manufactured by a computer, but there was nothing. Every detail was authentic. It was uncanny. As with VISAR's command of English and the data needed to disguise the perceptron as a Boeing, all the information must have been extracted from Earth's communications links; practically everything necessary had been communicated electronically from somewhere at some time or another. No wonder the Thuriens had been particular about keeping everything connected with this business out of the network!

He reached out and ran a finger experimentally down Lyn's arm. It felt warm and solid. The whole thing was exactly what he had said to VISAR—a *total* sensory stimulation process, probably acting on the brain centers directly and bypassing the neural inputs. It was astounding.

Lyn glanced down at his hand, then looked up and eyed him suspiciously. "I don't know if it's that authentic, either," she told him. "And right now I'm not that curious. Forget it."

Before Hunt could reply, the phone rang again. He answered it. It was Danchekker, looking ready to commit mayhem.

"This is monstrous! Outrageous!" The veins at his temples were throbbing visibly. "Have you any idea of the provocation to which I have been subjected? Where are you in this computerized lunatic asylum? What kind of—"

"Hold it, Chris. Calm down." Hunt held up a hand. "It's not as bad as you think. All that's—"

"*Not as bad?* Where in God's name are we? How do we get out of it? Have you talked to the others? By what right do these alien creatures presume to—"

"You're not anywhere, Chris. You're still on the ground at McClusky. So am I. We all are. What's happened is—"

"Don't be preposterous! It's quite evident that—"

"Have you talked to VISAR? It'll explain it all far better than I can. Lyn's with me and—"

"No I have not, and what's more I have no intention of doing anything of the kind. If these Thuriens do not possess the common courtesy to—"

Hunt sighed. "VISAR, take the professor home and straighten him out, could you. I don't think I'm up to dealing with him right now."

"I'll handle it," VISAR replied, and Danchekker promptly vanished from the screen leaving an empty room in the frame.

"Amazing," Hunt murmured. There were times, he thought, when he would have liked to be able to pull that stunt with Danchekker himself.

A knock sounded lightly on the door. Hunt and Lyn's heads jerked around to look at it, turned back to meet each other's questioning looks, then stared at the door again. Lyn shrugged and moved across the room toward it. Hunt switched off the terminal and looked up to find the eight-foot-tall figure of a Ganymean straightening up after ducking through the doorway. Lyn stood speechless with surprise as she held the door open.

"Dr. Hunt and Miss Garland," the Ganymean said. "First, on behalf of all of us, I apologize for the somewhat bizarre welcome. It was necessary for some very important reasons, which will be explained when we all get together very shortly. I hope that our leaving you on your own like this hasn't seemed too bad-mannered, but we thought that perhaps a short period of adjustment might be beneficial. I am Porthik Eesyan—one of those you were expecting to meet."

chapter ten

Eesyan was subtly different in form from the Ganymeans of the *Shapieron*, Hunt noticed as they walked. He had the same massive torso lines beneath his loose-fitting yellow jerkin and elaborately woven shirt of red and amber metallic threads, and the same six-fingered hands, each with two thumbs, but his skin was darker than the grays that Hunt remembered—almost black—and seemed smoother in texture; his build was lighter and more slender, his height slightly less than would have been normal, and his lower face and skull, though still elongated significantly, had receded and broadened into a more rounded head that was closer to the human profile.

"We can move objects from place to place instantaneously by means of artificially generated spinning black holes," Eesyan told them. "As your own theories predict, a rapidly spinning black hole flattens out into a disk, and eventually becomes a toroid with the mass concentrated at the rim. In that situation the singularity exists across the central aperture and can be approached axially without catastrophic tidal effects. The aperture affords an 'entry port' into a hyperrealm described by laws not subject to the conventional restrictions of ordinary space-time. Creating such an entry port also gives rise to a hypersymmetric effect that appears as a projection elsewhere in normal space, and which functions as a coupled exit port. By controlling the dimensions, spin, orientation, and certain other parameters of the initial hole, we can select with considerable accuracy the location of the exit up to distances in the order of several tens of light-years."

With Eesyan between Vic and Lyn, they were walking along a broad, enclosed, brightly illuminated arcade of soaring lines, gleaming sculptures, and vast openings, which led into other spaces. There were more Escher-like distortions and inversions here and there in the scene, but nothing as overwhelming as the sight they had first seen from the perceptron. Apparently Ganymean gravitic engineering tricks came with the architecture on Thurien. For this was Thurien. They had emerged from the room and walked through a series of galleries and a huge domed space bustling with Ganymeans, eventually to this place, the illusory blending so smoothly into reality that Hunt had missed the point along the way at which the switch from one to the other had taken place. The meeting between the two worlds was about to take place, Eesyan had informed them, and he had been assigned to escort them there personally. No doubt VISAR could have transferred them there instantly, Hunt thought, but this seemed a more natural way while they were still "acclimatizing." And having an opportunity to get to know at least one of the aliens informally in advance helped the process further. Probably that was the idea.

"That must be how you got the perceptron to Earth," Hunt said.

"Almost to Earth," Eesyan told him. "A black hole large enough to take a sizable object creates a significant gravitational disturbance over a large distance. Therefore we don't project things like that into the middle of planetary systems; it would disrupt clocks and calendars and so on. We exited the perceptron outside the Solar System, and it had to make the last lap in a more conventional way."

"So a round trip needs four conventional stages," Lyn commented. "Two one way, and two the other?"

"Correct."

"Which explains why it took something like a day to make it from Thurien to Earth," Hunt said.

"Yes. Instant planet-to-planet hopping is out. But *communications* is another matter entirely. We can send messages by beaming a gamma frequency microlaser into a microscopic black-hole toroid that can be generated in equipment capable of operating on planetary surfaces without undesirable side effects. So instant planet-to-planet datalinks are practicable. What's more, generating the microscopic black holes needed for them doesn't require the enormous amount of energy that holes big enough to send ships through do. So we don't do a lot of instantaneous people-moving unless we have to; we prefer moving *information* instead."

It fitted in with what Hunt already knew: he and Lyn were really at McClusky, and all the information they were perceiving was being transmitted there through VISAR. "That explains how the information gets sent," he said. "But what's the input to the system? How is it originated in the first place?"

"Thurien is a fully 'wired' planet," Ecsyan explained. "So are most of the other planets in the portions of the Galaxy where we have spread. VISAR exists all over those worlds, and in other places between, as a dense network of sensors located inside the structures of buildings and cities, distributed invisibly across mountains, forests, and plains, and in orbit above planetary surfaces. By combining and interpolating between its data inputs, it is able to compute and synthesize the complete sensory input that would be experienced by a person located at any particular place.

"VISAR bypasses the normal input channels to the brain and stimulates symbolic neural patterns directly with focused arrays of high-resolution spatial stress-waves. Thus it can inject straight into the mind all the information that would be received by somebody physically present at whatever place is specified. Also it monitors the neural activity of the voluntary motor system and reproduces faithfully all the feedback sensations that would accompany muscular movements and so forth. The net result is to create an illusion of actually being at a remote location which is indistinguishable from the real thing. Physically transporting the body would add nothing."

"Star travel the easy way," Lyn murmured. She gazed around as they came to the end of the arcade and turned off to begin walking across a curved, sweeping surface that had looked like a wall a minute ago, but now seemed to be pivoting slowly as they moved onto it and lifting the whole of the arcade and the structures connected to it up at an increasing angle behind them. "This is all real and twenty light-years away?" she said, still sounding disbelieving. "I really haven't come here?"

"Can you tell the difference?" Eesyan asked her.

"How about you, Porthik?" Hunt asked as a new thought struck him. "Are you actually here . . . there . . . whatever, in Vranix, or what?"

"I'm on an artificial world twenty million miles from Thurien," Eesyan replied. "Calazar is on Thurien, but six thousand miles from Vranix at a place called Thurios—the principal city of Thurien. Vranix is an old city that we keep preserved for sentimental and traditional reasons. Frenua Showm, whom you were also expecting to meet and will very shortly, is on a planet called *Crayses*, which is in a star system about nine light-years from Gistar."

Lyn was looking puzzled. "I'm not quite sure I get this," she said. "How do we all manage to get consistent impressions when we're in different places? How do I see you there, Vic next to you, and all this around us when it's scattered all over the Galaxy?" Hunt was still too boggled by what Eesyan had said a moment earlier to be able to ask anything.

"VISAR manufactures composite impressions from data originated in different places and delivers them as a total package," Eesyan replied. "It can combine visual, tactile, audile, and other details of an environment with data synthesized from monitoring the neural activity of other persons linked into the system, and provide each individual with a complete, personalized impression of being in that environment and interacting physically and verbally with the others. Hence we can visit other worlds, travel among other cultures, convene for meetings in other star systems, and make visits to artificial worlds out in space ... and be home in an instant. We do move around physically to some degree, of course, for example in recreation or for activities that require physical presence, but for the most part our long-range business and travel is conducted via electronics and gravitics."

The surface continued curving over and brought them out into a wide circular gallery that looked down over a railed parapet on a fairly busy plaza of some kind a level below. Between the flowing curves and surfaces enclosing the space from above, they could see part of the floor of the arcade that they had been walking along a few minutes earlier. At least, it had seemed like a floor at the time. But by now they were beginning to get used to that kind of thing.

"When we first sat down inside that planet at McClusky, all my senses went haywire for a while," Lyn said as she thought back. "What was that all about?"

"VISAR tuning in to your personal cerebral patterns and activity levels," Eesyan told her. "It was making adjustments until it obtained correct feedback responses. They vary somewhat from individual to individual. The process is a one-time thing. You could think of it as somewhat like fingerprinting."

"Porthik," Hunt said after they had continued for some distance in silence. "That stunt you pulled on me right at the beginning—you've been getting some mixed-up stories about Earth, and you needed to check them out. Right?"

"It was extremely important, as Calazar will explain," Eesyan answered.

"But was it necessary?" Hunt queried. "If VISAR can access symbolic neural patterns directly, why couldn't it have simply pulled whatever it wanted to know straight out of my memory? That way there wouldn't have been any risk of wrong answers."

"Technically that would be possible," Eesyan agreed. "However, for reasons of privacy such things are not permitted under our laws, and VISAR is programmed in a way that restricts it to supplying primary sensory inputs to the brain and monitoring motor and certain other terminal outputs only. It communicates only what would be seen, heard, felt, and so on; it does not read minds."

"How about the others?" Hunt inquired. "Do you have any idea how they're getting along? I wouldn't exactly recommend your welcoming ceremonies as the best way of making friends."

Eesyan's mouth puckered in the way that Hunt had long ago recognized as the Ganymean equivalent of a smile. "You needn't worry. They haven't all been getting to the bottom of VISAR as quickly as you did, so some of them are still a little confused, but apart from that they're fine."

The confusion had been intentional, Hunt realized suddenly. It was a deliberate measure calculated to defuse any animosity left lingering as a result of the initial shock tactics. Eesyan's showing up to escort them to wherever they were going was no doubt part of the plan too. "It didn't seem quite like that when I talked to Chris Danchekker on the phone a few minutes before you arrived," he said, grinning to himself as he caught the expression on Lyn's face.

"As a matter of fact, you and Professor Danchekker did have comparatively hard rides," Eesyan admitted. "We're sorry about that, but the two of you were unique in that you both possessed firsthand knowledge of certain events connected with the *Shapieron* that we were particularly anxious to obtain. The experiences of your companions were more in the nature of discussions concerning their various specialized fields. Their accounts corroborated one another's perfectly. It was very illuminating."

"What happened with you and Chris?" Lyn asked, looking across at Hunt.

"I'll tell you about it later," he replied. What they did might have been unconventional, but it had certainly worked, he told himself with grudging admiration. In those first few minutes the Ganymeans had obtained and verified more information than they could have in days of talking. If it was that important, he could hardly blame them after the way they had been messed around by the UN at Farside. He wondered if Caldwell and the others saw things the same way. It wouldn't be long before he found out, he saw as he looked ahead of them. They seemed to have arrived at their destination.

They were walking down a shallow, fan-shaped ramp that

was taking them through a final arch out into the open. They emerged into a descending arrangement of interlocking geometric forms, terraces, and esplanades that formed one side of a large circular layout echoing the same theme. The lowermost, central part, directly ahead of them, consisted of a forum of seats set in tiers and facing one another from all four sides of a rectangular floor. The whole place was a vast composition of color and form set among pools of liquid fluorescence fed by slow-motion rivers and fountains of shimmering light. A number of figures were assembled on three sides of the floor, all Ganymean. They were standing and seemed to be waiting. At the front and in the center of a raised section of seats on one side was Calazar, recognizable by his dark green tunic and silvery cape.

And then Hunt saw Caldwell's stocky frame emerge from another entrance on the far side of an open area to his right, accompanied by a Ganymean . . . and beyond Caldwell, Heller and Packard appeared with another Ganymean, Heller walking calmly and with assurance, Packard staring from side to side and looking bewildered. Hunt turned his head the other way in time to see Danchekker walking through an archway, waving his arms and remonstrating to a Ganymean on either side; evidently it was taking two of them to handle him. The arrivals had been synchronized perfectly. It couldn't have been accidental.

Suddenly Lyn gasped and stopped, her face raised to stare at something overhead. Hunt followed her gaze . . . and stopped . . . then gasped.

From three sides beyond the raised rim of the place they were in, three slim spires of pink ivory converged upward above their heads for an inestimable distance before blending into an inverted cascade of terraces and ramparts that broadened and unfolded upward and away for what must have been miles. Above it—it didn't make sense, but above it, where the sky should have been, the scene mushroomed out into a mind-defying fusion of structures of staggering dimensions that marched away as far as the eye could see in one direction, and fringed a distant ocean in the other. It had to be the city of Vranix. But it was all hanging miles over their heads and upside down.

And then the realization hit him. They had walked out into the sky. The three pink spires "rising" from around them in fact surmounted an enormous tower that projected upward from the city, supporting a circular platform that held the place they were in. But they had come out on the *underside* of it! Their senses had become sufficiently disoriented in the Ganymean labyrinth for them to have inverted without realizing it, and they had walked outside in some locally generated gravity effect to find themselves gazing down over the surface of Thurien stretching away over their heads.

Caldwell and the others had seen it too, and were just standing, staring. Even Danchekker had stopped talking and was looking upward, his mouth hanging half open. It was the Ganymeans' final trump card and master stroke, Hunt realized. Even if any of his companions had been harboring any lingering resentments, they would be too overwhelmed by this—timed precisely to hit them minutes before the meeting was due to begin—to protest very strongly. He liked these aliens, he decided, strange though the thought seemed in some ways at that particular moment. He always enjoyed seeing professionals in action.

One by one the dazed figures of the Terrans came slowly back to life and began moving again, down toward the central forum where the Ganymeans were waiting.

chapter eleven

"We owe you an apology," Calazar said bluntly as soon as the introductions had been completed. "I know that's not supposed to be the best way of starting a meeting by Earth's customs, but I've never really understood why. If it needs saying, let's say it and get it out of the way. As you no doubt appreciate by now, we needed to check some facts that are important to us, and to you too I would imagine. It seems just as well that we did."

It was going to be a far less formal affair than he had been half prepared for, Hunt noted with relief. He wondered if what he was hearing was an accurate translation of Calazar's words or a liberal interpretation concocted by VISAR. He had assumed that an opening on this note would be unavoidable, and was ready for some fireworks there and then. But as he looked around he could see that the Ganymean defusing tactics appeared to be having their desired effect. Caldwell and Heller seemed in command of themselves and were looking purposeful as if by no means ready to let the matter just go at that, but at the same time they were subdued sufficiently to wait and see what developed before making an issue out of anything. Danchekker had obviously come in spoiling for a fight, but the psychological left hook that the Ganymeans had delivered out of the blue— literally—at the last moment had temporarily knocked it out of him. Packard appeared to be in some kind of trance; in his case the tranquilizer had, perhaps, worked too well.

After pausing, Calazar continued, "On behalf of our entire race, we welcome you to our world and to our society. The threads that have traced the evolution of our two kinds, and which have remained separated until now, have at last crossed. We hope that from this point on they will continue to remain entwined for the benefit and greater learning of all of us." With that he sat down. It was simple, Hunt thought, and seemed a good way of getting things moving.

The Terran faces turned toward Packard, who was officially the most senior in rank and therefore the designated spokesman. It took him a few seconds to realize that the others were looking at him. Then he looked uncertainly from side to side, gripped the sides of his chair, moistened his lips, and rose slowly and somewhat unsteadily to his feet. "On behalf of the . . . government of . . ." The words dried up. He stood swaying slightly and staring dumbstruck at the rows of alien countenances arrayed before him, and then raised his head and shook it disbelievingly at the spectacle of the tower falling away into the metropolis of Vranix and the panorama of Thurien stretching off on every side beyond. For an instant Hunt thought he was going to collapse. And then he vanished.

"I regret that the Secretary of State appears to be temporarily indisposed," VISAR informed the assembly.

That was enough to break the spell. At once Caldwell was on his feet, his eyes steely and his mouth clamped in a downturned line. Heller had also started to rise, but she checked herself and sank back into her seat as Caldwell beat her to it by a split second. "This has gone too far," Caldwell grated, fixing his eyes on Calazar. "Save the niceties. We came here in good faith. You owe us an explanation."

Instantly everything changed. The forum, the tower, Vranix, and the overhead canopy of Thurien were gone. Instead they were all indoors in a fairly large but not huge room with a domed ceiling, which contained a wide, circular table of iridescent crystal and a centerpiece. The principal participants were placed around it in the same relative positions as before with Caldwell still standing; the other Ganymeans who had been present earlier were looking on from raised seats behind. Compared to the previous setting this one felt protective and secure.

"We underestimated the impact," Calazar said hastily. "Perhaps this will be closer to what you are used to."

"Never mind the Alice-in-Wonderland effects," Caldwell said. "Okay, you've made your point—we're impressed. But we came here at your request and somebody just flipped out as a consequence. We don't find it amusing."

"That was not intentional," Calazar replied. "We have already expressed our regrets. Your colleague will be back to normal very soon."

The exchange did not have the connotations that it would have if this confrontation were taking place on Earth, Hunt knew as he listened. Because of their origins Ganymeans simply didn't seek to intimidate nor did they respond to intimidation. They didn't think that way. Calazar was simply stating the facts of the matter, no more and no less. The standards and conditioning of human culture did not apply to this situation. Caldwell knew it too, but somebody had to be seen to set the limits.

"So let's get down to some straight questions and answer," Caldwell said. "You said that our two races have evolved separately until now. That's not entirely true—the two lines come together a long way back in the past. Since the story you've been getting about us seems to have become confused somewhere, it might help clear up a lot of uncertainty and save us some time if I sum up what we already know." Without waiting for a response he went on, "We know that your civilization existed on Minerva until around twenty-five million years ago, that you shipped a lot of terrestrial life there, possibly to attempt a genetic-engineering solution to the environmental problems, and that the Lunarians evolved from ancestors included among them after you left. We also know about the Lunarian war of fifty thousand years ago, about the Moon being captured by Earth, and about ourselves having descended from Lunarian survivors that came with it. Are we talking the same language so far?"

A ripple of murmurings broke out among the Ganymeans. They seemed surprised. Evidently the Terrans knew a lot more than they had expected. That could put an interesting new perspective on things, Hunt thought.

Frenua Showm, the female ambassador of Thurien, who had been introduced at the commencement of the proceedings, replied. "If you already know about the Lunarians, you shouldn't have any difficulty in finding the answer to one of the questions that you have no doubt been asking," she said. "Earth has been under surveillance because of our concern that it might go the way of its Lunarian ancestors and become a technically advanced, belligerent planet. The Lunarians destroyed themselves before they spilled out of the Solar System. Earth might not have. In other words we saw in Earth a potential threat to the other parts of the Galaxy, and perhaps, one day, to all of it." Showm gave the impression that she was far from convinced, even now, that it wasn't so. Definitely not a Terranophile, Hunt decided. The reason did not come as a surprise. With the Ganymeans being the way they were and the Lunarians having been the way they had, it had to be something like that.

"So why all the secrecy?" Heller asked from beside Caldwell. Caldwell sat down to allow her to take it from there. "You claim to represent the Thurien race, yet it's obvious that you don't speak for everybody. You don't want this dialogue brought to the attention of whoever is responsible for the surveillance. So are you what you say you are? If so, why do you need to conceal your actions from your own people?"

"The surveillance is operated by an autonomous . . . shall we say, 'organization' within our system," Calazar replied. "We had reason to suspect the accuracy of some of the information being reported. It became necessary for us to verify it . . . but discreetly, in case we were wrong."

"Suspect the accuracy!" Hunt repeated, spreading his hands in an imploring gesture around the table. "You're making it sound like just a minor aberration here and there. Christ . . . they didn't even tell you that the *Shapieron* had returned and was on Earth at all—your own ship with your own people in it! And the picture you got of Earth wasn't just inaccurate; it was systematically distorted. So what the hell's been going on?"

"That is an internal affair of Thurien that we will now be in a position to do something about," Calazar assured him. He seemed a little off balance, perhaps as a result of his having been unprepared for the Terrans knowing as much as Caldwell had revealed.

"It's not just an internal affair," Heller insisted. "It concerns our whole planet. We want to know who's been misrepresenting us, and why."

"We don't know why," Calazar told her simply. "That's what we're trying to find out. The first step was to get our facts straight. My apologies again, but I think we have now achieved that."

Caldwell was scowling. "Maybe you ought to let us talk to this 'organization' direct," he rumbled. "We'll find out why."

"That's not possible," Calazar said.

"Why?" Heller asked him. "Surely we've got a legitimate interest in all this. You've carried out your discreet checking of facts now, and you've got your answers. If you in fact represent this planet, what's to stop you acting accordingly?"

"Are you in a position to make such demands?" Showm challenged. "If our interpretation of the situation is correct, you do not constitute an officially representative group of the whole of Earth's society, either. That function surely belongs rightfully to the United Nations, does it not?"

"We've been communicating with them for weeks," Calazar said, taking Showm's point. "They have done nothing to dispel any wrong impressions of Earth that we may have, and they seem disinclined to meet us. But your transmissions were directed from another part of the Solar System entirely, suggesting perhaps that you did not wish our replies to become general knowledge, and therefore that you are equally concerned with preserving secrecy."

"What is the reason for the UN's curious attitude?" Showm asked, looking from one to another of the Terrans and allowing her eyes to rest finally on Heller.

Heller sighed wearily. "I don't know," she admitted. "Perhaps they're wary of the possible consequences of colliding with an advanced alien culture."

"And so it might be with some of our own race," Calazar said. It seemed unlikely since Earth was hardly advanced by

Thurien standards, but strange things were possible, Hunt supposed.

"So maybe we should insist on talking to that organization directly," Showm suggested pointedly. There was no response to that.

There was still something Hunt didn't understand when he sat back and tried to reconstruct in his mind the probable sequence of events as the Thuriens would have perceived them. For some time they had been building up a picture of a belligerent and militarized Earth from the accounts forwarded by the mysterious "organization," none of which had mentioned the *Shapieron*. Then a signal, coded in Ganymean, had suddenly come in direct to Calazar's side of the operation, advising that the ship was on its way home. After that, the further transmissions from Farside would have accumulated to hint of an Earth significantly different from that which the surveillance reports had described. But why had it been so important for the Thuriens to establish which version was correct? The measures that they had employed to find out said very clearly that the issue had been taken much more seriously than could be explained by mere academic curiosity or the need to straighten out some internal management problems.

"Let's start at the beginning with this relay device—or whatever you'd call it—that you've got outside the Solar System," he suggested when he had that much clear in his head.

"It's not ours," Eesyan said at once from his position next to Calazar, opposite Showm. "We don't know what it is, either. You see, we didn't put it there."

"But you must have," Hunt protested. "It uses your instant communications technology. It responded to Ganymean protocols."

"Nevertheless it's a mystery," Eesyan replied. "Our guess is that it must be a piece of surveillance hardware, not operated by us but by the organization responsible for that activity, which malfunctioned in some way and routed the signal through to our equipment instead of to its intended destination."

"But you replied to it," Hunt pointed out.

"At the time we were under the impression it was from the *Shapieron* itself," Calazar answered. "Our immediate concern was to let its people know that their message had been received, that they had correctly identified Gistar, and that they were heading for the right place." Hunt nodded. He would have done the same thing.

Caldwell frowned in a way that said he still wasn't clear about something. "Okay, but getting back to this relay—why didn't you find out what it was? You can send stuff from Thurien to Earth in a day. Why couldn't you send something to check it out?"

"If it was a piece of surveillance hardware that had gone faulty and given us a direct line, we didn't want to draw attention to it," Eesyan replied. "We were getting some interesting information through it."

"You didn't want this—'organization' to know about it?" Heller queried, looking puzzled.

"Correct."

"But they already knew about it. The reply from Gistar was all over Earth's newsgrid. They must have known about it if they run the surveillance."

"But they weren't picking up *your* signals *to* the relay," Eesyan said. "We would have known if they were." Suddenly Hunt realized why Gistar hadn't responded to the Farside transmissions that had continued for months after the *Shapieron*'s departure: the Thuriens didn't want to reveal their direct line via Earth's news network. That fitted in with their insistence on nothing being communicated via the net when at last they had elected to reopen the dialogue.

Heller paused for a moment and brought her hand up to her brow while she collected her thoughts. "But they couldn't have left it at that," she said, looking up. "From what they had picked up out of the newsgrid, they would have known that you knew about the *Shapieron*—something they hadn't been telling you about. They couldn't have just done nothing . . . not without arousing suspicion. They'd have to tell you about it at that point, because they knew if they didn't you'd be going to them and asking some awkward questions."

"Which is exactly what they did," Calazar confirmed.

"So didn't you ask them why they hadn't gotten around to it earlier?" Caldwell asked. "I mean—hell, the ship had been there for six months."

"Yes, we did," Calazar replied. "The reason they gave was that they were concerned for the *Shapieron*'s safety, and feared that attempts to interfere with the situation might only jeopardize it further. Rightly or wrongly, they had come to the decision that it would be better for us to know only after it was out of the Solar System."

Caldwell snorted, obviously not impressed by the mysterious "organization's" excuse. "Didn't you ask to see the records they had acquired through their surveillance?"

"We did," Caldwell answered. "And they produced ones that had every appearance of justifying their fears for the *Shapieron* completely."

Now Hunt knew where the phony depictions that he had witnessed of the *Shapieron*'s arrival at Ganymede had come from: the "organization" had faked them just as they had been faking their reports of Earth all along. Those were the versions that Calazar's people had been shown. If those scenes with their frighteningly authentic blending of reality and fantasy were typical of what had been going on, it was no wonder that the deception had gone unsuspected for years.

"I've seen some of those records," Hunt said. He sounded incredulous. "How did you ever come to suspect that they might not be genuine? They're unbelievable."

"We didn't," Eesyan told him. "VISAR did. As you may be aware, the drive method of the *Shapieron* creates a space-time deformation around the ship. It is most pronounced when main drive is operating, but exists to some extent even under auxiliary drive—sufficient to displace the apparent positions of background stars close to the vessel's outline by a measurable amount. VISAR noticed that the predicted displacements were present in some of the views we were shown, but completely missing from others. Hence the reports of the *Shapieron* were suspect."

"And not only those," Calazar said. "By implication, every other report that we had ever received of Earth was in doubt too, but we had no comparable way of testing them." He moved his eyes solemnly along the row of Terran faces. "Perhaps now you can see why we were concerned. We had two conflicting impressions of Earth, and no way of knowing how much of each might be true. But suppose that Earth was as aggressive and as irrational as we had been led to believe for years, and that the occupants of the *Shapieron* had indeed been received and treated in the ways described to us. . . ." He left the sentence unfinished. "Well, in our position what might you have thought?"

A silence descended around the table. The Thuriens

wouldn't have known what to believe, Hunt conceded inwardly. Their only way to check the facts would have been to reopen the dialogue with Earth secretly and establish face-to-face contact, which was precisely what they had done. So why had it been so important?

Suddenly Lyn's mouth dropped open, and she stared wide-eyed at Calazar. "You were afraid that we might have bombed the *Shapieron* or something!" she gasped, horrified. "If we were the way those stories said, we'd never have let that ship get to Thurien to tell anybody about it." The shocked looks coming from around her said that it suddenly all made sense to the others too. Even Caldwell seemed deflated for the moment. It was a shame about Jerol Packard, but nobody could blame the Thuriens for acting as they had.

"But you didn't have to wait to find out," Hunt said after a few seconds. "You can project black-hole ports across light-years. Why didn't you simply intercept the ship and get it here fast? Surely they'd have been the obvious people to check your surveillance reports with; they had been on Earth for six months."

"Technical reasons," Eesyan replied. "A Thurien vessel can clear a planetary system in about a day, but only because it carries on-board equipment that interacts with the transfer port and keeps the gravitational disturbance relatively localized. Naturally the *Shapieron* does not have such equipment. We needed to give it months if we were to avoid perturbing your planetary orbits. That would have been embarrassing if our fears were groundless. But we've been taking a risk. We finally reached the point where we had to know whether or not that ship was safe—*now*, without any further delays and obstructions."

"We had decided to go ahead anyway when it became clear that we were not making progress with the UN," Calazar told them. "Only when your messages from Jupiter started coming in did we decide to leave it a little longer. We had the necessary ships and generators ready then, and they have been standing by ever since. All they needed was one signal from us to commence the operation."

Hunt sank back in his chair and released a long breath. It had been a close thing. If Joe Shannon on *Jupiter Five* had not been thinking too clearly for a day or two, all of Earth's astronomical tables would have needed to be worked out all over again from square one.

"You'd better send the signal."

The voice sounded suddenly from one end of the Terran group. Everyone looked round, surprised, and found Danchekker directing a challenging look from one part of the table to another as if inviting them to make some obvious deduction. A score of Terran and Ganymean faces stared back at him blankly.

Danchekker removed his spectacles, polished them with a handkerchief, and then returned them to his nose in the manner of a professor allowing a class of slow students time to reflect upon some proposition he had put to them. There was no reason why VISAR would make lenses that existed only in somebody's head go cloudy, Hunt thought to himself; the ritual was just an unconscious mannerism.

At last Danchekker looked up. "It seems evident that this, er, 'organization' responsible for the surveillance activities, whatever its nature, would not see its interests served by the *Shapieron* reaching Thurien." He paused to let the full implication sink in.

"And now let me conjecture as to what might be my disposition now, were I in the position of the leaders of that organization," he resumed. "I assume that I know nothing about this meeting or that any dialogue between Thurien and Earth is taking place at all since my source of information would be the terrestrial communications network, and all references to such facts have been excluded from that system. Therefore I would have no reason to believe that my falsified accounts of Earth have been questioned. Now, that being so, if the *Shapieron* were to encounter an unfortunate, shall we say, accident, somewhere in the void between the stars, I would have every reason to feel confident that, if perchance the Thuriens should suspect foul play, Earth would top their list as the most likely culprit." He nodded and showed his teeth briefly as the appalled expressions around the table registered the impact of what he was driving at.

"Precisely!" he exclaimed, and looked across at Calazar. "If you have at your disposal the means of extracting that vessel from its present predicament, I would strongly advise that you proceed with such action without a moment of further delay!"

chapter twelve

Niels Sverenssen lay propped against the pillows in his executive-grade quarters at Giordano Bruno, watching the girl dress by the vanity on the far side of the room. She was young and quite pretty, with the clear complexion and open features typical of many Americans, and her loose black hair cut an intriguing contrast against her white skin. She should use the sunray facilities provided in the gymnasium more often, he thought to himself. As with most of her sex, her superficial layer of college-applied pseudointellectualism went no deeper than the pigment in her skin; beneath it she was as facile as the rest of them—a regrettably necessary but not unpleasant diversion from the more serious side of life. "You only want my body," they had cried indignantly down through the ages. "What else can you offer?" was his reply.

She finished buttoning her shirt and turned toward the mirror to run a comb hurriedly through her hair. "I know it's a strange time to be leaving," she said. "Trust me to be on early shift this morning. I'm going to be late again as it is."

"Don't worry about it," Sverenssen told her, putting more concern into his voice than he felt. "First things must come first."

She picked her jacket up off the back of a chair next to the vanity and slung it over her shoulder. "Have you got the cartridge?" she asked, turning back to face him.

Sverenssen opened the drawer of the bedside unit, reached inside, and took out a matchbook-size, computer micromemory cartridge. "Here. Remember to be careful."

The girl walked over to him, took the cartridge and folded it inside a tissue, then slipped it into one of the pockets of her jacket. "I will. When will I see you again?"

"Today will be very busy. I'll have to let you know."

"Don't make it too long." She smiled, stooped to kiss him on the forehead, and left, closing the door softly behind her.

Professor Gregor Malliusk, the Director of Astronomy at the Giordano Bruno observatory, was not looking pleased when she arrived in the main-dish control room ten minutes later. "You're late again, Janet," he grumbled as she hung her jacket in one of the closets by the door and put on her white working coat. "John had to leave in haste because he's going to Ptolemy today, and I've had to cover. I've got a meeting in less than an hour and things to do beforehand. This situation is becoming intolerable."

"I'm sorry, Professor," she said. "I overslept. It won't happen again." She walked quickly across to the supervisory console and began going through the routine of calling up the night's status logs with deft, practiced movements of her fingers.

Malliusk watched balefully from beside the equipment racks outside his office, trying not to notice the firm, slim lines of her body outlined by the white material of her coat and the raven black curls tumbling carelessly over her collar. "It's that Swede again, isn't it," he growled before he could stop himself.

"That's my business," Janet said without looking up, making her voice as firm as she dared. "I've already said—it won't happen again." She compressed her mouth into a tight line and stabbed savagely at the keyboard to bring another screen of data up in front of her.

"The check correlation on 557B was not completed yesterday," Malliusk said icily. "It was scheduled for completion by fifteen hundred."

Janet hesitated from what she was doing, closed her eyes momentarily, and bit her lip. "Damn!" she muttered beneath her breath, then louder, "I'll skip break and get it done then. There's not a lot of it left."

"John has already completed it."

"I'm . . . sorry. I'll do an extra hour off his next shift to make up."

Malliusk scowled at her for a few seconds longer, then turned on his heel abruptly and left the control room without saying anything more.

When she had finished checking the status logs, she switched off the screen and walked over to the transmission

subsystem communications auxiliary processor cabinet, opened
a cover panel, and inserted the cartridge that Sverenssen had
given her into an empty slot. Then she moved around to the
front of the system console and ran through the routine of integrating the contents of the cartridge into the message buffer
already assembled for transmission later that day. Where the
transmission was intended for she didn't know, but it was part
of whatever had brought the UN delegation to Bruno. Malliusk
always took care of the technical side of that personally, and he
never talked about it with the rest of the staff.

Sverenssen had told her that the cartridge contained some
mundane data that had come in late from Earth for appending to
the transmission that had been already composed; everything
that went out was supposed to be approved formally by all of
the delegates, but it would have been silly to call them all together merely to rubber-stamp something as petty as this. But a
couple of them could be touchy, he had said, and he cautioned
her to be discreet. She liked the feeling of being confided in
over a matter of UN importance, even if it had only to do with
some minor point, especially by somebody so sophisticated and
worldly. It was so deliciously romantic! And, who knew? From
some of the things that Sverenssen had said, she could be doing
herself a really big favor in the long run.

"He is a guest here, like the rest of you, and we have done
our best to be accommodating," Malliusk told Sobroskin later
that morning in the Soviet delegate's offices. "But this is interfering with the observatory's work. I do not expect to have to
be accommodating to the point of having my own work disrupted. And besides that, I object to such conduct in my own
establishment, particularly from a man in his position. It is not
becoming."

"I can hardly intervene in personal matters that are not part
of the delegation's business," Sobroskin pointed out, doing his
best to be diplomatic as he detected more than merely outraged
propriety beneath the scientist's indignation. "It would be more
appropriate for you to try talking to Sverenssen directly. She is
your assistant, after all, and it *is* the department's work that is
being affected."

"I have already done that, and the response was not satisfactory," Malliusk replied stiffly. "As a Russian, I wish my com-
plaint to be conveyed to whichever office of the Soviet

Government is concerned with the business of this delegation, with the request that they apply some appropriate influence through the UN. Therefore I am talking to you as the representative here of that office."

Sobroskin was not really interested in Malliusk's jealousies, and he didn't particularly want to stir up things in Moscow over something like this; too many people would want to know what the delegation was doing on Farside in the first place, and that would invite all kinds of questions and poking around. On the other hand, Malliusk obviously wanted something done, and if Sobroskin declined there was no telling whom the professor might be on the phone to next. There really wasn't a lot of choice. "Very well," he agreed with a sigh. "Leave it with me. I'll see if I can talk to Sverenssen today, or maybe tomorrow."

"Thank you," Malliusk acknowledged formally, then marched out of the office.

Sobroskin sat there thinking for a while, then reached behind himself to unlock a safe, from which he took a file that an old friend in Soviet military intelligence had sent up to Bruno unofficially at his request. He spent some time thumbing through its contents to refresh his memory, and as he thought further, he changed his mind about what he was going to do.

There were a number of strange things recorded in the file on Niels Sverenssen—the Swede, supposedly born in Malmo in 1981, who had vanished while serving as a mercenary in Africa in his late teens and then reappeared ten years later in Europe with inconsistent accounts of where he had been and what he had been doing. How had he suddenly reemerged from obscurity as a man of considerable wealth and social standing with no record of his movements during that time that could be traced? How had he established his international connections without it being common knowledge?

The pattern of womanizing was long and clear. The affair with the German financier's wife was interesting . . . with the rival lover who had publicly sworn vengeance and then met with a skiing accident less than a month later in dubious circumstances. A lot of evidence implied people had been bought off to close the investigation. Yes, Sverenssen was a man with connections he would not like to see aired publicly and the ruthlessness to use them without hesitation if need be, Sobroskin thought to himself.

And more recently—within the last month, in fact—why

had Sverenssen been communicating regularly and secretly with Verikoff, the space-communications specialist at the Academy of Sciences in Moscow who was intimately involved with the top-secret Soviet channel to Gistar? The Soviet Government did not comprehend the UN's apparent policy but it suited them, and that meant that the existence of the independent channel had to be concealed form the UN more than from anybody else; the Americans had doubtless deduced what was happening, but they were unable to prove it. That was their loss. If they insisted on tying themselves down with their notions of fair play, that was up to them. But why was Verikoff talking to Sverenssen?

And finally, in years gone by Sverenssen had always been a prominent figure in leading the UN drive for strategic disarmament, and a champion of world-wide cooperation and increased productivity. Why was he now vigorously supporting a UN policy that seemed opposed to seizing the greatest opportunity the human race had ever had to achieve those very things? It seemed strange. Everything to do with Sverenssen seemed strange.

Anyhow, what was he going to do about Malliusk's assistant? She was an American girl, Malliusk had said. Perhaps there was a way in which he could clear this irritating business up without inviting Sverenssen's close attention at a time when he was particularly anxious to avoid it. Their national loyalties aside, he admired the way in which Pacey had continued battling to promote his country's views after Heller left, and he had got to know the American quite well socially. In fact it was a shame in some ways that over this particular issue the U.S.S.R. and the U.S.A. were not together on the same side of the table; at heart they seemed to have more in common with each other than with the rest of the delegation. Very probably it wouldn't make much difference for a lot longer anyway, he admitted to himself. As Karen Heller had said on one occasion, it was the future of the whole race they should be thinking about. As a man he tended to agree with her; if the contact with Gistar meant what he thought it meant, there would be no national differences to worry about in fifty years' time, nor maybe even any nations. But that was as a man. In the meantime, as a Russian, he had a job to do.

He nodded to himself as he closed the file and returned it to the safe. He would talk to Norman Pacey and see if Pacey would talk to the American girl quietly. Then, with luck, the whole thing would resolve itself with no more than a few ripples that would soon die away.

chapter thirteen

Framed in the screen that took up most of one wall of the room was the image of a planet, captured from several thousand miles out in space. Most of its surface was ocean blue or stirred into spirals of curdled clouds through which its continents varied from yellowy browns and greens at its equator to frosty white at the poles. It was a warm, sunny, and cheerful world, but the image failed to re-create the sense of wonder at the energy of the life teeming across its surface that Garuth had felt at the time the image was captured months earlier.

As Garuth, commander of the long-range scientific mission ship *Shapieron*, sat in his private stateroom staring at the last view to be obtained of Earth, he pondered on the incredible race of beings that had greeted the return of his ship from its long exile in the mysterious realm of compoundly dilated time. Twenty-five million years before, although only a little over twenty by the *Shapieron*'s clocks, Garuth and his companions had left a flourishing civilization on Minerva to conduct a scientific experiment at a star called Iscaris; if the experiment had gone as planned, they would have been gone for twenty-three years of elapsed time back home, having lost less than five years from their own lifetimes. But the experiment had not gone as planned, and before the *Shapieron* was able to return, the Ganymeans had vanished from Minerva; the Lunarians had emerged, built their civilization, split into opposing factions, and finally destroyed themselves and the planet; and *Homo sapiens* had returned to Earth and written several tens of thousands of years of history.

And so the *Shapieron* had found them. What had been a pathetically deformed mutant left by the Ganymeans to fend for itself against hopeless odds in a harsh and uncompromising environment had transformed itself into a creature of pride and defiance that had not only survived, but laughed its contempt at every obstacle that the universe had tried to throw in its path. The Solar System, once the exclusive domain of the Ganymean civilization, had become rightfully the property of the human race. And so the *Shapieron* had departed once more into the void on a forlorn quest to reach the Giant's Star, the supposed new home of the Ganymeans.

Garuth sighed. Supposed for what reasons? Speculations based upon nothing that even the most elementary student of logic would accept as evidence; a frail straw of possibility clutched at to rationalize a decision taken in reality for reasons that only Garuth and a few of his officers knew about; a fabrication in the minds of Earthmen, whose optimism and enthusiasm knew no bounds.

The incredible Earthmen . . .

They had persuaded themselves that the myth of the Giants' Star was true and gathered to wish the Ganymeans well when the ship departed, believing, as most of Garuth's own people still believed, the reason he had stated—that Earth's fragile civilization was still too young to withstand the pressures of coexistence with an alien population that would have grown in numbers and influence. But there must have been a few, like the American biologist Danchekker, and the Englishman Hunt, who had guessed the real reason—that long ago the Ganymeans had created the ancestors of *Homo sapiens*. The human race had survived and flourished in spite of all the handicaps that the Ganymeans had inflicted upon them. Earth had earned its right to freedom from Ganymean interference; the Ganymeans had already interfered enough.

And so Garuth had allowed his people to believe the myth and follow him into oblivion. The decision had been hard, but they deserved the comfort of hope, at least for a while, he told himself. Hope had sustained them through the long voyage from Iscaris; they trusted him again now as they had then. Surely it was not wrong to allow them that until the time came when they would have to know what only Garuth and a select few knew at present, and probably what Earthmen like Danchekker and Hunt already knew. But he would never be certain how much those two friends from that astounding race of impetuous and at times aggressively inclined dwarves had really known. He would never see them again.

Garuth had stared silent and alone at this image many times since the ship's departure from Earth, and at the star maps showing its distant destination, still many years away and gleaming as just another insignificant pinpoint among millions. There was a chance, of course, that the scientists of Earth had been right. There was always a shred of hope that— He checked himself abruptly. He was allowing himself to slip into wishful thinking. It was all nothing but wishful thinking.

He straightened up in his chair and returned from his reverie. There was work to do. "ZORAC," he said aloud. "Delete the image. Inform Shilohin and Monchar that I would like to see them later today, immediately after this evening's concert if possible." The image of Earth disappeared. "Also I'd like to have another look at the proposal for revising the Third Level Educational curriculum." The screen came to life at once to present a table of statistics and some text. Garuth studied it for a while, voiced some comments for ZORAC to record and append, then called up the next screen in the sequence. Why was he worried at all about an educational curriculum that was nothing more than part of a pattern of normality that had to be preserved? Condemned by his decision along with the rest of his people, the children were destined to perish ignominiously and unmourned in the emptiness between the stars, knowing no home other than the *Shapieron*. Why did he concern himself with details of an educational curriculum that would serve no purpose?

He pushed the thought firmly from his mind and returned his attention fully to the task.

chapter fourteen

"Look, I know I don't have any right to interfere in your private life, and I'm not trying to," Norman Pacey said from an armchair in his private room at Bruno some hours after Sobroskin had talked to him about Janet. He tried to make his voice reasonable and gentle, but at the same time firm. "But when it gets to the point where I get dragged in and it affects the delegation's business, I have to say something."

From the chair opposite, Janet listened without changing expression. There was just a trace of moisture in her eyes, but whether that was due to remorse, anger, or to a sinus condition that had nothing to do with either, Pacey couldn't tell. "I suppose it was a bit silly," she said at last in a small voice.

Pacey sighed inwardly and did his best not to show it. "Sverenssen should have known better anyway," he said, hoping that it might be a consolation. "Hell—look, I can't tell you what to do, but at least be smart. If you want my advice for what it's worth, I'd say forget the whole thing and concentrate on your job here. But it's up to you. If you decide not to, then keep things so that they don't give Malliusk anything to come bitching about to us. There—that's as frank as I can be."

Janet stroked her lip with a knuckle and smiled faintly. "I'm not sure if that would be possible," she confided. "If you want the real reason why it's bugging him, it's because he's had this thing about me ever since I came up here."

Pacey groaned under his breath. He had felt himself slipping into a father role, and her responding to it. Now her whole life story was about to come pouring out. He didn't have the time. "Oh Jesus . . ." He spread his hands appealingly. "I really don't want to get too involved in your personal life. I just felt there was an aspect that I ought to say something about purely as the U.S. member of the delegation. Suppose we simply leave it at that and stay friends, huh?" He pushed his mouth into a grin and looked at her expectantly.

But she had to explain everything. "I guess it was just that everything here was so strange and different . . . you know . . . out here on the back of the Moon." She looked a little sheepish. "I don't know . . . I suppose it was nice to meet someone friendly."

"I understand." Pacey half-raised a hand. "Don't imagine you're the first—"

"And he was such a different kind of man to talk to. . . . He understood things too, like you." Her expression changed suddenly, and she looked at Pacey in a strange way, as if unsure about voicing something that was on her mind. Pacey was about to stand up and bring the matter to a close before she turned the room into a private confessional, but she spoke before he could move. "There's something else I've been wondering about . . . whether I ought to mention it to somebody or not. It seemed okay at the time, but . . . oh, I don't know—it's been kind of bothering me." She looked at him as if waiting for a signal to go on. Pacey stared back without the slightest indication of interest. She went on anyway. "He gave me some micromemories with some additional data in for appending to the transmissions that Malliusk has been handling. He said it was just some extra trivial stuff, but . . . I don't know . . . there was something strange about the way he said it." She released her breath sharply and seemed relieved. "Anyhow, there—now you know about it."

Pacey's posture and manner had changed abruptly. He was leaning forward and staring at her, a shocked look on his face. Her eyes widened in alarm as she realized that what she said was more serious than she thought. "How many?" he demanded crisply.

"Three . . . The last was early this morning."

"When was the first?"

"A few days ago . . . more maybe. It was before Karen Heller left."

"What did they say?"

"I don't know." Janet shrugged helplessly. "How would I know that?"

"Aw, come on." Pacey waved a hand impatiently. "Don't tell me you weren't curious. You've got the equipment to read a memory onto a screen."

"I tried to," she admitted after a few seconds. "But they had a lockout code that wouldn't permit a read from the console routine. They must have had a built-in, one-time activating sequence from the transmission call. They'd self-erased afterward."

"And that didn't make you suspicious?"

"At first I thought it was just some kind of routine UN security procedure. . . . Then I wasn't so sure. That was when it started bothering me." She looked across at Pacey nervously for a few seconds, then added timidly, "He did say it was only some trivial additions." Her tone said she didn't believe that now, either. Then she lapsed into silence while Pacey sat back with a distant expression on his face, gnawing unconsciously at the knuckle of his thumb while his mind raced through the possible meaning of what she had said.

"What else has he said to you?" he asked at last.

"What else?"

"Anything. Try and remember anything strange or unusual that he might have done or talked to you about—even things that sound stupid. This is important."

"Well . . ." Janet frowned and stared at the wall behind him. "He told me about all the work he did for disarmament and how he was mixed up in turning the UN into an efficient global power since then . . . all the people in high places that he knows all over."

"Uh huh. We know about that. Anything else?"

A smile flickered on Janet's mouth for a second. "He gets mad because you seem to give him a hard time at the delegation meetings. I get the impression he thinks you're a mean bastard. I can't think why, though."

"Yes."

Her expression changed suddenly. "There was something else, not long ago. . . . Yesterday, it was." Pacey waited and said nothing. She thought for a moment. "I was in his quarters—in the bathroom. Somebody else from the delegation came in the front door suddenly, all excited. I'm not sure which one it was. It wasn't you or that little bald Russian guy, but somebody foreign. Anyhow, he couldn't have known I was in there and started talking straight away. Niels shut him up and sounded really mad, but not before this other guy had said something about some news coming in that something out in space a long way off would be destroyed very soon now." She wrinkled her brow for a moment, then shook her head. "There wasn't anything else . . . not that I could make out, anyway."

Pacey was staring at her incredulously. "You're sure he said that?"

Janet shook her head. "It sounded like that . . . I can't be sure. The faucet was running and . . ." She let it go at that.

"You can't remember hearing anything else?"

"No . . . sorry."

Pacey stood up and walked slowly over to the door. After pausing for a while he turned and came back, halting to stand staring down in front of her. "Look, I don't think you realize what you've got yourself into," he said, injecting an ominous note into his voice. She looked up at him fearfully. "Listen hard to this. It is absolutely imperative that you tell nobody else about this. Understand? *Nobody!* If you're going to start being sensible, the time is right now. You must *not* let one word of what you've told me go a step further." She shook her head mutely. "I want your word on that," he told her.

She nodded, then after a second or two asked, "Does that mean I can't see Niels?"

Pacey bit his lip. The chance to learn more was tempting, but could he trust her? He thought for a few seconds, then replied, "If you can keep your mouth shut about what you heard and what you've said. And if anything else unusual happens, let me know. *Don't* go playing at spies and looking for trouble. Just keep your eyes and ears open, and if you see or hear anything strange, let me know and nobody else. And don't write anything down. Okay?"

She nodded again and tried to grin, but it didn't work. "Okay," she said.

Pacey looked at her for a moment longer, then spread his arms to indicate that he was through. "I guess that's it for now. Excuse me, but I've got things waiting to get done."

Janet got up and walked quickly to the door. She was just about to close it behind her when Pacey called, "And Janet . . ." She stopped and looked back. "For Christ's sake try to get to work on time and stay out of the hair of that Russian professor of yours."

"I will." She managed a quick smile, and left.

Pacey had noted for some time that, like himself, Sobroskin seemed excluded from the clique that revolved around Sverenssen, and he had come to believe increasingly that the Russian was playing a lone game on behalf of Moscow and merely finding the UN policy expedient. If so, Sobroskin would not be a party to whatever information Janet had caught a snippet of. Unwilling to break radio silence on Thurien-related matters with Earth, he decided to risk playing his hunch and arranged to meet the Russian later that evening in a storage room that formed part of a rarely frequented section of the base.

"Obviously I can't be sure, but it could be the *Shapieron*," Pacey said. "There seem to be two groups of Thuriens who aren't exactly on open terms with each other. We've been talking to one group, who appear to have the best interests of the ship at heart, but how do we know that other people back here haven't been talking to the other group? And how do we know that the other group feels the same way?"

Sobroskin had been listening attentively. "You're referring to the coded signals," he said. As expected, everybody had denied having anything to do with them.

"Yes," Pacey answered. "We assumed it was you because we know damn well it isn't us. But I'm willing to concede that we might have been wrong about them. Suppose the UN has set up this whole thing at Bruno for appearance's sake while it plays some other game behind the scenes. They could be stalling both of us while all the time they're talking behind our backs to . . . I don't know, maybe one Thurien side, maybe the other, or maybe even both."

"What kind of game?" Sobroskin asked. He was obviously fishing for ideas, probably through having few of his own to offer just then.

"Who knows? But what I'm worried about is that ship. If I'm wrong about it I'm wrong, but we can't just do nothing and hope so. If there's reason to suppose that it might be in danger, we have to let the Thuriens know. They might be able to do something." He had thought for a long time about risking a call to Alaska, but in the end decided against it.

Sobroskin thought deeply for a while. He knew that the coded signals were coming in in response to the Soviet transmissions, but there was no reason to say so. Yet another oddity had come to light concerning the Swede, and Sobroskin was anxious to follow it through. Moscow wished for nothing other than good relations with the Thuriens, and there was nothing to be lost by cooperating in warning them by whatever means Pacey had in mind. If the American's fears proved groundless, no permanent harm would result that Sobroskin could see. Either way, there was no time to consult with the Kremlin. "I respect your confidence," he said at last, and meant it, as Pacey could see he did. "What do you want me to do?"

"I want to use the Bruno transmitter to send a signal," Pacey replied. "Obviously it can't go through the delegation, so we'd have to go to Malliusk directly to take care of the technical side. He's a pain, but I think we could trust him. He wouldn't respond to an approach from me alone, but he might from you."

Sobroskin's eyebrows raised a fraction in surprise. "Why did you not go to the American girl?"

"I thought of it, but I'm not convinced she's reliable enough. She's too close to Sverenssen."

Sobroskin thought for a moment longer, then nodded. "Give me an hour. I'll call you in your room then, whatever the news." He sucked his teeth pensively as if weighing up something in his mind and then added, "I would suggest taking things easy with the girl. I have reports on Sverenssen. He can be dangerous."

They met Malliusk in the main-dish control room after the evening shift was over and while the astronomers booked for the night were away having coffee. Malliusk agreed to their request only after Sobroskin had consented to sign a disclaimer stating that the action was requested by him, acting in his official capacity as a representative of the Soviet Government. Malliusk locked the statement among his private papers. He then closed the control-room doors and used the main screen of the supervisory console to compose and transmit the message that Pacey dictated. Neither of the Russians could understand why Pacey insisted on appending his own name to the transmission. There were some things that he was not prepared to divulge.

chapter fifteen

Monchar, Garuth's second-in-command, was visibly tense when Garuth arrived in response to the emergency call to the *Shapieron*'s Command Deck. "There's something we've never seen before affecting the stressfield around the ship," he said in answer to Garuth's unvoiced question. "Some kind of external bias is interfering with the longitudinal node pattern and degrading the geodesic manifolds. The gridbase is going out of balance, and ZORAC can't make sense of it. It's trying to recompute the transforms now."

Garuth turned to Shilohin, the mission's chief scientist, who was in the center of a small group of her staff, taking in the information appearing on a battery of screens arrayed around them. "What's happening?" he asked.

She shook her head helplessly. "I've never heard of anything like this. We're entering some kind of space-time asymmetry with coordinates transforming inversely into an exponential frame. The whole structure of the region of space that we're in is breaking down."

"Can we maneuver?"

"Nothing seems to work. The divertors are ineffective, and the longitudinal equalizers can't compensate even at full gain."

"ZORAC, what's your report?" Garuth called in a louder voice.

"Impossible to construct a gridbase that couples consistently into normal space," the computer replied. "In other words I'm lost, don't know where we are, where we're going, or even if we're going anywhere, and don't have control anyway. Otherwise everything's fine."

"System status?" Garuth inquired.

"All sensors, channels, and subsystems checked and working normally. No—I'm not sick, and I'm not imagining it."

Garuth stood nonplussed. Every face on the Command Deck was watching and waiting for his orders, but what order could he give when he had no idea what was happening and what, if anything, could be done about it. "Call all stations to emergency readiness and alert them to stand by for further instructions," he said, more to satisfy expectations than for any definite reason. A crewman to one side acknowledged and turned toward a panel to relay the order.

"Total stressfield dislocation," Shilohin murmured, taking in the latest updates on the screens. "We're dissociated from any identifiable reference." The scientists around her were looking grim. Monchar nervously gripped the edge of a nearby console.

Then ZORAC's voice sounded again. "The trends reported have begun reversing rapidly. Coupling and translation functions are reintegrating to a new gridbase. References are rotating back into balance."

"We might be coming out of it," Shilohin said quietly. Hopeful mutterings broke out all around. She studied the displays again and appeared to relax somewhat.

"Stressfield not returning to normal," ZORAC advised. "The field is being externally suppressed, forcing reversion to subgravitic velocity. Full spatial reintegration unavoidable and imminent." Something was slowing the ship down and forcing it to resume contact with the rest of the universe. "Reintegration complete. We're in touch with the universe again . . ." An unusually long pause followed. "But I don't know which part. We seem to have changed our position in space." A spherical display in the middle of the floor illuminated to show the starfield surrounding the ship. It was nothing like that visible from the vicinity of the Solar System, which should not have altered beyond recognition since the *Shapieron*'s departure from Earth.

"Several large, artificial constructions are approaching us," ZORAC announced after a short pause. "The designs are not familiar, but they are obviously the products of intelligence. Implications: we have been intercepted deliberately by a means unknown, for a purpose unknown, and transferred to a place unknown by a form of intelligence unknown. Apart from the unknowns, everything is obvious."

"Show us the constructions," Garuth commanded.

Three screens around the Command Deck displayed views obtained in different directions of a number of immense craft, the like of which Garuth had never seen, moving slowly inward from the background of stars. Garuth and his officers could only stand and stare in silent awe. Before anybody could find words, ZORAC informed them, "We have communications from the unidentified craft. They are using our standard high-spectrum format. I'm putting it on the main monitor." Seconds later, the large screen overlooking the floor presented a picture. Every Ganymean in the Command Deck froze, stupefied by what they saw.

"My name is Calazar," the face said. "Greetings to you who went to Iscaris long ago. Soon you will arrive at our new home. Be patient, and all will be explained."

It was a Ganymean—a slightly modified Ganymean, but a Ganymean sure enough. Elation and joy mixed with disbelief surged in the confused emotions exploding in Garuth's head. It could only mean that . . . the signal that the Earthmen had beamed outward from their Moon had been received. Suddenly his heart went out to the impetuous, irrepressible, unquenchable Earthmen. They had been right after all. He loved them, every one.

Gasps of wonder were erupting on every side as one by one

the others realized what was happening. Monchar was turning circles and waving his arms in the air in an uncontrollable release of emotion, while Shilohin had sunk into an empty seat and was just gaping wide-eyed and speechless up at the screen.

Then ZORAC confirmed what they already knew. "I've matched the starfield with extrapolations from records and fixed our location. Don't ask me how, but it seems that the voyage is over. We're at the Giants' Star."

Less than an hour later, Garuth led the first party of Ganymeans out of the lock of one of the *Shapieron*'s daughter vessels and into a brilliantly lit reception bay in one of the craft from Thurien. They approached the line of figures that were waiting silently, and went through a short welcoming ritual in which the dam finally broke and all the pent-up anguish and hope that the wanderers had carried with them burst forth in a flood of laughter and not a few tears. It was over. The long exile was over, and the exiles were finally home.

Afterward the new arrivals were conducted to a side chamber and required to recline on couches for a few minutes. The purpose of this was not explained. The Ganymeans experienced a strange sequence of sensory disturbances, after which all was normal again. They were then told that the process was complete. Minutes later, Garuth left the side chamber with his party to reenter the area where the Thuriens were assembled . . . and suddenly stopped dead in his tracks, his eyes popping in disbelief.

Slightly ahead of the Thuriens, grinning unashamedly at the Ganymeans' total bemusement, stood a small group of familiar pink dwarves. Garuth's mouth fell open, hung limply for a moment, and then closed again without making any sound. For the two figures moving toward him, ahead of the other humans, were none other than—

"What kept you, Garuth?" Hunt asked cheerfully. "Did you miss a sign somewhere along the way?"

"Do forgive my amusement at your expense," Danchekker said, unable to suppress a chuckle. "But I'm afraid the expression on your face is irresistibly provocative."

Behind them Garuth could see another familiar figure—stocky and broad, with wiry hair streaked with gray and deeply etched features; it was Hunt's superior from Houston, and next to him was the red-haired girl who also worked there. Beside them were another man and woman, neither of whom he recognized. Garuth forced his feet to move again, and through his daze saw that Hunt was extending a hand in the customary manner of greeting of Earth. Garuth shook hands with him warmly, then with the others. They were not optical images of some kind; they were real. The Thuriens must have brought them from Earth for this occasion by methods unknown at the time of Minerva.

As he stood back to allow his companions to surge forward toward the Terrans, Garuth spoke quietly into the throat microphone that still connected him with the *Shapieron*, riding not far away from the Thurien vessel. "ZORAC, I am not dreaming? This is really happening?" ZORAC could monitor visual scenes via the miniaturized TV-camera headbands that Ganymeans from the ship wore most of the time.

"I don't know what you mean," ZORAC's voice replied in the earpiece that Garuth was also wearing. "All I can see is a ceiling. You're all lying in chairs of some kind in there, and you haven't moved for almost ten minutes."

Garuth was at a loss. He looked around and saw Hunt and Calazar making their way toward him through the throng of Ganymeans and Terrans. "Can't you see them?" he asked, mystified.

"See who?"

Before Garuth could answer, another voice said, "Actually that wasn't ZORAC. It was me, repeating and imitating ZORAC. Allow me to introduce myself—my name is VISAR. Perhaps it's time we explained a few things."

"But not in the lobby," Hunt said. "Let's go on through into the ship. There's quite a lot that needs explaining." Garuth was even more perplexed. Hunt had heard and understood the exchange even though he was not wearing communications accessories and the exchange had been in Ganymean.

Calazar stood waiting until the rest of the welcomes and introductions had been completed. Then he beckoned and led the mixed group of Ganymeans and Terrans into the body of the huge spacecraft from Thurien, now only a matter of hours away.

chapter sixteen

Hunt and Danchekker were somewhere out in the vastness of space. Around them was a large, darkened area made up of walled enclosures that looked like booths and interconnecting stretches of open floor, extending away beneath pools of subdued local lighting into the shadows on all sides. The dominant light was a soft, ghostly whiteness coming from the stars overhead, every one bright and unblinking.

After the reception of the *Shapieron* some distance outside the system of Gistar, Jerol Packard, by then his normal self once more, had decided to leave the two groups of Ganymeans alone for some time without Terran intrusion. The others had agreed. They seized the opportunity thus presented to make some instant "visits," courtesy of VISAR, to experience other parts of the Thurien civilization. Packard and Heller went to Thurios to learn more of the system of social organization while Caldwell and Lyn were taken on a tour of light-years between stops to observe more of Thurien space engineering in action. Hunt and Danchekker, intrigued after following the operation that had been mounted to intercept the *Shapieron*, were curious about how the energy had been generated to form the enormous black-hole toroid thrown in the ship's path, and how it was hurled across such an immense distance. VISAR had offered to show them a Thurien power plant, and an instant later they had found themselves here.

They were beneath a huge, transparent blister that formed part of some form of construction hanging in space. But what scale of construction was this? To left and right outside the blister, and in front and behind, the external parts of the structure swept away and upward in four gently curving arms of intricately engineered metal architecture that shrank into the distance to give an impression of immensity that was almost frightening. They seemed to be standing at the crossover point of two shallow crescents that met at right angles like sections of the equator and a longitude line drawn on a globe. The tips of the four crescent arms carried four long, narrow, cylindrical forms whose axes seemed to converge on some distant point like those of four gigantic gun barrels trained to concentrate fire on a remote target. How far away they were was impossible to guess since there was nothing familiar to give any visual cue of size.

Farther away and to one side, positioned almost edge-on to their vantage point, was another structure identical to the one they were in, comprising a similar cruciform of two crescents and carrying its own quadruplet of cylinders, details of its far side losing themselves in foreshortening and distance. And on the other side of the view was another, also edge-on, and another above, and yet another below. The whole set of them, Hunt realized as he looked, was positioned symmetrically in space around a common center to form sections of an imaginary spherical surface like parts of an engineer's exploded drawing, and the gun barrels were pointing inward radially. And far away at the focus of this configuration, an eerie halo of blurred, scrambled starlight was hanging in the void, tinted with a dash of violet.

After giving them some time to take in the scene VISAR informed them, "You are now something like five hundred million miles outside the system of Gistar. You're standing in something called a *stressor*. There are six of them, and together they define a boundary around a spherical volume of space. Each of the arms outside is of the order of five thousand miles long. That's how far away those cylinders are, which should give you some idea of their size."

Danchekker looked at Hunt dumbfounded, raised his head again to take in the scene above, then looked at Hunt once more. Hunt just stared back glassy-eyed.

VISAR continued, "The stressors induce a zone of enhanced space-time curvature that increases in intensity toward the center until, right at the focus, it collapses into a back hole." A bright red circle, obviously superposed on their visual inputs by VISAR, appeared from nowhere to surround the hazy region. "The hole is in the center of the circle," VISAR told them. "The halo effect is distorted light from background stars—the region acts like a gravitic lens. The hole itself is about ten thousand miles from you, and the space you're in is actually highly distorted. But I can censor confusing data, so you feel and act normal.

"Behind the shell defined by the stressors are batteries of projectors that create intense beams of energy by matter annihilation and direct them between the sensors and into the hole. From there the energy is redirected and distributed through a higher-order dimension grid and extracted back into ordinary space wherever it's needed. In other words this whole arrangement forms the input into an h-space distribution grid that delivers to anywhere you like, instantaneously, and over interstellar distances. Like it?"

A while went by before Hunt found his voice. "What kinds of things hook on the other end?" he asked. "I mean, would this feed a whole planet . . . or what?"

"The distribution pattern is very complex," VISAR replied. "Several planets are being fed from Garfalang, which is what the place you're at is called. So are a number of high-energy projects that the Thuriens are engaged in at various places. But you can hook smaller units into the grid wherever they happen to be, such as spacecraft, other vehicles, machines, dwellings—anything that uses power. The local equipment needed to tap into the grid is not large in size. For instance the perceptron that we landed in Alaska was powered from the grid on the conventional stage from its exit port to Earth. It would have had to be much larger if it carried its own on-board propulsion source. Hardly any of our machines have local, self-contained power sources. They don't need them. The grid feeds everything from large centralized generators and redirectors, like the one you're in, located far out in space."

"This is unbelievable," Danchekker breathed. "And to imagine, fifty years ago people were frightened of their energy sources being exhausted. This is stupefying . . . quite stupefying."

"What's the prime source?" Hunt asked. "You said the input beams were produced by matter annihilation. What gets annihilated?"

"Mainly the cores of burned-out stars," VISAR answered. "Part of the energy generated is tapped off to drive a network of transfer ports for conveying material from the remote sites, where the cores are dismantled, to the annihilator batteries. The net production of useful energy fed into the grid from Garfalang is equivalent to about one lunar mass per day. But there's plenty of fuel around. We're a long way from any crisis. Don't worry about it."

"And you can concentrate the energy from here across light-years of space through some kind of . . . hyperdimension and create a transfer toroid remotely," Hunt said. "Is it always as elaborate as the operation we watched?"

"No. That was a special case that required exceptionally precise control and timing. An ordinary transfer is pretty simple by comparison, and just routine."

Hunt fell silent while he took in more of the spectacle overhead, and went back in his mind over the details of the operation he had witnessed.

Calazar had decided to go ahead with the interception of the *Shapieron* without further delay when a baffling message, signed personally by Norman Pacey, came in from Bruno to warn of a possibility that the ship could be in some kind of danger. How Pacey could have known about a risk that had been recognized on Thurien only with the benefit of information that Pacey couldn't possibly have possessed was a mystery.

Apparently the "organization" possessed equipment capable of tracking the *Shapieron* just as Calazar's people did, and Calazar had been unwilling to reveal his actions by simply allowing the ship to vanish from the course it had been following. Therefore he had called upon Eesyan's engineers to modify the operation to cover not only the fishing of a vessel out of the void twenty light-years away, but also the substitution of a dummy object constructed to give identical readings on the "organization's" tracking instruments. There was a risk that the gravitational disturbance produced in the process might itself be detected, but since continuous monitoring was not practicable for technical reasons, there was a good chance that the substitution could be made invisible provided the operation was pulled off in minimum time. As planned, the switch had gone quickly and smoothly, and if all had gone well the "organization" would by now be receiving tracking-data updates originating from the decoy while the *Shapieron* was in fact light-years away and almost at Thurien. Time would no doubt tell if the switch had gone quickly and smoothly enough.

Hunt didn't know what to make of this game of deception and counterdeception between two, possibly rival, groups of Ganymeans. As Danchekker had maintained from the beginning, the response simply did not fit with the way Ganymean minds worked. Hunt had tried several times to squeeze a hint of what was behind it all out of VISAR, but the machine, evidently acting under a firm directive not to discuss the matter, merely reaffirmed that Calazar would broach the subject himself at the appropriate time.

But whatever the reasons, the *Shapieron* had not been attacked or interfered with in whatever way Pacey had feared, and it was now in safe hands. The only conclusion Hunt could draw was that Pacey had totally misinterpreted something and overreacted, which seemed strange for the kind of person Hunt had judged Pacey to be. To be fair, Hunt conceded as he thought about it again, Pacey hadn't actually said for certain that it was the *Shapieron* that was threatened; what he had said was that he had reason to believe that *something* well out in space was in danger of destruction, and he had expressed concern that it might be the *Shapieron*. Calazar had decided not to take any chances, and Hunt couldn't blame him for that. What the warning did seem to indicate was that Pacey had been hopelessly wrong about something. Or had he? Hunt wondered.

Suddenly Hunt realized he was feeling physically uncomfortable. Surely not, he thought. Surely the package of sensations that made up his computer-simulated body couldn't be that complete. What would be the point?

He looked around him instinctively and discovered he was back in his own body in the recliner inside the perception. "Facing you at the back end of the corridor," VISAR's voice informed him. Hunt sat up, shaking his head in wonder. As always, the Ganymeans had thought of everything. So *that* was what the mysterious door was for.

He was back at Gistar a few minutes later, and found Danchekker waiting for him wearing a grave expression. "Some alarming news has come through while you were absent," the professor informed him. "It appears that our friend at Giordano Bruno was not quite as mistaken as we had supposed."

"What's happened?" Hunt asked.

"The device that has been relaying the communications between Farside and Thurien has ceased operating. According to VISAR, indications are that something destroyed it."

chapter seventeen

How could Norman Pacey, isolated and incommunicado on lunar Farside, have known that the relay was about to be destroyed? His only source of information from outside the solar system was the signals coming in from the Thuriens at Gistar, and the Thuriens themselves hadn't known about it. And why had Pacey apparently acted independently of the official UN delegation on Farside in sending the warning? Furthermore, how had he gained access to the equipment there, and how had he been able to operate it? In short, just what was going on at Farside?

Jerol Packard requested from the Thuriens a complete set of their versions of all the messages that had been exchanged with Earth since the whole business began. Calazar agreed to supply them, and VISAR hard-copied them through to McClusky by means of equipment contained in the perceptron. When the team there compared the Thuriens' transcripts with their own, some peculiar discrepancies emerged.

The first set comprised one-way traffic from Earth and were from the period immediately following the *Shapieron*'s departure, when scientists at Bruno had resisted UN pressure and continued transmitting in the hope of renewing the dialogue that the first brief, unexpected signal from the Giants' Star had initiated. These messages contained information regarding Earth's civilization and state of scientific progress that over the months had begun adding up to form a picture which was not at all consistent with that reported to the Thuriens for years by the still mysterious and undefined "organization." Perhaps these inconsistencies had been the cause of the Thuriens becoming suspicious about the reports in the first place. In any event, the two sets of transcripts of these messages matched perfectly.

The next group of exchanges dated from the time that

Thurien began talking again, and the UN stepped in to handle Earth's end. At this point the tone of the transmissions from Farside took on a distinctly different flavor. As Karen Heller had told Hunt at his first meeting with her in Houston, and as he had verified for himself since, the messages became negative and ambivalent, doing little to dispel the Thuriens' notions of a militarized Earth and rejecting their overtures for a landing and direct talks. Among these transmissions the first discrepancies appeared.

Every one of the communications sent during the period in which Heller was on Farside was reproduced faithfully in the Thuriens' records. But there were two additional ones—identifiable by their format and header conventions as having undoubtedly originated from Bruno—that she had never seen before. What made these even more mysterious was that their contents were overtly belligerent and hostile to a degree that the UN delegation would never have condoned even with its negative attitude. Some of the things they said were simply untrue, the gist of them being that Earth was capable of managing its own affairs, didn't want and wouldn't tolerate alien interference, and would respond with force if any landing was attempted. More inexplicable still was the fact that some of the details correlated with and reinforced the falsified picture of Earth that Hunt and the others had learned of only after meeting the Thuriens. How could anyone at Bruno have known anything about that?

Then Hunt's signals had started coming in from Jupiter—coded in Ganymean, welcoming the suggestion for a landing, suggesting a suitable location, and projecting a different image completely. No wonder the Thuriens had been confused!

After that came the Soviet signals, complete with details of the security code to be used for replies. Packard had persuaded Calazar to include them by playing up the grilling that the Terrans had been put through and especially its effect on him personally. The Soviets, too, had expressed interest in a landing, though in a manner distinctly more cautious than Hunt's messages from Jupiter. This theme traced consistently through most of the Soviet signals, but again there were some, in this case three, that stood out as exceptions and conveyed similar sentiments to those of the "unofficial" transmissions from Bruno. And even more amazingly, they tallied in some significant details with the Bruno exceptions in ways that couldn't have been coincidental.

How could the Soviets have known about unofficial signals from Bruno that even Karen Heller hadn't known about when she was there? The only way, surely, was if the Soviets were responsible for them. Did that mean that the Kremlin was so dominating the UN that the whole Bruno operation had been simply a sham to distract the U.S. and other prominent nations that knew about Gistar, and that the delegation's ostensibly mild but nevertheless counterproductive actions had been secretly derailed, presumably by somebody put there for the purpose—perhaps in the form of Sobroskin? That the Director of Astronomy at Bruno was also a Russian gave further credibility to the thought, but against it was the unavoidable fact that the Soviets' own effort had been sabotaged in exactly the same manner. Again nothing made sense.

Later a third unofficial message from Bruno, sent after Karen Heller had left, reached a new peak of aggressiveness, announcing that Earth was severing relations and had taken steps to insure that the dialogue would be discontinued permanently. Finally there was Norman Pacey's warning of something about to be destroyed out in space, and shortly afterward the relay had ceased operating.

The answers to these riddles would not be found in Alaska. Packard waited until a State Department courier arrived at McClusky with the official news that communications with Gistar had ceased and the UN delegation was returning to Earth, and then left for Washington with Caldwell. Lyn went with them for the purpose of returning to McClusky with an update as soon as they had talked to Pacey.

Hunt and Danchekker stood on the apron at McClusky, watching the UNSA jet that had just lifted off to take Packard, Caldwell, and Lyn to Washington turn and begin climbing away steeply toward the south. Not far from them, a ground crew was busy shoveling snow over the holes in the concrete left by the landing gear of the perceptron, which had moved itself into line with the other UNSA aircraft parked along one side of the apron in order to provide a more natural scene for the "organization's" surveillance instruments. Although the black hole contained in the vessel's communications system was microscopic, it still had the equivalent mass of a small mountain; McClusky's apron hadn't been designed for that.

"It's funny when you think about it," Hunt remarked as the plane shrank to a dot above the distant ridgeline. "It's twenty light-years from Vranix to Washington, but the last four thousand miles take all the time. Maybe when we get this business cleared up, we could think about wiring a few parts of this planet into VISAR."

"Maybe." Danchekker's voice was noncommittal. He had been noticeably quiet since breakfast.

"It would save Gregg a lot of charges from Transportation Services."

"I suppose so."

"How about wiring up Navcomms HQ and Westwood? Then we'd be able to go straight to Thurien from the office and be back for lunch."

"Mmm . . ."

They turned and began walking back toward the mess hall. Hunt glanced sideways to give the professor a curious look, but Danchekker appeared not to notice and kept walking.

Inside they found Karen Heller hunched over a pile of communications transcripts and notes she had made while at Bruno. She pushed the papers away and sat back in her chair as they entered. Danchekker moved over to a window and stared silently out at the perceptron; Hunt turned a chair around and straddled it to face the room from a corner. "I just don't know what to make of this," Heller said with a sigh. "There just isn't any way that some of this information could have been known to anybody here or on the Moon except us—unless they've been in contact with Calazar's 'organization.' Could that be possible?"

"I wondered the same thing," Hunt replied. "How about the coded signals? Maybe Moscow wasn't transmitting to Calazar's bunch at all."

"No, I've checked." Heller gestured toward the papers around her. "Every one that we picked up was sent by Calazar's aide. They're all accounted for."

Hunt shook his head and folded his arms on the backrest of the chair. "It's got me beat too. Let's wait and see what they find out from Norman when he gets back." A silence descended. Lost in thoughts of his own, Danchekker continued staring out through the window. After a while Hunt said, "You know, it's funny—sometimes when things become so confusing that you think you'll never make any kind of sense out of them, it just needs one simple, obvious thing that everybody's overlooked to make everything come together. Remember a couple of years back when we were trying to figure out where the Lunarians came from. Nothing added up until we realized that the Moon must have moved. Yet looking back, that should have been obvious all along."

"I hope you're right," Heller said as she collected papers and returned them to their folders. "Something else I don't understand is all this secrecy. I thought Ganymeans weren't supposed to be like that. Yet here we are with one group doing one thing, another doing something else, and neither wanting to let the other know anything about it. You know them better than most people. What do you make of it?"

"I don't know," Hunt confessed. "And who bombed the relay? Calazar's bunch didn't, so it must have been the other bunch. If so, they must have found out about it despite all the precautions, but why would they want to bomb it, anyway? It's definitely a strange way for Ganymeans to be carrying on, all right . . . or at least, it is for the kind of Ganymeans that existed twenty-five million years ago." He turned his head unconsciously and directed his last words at Danchekker, who still had his back to them. Hunt had not yet been convinced that such a span of time couldn't have been sufficient to bring about some fundamental change in Ganymean nature, but Danchekker had remained intractable. He thought that Danchekker hadn't heard, but after a few seconds the professor replied without moving his head.

"Perhaps your original hypothesis deserved more consideration than I was prepared to give it at the time."

Hunt waited for a few seconds, but nothing further happened. "What hypothesis?" he asked at last

"That perhaps we are not dealing with Ganymeans at all." Danchekker's voice was distant. A short silence fell. Hunt and Heller looked at each other. Heller frowned; Hunt shrugged. Of course they were dealing with Ganymeans. They looked back at Danchekker expectantly. He wheeled around to face them suddenly and brought his hands up to clasp his lapels. "Consider the fact," he invited. "We are confronted by a pattern of behavior that is totally inconsistent with what we know to be true of the Ganymean nature. That pattern concerns the relationship between two groups of beings. One of these groups we have met and know to be Ganymean. The other group we have not been permitted to meet, and the reasons that have been offered, I have no hesitation in dismissing as pretexts. A logical conclusion to draw, therefore, would be that the second group is *not* Ganymean—would it not?"

Hunt just stared back at him blankly. The conclusion was so obvious that there was nothing to be said. They had all been assuming that the "organization" was Ganymean, and the Thuriens had said nothing to change their minds. But the Thuriens had never said anything to confirm it either.

"And consider this," Danchekker went on. "The structural organizations and patterns of neural activity at the symbolic level in human and Ganymean brains are quite dissimilar. I find it impossible to accept that equipment designed to interact in a close-coupled mode with one form would be capable of functioning at all with the other. In other words, the devices inside that vessel standing out on the apron cannot be standard models designed for use by Ganymeans, which, purely by good fortune, happen to operate effectively with human brains too. Such a situation is impossible. The only way in which those devices could operate as they do is by virtue of having been *specifically constructed to couple with the human central nervous system in the first place*! Therefore the designers must have been intimately familiar with the most detailed inner workings of that system—far more so than they could have been by any amount of study of contemporary terrestrial medical science through their surveillance activities. Therefore that knowledge could only have been acquired on Thurien itself."

Hunt looked across at him incredulously. "What are you saying, Chris?" he asked in a strained voice, although it was already plain enough. "That there are *humans* on Thurien as well as Ganymeans?"

Danchekker nodded emphatically. "Exactly. When we first entered the perceptron, VISAR was able, in a matter of mere seconds, to adjust its parameters to produce normal levels of sensory stimulation and to decode the feedback commands from the motor areas of our nervous systems. But how did it know what stimulation levels were normal for humans? How did it know what patterns of feedback were correct? The only possible explanation is that VISAR already possessed extensive prior experience in operating with human organisms." He looked from one to the other to invite comment.

"It could be," Karen Heller breathed, nodding her head slowly as she digested what he had said. "And maybe that explains why the Ganymeans haven't exactly been rushing themselves to tell us about it until they've got a better feel for how we might react—especially with the accounts they've been getting of what we're like. And it could make sense that if they *are* human, they got the job of running a surveillance program to keep an eye on Earth." She thought over what she had said and nodded again to herself, then frowned as something else occurred to her. She looked up at Danchekker. "But how could they have gotten there? Could they be from some independent family of evolution that already existed on Thurien before the Ganymeans got there . . . something like that maybe?"

"Oh, that's quite impossible," Danchekker said impatiently. Heller looked mildly taken aback and opened her mouth to object, but Hunt shot her a warning glance and gave a barely perceptible shake of his head. If she got Danchekker into a lecture on evolution, they'd be listening all day. She signaled her acceptance with a slight raising of an eyebrow and let it go at that.

"I don't think we have to search very far for the answer to that question," Danchekker informed them airily, drawing himself upright and tightening his hold on his lapels. "We know that the Ganymeans migrated to Thurien from Minerva approximately twenty-five million years ago. We also know that by then they had acquired numerous species of terrestrial life, including primates as advanced as any of the period. Indeed we discovered some of them ourselves in the craft on Ganymede, which we have every reason to believe was involved in that very migration." He paused for a moment as if doubting that the rest needed spelling out, then continued. "Evidently they took with them some representatives of early prehuman hominids, the descendants of which have since evolved and increased to become a human population enjoying full cocitizenship within the society of Thurien, as is evidenced by the fact that VISAR accommodates both them and Ganymeans equally." Danchekker dropped his hands to clasp them behind his back and thrust his chin out with evident satisfaction. "And that, Dr. Hunt, unless I am very much mistaken, would appear to be the simple and obvious missing factor that you were looking for," he concluded.

chapter eighteen

Norman Pacey held up his hand in a warning gesture and closed the door to cut off the room from the secretary giving directions to two UNSA privates who were loading boxes onto a cart in the outer office. Janet watched from a chair that she had cleared of a stack of papers and document holders waiting to be packed in preparation for the delegation's departure from Bruno. "Now start again," he told her, turning away from the door.

"It was last night, maybe early this morning . . . I'm not sure what time." Janet fiddled awkwardly with a button on her lab coat. "Niels got a call from somebody—I think it was the U.S. European, Daldanier—about something they needed to discuss right away. He started saying something about somebody called Verikoff, it sounded like, but Niels stopped him and said he'd go and talk to him at his place. I pretended I was still asleep. He got dressed and slipped out . . . kind of creepily, as if he were being careful not to wake me up."

"Okay," Pacey said with a nod. "Then what?"

"Well . . . I remembered he'd been looking at some papers earlier when I came in. He put them away in a holder, but I was sure he hadn't locked it. So I decided to take a chance and see what they were about."

Pacey clenched his teeth in the effort not to let his feelings show. That was exactly the kind of thing he had told her *not* to do. But the outcome sounded interesting. "And," he prompted.

Janet's face took on a mystified look. "There was a folder among the things inside. It was bright red around the edges and pink inside. What made me notice it was that it had your name on the front."

Pacey's brows creased as he listened. What Janet had described sounded like a standard UN-format document wallet that was used for highly confidential memoranda. "Did you look inside it?"

Janet nodded. "It was weird . . . the report criticized the way you'd been obstructing the meeting here and stated in a *Conclusions* section that the delegation would have made more progress if the U.S. had shown a more cooperative attitude. It didn't sound like you at all, which was why I thought it was weird." Pacey was staring at her speechlessly. Before he could find words to reply, she shook her head as if feeling a need to disclaim responsibility for what she was going to say next. "And there was this part about you and—Karen Heller It said that you two were . . ." Janet hesitated, then raised a hand with her index and second fingers intertwined, " . . . like that, and that such—how was it put?—such 'blatant and indiscreet conduct was not becoming to a mission of this nature, and possibly had some connection with the counterproductive contribution of the United States to the proceedings.' " Janet sat back and shook her head again. "I knew the report simply wasn't true . . . And coming from him, well . . ." She let the sentence trail away and left it at that.

Pacey sat down on the edge of a half-filled packing case and stared at her incredulously. A few seconds went by before he found his voice. "You actually saw all this?" he asked at last.

"Yes . . . I can't give you all of it word for word, but that was what it said." She hesitated. "I know it's crazy, if that helps. . . ."

"Does Sverenssen know you saw this report?"

"I don't see how he could. I put everything back exactly the way it was. I guess I could have got you more of it, but I didn't know how long he'd be away. As it turned out, he was gone quite a while."

"That's okay. You did the right thing not risking it." Pacey stared down at the floor for a while, feeling totally bewildered. Then he looked up again and asked, "How about you? Has he been acting strange now that we're leaving? Anything . . . ominous, maybe?"

"You mean sinister warnings to keep my mouth shut about the computer?"

"Mmm . . . yes, maybe." Pacey looked at her curiously.

She shook her head and smiled faintly. "Quite the opposite as a matter of fact. He's been very gentlemanly and said what a shame it is. He even hinted that we could get together again sometime back on Earth—he could fix me up with a job that pays real money, all kinds of interesting people to meet . . . stuff like that."

A smarter move, Pacey thought to himself. High hopes and treachery had never gone together. "Do you believe him?" he asked, cocking an eyebrow.

"No."

Pacey nodded in approval. "You *are* growing up fast." He looked around the office and massaged his forehead wearily. "I'm going to have to do some thinking now. I'm glad you told me about it. But you've got your coat on, which says you probably have to get back to work. Let's not start upsetting Malliusk again."

"He's off today," Janet said. "But you're right—I do have to get back." She stood up and moved toward the door, then turned back as she was about to open it. "I hope it was okay. I know you said to keep this away from the delegation offices, but it seemed important. And with everybody leaving . . ."

"Don't worry about it. It's okay. I'll see you again later."

Janet departed, leaving the door open in response to Pacey's wave request. Pacey sat for a while and began turning what she had told him over again in his mind, but was interrupted by the UNSA privates coming in to sort out the boxes ready for moving. He decided to go and think about it over a coffee in the common room.

The only people in the common room when Pacey entered a few minutes later were Sverenssen, Daldanier, and two of the other delegates, who were all together at the bar. They acknowledged his arrival with a few not overfriendly nods of their heads and continued talking among themselves. Pacey collected a coffee from the dispenser on one side of the room and sat down at a table in the far corner, wishing inwardly that he had picked somewhere else. As he studied them surreptitiously over his cup, he listed in his mind the unanswered questions that he had collected concerning the tall, immaculately groomed Swede who was standing in the center of the vassals gathered around him at the bar.

Perhaps Pacey's fears about the *Shapieron* had been misplaced. Could what Janet had overheard have been connected with the communications from Gistar ceasing so abruptly? It had happened suspiciously soon afterward. If so, how could

Sverenssen and at least one other member of the delegation have known about it? And how were Sverenssen and Daldanier connected with Verikoff, whom Pacey knew from CIA reports to be a Soviet expert in space communications? If there were some conspiracy between Moscow and an inner clique of the UN, why had Sobroskin cooperated with Pacey? Perhaps that had been part of some even more elaborate ruse. He had been wrong to trust the Russian, he admitted to himself bitterly. He should have used Janet and kept Sobroskin and Malliusk out of it.

And last of all, what was the motive behind the attempt to character-assassinate him personally, compromise Karen Heller, and misrepresent the role they had played at Bruno? It seemed strange that Sverenssen had expected the plan to work, because the document Janet had described would not be substantiated by the official minutes of all the delegation's meetings, a copy of which would also be forwarded to UN Headquarters in New York. Furthermore, Sverenssen knew that as well as anybody; and whatever his other faults, he was not naive. Then a sick feeling formed slowly in his stomach as the truth dawned on him—he had no way of being certain that the minutes which *he* had read and approved, which had recorded the debates verbatim, would be the versions that would go to New York at all. From what Pacey had glimpsed of whatever strange machinations were in progress behind the scenes, anything was possible.

"In my opinion it would be a good thing if the South Atlantic deal did go to the Americans," Sverenssen was saying at the bar. "After the way the United States almost allowed its nuclear industry to be wrecked just before the turn of the century, it's hardly surprising that the Soviets gained a virtual monopoly across most of Central Africa. An equalizing of influence in the general area and the stiffening of competition it would produce could only be in the better long-term interests of all concerned." The three heads around him nodded obediently. Sverenssen made a casual throwing-away motion. "After all, in my position I can hardly allow myself to be swayed by mere national politics. The longer-term advancement of the race as a whole is what is important. That is what I have always stood for and shall continue to stand for."

After everything else this was too much. Pacey choked down his mouthful of coffee and slammed his cup down hard on the table. The heads at the bar turned toward him in surprise. "Hogwash!" he grated across the room at them. "I've never heard such garbage."

Sverenssen frowned his distaste for the outburst. "What do you mean?" he asked coldly. "Kindly explain yourself."

"You had the biggest opportunity ever for the advancement of the race right in your hand, and you threw it away. That's what I mean. I've never listened to such hypocrisy."

"I'm afraid I don't follow you."

Pacey couldn't believe it. "Goddammit, I mean this whole farce we've been having here!" He heard his voice rising to a shout, knew it was bad, but couldn't stop himself in his exasperation. "We were talking to Gistar for weeks. We said nothing, and we achieved nothing. What kind of 'standing for advancement' is that?"

"I agree," Sverenssen said, maintaining his calm. "But I find it strangely inappropriate that *you* should protest in this extraordinary fashion. I would advise you instead to take the matter up with your own government."

That didn't make any sense. Pacey shook his head, momentarily confused. "What are you talking about? The U.S. policy was always to get this moving. We wanted a landing from the beginning."

"Then I can only suggest that your efforts to project that policy have been singularly inept," Sverenssen replied.

Pacey blinked as if unable to believe that he had really heard it. He looked at the others, but found no sympathy for his predicament on any of their faces. The first cold fingers of realization as to what was going on touched at his spine. He shifted his eyes rapidly across their faces in a silent demand for a response, and caught Daldanier's gaze in a way that the Frenchman couldn't evade.

"Let us say it has been apparent to me that the probability of a more productive dialogue would have been improved considerably were it not for the negative views persistently advanced by the representative of the United States," Daldanier said, avoiding the reference to Pacey by name. He spoke in the reluctant voice of somebody who had been forced to offer a reply he would have preferred left unsaid.

"Most disappointing," Saraquez, the Brazilian, commented. "I had hoped for better things from the nation that placed the first man on the Moon. Hopefully the dialogue might be resumed one day, and the lost time made good."

The whole situation was insane. Pacey stared at them dumbfounded. They were all part of the plot. If that were the version that was going to be talked about back on Earth, backed by documentary records, nobody would believe his account of what had happened. Already he wasn't sure if he believed it himself, and he hadn't left Bruno yet. His body began shaking uncontrollably as a rising anger took hold. He got up and moved forward around the table to confront Sverenssen directly. "What is this?" he demanded menacingly. "Look, I don't know who you think you are with the high-and-mighty act and the airs and graces, but you've been making me pretty sick ever since I arrived here. Now let's just forget all that. I want to know what's going on."

"I would strongly advise you to refrain from bringing personal issues into this," Sverenssen said, then added pointedly, "*especially* somebody of your inclination toward the . . . indiscreet."

Pacey felt his color rising. "What do you mean by that?" he demanded.

"Oh, come . . ." Sverenssen frowned and looked away for an instant like somebody seeking to avoid a delicate subject. "Surely you can't expect your affair with your American colleague to have escaped notice completely. Really . . . this kind of thing is embarrassing and uncalled for. I would rather we dropped the matter."

Pacey stared at him for a moment in frank disbelief, then turned his gaze toward Daldanier. The Frenchman turned to pick up his drink. He looked at Saraquez, who avoided his eyes and said nothing. Finally he turned to Van Geelink, the South African, who had only been listening so far. "It was very unwise," Van Geelink said, almost managing to sound apologetic.

"*Him!*" Pacey gestured in Sverenssen's direction and swept his eyes over the others again, this time offering a challenge. "You let *him* stand there and spew something like that? Him of all people? You can't be serious."

"I'm not sure that I like your tone, Pacey," Sverenssen said. "What are you trying to insinuate?"

The situation was real. Sverenssen was actually brazening it out. Pacey felt his fist bunch itself against his side but resisted the urge to lash out. "Are you going to try and tell me I dreamed that too?" he whispered. "Malliusk's assistant—it never happened? Are these puppets of yours going to back you up on that too?"

Sverenssen made a good job of appearing shocked. "If you are suggesting what I think you are suggesting, I would advise you to retract the remark at once and apologize. I find it not only insulting, but also demeaning to somebody in your position. Pathetic fabrications will not impress anybody here, and are hardly likely to do anything to restore the doubtlessly somewhat tarnished image that you will have made for yourself on Earth. I would have credited you with more intelligence."

"Bad, very bad," Daldanier shook his head and sipped his drink.

"Unheard of," Saraquez muttered.

Van Geelink stared uncomfortably at the floor, but said nothing.

At that moment a call from the speaker concealed in the ceiling interrupted. "Calling Mr. Sverenssen of the UN Delegation. Urgent call holding. Would Mr. Sverenssen come to a phone, please."

"You must excuse me, gentlemen," Sverenssen sighed. He looked sternly at Pacey. "I am prepared to attribute this sad exhibition to an aberration occasioned by your having to acclimatize to an extraterrestrial environment, and will say no more about it." His voice took on a more ominous note. "But I must warn you that should you persist in repeating such slanderous accusations when we leave the confines of this establishment, I will be obliged to take a far more serious view. If so, you would not find the consequences beneficial either to your personal situation or to your future prospects professionally. I trust I make myself clear." With that he turned and conveyed himself regally from the room. The other three drank up quickly and left in rapid succession.

That night, his last at Bruno, Pacey was too bewildered, frustrated, and angry to sleep. He stayed up in his room and paced about the floor going over every detail of all that had happened and examining the whole situation first from one angle and then from another, but he could find no pattern that fitted everything. Once again he was tempted to call Alaska, but resisted.

It was approaching 2 A.M. local time when a light tap sounded on the door. Puzzled, Pacey rose from the chair in which he had been brooding and went over to answer it. It was Sobroskin. The Russian slipped in quickly, waited until Pacey closed the door, then reached inside his jacket and produced a large envelope that he passed over without speaking. Pacey opened it. Inside was a pink wallet with a bright red border. The title label on the front read: CONFIDENTIAL. REPORT 238/2G/NTS/FM. NORMAN H. PACEY—PERSONAL PROFILE AND NOTES.

Pacey looked at it incredulously, opened it to ruffle quickly through the contents, then looked up. "How did you get this?" he asked in a hoarse voice.

"There are ways," Sobroskin said vaguely. "Did you know of it?"

"I . . . had reason to believe that something like it might exist," Pacey told him guardedly.

Sobroskin nodded. "I thought you might wish to put it somewhere safe, or perhaps burn it. There was only one other copy, which I have already destroyed, so you may rest with knowledge that it will not get to where it was supposed to go." Pacey looked down at the wallet again, too stunned to reply. "Also, I came across a very strange volume of minutes of the delegation's sessions—nothing at all like what I remembered. I substituted a set of the copies that you and I both saw and approved. Take my word for it that those are the ones that will reach New York. I resealed them myself in the courier's bag just before it was taken to Tycho."

"But . . . how?" was all Pacey could say.

"I have not the slightest intention of telling you." The Russian's voice was curt, but his eyes were twinkling.

Suddenly Pacey grinned as the message at last got through that not everybody in the world was his enemy. "Perhaps it's about time we sat down and compared notes," he said. "I guess I don't have any vodka in the place. How about gin?"

"Precisely the conclusion that I have come to also," Sobroskin said, extracting a sheaf of notes from an inside pocket. "Gin would be fine—I'm very partial to it." He hung his jacket by the door and sat down to make himself comfortable in one of the armchairs while Pacey went into the next room for some glasses. While he was there he checked to make sure the ice maker was well stocked. He had a feeling it was going to be a long night.

chapter nineteen

Garuth had spent twenty-eight years of his life with the *Shapieron.*

A group of scientists on ancient Minerva had advocated a program of extensive climatic and geological engineering to control the predicted buildup of carbon dioxide. The project would have been extremely complicated, however, and simulation models revealed a high risk of rendering the planet uninhabitable sooner rather than later by disrupting the greenhouse effect that enabled Minerva to support life at its considerable distance from the Sun. As an insurance against this risk, another group proposed a method for increasing the Sun's radiation output by modifying its self-gravitation, the idea being that the climatic-engineering program could go ahead, and if instabilities did set in to the point of destroying the greenhouse effect, the Sun could be warmed up to compensate. Thus, overall, Minerva would be no worse off.

As a precaution, the Minervan government decided to test the latter idea first by dispatching a scientific mission aboard the *Shapieron* to conduct a full-scale trial on a sunlike star called Iscaris, whose planets supported no life of any kind. It was as well that they did. Something went wrong that caused Iscaris to go nova, and the expedition had been forced to flee without waiting for completion of the repairs to the ship's main-drive system, which were in progress at the time. Hurled to maximum speed and with its braking system inoperative, the *Shapieron* returned to the vicinity of the Solar System and circled for over twenty years by its own clocks under conditions of compounded time dilation while a million times that amount sped by in the rest of the Universe. And so, eventually, the ship had come to Earth.

As Garuth stood in the doorway of one of the lecture theaters of the ship's school and gazed across the rows of empty seats and scratched worktops to the raised dais and array of screens at the far end, his mind recalled those years. Many who had left Minerva with him had not survived to see this day. At times he had believed that none of them would ever see it. But, as was the pattern of life, a new generation had replaced those who were gone—a generation born and raised in the emptiness of space, who, apart from the brief stay on Earth, had known no other home than the inside of the ship. In many ways Garuth felt like a father to all of them. Although his own faith had wavered at times, theirs had not, and as they had never thought to doubt, he had brought them home. What would happen to them now? he wondered.

Now that the day had arrived, he found he had mixed feelings. The rational part of him was joyful, naturally, that the long exile of his people was over, and they were at last reunited with their kind; but at a deeper level, another part of him would miss this miniature, self-contained world, which for so long now had been the only one he had known. The ship, its way of life, and its tiny, close-knit community were as much part of him as he was part of them. Now all that was over. Would he ever be able to belong in the same way in the mind-defying, overwhelming civilization of Thurien with technologies that bordered on magic and a population of hundreds of billions flung across light-years of stars and space? Could any of them? And if not, could they ever belong anywhere again?

After a while he turned away and began walking slowly through the deserted corridors and communications decks toward an access point into a transfer tube that would take him back to the ship's command section. The floors were worn by years of treading feet; the corners of the walls abraded and smoothed by the passings of innumerable bodies. Every mark and score had its own tale to tell of some event that had occurred somewhere in the course of all those years. Would all that now be forgotten?

In some ways he felt that it already had been. The *Shapieron* was in high orbit over Thurien, and most of its occupants had been taken down to accommodations prepared for them on the surface. There had been no public celebrations or welcoming ceremonies; the fact that the ship had been intercepted still had to be concealed. Only a handful of Thuriens were aware that Garuth and his people existed at all.

Shilohin was waiting on the Command Deck when he arrived, studying information on one of the displays. She looked around as he approached. "I had no idea just how complex the operation to intercept the ship was," she said. "Some of the physics is quite remarkable."

"How so?" Garuth inquired.

"Eesyan's engineers created a composite hyperport—a dual-purpose toroid that functioned as an entry port in one direction and an exit in the other at the same time. That was how they made the substitution so quickly: the dummy came out of one side as we went into the other. But to control it, they had to get their timing down to picoseconds." She paused and gave him a searching look. "You seem sad. Is something wrong?"

He gestured vaguely in the direction he had just come from. "Oh, it's just . . . walking through the ship . . . empty, with nobody around. It takes some getting used to after so long."

"Yes, I know." Her voice fell to an understanding note. "But you shouldn't feel sad. You did what you promised. They will all have their own lives to live again soon. It will be for the better."

"I hope so," Garuth said.

At that moment ZORAC spoke. "I've just received another message through VISAR: Calazar is free now and says he'll see you as soon as you're ready. He suggests meeting at a planet called Queeth, approximately twelve light-years from here."

"We're on our way," Garuth said. He shook his head wonderingly at Shilohin as they left the Command Deck. "I'm not sure I'll ever get used to this."

"The Earthpeople seem to be adapting well," she replied. "The last time I talked to Vic Hunt, he was trying to find a way of getting a coupler installed in his office."

"Earthpeople can adapt to anything," Garuth said with a sigh.

They entered the room in which the Thuriens had installed a row of four portable percepto-coupling cubicles, which represented the only means of using the Thurien system since the Shapieron was not wired for VISAR; hence Calazar could not "visit" the ship. Had the ship not been in orbit and therefore in free-fall, the weight of the microtoroid contained in the communications module of the equipment would have buckled the deck at best. Garuth entered one of the cubicles as Shilohin selected another, and he settled back in the recliner to couple his mind into VISAR. An instant later he was standing alongside Calazar in a large room that was part of an artificial island floating fifty miles above the surface of Queeth. Shilohin appeared next to him a few seconds later.

"Terrans are shrewder than you give them credit for," Garuth stated after the three of them had been talking for some time. "We lived among them for six months, and we know. What is difficult for the Ganymean mind to grasp is that deception and the recognition of deception are parts of their way of life. They have a natural feel for it and will soon get to the truth. Trying to conceal it any longer will only make the situation more embarrassing for all of us when they do. You should be frank with them now."

"And besides, this is not the Ganymean way," Shilohin said. "We have told you the true situation on Earth and how we were made welcome and helped there in every way possible. Your earlier doubts were justified because of the lies reported to you by the Jevlenese, but that no longer holds. You owe it to the Terrans, and to us, to tell them the whole truth now."

Calazar moved away a short distance and turned to stand with his hands clasped behind his back while he considered what they had said. The room they were in formed an oval projection hanging from the underside of the island. Its interior comprised a sunken floor surrounded by a continuous, sloping transparent wall that looked down over the purple, cloud-flecked surface of Queeth in every direction. Outside the wall and above, the mass of the island loomed in a series of metallic contours, blisters, and prominences converging together as they curved away out of sight overhead. "So . . . we won't be able to keep the truth from them," Calazar said at last without turning his head.

"Remember it was the Terrans who first recognized the risk that the Jevlenese could have planned to destroy the *Shapieron* with Earth set up to take the blame," Garuth reminded him. "The Thuriens would never have thought of it. Let's be honest—Terran and Jevlenese minds think very much alike, and Ganymean minds think very differently. We are not predators, and we have not evolved the art of sensing predators."

"And for the same reason you might well find you *need* the Terrans to help get to the bottom of exactly what the Jevlenese are up to," Shilohin added. "Are you any nearer to finding out why they have been systematically falsifying their reports of Earth for years?"

Calazar turned from the viewing wall and faced them again. "No," he admitted.

"Years," Garuth repeated pointedly. "And you suspected nothing until you began receiving the communications from Farside."

Calazar thought for a while, then sighed and nodded in resignation. "You are right—we suspected nothing. Until recently we believed the Jevlenese had integrated well into our society as enthusiastic students of our science and culture. We saw them as cocitizens who would spread outward with us to other worlds. . . ." He gestured behind him and downward. "This one, for example. We even helped them to establish their own autonomously administered and completely self-governed planet as the cradle of a new civilization that would cross the Galaxy in partnership with our own."

"Well, something has obviously gone badly wrong somewhere," Shilohin commented. "Maybe it needs a Terran mind to fathom out what and why."

Calazar looked at them for a moment longer, then nodded again. "Officially Frenua Showm is responsible for our dealings with Earth," he said. "We should talk to her about this. I'll see if I can get her here now." He turned his face away and called in a slightly raised voice, "VISAR, find out if Frenua Showm is available. If she is, show her a replay of our conversation here and ask if she'd join us when she has seen it."

"I'll see to it," VISAR acknowledged.

After a short silence Shilohin remarked, "She didn't strike me as being overfond of Earthpeople in the replay of the Vranix meeting."

"She has never trusted the Jevlenese," Calazar answered. "Her sentiments apparently extend to include Terrans also. Maybe it's not surprising." After another silence he commented, "Queeth is an interesting world, with an emergent intelligent race spread across much of its surface. The Jevlenese have cooperated in bringing many similar planets into our system in the past. They seem to possess a natural aptitude for dealing with primitive races in a way that would not come easily to Ganymeans. I'll show you an example of what I mean. VISAR, let's have another view of the place I was looking at earlier."

A solid image appeared above the open area in the center of the floor. It was of a view looking down on a township in which blocks of hewn rock or baked clay had been built into crude buildings of strangely curved designs. They were huddled around the base of a larger and more imposing edifice of ramps and columns set at the top of an arrangement of broad flat steps ascending on all of its six sides. As Garuth looked at the structure, it reminded him in a vague way of the depictions of ancient temples that he had seen while he was on Earth. The space at the foot of the steps on one side was densely packed with figures.

"Queeth is not integrated into VISAR yet," Calazar informed them as they watched. "Therefore we can't go down there. The view is being captured under high resolution from orbit and injected into your visual cortexes."

The view narrowed, and the magnification increased. The crowd consisted of beings who were bipeds with two arms and a head, but the parts not covered by their roughly cut clothes seemed to be formed from what looked like a pink, glinting crystal rather than skin. Their heads were elongated vertically and covered with reddish mats on top and behind, their limbs were long and slender, and they moved with a flowing grace that Garuth found strangely captivating.

What made his eyes open wider in surprise was the group of five figures posing above the crowd at the top of the steps, standing motionless and erect in flowing garments and high, elaborate headdresses. They seemed aloof and disdainful. And then Garuth realized suddenly what the movements of the slender, pink aliens meant. The movements were signaling supplication and reverence worship, almost. The starship commander turned his head sharply to direct a questioning look at Calazar.

"The Queeths think that the Jevlenese are gods," Calazar explained. "They come down from the sky in magic vessels and work miracles. The Jevlenese have been experimenting with the technique for some time as a means of pacifying primitive races and instilling respect and trust in them before moving them from barbarism toward civilization. Apparently they got the idea from Earth—from their surveillance observations of long ago."

Shilohin seemed concerned. "Is it wise?" she asked. "How could a race hope to advance toward rational methods and effective control of its environment if its foundations are built on such unreason? We know what happened on Earth."

"I was wondering if you'd say something like that," Calazar said. "I myself have been wondering the same thing. Perhaps, before these recent developments, we have been altogether too trusting of the Jevlenese." He nodded soberly. "I think we will see some big changes in the not-too-distant future."

Before either of the others could reply, VISAR informed them, "Frenua Showm will join you now."

"We don't need the view anymore," Calazar said. The image of Queeth vanished, and a second or two later Showm was standing by Calazar.

"I don't like it," she said frankly. "The Terrans will want a confrontation with the Jevlenese, and that would mean all kinds of problems. The whole situation is complicated enough as it is."

"But we did set the Jevlenese up to handle the surveillance of Earth," Calazar pointed out. "Why shouldn't we expect to accept the consequences?"

"We didn't set them up," Showm said. "They argued and pressed demands until the Thurien administration of the time conceded. They practically took it over." She shook her head apprehensively. "And the idea of the Terrans getting involved in our investigations makes me nervous. I don't like the thought of them gaining access to Thurien-level technology. Remember what happened to the Lunarians. And look at what the Jevlenese have been doing since they acquired their own version of VISAR. It's simply a fact with all their kind—if they get their hands on advanced technology, they abuse it." She glanced at Garuth and Shilohin and then looked back at Calazar. "Our concern was for the *Shapieron*. It is now safely at Thurien. If the rest were up to me alone, I'd break off contact with Earth now and leave them out of it completely while we straighten out the situation with the Jevlenese. We don't need Terrans. They've served their purpose."

"I must protest!" Garuth exclaimed. "We regard them as close friends. If it hadn't been for their help, we would never have reached Thurien at all. We cannot simply disregard them. It would be an insult to every Ganymean on the *Shapieron*."

Before Calazar could reply, VISAR interrupted with another announcement. "Excuse me again, but Porthik Eesyan is asking to join you. He says it's urgent."

"Well, we're not going to resolve this in minutes," Calazar said. "Very well, VISAR. We will receive him."

Eesyan materialized at once. "I've just left Hunt and Danchekker at Thurien," he said. The Thuriens took VISAR so much for granted that they never bothered with preliminaries. "I was half expecting it—they've found out about the Jevlenese. They're demanding to talk to us all about them."

Calazar stared at him in astonishment. The others looked equally taken aback. "How?" Calazar asked. "How could they? VISAR has been censoring all references to them from the datastream beamed to Earth. They couldn't have witnessed one scene with a single Jevlenese in it."

"They've deduced that humans are here," Eesyan replied, modifying his previous statement. "They've worked out that the surveillance has to have been run by humans. We'll have to do something. I don't think I can stall them much longer—especially Danchekker."

Garuth turned toward Calazar and Showm, at the same time spreading his hands wide. "I hate to say I told you so, but it is as I said—you *can't* keep secrets from Terrans. Now you've got to talk to them." Calazar looked inquiringly at Showm.

Showm searched her mind for an alternative but couldn't find one. "Very well," she agreed wearily. "If it must be. Let's bring them here while we're together and tell them the facts."

"What about Karen Heller, VISAR?" Calazar asked. "Is she coupled into the system at this moment too?"

"She's at Thurien examining surveillance reports from earlier years," VISAR replied.

"In that case invite her to join us," Calazar instructed. "Then bring them all here as soon as they're ready."

"One second." A short pause followed. Then, "She's just finishing hardcopying some notes through to McClusky. She'll be here in half a minute." Simultaneously Hunt and Danchekker materialized in the middle of the floor.

"I still say I'll never get used to this," Garuth muttered to Shilohin.

chapter twenty

"We have conducted surveillance of Earth since the beginning of human civilization," Calazar declared. "For most of that time the operation has been entrusted to a race within our society known as the Jevlenese, which until now we have not brought to your attention. As you appear to have deduced for yourselves already, the Jevlenese are fully human in form."

"*Homo sapiens* are somewhat . . . volatile," Frenua Showm added, as if feeling that some additional explanation was called for. "Humans possess an intense instinct for rivalry. We felt that the issue was potentially sensitive. It could always be revealed tomorrow, but never unsaid again once said today."

"You see," Danchekker pronounced, looking toward Hunt with some evident satisfaction from where he was standing on the far side of Karen Heller. "As I maintained—an independent hominid line descended from ancestral primates taken to Thurien at the time of the migration from Minerva."

"Er . . . no," Calazar said apologetically.

Danchekker blinked and stared at the alien as if he had just uttered a blasphemy. "I beg your pardon."

"The Jevlenese are far more closely related to *Homo sapiens* than that. In fact they are descended from the same Lunarian ancestors as yourselves—of fifty thousand years ago." Calazar glanced anxiously at Showm, then looked back at the Terrans to await their reactions. Garuth and Shilohin waited in silence; they knew the whole story already.

Hunt and Danchekker looked at each other, equally confused, and then at the Ganymeans again. The Lunarian survivors had reached Earth from the Moon; how could any of them have got to Thurien? The only possible way was if the Thuriens had taken them there. But where could the Thuriens have taken them from? There couldn't have been any survivors on Minerva itself. All of a sudden so many questions began boiling inside Hunt's head that he didn't know where to begin. Danchekker seemed to be having the same problem.

Eventually Karen Heller said, "Let's go back to the start of it all and check some of the basics." She was still looking at Calazar and directing her words to him. "We've been assuming that the Lunarians evolved on Minerva from terrestrial ancestors that you left behind when you went to Thurien. Is that correct, or have you been leaving out something?"

"No, that is correct," Calazar replied. "And by fifty thousand years ago they had developed to the level of a fairly advanced technological civilization very much as you supposed. Up to that point all was as you reconstructed."

"That's good to know, anyhow." Heller nodded and sounded relieved. "So why don't you take the story from there and fill in what happened after that, in the order it happened," she suggested. "That'll save a lot of questions."

"A good idea," Calazar agreed. He paused to collect his thoughts, then looked from side to side to address all three of them, and went on, "When the Ganymeans migrated to Thurien, they left behind an observation system to monitor developments on Minerva. At that time they did not possess the sophisticated communications that we have today, so the information they received was somewhat sporadic and incomplete. But it was enough to give a reasonably complete account of what took place. Perhaps you would like to see Minerva as captured by the sensors operating at that time." He gave an instruction to VISAR, moved back a few paces, and looked expectantly at the center of the floor. A large image appeared, looking solid and real enough to touch. It was an image of a planet.

Hunt knew every coastal outline and surface feature of Minerva by heart. One of the most memorable discoveries of recent years—in fact the one that had started off the investigations which had culminated in proof of Minerva's and the Ganymeans' existence even before the *Shapieron* appeared—had been that of "Charlie," a space suit–clad Lunarian corpse uncovered in the course of excavations on the Moon. From maps found on Charlie, the researchers at Navcomms had been able to reconstruct a six-foot-diameter model of the planet. But the image that Hunt was examining now did not exhibit the enormous ice caps and narrow equatorial belt that Hunt remembered from the model. The two land masses were there, though changed appreciably in outline, but as parts of a more extensive system of continents that stretched north and south to ice caps much smaller—not much larger than those of contemporary Earth. For this was not the Minerva of the Lunarians of fifty thousand years back; it was the Minerva of twenty-five million years before the Lunarians existed. And it was captured live, as it had been; it was no mere model reconstructed from maps. Hunt looked around at Danchekker, but the professor was too spellbound to respond.

For the next ten minutes they watched and listened as Calazar replayed a series of close-ups captured from orbit that showed the imported terrestrial animal species evolving and spreading, extinguishing the native Minervan forms, adapting and radiating at the rate of over two million years per minute, until eventually the first social man-apes emerged from a line that had begun with an artificially modified type of the originally imported primates.

The pattern was very much as had been conjectured for many years on Earth, except that until 2028 it had all been assumed to have taken place on the wrong planet, or at least the fossils discovered from the pre-fifty-thousand-less-a-bit years B.C. period had been attributed to the wrong hominid family. But there was a completely unexpected phase that had never appeared in the story put together by the anthropologists on Earth: early in the man-ape era, the species had returned for a period to a semiaquatic environment, mainly as a consequence of not being equipped physically to deal with predators on land. Thus they had commenced the path that whales and other aquatic mammals had taken, but they reversed it and came out of the water again when their increasing intelligence provided them with other means of protecting themselves, which happened before any significant physical adaptations had developed. This phase accounted for their upright posture, loss of body hair, rudimentary webbing between thumb and index finger, the salt-excreting function of their tear ducts, and several other peculiarities that experts on Earth had been arguing about for years. Danchekker would have spent the rest of the week talking about that alone, but Hunt persuaded him to take it up again with Eesyan at some other time.

After that came the discovery of tools and fire, tribalization, and the sequence of evolving social order that led from primitive hunter-gatherer economies through agriculture and city-building to the discovery of the sciences and the beginnings of industrialization. And there was something about this part of their history too that set them apart from terrestrial humans in Hunt's eyes: the practical and realistic approach that the Lunarians had adopted to everything they did. They had exploited their resources and talents efficiently, without drifting off into fruitless reliance on superstitions and magic to solve their problems as had so many millennia of Earth people. For the early hunters, better weapons and greater skill decided success, not the whims of imaginary gods who needed to be placated. For the crop growers, better knowledge of plants, the land, and the elements improved yields; rituals and incantations did not, and were soon abandoned. And not very long afterward it was measurement, observation, and the powers of reason that uncovered the laws governing the universe and opened up new horizons for the harnessing of energy and the creation of wealth. As a result the Lunarian sciences and industries had mushroomed almost overnight in comparison with the halting, faltering groping toward enlightenment that had come later when the same general pattern repeated itself on Earth.

The scientists on Earth who had recovered the information on the Lunarians had pictured them as an incurably aggressive and warlike breed whose discoveries of advanced technology had inevitably spelled their eventual self-destruction. Hunt and the others now learned that this picture was not really accurate. There had been some feuding and fighting in the earlier periods of Lunarian history, it was true, but by the time of the early industrial period such things had become rare. A greater common cause had united the Minervan nations. Their scientists recognized the deteriorating conditions that were descending with the coming Ice Age, and the whole race embarked on a feverish development of the sciences that would enable them to move to a warmer planet in the centuries ahead. The astronomers of the time singled out Mars and Earth as the most promising candidates. The stakes were survival, and there were no resources to be squandered on internal conflicts, until . . .

About two hundred years before the final, catastrophic war, something happened to change all that. Calazar explained, "It could have been a result of extreme genetic instabilities still inherent in the race. At about the time they had learned to harness steam and were just beginning to explore electricity, a superbreed of Lunarians appeared quite suddenly and advanced a quantum leap ahead of anything else in existence anywhere on the planet. Exactly where or when they appeared we don't know. Numerically they were few to begin with, but they spread and consolidated rapidly."

"Was that when the planet started to polarize?" Heller asked.

"Yes," Calazar replied. "The superbreed became the Lambians. They were totally ruthless. They militarized and formed a totalitarian regime that imposed itself by force on a large portion of the planet before the other nations could muster the strength to resist. Their aim was to gain control of Minerva's industrial and technical capabilities totally and exclusively to guarantee their own move to Earth, which meant taking over the nations that had been pursuing that goal collectively. Submission would have meant extinction. The other nations had no choice but to unite, arm, and defend their security. They became the Cerians. The course was set irrevocably toward a struggle to the death between the two factions."

Hunt watched more scenes showing the gradual transformation of Minerva into one enormous military and manufacturing machine dedicated to preparations for war. The tragedy of what had happened appalled him. There had been no need for it. More effort had gone into armaments than would have been needed to move the whole Lunarian race to Earth twice over. If the Lambians hadn't appeared on the scene when they did, the people on Minerva would have done it. After millennia they had gotten to within two hundred years of achieving the goal that would have saved them from extinction and preserved their civilization, and then they had thrown it all away.

VISAR began showing scenes from the war itself. A world quaked under the shocks of miles-high fireballs that vaporized cities; oceans boiled, and forests flared into carpets of sterile ash writhing and twisting in an atmosphere in turmoil. Then blankets of smoke and dust blotted out the surface and turned the planet into a murky ball of black and brown. Spots of red and slowly pulsating yellow appeared, isolated and glowing dimly at first, but becoming brighter and spreading, then merging as continents ruptured and the planet's interior exploded through and hurled fragments of crust into the void. The asteroids were being born, and what would eventually become Pluto was being carved into a tombstone for a whole race, destined to drift forever far from the Sun. Although Garuth and Shilohin had watched these scenes before, they became very quiet; they alone among all those present had known Minerva as home.

Calazar waited a while for the mood to lighten, then resumed, "The Ganymeans had long been troubled by their consciences over their genetic interference with the early Lunarian ancestors. Therefore their policy toward Minerva had been one of nonintervention in its affairs. You've just seen the result of that. After the calamity a few survivors were left stranded on the Moon with no hope of survival. By that time Thurien had perfected the black-hole technology that made instant communications and transfers of objects possible, so the Ganymeans were aware of events in real time, and they were in a position to intervene. After witnessing the results of their policy, they could not simply stand aside and allow the survivors to perish. Accordingly, they organized a rescue mission and sent several large vessels to the close vicinity of Luna and Minerva."

It took Hunt a few seconds to see the implications of what Calazar had just said. He stared at the Ganymeans in sudden surprise. "Not outside the Solar System?" he queried. "I thought you said you didn't establish large toroids inside planetary systems."

"It was an emergency," Calazar replied. "The Ganymeans decided to forget their rules for once. They didn't have any time to spare."

Hunt's eyes opened wider as the implication hit him: *that* was how Pluto had gotten to where it was! And *that* was what had broken the gravitational coupling between Minerva and its moon. One simple statement had put half his people at Navcomms out of business.

"So the Lunarian ancestors of the human race never came to Earth with the Moon at all," Karen Heller said. "They were *taken* here—by the Ganymeans. The Moon only showed up later."

"Yes," Calazar replied simply.

That answered another mystery. All the math models of the process had required a long transit time for the Moon to get from Minerva to the orbit of Earth. A lot of doubt had been expressed that a handful of Lunarian survivors could have lasted for any length of time at all, let alone with the resources necessary to reach Earth. But with Ganymean intervention added into the equation, all that changed. With some Ganymean help that handful would have established a secure settlement for themselves and been able to make a viable start at rebuilding their culture. So why had they plunged back into a barbarism that had taken tens of thousands of years to recover from? The only answer could be the upheavals caused by Luna being captured later. The truth was so ironic, Hunt thought: if they hadn't been stabbed in the back by their own Moon, they could have been back into space by 45,000 B.C., if not sooner.

"But not all were taken to Earth," Danchekker concluded. "Another group was taken back to Thurien, and have since become the Jevlenese."

"It was so," Calazar confirmed.

"Even after all that had happened," Showm explained, "the Cerians and the Lambians were unmixable. Since the Lambians had been the cause of the trouble, the Ganymeans of that time considered that more good would come out of the Lambians being taken to Thurien and—it was hoped—being integrated into Ganymean ways and society. The Cerians were taken to Earth at their own request. They were offered ongoing aid to rebuild, but they declined. So a surveillance system was set up instead to keep an eye on them—as much for their own protection as anything." Hunt was surprised. If the surveillance system had been in place that long, the Ganymeans would have known about the collapse of the colony which they themselves had helped found. Why had they let it happen?

"So how did the others make out—the Lambians?" Heller asked. "They couldn't have been running the surveillance that far back. How did they get their hands on it?"

Calazar emitted a heavy sigh. "They caused a lot of problems for the Thuriens of that time, so much so that when Luna came to be captured by Earth and caused widespread catastrophes that demolished the fragile beginnings of the new Cerian society that had started to take root there, it was decided to leave things be. With troubles of their own at home, the Thuriens were not eager to see another human civilization rushing headlong toward advancement, perhaps to repeat the Minervan disaster." He shrugged as if to say that right or wrong, that was the way it had been, then resumed, "But as time went by and further generations of Lambians came and went, the situation seemed to improve. Signs appeared that they could be integrated fully into Ganymean society, so the Ganymean leaders adopted a policy of appeasement in an attempt to accelerate the process. As a result the Jevlenese, as the descendants of the Lambians were called by then, acquired control of the surveillance program."

"A mistake," Showm commented. "They should have been exiled."

"With hindsight, I think I agree," Calazar said. "But that was long before either my time or yours."

"How about telling us something about this system," Hunt suggested. "How does it work?"

Eesyan answered. "Mostly from space. Until about a century ago, it was comparatively simple. Since Earth entered its electronics and space era, the Jevlenese have had to be more careful. Their devices are very small and virtually undetectable. Most of their information comes from intercepting and retransmitting your communications, such as the laser links between Jupiter and Earth. At one time in the early years of your space program they manufactured instrument packages to resemble pieces of your own space debris, but they had to stop when you started clearing things up. That experiment had its uses though; that was where we got the idea of building a perceptron that looked like a Boeing."

"But how could they fake the reports as well as they did?" Hunt asked. "They must have something of their own like VISAR. No Mickey Mouse computer did that."

"They have," Eesyan told him. "Long ago, when there seemed reason to feel optimistic about the Jevlenese, the Thuriens helped them establish their own autonomous world. It's called Jevlen, on the fringe of our developed region of space, and it's equipped with a system known as JEVEX, which is VISAR-like but independent of VISAR. Like VISAR, JEVEX operates across its own system of many stars. The surveillance system from Earth is coupled into JEVEX, and the reports that we receive are transmitted indirectly from JEVEX through VISAR."

"So it isn't difficult to understand how the fabrications and distortions were engineered," Showm said. "So much for philanthropy. They should never have been allowed to operate such a system."

"But why did they do it?" Karen Heller asked. "We still don't have an answer. Their reports were pretty accurate up until about the time of World War II. The problems of the late twentieth century were somewhat exaggerated, but for the last thirty years it's turned into pure fiction. Why would they want you to think we were still heading for World War III?"

"Who can understand the contortions of human minds?" Showm asked, using the general term unconsciously.

Hunt just caught the look that she flashed involuntarily at Calazar as she spoke. There was something more behind it all, he realized—something that the Thuriens were not divulging even now. Whatever it was, he was just as certain in that same split second that Garuth and Shilohin didn't know about it, either. But he didn't feel this was the time to force a confrontation. Instead he steered the discussion back into technicalities as he remembered something else. "What kind of archives does JEVEX have?" he asked. "Do they go all the way back to the Ganymean civilization on Minerva, like VISAR's?"

"No," Eesyan replied. "JEVEX is of much more recent vintage. There was no need to load it with VISAR's complete archives, which concerned only Ganymeans." He studied Hunt curiously for a few seconds. "Are you thinking about the anomalies in the displacements of background stars that VISAR noticed in the shots of the *Shapieron*?"

Hunt nodded. "That explains it, doesn't it. JEVEX couldn't have known about the displacements. VISAR had access to the original design data for the ship; JEVEX didn't."

"Correct," Eesyan said. "There were a few other anomalies too, but all similar—all to do with an old Ganymean technology that JEVEX couldn't have known very much about. That was when we became suspicious." At which point everything that had ever come from JEVEX would be suspect, Hunt saw. But there would have been no way of checking any of the rest without bypassing the Jevlenese completely and going straight to the source of the information—Earth. And that was precisely what the Thuriens had done.

Calazar seemed anxious to move them away from the whole topic. When a lull presented itself, he said, "Garuth wanted me to show you another sequence that he thought you would find interesting. VISAR, show us the Ganymean landing at Gorda."

Hunt jerked his head up in surprise. The name was familiar. Danchekker was looking incredulous as well. Heller was looking from one to the other of the men with a puzzled frown; she was less conversant with Charlie's story than they were.

Don Maddson's linguistics team at Navcomms had eventually succeeded in deciphering a notebook of Charlie's that had re-

mained a mystery for a long time. It gave a day-to-day account
of Charlie's experiences as one member of a rapidly diminishing
band of Cerian survivors making a desperate trek across the lunar surface to reach a base that offered their last hope of escape
from the Moon, if any hope remained at all. The account had
covered events up to the point of Charlie's arrival at the place
at which he had been found, by which time attrition of various
kinds had reduced his band to just two—him, and a companion
whose name had been Koriel. Charlie had collapsed there from
the effects of a malfunctioning life-support system, and Koriel
had left on a lone bid to reach the base. Apparently he had
never returned. The base was called Gorda.

A new image appeared above the center of the floor. It was
of a wilderness of dust and boulders etched harshly beneath a
black sky thick with stars. The landscape had been seared and
churned by forces of unimaginable violence to leave just the
twisted and mutilated wreckage of what could once have been
a vast base. Amid the desolation stood a single structure that
appeared to have survived almost intact—a squat, armored
dome or turret of some kind, blown open on one side. Its interior was in darkness.

"That was all that was left of Gorda," Calazar commented.
"The view you are seeing is from a Thurien ship that had
landed a few minutes before."

A small vehicle, roughly rectangular but with pods and other
protuberances cluttering its outside, moved slowly into view
from behind the camera, flying twenty feet or so above the
ground. It landed near the dome, and a group of Ganymeans
wearing space suits emerged and began moving cautiously
through the wreckage toward the opening. Then they stopped
suddenly. There were movements in the shadows ahead of them.

A light came on from somewhere behind to light up the
opening. It revealed more figures, also in suits, standing in
front of what looked like an entrance leading down to an underground section of whatever the dome had been part of.
Their suits were different, and they stood a full head and
shoulders shorter than the Ganymeans facing them from a few
yards away. They were carrying weapons, but they appeared
unsure of themselves as they looked nervously at one another
and at the Ganymeans. None of them seemed to know what to
do or what to expect. None of them, except one . . .

He was standing in front of the others in a blue space suit

that was plastered with dust and grotesquely discolored by scorch marks, his feet planted firmly astride, and a rifle-like weapon held unwaveringly in one hand to cover the leading Ganymean. With his free arm he made a gesture behind him to wave the others forward. The movement was decisive and commanding. They obeyed, some moving up to stand on either side of him, others moving out to cover the aliens from protected positions among the surrounding debris. He was taller than the others and heavy in build, and the lips of the face behind his visor were drawn back in a snarl to reveal white teeth that contrasted sharply with his dark, unshaven chin and cheeks. Something unintelligible came through on audio. Although the words meant nothing, the tone of challenge and defiance was unmistakable.

"Our surveillance methods were not as comprehensive then," Calazar commented. "The language was not known."'

In the scene before them, the Ganymean leader was replying in his own tongue, evidently relying on intonation and gesture to dispel alarm. As the exchange continued, the tension seemed to ease. Eventually the human giant lowered his weapon, and the others who had taken cover began emerging again. He beckoned for the Ganymeans to follow, and as the ranks behind him opened to make way, he turned away to lead them down into the inner entrance.

"That was Koriel," Garuth said.

Hunt had already guessed that. For some reason he felt very relieved.

"He succeeded!" Danchekker breathed. Elation was showing on his face, and he swallowed visibly. "He *did* get to Gorda. I'm—I'm glad to know that."

"Yes," Garuth said, reading the further question written across Hunt's face. "'We have studied the ship's log. They did return, but Koriel's companion had already died. They left him as they found him. They did manage to rescue some of the others who had been left strung out along the way, however."

"And after that?" Danchekker queried. "Another thing we have often wondered is whether or not Koriel was among those who finally reached Earth. It seems now that he may well have been. Do you happen to know if he in fact was?"

In reply Calazar called up another image. It was a view of a settlement formed from a dozen or so portable buildings of unfamiliar design, situated on a river bank against a back-

ground of semitropical forest with the hazy outline of mountains rising in the distance beyond. On one side was what
looked like a supply dump, with rows of stacked crates, drums,
and other containers. A crowd of two or three hundred figures
was assembled in the foreground—human figures, dressed
mainly in simple but serviceable-looking shirts and pants, and
many of them carrying weapons either holstered at the waist or
slung across the shoulder.

Koriel was standing ahead of them, huge, broad-shouldered,
with dense, black hair, unsmiling features, and his thumbs
hooked loosely in his belt. Two lieutenants were standing on
either side and a pace behind him. Some of the arms in the
crowd began rising in a farewell salutation.

Then the view began to fall away and tilt. The settlement
shrank quickly and lost itself among a carpet of treetops, which
in turn faded to become just a hazy area of green on a patch-
work of colors taking form as the scale reduced and more of
the surrounding landscape flowed into view from the sides.
"The last view from the ship as it departed from Earth to return to Thurien," Calazar said. A coastline that was recognizable as part of the Red Sea moved into the picture and shrank
to become part of a familiar section of Middle East geography
despite being distorted at the periphery by perspective. Finally
the edge of the planet itself appeared, already looking distinctly curved.

They watched in silence for a long time. Eventually
Danchekker murmured, "Imagine . . . the whole human race
began with that tiny handful. After all that they had endured,
they conquered a whole world. What an extraordinary race
they must have been."

This was one of the few occasions on which Hunt had seen
Danchekker genuinely moved. And he felt it too. He thought
back again to the scenes from the Lunarian war and the visions
that the Jevlenese had created of Earth stampeding toward exactly the same catastrophe. And yet it had almost come true. It
had been close—far too close. If Earth had not changed course
when it did, just two or three decades more would have made
that come true. And then Charlie, Koriel, Gorda, the efforts of
the Thuriens, the struggles of the handful of survivors that he
had just seen—and all that they endured after that—would
have been for nothing.

It brought to mind Wellington's words after Waterloo: "It

was a close-run thing, a damned close-run thing—the closest-
run thing you ever saw in your life."

chapter twenty-one

After hearing Norman Pacey's account of the events at Bruno,
Jerol Packard lodged a confidential request with an office of
the CIA for a compendium of everything that had accumulated
in its files over the years concerning Sverenssen and, for good
measure, the other members of the UN Farside delegation as
well. Cliifford Benson, the CIA official who had dealt with the
request, summarized the findings a day later at a closed-door
session in Packard's State Department office.

"Sverenssen reappeared in Western Europe in 2009 with a
circle of social and financial contacts already established. How
that happened is not clear. We can't find any authenticated
traces of him for about ten years before then—in fact from the
time he was supposed to have been killed in Ethiopia." Benson
gestured at a section of the summary charts of names, photographs, organizations, and interconnecting arrows pinned to a
wallboard. "His closest ties were with a French-British-Swiss
investment-banking consortium, a big part of which is still run
by the same families that set up a network of financial operations around Southesast Asia in the nineteenth century to laun-
der the reveneues from the Chinese opium trade. Now here's
an interesting thing—one of the biggest names on the French
side of that consortium is a blood relative of Daldanier. In fact
the two names have been connected for three generations."

"Those people are pretty tightly knit," Caldwell commented.
"I don't know if I'd attach a lot of significance to something
like that."

"If it were an isolated case, I wouldn't, either," Benson
agreed. "But look at the rest of the story." He indicated another
part of the chart. "The British and Swiss sides control a sizable part of the world's bullion business and are connected

through the London gold market and its mining affiliations to South Africa. And look what name we find prominent among the ones at the end of that line."

"Is that Van Geelink of the same family as Sverenssen's cohort?" Lyn asked dubiously.

"It's the same," Benson said. "There are a number of them, all connected with different parts of the same business. It's a complicated setup." He paused for a moment, then resumed, "Up until around the first few years of this century, a lot of Van Geelink–controlled money went into preserving white dominance in the area by undermining the stability of black Africa politically and economically, which is one reason why nobody seemed interested in backing resistance to the Cuban and Communist subversions that were going on from the '70s through '90s. To maintain their own position militarily in the face of trade embargoes, the family organized arms deals through intermediaries, frequently South American regimes."

"Is this where the Brazilian guy fits in?" Caldwell asked, raising an eyebrow.

Benson nodded. "Among others. Saraquez's father and grandfather were both big in commodity financing, especially to do with oil. There are links from them as well as from the Van Geelinks to the prime movers behind the destabilization of the Middle East in the late twentieth century. The main reason for that was to maximize short-term oil profits before the world went nuclear, which also accounts for the orchestrated sabotage of public opinion against nuclear power at around the same time. A side effect that worked in the Saraquezes' interests was that it boosted the demand for Central American oil." Benson shrugged and tossed out his hands. "There's more, but you can see the gist of it. The same kind of thing shows up with a few more who were on that delegation. It's one happy family, in a lot of cases literally."

Caldwell studied the charts with a new interest once Benson had finished. After a while he sat back and asked, "So what does it tell us? What's the connection with what went on at Farside? Figured that out yet?"

"I just collect facts," Benson replied. "I leave the rest to you people."

Packard moved to the center of the room. "There is another interesting side to the pattern," he said. "The whole network represents a common ideology—feudalism." The others looked at him curiously. He explained, "Cliff's already mentioned their involvemnt in the antinuclear hysteria of thirty or forty years ago, but there's more to it than that." He waved a hand at the charts that Benson had been using. "Take the banking consortium that gave Sverenssen his start as an example. Throughout the last quarater of the 1900s they provide a lot of behind-the-scenes backing for moves to fob the Third World off with 'appropriate technologies,' for various antiprogress, antiscience lobbies, and that kind of thing. In South Africa we had another branch of the same net pushing racism and preventing progressive government, industrialization, and comprehensive education for blacks. And across the ocean we had a series of right-wing fascist regimes protecting minority interests by military takeovers and at the same time obstructing general advancement. You see, it all adds up to the same basic ideology—preserving the feudal privileges and interests of the power structure of the time. What it says, I guess, is that nothing's changed all that much."

Lyn appeared puzzled. "But it has, hasn't it?" she said. "That's not the way the world is these days. I thought this guy Sverenssen and the rest were committed to just the opposite—advancing the whole world all over."

"What I meant was that the same people are still there," Packard replied. "But you're right—their underlying policy seems to have shifted in the last thirty years or so. Sverenssen's bankers provided easy credit for Nigerian fusion and steel under a gold-backed standard that couldn't have worked without the cooperation of people like the Van Geelinks. South American oil helped defuse the Middle East by leading the changeover to hydrogen-based substitutes, which was one of the things that made disarmament possible." He shrugged. "Suddenly everything changed. The backing was there for things that could have been done fifty years earlier."

"So what about their line at Bruno?" Caldwell asked again, looking mystified. "It doesn't fit."

There was a short silence before Packard proceeded. "How's this for a theory? Controlling minorities never have anything to gain from change. That explains their traditional opposition to technology all through history, unless it offered something to advance their interests. That meant it was okay as long as they controlled it. Hence we get the traditional stance of their kind through to the end of the last century. But by that time it

was becoming obvious from the way the world was going that
if something didn't change soon, somebody was going to start
pressing buttons, and then there wouldn't be any kind of pond
left to be a fish in. The only choice was nuclear reactors or nuclear bombs. So this revolution they made happen, and they
managed to maintain control in the process—which was neat.

"But Thurien and everything it could mean was something
else. This group would have been swept away by the time the
dust from that kind of revolution finally settled. So they cor-
nered the UN handling of the matter and put up a wall until
they got some ideas about where to go next." He threw out his
hands and looked around the room to invite comment.

"How did they find out about the relay?" Norman Pacey
asked from a corner. "We know from what Gregg and Lyn said
that the coded signals had nothing to do with it. And we know
Sobroskin wasn't mixed up with it."

"They must have been involved with getting rid of it,"
Packard replied. "I don't know how, but I can't think of anything else. They could have used some personnel of UNSA
who they knew wouldn't talk, or maybe a government or commercial outfit that operates independently to send a bomb or
something out there . . . probably as soon as the first signal
from Gistar came in months ago. So what they've been doing
is stalling things until it got there."

Caldwell nodded. "It makes sense. You've got to hand it to
them—they almost had it tied up. If it wasn't for McClusky . . . who knows?"

A solemn silence descended and persisted for a while. Eventually Lyn looked inquiringly from one man to another. "So
what happens now?" she asked.

"I'm not sure," Packard replied. "It's a complicated situation
all around."

She looked at him uncertainly for a second. "You're not
saying they might get away with it?"

"It's a possibility."

Lyn stared as if she couldn't believe her ears. "But that's ridiculous! You're telling us that for . . . I don't know how many
years, people like this have been keeping whole nations backward, sabotaging education, and supporting all kinds of idiot
cults and propaganda to stay on top of the pile, and there's
nothing anybody can do? That's crazy!"

"I didn't put the situation as definitely as that," Packard

said. "I said it's complicated. Being pretty sure of something and being able to prove it are two different things. We're going to have to do a lot more work to make a case out of it."

"But, but . . ." Lyn searched for words. "What else do you need? It's all wrapped up. Bombing that relay outside Pluto has to be enough on its own. They weren't acting for the whole planet when they did that, and certainly not in its interests. There has to be enough in that to nail them."

"We don't have any way of *knowing* for sure that they did it," Packard pointed out. "It's pure speculation. Maybe the relay just broke down. Maybe Calazar's organization did it. You couldn't pin anything on Sverenssen that'd stick."

"He knew it was going to happen," Lyn objected. "Of course he was mixed up in it."

"Knew on whose say-so?" Packard countered. "One little girl at Bruno who thinks she might have overheard something that she didn't understand, anyway." He shook his head. "You heard Norman's story. Sverenssen could produce witnesses lined up all down the hall to state that he never had anything to do with her. She became infatuated, then went running to Norman with a silly story to get even when Sverenssen wasn't interested. Such things happen all the time."

"What about the fake signals he got her to send?" Lyn persisted.

"What fake signals?" Packard shrugged. "All part of the same game. She made up that story. They never existed."

"But the Thurien records say they did," Lyn said. "You don't have to tell the whole world about Alaska right now, but when the time's right you can wheel in a whole planet of Ganymeans to back you up."

"True, but all they confirm is that some strange signals came in that weren't sent officially. They don't confirm where they came from or who sent them. The header formats could have been faked to resemble Farside's." Packard shook his head again. "When you think it through, the evidence is not anywhere near conclusive."

Lyn turned an imploring face toward Caldwell. He shook his head regretfully. "He's got some good points. I'd like to see them all go down just as much as you would, but it doesn't look as if the case to do it is there yet."

"The problem is you can never get near them," Benson said, coming back into the conversation. "They don't make many slips, and when they do you're never around. Now and again you get something leaking out like what happened at Bruno, but it's never enough to be a clincher. That's what we need— something to clinch it. We need to put somebody on the inside, close to Sverenssen." He shook his head dubiously. "But something like that needs a lot of research and planning, and it takes a long time to select the right person for the job. We'll start working on it, but don't hold your breath waiting for results."

Lyn, Caldwell, and Pacey were all staying at the Washington Central Hilton. They ate dinner together that evening, and over coffee Pacey talked more about what they had learned in Packard's office.

"You can trace the same basic struggle right down through history," he told them. "Two opposed ideologies—the feudalism of the aristocracies on one side, and the republicanism of the artisans, scientists, and city-builders on the other. You had it with the slave economies of the ancient world, the intellectual oppression of the Church in Europe in the Middle Ages, the colonialism of the British Empire, and, later on, Eastern Communism and Western consumerism."

"Keep 'em working hard, give 'em a cause to believe in, and don't teach 'em to think too hard, huh?" Caldwell commented.

"Exactly." Pacey nodded. "The last thing you want is an educated, affluent, and emancipated population. Power hinges on the restriction and control of wealth. Science and technology offer unlimited wealth. Therefore science and technology have to be controlled. Knowledge and reason are enemies; myth and unreason are the weapons you fight them with."

Lyn was still thinking about the conversation an hour later when the three of them were sitting around a small table in a quiet alcove that opened off one end of the lobby. They had opted for a last drink before calling it a night, but the bar had seemed too crowded and noisy. It was the same war that Vic, consciously or not, had been fighting all his life, she realized. The Sverenssens who had almost shut down Thurien stood side by side with the Inquisition that had forced Galileo to recant, the bishops who had opposed Darwin, the English nobility who would have ruled the Americans as a captive market for some industry, and the politicians on both sides of the Iron Curtain who had seized the atom to hold a world to ransom with bombs. She wanted to contribute something to his war, even if only a token gesture to show that she was on his side. But what? She had never felt so restless and so helpless at the same time.

Eventually Caldwell remembered an urgent call that he needed to make to Houston. He excused himself and stood up, saying he would be back in a few minutes, then disappeared into the arcade of souvenir and menswear shops that led to the elevators. Pacey lounged back in his seat, put his glass down on the table, and looked across at Lyn. "You're being very quiet," he said. "Eat too much steak?"

She smiled. "Oh . . . just thinking. Don't ask what about. We've talked too much shop today already."

Pacey stretched out an arm to pick up a cracker from the dish in the center of the table and popped it into his mouth. "Do you get up to D.C. much?" he asked.

"Quite a bit. I don't stay here very often, though. I usually put up at the Hyatt or the Constitution."

"Most UNSA people do. I guess this is one of the two or three favorite places for political people. It's almost like an after-hours diplomatic club at times."

"The Hyatt's pretty much like that for UNSA."

"Uh huh." Pause. "You're from the East Coast, aren't you?"

"New York originally—upper East Side. I moved south after college to join UNSA. I thought I was going to be an astronaut, but I ended up flying a desk." She sighed. "Not complaining though. Working with Gregg has its moments."

"He seems quite a guy. I imagine he'd be an easy boss to get along with."

"He does what he says he's going to do, and he doesn't say he's going to do what he can't. Most of the people in Navcomms respect him a lot, even if they don't always agree with him. But it's mutual. You know, one of the things he always—"

A call from the paging system interrupted. "Calling Mr. Norman Pacey. Would Norman Pacey come to the front desk, please. There is an urgent message waiting. Urgent message for Norman Pacey at the front desk. Thank you."

Pacey rose from his chair. "I wonder what the hell that is. Excuse me."

"Sure."

"Want me to order you another drink?"

"I'll do it. You go ahead."

Pacey made his way across the lobby, which was fairly busy with people coming and going and parties assembling for late dinner. One of the clerks at the desk raised his eyebrows inquiringly as he approached. "My name is Pacey. You paged me just now. There should be a message here somewhere."

"One moment, sir." The clerk turned to check the pigeon-holes behind him, and after a few seconds turned back again holding a white envelope. "Mr. Norman Pacey, Room 3527?" Pacey showed the clerk his key. The clerk passed over the envelope.

"Thanks." Pacey moved a short distance away to open the envelope in a corner by the Eastern Airlines booth. Inside was a single sheet of paper on which was handwritten:

> *Important that I talk to you immediately. Am across lobby. Suggest we use your room for privacy.*

Pacey frowned, then looked up and from side to side to scan the lobby. After a few seconds he picked out a tall, swarthy man in a dark suit watching him from the far side. The man was standing near a group of half a dozen noisily chattering men and women, but he appeared to be alone. He gave a slight nod. Pacey hesitated for a moment, then returned it. The man glanced casually at his watch, looked around, and sauntered toward the arcade that led through to the elevators. Pacey watched him disappear, and then walked back to where Lyn was sitting.

"Something just came up," he told her. "Look, I'm sorry about this, but I have to meet somebody right away. Give Gregg my apologies, would you."

"Want me to tell him what it's about?" Lyn asked.

"I don't know myself yet. I'm not sure how long it'll take."

"Okay. I'll be fine just watching the world go by. See you later."

Pacey walked back across the lobby and entered the arcade just in time to miss a tall, lean, silver-haired and immaculately dressed figure turning away from the reception desk after collecting a room key. The man moved unhurriedly to the center of the lobby and stopped to survey the surroundings.

* * *

The swarthy man was waiting a short distance from the elevators when Pacey emerged a minute or so later on the thirty-fifth floor. As Pacey approached him, he turned silently and led the way to 3527, then stood aside while Pacey unlocked the door. Pacey allowed him to enter first, then followed and closed the door behind them as the other turned on the light. "Well?" he demanded.

"You may call me Ivan," the swarthy man said. He spoke in a heavy European accent. "I am from the Soviet Embassy here in Washington. I have a message that I have been instructed to deliver to you in person: Mikolai Sobroskin wishes to meet with you urgently concerning matters of some considerable importance which, I understand, you are aware of. He suggests that you meet in London. I have the details. You may convey your response back to him through me." He watched for a few seconds while Pacey stared back uncertainly, not knowing what to make of the message, then reached inside his jacket and drew out what looked like a folded sheet of stiffened paper. "I was told that if I gave you this, you would be satisfied that the message is genuine."

Pacey took the sheet and unfolded it. It was a blank sample of the pink, red-bordered document wallet used by the UN for confidential information. Pacey stared at it for a few seconds, then looked up and nodded. "I can't give you an answer on my own authority right at this moment," he said. "I'll have to get in touch with you again later tonight. Could we do that?"

"I had expected as much," Ivan said. "There is a coffee shop one block from here called the Half Moon. I will wait there."

"I may have to take a trip somewhere," Pacey warned. "It could take a while."

Ivan nodded. "I will be waiting," he said, and with that, he left.

Pacey closed the door behind him and spent a few minutes walking thoughtfully back and forth across the room. Then he sat down in front of the datagrid terminal, activated it, and called Jerol Packard's private home number.

Downstairs in the alcove to one side of the lobby, Lyn was thinking about Egyptian pyramids, medieval cathedrals, British dreadnoughts, and the late-twentieth-century arms race. Were they all parts of the same pattern too? she wondered. No matter how much more wealth per capita improving technology made possible, always there had been something to soak up the surplus and condemn ordinary people to a lifetime of labor. No matter how much productivity increased, people never seemed to work less, only differently. So if they didn't reap the fruits, who did? She was beginning to see lots of things in ways she hadn't before.

She didn't really notice the man in the seat that Pacey had vacated a few minutes earlier until he started speaking. "May I sit with you? It is so relaxing to do nothing for a few minutes at the end of a hectic day and just watch the human race going about its business. I do hope you don't mind. The world is so full of lonely people who insist on making islands of themselves and a tragedy of life. It always strikes me as such a shame, and so unnecessary."

Lyn's glass nearly dropped from her hand as she found herself looking at a face that she had seen only hours before on one of the charts that Clifford Benson had hung on the wall in Packard's office. It was Niels Sverenssen.

She downed the rest of her drink in one gulp, almost choking herself in the process, and managed, "Yes . . . it is, isn't it?"

"Are you staying here, if you don't mind my asking?" Sverenssen inquired. She nodded. Sverenssen smiled. There was something about his aristocratic bearing and calculated aloofness that set him apart from the greater part of the male half of the race in a way that many women find alluring, she admitted to herself. With his elegant crown of silver hair and well-tanned noble features, he was . . . . well, not exactly handsome by *Playgirl* standards, but intriguing in some undeniable way. And the distant look in his eyes made them almost hypnotic. "On your own?" he asked.

She nodded again. "Sort of."

Sverenssen raised his eyebrows and motioned his head in the direction of her glass. "I see you are empty. I was on my way to have an unwinder myself in the bar. It seems that, temporarily at least, we are both islands in a world of nine billion people—a most unfortunate situation, and one which I am sure we could do something to correct. Would you consider it an impertinence if I invited you to join me?"

Pacey stepped into the elevator and found Caldwell there, evidently on his way back down to the lobby.

"It took longer than I thought," Caldwell said. "There's a lot of hassle going on at Houston about budget allocations. I'm going to have to get back there pretty soon. I've been away too long as it is." He looked at Pacey curiously. "Where's Lyn?"

"She's downstairs. I got called away." Pacey stared at the inside of the doors for a second. "Sobroskin's been in touch via the Soviet Embassy here. He wants me to meet him in London to talk about something."

Caldwell raised his eyebrows in surprise. "You're going?"

"I'll know later. I just called Packard, and I'm going to take a cover over to his place right now to tell him about it. I've arranged to meet somebody later tonight to let them know." He shook his head. "And I thought this would be a quiet night."

They came out of the elevator and walked through the arcade to where Pacey had left Lyn. The alcove was empty. They looked around, but she was nowhere in sight.

"Maybe she went to the little girls' room," Caldwell suggested.

"Probably."

They stood for a while talking and waiting, but there was no sign of Lyn. Eventually Pacey said, "Maybe she wanted another drink, couldn't get served out here, and went into the bar. She might still be in there."

"I'll check it out," Caldwell said. He about-faced and stumped away across the lobby.

A minute later he returned, wearing the expression of somebody who had been hit from behind by a tramcar while minding his own business in the middle of the Hilton. "She's in there," he announced in a dull voice, slumping down into one of the empty seats. "She's got company. Go see for yourself, but stay back from the door. Then come back and tell me if it's who I think it is."

A minute later Pacey thudded down into the chair opposite. He looked as if he had been hit by the same tram on its return trip. "It's him," he said numbly. A long time seemed to pass. Then Pacey murmured, "He's got a place up in Connecticut somewhere. He must have stopped off in D.C. for a few days on his way back from Bruno. We should have picked some other place."

"How'd she look?" Caldwell asked.

Pacey shrugged. "Fine. She seemed to be doing most of the talking, and looked quite at home. If I hadn't known any better, I'd have said it was some guy swallowing a line and well on his way to ending up a few hundred poorer. She looks as if she can take care of herself okay."

"But what the hell does she think she's trying to do?"

"You tell me. You're her boss. I hardly know her."

"But Christ, we can't just leave her there."

"What can we do? She walked in there, and she's old enough to drink. Anyhow, I can't go in there because he knows me, and there's no point in making problems. That leaves you. What are you going to do—make like the boss who can't see when he's being a wet blanket, or what?" Caldwell scowled irritably at the table but seemed stuck for a reply. After a short silence Pacey stood up and spread his hands apologetically. "Look, Gregg, I know this sounds kind of bad, but I'm going to have to leave you to handle it in whatever way you want. Packard's waiting for me right now, and it's important. I have to go."

"Yeah, okay, okay." Caldwell waved a hand vaguely. "Call me when you get back and let me know what's happening."

Pacey left, using a side entrance to avoid crossing the lobby in front of the bar. Caldwell sat brooding for a while, then shrugged, shook his head perplexedly, and went back up to his room to catch up on some reading while he waited for a call from Pacey.

chapter twenty-two

Danchekker gazed for a long time at the two solid images being displayed side by side in a laboratory in Thurien. They were highly magnified reproductions of a pair of organic cells obtained from a species of bottom-dwelling worm from an ocean on one of the Ganymean worlds, and showed the internal structures color-enhanced for easy identification of the nuclei and other components. Eventually he shook his head and looked up. "I'm afraid I am obliged to concede defeat. They both appear identical to me. And you are saying that one of them does not belong to this species at all?" He sounded incredulous.

Shilohin smiled from a short distance behind him. "The one on the left is a single-cell microorganism that contains enzymes programmed to dismantle the DNA of its own nucleus and reassemble the pieces into a copy of the host organism's DNA," she said. "When that process is complete, the whole structure is rapidly transformed into a duplicate of whatever type of cell the parasite happens to be residing in. From then on the parasite has literally become a part of the host, indistinguishable from the host's own naturally produced cells and therefore immune to its antibodies and rejection mechanisms. It evolved on a planet subject to intense ultraviolet radiation from a fairly hot, blue star, probably from a cell-repair mechanism that stabilized the species against extreme mutation. As far as we know it's a unique adaptation. I thought you'd be interested in seeing it."

"Extraordinary," Danchekker murmured. He walked across to the device of gleaming metal and glass from which the data to generate the image originated, and stooped to peer into the tiny chamber containing the tissue sample. "I would be most interested in conducting some experiments of my own on this organism when I get back. Er . . . do you think the Thuriens might let me take a sample of it?"

Shilohin laughed. "I'm sure you'd be welcome to, Professor, but how do you propose carrying it back to Houston? You're forgetting that you're not really here."

"Tch! Stupid of me." Danchekker shook his head and stepped back to gaze at the apparatus around them, the function of most of which he still failed to comprehend. "So much to learn," he murmured half to himself. "So much to learn . . ." He thought for a while, and his expression changed to a frown. Eventually he turned to face Shilohin again. "There's something about this whole Thurien civilization that has been puzzling me. I wonder if you can help."

"I'll try. What's the problem?"

Danchekker sighed. "Well . . . I don't know . . . after twenty-five *million* years, it should be even *more* advanced than it is, I would have thought. It is far ahead of Earth, to be sure, but I can't see Earth requiring anywhere near that amount of time to reach a level comparable to Thurien's today. It seems . . . strange."

"The same thought occurred to me," Shilohin said. "I talked to Eesyan about it."

"Did he offer a reason?"

"Yes." Shilohin paused for a long time while Danchekker looked at her curiously. Then she said, "The civilization of Thurien came to a halt for a very long time. Paradoxically it was as a result of its advanced sciences."

Danchekker blinked uncertainly through his spectacles. "How could that be?"

"You have studied Ganymean genetic-engineering techniques extensively," Shilohin replied. "After the migration to Thurien, they were taken even further."

"I'm not sure I see the connection."

"The Thuriens perfected a capability that they had been dreaming of for generations—the ability to program their own genes to offset the effects of bodily aging and wasting . . . indefinitely."

A moment or two went by before Danchekker grasped what she was saying. Then he gasped. "Do you mean immortality?"

"Exactly. For a long time it seemed that Utopia had been achieved."

"Seemed?"

"Not all the consequences were foreseen. After a while all their progress, their innovation, and their creativity ceased. The Thuriens became too wise and knew too much. In particular they knew all the reasons why things were impossible and why nothing more could be achieved."

"You mean they ceased to dream." Danchekker shook his head sadly. "How unfortunate. Everything that we take for granted began with somebody dreaming of something that couldn't be done."

Shilohin nodded. "And in the past it had always been the younger generations, too naive and inexperienced to recognize the impossible when they saw it, who had been foolish enough to make the attempt. It was surprising how often they succeeded. But now, of course, there were no more younger generations."

Danchekker was nodding slowly as he listened. "They turned into a society of mental geriatrics."

"Exactly. And when they realized what was happening, they went back to the old ways. But their civilization had stagnated for a very long time, and as a result most of their spectacular breakthroughs have occurred only comparatively recently. The instant-transfer technology was developed barely in time for them to be able to intervene at the end of the Lunarian war. And things like the h-space power-distribution grid, direct neural coupling into machines, and, eventually, VISAR came much later."

"I can imagine the problem," Danchekker murmured absently. "People complain that life is too short for the things they want to do, but without that restriction perhaps they would never do anything. The pressure of finite time is surely the greatest motivator. I've often suspected that if the dream of immortality were ever realized, the outcome would be something like that."

"Well, if the Thuriens' experience was anything to go by, you were right," Shilohin told him.

They talked about the Thuriens for a while longer, and then Shilohin had to return to the *Shapieron* for a meeting with Garuth and Monchar. Danchekker remained in the laboratory to observe some more examples of Thurien biological science presented by VISAR. After spending some time at this he decided he would like to discuss some of what he had seen with Hunt while the details were fresh in his mind, and asked VISAR if Hunt was currently coupled into the system.

"No, he's not," VISAR informed him. "He boarded a plane that took off from McClusky about fifteen minutes ago. If you want, I could put you through to the control room there."

"Oh, er . . . yes, if you would," Danchekker said.

An image of a communications screen appeared in mid-air a couple of feet in front of Danchekker's face, framing the features of the duty controller at McClusky. "Hello, Professor," the controller acknowledged. "What can I do for you?"

"VISAR just told me that Vic has left for somewhere," Danchekker replied. "I wondered what was happening."

"He left a message for you saying he's gone to Houston for the morning. It doesn't go into any details, though."

"Is that Chris Danchekker? Let me talk to him." Karen Heller's voice sounded distantly from somewhere in the background. A few seconds later the controller moved off one side of the screen, and she came into view. "Hello, Professor. Vic got fed up waiting for Lyn to get back from Washington with some news, so he called Houston. Gregg is back there, but Lyn isn't. Vic's gone to find out what's going on. That's really about all I can tell you."

"Oh, I see," Danchekker said. "How strange."

"There was something else that I wanted to talk to you about," Heller went on. "I've been doing a lot of looking into some parts of Lunarian history with Calazar and Showm, and it's becoming rather interesting. We've some questions I'd like your answers to. How soon do you think you'll be back?"

Danchekker muttered under his breath and looked wistfully around the Ganymean laboratory, then realized that he was getting signals through VISAR that his body was getting hungry again. "Actually, I'll be coming back now," he replied. "Perhaps I could talk to you in the canteen, ten minutes from now, say?"

"I'll see you there," Heller agreed and disappeared with the image of the screen.

Ten minutes later Danchekker was heartily demolishing a plate of bacon, eggs, sausage, and hash browns at McClusky while Heller talked over a sandwich from the opposite side of the table. Most of the UNSA people were busy refitting one of the other buildings to afford more permanent storage facilities, and apart from some clatterings and bangings from the adjoining kitchen there were no signs of life in their immediate vicinity.

"We've been analyzing the rates of development of the Lunarian civilization and Earth's," she said. "The difference is staggering. They were into steam power and machines in a matter of a few thousand years after starting to use stone tools. We took something like ten times as long. Why do you think that was?"

Danchekker frowned while he finished chewing. "I thought that the factors responsible for the accelerated advancement of the Lunarians were already quite obvious," he replied. "For one thing, they were closer chronologically to the original Ganymean genetic experiments. Therefore they possessed a great genetic instability, and with it a tendency to a more extreme form of mutation. The sudden emergence of the Lambians is doubtless a case in point."

"I'm not convinced that it explains it," Heller replied slowly. "You've said yourself a few times that tens of thousands of years isn't enough to make a lot of difference. I got VISAR to do some calculations based on human genetic data that ZORAC acquired when the *Shapieron* was on Earth. The results seem to bear it out. And the pattern was already established long before the Lambians appeared. That was only two hundred years before the war."

Danchekker sniffed as he buttered a piece of toast. Politicians had no business playing at being scientists. "The Lunarians would have found a profusion of remnants of the earlier Ganymean civilization on Minerva," he suggested. "The knowledge gained from sources of that nature gave them a flying start over Earth."

"But the Cerians who came to Earth were from a civilization that was already advanced," Heller pointed out. "So that balances. What else made the difference?"

Danchekker wrinkled his nose up and scowled. *Female* politicians playing at being scientists were intolerable. "The Lunarians culture developed during the deteriorating environmental conditions of the approaching Ice Age," he said. "That provided additional pressures."

"The Ice Age was here when the Cerians arrived, and it lasted for a long time afterward," Heller reminded him. "So that balances too. So again—what caused the difference?"

Danchekker stabbed his fork into his meal in a show of exasperation. "If you wish to doubt my word as a biologist and an anthropologist, you have of course every right to do so, madam," he said airily. "For my part, I see no justification whatsoever for elaborating any hypothesis beyond the simple minimum required to account for the facts. And what we already know is perfectly adequate for that purpose."

Heller seemed to have been expecting something like that, and didn't react. "Maybe you're thinking too much like a biologist," she suggested. "Try looking at it from a sociological angle, and asking the question the other way around."

Danchekker's expression said that there couldn't be any other way around. "What do you mean?" he demanded.

"Instead of telling me what speeded the Lunarians up, try asking what slowed Earth down."

Danchekker stared darkly down at his plate for a few seconds, then raised his head and showed his teeth. "The upheavals caused by the Moon's capture," he pronounced.

Heller looked at him in open disbelief. "And regressed them to a point that needed tens of thousands of years to recover from? No way! A few centuries at the most, maybe, but not *that* much. I couldn't buy it. Neither could Showm. Neither could Calazar."

"I see." Danchekker looked a bit taken aback. He attacked his bacon in silence for a while and then said, "And what alternative explanation, if any, are you offering, might I ask?"

"Something you haven't mentioned so far," Heller answered. "The Lunarians developed rational, scientific thinking early on, and relied on it totally from the beginnings of their civilization. By contrast Earth went off into thousands of years of believing that magic, mysticism, Santa Claus, the Easter Bunny, and the Tooth Fairy would solve its problems. It only started to change comparatively recently, and even today there's still a lot of that around. We got VISAR to estimate the effects, and it eclipses all the other factors put together. *That's* what caused the difference!"

Danchekker thought about it for a while, then replied a trifle grudgingly, "Very well." He thrust his chin out defensively. "But I fail to see the need for any melodramatic suggestion that it poses a different question. It's as valid to argue that the early adoption of rational methods accelerated one race as it is to say that its absence retarded the other. What point are you making?"

"I've been thinking a lot about it since I talked to Calazar and Showm, and asking what the reason was. Vic says everything has to have a reason, even if it takes some digging to find it. So what would the reason be for a whole planet clinging obstinately to a lot of nonsense and superstitions for thousands of years when even a little bit of observation and common sense should have shown it doesn't work?"

"I think perhaps you underestimate the complexities of scientific method," Danchekker told her. "It takes centuries . . . scores of generations to evolve the techniques necessary to distinguish reliably between facts and fallacies, and truth and myth. Certainly it couldn't happen overnight. What else did you expect?"

"So why didn't that stop the Lunarians?"

"I have no idea. Have you?"

"That was the question I was leading up to." Heller leaned forward to look at him intently across the table. "What do you think of this for a suggestion: The reason that belief in myths and magic became so deeply rooted in Earth's cultures and persisted for so long could be that, in the earliest stage of our first civilizations, it *did* work?"

Danchekker gagged over the mouthful of food that had been

about to swallow and colored visibly. "*What*? That's preposterous! Are you suggesting that the laws of physics that dictate the running of the Universe could have changed in the last few thousand years?"

"No, I'm not. All I'm—"

"I've never heard such an absurd suggestion. This whole matter is already complicated enough without introducing attempts to explain it by astrology, ESP, or whatever other inanities you have in mind." Danchekker looked about him impatiently and sighed. "Really, it would take far too long to explain why if you are unable to distinguish between science and the banalities dispensed in adolescent magazines. Just take my word that you are wasting your time . . . mine too, I might add."

Heller maintained her calm with some effort. "I am *not* suggesting anything of the kind." An edge of strain had crept into her voice. "Kindly listen for two minutes." Danchekker said nothing and eyed her dubiously across the table as he continued eating. She went on, "Think about this scenario. The Jevlenese have never forgotten that they're Lambians, and we're Cerians. They still see Earth as a rival and always have. Now put them in the situation where they've been taken to Thurien and are making the most of the opportunity to absorb all that Ganymean technology, and the rivals on Earth have just been sent back to square one by the Moon showing up. They've gained control of the surveillance operation, and probably by this time they can do their own instant moving of ships and whatever around the Galaxy because they've got their own independent computer, JEVEX, on their own independent planet. Also they're *human* in form—physically indistinguishable from their rivals." Heller sat back and looked at Danchekker expectantly, as if waiting for him to fill in the rest himself. He stopped with his fork halfway to his mouth and gaped at her incredulously.

"They could have *made* magic and miracles work," Heller went on after a few seconds. "They could have put their own, shall we say, 'agents' into our culture way back in its ancient history and deliberately instilled systems of beliefs that we still haven't entirely recovered from—beliefs that were guaranteed to make sure that the rival would take a long, long time to rediscover the sciences and develop the technologies that would make it an opponent worth worrying about again. Meanwhile the Jevlenese have bought themselves a lot of time to become established on their own system of worlds, expand JEVEX, milk off more Ganymean know-how, and whatever else they've been up to." She sat back, spread her hands, and looked at Danchekker expectantly. "What do you think?"

Danchekker stared at her for what seemed a long time. "Impossible," he declared at last.

Heller's patience finally snapped. "Why? What's wrong with that theory?" she demanded. "The facts are that something slowed Earth's development down. This accounts for it, and nothing that you came up with does. The Jevelenese had the means and the motive, and the answer fit the evidence. What more do you want? I thought science was supposed to be open-minded at least."

"Too farfetched," Danchekker retorted. He became openly sarcastic. "Another principle of science, which you appear to have overlooked, is that one endeavors to test one's hypotheses by experiment. I have no idea how you intend testing this far-flung notion of yours, but for suggestions I recommend that you might try consulting the illustrators of *Superman* comics or the authors of the articles one finds in those housewives' journals found on sale in supermarkets." With that he returned his attention fully to his meal.

"Well if that's your attitude, enjoy your lunch." Heller rose indignantly to her feet. "I heard that Vic had a hell of a time getting you to accept that the Lunarians existed at all. I can see why!" She turned and marched out of the room.

Karen Heller was still fuming thirty minutes later as she stood by one of the buildings on the edge of the apron watching a UNSA crew installing a more permanent generator facility. Danchekker came out of the door of the mess hall some distance away, saw her, then walked slowly off in the opposite direction, his hands clasped behind his back. He stopped at the perimeter fence and stood for a long time staring out across the marshes, turning his head every now and then to glance back at where Heller was standing. Eventually he turned and paced thoughtfully back to the door of the mess hall. When he was almost there he stopped, looked across at her again, hesitated for a few seconds, then changed direction and came over to her.

"I, er—I apologize," he said. "I think you may have something. Certainly your conclusions warrant further investigation.

We should contact the others and tell them about it as soon as possible."

chapter twenty-three

"She what?!"

Hunt caught Caldwell's arm and drew him to a halt halfway along the corridor leading toward Caldwell's office at the top of the Navcomms Headquarters Building.

"He told her to give him a call next time she was in New York to see her mother," Caldwell said. "So I told her to take some vacation and go see her mother." He lifted Hunt's fingers from the sleeve of his jacket and resumed walking.

Hunt stood rooted to the spot for a second, then came to life once more and caught up in a few hurried paces. "What in hell? . . . You can't do that! She happens to be very special to me."

"She also happens to be my assistant."

"But . . . what's she supposed to do when she sees him—read poetry? Gregg, you can't do that. You've got to get her out of it."

"You're sounding like a maiden aunt," Caldwell said. "I didn't do anything. She set it up herself, and I didn't see any reason not to use the chance. It might turn up something useful."

"Her job description never said anything about playing Mata Hari. It's a blatant and inexcusable exploitation of personnel beyond the limits of their contractual obligations to the Division."

"Nonsense. It's a career-development opportunity. Her job description stresses initiative and creativity, and that's what it is."

"What kind of career? That guy's only got one track in his head. Look, it may come as kind of a surprise, but I don't go for the idea of her being another boy-scout badge for him to stitch on his shirt. Maybe I'm being old-fashioned, but I didn't think that that was what working for UNSA was all about."

"Stop overreacting. Nobody said a word about anything like that. It could be a chance to fill in some of the details we're missing. The opportunity came out of the blue, and she grabbed it."

"I've heard enough details already from Karen. Okay, we know the rules, and Lyn knows the rules, but he doesn't know the rules. What do you think he's going to do—sit down and fill out a questionnaire?"

"Lyn can handle it."

"You can't let her do it."

"I can't stop her. She's on vacation, seeing her mother."

"Then I want to take some special leave, starting right now. I've got personal emergency matters to attend to in New York."

"Denied. You've got too much to do here that's more important."

They fell silent as they passed through the outer office and into Caldwell's inner sanctum. Caldwell's secretary looked up from dictating a memo to an audiotranscriber and nodded a greeting.

"Gregg, this is going too far," Hunt began again when they got inside. "There's—"

"There's more to it than you think," Caldwell told him. "I've heard enough from Norman Pacey and the CIA to know that the opportunity was worth seizing when it presented itself. Lyn knew it too." He draped his jacket on a hanger by the door, walked around the other side of his desk, and dumped the briefcase that he had been carrying down on top of it. "There's a hell of a lot about Sverenssen that we never dreamed of, and a lot more we don't know that we'd like to. So stop being neurotic, sit down and listen for five minutes, and I'll give you a summary."

Hunt emitted a long sigh of capitulation, threw out his hands in resignation, and slumped down into one of the chairs. "We're going to need a lot more than five minutes, Gregg," he said as Caldwell sat down facing him. "You wait till you hear about the things we found out yesterday from the Thuriens."

Four and a half thousand miles from Houston, Norman Pacey was sitting on a bench by the side of the Serpentine lake in London's Hyde Park. Strollers in open-necked shirts and summery dresses making the best of the first warm days of the year added a dash of color to the surrounding greenery topped by distant frontages of dignified and imposing buildings that had not changed appreciably in fifty years. That was all they had ever wanted, he thought to himself as he took in the sights and sounds around him. All that people the world over had ever wanted was to live their lives, pay their way, and be left alone. So how had the few with different aspirations always been able to command the power to impose themselves and their systems? Which was the greater evil—one fanatic with a cause, or a hundred men free enough not to care about causes? But caring about freedom enough to defend it made it a cause and its defenders fanatics. For ten thousand years mankind had wrestled with the problem and not found an answer.

A shadow fell across the ground, and Mikolai Sobroskin sat down on the bench next to him. He was wearing a heavy suit and necktie despite the fine weather, and his head was glistening with beads of perspiration in the sunlight. "A refreshing contrast to Giordano Bruno," he commented. "What an improvement it would be if the *maria* were really seas."

Pacey turned his head from staring across the lake and grinned. "And maybe a few trees, huh? I think UNSA has got its work cut out for a while with the proposals for cooling down Venus and oxygenating Mars. Luna's way down the list. Even if it weren't, I'm not sure that anybody has come up with any good ideas for what they could do about it. But who knows? One day, maybe."

The Russian sighed. "Perhaps we had such knowledge in the palm of our hand. We threw it away. Do you realize that we have witnessed what could be the greatest crime in human history? And perhaps the world will never know."

Pacey nodded, waiting for a second to assume a more businesslike manner, and asked, "So? . . . What's the news?"

Sobroskin drew a handkerchief from his breast pocket and dabbed his head. "You were right about the coded signals from Gistar when you suspected that they were in response to an independent transmitting facility established by us," he replied.

Pacey nodded without showing surprise. He knew that already from what Caldwell and Lyn Garland had revealed in Washington, but he couldn't say so. "Have you found out how Verikoff and Sverenssen fit in?" he asked.

"I think so," Sobroskin said. "They seem to be part of a global operation of some sort that was committed to shutting down communications of any kind between this planet and Thurien. They used the same methods. Verikoff is a member of a powerful faction that strongly opposed the Soviet attempt to open another channel. Their reasons were the same as the UN's. As it turned out, they were taken by surprise before they could organize an effective block, and some transmissions were sent. Like Sverenssen, Verikoff was instrumental in causing additional messages to be sent secretly, designed to frustrate the exercise. At least we think so. . . . We can't prove it."

Pacey nodded again. He knew that too. "Do you know what they said?" he inquired out of curiosity, although he had read Caldwell's transcripts from Thurien.

"No, but I can guess. These people knew in advance that the relay to Gistar would deactivate. That says to me that they must have been responsible. Presumably they arranged it months ago with an independent launching organization, or maybe a part of UNSA that they knew they could trust . . . I don't know. But my guess is that their strategy was to delay the proceedings via both channels until the relay was put out of action permanently."

Pacey stared across the lake to an enclosed area of water on the far side in which crowds of children were swimming and playing in the sun. The sounds of shouting and laughter drifted across intermittently on the breeze. Apart from the confirmation of Verikoff's involvement, he hadn't learned anything new so far. "What do you make of it?" he asked without turning his head.

After a long, heavy silence, Sobroskin replied, "Russia had a tradition of tyranny through to the early years of this century. Ever since it threw off the yoke of Mongol subjugation in the fifteenth century, it was obsessed with preserving its security to the point that the security of other nations became a threat that could not be tolerated. It expanded its borders by conquest and held on to its acquired territories by oppression, intimidation, and terror. But the new lands in turn had borders, and there was no end to the process. Communism changed nothing. It was merely a banner of convenience for rallying gullible idealists and rationalizing sacrifice. Apart from a few brief months in 1917, Russia was no more Communist than the Church of the Middle Ages was Christian."

He paused to fold his handkerchief and return it to his pocket. Pacey waited without speaking for him to continue.

"We thought that all that began to change in the early decades of this century with the end of the threat of thermonuclear war and a more enlightened view of the internationalism. And superficially it did. Many like myself dedicated themselves to creating a new climate of understanding and common progress with the West as it emerged from its own style of tyranny." Sobroskin sighed and shook his head sadly. "But the Thurien affair has revealed that the forces that plunged Russia into its own Dark Age did not go away, and their purpose has not changed." He looked at Pacey sharply. "And the forces that brought religious terror and economic exploitation to the West have not gone away, either. On both sides they have merely modified their stance to avert what would have guaranteed their destruction along with everything else. There is a web across this whole planet that connects many Sverenssens with many Verikoffs. They pose behind banners and slogans that call for liberation, but the liberation they seek is their own, not that of the people who follow them."

"Yes, I know," Pacey said. "We've uncovered some of it too. What's the answer?"

Sobroskin raised an arm and gestured at the far side of the lake. "For all we know, those children might have grown up to see other worlds under other suns. But the price of that would have been knowledge, and knowledge is the enemy of tyranny in any disguise. It has freed more people from poverty and oppression than all of the ideologies and creeds in history put together. Every form of serfdom follows from serfdom of the mind."

"I'm not sure what you're saying," Pacey said. "Are you saying you want to come over to us or something?"

The Russian shook his head. "The war that matters has nothing to do with flags. It is between those who would set the minds of children free, and those who would deny them Thurien. The latest battle has been lost, but the war will continue. Perhaps one day we will talk to Thurien again. But in the meantime another battle is looming in Moscow for control of the Kremlin, and that is where I must be." He reached behind him for a package that he had placed on the bench behind him and passed it to Pacey. "We have a tradition of ruthlessness in handling our internal affairs that you do not share. It is possible that many people will not survive the next few months, and I could be one of them. If so, I would like to think that my work has not been for nothing." He released the package and withdrew his arm. "That contains a complete record of all that I know. It would not be safe with my colleagues in Moscow since their future, like my own, is full of uncertainties. But I know that you will use the information wisely, for you understand as well as I do that in the war that really matters we are on the same side." With that he stood up. "I am glad that we met, Norman Pacey. It is reassuring to see that on both sides, bonds exist that are deeper than the colors on maps. I hope that we meet again, but in case that is not to be . . ." He let the words hang and extended a hand.

Pacey stood up and grasped it firmly. "We will. And things will be better," he said.

"I hope so." Sobroskin released his grip, turned, and began walking away along the side of the lake.

Pacey's finger tightened around the package as he stood watching the short, stocky figure marching jerkily off to keep its appointment with fate, possibly to die so that children might laugh. He couldn't let him, he realized. He couldn't let him walk away without knowing. "Mikolai!" he called.

Sobroskin stopped and looked back. Pacey waited. The Russian retraced his steps.

"The battle was not lost," Pacey said. "There's another channel to Thurien operating right now . . . in the United States. It doesn't need the relay. We've been talking to Thurien for weeks. That was why Karen Heller returned to Earth. It's okay. All the Sverenssens in the world can't stop it now."

Sobroskin stared at him for a long time before the words seemed to register. At last he moved his head in a slow, barely perceptible nod, his eyes expressionless and distant, and murmured quietly, "Thank you." Then he turned away and began walking again, this time slowly, as if in a trance. When he had covered twenty yards or so he stopped, stared back again, and raised his arm in a silent salutation. Then he turned away and began walking once more, and after a few steps his pace lightened and quickened.

Even at that distance Pacey had seen the exultation in his expression. Pacey watched until Sobroskin had vanished among the people walking by the boathouses farther along the shoreline, then turned away and walked in the opposite direction, toward the Serpentine bridge.

chapter twenty-four

Niels Sverenssen's million-dollar home was situated in Connecticut, forty miles from New York City, on the shore side of a two-hundred-acre estate of parkland and trees that overlooked Long Island Sound. The house framed two sides of a large, clover-leaf pool set among terraced banks of shrubs. A tennis court on one side and outbuildings on the other completed the pool's encirclement. The house was fashionably contemporary, spacious, light, and airy, with sections of roof sweeping in clean, unbroken planes from crest almost to ground level in some places to give the complete structure the lines and composition of an abstract sculpture, and drawing back in others to reveal vertical faces and slanted panels of polished brownstone, tiled mosaic, or glass. The imposing central structure rose two levels and contained the larger rooms and Sverenssen's private quarters. One wing fell to single level and comprised six extra bedrooms and additional living space to accommodate the guests of his frequent weekend parties and other functions. The other was two-storied, though not as high as the central portion; it contained offices for Sverenssen and a secretary, a library, and other rooms dedicated to his work.

There was something odd about the history of Sverenssen's house.

Lyn had flown up to New York accompanied by one of Clifford Benson's agents, who had introduced her to a local office of the CIA to examine their records for additional information on Sverenssen. It turned out that his house had been built for him ten years previously by the construction division of Weismand Industries, Inc., a large, diversified corporation. The company was a builder of industrial premises, not private dwellings, which was no doubt why they had called in several outside architects and designers as consultants. What made the project even stranger was that Weismand was based in Califor-

nia; why would Sverenssen have used them when any number
of qualified firms existed in the area?

Further checks revealed that Weismand Industries stock was
held mainly by a Canadian insurance consortium that was
closely linked to the same British banking fraternity that, along
with its French and Swiss connections, had launched Sverenssen's spectacular career upon his sudden return from obscurity. Had Sverenssen simply been repaying a favor, or were
there other reasons why he felt it necessary to build his house
using a company with which he had close, and presumably
confidential, connections?

Lyn asked herself the question again as she reclined in a bikini on a chaise by the pool and studied the house through the
intervening flower beds and shrubs. Sverenssen, wearing sun-
glasses and clad in a pair of scarlet bathing trunks, was sitting
a few feet away at an umbrellaed table drinking iced lemonade
and talking with a man he had introduced as Larry. A blonde
named Cheryl was basking face-down and naked on another
chaise a short distance away, while two other girls, Sandy and
Carol, were laughing and shouting in the pool with a
Mediterranean-looking character by the name of Enrico. Sandy
was topless, and the object of the mêlée in progress was evidently to render her bottomless as well. Another couple had
been around earlier, but had been gone for the last hour or so.
It was Friday afternoon, and more people were expected to arrive as the evening wore on, plus a few the next morning.
Sverenssen had described the occasion as "a pleasant get-
together of some interesting friends" when Lyn called him on
Thursday morning.

The only thing that seemed even slightly unusual about the
house was the office wing, she decided as she looked at it.
Sverenssen had stressed that it was not open to visitors when
he showed her around earlier. That seemed reasonable enough,
but something was different about it, she realized. This part of
the building wasn't built to the same airy and open design as
the rest of the place, with yards of plate-glass windows and
sliding glass doors that led through to the inside. Instead it was
solid, with small windows set high off the ground. They
looked thick and seemed more suited to keeping sunlight out,
along with everything else. As she looked closer, she was sure
that what had seemed at first to be ornamental trim across the
windows was in fact carefully disguised bars guaranteed to ex-

clude any possibility of entry—not just by burglars, but by a tank. There were no doors to the outside at all; the only access to the wing was from inside the house. If she hadn't been look-ing specifically, she would never have noticed it, but the office wing, beneath its veneer of tiled designs and paintwork to match the rest of the house, was virtually a fortress.

The noise from the pool rose to a crescendo that culminated in a shriek as Enrico emerged from a flurry of water and bod-ies waving the lower half of Sandy's swimsuit triumphantly over his head. "One down, one to go," he yelled.

"Not fair!" Sandy screamed. "I was drowning. That's an un-fair advantage."

"Carol's turn," Enrico shouted.

"Like hell," Carol laughed. "That's inequality. Sandy, give me a hand and let's get the bastard." The commotion started all over again.

"It sounds as if they could use some help," Sverenssen said, turning his head to look across at Lyn. "Go ahead and join in. There aren't any restrictions on how you enjoy yourself here, you know."

She let her head fall back on the raised end of the chaise and forced a smile. "Oh, sometimes spectator sports are just as much fun. Anyway, they seem to be managing okay. I'll be the reserve division."

"She's being smart and saving her energy," Larry said, speaking to Sverenssen and sending Lyn a broad wink. She did a good job of pretending not to notice.

"Very wise," Sverenssen said.

"The real fun starts later," Larry explained, grinning. Lyn managed a half-smile, at the same time wondering how she was going to handle that. "We'll find you lots of new friends. They're great people here."

"I can't wait," Lyn said drily.

"Isn't she charming," Sverenssen said, glancing at Larry and looking approvingly back at Lyn. "I met her in Washington, you know—a most fortunate encounter. She has people that she visits here in New York." It made her feel like a piece of merchandise, which was probably a pretty close assessment of her situation. She wasn't especially surprised; if she hadn't been prepared to play along for appearance's sake, she wouldn't have come in the first place.

"I get to Washington a lot," Larry said. "You work there or something?"

Lyn shook her head. "Uh uh. I'm with the Space Arm in Houston—computers, lasers, and people who talk numbers all day . . . but it's a living."

"Ah, but we're going to change that, aren't we, Lyn," Sverenssen said. He looked at Larry. "As a matter of fact I was thinking of something in Washington that would suit her perfectly, and prove far more interesting, I'm sure. Do you remember Phil Grazenby? I had lunch with him one day while I was there recently, and he wants somebody bright and attractive to manage the new agency he's opening. And he is talking about really worthwhile money."

"We'll have to get together there if you make it," Larry said to Lyn. He made a face. "Aw, but that's business, and it's a long time away. Why wait until Washington? We can get to know each other right here. Are you here alone?"

"Yes, she's free," Sverenssen murmured.

"That's great!" Larry exclaimed. "Me too, and I'm the perfect guy for introducing new faces around here. Believe me, honey, you've made the right choice. You must have good taste. Tell you what—you can partner me in one of the games later. So we've got a deal, right?"

"I live for the present," Lyn said. "Suppose we let later take care of itself later, okay?" She stretched to squint up at the sun, then looked at Sverenssen. "Right now all I'm going to be good for is a case of radiation sickness if I don't cover up. I'm going to go inside in the shade and put on something else until it cools down a bit. I'll see you later?"

"By all means, my dear," Sverenssen said. "The last thing we want is for you to end up on the casualty list." Lyn unfolded herself from the chaise and walked toward the house. "I think you may have a little game of playing hard to get to win before—" she heard Sverenssen murmur. The rest was drowned out by another burst of screaming from the pool.

Cheryl raised her head and watched as Lyn disappeared between the shrubs. "You've got nothing to offer, Larry," she said. "Now *I* could show her a good time that's really different."

"So what's wrong with both of us?" Larry asked.

Lyn's room contained twin king-size beds and was as luxuriously furnished and fitted as every other part of the house.

She was supposed to be sharing it with somebody called Donna, who hadn't arrived yet. Inside, she took off her bikini and put on a shirt and shorts. Then she stood by the window thinking for a while.

There was a datagrid screen in the room, but she didn't want to make any calls since there was a good chance it was bugged. Anyway she didn't need to if she wanted to get out because Clifford Benson's people had already anticipated that. Inside her shoulder bag in the closet was a microelectronic transmitter that looked like a powder compact but would send out a signal when she unlocked a safety catch and pressed a disguised button. If she pressed it once, a CIA agent would call the house within seconds, posing as a brother with news of a family emergency and stating that a cab was on its way to collect her. If she pressed it three times, the two agents in the airmobile parked a mile down the road from the front gate would arrive in under half a minute, but that option was for use only if she got into real trouble. But she didn't want to get out just yet. The house was empty and quieter than it would be at any time for the rest of the weekend. There would never be another chance like this for a look around the place with little risk of being disturbed. She sure-as-hell wasn't going to chicken out after a couple of hours with nothing to report, she told herself.

She took a deep breath, bit her lip nervously, walked over to the door, inched it open, and listened. Everything seemed still. As she let herself out into the passage a half-stifled giggle came from behind the door opposite. She stopped for a second; there was no other sound, and she moved quietly on toward the central part of the house.

The passage led through a small den into a large, central, open room that rose the full height of the building, one side a sloping wall of glass panels facing the rear of the house. The room was elbow-shaped, thickly carpeted, and had a sunken floor in front of a large fireplace of brickwork, with areas of raised floors around it angling away to openings and stairways which gave access to other parts of the house.

Muffled voices and kitchen noises were coming from one of the corridors, but she didn't detect any sign of Sverenssen's domestic staff in her immediate vicinity. She slowly examined the furnishings, ornaments, the pictures on the walls, and the fittings overhead, but found nothing that looked out of place.

After pausing to replay her mental model of the layout, she picked out a narrow corridor that seemed to lead toward the office wing and followed it.

Eventually, after exploring the system of rooms that the corridor brought her to, most of which she had already seen in the course of the quick tour that Sverenssen had given her, she came back to what seemed to be the only door anywhere that opened through into the office wing. She tried the handle gently, but it was locked, as she had expected. When she tapped it with a knuckle, the sound it produced was flat and solid, even from the parts that looked like ordinary wood panels. They might have been wood on the surface, but there was a lot of something else underneath; that door had been put there to keep out a lot more than just drafts. Without a rock drill or an army demolition squad, she wasn't going to get any farther in that direction, so she turned to go back to the center part of the house. As she began moving, she recalled one of the sculptures that she had seen in the central room. It hadn't really struck her at the time, but now as she thought about it again, she realized that there had been something vaguely familiar about it. Surely not, she thought as she tried to visualize it again in her mind. There was no way it could be possible. She frowned and her pace quickened a fraction.

The piece was standing in an illuminated recess of one side of the brick fireplace—an abstract form rendered in some kind of silver and gold translucent crystal, about eight inches high and mounted on a solid black base. At least, when she glanced over it casually a few minutes earlier she had thought it to be abstract. But now as she picked it up and turned it slowly over in her hands, she became more convinced than ever that its form couldn't be simply a coincidence.

Its lowermost part was a composition of surfaces and shapes that could have meant anything, but projecting up from the center to form the main body of the design was a tapering column of finely carved terraces, levels, and intervening buttresses flowing upward in distinctive curves. Could it represent a tower? she wondered. A tower that she had seen not long ago. Three slim spires continued upward from the top of the main column—three spires supporting a circular disk just below their apexes. A platform? The disk had more finely cut details on its surface. She turned the sculpture over . . . and gasped. There were more details, defining a readily discernible pattern of concentric rings—on the *underside* of the platform! She was looking at a representation of the central tower of the city of Vranix. It couldn't possibly be. But it couldn't be anything else.

Her hand was shaking as she carefully replaced the sculpture in its recess. What the hell had she gotten herself into? she asked herself. Her first urge was to go back to her room, collect her things, and get out fast; but as she forced herself to calm down and her mind to think more clearly, she fought back the feeling. The opportunity to learn more was unique, and it would never present itself again. If there were more, nobody might ever know unless she found it now. She closed her eyes for a second and took a deep breath to summon up her reserves of nervous energy to see it through.

She had to find out more about the office wing, but there seemed no way to get inside. Maybe she could get nearer in some other way . . . under it, perhaps? A house like this would surely have cellars. There would probably be stairs somewhere in the direction of the kitchen. She moved across to the end of the corridor leading that way; voices were still audible, but they sounded closed off. Two doors proved to be closets. The third that she tried revealed a flight of wooden stairs going down. She entered, eased the door shut behind her, and descended.

The cellar that she found herself in looked ordinary, with a bench and some tool racks, a storage space, and lots of pipes and conduits. Machinery of some kind, probably a central air conditioner, was humming behind a louvered door to one side. Two other cellars opened off from this one, one in each direction of the two arms of the house; she moved on into the one leading toward the office wing. It was another storage area, full of boxes and leftover decorating materials. A partition wall with a gap in its center screened off the far end. Lyn crossed the area and peered through the gap. The cellar did not continue on beneath the office wing, but ended at a bare wall on the far side of the small space behind the partition. As Lyn looked around and studied the surroundings, she realized that the part of the cellars she had entered was strangely different from the rest structurally, particularly the blank wall facing her.

The line where the wall and ceiling met was formed by a steel girder that must have measured fifteen inches across the flange at least, and it was supported by two more, equally massive members running down the corners and terminating in what looked like solid concrete foundations partly visible along the lower part of the walls and going down into the floor. The ceiling, too, was reinforced with girders and cross ties gusseted at the angles. All was painted white to blend in with the general background of the other cellar rooms, and the casual visitor would probably never have noticed; but to somebody who was looking for the unusual and who had a special interest in that end of the house, the heavy structures stood out unmistakably.

So the office wing itself was not over any part of the cellars but was built on solid ground, and she was looking at one side of its foundation and underpinning. It was built from materials and in a fashion that would have supported a battleship. What could there be upstairs that would have crushed the foundations of an ordinary house and had made all this necessary? she wondered.

And then she remembered the holes she had seen punched through the concrete at McClusky.

A Thurien interstellar communications system contained a microscopic, artificially generated, black-hole toroid when it was switched on and operating.

But that idea was even more insane. The house had been built ten years before. Nobody had heard of the Ganymeans, let alone Thurien, in 2021.

She backed slowly away from the partition and turned dazedly back toward the stairs.

At the top of the stairs she stopped for a while to give the thumping in her chest time to slow down and to bring her reeling mind under some kind of control. Then she opened the door a fraction and brought her eye close to it just in time to catch a glimpse of Sverenssen moving out of sight behind an angle in the wall back near the corner room. He had been turning his head from side to side as he moved, as if he were looking for something . . . or somebody. Lyn immediately erupted into a new spasm of shaking and shivering. Suddenly Navcomms and Houston seemed very far away. If she ever got out of this, she'd never want to leave the coziness of her own office again.

If Sverenssen was looking for her, he would already have tried knocking on the door of her room. The part of her that felt guilty told her that she needed a reason for not being there. She thought for a few seconds, then let herself out into the corridor and went the other way, into the kitchen. A minute later she reemerged holding a cup of coffee and began making her way back to the guest section of the house.

"Oh, *there* you are." Sverenssen's voice sounded from behind her when she was halfway across one of the raised floors around the periphery of the corner room. She froze; had she done anything else, the coffee and the cup would have been all over the carpet. Sverenssen came out of one of the side rooms as she turned to face him. He was still wearing his bathing trunks, but had put sandals on his feet and thrown a shirt loosely over his shoulder. He was eyeing her uncertainly, as if he were mildly suspicious about something but not sufficiently sure of himself to be direct.

"I went to get some coffee," she said, as if it weren't obvious. Immediately she felt like the classic dumb broad; but at least she managed to stop herself from following up her statement with an inane laugh. She was certain that Sverenssen was looking past her shoulder at the sculpture in its recess. She could picture it in her mind's eye with a neon sign in six-inch letters above shouting, "I HAVE BEEN MOVED." Somehow she resisted the compulsion to turn her head.

"I wouldn't have thought that somebody from Houston would be bothered by the sun," he remarked. "Especially somebody with a tan like yours." His voice was superficially casual, but had an undertone that invited an explanation.

For a second or two she felt trapped. Then she said, "I just wanted to get away for a while. Your friend . . . Larry, was starting to come on a bit strong. I guess I need time to get used to this."

Sverenssen looked at her dubiously, as if she had just confirmed his fears about something. "Well, I do hope you manage to loosen up a little before too much longer," he said. "I mean, the whole idea of being here is to enjoy oneself. It would be such a shame if one person allowed her inhibitions to ruin the atmosphere for everyone else, wouldn't it."

Despite her confusion, Lyn couldn't keep a sharp edge out of her voice. "Look . . . I didn't exactly come here expecting this," she told him. "You never said anything about playing musical people."

A pained expression came over Sverenssen's face. "Oh dear, I do hope you're not going to start preaching any middle-class morals. What did you expect? I said I would be entertaining some friends, and I expect them to be entertained and made to feel welcome in a manner appropriate to their tastes."

"*Their* tastes? That's very nice of you. They must love you for it. What about my tastes?"

"Are you suggesting that *my* acquaintances fail to come up to *your* standards? How amusing. You've already made your tastes quite plain—you aspire to luxury and the company that goes with it. Well, you have them. Surely you don't expect anything in this life to come free."

"I didn't expect to be treated like a piece of candy to be dangled in front of those overgrown kids out there."

"You're talking like an adolescent. Do I not have a right to expect you, as my guest, to behave sociably in return for my hospitality? Or did you imagine that I was some kind of a philanthropist who opens his home to the world for reasons of pure charity? I can assure you that I am nothing of the kind, and neither is anybody else who has the intelligence to understand the realities of life."

"Who said anything about charity? Doesn't respect for people come into it anywhere?"

Sverenssen sneered. Evidently it didn't. "Another middle-class opiate. All I can say to you is that whatever fantasies you have been harboring appear to have been sadly unfounded." He sighed and shrugged, apparently having already dismissed the matter as a lost cause. "The opportunity is yours to enjoy a life quite free from worries financial or otherwise, but seizing it requires that you throw off a lot of silly protective notions left over from childhood and make a pragmatic assessment of your situation."

Lyn's eyes blazed, but she managed to keep her voice under control. "I think I just made it." Her tone said the rest.

Sverenssen appeared indifferent. "In that case I suggest that you call yourself a cab without further delay and return to your world of misplaced romanticism and unfulfillable dreams," he said. "It really makes no difference to me. I can get somebody else here within the hour. The choice is entirely yours."

Lyn stood absolutely still until she had fought down the urge to hurl her coffee in his face. Then she turned away and, mustering the effort to maintain her calm, walked off in the direction of her room. Sverenssen followed her coldly with his eyes for a few seconds, then shrugged contemptuously and hurried out through a side door to rejoin the others at the pool.

* * *

Two hours later Lyn was sitting in a Washington-bound plane beside the CIA agent who had accompanied her to New York. Around them sat families, couples, people alone, and people together; some were dressed in business suits, some in jackets, and others in casual shirts, sweaters, and jeans. They were talking, laughing, reading, and sleeping—just ordinary, sane, civilized people, minding their own business. She wanted to hug every one of them.

chapter twenty-five

In the illusory world of VISAR's creations, Karen Heller was half a billion miles tall and floating in space. A loosely coupled binary system of Ping-Pong-ball-size stars, one yellow and one white, was revolving slowly in front of her while a myriad more glowed as pinpoints of light in the infinite blackness stretching away on every side. The center of mass of the two stars was located at one of the foci of a highly elongated ellipse, superposed on the view by VISAR, tracing the orbit of the planet Surio.

Hanging in space beside Heller and looking like some cosmic god contemplating the material universe as if it were a plaything, Danchekker extended an arm to point at the planet sliding along its trajectory in VISAR's speeded-up simulation. "The conditions that Surio encounters at opposite ends of the ellipse are completely different," he said. "At one end it's in close proximity to both its suns and therefore very hot; at the other it's remote from them and therefore quite cool. Its year alternates between a long oceanic phase during the cool period, and an equally long hot phase during which Surio possesses practically no hydrosphere at all. Eesyan tells me it's unique among the worlds that the Thuriens have discovered so far."

"It's fascinating," Heller said, enthralled. "And you're saying that life has emerged there despite those conditions. It sounds impossible."

"I thought so too," Danchekker told her. "Eesyan had to show me this before I'd believe otherwise. That was what I wanted to show you. Let's go down and take a closer look at the planet itself."

They seemed to be rushing toward Surio as VISAR responded to the verbal cue. The stars vanished away behind them, and the planet grew rapidly and swelled into a sphere that flattened out beneath them as they descended from the sky. It was in a cool, oceanic phase, and as they plunged downward they shrank in size so that the sea stretching from horizon to horizon looked normal. Then they were underwater, with strange alien life forms swimming and twisting the ocean around them.

A black, fishlike creature, vaguely reminiscent of some shark species, seemed to single itself out, their viewpoint moving progressively as they followed it. Then, as VISAR altered the content of the information being injected into their visual systems, the body and soft tissues of the creature became a translucent haze to reveal clearly the structure of its skeleton. The light filtering through the water from above went out suddenly, then came on again, then continued to flicker steadily like a slow-motion stroboscope. The image of the fish remained motionless in front of them. "Day and night cycles," Danchekker explained in answer to Heller's questioning look. "VISAR is speeding them up and freezing this image artificially so that we can observe it. Have you noticed yet that the intensity of the daylight periods is increasing?"

Heller had. She also noticed that the creature's skeleton was beginning to change subtly. Its spine was shortening and getting thicker, and the bones inside its fins were elongating and differentiating into clearly discernible jointed segments. Also, the fins were slowly migrating toward the creature's underside. "What's happening there?" she asked, pointing.

"It's an adaptation that I thought you might be interested in seeing," Danchekker replied. "The year is growing warmer, and the oceans around us have begun evaporating rapidly." VISAR obligingly raised them high above the surface again to confirm the statement. The face of the planet had already changed beyond recognition since their arrival. The oceans had retreated to a series of steep-sided basins, uncovering broad shelves that now connected into vast land masses what had previously been scattered islands and minor continents. Carpets of vegetation were creeping outward behind the receding shorelines and upward into what had been barren mountainous regions. A dense cloud blanket had formed, from which continuous rains were drenching the highlands.

They watched the surface transformation continue for a while, and then descended once more to follow local events in a shallow estuary formed where a river draining water from the rainy areas inland had carved a trench across the exposed continental shelf to one of the diminishing ocean basins. The creature that they had studied previously was now an amphibian living on the mud flats, with rudimentary legs already functioning and a fully differentiated mobile head. "It dissolves its bones by means of specially secreted fluids triggered by environmental cues, and grows a new skeleton more suited to an existence in its changed environment," Danchekker commented. "Quite remarkable."

To Heller this seemed an overly drastic solution. "Couldn't it stay a fish and simply move out into the oceans?" she asked.

"Very soon there won't be any oceans," Danchekker told her. "Wait and see."

The oceans shrank into isolated pools surrounded by mud, and then dried up completely. As the climate grew hotter the rivers from the highlands became trickles as they flowed downhill, finally evaporating away before reaching the basins, and what had been the seabeds turned into deserts. The vegetation receded across the shelves until it had been reduced to scattered oases of life clinging doggedly to the highest plateaus and mountain peaks. The creature had migrated upward and was now a fully adapted land dweller with a scaly skin and prehensile forelimbs, not unlike some of the earliest terrestrial reptiles. "Now it's in its fully transformed state," Danchekker said. "As Surio goes through a year, the animal cycles are repeated from one extreme of morphology to the other. An amazing example of how tenacious life can be under adverse conditions, wouldn't you agree."

The day lengthened as light periods from the two suns overlapped, and then shortened again as Surio came around the tip of its orbit and began its long swing outward into another cold phase. The vegetation began advancing down the mountainsides, the creature's limbs commenced reducing, and the whole sequence went slowly into reverse. "Do you think intelligence could ever emerge in a place like this?" Heller asked curiously.

"Who can say?" Danchekker replied. "A few days ago I would have said that what we have just witnessed was unthinkable."

"It's fantastic," Heller murmured in awe.

"No, it's reality," Danchekker said. "Reality is far more fantastic than anything that unaided human imagination could ever devise. The mind could not, for example, visualize a new color, such as infrared or ultraviolet. It can only manipulate combinations of elements that it has already experienced. Everything that is truly new can only come from the Universe outside. And uncovering the truth that lies out there is, of course, the function of science."

Heller looked at him suspiciously. "If I didn't know you better, I'd think you were trying to start an argument," she teased. "Let's get back before this conversation goes any further and see if Vic's called in yet."

"I agree," Danchekker said at once. "VISAR, back to McClusky, please."

He got up from the recliner, moved out into the corridor of the perceptron, and waited for a moment until Heller emerged from one of the other cubicles. They exited through the antechamber, were conveyed down to ground level, and a few seconds later were walking along the side of the apron toward the mess hall.

"I'm not going to let you get away with that," Heller began after a short silence. "I started out in law, which has a lot to do with uncovering the truth too, you know. And its methods are just as scientific. Just because you scientists need computers to do your work for you, that doesn't give you a monopoly on logic."

Danchekker thought for a moment. "Mmm . . . very well. If one is hampered by mathematical illiteracy, law does provide something of an alternative, I suppose," he conceded loftily.

"Oh really? I would say it demands far more ingenuity. What's more, it taxes the intellect in ways that scientists never have to bother about."

"What an extraordinary statement! And how would that be, might I ask?"

"Nature is often complex, but never dishonest, Professor. How often have you had to contend with deliberate falsification of the evidence, or an opponent with as much vested interest in obscuring the truth as you have in revealing it?"

"Hmph! And when was the last time that you had to subject your hypotheses to the test of rigorous proof by experiment, eh? Answer me that," Danchekker challenged.

"We do not enjoy the luxury of repeatable experiments," Heller responded. "Not many criminals will oblige by recommitting their crimes under controlled laboratory conditions. So, you see, we have to keep our wits sharp enough to be right the first time."

"Hmm, hmm, hmm . . ."

They had timed their return to McClusky well. Hunt called just as they entered the control room. "How quickly can you get back here?" Danchekker asked him. "Karen has had some remarkable thoughts which after some reflection I find myself forced to agree with. We need to discuss them at the earliest opportunity."

"Gregg and I are leaving right away," Hunt told him. "We've just heard about John's visit to the city. It puts a whole new light on everything. We need to talk to the board ASAP. Can you fix it?" It meant that Packard's report of Pacey's meeting with Sobroskin had arrived in Houston, and a meeting with Calazar and the Thuriens was urgently called for.

"I'll see to it immediately," Danchekker promised.

An hour later, while Hunt and Caldwell were still on their way and after Danchekker had made arrangements with Calazar, Jerol Packard called from Washington. "Hold everything," he instructed. "Mary's back. We're putting her on a plane up to you right now. Whatever you think you already know, I guarantee it's not half of it. She just blew our minds here. Don't do anything until she's talked to you."

"I'll see to it immediately," Danchekker sighed.

chapter twenty-six

For Imares Broghuilio, Premier of the Federation of Jevlenese Worlds and head of the Thurien civilization's Jevlenese component, the past few months had been beset with unexpected crises that had threatened to disrupt the carefully laid plans of generations.

First there had been the sudden and completely unpredictable reappearance of the *Shapieron* on Earth. The Thuriens had known nothing about that until the signal sent out by the Terrans at the time of the ship's departure was somehow relayed directly to VISAR without going through JEVEX. How that had happened had been, and still was, a mystery. Broghuilio had been left with no choice but to preempt awkward questions by going to Calazar first with the Jevlenese account of what had transpired, namely that the Jevlenese had felt apprehensive at the thought of inviting Thurien intervention in a situation already made precarious by the belligerence and instability of the Terrans and therefore, rightly or wrongly, had decided to postpone announcing any news until the ship was safely clear of Earth. The explanation had by necessity been hastily contrived, but at the time Calazar had seemed to accept it. The device that had relayed the signal was not something that the Thuriens had placed near the Solar System, Calazar had insisted in response to Broghuilio's accusation; the Thuriens had not broken their agreement to leave Earth surveillance to the Jevlenese. Privately, however, Broghuilio's experts had been able to suggest no other explanation for the relay. It seemed possible, therefore, that the Thuriens were, after all, more prudent than he had given them credit for.

This suspicion had been reinforced some months later when the Thuriens secretly reopened their dialogue with Earth for the unprecedented purpose of double-checking information supplied by JEVEX. Broghuilio had been unable to challenge this development openly since doing so would have revealed the existence of information sources on Earth that the Thuriens could not be allowed to discover, but with some fast footwork he had neutralized the attempt, at least for the time being, by securing control of the Earth end of the link. His bid to counter the surprise Soviet move of opening a second channel had not proved as successful, and he had been forced to resort to more desperate measures by having the link put out of action—something which he had avoided until that point because of the risk of the Thuriens electing to continue the dialogue by more direct means. He had calculated that they would hesitate for a long time before breaking their agreement in so open a fashion.

The Thuriens had not chosen to divulge their contact with Earth by mentioning the incident. Broghuilio's advisors had interpreted this as confirmation that the measures taken to persuade the Thuriens that Earth was responsible for the destruction of the relay had succeeded. A further implication was that the image that had been created of a hostile and aggressive Earth had survived intact, which, it was felt, would suffice to dissuade the Thuriens from taking things further by contemplating a landing.

After some anxious moments, therefore, the gamble appeared to have paid off. The only remaining problem was the *Shapieron*, outward bound from the Solar System and already beyond the point where an interception could be staged with only a moderate risk of disturbing planetary orbits. Broghuilio had guessed that the Thuriens, being the cautious breed that they were, would play safe and allow an ample safety margin. Accordingly he had put the relay first in order of priority, using it as a test of how easily the Thuriens would accept a suggestion of an overtly hostile act on the part of the Terrans. If they did accept it, then the odds would be acceptable they would hold Earth responsible for the destruction of the *Shapieron* as well. The Thuriens had passed the test, and now only a matter of minutes stood between Imares Broghuilio and the elimination of the last element of a problem that had been plaguing him for too long.

He felt a deep sense of satisfaction at a difficult challenge met as he stood at one end of the War Room, deep below a mountain range on Jevlen, surrounded by his entourage of advisors and military strategists, following the reports coming in through JEVEX from the instruments tracking the *Shapieron* many light-years away. As he looked slowly around at the ranks of generals in the all-black uniforms of the Jevlenese military and at the arrays of equipment bringing information from and carrying his directions to every corner of his empire, he felt a deep and stirring anticipation of fulfillment at the approaching appointment that destiny had set for him. It was a manifestation of the Jevlenese superiority and iron willpower of which he was both the last in a long succession of architects and the ultimate personification, and which would soon assert itself across the Galaxy.

The uniforms were not yet worn openly, and this place was not known to the Ganymeans who visited Jevlen and on occasion remained for protracted periods for various reasons. Organization, planning, and training operations were still conducted in secret, but already an embryonic officer corps was ready to emerge with an established command chain to a nucleus of trained active units upon which a carefully worked-out recruitment program could begin building at short notice. The factories hidden deep beneath the surface of Uttan, one of the remote worlds controlled by Jevlen, had been steadily accumulating weapons and munitions for several years, and the plans to switch the whole Jevlenese industrial and economic machine fully to a war footing were in an advanced stage.

But the time was not yet quite right. On one or two occasions the events of the past few months had almost prompted him into being swayed by the overreactions and panickings of his lesser aides and acting prematurely. But by thinking clearly and with courage and sheer willpower he had steered them through the obstacles and annihilated the problems one by one until finally only the matter of the *Shapieron* remained. And that would be disposed of very soon now. He had been tested and found not to be lacking, as the Cerians would discover for themselves as soon as the inhibiting yoke of Thurien had been cast off. But not yet . . . not quite yet.

"Target closed to within one scan period," JEVEX announced. The atmosphere in the room was tensely expectant. The *Shapieron* was approaching the device that had been transferred into its path via a toroid projected several days earlier in order for the gravitational disturbance to be outside the range of any Thurien tracking instruments following the ship at the time. The device itself, packing a nucleonic punch of several gigatons and programmed to detonate automatically on proximity, was gravitationally passive and would not register on the Thurien tracking system, which operated by computing the spatial location of the stressfield produced by the ship's drive. JEVEX's statement meant that the bomb would go off before the tracking system delivered its next update.

Garwain Estordu, one of Broghuilio's scientific advisors, seemed nervous. "I don't like it," he muttered. "I still say we should have diverted the ship and interned it at Uttan or somewhere. This . . ." He shook his head. "It's too extreme. If the Thuriens find out, we'll have no defense."

"This is a unique opportunity. The Ganymeans are psychologically ready to blame Earth," Broghuilio declared. "Such an opportunity will not come again. Such moments are to be seized and exploited, not wasted by timidity and indecision." He looked at the scientist disdainfully. "That is why I command and you follow. Genius is knowing the difference between acceptable risk and rashness, and then being willing to play for high stakes. Great things were never achieved by half-measures." He snorted. "Besides, what could the Thuriens do? They cannot match strength with strength. Their heritage has left them sadly ill-equipped to deal with the realities of the Universe on the terms that the Universe dictates."

"They have survived for a long time, nevertheless," Estordu observed.

"Artificially, because they have never faced the test of opposition," General Wylott declared, taking up the party line from one side of Broghuilio. "But trial by strength is the Universe's natural law. When the more natural course of events unfolds, they will not prevail. They are not tempered to spearhead the advance into the unknowns of the Galaxy."

"There speaks a soldier," Broghuilio said, scowling balefully at Estordu and the rest of the scientists. "You bleat like Ganymean sheep while you are in the safety of the fold, but who will protect you when you go out onto the mountain to face the lions?"

At that moment JEVEX spoke again: "Latest update now analyzed." A hush fell at once across the Jevlenese War Room. "Target no longer registering in scan data. All traces have vanished. Destruction effected with one-hundred-percent success. Mission accomplished."

The tension lifted abruptly, and a flurry of relieved murmurings broke out on all sides. Broghuilio permitted a grim smile of satisfaction as he drew himself up to his full height to acknowledge the congratulations being directed toward him from around the floor. His chest swelled with the feeling of power and authority that his uniform symbolized. Wylott turned and threw his arm out in a crisp Jevlenese salute acknowledging the leader. The rest of the military followed suit.

Broghuilio made a perfunctory return, waited a few moments for the excitement to subside, then raised an arm. "This is but a small foretaste of what is to come," he told them, his voice booming to carry to the far corners of the room. "Nothing will stand in our path when Jevlen marches forward to its destiny. The Thuriens will be wisps of straw lost in the hurricane that will sweep across first the Solar System, and then the Galaxy. DO YOU DARE TO FOLLOW ME?"

"WE DARE!" came the response.

Broghuilio smiled again. "You will not be disappointed," he promised. He waited for the room to quiet and then said in a milder tone, "But in the meantime we have our good *duty* to perform for our Ganymean masters." His mouth writhed in sarcasm as he wrung out the final word, causing grins to appear on the faces of some of his followers. He raised his head a fraction. "JEVEX, contact Calazar through VISAR and request that Estordu, Wylott, and I see him at once on a matter of gravest urgency."

"Yes, Excellency," JEVEX acknowledged. A short delay followed. Then JEVEX reported, "VISAR informs me that Calazar is currently in conference and asks if the matter can wait."

"I have just received news of the most serious nature," Broghuilio said. "It cannot wait. Convey my apologies to Calazar and inform VISAR that I must insist on going to Thurien immediately. Tell VISAR we have reason to believe that the *Shapieron* has met with a catastrophe."

A minute or two went by. Then JEVEX announced, "Calazar will receive you immediately."

chapter twenty-seven

At Houston, Caldwell had described to Hunt the network of real power that had lain hidden across the world possibly for centuries, operating to preserve privilege and promote self-interest by opposing and controlling scientific progress. The attempt first to frustrate and then to shut down communications with Thurien had seemed consistent with such a power structure and policy.

Then Danchekker had called in a visibly excited state from McClusky with the news that Karen Heller had opened up a completely new dimension to the whole situation. On arriving in Alaska hours later, Hunt and Caldwell learned of the evidence for supposing that the Jevlenese had been interfering with Earth's technological development since the dawn of its history while they grew in numbers, reorganized, and profited from their access to Ganymean knowledge. This notion had proved so astonishing that nobody made the connection between the two sets of information until Lyn arrived from Washington with the staggering announcement that not only was Sverenssen in communication with the Jevlenese, as he apparently had been for many years, but that, from the evidence of the sculpture, the Jevlenese were still staging physical visits to Earth, at least intermittently. In other words the Jevlenese had not been interfering merely way back in early times; what Pacey and Sobroskin had started to uncover parts of right now was a Jevlenese-controlled operation.

This news immediately threw up a host of whole new questions. Was Sverenssen simply a native Terran working as a collaborator, or was he actually a Jevlenese agent injected into Earth's society and using the identity of a Swede killed in Africa years before? Whatever the answer, how many more like him were there and who were they? Why had the Jevlenese been distorting their reports to make Earth appear warlike? Could the reason be that they wanted a pretext to justify to the Ganymeans their maintaining a military strength of their own as an "insurance" against the possibility of future terrestrial aggression beyond the Solar System? If so, who had the Jevlenese been intending to direct the military strength against—the Thuriens, to end what was seen as an era of Ganymean domination; or Earth, to settle an account that went back fifty thousand years? If Earth, had the activities of Sverenssen's network to promote strategic disarmament and peaceful coexistence during recent decades been a deliberate ploy calculated to render Earth defenseless and set it up to be taken over as a going industrial and economic concern instead of the ball of smoking rubble that would have been left had it been able to offer resistance? And if this were true, how had the Jevlenese then intended to deal with the Thuriens, who would hardly have just sat and done nothing while it all happened?

There had been more than enough reasons to talk straight away to the Ganymeans, so Calazar had called everybody together at Thurios—including Garuth, Shilohin, and Monchar from the *Shapieron*. After the ensuing debate had droned on for over two hours, VISAR interrupted to announce that something had just destroyed the object substituted for the *Shapieron*. Minutes later Imares Broghuilio, Premier of the Jevlenese group of worlds, contacted Calazar to request an immediate appointment.

Sitting off to one side of a room in the Government Center at Thurios with the others from McClusky, Hunt waited tensely for the confrontation with the first Jevlenese they would meet face to face, who were due to appear at any second. Garuth and his two companions from the *Shapieron* formed another small group on the far side; and Calazar, Eesyan, Showm, and a few more Thuriens were clustered at one end. The Ganymeans were still somewhat shaken by what they had learned of deception and subterfuge that went beyond their wildest imaginings. Even Frenua Showm had conceded that without the apparently uniquely human ability to penetrate such deviousness, it was doubtful that the Ganymeans would ever have reached the bottom of it. It seemed that being suspicious of another's motives was something that came with the conditioning of predatorial thinking, and Ganymeans simply were not predators. "On Earth they say you must set a thief to catch a thief," Garuth had remarked. "It appears just as true that to catch a human you must set a human."

"They might be great scientists, but they'd make lousy lawyers," Karen Heller murmured in Danchekker's ear. Danchekker snorted and said nothing.

Calazar was curious to see how far the Jevlenese would go in their fabrications if fed sufficient rope; also, there was more that he hoped to learn from them before exposing just how much he knew. For these reasons he did not want to confront them immediately with the presence of the Terrans and the *Shapieron* Ganymeans. He therefore instructed VISAR to edit out of the datastream sent to JEVEX, and hence to the participants on Jevlen, all information pertaining to those two groups. It meant that Hunt, Garuth, and their companions would, after a fashion, be there, but remain completely invisible to the Jevlenese. Such a tactic was a flagrant violation of good manners and Thurien law, and unprecedented throughout the many centuries for which VISAR had been in use. Nonetheless Calazar decreed that by their own actions the Jevlenese had warranted making this occasion an exception. Hunt was looking forward to the consequences.

"Premier Broghuilio, Secretary Wylott, and Scientific Adviser Estordu," VISAR announced. Hunt stiffened. Three figures materialized at the end of the room opposite Calazar and the Thuriens. The one in the center had to be Broghuilio, Hunt decided at once. He stood six-foot-three at least, and had dark eyes that blazed fiercely from a face made all the more intimidating by a mane of thick, black hair and a pugnacious mouth surrounded by a short, cropped beard. His body was clad in a short coat of gold sheen worn over a mauve tunic covering a barrel-like chest and powerful torso.

"What of the *Shapieron*?" Calazar demanded in an unusually clipped voice. Hunt would have expected that for one of Broghuilio's rank some form of opening formality would have been appropriate. The flicker of surprise that he caught on the faces of the other two Jevlenese seemed to say so too. One of them looked directly at where Hunt was sitting and stared straight through. It was a strange feeling.

"I regret the intrusion," Broghuilio began. His voice was deep and harsh, and he spoke stiffly, in the manner of somebody performing a duty that demanded a greater show of feeling than he could muster readily. "We have just received news of the most serious nature: all traces of the ship have disappeared from our tracking data. We can only conclude that it has been destroyed." He paused and cast his eyes around the room for effect. "The possibility that this could be the result of a deliberate act cannot be dismissed."

The Thuriens stared back in silence for what seemed a long time. They did not attempt playacting any show of concern or dismay . . . or even surprise. The first glimmer of uncertainty crept into Broghuilio's eyes as he searched the Ganymean faces for a reaction. Evidently this was not going as he had anticipated.

One of the other two, also tall, dressed somberly in dark blue and black, with icy blue eyes, slicked-back silver hair, and a florid face that tended toward puffiness, seemed not to have read the signs. "We tried to warn you," he said, spreading his hands imploringly in a good imitation of sharing the anguish that the Thuriens were presumably supposed to be feeling at that moment. "We urged you to intercept the ship before now." That was hardly true; possibly he placed a lot of faith in his powers of suggestion. "We told you that Earth would never allow the *Shapieron* to reach Thurien."

Across the room Garuth's eyes turned steely, and his expression was about as close to malevolence as that of a Ganymean could get. "Patience, Garuth," Hunt called out. "You'll get your shots in before long."

"Luckily Ganymeans possess plenty of that," Garuth replied. The Jevlenese didn't hear a thing. It was uncanny.

"Really?" Calazar responded after a pause. He sounded neither convinced nor impressed. "Your concern is most touching, Secretary Wylott. You almost sound as if you believe your own lies."

Wylott froze with his mouth hanging half open, obviously taken completely aback. The third Jevlenese, who had to be Estordu, was a lean, thin-faced man with a hooked nose, wearing an elaborate two-piece garment of light green embroidered with gold over a yellow shirt. He threw up his hands in shock. "Lies? I don't understand. Why do you say that? You have been tracking the ship yourselves. Hasn't VISAR confirmed the data?"

Broghuilio's expression darkened. "You have insulted us," he rumbled ominously. "Are you telling us that VISAR does not corroborate what we have said?"

"I'm not disputing the data," Calazar told him. "But I would advise you to think again about your explanation for it."

Broghuilio drew himself up to his full height to face the Thuriens squarely. Evidently he was going to brazen it out. "Explain yourself, Calazar," he growled.

"But we are waiting for *you* to explain *yourself*," Showm said from one side of Calazar. Her voice was low, little more than a whisper, but it held the tension of a tightly wound spring. Broghuilio jerked his face around to look at her, his eyes darting suspiciously from side to side as a sixth sense told him he had walked into a trap. "Let's forget the *Shapieron* for a moment," Showm went on. "How long has JEVEX been falsifying its reports of Earth?"

"What?" Broghuilio's eyes bulged. "I don't understand. What is the—"

"How long?" Showm asked again, her voice rising suddenly to cut the air sharply. Her tone and the expressions of the other Thuriens spelled out clearly that any attempt at a denial would have been futile. The hue of Broghuilio's face deepened to purple, but he seemed too stunned to form a reply.

"What grounds do you have for such an accusation?" Wylott demanded. "The department that conducts the surveillance is responsible to me. I consider this a personal attack."

"Evidence?" Showm uttered the word offhandedly, as if the demand were too absurd to take seriously. "Earth disarmed strategically in the second decade of its current century and has pursued peaceful coexistence ever since, but JEVEX has never mentioned it. Instead JEVEX has reported nucleonic weapons deployed in orbit, radiation projectors sited on Luna, military installations across the Solar System, and a whole concoction of fictions that have never existed. Do you deny it?"

Estordu was thinking frantically as he listened. "Corrections," he blurted suddenly. "Those were corrections, not falsifications. Our sources led us to believe that Earth's governments had discovered the surveillance, and they had conspired to conceal their warlike intentions. We instructed JEVEX to apply a correction factor by extrapolating the developments that would have taken place if the surveillance had not been discovered, and we presented these as facts in order to insure that our protective measures would not be relaxed." The stares coming from the Thuriens were openly contemptuous, and he finished lamely, "Of course, it is possible that the corrections were . . . somewhat exaggerated unintentionally."

"So I ask you again, how long?" Showm said. "How long has this been practiced?"

"Ten, maybe twenty years . . . I can't remember."

"You don't know?" She looked at Wylott. "It's your department. Have you no records?"

"JEVEX keeps the records," Wylott replied woodenly.

"VISAR," Calazar said. "Obtain the records from JEVEX for us."

"This is outrageous!" Broghuilio shouted, his face turning black with anger. "The surveillance program is entrusted to us by long-standing agreement. You have no right to make such a demand. It has been negotiated."

Calazar ignored him. A few seconds later VISAR informed them, "I can't make any sense of the response. Either the records are corrupted, or JEVEX is under a directive not to release them."

Showm did not seem surprised. "Never mind," she said, and looked back at Estordu. "Let's give you the benefit of the doubt and say twenty years. Therefore anything reported by JEVEX before that time will not have been altered. Is that correct?"

"It might have been more," Estordu said hastily. "Twenty-five . . . thirty, perhaps."

"Then let's go back farther than that. The Second World War on Earth ended eighty-six years ago. I have examined some of the accounts of events during that period as reported by JEVEX at the time. Let me give you some examples. According to JEVEX, the cities of Hamburg, Dresden, and Berlin were devastated not by conventional saturation bombing but by nuclear weapons. According to JEVEX, the Korean conflict in the 1950s escalated into a major clash of Soviet and American forces; in fact, nothing of the kind took place. Neither were tactical nuclear devices used in the Middle East wars of the '60s and '70s, nor was there an outbreak of Sino-Soviet hostilities in the 1990s." Showm's voice became icy as she concluded, "And neither was the *Shapieron* taken into captivity by a United States military garrison on Ganymede. The United States has never had a military garrison on Ganymede."

Estordu had no answer. Wylott remained immobile, staring straight in front of himself. Broghuilio seemed to swell with indignation. "We asked for *evidence!*" he thundered. "That is not evidence. Those are allegations. Where is your proof? Where are your witnesses? Where is your justification for this intolerable behavior?"

"I'll take it," Heller said, rising to her feet beside Caldwell. There was no way she was going to let him beat her to it this time. From where Hunt was sitting nothing appeared to change, but the way the three Jevlenese heads snapped around to gape at her left no doubt that VISAR had suddenly put her on stage.

Before any of them could say anything, Calazar spoke. "Allow me to introduce somebody who might satisfy your requirement—Karen Heller, Special Envoy to Thurien from the State Department of the United States."

Estordu's face had turned white, and Wylott's mouth was opening and closing ineffectively without producing any sound. Broghuilio was standing with his fists clenched and paroxysms of rage sweeping in visible tremors through the length of his body. "We have many witnesses," Calazar said. "Nine billion of them, in fact. But for now, a few representatives will suffice." The Jevlenese's eyes opened wider as the remainder of the Terran delegation became visible. None of them glanced in the opposite direction, indicating that Calazar had not yet instructed VISAR to reveal Garuth and the others from the *Shapieron.*

Karen Heller had compiled a long list of suspicions concerning Jevlenese manipulations of events on Earth, none of which she could prove. The opportunity for bluffing the confirmation from the Jevlenese would never again be quite what it was at that moment, and she plunged ahead without giving them a second's respite. "Ever since the Lambians were taken from Luna to Thurien after the Minervan war, they have never forgotten their rivalry with the Cerians. They have always seen Earth as a potential threat that would one day have to be eliminated. In anticipation of that day, they took advantage of their access to Ganymean sciences and devised an elaborate scheme to insure that their rival would be held in a state of backwardness and prevented from reemerging to challenge them until they had absorbed the last ounce of the knowledge and technologies that they thought would make them invincible." She was unconsciously addressing her words to Calazar and the Thuriens as if they were judge and jury, and the proceedings were a trial. They remained silent and waiting as she paused for a moment to shift to a different key.

"What is knowledge?" she asked them. "*True* knowledge, of reality as it is, as opposed to how it might appear to be or how one might wish it to be? What is the only system of thought that has been developed that is effective in distinguishing fact from fallacy, truth from myth, and reality from delusion?" She paused again for a second and then exclaimed, "*Science!* All the truths that we *know*, as opposed to beliefs which some choose blindly to adopt as if the strength of their convictions could affect facts, have been revealed by the rational processes of applied *scientific method*. Science alone yields a basis for the formulation of beliefs whose validity can be *proved* because they predict *results* that can be *tested*. And yet . . ." Her voice fell, and she turned her head to include the Terrans sitting around her. "And yet, for thousands of years the races of Earth clung persistently to their cults, superstitions, irrational dogmas, and impotent idols. They refused to accept what their eyes alone should have told them—that the magical and mystical forces in which they trusted and which they aspired to command were fictions, barren in their yield of results, powerless in prediction, and devoid of useful application. In a word, they were *worthless*, which of course made any consequences *harmless*. And this, from the Lambian, or Jevlenese, viewpoint, constituted a remarkably convenient situation. It was too convenient to be just a coincidence." Heller turned her head to look coldly at the Jevlenese. "But we know that it was not merely a coincidence. Far from it."

Danchekker turned an astonished face to Hunt, leaned closer, and whispered, "How extraordinary! I'd never have believed I'd hear *her* make a speech like that."

"I'd never have believed it, either," Hunt muttered. "What have you been doing to her?"

Still looking at the Jevlenese, Heller went on, "We know that the early beliefs in the supernatural were established by miracle workers whom *you* recruited and trained, and injected as agents to found and popularize mass movements and counter cultures based on myth, and to undermine and discredit any tendencies toward the emergence of the rational systems of thought that could lead to advanced technology, mastery over the environment, and a challenge to your position. Can you deny it?" She could read on their faces that her bluff had succeeded. They were standing rigid and unmoving, too numbed with shock to respond. Feeling more confident, Heller looked over at the Thuriens and resumed, "The superstitions and religions of Earth's early cultures were carefully contrived and implanted. The beliefs of the Babylonians, the Mayas, the ancient Egyptians, and the early Chinese, for example, were based on notions of the supernatural, magic, legend, and folklore, to sap them of any potential for developing logical methods of thought. The civilizations that grew upon those foundations built cities, developed arts and agriculture, and constructed ships and simple machines, but they never evolved the sciences that could have unlocked true power on any significant scale. They were harmless."

Low mutterings and murmurs were rippling among the Thuriens as some of them only began to realize for the first time the full extent of what the Terrans had uncovered. "And what of Earth's later history?" Calazar asked, mainly for the benefit of those Thuriens who had not been as involved in everything as he.

"The same pattern traces through to modern times," Heller replied. "The saints and apparitions who created legends by conveying messages and performing miracles were agents sent from Jevlen to reinforce and reassure. The cults and movements that perpetuated beliefs in spiritualism and the occult, in paranormal sciences and other such nonsenses that were in vogue in Europe and North America in the nineteenth century, were manufactured in an attempt to dilute the progress of true science and reason. And even in the twentieth century, the so-called popular reactions against science, technology, positive economic growth, nuclear energy, and the like were in fact carefully orchestrated."

"Your answer?" Calazar demanded curtly, staring at Broghuilio.

Broghuilio folded his arms, drew a long breath, and turned slowly to face directly toward where Heller was standing. He seemed to have recomposed himself and was apparently far from conceding defeat yet. He glared defiantly at the Terrans for a few seconds and then turned his head toward Calazar. "Yes, it was so. The facts are as stated. The motive, however, was not as described. Only a *Terran* mind could conceive of such motives. They are projecting into us their own evils." He threw out an arm to point at the Terrans accusingly. "You

know the history of their planet, Calazar. All the violence and
bloodthirstiness that destroyed Minerva is preserved today on
Earth. I do not have to repeat to you their unending history of
quarrels, wars, revolutions, and killing. And that, mark you,
was *despite* our efforts to contain them! Yes, we planted agents
to steer them away from the sciences and from reason. Do you
blame us? Can you imagine the holocaust that would be
sweeping across the Galaxy today if they had been allowed to
return into space tens of thousands of years ago? Can you
imagine the threat that it would have posed to you as well as
to us?" He looked again at where the Terrans were sitting, and
scowled distastefully. "They are primitives. Insane! They always will be. We kept their planet backward for the same rea
son that we would not give fire to children—to protect them as
well as ourselves, and you too. We would do the same again.
I have no apologies to offer."

"Your actions betray your words," Frenua Showm retorted.
"If you believed that you had pacified a warlike planet, you
would have been proud of the achievement. You would not
have concealed the fact. But you did the opposite. You presented a falsified picture of Earth that showed it as warlike
when in fact it was moving in exactly the direction that you
should have considered desirable. You successfully delayed its
advancement until its Minervan inheritance had been diluted
sufficiently for it to advance wisely. But not only did you conceal that fact, you distorted it. How do you explain that?"

"A temporary aberration," Broghuilio replied. "Underneath
nothing has changed. We altered the more recent developments
so that you would not be misled. A final solution to the
problem was still called for."

Heller was thinking rapidly as she listened. The "final solution" had to mean that the Jevlenese had used Earth's belligerence as an excuse to maintain their own military forces as she
had suspected. It seemed to support another line of thought
that her researches had caused her to wonder about, and here
was an opportunity to test it. But to do so she would have to
resort to bluff again. "I challenge that explanation," she said.
"What I have described so far is only part of what the
Jevlenese have been doing. "All the heads in the room turned
toward her. "By the time of the nineteenth century, it was obvious that Western civilization was rapidly spreading science
and industrial technology across the globe in spite of all their

efforts. At that point the Jevlenese changed their tactics. They actually began to stimulate and accelerate scientific discovery by leaking information in various quarters that precipitated major breakthroughs." She turned her head a fraction. "Dr. Hunt. Would you like to comment, please?"

Hunt had been expecting the question. He stood up and said, "The sharp discontinuities and nonlinearities that attended the major breakthroughs in physics and mathematics in the late nineteenth and early twentieth centuries have been a mystery for a long time. In my opinion, such conceptual revolutions could not have happened in the time they did without some external influence."

"Thank you," Heller said. Hunt sat down. She looked back at the Thuriens, more than a few of whom appeared puzzled. "Why would the Jevlenese do such a thing when their policy up until then had been to retard their rival? Because they were forced to accept the fact that they would not be able to keep Earth back any longer. Therefore, if Earth was about to become a high-technology planet anyway, the Jevlenese decided to use their already established infrastructure of influence to steer that advancement in such a direction that their rival would eliminate itself. In other words they set out to engineer events in such a way that the sciences which they themselves had helped develop would be used not to eradicate the scourges that had plagued mankind throughout history, but to wage war on a global scale and with unprecedented ferocity." She watched Broghuilio carefully as she spoke, and saw that she had hit the mark. Now was the moment to go for the kill.

"Deny that it was Jevlenese agents who infiltrated the European nobility at the end of the nineteenth century and created the rash of internecine jealousies that culminated in the horrors of the First World War," she challenged in a suddenly loud and cutting voice. "Deny that it was a Jevlenese-controlled organization that seized control of Russia after the 1917 revolution and developed the prototype for the totalitarian police state. And deny that you set up a Jevlenese group in the wreckage of postwar Germany to resurrect the hatreds that the League of Nations was formed to resolve by peaceful means. They were led by some very carefully selected and trained individuals, weren't they? What happened to the real Adolf Hitler? Or perhaps you operated from behind the throne—Alfred Rosenberg, perhaps?" The three Jevlenese did not have to say anything.

Their frozen postures and stunned expressions provided all the confirmation needed. Heller turned her head toward the Thuriens and explained, "World War II was supposed to be nuclear. The necessary scientific, political, social, and economic prerequisites had all been taken care of. It didn't quite work as planned, but it came frighteningly close."

A new wave of mutterings broke out among the Thuriens. Heller waited for it to subside and then concluded in a quieter voice, "The tensions continued for over half a century, but despite the continuing Jevlenese efforts, the global catastrophe that they sought never quite took place." The next part was pure guesswork, but she continued without any change of tone. "They concluded that one day they would have to confront their rival themselves, and so embarked on a program of exaggerating Earth's wars and armament developments to justify to the Thuriens their creation of a 'protective' strength of their own. At the same time they reversed their policy on Earth and used their network to defuse tensions, promote disarmament, and permit its people to develop their talents and resources creatively in the ways they had always wanted to. The object of this, of course, was to turn Earth into a defenseless target. To maintain the justification for increasing their own armed forces, they supplied the Thuriens with what gradually became a total fantasy manufactured inside JEVEX."

Heller paused again, but this time there was no sound. She wheeled around to point at the Jevlenese, and her voice rose to an accusing shout. "*They* accuse *us* of killing each other, when all the time they know full well that *their agents* have orchestrated the worst episodes of havoc and bloodshed in Earth's history. *They* have murdered more people than all the leaders of planet Earth put together." Her voice fell to an ominous whisper. "But the unexpected arrival of the *Shapieron* threw all those plans into confusion. Here was a group of Ganymeans who would expose the lie if they were allowed to make contact with Thurien. Now we see the *real* reason why its existence was never disclosed." The color was draining from Broghuilio's face. Wylott had turned scarlet and seemed to be having difficulty breathing, while on Broghuilio's other side Estordu was dripping with perspiration and shaking visibly. Across the room Garuth, Shilohin, and Monchar were sitting forward tensely as they sensed the moment approaching for them to reveal themselves.

"And now we come to the question of the *Shapieron*," Heller said. Her tone was almost soft, but menace was glittering in her eyes as she fixed them upon the Jevlenese. "We heard earlier a suggestion that Earth had sabotaged it. The suggestion is based on what we have seen to be lies. The *Shapieron* was never in any jeaporady at any time during the six months it was on Earth. On the contrary, our relationship with the Ganymeans was very friendly. We have ample records to prove that." She paused for a second. "But we do not have to rely on those records to prove that Earth did nothing to harm that ship or its occupants. We have far more convincing evidence than that." Across the room Garuth and his companions stiffened. Calazar was about to give the instruction to VISAR.

And the Jevlenese vanished.

The floor where they had been standing was suddenly empty. Surprised murmurs broke out on all sides. After a few seconds VISAR announced, "JEVEX is cutting all its links. I have no access to it at all. It is ignoring requests to reconnect."

"What do you mean?" Calazar asked. "You have no communications to Jevlen at all?"

"The whole planet is isolating itself," VISAR replied. "All the Jevlenese worlds are disconnecting. JEVEX has detached and become an independent system. No further communications or visits within its operating zone are possible."

The consternation breaking out among the Thuriens meant that something very unusual was happening. Hunt turned to meet an inquiring look from Danchekker and shrugged. "It looks as if JEVEX has broken off diplomatic relations," he said.

"What do you suppose it means?" Danchekker asked.

"Who knows? It sounds like a siege. They're inside their own zone controlled by JEVEX, and JEVEX isn't talking to anyone. So I guess that short of sending ships in there's no way anyone can get at them now."

"It might not be that easy," Lyn said from Hunt's other side. "If they've been setting themselves up as a Galactic police force, there could be a problem there."

A strange silence fell over the Thuriens. Calazar and Showm looked uneasily at each other; Eesyan looked down and fiddled awkwardly with his knuckles. The Terrans and the *Shapieron* Ganymeans looked at them curiously. Eventually Calazar looked up with a sigh. "Your demonstration of how to get truth from the Jevlenese was remarkable. You were wrong on one of your assumptions, however. We have never agreed to any proposal by the Jevlenese that they maintain a military force either to counter possible aggressive expansionism by Earth or for any other reason."

Heller didn't seem too reassured by the statement as she sat down. "You know now what they're like," she said. "How can you be certain that they haven't been secretly arming themselves."

"We can't," Calazar admitted. "If they have, the implications of the situation that would confront both of our civilizations are serious."

Caldwell was puzzled. He frowned for a moment as if to check over what was going through his mind, stared at Heller for a second, then looked across at Calazar. "But we assumed that was why they invented the phony stories," he said. "If that wasn't the reason, then what was?"

The Thuriens looked even more uncomfortable. Showm turned to Calazar and spread her hands as if conceding there was something that couldn't be concealed any longer. Calazar hesitated, then nodded. "It is clear to us now why the Jevlenese falsified their reports," Showm said, turning her head to address the whole room. An expectant hush fell as she paused. She took a long breath and resumed, "There is more to this, which up until now we have felt it wiser not to talk about . . ." She turned her head momentarily sideways to glance at Garuth and his colleagues, ". . . to any of you." They waited. She went on, "For a long time the Ganymeans have been haunted by the specter of Minerva repeating itself, and this time possibly spilling out into the Galaxy. Just under a century ago, the Jevlenese persuaded our predecessors that Earth was on the verge of doing just that, and urged a solution to contain Earth's expansion permanently. The Thuriens commenced working on a contingency plan accordingly. Because of the false picture that we were given by the Jevlenese, we have continued with the preparations to implement that plan. If we had known the true situation on Earth, we would have abandoned the idea. Clearly the Jevlenese were misleading us in order to harness our technology to contain their rival permanently and eliminate it from competing with them across the Galaxy in times to come. That was what Broghuilio meant when he referred to the final solution."

The Terrans needed a few seconds to digest what Showm

was saying. "I'm not sure I follow what you mean,"
Danchekker said at least. "Contained Earth's expansion by
what means? You don't mean by force, surely."

Calazar shook his head slowly. "That would not be the
Ganymean way. We said contain, not oppose. The choice of
word was deliberate."

Hunt frowned as he tried to fathom what Calazar was driving at. Contain Earth? It was too late for that; mankind's civilization had already spread a long way beyond Earth. Then it
could only mean . . . His eyes widened suddenly in disbelief.
Surely not even Thurien minds could think on a scale as vast
as that. "Not the Solar System!" he gasped, staring at Calazar
in awe. "You're not telling us you were going to shut in the
whole Solar System."

Calazar nodded gravely. "We devised a scheme for using
our gravitic science to create a shell of steepened gravitational
gradient that nothing—not Earthmen, nor Earthmen's aggression, nor even light itself, would escape from. Inside the shell
conditions would be normal, and Earth would be free to pursue
whatever way of life it chose. And beyond the shell, so would
we." Calazar looked around and took in the appalled stares
coming back at him. "That was to have been our final solution," he told them.

chapter twenty-eight

And so for the first time in the long history of their race the
Ganymeans found themselves at war, or at least in a situation
so akin to war that the differences were academic. Their response to the Jevlenese was swift and devastating. Calazar
ordered VISAR to withdraw all its services from the Jevlenese who were physically present on Thurien and the other
Ganymean-controlled worlds. A whole population who
throughout their lives had taken for granted the ability to communicate or travel instantly anywhere at any time, to have in-

formation of every description available on request, and who had relied completely on machines for every facet of their existence, found themselves suddenly cut off from the only form of society that they knew how to function in. They were isolated, powerless, and panic-stricken. Within hours they had been reduced to helplessness and were speedily rounded up and detained, as much for their own safety and sanity as to keep them out of any unlikely mischief, until the Ganymeans decided what to do with them. The whole Jevlenese contingent scattered across all the Ganymean worlds had thus been eliminated in a single lightning blow that left no survivors.

That left the enemy headquarters planet of Jevlen together with its system of allied worlds, which were serviced by JEVEX and not by VISAR. This, it turned out, was going to be a far harder nut to crack since it was unassailable by simply sending in ships as Hunt had thought of doing earlier.

The problem was that Jevlen was light-years away from Gistar, and the only way of getting ships there was through black-hole toroids projected by VISAR. But when VISAR attempted to project a few test beams into JEVEX's operating zone, it found that JEVEX was able to disrupt the beams easily; evidently the Jevlenese had been planning to break from Thurien for some time. Neither was it feasible for VISAR to transfer ships through toroids projected to just beyond the fringe of JEVEX's effective jamming radius to make their own way to Jevlen from there. The problem in this case was that all the Thurien vessels relied on power, as well as navigational and control signals, beamed through the Thurien h-grid from centralized generating and supervisory centers, and JEVEX could disrupt those beams just as easily. In other words, nothing could get into the Jevlenese system as long as JEVEX was operating, and the only way to stop it from operating was to send something in. It was a deadlock.

More serious was the possibility that the Jevlenese might have been amassing weapons secretly for a long time, and, in anticipation of exactly the kind of situation that now existed, building vessels to transport them that operated with self-contained propulsion and control capability. If so, they would be in a position to move their forces with impunity into VISAR-controlled regions and proceed unopposed with whatever threats or actions they had been planning. Time was crucial. The events at Thurios had clearly forced the Jevlenese to make their break sooner than they had intended, and the more swiftly the Thuriens reacted, the better the chances would be of catching the Jevlenese at a disadvantage with their preparations incomplete. But what kind of reaction was possible from a race that had no experience of resisting an armed opponent, possessed no weaponry to react with even if they had, and couldn't get near their opponent anyway? Nobody had any solution to offer until a day after the confrontation in Thurios, when Garuth, Shilohin, and Eesyan requested a private audience with Calazar.

"No disrespect, but your experts are missing the obvious," Garuth said. "They've taken advanced Thurien technology for granted for so long that they can't think in any other terms."

Calazar raised his hands protectively. "Calm down, stop waving your arms about, and tell me what you're trying to say," he suggested.

"The way to get in at Jevlen is in orbit over Thurien right now," Shilohin said. "The *Shapieron*. It might be obsolete by your standards, but it's got its own on-board power, and ZORAC flies it perfectly well without any need for anybody's h-grid."

For a few seconds Calazar stared mutely back at them in astonishment. What they had said was true—none of the scientists who had been debating the problem without a break since JEVEX had severed its connections had even considered the *Shapieron*. It seemed so obvious that Calazar was convinced there had to be a flaw. He looked questioningly at Eesyan.

"I can't see why not," Eesyan said. "As Shilohin says, there's no way JEVEX could stop it."

There was something deeper behind this proposal, Calazar sensed as he searched Garuth's face. What was equally obvious, and had not been said, was that even if JEVEX could not prevent the *Shapieron* from physically entering its operating zone, it might well have plenty of other means at its disposal for stopping the ship once it got in there. Garuth had been itching to confront the Jevlenese yesterday, and had been frustrated at the last moment. Was he now ready to risk himself, his crew, and his ship in recklessly settling something that he saw as a personal vendetta against Broghuilio? Calazar could not permit that. "The *Shapieron* would still be detected," he pointed out. "The Jevlenese will have sensors and scanners all over their star system. You could be walking into anything. A ship on its own, isolated from any communications with Thurien, with no defensive equipment of any kind? . . ." He let the sentence hang and allowed his expression to say the rest.

"We think we have an answer to that," Shilohin said. "We could fit the ship's probes with low-power h-link communicators that wouldn't register on JEVEX's detectors and deploy them as a covering screen twenty miles or so out from the *Shapieron*. That would give them, effectively, faster-than-light communications back to the ship's computers. ZORAC would be able to generate cancellation functions that the probes would relay outward as out-of-phase signals added to the optical and radar wavelengths reflected from the ship so that the net readings registered at a distance in any direction would be zero. In other words it would be electromagnetically invisible."

"It would still show up on h-scan," Calazar objected. "JEVEX could detect its main-drive stressfield."

"We don't have to use main drive at all," Shilohin countered. "VISAR could accelerate the ship in h-space and eject it from the exit port with sufficient momentum to reach Jevlen passively in a day. When it got near, it could retard and maneuver on its auxiliaries, which radiate below detection threshold."

"But you'd still have to project an exit port outside the star system," Calazar said. "You couldn't hide that scale of disturbance from JEVEX. It would know that something was going on."

"So we send another ship or two as decoys . . . unmanned ships," Shilohin replied. "Let JEVEX jam those and think that's all there is to it. In fact that would be a good way of diverting its attention from the *Shapieron*."

Calazar still didn't like the proposal. He turned away, clasped his hands behind his back, and paced slowly across the room to stare at the wall while he thought it over. He was not a technical expert, but from what he knew, the scheme was workable theoretically. Thurien ships carried on-board compensators that interacted with a projected toroid, compacting it and minimizing the gravitational disturbance created around it. That was why Thurien ships could travel out of a planetary system and transfer into h-space after only a day of conventional cruising. The *Shapieron* had not been built with such compensators, of course, which was why months had been necessary for it to clear the Solar System. But even as the thought struck him, Calazar realized there was a simple answer to that too: the *Shapieron* could be equipped with a Thurien compensator system in a matter of days. Anyway, if there were serious technical difficulties, Eesyan would already have found them.

Calazar did not have to ask what the purpose of the exercise would be. JEVEX consisted of a huge network similar to VISAR, and in addition to its grid of h-communications facilities possessed a dense mesh of conventional electromagnetic signal beams that it employed for local communications over moderate distances around Jevlen. If the Thuriens could intercept one, or preferably several, of those beams, simulating regular traffic in order to be inconspicuous, there was a chance that they might be able to gain access to the operating nucleus of JEVEX and crash the system from the inside. If they succeeded, the whole Jevlenese operation would come down with it, and the same thing would happen to the whole empire that had happened on a smaller scale to the Thurien Jevlenese a day earlier. But the problem was how to get the necessary hardware physically into a position to intercept the beams. Eesyan's scientists had been debating it for over a day and so far had produced no usable suggestions.

At last Calazar wheeled around to face the others again. "Very well, you seem to have that side of it all figured out," he conceded. "But tell me if I'm missing something. There's something else that you haven't mentioned: the kind of computing power you'd need to bring down a system like JEVEX would be phenomenal. ZORAC could never do it. The only system in existence that would stand a chance is VISAR, but you couldn't couple VISAR into ZORAC because that would require an h-link, and you couldn't close an h-link while JEVEX is running."

"That's a gamble," Eesyan admitted. "But ZORAC wouldn't have to crash the whole JEVEX system. All it would have to do is open up a channel to let VISAR in. Our idea is to equip the *Shapieron* and a set of its daughter probes with h-link equipment that VISAR can couple in through, and disperse them to intercept a number of channels into JEVEX. Then if ZORAC can just get far enough into JEVEX to block its jamming capability, we can throw the whole weight of VISAR in behind ZORAC and hit JEVEX from all directions at once. VISAR would do the rest."

There was a chance, Calazar admitted to himself. He didn't know what the plan's odds of success were, but it was a chance;

and Garuth's idea was more than anybody else had been able to come up with. But the vision in his mind's eye of the *Shapieron* venturing alone into a hostile region of space, unarmed and defenseless, and the tiny ZORAC pitting itself against the might of JEVEX, was chilling. He walked slowly back to the center of the room while the other three Ganymeans watched him intently. It was clear from their expressions what they wanted him to say. "You realize, of course, that this could mean subjecting your ship to what could be a considerable risk," he said gravely, looking at Garuth. "We have no idea what the Jevlenese have waiting there. Once you are in, there will be no way for us to get to you if you encounter difficulties. You would not even be able to contact us without revealing your presence, and even then the channel would immediately be jammed. You would be entirely on your own."

"I know that," Garuth answered. His expression had hardened, and his voice was uncharacteristically tense. "*I* would go. I would not ask any of my people to follow. It would be for them to decide individually."

"I have already decided," Shilohin said. "A full crew would not be necessary. More would come forward than would be needed."

Inside, Calazar was beginning to yield to the irrefutable logic of their argument. Time was precious, and the effectiveness of anything that could be done to thwart the Jevlenese ambitions would be amplified by an enormous factor with every day saved. But Calazar knew, too, that Garuth's scientists and ZORAC would not possess the knowledge of Thurien computing techniques viably to wage a war of wits with JEVEX; the expedition would have to include some expertise from Thurien as well.

Eesyan seemed to reach his mind. "I will go too," he said quietly. "And there will also be more volunteers among my experts than we will require. You can count on it."

After a long, heavy silence, Shilohin said, "Gregg Caldwell has a method that he uses sometimes when he has to make a difficult decision quickly: forget the issue itself and consider the alternatives; if none of them is acceptable, the decision is made. It fits this situation well."

Calazar drew a long breath. She was right. There were risks, but doing nothing and having to face at some later date what the Jevlenese had been preparing anyway, with their plans correspondingly more advanced, might be taking a greater risk in the long run. "Your opinion, VISAR?" he said.

"Agreed on all points, especially the last," VISAR replied simply.

"You're confident about taking on JEVEX?"

"Just let me at it."

"You could operate effectively with access only through ZORAC? You could neutralize JEVEX on that basis?"

"Neutralize it? I'll tear it apart!"

Calazar's eyebrows lifted in surprise. It sounded as if VISAR had been talking with Terrans too much. His expression grew serious again as he thought for a few seconds longer, then nodded once. The decision was made. At once his manner became more businesslike. "The most important thing now is time," he told them. "How much thought have you given to that? Do you have a schedule worked out yet?"

"A day to select and brief ten of my scientists, five days to equip the *Shapieron* with entry compensators for it to clear Gistar in minimum time, and five days to fit the ship and probes with h-link and screening hardware," Eesyan replied at once. "But we can stage those jobs in parallel and conduct testing during the voyage. We'll need a day to clear Gistar and another to make Jevlen from the exit port, plus an extra day to allow for Vic Hunt's Murphy Factor. That means we could be leaving Thurien in six days."

"Very well," Calazar said, nodding. "If we are agreed that time is vital, we must not waste any. Let us begin immediately."

"There is one more thing," Garuth said, then hesitated.

Calazar waited for a few seconds. "Yes, Commander?"

Garuth spread his hands, then dropped them to his sides again. "The Terrans. They will want to come too. I know them. They will want to use the perceptron to come physically to Thurien to join us." He looked appealingly at Shilohin and Eesyan as if for support. "But this . . . war will be fought purely with advanced Ganymean technologies and techniques. The Terrans would be able to contribute nothing. There is no reason why they should be allowed to place themselves at risk. On top of that, we have been helped enormously so far by information from Earth, and we might well be again. In other words we cannot afford to be without the communications channel to McClusky at a time like this. They have a more valuable function to perform there. Therefore I would rather we deny any such request . . . for their own good as much as anything else."

Calazar looked into Garuth's eyes and saw again the hardness that he had glimpsed at the moment when Broghuilio had announced the *Shapieron*'s destruction. It was as Calazar had suspected—a personal score to be settled with Broghuilio. Garuth wanted no outsiders, not even Hunt and his colleagues. It was a strange reaction to find in a Ganymean. He looked at Shilohin and Eesyan and could see that they had read it too. But they would not offend Garuth's pride and dignity by saying so. And neither would Calazar.

"Very well," he agreed, nodding. "It will be as you request."

chapter twenty-nine

Night surrounded the Soviet military jet skimming northward over the ice between Franz Josef Land and the Pole. The clash that had occurred inside the Kremlin and throughout the ruling hierarchy of the Soviet Union was still far from resolved, and the loyalties of the nation's forces were divided; the flight was therefore being made secretly to minimize risks. While Verikoff sat rigidly between two armed guards at the back of the darkened cabin and the half-dozen other officers dozed or talked in lowered voices in the seats around him, Mikolai Sobroskin stared out at the blackness through the window beside him and thought about the astounding events of the past forty-eight hours.

The aliens didn't stand up very well under interrogation, he had discovered. At least, the alien Verikoff hadn't. For that was what Verikoff was—a member of a network of agents from the fully human contingent of Thurien that ran the surveillance operation, and who had been infiltrating Earth's society all through history. Niels Sverenssen was another. The demilitarization of Earth had been engineered in preparation for their emergence as a ruling elite to be established by the Jevlenese, with Sverenssen as planetary overlord. Earth would eventually be deindustrialized to provide a playground for the aristocracy of Jevlen and extensive rural estates as rewards for its more faithful servants. How a planet reduced to this condition would support the portion of its population not required for labor and services had not been explained.

Once this much had been established, the value of Verikoff's skin had fallen markedly. To save it he had offered to cooperate, and to prove his credibility he had divulged details of the communications link between Jevlen and its operation on Earth, located at Sverenssen's home in Connecticut and installed by Jevlenese technicians employed by a U.S. construction company set up as a front for some of the Jevlenese's other activities. Through this link Sverenssen had been able to report details of the Thurien attempt to talk to Earth secretly via Farside and had received his instructions for controlling the Earth end of the dialogue. Sobroskin had detected no hint that Verikoff knew anything about the U.S. channel that Norman Pacey had mentioned. Despite the elaborate Jevlenese information-gathering system, therefore, Sobroskin had concluded that at least that secret had been kept safe.

Sobroskin had decided that the first step toward breaking up the network would have to be the severing of the link through Connecticut while its discovery was still unknown, and the Jevlenese were therefore off guard and vulnerable. Obviously that could only be accomplished with the help of somebody in Washington, and since nobody, not even Verikoff, knew the full extent of the network or who might be among its members, that had meant Norman Pacey. Sobroskin had called "Ivan" at the Soviet embassy and, using a prearranged system of innocuous-sounding phrases, conveyed a message for relaying to Pacey. A call from the U.S. State Department to an office in Moscow eight hours later, stating that hotel reservations had been made for a group of visiting Russian diplomats, confirmed that the message had been received and understood.

"Five minutes to touchdown," the pilot's voice sounded from an intercom in the darkness overhead. A low light came on in the cabin, and Sobroskin and the other officers began collecting the cigarette packages, papers, and other items strewn around them, then put on heavy arctic coats in preparation for the cold outside.

Minutes later the plane descended slowly out of the night and settled in the center of a dim pool of light that marked the landing area of an American scientific research base and arctic weather station. A U.S. Air Force transport stood in the shadows to one side with its engines running and a small group of heavily muffled figures huddled in front of it. The door forward of the cabin swung open, and a set of steps telescoped downward. Sobroskin and his party descended and walked quickly across the ice with Verikoff and the two officers escorting him making up the middle of the group. They halted briefly in front of the waiting Americans.

"You see, it wasn't such a long time, after all," Norman Pacey said to Sobroskin as they shook hands through the thick gloves they were wearing.

"We have much to talk about," Sobroskin said. "This whole thing goes further than your wildest imaginings."

"We'll see," Pacey replied, grinning. "We haven't exactly been standing still, either. You may have some surprises coming too."

The group began boarding while behind them the engine note of the Soviet jet rose, and the plane disappeared back into the night. Thirty seconds later the American transport lifted off, its nose swinging northward onto the course that would take it over the Pole and down across eastern Canada to Washington, D.C.

It was late evening at McClusky. The base was quiet. A short distance from the line of parked aircraft brooding silently in the subdued orange glow cast by lamps spaced at intervals along the perimeter fence, Hunt, Lyn, and Danchekker were staring in the direction of the constellation Taurus.

They had argued, inveigled, and protested that the business was as much Earth's as anybody's, and that if Garuth and Eesyan were risking themselves, honor and justice demanded that Earthpeople should also be there to share whatever consequences were in store, but to no avail; Calazar had been adamant that the perceptron could not be moved. They had not dared call in higher authority in the form of the UN or the U.S. Government to back their case because there was no way of knowing who might be working for the Jevlenese. Therefore they could do nothing but resign themselves to hoping and waiting.

"It's crazy," Lyn said after a while. "They've never fought a war in their history, and now they're going in on a commando raid to try and take out a whole planet. I never knew Ganymeans were like that. Do you think Garuth has flipped out or something?"

"He just wants to fly his ship one more time," Hunt murmured and snorted humorlessly. "You'd think that after twenty-five million years of it he'd have had enough." The thought had also crossed Hunt's mind that perhaps Garuth had decided to go down with it like the proverbial captain. He didn't say so.

"A noble gesture, nevertheless," Danchekker said. He shook his head with a sigh. "But I feel uneasy. I don't see why the perceptron had to remain here. That sounded like an excuse. Even if we could not have contributed anything technically, we could still contribute something else which I fear Garuth and his friends might well find themselves in need of if they encounter difficulties."

"How do you mean?" Lyn asked.

"I'd have thought it was obvious," Danchekker answered. "We have seen already how differently Ganymean and human minds function. The Jevlenese may possess some talent for intrigue and deception, but they are not the masters of the art that they appear to imagine. It requires a human insight, however, to recognize and exploit their blunders."

"They've only had Ganymeans to deal with," Hunt said. "We've had a few thousand years of practice handling one another."

"My point entirely."

A short period of silence elapsed, then Lyn said absently, "You know what I'd like to see? If those Jevlenese guys think they're so smart, I'd like to see them come up against some real professionals and find out what deception is all about. And with VISAR on our side, we ought to have the right equipment to do it with, too."

Hunt looked at her and frowned. "What are you talking about?"

"I'm not sure really." She thought for a moment and shrugged. "I was just thinking that with JEVEX faking all that information for years and feeding it to the Thuriens, it would be kind of nice if we did something like that to them . . . just for the hell of it."

"Did something such as what?" Hunt asked, still puzzled.

Lyn looked back up at the night sky with a distant expression. "Well, imagine this as a for-instance. JEVEX must have all those stories about weapons and bombs and things that it's been inventing stored away someplace in its records, right? And someplace else in its records, it must have all the genuine information about Earth that it's collected through its surveillance system—in other words, all the stuff about Earth that it knows is true. But how does it know which is which? How does it know which records are real and which are phony?"

"I don't know." Hunt shrugged and reflected for a second. "I suppose it'd have to tag them with some kind of header-label system."

"That's what I thought," Lyn said, nodding. "Now suppose VISAR did manage to get inside JEVEX, and it scrambled those labels around so that JEVEX couldn't tell the difference anymore. It would make JEVEX really believe all those stories were true. Imagine what would happen if it started saying things like that. Broghuilio and his bunch would go bananas. See what I mean—it'd be nice to watch."

"What a delightful thought," Danchekker murmured, intrigued. An evil smile crept across his face as he pictured it. "How unfortunate that we never mentioned it to Calazar. War or not, the Ganymeans would have been unable to resist it."

Hunt was smiling distantly too as he thought about it. The idea could be taken a lot farther than Lyn had suggested. If VISAR got into JEVEX's memory system sufficiently to change the labels, it would only be a short step from there for it to add in some extra fiction of its own devising. For example, if it could gain access to the part of JEVEX that handled the incoming surveillance data from Earth, VISAR could probably make JEVEX think anything it wanted about what was happening on Earth—such as a whole armada being readied to blow Jevlen out of the Galaxy. As Danchekker had said, a delightful thought.

"You could fake an agreement with Thurien to use their toroids to transport a strike force to Jevlen," Hunt said. "That way you could have JEVEX saying it would arrive in days. And if you'd already scrambled its records from way back, that would be fully consistent with what it would think it had been reporting for years. The Jevlenese would know it hadn't . . . but then if they've never questioned it all their lives, maybe they wouldn't know what to think. What do you think Broghuilio would make of that?"

"He'd have a heart attack," Lyn said. "What do you think, Chris?"

Danchekker turned serious all of a sudden. "I have no idea," he replied. "But this is an example of precisely the kind of thing I was referring to. The idea of finding ways to bewilder a foe is something that comes naturally to humans but not to Ganymeans. They are going to attempt the straightforward approach of simply crashing JEVEX—direct, logical, and without any thought of deviousness. But suppose that the Jevlenese have prepared themselves by providing backup systems capable of operating autonomously even without JEVEX. If so, the *Shapieron* could still find itself exposed to considerable dangers when it reveals itself by bringing down JEVEX, assuming it succeeds. I trust you see my point." Danchekker directed a solemn stare at the other two, then continued: "But on the other hand, if their plan had been to *control* JEVEX rather than disable it, and to disorient the Jevlenese by subterfuge of the kind you have been describing, then perhaps all manner of opportunities to exploit and exacerbate the resulting situation further might have presented themselves, which as things stand will never be created." He looked up at the sky again and shook his head sadly. "I can't for a moment imagine our Ganymean friends adopting such a tactic, I'm afraid."

The amusement of a few minutes earlier had drained from Hunt's face as he listened. He had tried, Caldwell had tried, and Heller had tried, but still he couldn't escape the lingering discomfort that perhaps they could have tried harder still. Now that Danchekker had voiced them, he recognized the same thoughts that he had been suppressing. "We should have gone with them," he said in a heavy voice. "We should have made Gregg bully them into it."

"I doubt that it would have made any difference," Danchekker said. "Couldn't you see that Garuth had a personal score to settle with Broghuilio? He didn't want anybody else involved as a matter of principle. Calazar knew it too. Nothing we could have said would have made any difference."

"I guess you're right." Hunt sighed. He looked toward Taurus again, stared at it for a while, then suddenly snapped out of his reverie and looked from side to side at the others. "It's getting cold," he said. "Let's go inside and get some coffee."

They turned and began walking slowly back across the apron toward the mess hall.

Many light-years away, the *Shapieron* slipped quietly out of orbit above Thurien. For a little over a day VISAR tracked it to beyond the Gistar system and monitored its transfer through h-space to a point just outside JEVEX's zone of control on the fringe of the Jevlenese star system. The power and control beams to the two unmanned decoy ships sent with it were promptly jammed, and while they drifted helplessly on the edge of JEVEX-space, the *Shapieron* continued moving inward and vanished from the view of VISAR's instruments into the cloak of impenetrability that surrounded the enemy star.

chapter thirty

The construction floating in space was in the form of a hollow square. It measured over five hundred miles along a side. From each of its corners a bar, twenty miles thick, extended diagonally inward to support the two-hundred-mile-diameter sphere held in the center. The surfaces of the outer square bristled with angular protuberances, sections of ribbing, and domed superstructures, all etched harshly in black and shades of metallic gray, and immense winding girded parts of the central sphere and its supporting members. Receding away into space behind it, a line of identical objects spaced at two-thousand-mile intervals diminished in size with distance until they were lost in the background of stars.

Imares Broghuilio, formerly Premier of the Jevlenese faction of Thurien and now Overlord of the recently proclaimed Independent Protectorate of Jevlenese Worlds, stood in his black Supreme Military Commander's uniform, his arms folded across his chest, and scowled out at the scene from inside a blisterdome on the hull of a spacecraft riding several thousand miles off. Low to one side, the dark, rugged sphere of the planet Uttan hung as a crescent against the blackness, appearing the size of a tennis ball held at arm's length. Wylott and a number of generals from various commands of the Jevlenese military were standing behind him with Estordu and a handful of civilian advisors. To one side, not looking very happy, were Niels Sverenssen and Feylon Turl, technical coordinator of the quadriflexor construction program.

Broghuilio waved an arm at the scene outside. "*We* have been forced to revise *our* timetables just as drastically and in just as little time," he said curtly, glaring at Turl. "I expect you to do at least as well."

"But engineering on this scale can't be accelerated by that kind of factor simply by ordering it to be," Turl protested. "We are still short by fifty units. It will take two years at least, even with round-the-clock shifts in all critical—"

"Two years is unacceptable," Broghuilio said flatly. "I've given you our requirement, and I want your confirmation, today, that it will be met as stipulated. Tell me what *can* be done for a change. The Protectorate is now operating on a war economy, and whatever resources are needed will be made available."

"It isn't simply a question of production resources," Turl insisted. "The power to transfer that number of quadriflexors to the target won't be available for two years. Crallort's latest estimates show that—"

"Crallort has been removed," Broghuilio informed him. "That office is now under military control. The generator battery will be expanded under an emergency program that is already in effect, and the power requirement will be met as stipulated."

"I—" Turl began, but Broghuilio cut him off with an impatient motion of his hand.

"You have until twenty-four hours from now to discuss the revisions with your staff. I shall expect you at the Directorate of Strategic Planning on Jevlen at that time to report. I will *not* expect to hear lame excuses. Do I make myself understood?"

"Yes, Excellency," Turl mumbled.

Subvocally Broghuilio instructed JEVEX to remind him later in the day to review possible candidates for Turl's replacement at Uttan, then turned his eyes contemptuously toward Sverenssen. "And it appears that my 'able lieutenant' who was supposed to have had the situation on Earth 'well under control' is equally incompetent," he sneered. "Well, what have you been able to find out? How did the Thuriens manage to communicate with Terrans right under your noses? Where is their facility located? What is your plan to eliminate it? How did they penetrate your operation? Who has been betraying it? I hope you have good answers, Sverenssen."

"I must protest," Sverenssen said in a shocked voice. "Yes, I admit that the Thuriens did establish a link somehow. But the accusation that we have allowed our operation to be penetrated is without foundation. There is no evidence to—"

"Then you are either blind or stupid!" Broghuilio spat. "I was there, in Thurios. You were not. I tell you they knew everything. The Terrans must have turned half the imbeciles in your organization and had them working against us for years. How long have they had a link on Earth direct into VISAR?"

"We ... have not been able to ascertain that yet, Excellency," Sverenssen admitted.

"Obviously since long before they started anything on Farside," Broghuilio said. "The whole Bruno operation was a façade to fool you and keep you occupied, and you swallowed every inch of it." He screwed up his face and mimicked a fawning tone. " 'We have gained complete control, Excellency,' I was told. Pah!" Broghuilio slammed a fist into his other palm. "Control! They were manipulating you like a puppet. They probably have been for years. Overlord of Earth? You'd be a laughingstock trying to govern a kindergarten." Sverenssen paled, and his jaw strained, but he said nothing.

Broghuilio raised his arms in front of the rest of the company as if inviting them to witness his predicament. "You see what I have to contend with—imbecile engineers and imbecile agents. And what of you? Clearly the enemy will not sit idly by and do nothing while we complete our preparations. But we are told that it will take two years. Thus we have a problem situation that demands some form of action now, while we retain the initiative. What are your plans?"

Some of the generals looked uncertainly at one another. Eventually Wylott replied hesitantly, "We are still analyzing the latest developments. The situation calls for a complete revision of every—"

"Never mind your academic analyses and evaluations. Do you have firm *plans* drawn up for offensive *action, now*, to secure our position while the quadriflexor program is being completed?"

"No, but we've never—"

"The general does not have a plan," Broghuilio told the rest of them. "You see—on all sides I have to deal with imbeciles. But fortunately for all of us, I do have a plan. Our weapons production program here at Uttan has begun showing results, has it not? We have ships, armaments, and sufficient generating capacity to transfer them to Gistar at once, while the Thuriens have nothing. It is a time for boldness."

Wylott seemed worried. "That is not the way we have always intended," he said. "Our plans have never included launching an unprovoked assault on Thurien. The weapons were to be used against the Cerians. We would find it hard to justify such an action to the people. It would not be popular."

"Did I say anything about attacking Thurien?" Broghuilio asked. "Can you conceive of no methods other than brute force and clumsiness? Have you no sense of subtlety?" He turned his head to address all present. "War is as much a matter of psychology as it is of weapons, and in particular of understanding the psychology of one's enemy. Study the history of Earth, or even of Minerva. Many great victories have been won by seizing an opportune psychological moment. And such a moment presents itself to us now."

"What are you proposing?" Estordu asked uneasily. "That we might intimidate Thurien into submission?"

Broghuilio looked at him in surprise and with unconcealed approval. "For a scientist you are thinking quickly for once," he said. He raised his voice. "You hear? The scientist is thinking more like a general than any of you. The Thuriens have no taste for war, nor even any concept of it. At this moment they believe that we have retreated into a shell and will not trouble them for a long time to come. They feel secure for the time being, and that is why they are vulnerable."

He strode slowly to one side of the dome and stared out at the distant ball of Uttan for a few seconds. Then he came back to the center and resumed, "I will tell you what the Thuriens are thinking at this moment. They realize that we present a threat which they do not have the stomach to face, but which the Terrans do. On the other hand they possess the technology necessary to counter that threat, whereas the Terrans do not. So what will be their obvious strategy?"

Wylott was beginning to nod slowly. "To arm and equip the Terrans as proxy troops," he said. "Thurien will enlist Earth to fight on its behalf."

"Exactly!" Broghuilio exclaimed. "But Earth is demilitarized and not competent to match us technically anyway, and at this moment the Thuriens have nothing to arm them with." He looked around with a triumphant glint in his eyes. "In other words their solution will require *time*. But we do not need time because right now we have something, and they have nothing. Our forces might be small compared to what they will be in times to come, but that situation gives us a ratio of something to zero, which equates to infinite superiority. That advantage will not exist indefinitely, and it will never again be in our favor to the extent that it is now. And *that* is why the time to act is *now*, and not later."

Wylott's eyes gleamed as he began to see what Broghuilio was driving at. "With self-powered ships we can send a task force in and issue an ultimatum to the Thuriens to place VISAR under our control," he said. "Being Ganymeans, they will have no choice. Then they'd be helpless, and we would assume full control of the combined empires of JEVEX and VISAR."

"And the Terrans will be deprived of their armorers," Broghuilio completed. "In two years they could never hope to match us without the Thuriens. Thus we will have bought the time we need to complete our preparations for dealing with Earth, and for neutralizing Thurien permanently." He turned to confront Wylott squarely, folded his arms across his chest, and stuck out his chin. "That, General, is the plan—*my* plan."

"A stroke of genius," Wylott declared. A chorus of murmurs from the ranks behind endorsed the statement. "We will commence detailed preparations at once."

"See to it," Broghuilio ordered. He turned and glowered at Sverenssen. "And you, if you think you have the ability to redeem yourself, go back to Earth. I want every one of the traitors in your organization uncovered, tracked down, and dealt with. All except Rank B2 and above. *Those* are to be held while we arrange a landing to bring them back to Jevlen. I will deal with *them* personally." His voice fell to an ominous growl, and his eyes smoldered. "And if you fail in this, Sverenssen, *you* will certainly be brought back, even if I have to come physically to Earth myself to do it."

chapter thirty-one

Several days went by without news from the *Shapieron*. VISAR analyzed all the available data on the design of JEVEX and gave ZORAC a five-percent chance of electronically lock-picking its way through the layers of security checks and access restrictions protecting the enemy system. The problem was that JEVEX's Ganymean-designed molecular circuits worked at subnanosecond speeds, enabling an enormous amount of self-checking to be interleaved with its regular operations. The odds were overwhelming that any chink in JEVEX's armor that ZORAC managed to slip a wedge into would be detected and closed before VISAR could be brought in to drive the wedge home. In other words JEVEX could scan its own internal processes too rapidly, or as Hunt put it to Caldwell, "It's got too much instant-to-instant awareness of what's going on inside itself. If we could distract its attention somehow, even for a few seconds, at the speeds those machines work at, ZORAC might be able to neutralize the jamming system and let VISAR in." But how could they distract JEVEX when the only channel they had to it was through ZORAC, and ZORAC couldn't get in until JEVEX had been distracted?

And then VISAR reported a series of gravitational disturbances outside Gistar's planetary system, followed by a steady accumulation of objects that seemed to be ships of some kind being transferred through from somewhere. Shortly afterward, the objects began moving toward Thurien. VISAR could detect no h-grid power or control beams and was unable to check their progress. They were self-powered, heavily armed Jevlenese war vessels, and there were fifty of them. As they fanned out to maneuver into positions around Thurien, JEVEX reopened contact briefly with VISAR to deliver the Jevlenese ultimatum: the Thuriens had forty-eight hours to place their entire world system under Jevlenese control. If at the end of that period they had not agreed, obliteration of Thurien cities one at a time would commence, starting with Vranix. Those were the terms. There was nothing to discuss.

The atmosphere inside the Government Center at Thurios was strained and tense. All of the Terran group from McClusky were present with Calazar, Showm, and a selection of engineering and technical experts that included Eesyan's deputy, Morizal. They were already six hours into the ultimatum period.

"But there must be something you can do," Caldwell protested, stamping backward and forward across the center of the room in frustration. "Couldn't you try using remote-controlled ships to ram them? Couldn't VISAR make a few black holes to suck them into or something? There has to be a way."

"I agree," Showm said, looking at Calazar. "We should try. I know it's distasteful, but the Jevlenese have made the rules. Have you considered the alternatives?"

"They could pick off ramships long before they even got near," Morizal said. "And they could detect a black hole forming and evade it long before it could trap them. And even then you could only hope to get a few at the most. The rest would incinerate Thurien then and there without waiting for the deadline."

"And besides, that's not the way," Calazar said at last, throwing up his hands. "Ganymeans have never sought solutions by war or violence. I couldn't condone anything like that. We will not descend to the level of Jevlenese barbarism."

"You've never faced this kind of threat before," Karen Heller pointed out. "What other way is there to meet it?"

"She's right," Showm said. "The Jevlenese force is not large. There's a good chance that it's all they possess right now. Six months from now that could change. Earth's logic is harsh, but nevertheless realistic in this kind of situation: losing some people now could buy the time to save many more later. It's a lesson they have learned, and we may have to as well."

"It's not the way," Calazar said again. "You've seen Earth's history. That kind of logic always leads to escalation without limits. It's insane. I won't allow us to start down that road."

"Broghuilio is insane," Showm insisted. "There's no other way."

"There must be. We need time to consider."

"We don't have any time."

A heavy silence descended. On one side of the room, Hunt caught Lyn's eye and shrugged hopelessly. She raised her eyebrows and sighed. There was nothing to say. The situation didn't look good. A short distance away Danchekker was becoming restless. He removed his spectacles, squinted through them while he twisted them first this way and then that in front of his face, then replaced them and began pinching his nose with his thumb and forefinger. Something was going through his mind. Hunt watched him curiously and waited.

"Suppose . . ." Danchekker began, thought for a second longer, then swung his head toward Calazar and Morizal. "Suppose we could induce the Jevlenese to postpone their offensive intentions and switch their force to the defensive . . . in other words take it back to Jevlen," he said. "That would gain us some time."

Calazar looked at him, puzzled. "Why should they do that? To defend against what? We have nothing to threaten any attack against them with, and neither have you."

"Agreed," Danchekker said. "But perhaps there is a way in which we could persuade them that we do." The Ganymeans stared back at him nonplussed. He explained, "Lyn and Vic were talking recently about an idea to *simulate* an all-out assault on Jevlen inside VISAR and inject it into JEVEX, assuming ZORAC gains access of course. And by suitably manipulating JEVEX's internal records, VISAR could, perhaps, then instill in JEVEX the conviction that the existence of such forces was consistent with what it has been observing for years. You see my point? Such a ruse might create enough confusion inside the Jevlenese camp for them to withdraw their forces. And given a sufficient level of uncertainty, they would probably not risk firing upon Thurien until they had determined the true situation. What we would do then I have no idea, but it would at least gain us some respite from the current predicament."

Showm was listening with a strange look on her face. "That would be almost identical to what they did to us," she murmured. "We'd be turning their own tactic right back at them."

"Yes, it does have a certain appeal of that nature about it," Danchekker agreed.

In response to some questions from Morizal, Danchekker went on to describe the idea in greater detail. When he had finished, the Ganymeans looked at one another dubiously, but none of them could pick out a fatal flaw in the argument. "What do you say, VISAR?" Calazar asked after they had talked for some time.

"It might work, but it still rests on a five-percent probability at best," VISAR replied. "It's still the same problem: the only way I could get into JEVEX is if ZORAC can switch off its jamming system, and so far ZORAC doesn't seem to be having much luck. I still haven't heard a thing from it."

"What else can you suggest?" Calazar asked.

A few seconds went by. "Nothing," VISAR admitted. "I could get to work and manufacture the information with some help from the Terrans and have it ready to beam through on the off-chance ZORAC does get me in, but its still five percent. In other words don't bank on it."

A faraway look had been coming into Hunt's eyes while the discussion was going on. One by one the heads in the room turned toward him curiously as they noticed. "It's this problem about distracting JEVEX's attention again," he said, "isn't it? If we could just freeze its self-checking functions for the couple of seconds ZORAC would need to switch off the jamming routines and open an h-link, VISAR would be able to hold that link open permanently and do the rest."

"True, but what's the point?" VISAR said. "We've already been through all this. We can't do anything like that because the only way in is through ZORAC in the first place."

"I think maybe we can," Hunt said in a distant voice. The room became very still. His eyes cleared suddenly as he gazed around at the others. They waited. "We can't create a diversion through ZORAC because ZORAC is outside the system trying to get in," he said. "But we've got another channel that goes straight through to the *inside* direct into the core of JEVEX "

Caldwell shook his head and looked puzzled. "What are you talking about? What channel? Where?"

"In Connecticut," Hunt told them. He glanced at Lyn for a second and then looked back at the others. "I'm betting that what's inside Sverenssen's house is a complete communications facility into JEVEX—probably one with its own neural coupler. What else could it be? We could get at it through that."

A few seconds elapsed before what he had said registered fully. Morizal seemed mystified. "Get at it and do what?" he asked. "How would you use it?"

Hunt shrugged. "I haven't really thought about it yet, but

there has to be something. Maybe we could use it to tell JEVEX all the things that VISAR's inventions will corroborate—Earth is fully armed and has been for years; an attack is on its way to wipe Jevlen out now ... supporting evidence, that kind of thing. That ought to shake it up for a second or two."

"That's the craziest thing I ever heard." Caldwell shook his head helplessly. "Why would it believe you? It wouldn't even know who you were. And anyhow, would you sit down in that thing and let JEVEX inside your head?"

"No, I wouldn't," Hunt said. "But JEVEX knows Sverenssen. And it would believe what he told it. That would really shake it up."

"Why would Sverenssen ever do something like that?" Heller asked. "What makes you think he'd want to cooperate?"

Hunt shrugged. "We put a gun to the bastard's head and make him," he replied simply.

Silence fell once again. The suggestion was so outrageous that nobody had a ready comment to offer. The Ganymeans were looking at each other in amazement, all except Frenua Showm, who seemed ready to go along with the scheme without further ado. "How would you get in?" Caldwell asked dubiously at last. "Lyn said it'd take an army."

"So use the Army," Hunt said. "Jerol Packard and Norman Pacey must know some people who could pull it off."

The idea was taking root as they thought about it. "But how do you know you could force him to do something like that without JEVEX knowing you were there doing it?" Heller asked. "I mean, VISAR can see somebody in the perceptron at McClusky even before they sit down in a recliner. How do you know Sverenssen's place isn't the same?"

"I don't," Hunt conceded. He spread his hands appealingly. "It's a risk. But it's a hell of a lot less of a risk than the one you were asking Calazar to take. And besides, the Ganymeans have taken enough of the risks already."

Caldwell nodded curtly as soon as Hunt said this. "I agree. Let's do it."

"VISAR?" Calazar inquired, still somewhat dazed by the sudden turn of events.

"I've never heard of anything like it," VISAR declared. "But if it increases the odds above five percent, it's worth a try. How soon can I start working on the movies?"

"Right away," Caldwell said. He moved to the center of the

group and suddenly felt the old, familiar feeling of being in command once again. "Karen and I will stay here to help out with that side of it. You'd better stay too, Chris, to explain the whole idea again. Vic needs to go to Washington to tell Packard what we want, and Lyn had better go with him because she knows the layout of the house."

"It sounds as if we should consider you in charge of this operation," Calazar said.

"Thanks." Caldwell nodded and looked around the room. "Okay," he said. "Let's go through the whole thing in detail from the beginning and work out as much as we can to synchronize the two ends of it."

Hunt and Lyn arrived in Washington late that afternoon. Caldwell had already called Packard from Alaska, so they were expecting to find Packard, Pacey, and Clifford Benson of the CIA waiting for them. What they were not expecting to find was a contingent of Soviet military officers there too, headed by Mikolai Sobroskin. To their further and total amazement they learned that a Jevlenese defector in the form of the scientist Verikoff was also present in another part of the building.

Most of the Russians were too stunned by what they heard from Hunt and Lyn to be capable of contributing very much to the proceedings. Sobroskin, however, digested their story quickly and confirmed—from what Verikoff had already told him—that the office wing of Sverenssen's house did indeed contain a full communications system into JEVEX, including a neural coupler. In fact Verikoff himself had used it on numerous occasions to make quick visits to Jevlen. This led Sobroskin to propose a means of simplifying considerably the plan that Hunt and Lyn had described. "As you say, the big risk in forcing Sverenssen to do it is that JEVEX might be able to observe what is happening," he said. "But perhaps there is no need for that at all. If we could just gain access to the device, Verikoff might be persuaded to do what is required voluntarily. JEVEX already knows Verikoff. It would have no reason to see anything amiss."

Ten minutes later they all left the room and descended one story of the building to enter a door that had two armed guards stationed outside it. Verikoff was inside with two more of Sobroskin's officers. At Sobroskin's request, Verikoff sketched a plan of Sverenssen's house on a mural display, indicating the location of the communications room and the access door into the wing in which it was located, as well as describing the building's protective features. "What's your verdict?" Pacey asked, looking at Lyn, when Verikoff had finished.

She nodded. "One-hundred-percent accurate. That's it, just the way it is."

"He seems to be telling the truth," Packard said, sounding satisfied. "And everything else he told Sobroskin checks with what Vic Hunt has told us. I think we can trust him."

Verikoff's eyes widened in surprise. He waved a hand at the sketch he had drawn, and then at Lyn. "She knows this already? How could that be? How could she know about the coupler?"

"It would take too long to explain," Sobroskin said. "Tell us what kind of visual sensors JEVEX has around the house. Are there some in all rooms, outside, inside the communications room, or what?"

"Only inside the communications room itself," Verikoff answered. He was looking from side to side uncomprehendingly.

"So JEVEX would not know about anything that was happening in the rest of the house outside that room," Sobroskin said.

Verikoff shook his head. "No."

"How about conventional intruder alarms around the grounds?" Pacey inquired. "Is the place equipped with anything like that? Would it be possible to get in over the walls and fences without being detected?"

"It's extensively wired," Verikoff replied. His expression became alarmed as he realized the implication of the questions. "Detection would be certain."

"Is the place watched from orbit by Jevlenese surveillance?" Hunt asked. "Could it be assaulted without it being reported?"

"As far as I know it is checked periodically, but not continuously."

"How frequently?"

"I don't know."

"How about Sverenssen's domestic staff?" Lyn asked. "Are they Jevlenese too, or just help that he hires locally? How much do they know?"

"Specially picked Jevlenese guards—all of them."

"How many?" Sobroskin demanded. "Are they armed? What armaments do they have?"

"Ten of them. There are always at least six in the house. They are armed at all times. Conventional Terran firearms."

Packard looked over at the others. One by one they returned slow nods. "It looks as if we could be in with a chance," he said. "It's time to bring in the professionals and see what they think."

Verikoff suddenly seemed apprehensive. "What is this talk of an assault?" he asked. "You are going in there?"

"*We* are going in there," Sobroskin told him.

Verikoff started to protest but stopped when he saw the menace in Sobroskin's eyes. He licked his lips and nodded. "What do you want me to do?" he asked.

An hour later a VTOL personnel carrier flew the whole party across the Potomac to the army base at Fort Myer. They were met by a Colonel Shearer, who commanded a Special Forces antiterrorist unit that had already been called to alert and was standing by. The planning and briefing session that followed went on until the early hours of the morning. The first gray light of dawn was showing in the east as an Air Force transport took off from Fort Myer and followed the coast toward New England. It landed with a whisper less than thirty minutes later at an out-of-the-way military supply depot situated among wooded hills twenty miles or so outside Stamford, Connecticut.

chapter thirty-two

The Jevlenese were still tapping into Earth's communications net. Earth knew they were, and the Jevlenese knew that Earth knew. Therefore, Caldwell reasoned, the Jevlenese would expect any high-level communications between Earth's governments, especially anything to do with an impending attack on Jevlen, to be encoded by methods that were generally thought to be unbreakable; anything else would not look authentic. But if the codes were indeed unbreakable, little purpose would be served by planting authentically encoded information in JEVEX since JEVEX wouldn't be able to unravel what it said.

At Caldwell's request the scientists at McClusky beamed details of the coding algorithms currently used for high-security terrestrial communications through to the perceptron. VISAR studied them and announced that JEVEX would have no problem. The scientists were skeptical. As a test VISAR invited them to compose an encoded message and send it over the beam, which they did. VISAR returned the plaintext translation less than a minute later. The stunned scientists decided that they still had a lot to learn about algorithms. But the implication was satisfactory: JEVEX could be led plausibly to believe that it was eavesdropping on Earth's highest-level secure communications.

Since then VISAR had been busy manufacturing a revised history of the last few decades on Earth in which the superpowers had not disarmed but gone on to escalate their strategic forces to insane levels of overkill capability, concluding with an account of Earth's leaders meeting secretly and agreeing to a hasty alliance to hurl their combined strength at Jevlen with the Thuriens transporting the force to within striking distance. Its latest creation, being previewed in the Government Center in Thurios, showed a conference hookup in which some of the senior officers engaged in the joint planning of the operation were delivering a preliminary briefing to their staffs. A General Gearvey, whom VISAR had already appointed as the American Supreme Commander, began speaking.

"We are about to engage an enemy who possesses a technology incalculably ahead of our own, and of unknown strength and retaliatory capability. But against that we have two factors in our favor that could redress the balance—*time* and *preparedness*. We are in a position to move now, while all our intelligence from the Thuriens leads us to believe that the enemy is not. Our strategy is therefore based on exploiting these factors to the fullest. We will forgo detailed planning and rely heavily on the initiative of local commanders in order to move fast and aim at total devastation of the enemy in a single, surprise, all-out, lightning strike with no compromises. This is not a time to ponder about morality. We might not have a second chance."

A Russian general leaned forward and took it from there. "The opening phase of the assault is designated OXBOW. Fifteen long-range radiation projectors will commence area-obliteration of selected targets on Jevlen, firing from one million miles standoff behind screens of destroyers and close-support tactical units. Five more will be held in reserve at ten million miles. The bombardment is intended to draw and engage the defensive forces while the spearheads move in to commence operations around the planet itself."

A European Air Force chief continued, "Phase BANSHEE will begin with a high-level sweep of Jevlenese nearspace to clear it of all enemy hardware. This will be followed immediately by rapid deployment of a mixed-strike orbital system to neutralize major military installations and observed ground concentrations. A secondary force will concentrate on population centers and administrative focal points to dislocate the defenses by creating panic and disrupting communications. Simultaneously, lower-altitude intercept units and killsats will contest Jevlenese air space, with carrier-based tactical groups operating in selective ground-strike and counterfire roles. Our objective here is to gain complete control above the surface within twelve hours of the spearheads going in. The codeword CLAYMORE will be issued upon the successful completion of this phase."

A Chinese general summed up the last part. "When CLAYMORE is declared, conditions will have been established to permit the seizure of bridgeheads on the surface. This phase is designated DRAGON. The first descents will be made by remote-controlled decoy landers to enable surviving defensive installations to be identified and destroyed by a portion of the orbital bombardment groups held in reserve for that purpose. The remaining orbiting groups will redeploy to provide close-support fire for the landings, and the carrier groups assigned to ground suppression will commence launching aircraft. When descent corridors have been cleared, the ground forces will be landed initially at twelve strategic points. Details of those operations are currently being finalized with the respective bridgehead commanders. Strategic bombardment from high level will continue throughout to prevent the defenses from concentrating on the landing areas."

"That concludes the overview," Gearvey said. "Individual unit assignments, timetabling, and call signs will follow immediately. Remain on standby."

"What do you think?" Caldwell asked as the image cut out.

"I'm impressed," Heller said. "It'd sure scare the hell out of me."

"Horrifying," Calazar pronounced numbly. "It is just as well that you did not go with the *Shapieron*. We would never have conceived anything like that."

Danchekker did not seem completely happy. "It still doesn't contain the sense of urgency that we have to convey," he said. "It doesn't mention any specific dates."

"I did that on purpose," Caldwell told him. "If we're going to be credible, we'd have to allow Earth ships months to get out of the solar system. The best thing seemed to be to leave it uncertain. What other way is there?"

"I don't know, but I still don't like it," Danchekker said.

Nobody spoke for a few seconds, then Morizal said, "Well, we've already got the Thuriens providing the transfer ports outside the Solar System. We could take it a step further and have the Terran vessels fitted with Thurien-supplied h-grid boosters. That way we could get them out of the Solar System in a day."

"A whole fleet?" Heller said dubiously. "Could a whole fleet be fitted out that quickly?"

"Conceivably yes," Morizal replied. "It's quite a simple job. With unlimited assistance from Ganymean engineers, it would be feasible."

"How does that sound?" Caldwell asked, looking at Danchekker.

"It sounds more like what we want," Danchekker agreed, nodding.

"Suppose I change the last part to this," VISAR offered. The image reappeared and showed General Gearvey again, just about to sum up.

"That concludes the overview," he said. "There are no major revisions to the schedule to report. The h-beam boosters are currently being fitted by the Thuriens, and the first assault elements should commence moving out from Earth, on time, at eighteen hundred hours today. Current indications are that the full force will complete its assembly outside the enemy star system three days from now as planned. The force will then reenter h-space and be accelerated to reexit into normal space at a velocity that will move it to Jevlen in twenty-two hours. Therefore we should be going into action four days from now. Good luck to you all. Individual unit assignments, timetabling, and call signs will follow immediately. Remain on standby." The image vanished.

"Excellent," Danchekker murmured.

"The next thing I need to start working on is some surveillance data from Earth to back it all up," VISAR said. "But first I need some reference information on contemporary Terran military hardware and installations. Can you get it beamed in through McClusky?"

"Give me a line," Caldwell said. "I'll get something moving right away." He turned his head away and stared grimly for a few seconds at another view, constructed from VISAR's locally collected data, of the pattern of Jevlenese warships positioned around Thurien. "Any news about the *Shapieron* yet?" he asked.

"Nothing," VISAR told him. Its tone was neutral.

An image in the form of a frame enclosing the features of the controller at McClusky appeared in the air a few feet in front of Caldwell's face. Caldwell turned his head away from the view of the Jevlenese threat and returned his attention to the matter at hand.

chapter thirty-three

"Damn! Damn! Damn!" Niels Sverenssen hammered savagely at the touchboard of the datagrid terminal, then brought his fist down heavily on top of the unit as the screen remained dead. He turned away and marched furiously toward the L-shaped central room. "Vickers!" he shouted. "Where are you, for God's sake? I thought those confounded dataphone people were supposed to be here by now."

Vickers, the heavily built and swarthy chief of Sverenssen's domestic staff, appeared from one of the passages. "I only returned ten minutes ago. They said they'd be right over."

"Well, why aren't they?" Sverenssen demanded irritably. "I have calls waiting that must be made immediately. The service *must* be restored at once."

Vickers shrugged. "I already told 'em that. What else was I supposed to do?"

Sverenssen began massaging a fist with his other hand and pacing to and fro, cursing beneath his breath. "Why do such things always have to happen at a time like this? What kinds of buffoon are unable to maintain a simple communications service competently? Oh, the whole thing is intolerable!"

The first faint hum of an approaching aircar drifted in from the direction of the window. Vickers cocked his head to listen for a second, then walked over to peer out through one of the sliding glass panels that formed part of a wall. "It's a cab," he said over his shoulder, "coming down over the roof." They heard the cab land on the other side of the house, in the front driveway. The door chime sounded shortly afterward, followed by the footsteps of one of the maids as she hurried to the front hallway. He heard a muted exchange of female voices, and a few moments later the maid ushered in a smiling Lyn Garland. Sverenssen's' mouth dropped open in a mixture of surprise and dismay.

"Niels!" she exclaimed. "I tried to call you, but you seem to be having problems with the line. I thought you wouldn't mind me showing up, anyway. I've been thinking about what you said. You know, maybe you were right. I thought maybe we could patch things up a little." Her hand was resting casually on the top of her shoulder bag as she spoke. Sverenssen was not inside the communications room, which was the one thing Colonel Shearer had insisted on before he could move in. Inside the top of the bag, Lyn's finger found the button on the microtransmitter and pressed it three times.

"Oh, not now!" Sverenssen groaned. "You should know better than to barge in like this. I am an extremely busy man, and I have things to attend to. Anyway, I thought I made myself perfectly clear on the not-so-memorable occasion of our last meeting. Good day. Vickers, kindly show Miss Garland back to her cab."

"This way," Vickers said, taking a step forward and nodding his head toward where the maid was still hovering.

"Oh, but you did," Lyn said, looking at Sverenssen and ignoring Vickers. "You made it very clear. And I was being so silly, wasn't I, just like you said. But now I've had a chance to think about it, it sounds so—"

"Get her out of here," Sverenssen muttered, turning away. "I don't have time to waste listening to any inane female prattling today." Vickers gripped Lyn's upper arm and steered her firmly back along the corridor to the front hall while the maid ran on ahead to hold the door open. The cab was still there. Just as they reached the door, a Southern New England Dataphones repair truck rounded the bend in the driveway and drew up in front of the house, halting so close to the cab that the ladders slung on its side overhung and blocked its ascent path.

The cabbie wound down his window and leaned out to yell in the direction of the front end of the truck. "Hey, asshole! Who taught ya ta drive dat thing? How the hell am I supposed to get outa here?" Two repairmen had jumped out of the passenger-side door of the truck, and another was emerging from the rear. The truck's engine came to life again in a series of laboring electric whines, then shuddered and died.

"I've got problems," a voice shouted through the open driver's window of the truck. "The same thing happened just now when we left the office."

"Well, do something with the goddam thing, willya. I've got a living ta make."

Vickers had released Lyn's arm and was growling profanities beneath his breath. With what was going on in the driveway, neither he nor the maid noticed her backing quietly away across the hall.

"Back up for Chrissakes. What's the matter? Don't you know how to reverse a cab?"

"How can I back up? Don't those look like flowers behind me to you? You need lenses or sump'n?"

Another technician was coming out of the back of the truck. There were already more of them than would have been sent on a simple domestic repair job, but Vickers and the maid were too preoccupied with the argument to register the fact for a few vital seconds. Also they failed to notice the sound of air engines growing steadily louder from beyond the treetops flanking the driveway.

When Lyn reappeared in the corner room Sverenssen was on the far side at one of the windows, peering out and upward as sound deluged the house suddenly, seemingly from all directions. All in the same moment, two Army assault landers dropped into sight from above and came down on the terrace by the pool with khaki-clad figures already bursting from their doors, explosions and the sounds of shattering glass came from the upper part of the house, and there was a brief glimpse of Vickers and the maid being bowled over by more figures pouring into the front hall before additional concussions followed by clouds of smoke blotted out the view along the corridor.

Lyn snatched the respirator from her bag, clamped it over her face and eyes, and snapped its retaining band into position behind her head just as the barrage of stun grenades and gas bombs crashed in through the ground-floor windows of the house. Detonations and smoke were everywhere, punctuated by shouting, splintering glass, the thuds of doors being smashed down, and a few scattered shots. One of the domestics appeared in the archway that led through to the main stairs, gesticulating frantically upward and behind him. "They're on the roof! There's soldiers coming in off the roof! They're—" The rest was drowned by more explosions, and he was engulfed by a cloud of smoke and gas erupting behind him.

Sverenssen had recoiled from the window, and Lyn could see him clawing at his eyes in the middle of the room as he tried to get his bearings. Whatever happened, he couldn't be allowed to get to the communications room now. She began picking her way cautiously around the wall to get between him and the passageway leading to the office wing. He saw the movement through the smoke and came nearer. *"You!"* His face twisted into a mask of fury as he recognized her, made even more grotesque by the watery streaks cutting through the smoke grime on his cheeks. Lyn's heart did a backflip in her chest. She backed away, but kept moving toward the passageway. Sverenssen's shape came looming through the smoke, straight at her.

Then barked military commands sounded inside the house, seemingly from not far away in the direction of the guest annex. Sverenssen threw a glance back over his shoulder and hesitated. Shadowy figures were struggling in the corridor outside the kitchen, and there was more movement on the side of the house facing the pool. He changed direction and made a bolt toward the office wing. Without realizing what she was doing, Lyn scooped up a wicker chair and hurled it across the floor at his legs. Sverenssen went down heavily and struck his head on the wall as he sprawled full-length on the floor.

But through the smoke Lyn could see he was still moving. She looked around desperately, picked up a large vase from a side table, swallowed hard and tried to stop her hands from shaking, and forced herself to move nearer. Sverenssen was half sitting up, one hand clutching at his head, a small trickle of blood oozing through his fingers. He braced a foot beneath himself, stretched out an arm to steady himself against the wall, and started to haul himself up. Lyn raised the vase high with both hands. But Sverenssen's legs had turned to jelly. He swayed for a second, groaned aloud, and then collapsed back against the baseboard. Lyn was still standing paralyzed in the same position when the first figures wearing respirators and Army combat uniforms and carrying assault rifles materialized out of the fumes around her. One of them took the vase lightly from her hands. "We'll take care of him," a gruff voice told her. "Are you okay?" She nodded mutely while in front of her two Special Forces troopers lifted Sverenssen roughly to his feet.

"Bloody good show that," an English voice commented from somewhere behind her. "You know, if you worked at it, you might even get a job with the SAS." She turned and found Hunt looking at her approvingly. Shearer stood next to him. Hunt moved beside her, slipped an arm around her waist, and squeezed reassuringly. She pressed the side of her head against his shoulder and clung tightly as the tension released itself in a spasm of trembling. Talking could wait until later.

Around them the noise had subsided, and the smoke was clearing to reveal Sverenssen's domestic staff being brought into the corner room to be searched and relieved of their weapons before they were herded away into the guest annex. As the assault troops and the others already inside the house removed their respirators, a knot of American and Soviet officers came in through the wreckage. They were accompanied by men wearing civilian clothes beneath combat jackets. Sverenssen's eyes bulged in disbelief as they refocused. "Hi," Norman Pacey said, with a trace of deep satisfaction. "Remember us?"

"For you the war is over, my friend," Sobroskin informed him. "In fact, everything is over. It's a shame that you did not find Bruno up to your standards. It's quite luxurious compared to where you will be going." Sverenssen's face withered with anger, but he still seemed too dazed to make any reply.

A sergeant crossed the room, saluted, and reported to Shearer. "No casualties, sir. Just some cuts and bruises, mainly on the other side. None of them got away. The whole house is secured."

Shearer nodded. "Start getting them out right away. Let's get those landers away before they're spotted by the surveillance. Where are Verikoff and the CIA people?" Even as he spoke, another group of figures pushed into the room. Sverenssen's head jerked around, and his jaw dropped as he heard the name. Verikoff halted a few feet away from him and stood eying him defiantly.

"So, it's you . . ." Sverenssen hissed. "You . . . *traitor*!" He lunged forward instinctively and was promptly doubled over by a sharp blow delivered to the solar plexus by a rifle butt. As he sagged two of the troopers caught him and held him.

"He carries the key to the facility on him at all times," Verikoff said. "It should be on a chain around his neck." Shearer ripped open the front of Sverenssen's shirt, found the key, removed it, and passed it to Verikoff.

"You'll pay for these atrocities, Colonel," Sverenssen wheezed weakly. "Mark my words. I've ruined bigger men than you."

"Atrocities?" Shearer turned his head aside quizzically. "Do you know what he's talking about, Sergeant?"

"I've no idea, sir."

"Did you see anything?"

"Didn't see a thing, sir."

"Why do you think this man is holding his stomach?"

"Probably indigestion, sir."

As Sverenssen was hustled away to join his staff, Shearer turned to Clifford Benson. "I'm pulling my men out right away, apart from ten that I'll leave as guards for the house. I guess it's ready for you to take over."

"You did a fine job, Colonel," Benson acknowledged. He turned to the others. "Well, time's precious. Let's get on with it."

They stood aside while Verikoff led the way into the passage toward the office wing, and followed a few paces behind. At the end of the passage he came to a large, solid-looking, wooden door. "I am not sure how far JEVEX's visual field extends," he called to them. "It would be better if you kept well back." The others fell back into a small dense huddle with Hunt, Sobroskin, Lyn, Benson, and Pacey together at the front. "I need a minute to compose myself," Verikoff told them. They waited while he brushed a few specks of soot from his clothes, smoothed his hair, and wiped his face with a handkerchief. "Do I look as if all is normal?" he asked them.

"Fine," Hunt called back.

Verikoff nodded, turned to face the door, and unlocked it. Then he drew a deep breath, grasped the handle, and pushed the door open. The others caught a glimpse of elaborate instrumentation panels and banks of gleaming equipment, and then Verikoff stepped inside.

chapter thirty-four

The strain on the Command Deck of the *Shapieron* had been hovering around breaking point for days. Eesyan was standing in the center of the floor gazing up at the main display screen, where an enormous web of interconnected shapes and boxes annotated with symbols showed the road map into JEVEX that ZORAC had laboriously pieced together from statistical analyses and pattern correlations of the responses it had obtained to its probe signals. But ZORAC was not getting through to the nucleus of the system, which it would have to penetrate if it was going to disrupt JEVEX's h-jamming capability. Its attempts had been repeatedly detected by JEVEX's constantly running self-checking routines and thwarted by automatically initiated correction procedures. The big problem now was trying to decide how much longer they could allow ZORAC to try before the tables of fault-diagnostic data accumulating inside JEVEX alerted its supervisory functions that something very abnormal was happening. Opinions were more or less evenly divided between Eesyan's scientists from Thurien, who already wanted to call the whole thing off, and Garuth and his crew, who seemed willing to risk almost anything to pursue what was beginning to look, the more Eesyan saw of it, like some kind of death wish.

"Probe Three's function directive has been queried for the third time," one of the scientists announced from a nearby station. "Header response analysis indicates we've triggered a veto override again." He looked across at Eesyan and shook his head. "It's too dangerous. We'll have to suspend probing on this channel and resume regular traffic only."

"Activity pattern correlates with a new set of executive diagnostic indexes," another scientist called. "We've initiated a high-level malfunction check."

"We have to shut down on Three," another, standing by Eesyan, pleaded. "We're too exposed as it is."

Eesyan stared grimly up at the main screen as a set of mnemonics unrolled down one side to confirm the warning.

"What's your verdict, ZORAC?" he asked.

"I've reduced interrogation priority, but the fault flags are still set. It's tight, but it's the nearest we've come so far. I can try it one more time and risk it, or back off and let the chance go. It's up to you."

Eesyan glanced across to where Garuth was watching tensely with Monchar and Shilohin. Garuth clamped his mouth tight and gave an almost imperceptible nod. Eesyan drew a long breath. "Give it a try, ZORAC," he instructed. A hush fell across the Command Deck, and all eyes turned upward toward the large screen.

In the next second or two a billion bits of information flew back and forth between ZORAC and a Jevlenese communications relay hanging distantly in space. Then, suddenly, a new set of boxes appeared in the array. The symbols inside them were etched against bright red backgrounds that flashed rapidly. One of the scientists groaned in dismay.

"*Alarm condition,*" ZORAC reported. "General supervisor alert triggered. I think we just blew it." It meant that JEVEX knew they were there.

Eesyan looked down at the floor. There was nothing to say. Garuth was shaking his head dazedly in mute protest as if refusing to accept that this could be happening. Shilohin moved a step nearer and rested a hand on his shoulder. "You tried," she said quietly. "You had to try. It was the only chance."

Garuth was staring around him as if he had just awakened from a dream. "What was I thinking?" he whispered. "I had no right to do this."

"It had to be done," Shilohin told him firmly.

"Two objects a hundred thousand miles out, coming this way fast," ZORAC reported. "Probably defensive weapons coming to check out this area." It was serious. The screen hiding the *Shapieron* would never stand up to probing at close range.

"How long before we register on their instruments?" Eesyan asked hoarsely.

"A couple of minutes at most," ZORAC replied.

In the Jevlenese War Room, Imares Broghuilio stood gazing at a display showing the deployment of his task force in the vicinity of Thurien. Although the ships were in VISAR-controlled space, VISAR had not jammed their communications beams to Jevlen. No doubt the Thuriens had guessed that the force had standing orders to commence offensive action automatically if it was interfered with in any way. At least, they hadn't risked it, which was precisely the kind of reaction he had expected from a timid and overcautious race like the Ganymeans. Again his instincts had proved infallible. Exposed at last for what they were, the Thuriens had shown again that they had nothing with which to oppose the combination of nerve, strength, and willpower that he had forged. A deep sense of satisfaction and fulfillment swept through him with the realization that the issue was already as good as decided.

If a response had not been received by a certain time, the plan called for some selected uninhabited areas of Thurien's surface to be devastated as a demonstration that the ultimatum was serious. That time had now arrived, and Broghuilio's aides were waiting with a tense expectancy. "Report the current status of the fleet," he instructed curtly.

"No change," JEVEX replied. "Bombardment squadron standing by and awaiting orders. Secondary beams unlocked and primed for area saturation. Coordinates programmed for targets as selected."

Broghuilio gazed around his circle of generals to savor the moment for a while longer, then opened his mouth to issue the command. At that instant JEVEX spoke again. "I have to interrupt, Excellency. A channel has just opened from Earth, top priority. Your response is requested at once."

The smirk vanished from Broghuilio's face. "I have nothing to talk to Sverenssen about. He has his instructions. What does he want?"

"It isn't Sverenssen, Excellency. It's Verikoff."

Broghuilio's expression changed to an angry frown. "Verikoff? What business does he have there at this time? He should be handling the situation in Russia. What does he mean by ignoring protocols in this fashion?"

JEVEX seemed to hesitate for a moment. "He . . . says he has an ultimatum to deliver to you personally, Excellency."

Broghuilio looked as if he had suddenly been punched in the face. He stood absolutely motionless for a few seconds while an ominous tide of deep purple crept slowly upward behind his beard, starting at his collar and eventually finding its way to his scalp. The generals around him were exchanging shocked, uncomprehending looks. Broghuilio licked his lips, and his fist opened and closed by his sides. "Get him here," he growled. "And JEVEX, do *not* disconnect him until *I* say so."

"I regret that is impossible, Excellency," JEVEX replied. "Verikoff is not coupled neurally into the system. I have audio and visual contact only." A screen on one wall of the room came to life to show Verikoff standing in the center of Sverenssen's communications room, evidently having thought better of committing himself to the recliner that was partly visible behind him. Something had happened to him since he had entered the room. He was staring out from the screen with his arms folded solidly across his chest, and he looked calm and assured.

"Behold, the textbook warlord," Verikoff allowed his lip to curl into a contemptuous sneer. "You should not have sent us to Earth, Broghuilio. It has been an honor and an education to meet *real* warriors. Believe my words—you would be even more of a fool than the fool you are to pit your rabble of amateurs against the Terrans. If you do, they will destroy you. That is my message."

Broghuilio's eyes widened. The veins at the sides of his neck began pulsating. "*You* are the traitor!" he spat. "Now we see the vermin exposing himself at last. What is this talk of an ultimatum?"

"Traitor? No." Verikoff remained unperturbed. "Merely a question of calculating the winning odds, which after all is your own dictum. You have set us up well to assume control of Earth very soon, and we thank you for it, but unfortunately for you that puts us on the winning side. Which do you think we'd rather be—caretakers of an outpost of your empire, or rulers of our own? The answer should not be difficult."

"What do you mean by *we*?" Broghuilio demanded. "How many of you are behind this?"

"All of us, of course. We manipulate all of Earth's major national governments and therefore have control over its strategic

forces. And we have enjoyed the cooperation of the Thuriens
for a long time now. How else do you think they've been able
to talk to the Terrans without your knowing anything about it?
They know that you, not the Terrans, are the real threat to the
Galaxy, and we have persuaded them to allow us a free hand
to deal with it. So we command a fully armed planet, backed
by Thurien technology. It's all over, Broghuilio. All you have
left to save now is your skin."

A short distance back from the open door through which
Verikoff was speaking, Hunt turned an astounded face toward
Lyn and leaned close to whisper in her ear. "I didn't think he
had it in him. The guy deserves an Oscar." Beside them,
Sobroskin, looking as if he didn't really believe it either, had
lowered the automatic with which he had been covering
Verikoff from the passageway.

Broghuilio was looking bewildered. "Strategic forces? What
strategic forces? Earth doesn't have any strategic forces."

Then JEVEX interrupted again. "We have an alarm condition
in Sector Five. Something unidentified is attempting to penetrate the net. Two destroyers have been detached from station
and sent to investigate."

"Don't bother me with such things now," Broghuilio raged,
waving his arms impatiently. "Delegate to Sector Control and
report later." He looked back at Verikoff again. "Earth demilitarized years ago."

"Is that what you believe?" Verikoff leered openly. "You
poor simpleton. You don't really imagine we'd allow Earth to
disarm when we knew this day was coming, do you? That
story was purely for your consumption. Ironically you almost
changed it back into the truth. It has given the Thuriens a lot
of amusement."

Broghuilio still couldn't make any sense out of it. "Earth
has disarmed," he insisted. "Our surveillance . . . JEVEX has
shown us—"

"JEVEX!" Verikoff scoffed. "VISAR has been pumping fairy
tales into JEVEX for years." His expression became hard and
threatening. "Listen to me, Broghuilio, for I am in no mood to
repeat myself. This demonstration at Thurien has taken things
too far. The Ganymeans have seen now what you represent,
and they are not of a mind to hold us back by scruples. So this
is our ultimatum to you: either you withdraw from Thurien
now, and agree to place your entire military command under

our jurisdiction unconditionally, or the Thuriens will transfer through to Jevlen a combined Terran force that will blow you to stardust—you, your whole planet, and that laughable aggregation of scrap that you call a computer network."

Somewhere deep inside JEVEX something hiccuped. A million tasks that had been running inside the system froze in the confusion as directives coming down from the highest operating levels of the nucleus redefined the whole structure of priority assignments to force an emergency analysis of the new data. And in the middle of it all, the routines that had been scanning for inquisitive probes through h-space faltered. It was only for a few seconds, but . . .

On Thurien, VISAR spoke suddenly to end a long vigil that had been dragging silently by for hours. "Something's happened! I've got a link to ZORAC!" Even as Caldwell was jumping to his feet, and Heller and Danchekker were looking up with startled faces on the other side of the room, streams of binary were pouring across the gulf to the *Shapieron*, light-years away, and VISAR had begun analyzing the patterns assembled by ZORAC.

"What's the situation?" Calazar asked tensely. "Is the ship all right? How far into JEVEX have they penetrated?"

"They've got problems," VISAR said after a short delay. "Give me a few more seconds. This is going to need some fast footwork."

On the Command Deck of the *Shapieron*, a familiar voice that had not been heard for several days spoke suddenly to break the silence that had fallen with despair. "Say, you're in a bit of a mess here. Sit tight. I'll handle this."

Eesyan's jaw dropped in disbelief. Garuth looked up speechlessly from where he had sunk down into a chair at one of the empty crew stations. Around them a score of other dazed Ganymeans had heard it too, but didn't believe it, either. "VISAR?" Eesyan whispered, as if half fearing an aural hallucination. "ZORAC, was that VISAR?"

"It's busy," ZORAC's voice answered. "Don't ask me what's happened, but yes it was. Something deactivated the self-checking functions, and I've switched off the jamming routine. We're through to Thurien."

While ZORAC was speaking, VISAR decoded the access passwords into JEVEX's diagnostic subsystem, erased a set of data that it found there, substituted new data of its own, and reset the alarm indicators. Inside the Jevlenese Defense Sector Five control center, a display screen changed to announce a false alarm caused by a malfunctioning remote communications relay. Far off in space, the two destroyers turned away to return to their stations and resume routine patrolling. Already VISAR was pouring volumes of information into JEVEX that it had no time to explain, not even to ZORAC. At the same time it broke its way into JEVEX's communications subsystem and gained control of the open channel to Earth.

A voice that Verikoff recognized as VISAR's spoke suddenly in the communications room in Sverensscn's house. "Okay, we've done it. If Vic Hunt and the others are there somewhere, you can bring them in to watch what happens next. I can edit them out of the datastream to Jevlen on a one-way basis. Get off the line now as quick as you can."

Somehow Verikoff kept his astonishment from showing. Behind him Hunt and the others had heard and were slowly moving in through the door, too astounded to say anything. Broghuilio, obviously unaware of them, was still staring dumbstruck from one of the screens. Verikoff pulled himself together and reacted swiftly. "You have one hour to give your reply, Broghuilio," he said. "And hear this—if one of those ships at Thurien makes so much as anything that even looks like a hostile move, we will attack under an order that will be irrevocable once issued. You have one hour."

Nothing changed on the screen, but VISAR announced, "Okay, you're off the air." At once a bewildered Verikoff was assailed by congratulations and backslapping from all sides. Pacey and Benson were watching incredulously from the doorway, while just inside the room Sobroskin slipped his automatic surreptitiously back inside his jacket.

Another screen came to life to show the Command Deck of the *Shapieron* as VISAR continued to integrate the communications functions of JEVEX that it was taking over into its own network. A few seconds later another screen brought the view from the Government Center in Thurios. It had to be the most bizarre computer hookup ever, Hunt thought as his eyes jumped from side to side to take it all in. Caldwell, Heller, and Danchekker were physically in Alaska, yet he was seeing them through a link that extended from Connecticut to a Jevlenese star light-years away, back to the *Shapieron* and from there to a second star, and from Gistar back to the perceptron at McClusky.

"You . . . apparently believe in cutting things close," Eesyan said from the *Shapieron*, still looking distinctly shaken.

"You worry too much," Caldwell told him, addressing a point offscreen. "We know how to manage a business." He shifted his gaze to look straight out of the screen in Connecticut. "How'd it go? Is everybody okay? Where's Sverenssen?"

"We had a change of plans," Hunt replied. "I'll tell you about it later. Everybody's fine here."

On the screen that showed the Jevlenese War Room, Broghuilio had demanded a report from JEVEX on its current surveillance intercepts from Earth. JEVEX responded by producing accounts of Earth's leaders meeting secretly to agree on details of a combined attack on Jevlen. That was already historical, JEVEX declared in answer to questions from a completely stunned Broghuilio. Currently the plans for the assault were complete, and preparations were well advanced. JEVEX's latest intercept was a briefing from the senior officers of the joint Terran command staff, which it proceeded to replay. Broghuilio grew more perplexed and more flustered as he listened.

"Explain this, JEVEX," he demanded in a strangled voice. "What forces were those primitives talking about? What were those weapons?"

"My respect, Excellency, but it would appear to be self-explanatory," JEVEX answered. "The strategic forces that Earth has been building for some time. The weapons referred to are typical of those deployed by the various nations of Earth at the present time."

Broghuilio's brow knotted, and his beard quivered. He scowled at the nervous faces around him as if seized by the sudden suspicion that only he among all of them might be sane. "Typical of what weapons deployed by Earth at the present time? You have never informed us of such weapons."

Invisible fingers raced through JEVEX's memory, interchanging hundreds of thousands of record descriptors in a fraction of a second. "I regret that I must dispute the statement, Excellency. I have reported the details consistently."

The color of Broghuilio's face darkened even further. "What are you talking about? Reported details of what?"

"The sophisticated interplanetary offensive and defensive capabilities that Earth has been developing for several decades," JEVEX informed him.

"JEVEX, WHAT ARE YOU TALKING ABOUT?" Broghuilio exploded. "Earth disarmed years ago. You have reported *that* consistently. Explain this."

"There is nothing to explain. I have always reported what I have just said."

Broghuilio brought his hands up to massage his eyes, then wheeled around suddenly to throw out his hands in an imploring gesture to those around him. "Am I going mad, or is that idiot machine having some kind of a fit?" he demanded. "Will somebody tell me that I have been seeing and hearing what I think I have been seeing and hearing for all these years. Have I been imagining things? Were we told that Earth had disarmed, or were we not? Do those weapons that we just heard about exist, or do they not? Am I the only sane person in this room, or am I not? Somebody tell me what's happening."

"JEVEX reports the facts," Estordu said lamely, as if that explained everything.

"HOW CAN IT BE REPORTING FACTS?" Broghuilio shouted. "It's contradicting itself. Facts are facts. They can't contradict."

"I have contradicted nothing," JEVEX objected. "My records all indicate that—"

"Shut up! Speak when you are spoken to."

"My apologies, Excellency."

"What Verikoff said about VISAR must be true," Estordu muttered in a worried voice. "VISAR could have been manipulating JEVEX when they were coupled together, before JEVEX disconnected—for years, maybe. Now that JEVEX is isolated, possibly we're receiving the truth for the first time." A ripple of alarmed voices ran around the War Room.

Broghuilio licked his lips and looked suddenly less sure of himself. "JEVEX," he commanded.

"Excellency?"

"Those reports—they were received direct from the surveillance system?"

"Of course, Excellency."

"Those weapons exist? They are being mobilized now?"

"Yes, Excellency."

Wylott was looking uncertain. "How can we be sure?" he

objected. "JEVEX says first one thing and then another. How do we know what is true?"

"So, do we do nothing?" Broghuilio asked him. "Would you just sit there and hope that the Terran assault force doesn't exist? What would it take to convince you—a hundred thousand of them coming for your throat? And what would you do then? Imbecile!" Wylott fell silent. The others around the War Room looked at one another with apprehension.

Broghuilio clasped his hands behind his back and began pacing slowly. "We still have a card up our sleeve," he said after a few seconds. "We have decoded their top-level secure communications, and we know their plans. We may have fewer weapons, but we are immeasurably ahead of Earth technically. We command a vastly superior firepower." He looked up, and his eyes began to gleam. "You heard those primitives—the main advantage they were counting on was surprise. Well, they no longer have that advantage. So, Verikoff calls us a rabble, does he? Let him send in his horde of Terran primitives. We will be waiting for them. He will find out who are the rabble when they come up against *Jevlenese* weapons."

Broghuilio turned back to face Wylott. "The operation at Thurien must be suspended for the time being," he declared. "Recall our forces at once and redeploy them for defense of Jevlen. This is not a time to be concerned about upsetting orbits at Gistar. Project the transfer ports in to where the ships are now, and get them back here as soon as possible. I want them in position by this time tomorrow."

New orders went out to the commanders of the task force at Thurien, who prepared their vessels for immediate transfer back. But they were in VISAR-controlled space, and JEVEX reported that its attempts to project entry ports into that region were being jammed; the ships could not be brought back without getting clear of Gistar first. Broghuilio had no choice but to extend his deadline by an extra day and order his force to get away under its own power. An hour later it was streaming in full flight back toward the edge of the Thurien planetary system.

"Phase One completed successfully," Caldwell announced with satisfaction from Thurios as he watched the data displays being presented inside the Government Center. "We've got the bastards on the run. Now let's make sure we keep things going that way."

chapter thirty-five

The transfer ports were ready and waiting outside the system of Gistar as arranged, and the Jevlenese warships peeled out of formation to enter them in relays with crisp, disciplined, military precision. What they didn't know was that by then VISAR was controlling the transfer system, not JEVEX, and such were VISAR's manipulations of JEVEX's internal functions that JEVEX didn't know it, either. Upon exiting back into normal space, one squadron found itself at Sirius, another at Aldebaran, and another near Canopus, while the rest reappeared strewn in ones and twos across Arcturus, Procyon, Castor, Polaris, Rigel, and assorted other stars in between. Thus they were out of harm's way for the time being and could be rounded up later. That completed Caldwell's Phase Two.

With a cigarette in one hand and a cup of black coffee in the other, Hunt stood on the patio outside Sverenssen's house, watching a protesting group of people in brightly colored garb being herded into an Air Force personnel carrier by the pool while a vigilant semicircle of Special Forces troopers looked on from a short distance back. The most recent captives had arrived at Sverenssen's expecting a party, but had found the CIA waiting instead. With VISAR controlling the surveillance there was no longer any need to conceal the activity around the house from orbital observation, but Clifford Benson had decided to maintain a low profile all the same, mainly to take advantage of just this kind of opportunity to extend further his suspect list of Sverenssen's acquaintants. But that was really just a precaution to identify any collaborators that might have been recruited locally. VISAR had found included among JEVEX's records a complete organizational chart of the Jevlenese operation on Earth, and with that information now in

655

Benson's and Sobroskin's hands, the rest of the network would soon be mopped up.

A concentration of Ganymean spacecraft had been building up on the periphery of the Jevlenese planetary system, and at that point it would have been possible for VISAR to shut off all of JEVEX's services from the Jevlenese in the same way that it had done with the Jevlenese element across the Thurien-administered worlds. The problem, however, was that the Jevlenese had clearly been preparing for a war situation for some time, and there was no way of telling what other stand-alone and backup systems they might possess that were capable of operating without JEVEX. Hunt and Caldwell therefore decided that simply pulling the plug, sending in the Ganymeans, and hoping for the best was not the way to go. Instead they opted to continue applying pressure until either they obtained the unconditional surrender that Verikoff had demanded, or the Jevlenese operation somehow fell apart from the inside. Also they hoped that the reactions they observed inside the Jevlenese War Room would reveal whether or not, and if so to what degree, the Jevlenese could in fact carry on without JEVEX.

Behind Hunt, a flap opened in the plastic sheeting with which the back of the house had been temporarily repaired, and Lyn stepped out through what had been a glass-panel wall of the corner room. She moved over to where he was standing and slipped an arm lightly through his. "I guess this place is off the list for the party rounds from now on," she said, looking across at the VTOL down by the pool.

"Just my luck," Hunt murmured. "As soon as some of the girls I've been hearing about show up, they take 'em away again. Who ever deserved a life like this?"

"Is that all you were worried about?" she asked. Her eyes were twinkling, and there was an elusive, playfully challenging note in her voice.

"And to see pal Sverenssen off on his way, of course. What else?"

"Oh, really," Lyn said softly and mockingly. "That wasn't exactly the way I heard it from Gregg."

"Oh." Hunt frowned for a moment. "He, er . . . he told you about that, huh?"

"Gregg and I work pretty well together. You should know

that." She wriggled her arm more tightly inside his. "It sounded to me like somebody was pretty upset."

"Principles," Hunt said stiffly after a pause. "Fancy me being stuck up in a place like McClusky while somebody else was down here in the sun, getting all that action. It was the principle of it. I have very strong principles."

"Oh, you idiot," Lyn said with a sigh.

They walked back into the house. Sobroskin was standing nearby with a couple of his officers, and Verikoff was sitting on a couch on the far side of the room, talking with Benson and a mix of CIA officials and more Soviets. Norman Pacey was nowhere in sight; probably he was still in the communications room where Hunt had left him a while earlier. Hunt caught Sobroskin's eye and inclined his head slightly in Verikoff's direction. "That guy's done a good job, and he's trying hard," he muttered in a low voice. "I hope he gets a big remission."

"We'll see what we can do," Sobroskin said. His tone was noncommittal, but there was something deep down in it that Hunt found reassuring.

"WHAT?" A voice that sounded like Broghuilio's shrieked distantly from the direction of the passageway that led through to the communications room. "YOU'VE MANAGED TO LOCATE THEM WHERE?"

"Oh-oh. I think somebody's just found his fleet," Hunt said, grinning. "Come on. Let's go and watch the fun." They moved across toward the passageway, and all around the room figures began standing up and converging behind them. Nobody, it seemed, wanted to miss the excitement.

"There must have been a malfunction in JEVEX," the Supreme Commander of the Jevlenese task force pleaded, cringing as Broghuilio advanced menacingly toward him. "Everything has been premature. There was no time to test the transfer system thoroughly."

"It's true," a white-faced Wylott said from behind. "There wasn't enough time. An interplanetary operation could not be organized on such a schedule. It was impossible."

Broghuilio whirled around and pointed a finger at a screen showing the latest details of the Terran order of battle. "WELL THEY'VE DONE IT!" he raged. "Every bicycle and bedpan factory on the planet is making weapons." He turned to appeal to the whole room. "And what do my *experts* tell me? Two years to complete the quadriflexor program! Twelve months to bring the extra generators on line! 'But we have the overwhelming technical superiority, Excellency,' I'm told." He turned purple and raised his clenched fists over his head. "WELL WHERE IS IT? Do I have all the imbeciles in the Galaxy on my side? Give me a dozen of those Earthmen and I'd conquer the Universe." He wheeled upon Estordu. "Get them back here. Even if you have to exit them here in the middle of the planetary system, get them back here today."

"It . . . seems that it isn't quite that simple," Estordu mumbled bleakly. "JEVEX is reporting difficulties in controlling the transfer system."

"JEVEX, what is this oaf babbling about?" Broghuilio snapped.

"The central beam synchronization system is not responding, Excellency," JEVEX answered. "I am confused. I have not been able to interpret the diagnostic reports."

Broghuilio closed his eyes for a moment and fought to keep control of himself. "Then do it without JEVEX," he said to Estordu. "Use the standby transfer facility at Uttan."

Estordu swallowed. "The Uttan system is not general purpose," he pointed out. "It was only set up to handle supply transfers to Jevlen. The fleet is scattered across fifteen different stars. Uttan would have to recalibrate for every one. It would take weeks."

Broghuilio turned away in exasperation and began pacing furiously back and forth across the floor. He halted suddenly in front of the commanding general of the local defense system. "They've got their attack planned all the way down to who will dig the latrines after they've wiped out the last imbecile in your army. You have a direct line into their communications network, and you can decode their signals. You know their intentions. Where is your defense plan?"

"What? I . . ." the general faltered helplessly. "How do you—"

"YOUR PLAN OF DEFENSE. WHERE IS IT?"

"But . . . we have no weapons."

"You have no reserves? What kind of a general are you?"

"A few robot destroyers only, all controlled by JEVEX. Can they be relied upon? The reserves were sent to Thurien." That had been at Broghuilio's insistence, but nobody chose to remind him of the fact.

A deathly silence enveloped the Jevlenese War Room. At last Wylott said firmly. "A truce. There is no alternative. We must sue for a truce."

"What?" Broghuilio looked toward him. "The Protectorate has barely been declared, and already you are saying we should crawl to primitives? What kind of talk is this?"

"For time," Wylott urged. "Until Uttan is in full production and the stockpiles are built up. Give the army time to be brought up to strength and trained. Earth has been geared to war for centuries. We have not, and there is the difference. The break from Thurien was forced too soon."

"It looks as if it may be the only chance we have, Excellency," Estordu said.

"JEVEX has reopened a channel," VISAR announced. "Broghuilio wishes a private audience with Calazar." Calazar had been expecting the call and was sitting alone on one side of the room in the Government Center waiting for it, while Caldwell, Danchekker, Heller, and the Thuriens watched from the far side.

A head-and-shoulders image of Broghuilio appeared in a frame before Calazar. Broghuilio looked surprised and uncertain. "Why are we talking like this? I asked to come to Thurien."

"I do not feel that the intimacy of proximity would be appropriate," Calazar replied. "What did you wish to discuss?"

Broghuilio swallowed and forced his words with a visible effort. "I have had an opportunity to consider the recent . . . developments. On reflection, it seems that perhaps we were disoriented by the arrogance of the Terrans. Our reactions were, perhaps, a little . . . hasty. I would like to propose a debate to reconsider the relationship between our races."

"That is no longer an affair that concerns me," Calazar told him. "I have agreed with the Terrans to leave the matter to be settled between yourselves. They have given you their terms. Do you accept them?"

"Their terms are outrageous," Broghuilio protested. "We have to negotiate."

"Negotiate with the Terrans."

Alarm showed on Broghuilio's face. "But they are barbarians . . . savages. Have you forgotten what leaving them to settle things their way will mean?"

"I choose not to. Have you forgotten the *Shapieron*?"

Broghuilio paled. "That was an inexcusable error. Those responsible will be punished. But this . . . this is different. You are Ganymeans. We stood beside you for millennia. You can't stand aside and abandon us now."

"You deceived us for millennia," Calazar replied coldly. "We wanted to keep Lunarian violence from spreading into the Galaxy, but it is loose in the Galaxy already. Our attempts to change you have failed. If the only solution left lies with the Terrans, then so be it. The Ganymeans can do no more."

"We must discuss this, Calazar. You can't allow this."

"Will you accept the Terran terms?"

"They cannot be serious. There must be room for negotiation."

"Then negotiate with the Terrans. I have nothing more to say. Excuse me now, please." The image of Broghuilio vanished.

Calazar turned to confront the approving faces across the room. "How did I do?" he asked.

"Terrific," Karen Heller told him. "You should apply for a seat in the UN."

"How does it feel to be hard-nosed, Terran-style," Showm asked curiously.

Calazar stood up, drew himself up to his full height, and filled his lungs with air while he considered the question. "Do you know, I find it rather . . . invigorating," he confessed.

Caldwell turned his head toward an image showing the observers on Earth. "It's not looking so bad," he said. "They can't get their ships back, and they don't seem to have a lot else. We could pull the rug out now. What do you think?"

Hunt was looking dubious. "Broghuilio's shaky, but he hasn't cracked yet," he replied. "He might have enough there to turn nasty with, especially if only unarmed Thurien ships show up. I'd like to see him a bit more unhinged first."

"So would we," Garuth said from the *Shapieron*. His tone left no room for doubt about the matter.

Caldwell thought for a second, then nodded. "I'll go along with that." He stroked his chin and cocked an eye at Hunt. "And VISAR has done a helluva job preparing all this material. It'd be a shame to waste it, wouldn't it."

"A terrible shame," Hunt agreed solemnly.

chapter thirty-six

The scene being presented inside the Jevlenese War Room was a view of the combined Terran battle fleet forming up as it moved from Earth. In the foreground a formation of destroyers, sleek, gray, and menacing, was moving into position to become part of an unfolding armada that extended away as far as the eye could see. As the first shrank into the distance to merge into the array, more formations slid majestically inward from the sides of the view and were absorbed in turn into the growing panorama. The first groups carried the Red Star of the Soviet Union, the next ones the Stars and Stripes of the U.S.A., and after those came the emblems of U.S. Europe, Canada, Australia, and the Republic of China. Farther away, moving slowly behind the vessels maneuvering and turning in the foreground, were lines of immense warships, their stark, solid contours broken by sinister weapon housings and ominous clusters of externally mounted missile pods. And behind them were the task groups and supply convoys—carriers, bombardment platforms, battle cruisers, interceptor mother ships, ground-suppression orbiters, shuttle launchers, troop and armor carriers, transports, all attended by swarms of support and escort craft—diminishing away to become pinpoints that seemed to be hardly moving at all against the stars. But appearances were deceiving. The whole awesome constellation was speeding silently and relentlessly away from Earth—toward the Ganymean transfer ports.

JEVEX's comments came through on audio. "The first wave, moving out from its forming-up area near Luna. Measured acceleration is consistent with the arrival time that the Terrans have indicated."

Broghuilio turned a shade paler. "First wave?" he gasped. "There's more?"

In response the scene changed to show a view looking down

on what appeared to be a huge base of some kind, enclosed by a perimeter fence and surrounded by desolate, sandy terrain. Lines of dots along one side expanded rapidly as the view enlarged, and resolved themselves into rows of surface shuttles in the process of being loaded. The area in front of them was packed with lines of tanks, artillery, personnel carriers, and thousands of troops waiting in neat, geometric groupings. "Chinese regular divisions embarking to be ferried up for the second wave now assembling in orbit," JEVEX announced.

The view changed again to show a similar scene, but this time set among thickly forested hills. "Conventional low-level supersonic bombers and high-altitude interceptors being loaded in Siberia."

And another view. "Missile batteries and antitank laser units embarking in the western U.S.A. There're more coming in from all over. Contingency plans are being drawn up for a third wave."

Perspiration was showing on Broghuilio's face. He closed his eyes, and his lips moved soundlessly as he struggled to remain calm. "Might I suggest, Excellency, that—" Wylott began, but Broghuilio cut him off with a sharp wave of his hand.

"Quiet. I need time to think." Broghuilio brought his hand up to his chin and began tugging at his beard nervously. He clenched his other fist behind his back and paced to the far end of the War Room. Then he turned to face back again. "JEVEX."

"Excellency?"

"VISAR must have a link into the Terran communications net through the Thurien facility there. Get me a channel into it through VISAR. I want to talk to the President of the United States of America, the Soviet Premier, or anybody else in high authority that VISAR can get hold of. Do it immediately."

"How do you want me to play it?" VISAR asked in the Government Center at Thurios.

"We can't let the plan bog down," Caldwell said. "Unconditional surrender has to be his only way out. Fix it so that he thinks he's cut off from everybody except Verikoff."

Anxious and impatient, Broghuilio had started pacing again. Then JEVEX announced, "VISAR is denying the request. It has been directed to conform to Thurien policy, which is to dissociate itself from Terran-Jevlenese affairs."

Broghuilio's legs almost buckled beneath him. "The Thuriens are transferring those warships here to wipe us out!" he shouted. "What kind of dissociation policy is that? Tell VISAR I insist."

"VISAR has instructed me to advise you, with respect, Excellency, to go to hell."

Broghuilio was too numbed with shock to react violently. "Then tell VISAR to connect me to Calazar again," he choked.

"VISAR refuses."

"Then connect VISAR through to me."

"VISAR has severed all connections. I am unable to obtain further responses."

Broghuilio had begun trembling with a mixture of rage and fear. He spun his head wildly from side to side, his eyes white and staring. "Verikoff is your only choice," Wylott said. "You have to accept the ultimatum."

"Never!" Broghuilio shouted. "I'll never surrender my force intact. We still have two days. We can evacuate the entire officer corps, our scientists, our best engineers, and consolidate at Uttan. We will make our stand there. Uttan has permanent defenses that the Terrans will find themselves hard put to match. They will still have some surprises in store for them if they try to follow us there." He looked at Wylott. "Work out a schedule with JEVEX to evacuate the maximum of value from Jevlen in two days. Begin at once. Ignore all other tasks."

"I think we ought to try the switch," Hunt said, watching. "They're just about ready."

"Are you really going to try that?" Shilohin asked from the *Shapieron.* She sounded skeptical. "It's too illogical, surely."

"What do you think, Chris?" Caldwell asked, glancing over his shoulder.

"They have been conditioned to accept contradictions now," Danchekker said. "At this moment there is a good chance that they will be incapable of thinking sufficiently clearly to question it."

"And they are close to panic," Sobroskin observed from beside Hunt. "Panic and logic are impossible companions."

"I'm still not sure I understand this phenomenon you call panic," Eesyan said from the *Shapieron.*

"Let's see if we can show you," Caldwell said, and gave an instruction to VISAR.

"Pardon, Excellency," JEVEX queried. "But your figure of two days appears irrelevant."

"What?" Broghuilio stopped dead in his tracks. "What do you mean, irrelevant?"

"I don't understand why you have specified two days," JEVEX answered.

Broghuilio shook his head, nonplussed. "It's obvious, isn't it? The Terran attack will begin two days from now, will it not?"

"I don't follow, Excellency."

Broghuilio sent a puzzled frown around the room. His aides stared back at him equally bemused. "The attack is due in two days, is it not?" he said again.

"There has been no postponement, Excellency. The attack is still expected today, twelve hours from now."

Nothing happened for a few seconds.

Then Broghuilio brought his hand up to his face and beat it slowly and deliberately several times against his brow. "JEVEX," he said. His voice was quiet as his effort to control himself overcompensated. "You have just told us that the first wave is only now in the process of leaving Earth."

"Pardon, Excellency, but I have no record of saying any such thing."

It was too much. Broghuilio's voice began to rise and shake uncontrollably. "How can the Terrans be less than a day away?" he demanded. "Are they or are they not departing from Earth now?"

"They began departing from Earth two days ago," JEVEX replied. "They have entered Jevlenese planetary space and will commence their attack in twelve hours' time."

Broghuilio's color was deepening rapidly. "Those surveillance reports that you just presented. Were they or were they not live from Earth as of this moment, as you stated?"

"They were records obtained two days ago, as I stated."

"YOU DID NOT SAY THAT!" Broghuilio screamed.

"I did. My records confirm it. Shall I replay them?"

Broghuilio turned to appeal to the rest of the room. "You all heard it. What did that idiot machine say? Were those views live or were they not?" Nobody was listening. One of the aides was rushing back and forth and jabbering incoherently, another was clutching at his face and moaning, while among the rest consternation was breaking out on every side.

"They couldn't be from two days ago."

"How do you know? How do you know what's happening and what isn't? How do you know anything?"

"JEVEX said so."

"It said the opposite too."

"Maybe JEVEX is mad."

"But JEVEX said—"

"JEVEX doesn't know what it's saying. We can't trust anything."

"The Terrans are coming! They're only hours away!"

On one side of the room the scientist, Estordu, quietly vanished. In the confusion, nobody noticed.

Broghuilio was waving his arms and shouting above the clamor. "Twelve hours. *Twelve hours!* And you tell me you have no weapons! They'll be coming straight in for the kill because they don't know what opposition to expect. . . . AND WE HAVE NO OPPOSITION TO OFFER! A shipful of children could walk in and take us over, and the Terrans don't even know it. And what do I have to stop them? Imbecile generals, imbecile scientists, and an imbecile computer!"

Wylott shouldered his way through to where Broghuilio was standing. "There is no choice," he insisted. "You have to accept Verikoff's terms. At least that way there will come another day." Broghuilio turned his head and glowered, but the inevitability of what Wylott had said was written in his eyes. But still he could not bring himself to give the order. Wylott waited for a few seconds, then raised his head to call above the commotion still going on around them. "JEVEX. Call Earth via your own channel to Sverenssen. Get Verikoff on the line."

"At once, General," JEVEX acknowledged.

In the communications room in Connecticut, Hunt turned his head toward Verikoff, who was watching from the doorway. "You'd better come on in. It looks as if you'll be on again in a few seconds to accept the surrender. It's just about all over." Verikoff moved to the center of the room while the others fell back to clear a small circle around him. On the screen showing the Jevlenese War Room, Wylott and Broghuilio had turned to look directly out at the room and were waiting expectantly for JEVEX to make the connection. Verikoff folded his arms and assumed a domineering posture in readiness.

And suddenly the screen went blank.

Puzzled looks appeared all around the room. "VISAR?" Hunt said after a few seconds. "VISAR, what's happened?" There was no reply. The screens that had been connecting them to Thurien and the *Shapieron* had gone blank as well.

Verikoff moved quickly over to a bank of equipment on one side of the room and ran rapidly through a sequence of tests. "It's dead," he announced, looking up at the others. "The whole system is dead. We don't have any channels to anywhere, and I can't open any. Something has cut us off from JEVEX completely."

In the Government Center at Thurios, Caldwell was equally bewildered. "VISAR, what's happened?" he demanded. "Where did the views from Earth and Jevlen go? Have you lost them or something?"

A few seconds went by, then VISAR answered. "It's worse than that. I haven't only lost Connecticut and the War Room, I've lost everything from JEVEX. I don't have anything into it at all. The whole system has switched off."

"Don't you know anything that's happening at Jevlen at all?" Morizal asked, aghast.

"Nothing," VISAR said. "The only channel I've got to anywhere in the whole of the JEVEX-controlled world-system is the one through to the *Shapieron*. JEVEX seems to be dead. The whole system has just gone down."

Broghuilio found himself reclining in his private quarters deep underground in the complex that housed the Directorate of Strategic Planning. He sat up sharply, unsure of what had happened. A moment before he had been in the War Room with Wylott, waiting for a connection to Verikoff. Even as he remembered, he saw again in his mind's eye the armada from Earth, at that moment sweeping inward toward Jevlen. He looked around wildly. "JEVEX?"

No response.

"JEVEX, answer me."

Nothing.

Something cold and heavy turned over deep in his stomach. He leaped to his feet, fumbled his way into a robe to cover his shorts and undershirt, and hurried into the next room to check the status indicators of the suite's monitor panel. Lighting, air conditioning, communications, services . . . everything had reverted to emergency backup mode. JEVEX was not operating. He tried activating the communications console, but the only thing he could raise on the screen was a message stating that all channels were saturated. It meant that the condition was

general and not due simply to some local failure; the complex
was in panic. He rushed through into his bedroom and began
frantically tearing clothes out of a closet.

He was still buttoning his tunic when a tone sounded from
the outside door in the hallway. Broghuilio hastened out and
pressed his thumb against a printlock plate to dematerialize the
door. Estordu was there with two other aides. The sounds of
shouting and commotion came in from behind them.

"What's happened?" Broghuilio demanded. "The whole system is dead."

"I deactivated it," Estordu told him. "I threw the manual
override breakers in the master nucleus control room. I've shut
JEVEX down totally."

Broghuilio's beard quivered, and his eyes widened. "You
what—" he began, but Estordu waved a hand impatiently to silence him. The gesture was so out of character that Broghuilio
just stared.

"Can't you see what's happened?" Estordu said, speaking
rapidly and urgently. "JEVEX was not functioning coherently.
Something was affecting it from the *inside*. It could only have
been VISAR. Somehow VISAR gained access to it. That meant
that the Thuriens could have been watching every move we
made. We still have twelve hours, and if we move quickly we
can still get away. We still have emergency communications
channels to Uttan, and the standby transfer system can project
an entry port to Jevlen. With JEVEX inoperative and VISAR
therefore blind, we can make our arrangements without risking
interference from the Thuriens or the Terrans. The nearest
Terran ships are still twelve hours away. By the time they get
here we can be gone, and they'll have no way of knowing
where to. By the time they think of looking for us at Uttan, we
will be well prepared. Don't you see? It was the only way.
With JEVEX running we couldn't have planned a move without
them knowing."

Broghuilio thought rapidly as he listened. There was no time
for arguing, and anyway, Estordu was right. He nodded. "Everyone with their wits about them will go physically to the War
Room," he said. He looked at Estordu. "Find Lantyar and tell
him I want five reliable crews mustered and brought to
Geerbaine by eighteen hundred hours today. You . . ." He
directed his gaze at one of the two aides standing behind
Estordu. "Contact the operations commander at Geerbaine and

tell him I want five E-class transports ready for launch not one
minute later than then, and power standing by on-line at Uttan
to project ports as soon as the transports clear Jevlen." He gestured to the other aide. "And you, find General Wylott and tell
him to mobilize four companies of guards and organize air
transportation from here to Geerbaine, ready to leave by seventeen thirty hours. I'll need capacity for two thousand persons.
Commandeer it from wherever you need to, and don't hesitate
to use force. Do you understand?" Broghuilio straightened his
collar and went back through to the bedroom to buckle on his
belt and sidearm. "I am going to the War Room now," he
called out to them. "The three of you will report to me there
not later than one hour from now. Do as I say, and this time
tomorrow we will all be on Uttan."

chapter thirty-seven

The *Shapieron* had moved closer to Jevlen to await the arrival
of the Ganymean ships from Thurien, which had begun moving inward from the edge of the planetary system but were still
many hours away. The main screen on the Command Deck
was showing views of Jevlen's surface being sent back from
probes at lower altitudes. The planet seemed to be in chaos.
Nothing was flying anywhere, but in many places people had
begun leaving the cities on foot and in disorderly streams of
ground vehicles that had soon jammed solid on highway systems never intended for more than minor local or recreational
traffic. Disturbances and rioting had broken out in a few
places, but in most the populations were merely assembling in
the open spaces, leaderless and bewildered. Communications
traffic from the surface was garbled and revealed no organization for maintaining order or vital services. In short, the
Ganymeans were going to have a big job on their hands putting the pieces of the mess together again.

Garuth was tense and apprehensive as he stood in the center

of the Command Deck taking in the reports. VISAR had not crashed JEVEX, so the culprit had to have been the Jevlenese themselves. Somehow they had discovered they were the un-witting objects of surveillance through JEVEX, and had shut down the system to blind VISAR to what they were doing. In other words they were up to something, and there was no way of knowing what. Garuth didn't like it.

The other thing that was bothering him at a deeper level was the feeling that he had failed. Despite the reassurances of Eesyan, Shilohin, Monchar, and the others that his bringing the *Shapieron* to Jevlen had saved Thurien, Garuth was acutely conscious of how near to disaster he had brought them, and that only the fast action of Hunt and the others on Earth had saved things. He had risked his crew and Eesyan's scientists ir-responsibly, and others had bailed him out. Yes, the threat to Thurien had been removed; but Garuth didn't feel he deserved very much credit for that. He would have liked to have con-tributed more and the congratulations that had poured through from Thurien had only added to his discomfort.

On a smaller screen to one side, Hunt was talking over his shoulder to the others who were crowded into the room in the Connecticut house that had been the headquarters of the Jevlenese operation to infiltrate Earth. "Can you imagine the problems we might have created for lots of people on this planet in years to come?"

"What do you mean?" the voice of Norman Pacey, the American government representative, asked from somewhere in the background.

Hunt half turned to wave at the screen in front of him. "One day people might be sending their kids to college on Thurien. Suppose the kids figure out this stunt for themselves and start calling home collect."

After JEVEX had gone off the air and shut down the commu-nications facility, the group in Connecticut had reestablished contact by the simple expedient of telephoning the control room at McClusky and linking back into VISAR via the databeam to the perceptron. They had called on two lines from the datagrid terminals in Sverenssen's office, next door to the communications room, and had one screen to the *Shapieron* and another to the Government Center at Thurios.

"I still don't believe it," the CIA official, Benson, said from a chair by a window, partly visible over Hunt's shoulder.

"When I see somebody picking up the phone and calling talking computers in an alien spaceship out at some other star, I don't believe it." Benson turned his head to address somebody offscreen. "*Jeez!* The CIA should have had something like this years ago. We could even have tuned into what you guys were talking about in the men's room inside the Kremlin."

"I think the days of that kind of thing will very soon be over, my friend," a voice replied from somewhere in an accent that Garuth assumed was Russian.

It would have made no difference if they were physically present in the *Shapieron*, he thought to himself. They would banter and laugh in the same way whatever the risks and whatever the unknowns. They could try, fail, forget, laugh, and try again—and probably succeed. The thought that they had been within a hair's breadth of disaster didn't trouble them. They had won the round, now it was dismissed and in the past, and their only thoughts now were for the next. Sometimes Garuth envied Earthmen.

ZORAC spoke suddenly. Its tone was urgent. "Attention please. There is a new development. Probe Four has detected ships rising fast from the surface on the far side of Jevlen— five of them in tight formation." At the same instant the view on the main screen changed to show the curving, cloud-blotched surface of the planet with five dots creeping across the mottled background.

On the auxiliary screen Hunt was leaning forward while others crowded behind him. They had stopped talking. An adjacent screen showed Calazar and the observers at Thurios, all equally tense.

"It has to be Broghuilio and his staff," Calazar said after a few seconds. "They must be making a break for Uttan. Estordu said they've got a standby transfer system that operates between Jevlen and Uttan. That's what they've been planning! We should have thought of it."

Eesyan had joined Garuth in the center of the Command Deck. Shilohin, Monchar, and some of the scientists were gathering around from the sides of the room. "They have to be stopped," Eesyan said, sounding worried. "They could have Uttan prepared and defended as a fallback base. If they reach it and regroup, they could decide to fight it out. It would only be a matter of time before they realized that we don't have anything to challenge them with. With Uttan in their hands, we'd be in real trouble."

"What is Uttan?" Hunt asked from the screen.

Eesyan turned away from Garuth and answered in a faraway voice as he tried to think. "An airless, waterless ball of rock on the fringe of Jevlenese space, but very rich in metals. The Jevlenese were granted it long ago as a source of raw materials to build up their industries. It's obviously where their weapons came from. But if what we suspect is right, they've turned the whole planet into a fortified armaments factory. We've got to prevent Broghuilio's getting there."

While Eesyan was speaking to Hunt, Garuth quickly reviewed what he could recollect of the Thurien h-transfer system. VISAR or JEVEX could jam h-beams projected into their respective regions of space by virtue of the dense networks of sensors they possessed, which enabled them to monitor the field parameters of a transfer toroid just beginning to form, and disrupt the energy flow through from h-space. Without the sensors, jamming wouldn't work. But the only sensors that existed in the vicinity of Jevlen were JEVEX's and VISAR would not be able to use them since it could only do so through JEVEX, and JEVEX was dead. Hence a beam from Uttan couldn't be disrupted by VISAR. So *that* was why the Jevlenese had shut down the system.

"There's nothing we can do," Calazar was saying from the other screen. "We haven't got anything near there. Our ships are still eight hours away at least."

An agonized silence fell on the Command Deck. Calazar was looking helplessly from one side to another about him, while to one side of him Hunt and the Terrans on Earth had frozen into immobility. On the main screen the five Jevlenese vessels had cleared the edge of the planet's disk.

A feeling of composure and confidence that he had not known for a long time flowed slowly into Garuth's veins as the situation unfolded in sudden crystal clarity. There was no doubt about what he had to do. He was himself again, in control of himself and in command of his ship. "We are right here."

Eesyan stared for a second, then turned his head to gaze uncertainly at the five dots on the main screen, now diminishing rapidly into the starry background of space. "Could we catch them?" he asked dubiously.

Garuth smiled grimly. "Those are just Jevlenese planetary

transports," he said. "Have you forgotten? The *Shapieron* was built as a starship." Without waiting for a response from Calazar, he raised his head and called in a louder voice, "ZORAC, dispatch Probe Four in pursuit immediately, recover deployed probes, lift the ship into high orbit, charge all on-board probes for maximum range, and bring the main drives up to full-power readiness. We're going after them."

"And what will you do then?" Calazar asked.

"Worry about that later," Garuth replied. "The first thing is not to lose them."

"Tally ho!" ZORAC cried, mimicking a flawless English accent.

Hunt sat up and blinked in astonishment on one of the screens. "Where the hell did it pick that up?" he asked.

"Documentaries of World War II British fighter pilots," ZORAC announced. "That was for your benefit, Vic. I thought you'd appreciate it."

chapter thirty-eight

Broghuilio stood on the bridge of the Jevlenese flagship and scowled while the technicians and scientists clustered around a battery of datascreens in front of him took in the details of the report coming through from the long-range scanning computers. Gasps of disbelief sounded among the rising murmur of voices. "Well?" he demanded as his patience finally exhausted itself.

Estordu turned from the group. His eyes were wide with shock. "It can't be possible," he whispered. He made a vague gesture behind him. "But it's true . . . there's no doubt about it."

"What is it?" Broghuilio fumed.

Estordu swallowed. "It's . . . the *Shapieron*. It's pulling away from Jevlen and turning this way."

Broghuilio stared at him as if he had just gone insane, then snorted and pulled two of the technicians out of the way to see the screens for himself. For a second his mouth clamped tight, and his beard quivered as his mind refused to accept what his eyes were seeing. Then another screen came to life to show a magnified view from the long-range optical imagers that left no room for dissent. Broghuilio spun around to glare at Wylott, who was watching numbly from a few feet back. "HOW DO YOU EXPLAIN THIS?" he shouted.

Wylott shook his head in protest. "It can't be. It was destroyed. I *know* it was destroyed."

"THEN WHAT IS THAT COMING AT US RIGHT NOW?" Broghuilio whirled to the scientists. "How long has it been at Jevlen? What is it doing here? Why didn't any of you know about it?"

The captain's voice came from the raised section of the bridge above them. "I've never seen acceleration like it! It's vectoring straight after us. We'll never outrun it."

"They can't do anything," Wylott said in a choking voice. "It's not armed."

"Fool!" Broghuilio snapped. "If it wasn't destroyed, it must have been transferred to Thurien. And Terrans could have been transferred to Thurien. So it could have Terrans on board it with Terran weapons. They could blow us apart, and after your bungling, the *Shapieron*'s crew won't lift a finger to stop them." Wylott licked his lips and said nothing.

"Stressfield around the *Shapieron* building up rapidly," the long-range surveillance operator called from one of the stations above. "We're losing radar and optical contact. H-scan shows it's maintaining course and acceleration."

Estordu was thinking furiously. "We may have a chance, Excellency," he said suddenly. Broghuilio jerked his head around and thrust his chin out demandingly. Estordu went on, "The Ganymean ships from that period did not possess stressfield transmission correction, and h-scan equipment was unknown. In other words they have no means of tracking us while they're under main drive. They'll have to aim blind to intercept our predicted course and slow down at intervals to correct. We might be able to lose them by changing course during their blind periods."

At that instant another operator called out, "Gravitational anomaly building up astern and starboard, range nine eighty miles, strength seven, increasing. Readings indicate a Class Five exit port. H-scan shows conformal entry-port mapping to vicinity of *Shapieron*." The tension on the bridge rocketed. It meant that VISAR was projecting two beams to create a linked pair of transfer ports—a "tunnel" through h-space from the *Shapieron* to the Jevlenese vessels. A Class Five port would admit something relatively small. The operator's voice came again, rising with alarm. "An object has emerged at this end. It's coming this way, fast!"

"A bomb!" somebody screamed. *"They've exited a bomb!"* Consternation broke out around the bridge. Broghuilio was wide-eyed and sweating profusely. Wylott had collapsed onto a chair.

The operator's voice came again. "Object identified. It's one of the *Shapieron*'s robot probes . . . matching us in course and speed. The exit port has dissolved."

And the long-range surveillance operator: "*Shapieron* closing and still accelerating. Range two-twenty thousand miles."

"Get rid of it," Broghuilio barked up at the level above. "Captain, shake that thing off."

The captain gave a set of course-correction instructions, which the computers acknowledged and executed.

"Probe matching," came the report. "Evasion ineffective. *Shapieron* has corrected to a new vector and is still closing."

Broghuilio turned a furious face toward Estordu. "You said they'd be blind! They're not even slowing down." Estordu spread his hands and shook his head helplessly. Broghuilio looked at the rest of the group of scientists. "Well, how are they doing it? Can't any of you work it out?" He waited for a few seconds, then pointed a finger angrily at the screens showing the tracking data of the *Shapieron*. "Some genius on *that* ship has thought of something. Everywhere I am surrounded by imbeciles." He began pacing back and forth across the bridge. "How does this happen? They have all the geniuses, and I have all the imbeciles. Give me—"

"The probe!" Estordu groaned suddenly. "They must have fitted the probe and the *Shapieron* with h-links. The probe will be able to monitor every move we make and update the *Shapieron*'s flight-control system through VISAR. We'll never lose it now."

Broghuilio glared at him for a second, then looked across at the communications officer. "We have to make the jump to Uttan now," he declared. "What's the status there?"

"The generators are up to power and standing by," the officer told him. "Their director is locked onto our beacon, and they can throw a port here immediately."

"But what if that probe transfers through with us?" Estordu said. "VISAR would locate it when it reenters at Uttan. It would reveal our destination."

"Those geniuses will have guessed our destination already," Broghuilio retorted. "So what could they do? We can blow anything that comes near Uttan to atoms."

"But we're still too close to Jevlen," Estordu objected, looking alarmed. "It would disrupt the whole planet . . . chaos everywhere."

"So would you rather stay here?" Broghuilio sneered. "Hasn't it occurred to you yet that the probe was just a warning? The next thing they tunnel through at us *will* be a bomb." He sent a stare around the bridge that defied anybody to argue with him. Nobody did. He raised his head. "Captain. Transfer now, to Uttan."

The command was relayed to Uttan, and within seconds huge generators were pouring energy into a tiny volume of space ahead of the five Jevlenese ships. The fabric of space-time wrinkled, then buckled, heaved, and fell in upon itself to plummet out of the Universe. A spinning vortex began growing to open up the gateway to another realm, first as a faint circle of curdled starlight against the void, then getting stronger, thicker, and sharper, and expanding slowly to reveal a core of featureless, infinite blackness.

And then a counterspinning pattern of refractions materialized inside the first. The resultant composite of vortices shimmered and pulsated as filaments of space and time writhed in a tangle of knotted geodesics. Something was wrong. The port was going unstable. "What's happening?" Broghuilio demanded.

Estordu was turning his head frantically from side to side to take in the displays and data reports. "Something is deforming the configuration . . . breaking up the field manifolds. I've never seen anything like this. It can only be VISAR."

"That's impossible," one of the other scientists shouted. "VISAR can't jam. It has no sensors. JEVEX is shut down."

"That's not jamming," Estordu muttered. "The port began to form. It's doing something else. . . ." His eye caught the view of the *Shapieron* again. "The probe! VISAR is using the probe to monitor the entry-port configuration. It couldn't jam the beam, so it's trying to project a complementary pattern from Gistar to cancel out the toroid from Uttan. It's trying to neutralize it."

"It couldn't," the other scientist protested. "It couldn't get enough resolution through a single probe. It would be aiming virtually blind from Gistar."

"The Gistar and Uttan beams would interact constructively in the same volume," another pointed out. "If an unstable resonance developed, anything could happen."

"That *is* an unstable resonance," Estordu shouted, pointing at the display. "I tell you, that's what VISAR's doing."

"VISAR would never risk it."

Ahead of the ships, a maelstrom of twisting, convulsing, multiple-connected relativity was boiling under the clash of titanic bolts of energy materializing and superposing from two points, each light-years away. The core shrank, grew again, fragmented, then reassembled itself. And still they were heading directly for its center.

Broghuilio had listened enough. He turned his head up to where the captain was watching him, waiting. Then at the last second, something about Estordu pulled his attention away.

Estordu was standing absolutely still with a strange look on his face as he stared at the view of the *Shapieron*. He was mumbling to himself, and seemed to have forgotten everything going on around him. "H-links through the probes," he whispered. "That was how VISAR got into JEVEX." His eyes opened wider, and his face became ashen as the full realization hit him. "That was how . . . *everything* got into JEVEX! It never existed, any of it. They were doing it through the *Shapieron* all the time. . . . We're running away from a single unarmed ship."

"What is it?" Broghuilio snapped. "Why are you looking like that?"

Estordu looked at him with a bleak stare. "It doesn't exist. . . . The Terran strike force doesn't exist. It never did. VISAR wrote it into JEVEX through the *Shapieron*. The whole thing was a fabrication. There was nothing there but the *Shapieron* all the time."

The captain leaned over from above. "Excellency, we have to . . ." He stopped as he saw that Broghuilio was not listening, hesitated for a second, then turned away to call to somewhere behind him. "Disengage forward compensators. Cut in emergency boost and reverse at full power. Compute evasion function and execute immediately."

"*What?—What did you say?*" Broghuilio turned to face the

semicircle of cowering figures behind him. "Are you telling me the Terrans have been making fools out of all of you?"

From above the synthetic voice of a computer came tonelessly: "Negative function. Negative function. All measures ineffective. Ship accelerating on irreversible gradient. Corrective action now impossible. Repeat: Corrective action now impossible."

But Broghuilio didn't hear, even as the craft plunged into the knot of insanely tangled space-time looming around them. "You imbeciles!" he breathed. His voice rose and began shaking uncontrollably as he lifted his fists high above his head. "*Imbeciles!* IMBECILES! You *IM-BE-CILES!!*"

"My God, they're going straight into it!" Hunt gasped from a screen on the Command Deck of the *Shapieron.* The view on the main screen was being sent back from the probe two hundred thousand miles away, still clinging doggedly to the heels of the Jevlenese ships. A horrified silence had fallen all around.

"What's happening?" Eesyan whispered from the center of the floor.

"An oscillating instability is coupling positively to an h-frequency alias caused by discrepancies in the beam spectra," VISAR answered. "The properties of the region created are beyond analysis."

On another screen Calazar, openmouthed with shock, was shaking his head in protest. "I never intended this," he said in a strangled voice. "Why didn't they turn away? I just wanted to deny them the port."

"ZORAC, cut the main drives and decelerate," Garuth instructed in a voice that was clipped and expressionless. "Present an optical scan of the area as soon as we reintegrate."

A background of turbulent light and blackness now filled the entire main screen. The five dots grew smaller in front of it . . . and were suddenly swallowed up in the chaos. The turmoil seemed to rush out as the probe followed in after them, and then the view changed abruptly as the *Shapieron*'s stressfield dispersed and ZORAC switched through the long-range image from the ship's own scanners. "The instability is breaking down," VISAR reported. "The resonances are degenerating into turbulence eddies. If there was a tunnel there, it's caving in." On the screen the patterns broke up into swirling fragments of light that spiraled rapidly inward, at the same time growing smaller, dimmer, and redder. They faded, and then died. The region of the starfield that was left shimmered for a few seconds to mark where the upheaval had been, and then all was normal just as if nothing had happened.

For a long time an absolute silence gripped the Command Deck, and nobody moved. The faces on the screens showing Earth and Thurien were grim.

And then VISAR spoke again. There was a distinct note of disbelief in its voice. "I have a further report. Don't ask me how right now, but it looks as if they got through. The probe was still transmitting when the tunnel closed in behind it, and its last signal indicates that it reentered normal space." While surprise was still evident all over the Command Deck, the view on the main screen changed to show the last image transmitted by the probe. The five Jevlenese ships were hanging in ragged formation in what looked like ordinary space sure enough, studded with what looked like ordinary stars. And up near one corner was a larger speck that could have been a planet. The image froze at that point. "The transmission ceased there," VISAR said.

"They survived that?" Eesyan stammered. "Where is it? Where in space did they emerge?"

"I don't know," VISAR answered. "They must have been trying for Uttan, but anything could have happened. I'm trying to match the starfield background with projections from Uttan now, but it could take a while."

"We can't risk waiting," Calazar said. "Even though Uttan might be defended, I'll have to send in the reserve ships from Gistar to try and cut Broghuilio off before he reaches that planet." He waited for a few seconds, but nobody could disagree. His voice became heavier. "VISAR, connect me to the reserve-squadron commander," he said.

"There is nothing more for us to do here," Garuth said in a voice that had become very quiet and very calm. "ZORAC, return the ship to Jevlen. We will await the arrival of the Thuriens there."

While the *Shapieron* was turning to head back, a set of toroids opened up briefly some distance outside the planetary system of Gistar, and the squadron of Thurien vessels that had been held in reserve there transferred into h-space, then reemerged outside the system of Uttan. The Jevlenese long-range surveillance instruments detected them as a series of objects hurtling inward at a speed not much below that of light. The commander at Uttan decided that a portion of the Terran strike force had been diverted, and within minutes every emergency signal band was carrying frantic offers of unconditional surrender. The Thuriens arrived at Uttan some hours later and took over without opposition.

That result had been unexpected. The reason for it was even more unexpected: Broghuilio's ships had not, after all, appeared at Uttan, or anywhere near it. Uttan control had lost contact when they vanished from the vicinity of Jevlen, and had been unable to relocate them. Without their leaders, the defenders at Uttan opted to capitulate without a fight.

So where had the five Jevlenese ships gone? VISAR reported that they had not rematerialized anywhere inside the regions of space that it controlled, and when it projected small transfer ports to the scores of worlds previously run by JEVEX and sent search probes bristling with sensors and instruments, the ships were not to be found at any of those places, either. They seemed to have vanished entirely from the explored portion of the Galaxy.

The Thuriens did find something else at Uttan, however—something that left them shaken and mystified. Hanging in space, all at various stages of construction, they found lines of immense engineering structures. Each was in the form of a hollow square that measured five hundred miles along a side, and carried at its center a two-hundred-mile-diameter sphere supported by bars extending diagonally inward from the corners.

chapter thirty-nine

"I don't understand this," Calazar said as he stared out from one of the Thurien vessels floating near Uttan. "Those are full-scale quadriflexors, exactly as we designed them. The Jevlenese have been building hundreds of them."

"I don't know," Showm replied, shaking her head beside him. "It makes no sense."

Heller, Caldwell, and Danchekker looked at each other. "What's a quadriflexor?" Caldwell asked.

Calazar sighed. There was no point in being evasive. "They are the devices with which we were going to enclose the Solar System," he said. "They were to be positioned at a considerable distance outside Pluto at points defining a quasispherical surface around the system. Every quadriflexor would couple through h-fields to the four adjacent to it in the grid, and collectively they would create a cumulative deformation of spacetime at that boundary which would equate to an escape-proof gravitic gradient.

"We performed preproduction testing on some scaled-down prototypes, and we did in fact begin building some of the full-size versions, but we are still a long way from being in a position to implement the final plan." Calazar waved at the view outside the ship. "But the Jevlenese have obviously been copying our designs in secret, and their program was far more advanced. I can't understand why."

Danchekker was blinking behind his spectacles and frowning to himself while he wrestled with the riddle. Somehow he had the feeling that the last layer of the enigmatic onion that seemed to surround everything connected with the Jevlenese was about to be peeled away. By at first exaggerating Earth's aggressiveness and later manufacturing false evidence, the Jevlenese had persuaded the Ganymeans that Terran expansion had to be checked, and nothing short of physical containment would check it. The Ganymeans had, until very recently, been convinced, and had set the necessary preparations in motion accordingly. But the Jevlenese had embarked on an identical venture and concealed the fact from the Ganymeans. Why? What did it mean?

Danchekker looked over at the images that VISAR was presenting of the Command Deck of the *Shapieron* and Sverenssen's office in Connecticut, but there were no suggestions forthcoming from those directions. The Ganymeans in the *Shapieron* were preoccupied with something that was happening on the main screen inside the ship, while in the other view he could see only the backs of Hunt and the others as they crowded around the terminal on the other side of the room, which connected them to the *Shapieron*. A lot of excited talking was going on in both places, but what it was about was obscure.

"Could they have been planning to do the same thing themselves?" Karen Heller said at last.

"For what reason?" Calazar asked. "We were already working on it. What could they have stood to gain?"

"Time?" Caldwell offered.

Calazar shook his head. "If time was so critical to them, they could have persuaded us to accelerate our own program with a fraction of the effort that they must have put into this. Certainly we have the resources to have been able to beat any schedule they could have been aiming at."

Frenua Showm was looking thoughtful. "And yet it's strange," she mused. "On several occasions when we wanted to speed up our program, the Jevlenese actually seemed to play down the risks of Terran expansion. It was as if they were trying to keep our research moving, but weren't in a hurry to see us move into production."

"They were milking off the know-how," Caldwell grunted. "Making sure that their program stayed well ahead of yours." He paused for a few seconds, then asked, "Could those things be used for shutting in anything else apart from a star system?"

"Hardly," Calazar replied, then added, "Well, I suppose they could be used to close in anything of comparable size . . . or something smaller, come to that."

"Mmm . . ." Caldwell lapsed back into thought.

Heller shrugged and turned up her hands. "If they weren't going to enclose the Solar System, they must have been planning to enclose some other . . ." Her voice trailed away as the answer suddenly became plain, to her and to everybody else at the same time.

Calazar and Showm stared speechlessly at each other for a few seconds. "*Us?*" Calazar managed at last in a strained voice. "*The Thuriens?* They were going to shut in Gistar?" Showm brought her hand up to her brow and shook her head as she struggled to take in the implication of it. Caldwell and Heller were standing dumbstruck.

The whole thing slowly became clear in Danchekker's mind. "*Yes!*" he exclaimed. He moved forward to the center of the group and stood for a moment checking his thoughts, then began nodding his head vigorously. "Yes!" he said again. "Surely it's the only acceptable explanation." He looked excitedly from one to another of the others as if he expected them to agree with something there and then. They stared back at him blankly. Nobody knew what he was talking about. He waited for a moment and then elaborated. "I have never been able to accept fully that the obsessive Lambian–Cerian rivalry could have persisted in the minds of the Jevlenese for all that time, especially with their exposure to Ganymean influence. Did it never strike you as strange? Didn't any of you ever feel that there had to be something more behind it than just that?" He looked at the others questioningly again.

After a few seconds Caldwell said, "I guess not, Chris. Why? What are you getting at?"

Danchekker moistened his lips. "It's an interesting thought, wouldn't you agree, that there was one entity that was always there at the back of things, permanent and unchanging while generations of Jevlenese came and went."

There was a moment of silence. Then Heller stared at him and gasped. "JEVEX? Are you saying the computer was behind the whole thing?"

Danchekker nodded rapidly. "JEVEX was established a long time ago. Is it completely inconceivable that its basic design and programming couldn't somehow have embodied as some kind of innate driving instinct the ruthlessness and ambitions of its creators—the descendants of the original Lambians? And to realize those ambitions, could it not have harnessed the Jevlenese elite as its instruments? But if that were so, it would have found itself confronted by a serious obstacle in the form of the restraints imposed on it by the Thuriens."

Caldwell was beginning to nod. "It would have had to get the Thuriens out of the way somehow," he agreed.

"Precisely," Danchekker said. "But not too quickly. There was a lot that it wanted to learn from them first. And the really cunning part was that at the end of it all, the Thuriens' own ingenuity and technology would provide the means whereby the Jevlenese would get rid of them. Then, armed with stolen Ganymean science and with JEVEX as their leader, the Jevlenese would have had the Galaxy at their mercy. Think of all those developing worlds . . . and a technology that could cross light-years in moments. They would become the masters of every part of explored space, poised to expand their empire without limit, and the only potential opposition would be safely locked up inside a gravitic shell that nothing could get out of." Danchekker gripped his lapels and turned from side to side to take in the astounded expressions around him. "So now at last we see what was behind it all—the ultimate design that they had been working on, probably ever since Minerva. And how near they came to succeeding!"

"So the weapons at Uttan . . ." Calazar said falteringly, still struggling to grasp the enormity of it all. "They were never intended to be used against Thurien at all?"

"I doubt it," Danchekker said. "I suspect that they were for afterward, to add teeth to their expansion when the time came."

"Yes, and guess who'd have been first on the list," Heller said. "They were Lambians, and we were Cerians."

"Of course!" Showm whispered. "Earth would have been defenseless. *That* was why they concealed your demilitarization from us." She nodded slowly in grudging admiration. "It was neatly worked out. First they work to retard Earth's advancement while they grow strong and learn. Then they accelerate Earth's rate of discovery suddenly, engineer the results into a threat which they enlist Ganymean aid to eliminate. And finally they remove the threat to themselves but conceal the fact from the Ganymeans, and use the very technique that they have induced the Ganymeans to develop as the means of eliminating the Ganymeans instead. That would have left them in a position to settle the old score with the Cerians without interference, and with the odds overwhelmingly in their favor."

"We wouldn't have stood a chance," Caldwell breathed, for once genuinely staggered.

"And the Jevlenese would have repossessed the Solar System, which I suspect has always been their first goal," Danchekker said. "I would imagine they have always considered it rightly theirs. And they would no longer have had to play second fiddle to the Ganymeans, a position they clearly have never been able to come to terms with gracefully."

"It all makes sense," Calazar said in a resigned voice. "Why they were so insistent about administering their own, autonomous group of worlds . . . why they needed a system independent of VISAR, controlling its own volume of space." He looked at Showm and nodded. "A lot of things are beginning to make sense now."

He fell silent for a few seconds. When he spoke again his voice was lighter. "If all this is true, then our problem of what to do next could be eased considerably. If the roots of it all lay not so much in the Jevlenese people but in JEVEX, then maybe there is hope for them after all. Distasteful punitive measures may not be necessary."

A distant look came into Showm's eyes. "Ye-es," she said slowly, and began nodding. "Perhaps, given the right help, they might rebuild their civilization upon a new model and emerge from it all as a mature and benign race. All may not be lost yet."

"It does give us a positive goal to aim at and a task to accomplish," Calazar said, sounding more enthusiastic. "Despite all the setbacks, things might work out to a successful conclusion. As you say, all is not lost."

"Er, at present this is merely a hypothesis, you understand," Danchekker said hastily. "But there might be a way to test it. If the whole thing did in fact begin with JEVEX, it might be possible to trace the origins of some of the things we've been talking about back to conceptual subnets of some form buried in JEVEX's older archives." He looked at Calazar. "I assume that once your people are fully in control of Jevlen, it would be possible to reactivate parts of JEVEX in a controlled fashion and allow VISAR to examine its records thoroughly."

Calazar was already nodding. "I would have thought so. Eesyan is really the person we should talk to about that." He looked across at the view coming from the Command Deck of the *Shapieron*. "Isn't he free yet? What's happening there?"

Consternation was breaking out among the Ganymeans crowded below the main screen in the image. At the same time a chorus of shouts erupted from the other image, showing the view from Earth, in which Hunt and the others were bumping into each other in their haste to get back across the room to the terminal that connected them to the Thurien ship at Uttan. Danchekker, Calazar, and the others with them forgot their conversation of a few moments earlier and stared in astonishment. Hunt was almost incoherent with excitement as he got to the screen. "We've found them! ZORAC reprocessed the planet. We know where they went. It's impossible!"

Danchekker blinked at him. "Vic, what are you babbling about? Kindly calm down, and simply say whatever it is that you're trying to say."

Hunt recomposed himself with some effort. "The five Jevlenese ships. We know what happened to them." He paused for a second to get his breath back, then turned his head away to call over the people behind him to the terminal connecting them to the *Shapieron.* "ZORAC, pass that shot over to VISAR, would you. Tell VISAR to display it at Uttan." In the ship where Danchekker was, an image appeared of the final shot of the Jevlenese vessels sent back by the *Shapieron*'s probe just before the tunnel caved in. "Have you got it?" Hunt asked.

Danchekker nodded. "Yes. What about it?"

"The spot in the upper right-hand corner is a planet," Hunt said. "We asked ZORAC if there was any way it could reprocess that part of the image and enhance it to give us a better look at it. It did. We know what planet it is."

"Well?" Danchekker asked, puzzled, after a second or two. "Where is it?"

"A better question would be *when*?" Hunt told him.

Danchekker frowned and looked around him only to be met by expressions as confused as his own. "Vic, what are you talking about?" he asked.

"VISAR, show them," Hunt said in reply.

The speck enlarged in an instant to become a full disk occupying the whole frame. It was a world shining brightly against the stars with cloud formations and oceans. The resolution was not good, but there were continental outlines discernible on its surface. Calazar and Showm froze. A split second later, Danchekker realized why.

What he was looking at was not unfamiliar. Like Hunt, he had studied every island, isthmus, estuary, and coastline sandwiched between the two enormous ice caps of that planet many times—at Houston, in the course of the Lunarian investigations over two years earlier. He looked away. Calazar and Showm were still staring in silent awe, and now Caldwell too was wide-eyed with disbelief. Danchekker slowly turned his head to follow their gaze once again. It was still there. He hadn't imagined it.

The planet was Minerva.

chapter forty

Nobody could say for certain exactly how it had come about in those final few seconds as VISAR and the projector at Uttan fought for control of the same speck of space-time light-years away, and many believed that nobody ever would. But Hunt was forced at last to accept the truth of the claim that Paul Shelling had made at Houston on the day that Karen Heller and Norman Pacey had come to talk to Caldwell: the Ganymean physical equations that described the possibility of point-to-point transfers through space had solutions that admitted transfers through time too. Or both. For somehow the five Jevlenese ships had been hurled across light-years of space and backward through tens of thousands of years of time to emerge in the solar system when Minerva was still in existence. In fact, by careful measurement of the positions of background stars, the Ganymean scientists determined to a high degree of accuracy when; it came out to be about two hundred years before the final Lunarian war.

And that, of course, explained where the superbreed of Lambians, who had emerged seemingly overnight with a technology far in advance of anything else anywhere on the planet, had come from. And it explained why a planet that had, by and large, mended its warlike ways and commenced working constructively and cooperatively toward an eventual migration to Earth became divided into the two rival factions that in the end had destroyed each other. The Cerians were native, having evolved from the terrestrial primates transported to Minerva twenty-five million years earlier by the Ganymeans, while the Lambians were from Jevlen and fifty thousand years in the future. The Lambians never emerged at all; they *arrived*.

There were more than enough riddles in this for the scientists to argue over for many years to come. How, for example, could the Lambians have been the descendants of their own descendants? Their greed and power lust were seen at last as characteristic of them as a group rather than of the human race as a whole, but that being so, where had those characteristics originated? The Jevlenese had inherited them from the Lambians, who had inherited them from the Jevlenese that had landed on Minerva. So where and when had it started? Danchekker speculated that their passage through the zone of dislocated space-time might have induced some form of psychological aberration that had started the whole thing off, but the suggestion was not very satisfying since the meaning of the word "started" in this context was obscure to say the least.

Another enigma arose from the knowledge of subsequent events that the Jevlenese would presumably have taken back to Minerva with them. If they knew about the next two hundred years, the war, the millennia after that with the Thuriens, and their own eventual defeat at the hands of VISAR, why would they have allowed those very things to happen? Had they been powerless to change the sequence? Surely not. Had a whole new history somehow been written into the timeloop to erase and replace something else that had existed there "before," whatever that meant? Or had they perhaps taken few hard records with them in their haste and suffered some kind of stress-induced amnesia such that they arrived not knowing who they were or where they had come from, thus dooming themselves to launch again into an endless, unaltering cycle?

The Thuriens didn't know the answers to these questions either, which raised issues that were on the fringes of their own theoretical researches. Possibly, one day, future generations of Ganymean and Terran mathematicians and physicists would deduce the strange logic within which such things could happen. Then again, possibly no one would ever know.

But one mystery was solved that had been perplexing the Terrans, the Ganymeans, and the Jevlenese alike—the mystery of the device out beyond Pluto that had responded to that first message beamed from Farside in ancient Ganymean code, and relayed it directly to VISAR. The Thuriens had assumed it was something that the Jevlenese had positioned, the Jevlenese had assumed it was something that the Thuriens had emplaced, and because of the circumstances neither side had ever been able to challenge the other. And now that it had been destroyed, there was no way of investigating it. So what had it been, and how had it gotten there?

The answer could only be the probe that had gone through the tunnel on the heels of the Jevlenese ships. Naturally it had been programmed to respond to the communications protocols used by its own mother ship, and it had been fitted with an h-link to Thurien. By analyzing the log of messages exchanged during those last few seconds, Shilohin's scientists established that, just before the tunnel closed behind it, the probe had been in a passive mode awaiting its next command from the *Shapieron.* Apparently it had waited for a long time. After exiting near Minerva under the impetus that VISAR had imparted in accelerating it in pursuit of the Jevlenese ships, it climbed away from the Sun and eventually stabilized in a distant orbit out beyond Pluto. And it waited. And eventually it heard a command that it understood, and relayed it to VISAR because that was what its instructions told it to do. It didn't know that fifty thousand years had gone by in the meantime.

And so the full circle that linked Minerva and the early Ganymeans, the Lunarians both Lambian and Cerian, Charlie and Koriel, Earth and *Homo sapiens,* and the Giants' Star, was complete. It had begun with its own ending, and in the process JEVEX, Broghuilio, and the Lambians had become locked in an unbreakable loop that was firmly and permanently embedded in the past. Ironically their prison was even more escape-proof than the one that they themselves had devised.

Deprived of their corrupt element, the people of Jevlen turned out to be not so unlike human beings anywhere else after all, and set themselves to the task of rebuilding their society with a new mood of cooperation and optimism. This would require a great deal of physical hard work as well as social and political reforms because of the widespread damage, mainly from flooding, that had been caused by the gravitational upheaval of Broghuilio's spectacular departure, so Calazar installed Garuth as temporary planetary governor to supervise and coordinate the operation. Jevlen would be on probation for a while to come, and for some time there would be no planetwide system after the pattern of JEVEX; planning and other functions would require extensive information-processing capacity nevertheless, and fortunately a machine of just the right size presented itself in the form of ZORAC. The *Shapieron* was permanently based at Jevlen, and ZORAC became the nucleus of a new pilot network that one day would assume interplanetary dimensions and be merged into VISAR.

Furthermore the temporarily decomputerized world of Jevlen would provide an ideal environment for Garuth's people from the *Shapieron*, displaced twenty-five million years from their own civilization, to recuperate and readjust to the ways of the Thuriens. At the same time they would be able to play a key role in helping Garuth rebuild the planet and inaugurate a new system of Jevlenese government. So Garuth, his people, and ZORAC had a worthwhile job to do, a challenging future ahead, and a home of their own once again.

On Earth, Mikolai Sobroskin became the Soviet Foreign Minister under the new order that emerged from the wreckage of the previous regime. Through some machinations inside the Kremlin that would never be fully disclosed, Verikoff ended up as an advisor on extraterrestrial sciences, having made history as the first alien ever to apply for and be granted Terran citizenship.

In the U.S. State Department, Karen Heller and Norman Pacey headed a team assigned by Packard to draft a policy aimed at breaking down the barriers of East–West suspicions that had festered for over a century, and forging an era of universal prosperity from the combined economic and industrial might of the U.S. and Soviet giants, and the material and human resources of the emerging Third World. Already the international web that had precipitated World War I, financed both the Bolshevik Revolution and the rise of Hitler, manufactured the Middle East and Southeast Asian crises of later years, contrived for a whole world to fund its own blackmail through the nuclear arms race, and been behind a long list of other interesting things found recorded in great detail inside JEVEX, was well on its way to being broken up for good.

The UN, purged of the influences that would have manipulated it into a focal point of global power to be delivered wholesale into the hands of the Jevlenese, would be remolded into the instrument through which Earth would take its place in the interstellar community. And it would have an important role to play in that community—a role in which people like Clifford Benson, Colonel Shearer, and Sobroskin's generals would still have a place. For despite their sciences and their technology, the Ganymeans had learned the wisdom of preserving a strong right arm; there was no telling how many more Broghuilios might be waiting in the unexplored reaches of the Galaxy.

Such days would come, but they were still far in the future.

In the meantime there were preparations to be made—a whole planet to reeducate, and a whole system of natural sciences to be revised and brought up to date. UNSA drew up tentative plans for merging Navcomms into a new superdivision under Caldwell, who would move to Washington to begin the mammoth task of rewriting the long-range plans for the space program in the light of Ganymean technology and initiate studies for integrating selected parts of Earth's communications net into VISAR. Hunt would become Deputy Director of the new organization, and Danchekker, fired by the vision of unlimited access to scores of alien worlds each with its own alien biology and alien evolution, accepted an offer to go too as Director of Alien Life Sciences. At least, that was why Danchekker said he wanted to move to Washington. Caldwell reserved a box in the organization chart for Lyn too, of course.

But the real hero of the war, for which neither anybody nor anything else in existence anywhere could conceivably have substituted, was VISAR. Calazar agreed that VISAR would take over Uttan and run the planet exclusively, to enjoy its own measure of independence, and in the process be free to evolve further its own brand of intelligence in its own way and to its own design. But VISAR's ties to its creators would not be broken, and in the years and centuries ahead, the expansion into the Galaxy would manifest the same alliance of human and Ganymean, organic and inorganic instincts and abilities that had already proved to be a formidable combination.

epilogue

The procession of black limousines drew slowly to a halt before the military guard of honor and lines of foreign ambassadors standing by the side of the field of Andrews Air Force Base, Maryland, a few miles from Washington, D.C. The day was sunny and clear, and the thousands filling the area outside the boundary fence all around were strangely quiet.

Feeling somewhat odd and formal in his black pinstripe three-piece suit, stiffened cuffs and collar, and tightly knotted necktie, Hunt stepped out of the second car back from the one flying the presidential pennant on its hood, and helped Lyn out after him while the chauffeur held the door. Danchekker, similarly attired though nothing seemed to fit exactly as it was supposed to, came next, followed by Caldwell and a group of senior UNSA executives.

Hunt looked around and picked out the perceptron among a line of aircraft parked some distance away in the background. "It's not really like home, is it," he commented. "There aren't any windows boarded up, and it needs some snow and a few mountains around."

"I never thought you were sentimental," Lyn said. She looked up. "Blue sky, and lots of green. I'll stick with this."

"Not a romantic who hankers for old times, I perceive," Danchekker said.

Lyn shook her head. "After the amount of flying that I did back and forth to that place, I don't care if I never see McClusky again."

"We might be sending you a lot farther than that before very much longer," Caldwell grunted.

The Soviet Premier and his delegation had not yet emerged from the car immediately in front of them, but ahead of that the U.S. President and his entourage were assembling. Karen Heller and Norman Pacey detached themselves from the group and walked back. "Well, get used to it," Pacey said, making a sweeping gesture with his arm. "It's going to be your new home for a while. I've got a feeling this place will get to feel like your own private airport. You people are going to be pretty busy."

"We were just talking about it," Lyn said. "Vic seems to prefer McClusky."

"When will you be moving up to D.C.?" Heller inquired.

"It'll be a few months yet at least," Caldwell said.

She looked at Danchekker. "The first thing we'll have to do is have dinner somewhere, Chris. It'll make up for all those canteen meals in Alaska."

"An admirable suggestion," Danchekker replied. "And one with which I concur fully." Lyn nudged Hunt in the ribs. Hunt looked away and grinned.

Pacey glanced at his watch and looked over his shoulder.

Sobroskin was leading the Soviet party from the car ahead. "It's almost time," he said. "We'd better move on up." They walked forward to join the Soviet contingent, all of whom they had already met individually in the Executive Lounge earlier, and the whole group moved on to join the President and his party at the front of the cavalcade of limousines. Sobroskin moved closer to Pacey as they came to a halt. "The day has arrived, my friend," he said. "The children will see other worlds under other stars."

"And I told you you'd see it happen," Pacey said.

Packard was looking at Pacey curiously. "What did that mean?" he asked.

Pacey smiled. "It's a long story. I'll have to tell you about it sometime."

Packard turned his head toward Caldwell. "Well, at least I know what to expect this time, Gregg. You know, I don't think I'll ever live that down."

"Don't worry about it," Caldwell told him. "The rest of us were only a few seconds behind you."

They moved toward the open area of the base and came to a halt again, arranged in orderly rectangular groups with the McClusky team, including Jerol Packard, at the front, the U.S. and Soviet leaders alongside each other behind them with Pacey and Sobroskin standing ahead of their respective national delegations, and the UNSA and other groups from the remaining cars arrayed at the back. Every head was turned upward, waiting. And suddenly, sensed rather than heard, a wave of excitement rippled across the entire base and through the crowds packed outside.

The ship was already visible as a faint dot enlarging in the flawless blue above. As it grew larger, it took on a brilliant silvery sheen that glinted with reflected highlights in the sun, and resolved into a slender wedge with gracefully curved leading edges flaring to merge into two needle-pointed nacelles at the tips. And still it was getting larger.

Hunt's mouth dropped open as the raised bulges along its hull, ancillary housings swelling from its underside, fairings, pods, blisterdomes, and turrets gradually revealed themselves in a steadily unfolding hierarchy of detail to give the first real hint of the craft's awesome size. Gasps of wonder were coming from either side of him and behind, and the crowd outside seemed paralyzed. It must have been miles in length . . . tens of miles;

there was no way of telling. It expanded above their heads to fill half the sky like some huge, mythical bird that seemed to be hanging over the entire state of Maryland. And still it might have been in the stratosphere, or even beyond that.

He had seen the Thurien power generators and been told they were thousands of miles across, but that had been out in empty space where there were no references. His senses had been spared the impact of direct confrontation, leaving only his imagination to grapple with what the numbers had meant. This was different. He was standing on Earth, surrounded by trees, buildings, and everything else that made up the world of the familiar and the unquestioned, in which intrusions like this were forbidden. Even the distance from one horizon to another, which he sensed unconsciously although it was not visible directly, set a perspective that defined the permissible, imposed rules, and forced limits. The Thurien spaceship had no place in that scheme. It belonged to a different order of magnitude, breaking every known rule and making nonsense of the usual limits. He felt like an insect that had just grasped the meaning of the toenail in front of it, or a microbe that had glimpsed an ocean. His mind had no model to accommodate it. His senses rebelled from taking in the totality of what he was seeing. His brain fought to reconcile it with something that was manageable within a lifetime's stored experiences, couldn't, and gave up.

At last a light moving across his field of view against the underside of the ship broke the hypnotic trance that had taken hold of him. The figures that had been frozen into immobility around him began stirring as they saw it too. Something was coming down, and was already much nearer than the ship; it had to have been descending for some time, and had only just become visible. It moved swiftly and silently on a direct line toward the center of the base and turned into a flattened, highly elongated ellipsoid of pure gold, completely smooth except for two low, sharply swept fins projecting from its upper surface. It landed without a sound a short distance away, its nose pointing to where Hunt and the others were standing. For perhaps ten seconds not a sound or a movement disturbed the total stillness that had enveloped the base.

And then the forward section of the underside hinged slowly downward to form a broad, shallow ramp leading down to the ground. The point where the ramp entered the body was lost in a glow of brilliant yellow light. Lyn's fingers found Hunt's and squeezed as the first eight-foot-tall shapes appeared a dozen or so abreast out of the light and began moving down the ramp. At the bottom of the ramp, they halted to survey the waiting lines of Terrans.

In the center was Calazar, easily recognizable even without his familiar short silver cape and green tunic, and on one side of him were Frenua Showm, Porthik Eesyan, and Eesyan's deputy, Morizal. Garuth was at Calazar's other side, with Shilohin, Monchar, and other Ganymeans from the *Shapieron* whose light gray skins set them apart as a group from the darker, less heavily built Thuriens. The team that had gone to McClusky had been waiting a long time for this moment. For the first time since the perceptron's landing and their first hesitant entry into it, they were not seeing the Thuriens via neural stimulations transmitted from light-years away. This time the Thuriens were real.

Massed bands had begun playing in the background. The crowd, still overwhelmed by the spectacle filling the sky above their heads, was quiet. Then with orderly, unhurried dignity the Ganymeans started moving again, and Caldwell stepped forward to lead the McClusky team to meet them at the halfway point.

"It was a bit scary at times, but I think Earth has made it," Lyn whispered as they began moving.

"You're making it sound as if it's all over," Hunt murmured beside her. "This is just the start of it."

And it was. For the Ganymeans, it was the end of a task they had been working on for millennia; for the inhabitants of Jevlen, it was a change of heart and direction; and for VISAR, it was a new phase of existence.

But for *Homo sapiens*, it was a whole new beginning.

The heirs to the stars were about to claim their inheritance.

appendix

ANSWERS TO CROSSWORD

ACROSS

1 SHANNON—Irish river. (flow-er, not flower).

5 DECODE—find the meaning of. "Ode" (poem) added *to* "DEC."

9 INNOCENT—opposite of "guilty." "O" (zero) "cent" (money) *after* "inn" (pub).

10 BEACON—guiding light. Literally *in* "could *(be a con)*-fused."

12 DEEP END—profound conclusion. "Pen" (writer) jumping into (hint) "deed" (action).

13 EXTREME—ultimate. Literally *in* "t"*(ext reme)* dies.

14 EULER—Swiss mathematician. "E" (east, i.e., oriental) plus *changed* (anagram of) "rule."

16 INTRO—colloquial *short* form of "introduction," i.e., preamble. *Wild* (anagram of) "riot" *about* (around) "N" (compass point).

17 EXTRA—something more. "Ex" ("expert" less four letters of six) plus "tra," i.e., "art" *buck*(ward).

18 APART—separated. A-part (piece).

20 AFRICAN—continental. *Maybe* (anagram of) "i" (one) "fan car."

21 ANNULAR—ring-shaped, around. Annul (abolish) a "r" (right).

23 RETAIN—keep. "E" and "T" (head and tail of "elephant") *in*(side) "rain."

24 DISTRESS—heartache. Di's (Dianna's) tress (lock of hair).

25 YEMENI—type of Arab. "Men" and "I" *after* "ye" (half of "year," i.e., six months).

695

26 ENCASES—surrounds. "Ease" *surrounding* (double use) "NC" added *to* "S" (compass point).

DOWN

1 SWINDLE—something not fair. "Win" *in*(side) *perhaps* (anagram of) "sled."

2 ANNIE—noted (musical) lady. Advised to get a gun (arms).

3 NUCLEAR REACTION—*power*ful reaction (response) from nucleus (heart). Extra hint: "r" (right) taken *from* "heart" gives "heat."

4 NON-ADDICTING—not habit-forming. *Possibly* (anagram of) "did on gin can't."

6 ELECTROMAGNETIC—a (kind of) wave. Generated *from* charges of the kind (brigade) that produce light (i.e., accelerating electric ones).

7 ORCHESTRA—something that makes harmony. "H" (chemical symbol for hydrogen) *in*(side) *turbulent* (anagram of) "star core."

8 ERNIE—man's name. "N" (head of "Norman") *in*(side) "Erie" (lake).

11 TEST DATA FILE—experimental results. *Reorganized* (anagram of) "let's fit a date."

15 LOGARITHM—type of number. Phonetically similar to "logger" (lumberjack) "rhythm" (music).

19 THRUSTS—urges progress (mechanically, not politically). "H" (*initial* or "Hoover") *in*(side) "trust," *over* (literally) "S" (South).

20 ARRAY—matrix. "Ar" (chemical symbol for argon) plus "ray" (beam).

22 LOESS—geological deposit. "O" (nothing) *in*(side) "less" (smaller amount).